Lots of Love

FIONA WALKER

Lots of Love

Hodder & Stoughton

A CIP catalogue record for this title is
available from the British Library

Hardback ISBN 0 340 68230 2
Trade paperback ISBN 0 340 819650

Typeset in Plantin Light by Palimpsest Book Production Limited,
Polmont, Stirlingshire
Printed and bound in Great Britain by
Clays Ltd, St Ives plc

Hodder & Stoughton
A division of Hodder Headline
338 Euston Road
London NW1 3BH

For Hans and Christian,
who prove that some happy endings
begin a whole new chapter.

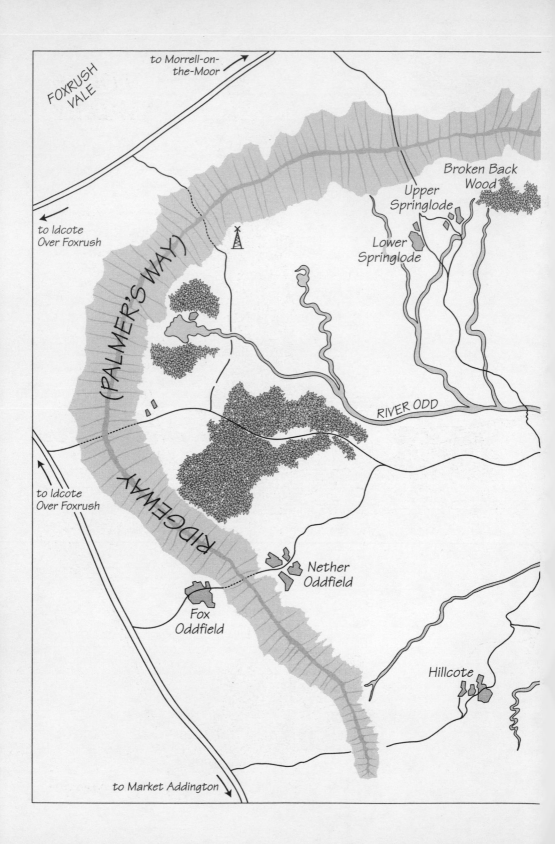

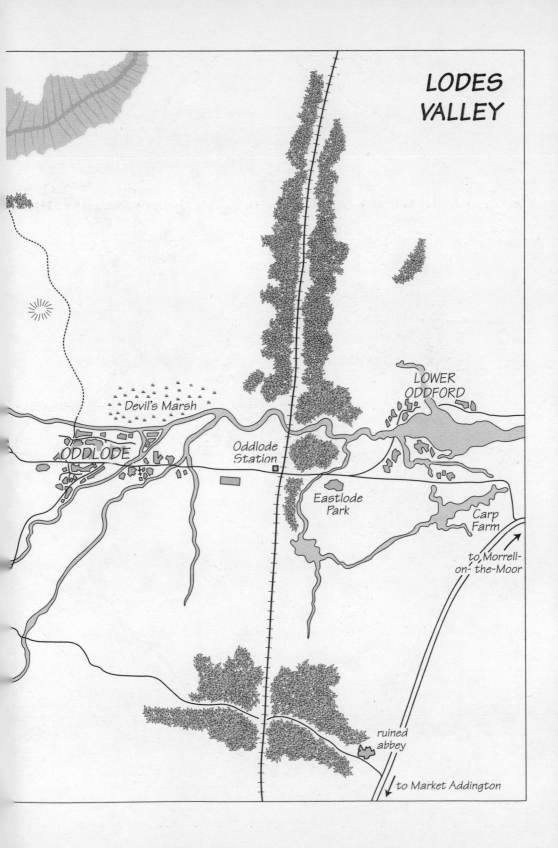

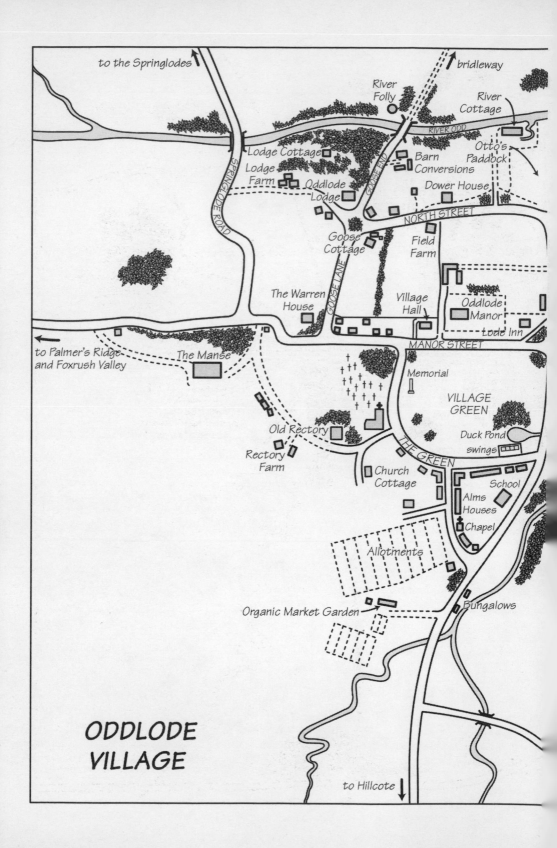

to the Springlodes

bridleway

River
Folly

River
Cottage

RIVER ODD

SPRINGLODE ROAD

Lodge Cottage

Lodge
Farm

Oddlode
Lodge

Barn
Conversions

Otto's
Paddock

Dower House

NORTH STREET

Goose
Cottage

GOOSE END

Field
Farm

GOOSE LANE

The Warren
House

Village
Hall

Oddlode
Manor

Lode Inn

to Palmer's Ridge
and Foxrush Valley

The Manse

MANOR STREET

Memorial

VILLAGE
GREEN

Old Rectory

Duck Pond

swings

Rectory
Farm

THE GREEN

Church
Cottage

School

Alms
Houses

Chapel

Allotments

Organic Market Garden

Bungalows

ODDLODE
VILLAGE

to Hillcote

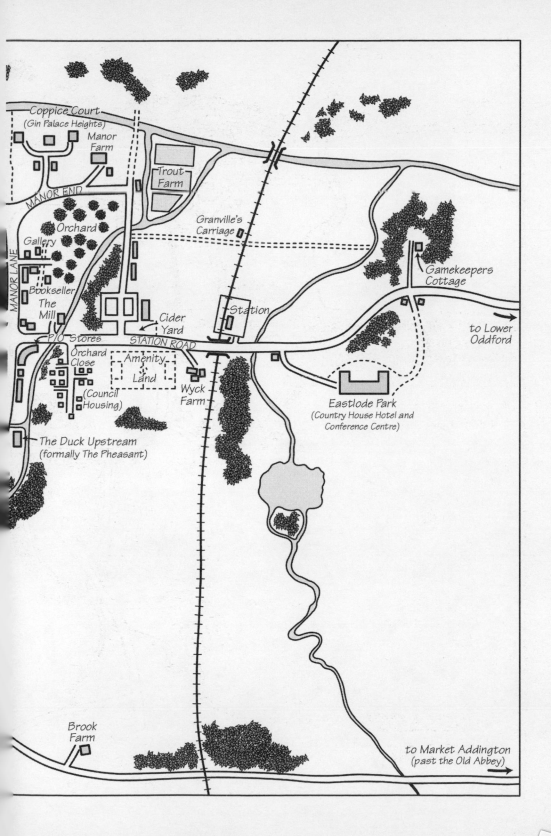

'Leave it – leave it. LEAVE IT!'

Ellen struggled to keep control of the jeep as Snorkel scrabbled around beneath her legs, trying to extract her ball from the footwell. A moment later, and a white clown's face looked up between her knees, red ball in mouth, mad blue eyes imploring.

'Not now, Snork,' she pleaded.

The ball was dropped lovingly on to her thigh, leaving a trail of wet slobber behind as it rolled down her bare leg and toppled into the footwell once more, settling under the brake pedal.

Having fallen asleep on the passenger seat after her ham sandwich and loo break at Taunton Deane Services two hours earlier, the collie had only just woken up again, and was desperate to have a run-around and play a game. But because they were so close to the end of their journey, Ellen didn't want to stop.

'Miaaaaaaaaeeeeeeecooooooow!' Fins complained from his wicker basket, redoubling his efforts to escape. He had been trying to chew his way out since setting off from Cornwall, with no loo break and no in-car ball game to break the monotony. The basket on the back seat positively vibrated from inside while at the same time rocking to and fro as Ellen negotiated the narrow, winding lane.

She'd forgotten just how many hairpins and illogical dog-legs there were in the lanes here, all relating to ancient rights of way and field systems that had long since been abandoned in the wake of modern farming. Unlike North Cornwall, with its twisting tunnels of high-banked lanes, the Cotswolds had low stone walls over which she caught regular glimpses of ripening crops and grazing stock, making it easy to lose concentration.

Even the woods were different, she noticed, as she dropped down a steep hill into a forest – the trees were tall and proud and let in far less light through their canopy. Compared to the bright sunshine outside, it was like driving into a cool, dark cathedral. She pushed her dark glasses up into her hair.

Snorkel let out a series of frustrated whines as she scratched frantically for her ball. Fins hissed and wailed as he munched at the wicker. To drown the din, Ellen turned on the radio, but the local station she'd tuned into hours earlier had long since faded to white noise. She pressed the scan button to find something else, then realised there was a tape in the deck and flipped it out to see what it was.

It was one of Richard's old compilations, lovingly put together to set the mood for long drives across Europe in search of surf.

Her eyes misted and she slotted it carefully back in, not pushing hard enough to engage the 'play' mechanism. She wasn't ready to listen to it yet. Nor was she ready for the song that started blasting out of the speakers when the auto-tracker found a station at last. It was Men at Work singing 'Land Downunder'. Ellen tetchily punched off the power switch.

At that moment, her phone started ringing. As she reached out to grab it from the dashboard, she glanced up at the road just in time to see the sharp right-hand bend appear through the dappled shadows. She was driving way too fast to take it safely, but it was too late to brake, so she was forced to wrench the steering-wheel round, bite her tongue and pray that they didn't hit a tree. With the car on two wheels, they bucketed round, kicking up leaf mulch and dirt from the verge, the back end of the jeep fighting to find any grip. The ringing mobile phone slid along the dash and fell into the passenger-door glovebox. Fins' basket fell on to its side with a furious squawk of protest from its occupant. Snorkel cowered in the footwell, bracing herself against the steering column and inadvertently sitting on the accelerator pedal.

Miraculously the car stayed on the road.

Ellen let out a whoop of exhilaration as they careered around. 'Sorry, guys!'

It was then that she spotted the tiny unmanned level-crossing just ahead. The warning lights were flashing red. The barriers were coming down.

She screamed and punched her foot hard on the brake only to encounter the hard, rubbery resistance of a ball trapped beneath it.

'Bugger, bugger, BUGGER!' Ellen tried to kick away the ball and kicked Snorkel by mistake.

Yelping and trembling, Snorkel threw up a partly digested ham sandwich on to Ellen's trainer.

'I am not going to die with dog sick on my foot!' Ellen screamed what might have been the last words of her life.

Left with no choice, she grabbed for the handbrake with both hands and hauled it back, immediately putting the car into a lurching, sideways, uncontrolled slide towards the lowering barriers. She closed her eyes and braced herself as the seatbelt punched the air from her lungs.

A moment later, she was aware of an unnerving silence. No wailing cat, whining dog or droning engine, and certainly no super-fast train rattling along the track to wipe her out – just a beep-beep-beep warning from the level-crossing and the ding-ingle jaunty tune of her mobile ringing.

Very cautiously, she opened her eyes. The jeep had come to a halt at an acute angle just a few inches short of the now-closed barriers, its engine stalled.

She wound down her window and took a deep breath of air, grateful to be alive. Outside, it smelt of pine needles and burning rubber. Just audible above the crossing warning and the phone ringing, she could hear wood pigeons purring fatly from a tree far overhead. From the depths of the upturned cat basket, Fins heard it too and managed a greedy if traumatised little hunting call.

Ellen started to laugh.

She reached for the phone, checking that Snorkel was still all right. The blue-eyed collie had her ears glued nervously to the back of her head and was still looking decidedly nauseous, but seemed in one piece, still sitting on the accelerator. Looking back between the front seats as she reached across them, Ellen saw that Fins' basket was now upside down behind the passenger seat, but four little white paws were already thrashing angrily out of four separate holes, so she guessed he hadn't broken anything. He was certainly giving full-blooded cries of protest once more.

'Miaaaaaaaaeeeeeeeeooooooow!'

'Yup?' She took the call.

'Hello? Hello? Ellen, is that you? What *is* that noise?'

Ellen gently shifted the wicker cat basket the right way up, rolling her eyes as she realised who was calling. She might have guessed.

'Hi, Mum.' She lifted the basket on to the back seat once more and slid her finger through the mesh door to give Fins a comforting stroke.

'Where are you?' demanded Jennifer.

Fins glared back at Ellen through his basket's door, shook himself all over as he adjusted to being the right way up again, then took a vicious swipe at her.

'At the railway crossing,' she picked up the roll of kitchen towel that had landed on the floor too and swung back into the driver's seat, 'on the lane that goes past the abbey, you know?' She was very proud that she had found the 'hidden' lane so easily after all these years.

'Why are you going that way?' The line crackled, but there was no mistaking her mother's critical tone, with which Ellen was all-too familiar having lived with it both as daughter and, at one time, as pupil too.

'I didn't want to get stuck in the traffic in Lower Oddford – there's always coachloads of tourists milling about and double-parked hire cars on the bridges.'

'Nonsense. It's never that busy. And it's much quicker that way.'

'Well, I'm here now.' Ellen unrolled a hunk of paper with one hand and reached down to scoop up the regurgitated ham sandwich, watched by two guilty blue eyes. She blew Snorkel a forgiving kiss before carefully putting the unpleasant bundle into the empty plastic wrapper. Then she fished around underfoot to find the ball, struggling to pull it from beneath the brake pedal.

'. . . always get stuck at the crossing that way,' her mother was saying. 'Your father says the signal that triggers the lights is just outside Addington Junction, so one has to wait ages unless it's an express. Then there's . . .'

As soon as she'd freed the ball, Ellen was almost flattened by Snorkel, who took this as her cue to leap out of the footwell and start playing again, trying to snap the ball from her hands. 'Get off, you soppy bitch!' She laughed.

'I beg your pardon?' Jennifer demanded archly in her ear.

'Not you, Mum, the dog.'

'Oh no – you haven't brought that smelly creature of Richard's with you?' Her horror was audible. 'Why didn't he take it with him?'

'To Australia?'

'Well, it can't stay in the house.' She sniffed.

'She'll have to.' Ellen ruffled the tufted ears, which had now sprung forward and were pointing at her jauntily as Snorkel stood bridging the gap between the two front seats, front paws on Ellen's leg.

'It must sleep in the old dovecote,' Jennifer insisted. 'A dog in the house will put purchasers off. They smell and they're unhygienic.'

Ellen said nothing, pressing her nose to Snorkel's soft coat. She still smelt of the sea from her early-morning swim at Treglin Mouth – brackish and salty. A few grains of sand remained trapped between her pads and in the feathers on the backs of her legs. Ellen closed her eyes and breathed deeply, tears worryingly close as she said another silent farewell to her beloved coast.

'You should really be heading into the village on the Oddford road, you know,' her mother was lecturing. 'You have to pick up the keys from Dot, remember? And the Orchard Close estate is on the way if you'd chosen that route.' Jennifer Jamieson was the sort of woman who drew maps of the supermarket aisles to plan the most efficient route from fresh fruit and veg to Ernest & Julio Gallo.

'I think I can spare the diesel to detour and pick them up,' Ellen said patiently.

'You're running very late. I told Dot you'd be there in the morning.'

Why was her mother such a worrier? she wondered. She could imagine her in Spain, checking the clocks every ten minutes, subtracting the hour difference, and looking critically at the phone waiting for it to ring.

'It's not yet midday.' She squinted up at the corridor of hot azure sky above the railway track, in the centre of which the sun blistered like a magnifying-glass on an inflatable blue lilo. 'We set out before seven, but we had to stop for a wee.'

'We?'

'It's a natural bodily function. C'mon, Mum, you're the biology teacher.'

Jennifer tutted irritably. 'You know exactly what I mean. *We* as in, you and . . . who else?'

'Me and the animals.'

'The animals and *I*,' Jennifer corrected automatically. But she was clearly relieved that her daughter hadn't brought one of her scruffy surfer friends along with her. 'Pets are such a bind. It's cruel to drag them from pillar to post. Honestly, Ellen, how you think you'll be able to go globe-trotting with the responsibility of—'

'I'll find them homes,' Ellen assured her, not wanting to get into this conversation while sharing a car with her beloved charges. 'We had someone lined up in Cornwall, but it fell through.'

'Hmmm.' Jennifer was unimpressed. 'Well, please do try to restrict any damage they might cause to the cottage. It's so important to maintain an atmosphere of clean, calm tranquillity.'

'Miaaaaaaaaeeeeeeeeooooooow!' Suddenly Fins' head popped out from one of the holes he'd been chewing, much to his own surprise, it seemed. Wide-eyed with fright, he gazed around the inside of the car, then decided to pull the rest of his body through. But being a distinctly overweight cat, he ended up thrashing around like an overheated health-spa client trying to escape from a steam cabinet.

There was a familiar two-toned toot in the distance. The train was approaching at last. Ellen started winding up the window. 'Mum, I have to go – I'll call you from the cottage, okay?'

'Don't forget the alarm code. Nine zero zero five three, as in Goose—'

'No, I won't.'

'And make sure Dot gives you the keys to the bunkhouse as well as the cottage.'

'Yes.'

'And—' Her mother's voice was drowned as a three-carriage train came clattering past. The volume it generated probably wasn't very great in the scale of things, but because the jeep was almost on the rails, it rattled and shook as though being attacked by a thousand baboons in a wildlife park.

Snorkel started barking excitedly, tail whirling. Fins' head promptly disappeared back into the basket. Ellen threw the phone back on to the dash and started the engine.

They were soon climbing back up through the woods and out on to the natural shelf half-way along the slope that ran from the Hillcote side of the ridgeway down into the Lodes valley. This was more familiar territory to Ellen. She remembered coming up here one long-ago white Christmas to toboggan, and another time to walk with her father when his doctor had advised him to take regular exercise after his first heart-attack – he had not imagined that Theo Jamieson would interpret this as ten-mile hikes three times a week. She recognised the strange, steepled barn belonging to Brook Farm and the little stone bridge that crossed the brook.

'Wooooooooof, wooooooahhhhhh! Wooooof! Woof. woof! Hoooooooeeeeeeaaaa! *WOOF!*'

Now that she'd started barking, Snorkel had decided singing

was a much more entertaining game than throwing her ball around under Ellen's feet. Sitting on the passenger seat, she barked and howled delightedly, revelling in the power of her own lungs.

'Okay – five minutes.' Ellen pulled up beside a little green footpath sign, engaged the four-wheel drive, and reversed the jeep right up on to the thick verge until it was under an ivy-clogged hedge, which would afford Fins some shade.

Snorkel spun round and round on her seat, barking all the more as Ellen reached for her baseball cap and jumped out of the car.

It was blindingly bright outside, the sun flame-throwing scorched heat on to the landscape. Although high up, only the faintest of breezes moved the sweltering air. Whichever way Ellen turned her face to catch it, it was nothing compared to the cool, briny wind of the Cornish coast.

The backs of her thighs felt sticky and creased from so long crammed into the leather seat. She rubbed them as she walked, tugging her shorts out of her bottom, then following suit with her knickers. The home-made frayed denim cut-offs were little more than hot pants and had a nasty tendency to ride up, but they were great for driving long distances because they had a tough seat yet left the whole length of her legs free.

As she climbed up the footpath behind an eager Snorkel, her T-shirt was soon wringing with sweat. She was about to tuck it under her bra when she remembered she wasn't wearing one, having over-efficiently packed it the night before. Instead, she gripped the hem and fanned in air as she walked, a habit she'd had since childhood.

The path ran alongside a huge field of ripening rape and up to a derelict Dutch barn. Ellen longed to run it to shake off the static of her long journey, but she didn't want to overexcite Snorkel who always took running to mean four miles along a beach and lots of stick-throwing.

Instead she let the dog pounce on butterflies in the hedgerow and trudged up to the barn before turning back to look across the valley, eyes shaded by baseball-cap peak, sunglasses and one hand, yet still narrowed against the light.

She couldn't deny its beauty, however landlocked and far from the place she thought of as home.

The horseshoe ridge, which curled round from behind her to wrap the entire valley in its sleeping dinosaur embrace, had a broad, bony back crested with the needles of distant woods and coppices, and a single tall aerial mast that she didn't remember from previous visits. High in those marl hills lay the multitude of springs that fed the twisting, curling river Odd. Here and there lay tiny honey-stone farms and hamlets, creamy brown snails clinging to the leafy flanks, changing little over the years and barely touched by development.

At this time of year the valley was a riot of acid greens and yellows. It reminded Ellen of the vegetable terrine Richard used to make on special occasions, a hundred contrasting horizontal stripes of pea-green pasture and yellow-pepper crops, divided by spinach-dark hedgerows and dotted with black-olive woods, all dusted with a sprinkling of paprika poppies.

Its sheer breadth always struck her afresh when she visited. In Cornwall, the valleys were smaller and deeper, like the bed Snorkel made from her green bean bag, twisting and twisting around until she'd formed a deep, comforting hollow into which she packed herself as tightly as possible.

But the Lodes Valley bed had been made by a huge pack of hounds that liked to sprawl out nose-to-tail on a vast, lumpy, green-striped mattress, stretching their legs along its many plateaux, burying their noses in the dips and hollows, chewing corners from the upholstery and hiding treats and bones among the pillows. And the juiciest bone lay in its green centre.

There was Oddlode, by far the biggest of the valley's few villages, lying on the crossroads that was formed by the wriggling Odd and the arrow-straight railway line – although the two were only distinguishable from where Ellen stood by the dark line of trees that flanked them. With its Cotswold-stone church spire and clusters of tawny cottages and grand houses, Oddlode looked, from a distance, like the ultimate cliché village jewel. Jennifer Jamieson certainly described it as such in her rather florid home-produced brochures that had, for many years, attracted families to holiday in Goose Cottage. 'Picture an exquisite brooch. At its centre is a sapphire set in a flawless emerald. That is Oddlode village green and its duck pond. Surrounding it is the gold filigree of tiny Cotswold stone cottages, breathtaking in their intricacy. That is the heart of Oddlode.'

Over the years Ellen had kept her visits to a minimum, but she knew it wasn't quite the crown jewel of the Cotswolds her mother made it out to be. Compared to picture-postcard Lower Oddford, Oddlode was an ungainly ugly sister – less touristy, hard-working, riddled with conflicts.

Her parents had moved there soon after she left her childhood home in the Quantock Hills to take up her place at Exeter University. It had long been Jennifer's dream to live in the Cotswolds, and the family had headed inland to holiday in the neighbouring Foxrush valley many times, always staying in the same guesthouse. For years, indulgent Theo Jamieson had assured his wife that they would live there one day. Having patiently waited until her daughter finished school, Jennifer bade farewell to Gorsemoor Comprehensive the same summer as Ellen, resigning as deputy head and taking a far less well-paid job teaching part-time at Market Addington sixth-form college.

This had hardly seemed to matter because the move was funded by Ellen's father finally agreeing to work from his company's London office, a transfer he'd long been offered but had thus far managed to resist.

When they lived near Taunton, it had taken Theo just fifteen minutes to drive to work. The train from Oddlode station to Paddington took an hour and a half, and then it was another half-hour by crowded tube to get to Chancery Lane. From the Cotswolds, the quickest journey into work he could hope for was over two hours.

Ellen calculated that her father, in transit for four hours a day five days a week, had spent over four thousand hours on a train before he had his first heart-attack on the six fifteen from Paddington to Hereford and Worcester. That was four years after the move, and he had spent five solid months of the time sitting on a train. By then Jennifer had spent just as much time – and a great deal of money – doing up the outdated if pretty Goose Cottage, converting the attics into bedrooms, having en-suites fitted and a utility extension added. It was to be her dream cottage.

It took a further thousand hours on a train for Theo to have his second heart-attack – the one that almost killed him on the Central Line between Oxford Circus and Tottenham Court Road; the crowds around him had thought he was drunk. By then Jennifer had converted Goose Cottage's thatched barn into a carport with a guest suite above, had spared no expense in getting the garden landscaped, and a fitted kitchen, complete with shiny blue Aga.

Ellen and Richard had been surfing off the Costa de la Luz when it happened, staying in a run-down Spanish campsite with a host of other travellers. It had been weeks before she found out how ill her father was. Tanned and impossibly healthy, she'd returned to find him sitting in a part-landscaped garden that he'd part paid for, reading the horror story that was his bank statement. The doctors had told him to find a less stressful job, take more holidays, take it easy – it was that, or take out life insurance in the certain knowledge that it would be cashed in before many more months were up.

Jennifer was haunted with guilt. While Theo recuperated, she took in paying holiday guests who stayed in the expensive barn guest suite and were fed full English breakfasts cooked on the expensive blue Aga. The money helped, but it wasn't enough for Theo to give up work.

Her father spent a further two thousand hours on a train before he retired. These journeys were mercifully uninterrupted by another heart-attack, although the doctors said this was more by luck than by design. He had finally stopped renewing his season ticket after he had spent six hours in an operating theatre undergoing a triple heart bypass. By then he had paid for his wife's dream cottage and saved up a small fund for early retirement.

He'd also managed to take a few more holidays, mostly in Spain, which he'd wanted to explore further after Ellen's vivid descriptions of the unspoiled coasts she and Richard had discovered far from the tourist trail. Like his daughter, Theo loved the sea. It was on one of these holidays that he had fallen in love with a ramshackle *finca* high in the hills above the Costa Verde, on the market for the same price as a second-hand Jaguar. Soon afterwards, the Jamiesons became a one-car couple with a second home. The same year, Market Addington sixth-form college was amalgamated with nearby St Jude's secondary school and Mrs Jamieson, commonly known as 'Bismarck' (because she always gave abysmal marks) was offered early retirement.

Which was when, by a curious twist of fate, Jennifer and Theo Jamieson's life took on uncanny parallels to their daughter's, although Ellen's mother refused to admit it. For the past four years, the couple had spent summers and Christmases in the Cotswolds, the rest of the year in Spain wrestling with local bureaucracy and builders as Theo created his dream retirement villa overlooking the sea. Goose Cottage was let as a holiday home while they were away and, because Jennifer's expensively enhanced dream cottage appealed to every tourist's idea of a Cotswold village idyll, it was rarely empty. The money paid the Spanish builders but, as always with the Jamiesons, there was little cash left in the pot.

Just days before Theo's beloved *finca* was declared fully restored, his restored heart staged a protest. It was only a minor attack, the Spanish doctors concluded. A warning bell. Enjoy your home, Señor, they said. Travel less. Put your feet up on your beautiful terrace beside your beautiful pool with the beautiful views across to the sea. Do what all the doctors have been telling you for years.

With their modest combined pensions topped up by holiday-rental income, the Jamiesons knew that they could not really afford to keep both the *finca* and the cottage, but neither wanted to relinquish their dream.

Jennifer wailed and cried and fought with everything in her

armoury to keep Goose Cottage, the lifelong fantasy that had almost killed her husband in the making.

Theo put up a sterling fight. He wanted to stay in Spain. He loved the climate, the golf and the people. He had never enjoyed the petty-mindedness of Oddlode and, because he had spent so much of his time there travelling to and from London, he'd never fully joined in village life as his wife had. To retire to Goose Cottage would mean continuing the B-and-B to provide an income, and he hated strangers tramping around when he was trying to read the *Telegraph* over breakfast.

He offered his wife a compromise. They would sell Goose Cottage and buy somewhere smaller in the village – perhaps one of the little cottages that nestled to the south of the green, once alms-houses and peppercorn-rent artisan cottages, now beloved of weekenders and young couples intent on turning a profit. Goose Cottage was far too large for them anyway, and Ellen and Richard showed no signs of starting a family . . .

That was when Jennifer woke up and realised that her dream had never really come true. She didn't particularly like Oddlode any more, either. Not modern Oddlode, with its unfamiliar faces, its youth drug problem, its constant threats of development and, most especially, the way she was now perceived as an old-guard bossyboots. She loved her dream cottage, and she loved the magnificent manor, the noble church, duck pond, post-office stores and olde-worlde pubs. It was the people she didn't like nowadays. So many old friends had moved away, and she'd alienated the few who remained by being absent so often that she missed the day-to-day gossip – also because her fabled archness and snobbery had ripened rather than mellowed with old age. Perhaps most tellingly, to be seen to 'downsize' to a smaller cottage in the village would crucify her. In Spain, high up on their hill in the beautifully restored *finca*, she and Theo were king and queen of the castle.

So when Jennifer found out how much Goose Cottage was worth – almost exactly ten times what they had paid for it eleven years earlier – she was left in no doubt that they should sell. If it went for the asking price, they could afford to visit Oddlode in pure luxury, staying in nearby Eastlode Park – one of the most expensive country-house hotels in England – for a fortnight every year for the rest of their lives without denting the capital in the investment accounts.

But Goose Cottage had not sold for the asking price: it hadn't sold at all. Nobody, it seemed, wanted to buy Jennifer Jamieson's dream.

At first, they blamed the market – putting a property up for sale in the first week of January was bound to mean a slow start, however much Jennifer had wanted to spend one last Christmas there before selling. Yet almost six months later, it had attracted just one laughable offer, so low that when he received the fax, Theo had suggested to the agents that they had mistakenly left off a zero.

The Jamiesons were baffled. Property in Oddlode was like gold dust because the railway station made it possible to commute to London. The junior school was reputedly the best in West Oxfordshire and had a ferocious waiting list: it was far too small to accommodate every pupil whose eager parents longed for their child to be taught there. For-sale signs rarely stayed up in Oddlode for more than a fortnight. Goose Cottage was often talked about as 'the prettiest in the village'. Why didn't anyone want it? The agent – the best in the area, everyone agreed – seemed equally baffled.

The Jamiesons needed to get to the bottom of the problem, but Theo's health made travelling difficult and neither relished the prospect of returning to Oddlode. In fact, now that her mind was made up, Jennifer flatly refused to return to see her dream cottage on the market. She had said her farewells at Christmas, contacted a reputable removals and shipping company, who were poised for action, and that, as far as she was concerned, was that. She refused to let Theo travel alone. But with no holiday rental from Goose Cottage now that it was for sale, things were desperate.

Which was where Ellen came in. Unlike Goose Cottage, the Shack (a far less des. res., built from a flat-pack and perched jauntily on a clifftop) had sold before the agent's brochures were printed. It had sold before either Richard or Ellen was ready, before they had divided up their few possessions, found homes for their pets or applied for their visas, in Richard's case to Australia, in Ellen's to the World.

Detouring via Oddlode *en route* to the World would not have been on Ellen's travel itinerary had she found time to write one, but saying no to her mother was not an easy option. She could use her time there to plan her trip, Jennifer pointed out. She could treat it as a holiday, enjoy the cottage – she'd hardly stayed there, after all.

They both knew why. Jennifer's hatred of Richard had made those few stays uncomfortable. Her obvious jubilation that the relationship was over was so infuriating that Ellen longed to tell her to get stuffed. She'd always disliked twee, over-perfect Goose Cottage and blamed it for her father's ill-health. She had eventually agreed to go there for her father's sake. She could have stayed in Cornwall with friends until she was better organised, but she had known that, sooner or later, Theo Jamieson would defy his wife and come home to try to sort things out. She hated to think of him away from his precious Spanish coast, stuck in a village he disliked, living in a house that had almost killed him in the making.

She planned to make her stay as short as possible. She would get the cottage sold, find homes for Snorkel and Fins, plot out her trip, book her first flight, pack her rucksack and leave. With any luck, it shouldn't take more than a fortnight.

Back at the jeep, Fins was looking out of the hole in his basket again, his swivelling head resembling a fluffy black and white periscope.

While Snorkel jumped back into the car, Ellen quickly checked the surfboards on the roof rack, still annoyed at herself for not taking the money that Foley's Sports in Bude had offered her for them. By telling them to shove their paltry hundred pounds where the sun didn't shine, she was still lumbered with the last thing that a Cotswold tourist needed. By contrast, she'd taken fifty pounds for her bike from Trisha at the pottery, and now wished she'd held on to it for a few more weeks. The lanes here were cycling heaven and she needed to stay fit.

Her T-shirt was dark with sweat now and felt disgustingly clammy. She grabbed the top bag from the boot and dug inside it for a fresh one. She checked around – there hadn't been a car in sight the entire time she'd been walking, so she was hardly worried – then quickly set about swapping, forgetting that she was still wearing a baseball cap, anchored to her head by the ponytail pulled through its back. With her face full of hot, wet cotton and her arms trapped above her shoulders, Ellen swung her head around irritably, trying to get the neck of the T-shirt beyond her ponytail and the cap's peak.

Of course, that was the exact moment when the first traffic the lane had seen for twenty minutes rounded the corner. And it wasn't any old traffic. It was a huge lorry with three surprised faces lined up at the windscreen. Ellen knew this because it drew level just as she broke free of her wrestling hold.

Amazingly, her dark glasses and baseball cap had stayed on, affording her a degree of anonymity, if little modesty. She had no choice but to brazen it out. Holding the T-shirt to her chest, she saluted them as they passed. She didn't even get a beep in return. On the rear of the lorry was emblazoned 'Horses'.

'Welcome to the Cotswolds,' Ellen told Snorkel and Fins, as she pulled on the fresh T-shirt, 'where legovers happen from mounting blocks, going out on the pull means clay pigeon shooting, and sharking is what American tourists call the prices in the antique shops.'

Orchard Close was a tidy, modern council estate built of Cotswold stone. The residents took a great deal of pride in it, and most of the immaculate little front gardens were a triumph of psychedelic geometry as rectangular flower-beds overflowed with primary-coloured blossoms, like ballpits in a children's playground. Which was why the few unkempt gardens stood out. And of those, the Wycks' was by far the most disorderly. Nettles and sedge swayed at waist height to either side of Ellen as she let herself through the broken gate and made her way gingerly up the uneven path, anxious not to get stung on her bare legs.

Loud drum 'n' bass was thumping out of a top window, which was, she saw, not open as she'd first thought but simply missing an entire pane of glass. When she knocked on the door, a thunderous bark made her step back. A moment later something that appeared to be the size of a small rhino started throwing itself bodily against the other side of the door, snarling madly.

Ellen decided to wait a safe distance away, noticing as she retreated that one of the downstairs windows was broken too, the smashed pane patched up with cardboard and gaffer-tape. Several ancient bicycle wheels and half a lawnmower were propped up against the wall.

The drum 'n' bass kept thumping, but nobody came to the door. Bracing herself, she knocked again, but there was no reply. The barking rhino let out a demented howl and tried to eat her through the letterbox, foiling Ellen's plan to take a peek through it.

She looked up at the glassless window and shouted, 'Hello,' a few times. Nothing.

A group of kids who'd been practising BMX tricks on the road when she arrived had cycled up and were now studying her thoughtfully as she hung around the Wycks' front door wondering what to do.

'You Wycky's new girlfriend?' asked one.

Ellen gave him an 'uh?' look over her shoulder. She hardly thought she looked like the type who would go for Reg Wyck who, from what little she remembered, was about sixty, wore the same stained overalls everywhere, looked like Lester Piggott and had the easy conversational patter to match. 'Is he in, do you know?' she asked, picking her way back towards the gate. 'Or Dot, maybe?'

'Dot ain't there – saw her leave a while back, din' we?' said one of the bikers, who was checking out the jeep. 'Nice motor – what are those things?'

'Surfboards.' Ellen grinned.

'Cool!' The boy dropped his bike so that he could climb up to take a better look, driving Snorkel mad as she jumped between the seats inside trying to scrabble her way out and make introductions.

'Oi – look all you like but don't touch, okay?' Ellen warned cheerfully, glancing back at the house. 'Is anyone in there?'

Another of the boys, who was staring at Ellen's long, tanned legs in the same awe-inspired way as his mate was staring at the surfboards, nodded mutely. Then, to prove a point, he put both little fingers in his mouth and let out a shrieking whistle. The rhino dog took this as a cue to throw itself at the door even more violently, growling and snarling so much it sounded as though it was ripping apart a mud hut. A moment later, the drum 'n' bass was cut and a head appeared through the missing window.

Ellen's memories of Dot and Reg might have been vague but she knew that neither had a buzz-cut, a pierced eyebrow and a home-made blue-ink tattoo on their neck.

'Whatdyawant, Kyle?' He glared at the boy.

'Lady here to see you, Wycky,' Kyle shouted. From the fear in his voice, Ellen thought, 'Wycky' was clearly a force to be reckoned with. And, having been asleep, he looked as though he was in a very bad mood.

'Eh?' He yawned widely, showing a lot of gold teeth, before noticing the jeep, then Ellen, and blinking hard to make sure he really was seeing what he thought he was.

'I'm Ellen Jamieson!' she called, hopping back down the path and trying to be heard over the rhino dog. 'I've come to col-lect—'

'SHUT THE FUCK UP, FLUFFY!' he yelled.

Ellen balked in surprise. Then, when the rhino dog suddenly stopped barking, she chewed back a wry smile because maybe she wasn't so unlike her mother, after all.

Fluffy wouldn't win any obedience classes at Crufts: within seconds he was barking again so loudly that the door rattled on its hinges.

'I've come to collect the keys,' Ellen called up to 'Wycky', miming unlocking a door. '*Goose Cottage*. Keys.'

'Eh?' he shouted, not hearing a word but using his high vantage-point to look down her T-shirt and decide that perhaps this was worth getting out of bed for. 'Hang on – I'll come out.'

Ellen turned away and lifted her face to the sun, anticipating a short wait. She almost jumped out of her skin when, the next moment, he landed beside her.

'Christ.' She looked from him to the window and back. It was certainly a novel route to the front garden, but she guessed it avoided dealing with Fluffy. And he clearly used it often because the BMX kids, who were still hanging round the jeep, didn't look remotely surprised.

'Saul Wyck,' he introduced himself, checking out her body slowly with the bluest pair of eyes Ellen had ever seen.

'Ellen Jamieson.' She eyed him through her shades in return. He was a few inches shorter than her, and built like a boxer with vast, muscular shoulders and a legion of small scars embossing his face. It was quite a handsome face, although its belligerent expression did it no favours. 'Are you Reg's son?'

'Grandson.' He narrowed one bright blue eye and studied her suspiciously. 'Why d'you want to know?'

'I've come for the Goose Cottage keys – I'm Theo and Jennifer's daughter.'

'First I've heard of it.' He crossed his arms defensively.

'Your grandmother's expecting me.'

'Nan's out – gone to the market. Won't be back till teatime now.'

Ellen glanced at her watch. It was only just after midday. Dot hadn't given her much grace to be late. 'Is Reg around, maybe?'

'In the pub.' He looked over his shoulder at the jeep, taking in the loaded roof racks and boot crammed high with bags and boxes. 'Always is on a Saturday.'

Ellen remembered her father telling her that Reg was a big drinker who rarely moved from the bar of the Lodes Inn from sundown on Friday until last orders on Sunday. Stories of his drunken antics were village folklore. 'Oh – right. Maybe I should pop over there and see if your nan's left the keys with him.'

Saul cackled delightedly. 'Won't get no sense out of him. Besides, Nan wouldn't trust him with them keys.'

Ellen took off her dark glasses and rubbed her eyes tiredly, not relishing the prospect of hanging around the village green until teatime with an overexcited dog and a furious cat. Even less waiting here with Saul and Fluffy. 'Do you know where they're kept?'

He rubbed his tongue over his teeth, blue eyes narrowed. 'Might do.'

Ellen cocked her head. She was starting to find his surly attitude seriously irritating. She knew that he was probably only protecting her parents' cottage by not trusting her word, but she hated being disbelieved. She mustn't start a fight. She always did this.

'Would you mind finding them for me?' she asked, as politely as she could.

Not budging an inch, Saul carried on the teeth-rubbing routine, which was clearly intended to intimidate but made him look as though a stubborn raspberry pip was wedged between his molars.

'You don't look much like Mrs J.' He took another long look at her legs and boobs. 'D'you know your T-shirt's on inside out?'

'Okay,' Ellen said impatiently. 'I admit my mother doesn't wear her clothes inside out. Nor does she bleach her hair, have three body piercings or a tattoo of the Burning Man on her shoulder – it's true. But we've got the same nose and I can show you my passport if you want proof.'

'I'd rather see your tattoo.' He grinned, flashing the gold teeth again and a few broken ones too. 'D'you like mine? Nice work, innit? Really detailed.'

For a moment Ellen thought he was referring to the stained blue blotch on his neck, which could have been anything from a spider to a swastika. But he was already pulling up his T-shirt sleeve proudly to reveal a colourful unicorn leaping across his biceps.

It was very nice work, Ellen had to admit, although too garish for her taste, and she wasn't too sure about the nubile vampire page three girl riding bareback on it, who was more like a busty Morticia Addams than Pamela Anderson.

'Lovely – really good work,' she said enthusiastically, eager to keep thawing him and get her hands on the keys. Mentioning the tattoo had clearly been an inspired move, if accidental.

'Show us yours, then.' He grinned, blue eyes gleaming like hot little gas flames. Perhaps he was thawing a little too quickly, Ellen worried.

Deliberately misunderstanding the suggestion, she turned and headed for the car to find her passport, her bottom now the subject of close examination. The bike kids, having become bored with looking at adults discussing keys, were winding up Snorkel by pulling faces at her. Fins had upped periscope again, and was glaring at them furiously.

'Blimey.' Saul cackled when she'd finally unearthed the little burgundy book and handed it to him. 'Bit different there, aintcha?'

'It was a few years ago.' Ellen glanced at the fresh-faced girl with braided, multicoloured hair and henna-tattoo choker.

'Ellen . . . Gabriella . . . Jamieson,' he read out, hamming up his security check in a bad Dixon of Dock Green impersonation. 'Sex . . . female. Mmm, I can see that. Born twelfth of the twelfth nineteen seventy-four. You're quite old, arencha?'

Ellen tried to snatch back the passport, but he held it up teasingly, still leafing through.

'Wow! Look at all these stamps.' He whistled.

'I travel a lot,' she muttered.

'I ain't never been abroad.' He snapped it shut and handed it back, surly and uncommunicative again, the tattoo's company moment gone as he eyed her broodily from beneath his pierced eyebrows.

'So is it okay if I take the keys now?' she asked carefully, trying hard not to put his back up further.

'Stay here.' He nodded curtly, and swaggered to the door

against which Fluffy had ceased hurling himself and was now just howling.

'Jesus.' Ellen held her breath as the door opened and something that looked like a giant sabre-toothed sheep flew outside with hackles raised. Saul grabbed its collar and hauled it back, slamming the door behind him.

'Al's Rottweiler got randy with the Old English Sheepdog that used to live at the Pheasant.' The kids were back, hanging over the gate, eager to fill Ellen in on Fluffy's lineage, which clearly fascinated them. 'All the other pups died and Al was going to drown Fluffy 'cos his mum din' want him, but Reg took him. He was only a few days old. My mum reckons Reg reared him on beer and that's why he's so mean. She says Fluffy's a public menace and that Al should've drowned him after all.'

'Who's Al?'

'Landlord at the Lodes Inn.'

So Fluffy was the result of a canine *Romeo and Juliet* union between Oddlode's two rival pubs. 'Doesn't look like a pub lick menace to me.' She glanced at the door, which was once again under assault. 'More likely to bite than lick, I'd say.'

'You not from round here, then?'

She shook her head.

'Saul can sort you out with anyfink,' they told her wisely. 'He's cool.'

'I'll bear that in mind.' She smiled weakly, and turned back to the house from which Saul was emerging, using the standard route this time rather than the window and fighting hard to keep Fluffy at bay.

He had a big bunch of keys in one hand – enough to access every house in Oddlode, it seemed – and set about peeling several off the ring.

'You sure they're the right ones?' she asked, wondering if he knew what he was doing.

'Yup,' he muttered, clearly not entirely happy to hand them over, and cursing as the bunch twisted round in his hands.

'Mum said to make sure the bunkhouse keys are with them.'

'That's these ones.' He was still trying to pull apart a stubborn fob with grubby fingernails.

Ellen waited patiently, batting away a wasp that had come buzzing up.

'You only staying a couple of days, yeah?' he asked over-casually.

'I said I'd stay until the house is sold, so I don't know how long that'll be.' She hoped he wasn't going to ask her on a date. However much she loved the idea of getting one over on her snobbish mother, who accused her of choosing men 'beneath herself' (Richard), she knew a dodgy and dangerous character when she saw one. Saul Wyck was not a man to encourage. Two glasses of house white and a bag of Scampi Fries in the local, and you could find yourself stalked for life.

But he seemed more interested in Goose Cottage.

'Someone'll want it soon enough, I reckon.' He tried to prise apart the ring with his gold teeth. 'Nice house, that. What's going to happen to all the stuff in it?'

'Most of it's getting shipped to Spain, I think. Not my problem.' She had only agreed to try to get a decent offer then wait until contracts were exchanged; she had no intention of overseeing another house move. 'I'm just here to spruce it up a bit – although I'm sure your grandparents keep it looking really nice,' she added quickly, realising this might cause offence. 'Mum wants it to look lived-in, that's all.'

He raised a scarred eyebrow and said nothing.

'D'you know what day they come? Only I'd better make sure I'm there to let them in now they won't have keys.'

'Dunno.' He handed over the keys, not looking at her. 'Depends.'

'That's okay – I can ask your nan another time. Thanks, I really appreciate this.'

'Sure.' He rubbed his chin on his shoulder, glancing up.

At that moment, Ellen felt an involuntary shudder rattle through her. The expression in those blue eyes was totally unexpected: he looked angry. Furiously, murderously angry.

But just as suddenly he smiled it away. 'Enjoy your stay.'

*   *   *

'We're so nearly there!' she promised her stir-crazy pets, as she turned left out of Orchard Close and back over the mill-chase bridge. The old mill was still in a terrible state, she noticed, its forecourt full of clapped-out cars and rusting tractors. She would have liked to stop off at the post-office stores for some cigarettes, but Fins' head was popping in and out of its peephole like a demented jack-in-the-box, and Snorkel was singing again. It wasn't fair on them to delay their escape a moment longer. She tried not to look at the shop's tempting Walls ice-cream board beside her as she waited to turn right opposite the wisteria-coated Lodes Inn and into Manor Lane.

The lane marked the start of the village's 'back loop', which ran round the walled gardens and grounds of Oddlode Manor. To the left, the manor towered in splendid isolation among its formal gardens. To the right, a tight huddle of old estate-workers' cottages and converted barns fought for space. As the lane swung round to become North Street, with the long drive to Manor Farm on the right, the cottages became much bigger and further apart. This was wealthy Oddlode, beloved of professional families and very rich weekenders. Most of the houses had at least one small paddock containing fat ponies or hobby sheep. Set back behind verges as deep and well-kempt as golf fairways, and shaded by a row of horse-chestnuts, North Street was *Country Living* heaven, lovingly tended by tens of Jennifers who had created their own dream houses and cottages over the decades.

At its far end, North Street forked into Goose End to the right, an unmade no-through-road leading past the Gothically decrepit old Lodge to the Odd river; and to the left, Goose Lane, which looped back to the main village road. And behind the deepest of plumped-up verges on the corner of North Street and Goose Lane, like little Miss Muffet sitting on her tuffet, was the 'prettiest cottage in Oddlode'.

Ellen's first impression as she swung into the gravel drive that had been cut into the verge was her usual one. How pretty. How twee. How Mum.

Under their neatly sculpted black thatched roofs, Goose Cottage, its dovecote and the converted barn always reminded Ellen of a raven-haired fairytale princess with two little sisters. Their black hair was braided and set, studded with tall chimneys like amber hairslides. Their tanned faces were exquisitely pretty with huge dark eyes blinking innocently in the sunlight. And those coy faces were covered with flowered veils – yellow climbing honeysuckle, purple wisteria, bright blue clematis, pink roses and white jasmine.

But Ellen knew these princesses were spoiled monsters. And they were looking surprisingly ragged, as though they'd had one too many late nights at society balls.

'Blimey.' She looked around her as she parked on the big gravel sweep between the garage barn and the cottage. She jumped out, letting Snorkel dash to the nearest patch of grass for a wee. The collie instantly disappeared into what had once been the Jamiesons' front lawn like an explorer into the Brazilian jungle.

The grass was knee-high.

Anxious not to let the dog out on to the lane, Ellen went to close the gates, which had been open when she arrived – another curiosity. Jennifer never allowed the gates to be left open: Theo had started and finished every one of his daily trips to the station by jumping out of the car to deal with the wrought-iron monsters.

She turned back and leaned against them, staring up at the cottage. Most of the leaded mullion windows were almost covered by the climbers. The unruly honeysuckle hung in fronds from the stone sills like false eyelashes. The windows themselves were so dusty and rain-marked behind their flowered awnings that they looked like opaque glass. Jennifer's 'herb trough' (as featured in *Cotswold Homes* magazine) was now frothing over with nothing but rampant sage and ground elder. There was litter everywhere – crisp packets, drinks bottles, empty cigarette boxes. A ripped blue tarpaulin had been discarded by the path, alongside a length of yellow hose-pipe and a compost bag crawling with wood lice. The potted bay trees that had once played sentry duty to the porch were lying on their sides, dead and brown-leafed.

When Ellen let herself into the porch there was a big bootmark on the lichen-green front door. She rushed to turn off the alarm, carrying Fins in his vibrating basket, but it wasn't set. Ellen stood still and looked about her.

The flagstone floor of the dining room was coated with dried muddy footprints and the table piled high with unopened mail. The house smelt unloved and unlived-in – dusty and stale, with an unexpected, familiar undertone of beer, cigarettes and greasy food, like a pub.

She soon found out why. As she turned left into the big kitchen, her mother's pride and joy, she saw several cigarette ends on the quarry tiles, ground underfoot by whoever had smoked them. Round the corner, the long, scrubbed pine table was loaded to breaking point with empty cans and bottles, and the remnants of several takeaways, which had attracted a haze of flies and a scattering of mouse droppings.

'Ugh – Jesus!' Ellen took the cat basket through to the utility room and rested it on the surface, making sure Fins had a good view out into the garden through the long, low windows. She'd let him out as soon as she had fetched his litter tray from the car, but first she had to check that the house was empty.

It was, if empty meant no human occupants. But there were mouse droppings in most rooms, and a dead pigeon in the attic study. Nothing appeared to have been stolen – just used and abused.

Whoever had been using Goose Cottage had confined themselves to three rooms and had taken full advantage of their plush surroundings. While the kitchen was clearly booze, food and party central, the sitting room was the 'cinema and games room', with the cabinet that housed the huge television and video gaping open and an unfamiliar PlayStation plugged in – Ellen was certain her parents didn't own such a thing. Oddly, there were no videos or game CDs in sight, just saucers brimming with yet more cigarette butts, another collection of soft-drink and beer cans and a lot of stains on Jennifer's cream furnishings.

Upstairs, the master bedroom was utter chaos. The bed had seen some serious action, and the culprits hadn't been too fussy about laundering sheets or clearing away used tissues and condoms. To get them in the mood, they'd burned tens of fat church candles, which had dripped wax all over the furniture, left smoky trails on the pale walls and at one point, it seemed, set light to both a corner of one curtain and an entire pillow.

'Oh, bugger.' Ellen rubbed her face. Her mother would be distraught if she knew.

It was hard to believe that the ancient, squabbling Wycks had been using Goose Cottage to spice up their marriage. But Dot certainly hadn't cleaned here in recent months, and Reg hadn't touched the riotous garden. Looking out at it from her parents' bedroom window, Ellen thought it looked more beautiful than she'd ever seen it, especially with Snorkel bounding through the overgrown flowerbeds like a spring lamb, white head tilting this way and that as she tried to snap at a bumble bee.

The mobile phone in her back pocket started ringing.

'Yup?'

'You *must* be there now, surely?' demanded Jennifer.

'Just arrived.' She chewed her lip, wondering what the hell to say.

'Everything okay?'

Ellen turned to look at the bed. One . . . two . . . three used condoms in sight from where she stood. It reminded her of some of the squalid places she and Richard had stayed in on the surf trail. In fact, it looked like their bedroom in the Shack during the first long, hot, loved-up summer they had lived there.

'Fine,' she said. 'Absolutely fine.'

'You haven't let that dog inside, have you?'

'No, she's in the garden.'

'For God's sake don't let it run around unsupervised out there. Reg is very particular about his beds.'

'Is he?' Ellen patted one column of the four-poster, noticing that long black silk scarves had been tied to each one. Kinky.

'And it mustn't be allowed to foul the lawns. There's nothing more offputting than a beautiful stretch of striped grass with a great dog plop in the middle of it.'

'Quite.' Ellen turned to look at the garden, which was as tall, wild and luscious as the Goose Cottage paddock beyond. For all she could see, the entire canine population of Oddlode could have been using this new meadow as a doggy loo. 'I'll make sure she goes out on her walks.'

'Be sure to scoop! Mr Gardner and I fought long and hard to get poop bins in the village.'

'Oh, I will,' she promised.

'And *do* try to enjoy yourself,' Jennifer added, as an afterthought.

'Yes.' Ellen watched as Snorkel rolled wantonly in something undoubtedly very smelly by the pond. 'You know, I think you're right, Mum. I might enjoy my stay here.'

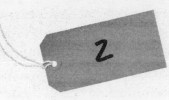

2

The village stores in Oddlode saw little action on a Saturday afternoon because the post-office section was closed. A traditional congregating place for the Oddlode pensioners to pass the time of day, the narrow counter was a shuttered, darkened corner when Ellen pinged her way into the store. But the four people inside were still quadruple the number she usually encountered in the tiny front-room Treglin shop, and she found herself smiling politely at the crowd as she would when entering Bude Safeway.

Two ramblers were choosing cold drinks at the chilled cabinet, and a pink-cheeked elderly woman was deep in conversation with a short, plump man in a loud shirt, both standing in front of the counter. 'Gone up to Lincolnshire with the rest of the hunters to turn them out to their summer grazing, she has. How she expects to get back in time, I have no idea, but she's left me to organise everything.'

'That's real mean,' her companion sympathised, in an American accent.

Looking around, Ellen barely recognised the interior of the shop. Outside it might be the same – a village institution for more than a century, forming the pretty, buttery cornerstone of the long terrace of cottages that clustered around the join of Station and School Lanes. But inside it had been gutted since her last visit. One wall now consisted entirely of cooled shelves and freezer cabinets, crammed full of classy delicatessen fare – fresh filled pasta, oak-smoked Cheddar, Ben and Jerry's ice-cream. There wasn't a Bird's Eye Ocean Pie or a Ginster's pasty in sight. Gone were the Blue Nuns and half-bottles of gin that had once gathered dust on shelves behind the till: a large wine and spirits selection offered discount bin ends and a one-week-only special offer on Pimm's. And as well as the usual range of stock staples, the shop now boasted freshly baked bread and cakes, magazines and newspapers, greetings cards and postcards, Cotswold souvenirs and even a video library offering the latest releases at an unbelievable one pound a night.

'. . . then them wine-merchant people phone to say they can't deliver today, and I tried to get Lady B on her module phone but after it rings a few times I see she's left it right on the desk in front of me . . .'

'What a nuisance.' The American nodded. Ellen guessed from the Hawaiian shirt and immaculate Bermuda shorts that he was an unfortunate tourist who had wandered in for a postcard or a film for his camera, and become trapped with the chatterbox shopkeeper. She didn't really want to relieve his shift, so hurriedly set about getting what she wanted.

She grabbed a bag of cat litter, a loaf of bread and a carton of milk to take to the counter. There, she waited to be served, but the pink-faced biddy was still mid-flow. 'So I called that lot at the Pheasant – I mean the Duck Upstream or whatever they call it now – and says, 'Can you help?' and that uppity madam says, 'I've already donated a meal for two, what do you want now? Blood?' and then she puts the phone down. I mean, how *rude* – of course Lady B would pay them, but I didn't have a chance to—'

'Excuse me?' Ellen waggled her milk politely. 'May I pay?'

The biddy patted her chest. 'Look at me, talking away when I've a hundred things to do. I am sorry, dear.' She flashed a sweet smile that puckered slightly as her gaze pressed carriage return on Ellen's hot-pants shorts and crop top. 'Mustn't keep you waiting.' Then, to Ellen's surprise, she walked out of the shop with a jaunty 'ping' of the door.

'Well, whaddaya know! I thought she'd never go.' The plump American chuckled, clapped his hands together and headed behind the till. 'Okay, young lady, let's ring these babies up.'

He grabbed a barcode reader and started waving it over Ellen's meagre purchases.

'Can I put a card up in your window?' she asked as he did so, feeling in her back pocket for the piece of paper she'd written out.

'Sure can – it's fifty pence a week.'

'I'll take a fortnight.' Ellen handed it over.

He read it at arm's length. 'Kind homes needed for well-behaved ten-month-old Border collie bitch and three-year-old black and white cat (male nutter). Can separate. Call Ellen on . . .'

'It's neuter,' Ellen pointed out. 'Male *neuter*, not nutter.'

'Ah!' He chuckled again, flipping it over to make a note of its expiry date on the back. 'Neuter, not nutter. That's kinda funny.'

'Well, actually he's both,' Ellen admitted.

'That's even funnier.' The round, cheerful face beamed, and Ellen realised that this was what Father Christmas would look like clean-shaven. 'We haven't seen you in here before, have we?'

'Not for years.' She dug through her purse for a fiver.

'We've only been here six months.' He thrust out a big, warm hand. 'Joel Lubowski. Swell to make your acquaintance, Ellen.'

'And yours. Hi. The shop looks great.' She smiled back, and turned as the door pinged again. A *bona fide* Goth swept in – female, black hair, white makeup and long black coat despite the sweltering day. Not looking at Joel, Ellen or the ramblers – who had now moved on to the postcards – she skulked over to the video display.

'Hi there, Godspell!' Joel called, and was ignored. He puffed out his fleshy cheeks and raised his eyebrows, looking ridiculously hurt as he packed Ellen's purchases into a bag. Joel was clearly a man who liked to spread happiness.

Godspell picked up the box for the latest Johnny Depp video and started reading the back, head bobbing.

'It's a real good movie!' Joel called, as he gave Ellen her change. 'Lily and I watched it last night.'

Godspell ignored him.

'Personal stereo,' Ellen pointed out kindly. 'She can't hear a thing.'

'Oh.' The big face perked up as Ellen winked and headed for the door. 'Hey – have an ice-cream on the house. Treat for pretty customers. Just beside you there.'

'Thanks.' Touched, Ellen helped herself to a Zoom. She really wanted the M and M Cornetto, but there was only one left and she didn't want to deny any of Joel's paying customers. 'See you around.'

'Call again soon!'

Grinning, because she had found the encounter quite bizarre, Ellen unhooked Snorkel's lead from the pegs outside and took her across the lane to eat the ice-cream on the green. Quite a few villagers were out, soaking up the sunshine, passing on gossip, kicking balls around or walking dogs. Ellen settled on a deserted bench overlooking the duck pond, under the shadow of three huge horse-chestnuts. She set Snorkel free to go and admire her reflection in the water and, hoicking one leg up on the bench, lapped up her Zoom and thought about the Goose Cottage Shaggers.

The more she thought about it, the more convinced she grew that it simply couldn't be Dot and Reg. They certainly weren't cleaning and gardening, but she had a pretty shrewd idea that neither were they doing the dirty in the flowered four-poster bed. What need would they have for condoms at their age? And they hardly sounded the sort to indulge in long Gran Turismo 5 battles on the alien PlayStation.

Which left either another member of the Wyck family – Saul was suspect number one in that camp – or the estate agent at Seaton's. First thing on Monday, Ellen planned to haul him over the coals. Even if he wasn't using the most desirable property on his books as a base for his illicit encounters, he had to know that the state of the place must be putting off potential purchasers. And, now she thought about it, why wasn't there a for-sale board up?

Sitting beside the sapphire eye of Jennifer Jamieson's jewelled brooch, Ellen had a perfect view of the gold filigree cottages lined up along one side of the oldest part of the village – a triangle formed by the green, Chapel Row and the Hillcote road along which she had driven into the village. More skips than cars were parked outside the tiny cottages, and many of the higgledy-piggledy line were decked out with scaffolding and rival builders' boards. One of the oldest, still wigged with moss-strewn thatch, had its face entirely hidden behind boarding on which a local vandal had charmingly spray-painted, 'Yuppies Fuck Off.'

Beyond the sagging roofs, most now tiled with slate or stone, Ellen could just make out the bell-tower of the old school that lay at the heart of the triangle and whose over-popularity was the cause of the village's great debate – a favourite bugbear of Jennifer's at one time. And beyond that she could see the hills in which she'd stopped to let Snorkel run earlier, now just another slice of the striped vegetable terrine. She squinted to pick out the rape field with the derelict Dutch barn, tapping her Zoom stick against her teeth. A moment later, she found herself spitting out something small and squirming.

That was when she discovered why her chosen bench had been deserted. Not only was it in the shade but the horse-chestnuts above it were raining down small, wriggling caterpillars. She shifted right up to one end to find a tiny spot not under the tree's canopy, twisting round to stretch out her legs and shake off those that had already landed.

'"Bevis Aspinall".' She read the inscription on the bench's brass plaque that she'd been leaning against when eating her ice-cream. '"Beloved son, dearly missed. 12.12.74–22.6.91". Oh!' She clasped her mouth with her hand as the connection registered. 'You poor bugger. Only sixteen.' It struck her as desperately sad.

She patted the weatherbeaten wooden arm beside her, feeling a curious affinity with Bevis in his shady corner by the pond. They shared the same birthday, and both liked to be close to water. Digging into her loaf to feed the ducks before she left, she told Bevis to keep an eye open for nefarious villagers with large private collections of console games.

As she and Snorkel headed home to start the clear-up operation, cutting a diagonal line across the green to Goose Lane, Ellen saw the pink-cheeked biddy who had been talking to Joel in the shop. She was now chatting to someone outside the tall wrought-iron gates to Oddlode Manor, on which Jennifer had pretentiously based the design for the Goose Cottage ones. Spotting Ellen and Snorkel, she nudged her companion and bobbed her head in their direction, her mouth still moving non-stop.

Ellen gave her a cheery wave and fanned air into her T-shirt, swinging her bag of shopping and wondering where she could get hold of a few PlayStation games.

By six, she'd had enough. The worst of the Shaggers' rubbish was in the three fat bin-bags that sat outside the door to the boot room, the bottles were in the recycling crate and the bedclothes were swooshing around in the washing-machine. After a long hunt for the keys, every grubby window in the house had been opened to air it, and bunches of lily of the valley, sweet rocket and French lavender sat in milk bottles in the kitchen and sitting room to disperse the smell of stale cigarettes.

Because Ellen had forgotten to buy cigarettes in the shop, and because she hated cleaning at the best of times, she was feeling twitchy and short-tempered. Poor Fins was yowling in his closed-barracks confinement of the utility and boot rooms. She longed to let him out, but she knew that he'd scarper and probably never be seen again. He had to stay there, at least for a few days.

To get away from the noise, guilt and dirt, she headed into the garden and contemplated the jungle. It would take her days to sort it out. The grass was so long that it needed to be strimmed or scythed before she could get a mower on to it. The rampant flowers clogging the beds looked rather spectacular, but docks and nettles that would take for ever to pull up were already bullying them out. The pond was a stagnant pit and had developed a repulsive-looking slime on its surface, which frothed ominously. And the paddock – once let to a local girl for her pony, as she recalled – was now a wild heath through which Snorkel was ploughing twisting furrows as she chased insects, followed enticing scents and sporadically stood stock still to look pleadingly at Ellen.

The collie was accustomed to running miles each day with Richard, swimming in the sea and clambering up and down the steep Cornish cliff paths like a mountaineer. Today's occasional loo breaks, playtime in the Goose Cottage garden and gander across the village were wholly inadequate.

'We could head back to the shop for cigarettes?' Ellen suggested, closing one eye as she tried not to give in to the nicotine temptation. 'Or I could quit today and take you to see the river.'

Snorkel just barked and bounded stupidly, blinking and sneezing as she sent up a cloud of pollen and grass seed.

Leaving the Goose Cottage doors unlocked and all the windows open – she was accustomed to Cornish isolation – Ellen set off across the lane towards Goose End, pausing under the big lime tree that formed a rural roundabout at the point where all the lanes and tracks met. Tarmac gave way to unkempt gravel as the long drive to Lodge Farm opened up ahead and Goose End swung to the right. Ellen took the latter, looking up at the top windows of the huge Lodge, just visible over its high stone wall.

If Goose Cottage had suffered six months of neglect, then the Lodge had suffered years. It had been empty and dilapidated for as long as Ellen remembered, those high garden walls only just holding back the impenetrable, enchanted forest that sprouted beyond. It was the sort of place that entranced children, their imaginations fired by ghost stories featuring deserted mansions or tales of enchanted gardens. Ellen remembered her father telling her that a famous sculptor had once lived there and that the grounds were full of his bronzes. She longed to open the arched wooden gate, which squatted like a magic porthole half-way along the garden wall, and take a peek inside.

With its mysterious, neglected Lodge and ancient barns, Goose

End had once been the forgotten corner of Oddlode, but now it, too, had been touched by modernisation. The barns had been converted into three luxurious houses; the tatty old farm-workers' cottages beside them had been sold on and spruced up. Yet as the village gave way to the bridlepath, which cut its way up through the hills, it still made Ellen think of the days in which all roads had been like this – simple tracks in which cartwheels got stuck and labourers' boots sank to the ankle as they walked.

The grassy bridge across the Odd marked the true start of the bridlepath. Despite the scorching heat of the day, the river was as high as Ellen remembered it. After an April where the showers had been non-stop torrents, one sunny, heatwave week in May had barely dissipated the gushing, bubbling force of the little river, which galloped its way through its high-banked winding trench to the north of the village like a bobsleigh along an Olympic course.

While Snorkel plunged into the gravel-bottomed shallows beside the bridge, Ellen climbed up the grassy arch and leaned on the stone wall, looking down into the clear, bubbling depths. Her father had brought her here a few times, excitedly showing off the gudgeon, dace and three-spined sticklebacks that took a patient eye to spot. Ellen had never had the heart to tell him that in the brooks around Treglin these fish were as common as minnows. But by far the most exciting residents of the river Odd were the crayfish that appeared every year for just a few days in such numbers you could catch them with your hands. Ellen couldn't boast that of Treglin. The crayfish were a well-kept village secret and fishing them was strictly limited, overseen by several self-appointed 'guardians' of which Ellen's mother had been one. Jennifer had been active on village committees. If there was a planning proposal to be fought or an amenity to be saved, she was always in the thick of the action. That well-meaning tenacity had been brought into play when she'd fought long and hard to stop Ellen seeing Richard 'for your own good'.

Ellen shook her head to stop herself going there. Plenty of time to think about Richard when she was riding across Mongolia or trekking in Tibet or spending time in any number of places that didn't make her think about him in relation to her mother.

Snorkel was still plunging around in the river's shallow gravel bed, trying to catch water fleas, her muzzle sending up great fans of drips as she nosed in and out like an ebullient duck.

Ellen crossed the bridge and tried to whistle her onwards, drawing level with a curious building that she'd never really understood – a pillared stone dome, covered with the man-made graffiti of spray paint and nature's vandalising ivy. Her father always claimed it was an Aphrodite temple, erected for villagers to conduct illicit affairs, but he was given to these flights of fancy, regularly quashed by a furious tut from Jennifer. Ellen doubted that many villagers used it for adulterous liaisons – especially not when they had Goose Cottage at their disposal. Overgrown with nettles and brambles, it would take a brave soul to get down to the buff in there.

'Horrid, isn't it?' said a voice just beside her. 'Even the glue-sniffers have abandoned it, these days.'

Ellen jumped and swung round to find a woman at her shoulder. She hadn't heard her approach but if she hadn't been so blinkered by the thick arms of her shades and the lowered peak of her baseball cap, she would certainly have seen her. Magnificently endowed and as broad-hipped as a lyre, she was an Aphrodite fit for a true Greek temple, albeit a mellow goddess in a slightly ruined one. From the mane of wild dark oak curls through the creased, floaty white smock dress to the camp gold flip-flops, she oozed scruffy sensuality.

'I hate it – nasty piece of neo-classical junk,' she told Ellen, in her wonderfully deep, euphonious voice, still looking at the 'temple'. 'Looks like a park bandstand or a bus shelter, doesn't it? I can't believe there's such a fuss going on about saving it.'

'What, actually, is it?' Ellen asked.

The wide, sunburned nose and cheeks tilted towards her, topped by mesmerising big green eyes. 'Well, it's known as the River Folly and the villagers would have you believe some romantic clap-trap about William Constantine building it as a love token for his wife in the eighteenth century, but . . .

Ophelia Gently, by the way – call me Pheely.' She thrust out
her hand.

'I'm Ellen.' She shook it, rather taken aback by the introduction,
made as suddenly as a sneeze and a 'bless you' in the middle of
the story.

'I happen to know,' Pheely carried on, huge eyes sparkling with
mischief, 'that one of the Constantines – a Victorian, so much
later – suffered from terrible constipation. He grew terribly bored
of sitting for hours on the manor bog and decided to build a loo
with a view. But the poor chap was killed in the Boer War before
he ever got a chance to use it. Ironic that half the village youth
have used it to piss in over the years.'

Ellen stared at the 'temple' and secretly agreed that it was
a bit of an elaborate eyesore compared to the rough-hewn
simplicity of the track, wild hedges and hills. But she didn't believe
a word of Pheely's story.

'Oh, God! Hamlet's raping your dog. Hang on!'

Ellen turned to watch in alarm as Pheely kicked off her flip-flops
and rushed down the bank to wade into the river and separate
a huge harlequin Great Dane from a very flirtatious Snorkel.
With her white smock soaking up water, and the dark curls
now full of snowy blossom from brushing past the hawthorns
on the bank, Ophelia Gently had been instantly transformed from
Greek princess to her Shakespearean namesake.

'Has she been spayed?' she shouted, as the Great Dane twisted
this way and that, refusing to leave his new girlfriend alone.

'Yes!' It was clearly Ellen's day to discuss her animals' repro-
ductive systems, she thought, as she waited on the bank beside
the gold flip-flops.

'In that case, I'll leave them to it.' Pheely waded out, smiling
widely. 'Sorry – Hamlet's totally debauched, but harmless. You
walking up the path? Shall we trundle together and hope the
lovers follow suit?'

She displayed such a disarming friendliness that Ellen found
herself liking her immediately. As they fell into step, she realised
suddenly that Pheely had set out for a dog walk in the white

shift and gold flip-flops. Eccentric and impractical only began to describe it, although on closer inspection the smock looked as though it had been far from pristine before she had taken her dunk. Where the fabric was still dry above the waist, it was covered in muddy red smears and was frayed at the neck. Yet Pheely herself wasn't as old, dishevelled or plump as Ellen had at first, unkindly, thought. Glancing across as they headed up the hill, she knocked ten years off the forty-something she'd originally taken her to be, and the flapping dress showed that between Pheely's buxom curves there was a near-Edwardian tiny waist.

'So you've bought Goose Cottage from the dreaded Jamiesons, I gather?' Pheely was shaking the drips and reeds from her dress, which was also coated with brown, soggy blossom picked up from the river.

'No.' She rolled her tongue beneath her bottom lip in amusement. 'I am a dreaded Jamieson. I'm their daughter.'

'Oops.' Pheely didn't seem remotely embarrassed and let out a throaty giggle that gurgled like the river. 'I thought I'd have heard about it if it had been sold, but Gladys has been telling everyone you moved in today.'

'Gladys?'

'You met her in the shop.'

'I only met an American called Joel.'

'GI Joel – he's a hoot.' Pheely pulled back her curtain of corkscrews and fixed Ellen with huge, thickly lashed eyes of the same pale green as copper verdigris. 'Was Lily with him?'

'Is that his wife?' Ellen remembered him telling the silent Goth girl that he and Lily had watched the movie together.

'Absolute *weirdo*, my dear,' Pheely whispered indulgently. 'You wait. Anyway, Gladys is about seventy and looks like a Cabbage Patch doll. Unmistakable.'

'The elderly lady?' Ellen raised her eyebrows. 'She only saw me for a nanosecond before leaving.'

'That's all Glad Tidings needs to assess your entire personal history.' Pheely tapped her nose. She was already panting as they started climbing up the cart track, her bare feet following the soft, grassy ridge in the centre because she'd left her flip-flops behind. 'She can tell your age, nationality, political persuasion, marital status, guilty secrets and likelihood to help out at the village fête from a two-second encounter at the bus stop. And she has eyes *everywhere*. She should work for the police.'

Ellen laughed. 'And what did she say about me?'

'Spotted moving into Goose Cottage at one with various animals. Spotted loitering in village shop at two thirty with just one animal in tow. Trying to get rid of all animals, it seems. The spotted-walking-with-Touchy-Feely-at-six bulletin is no doubt doing the rounds now, between frantic preparations for tonight's jamboree. And you are, I quote, "Not a natural blonde and one of them punky sorts with an earring through her belly button. She's a bit of a spiky madam – probably unmarried, poor thing."'

'Nosy old bitch,' Ellen said, without thinking.

Pheely snorted delightedly, then turned back to shout for Hamlet. 'Believe me, she's not as nosy or bitchy as I am. She's got a very sweet heart.' She carried on walking backwards beside Ellen. 'And she means – HAMLET! – well. Lord knows, we'd all need some entertainment after fifty years' working for the Bellings, and the Constantines before them.'

'That's the River Folly man, right?'

'His descendants, yes – HAMLET! – the lords of Oddlode Manor. Or so Hell's Bells – that's Isabel – would have you believe, but she was the first Constantine to bag a title. She's only Lady Belling now because – HAMLET! – St John got the ultimate gong when Her Maj tapped the chips on both his round shoulders with her sword. Sir St John! You can't imagine the trouble the locals have getting their tongues around that. Most call him the Surgeon.'

It was no wonder Pheely was so breathless, the rate at which that hypnotising voice divulged information.

'St John Belling the politician?' Ellen had recognised the name.

'The very same. HAMLET YOU GREAT OAF!' Having veered all over the bridlepath while walking backwards, Pheely decided to walk the right way round again.

'He's the one everyone says should have been PM, isn't he?'

'The nearly-man, yes. And so he would have been, were it not for that Godforsaken son of his,' Pheely muttered, with surprising bitterness. Then she laughed. 'Actually, I have very few things to thank Jasper Belling for, but perhaps that *is* one of them. The Surgeon would have taken this country back to the dark ages. When Jasper fucked up this village, he did the nation a favour. Such a noble gesture!'

Ellen was vaguely familiar with the story of St John Belling, long-tipped to succeed Thatcher and much admired by her mother. The owner of Oddlode Manor, one-time local Tory MP and a favourite cabinet minister of the Iron Lady with the soft spot for blue-eyed men, had fallen from grace when his son turned out to be a drug-smuggler or something like that. And that son was clearly Jasper Belling. But the rest of Pheely's chatter was already flying over her head.

'I might even force myself to go along tonight after all,' she was saying, pulling long grasses from the banks to wave around like a fairy wand. 'Glad Tidings was very miffed when I told her I wanted to withdraw my promise – she insisted that I couldn't do it without Lady B's permission. Can you imagine? That's when she told me all about you, no doubt trying to take my mind off the subject, which it did. I am such a butterfly.'

With her butterfly mind dancing from topic to topic, Pheely had a tendency to talk about people and things as though Ellen should know the subjects intimately. She was about to ask what was happening tonight but at that moment both dogs thundered up the path behind them, a golden flip-flop in each of their mouths.

'Oh, clever, clever darlings! What clever dogs! I do like your collie.' She collected the flip-flops, gracefully offered by Snorkel and wrestled from a reluctant Hamlet. 'Why do you want to get rid of her?'

'She's my ex-boyfriend's dog. He's moved to Australia. And I'm going abroad myself after the cottage here is sold.'

'Oh.' Curiously Pheely didn't ask any questions about this. For a woman who proclaimed herself 'nosy' and 'bitchy', she went rather shy. Now panting hard from trying to keep up with Ellen's brisk walking pace, she batted away midges, big green eyes downcast. 'Are your parents well?'

'Yes, fine.' Ellen stooped to throw a stick for Snorkel. Beside Hamlet's great stature, she looked minuscule, like a toy dog. 'Dad's heart is always a worry, but he seems to have found a life that suits him. And Mum's really taken to Spain. I didn't think she would, but she loves it there.'

'Giving them all hell about proposed green-belt developments and bypasses, no doubt.' Pheely winked.

'I think she's more worried about Dad's heart bypass these days,' Ellen said, more abruptly than she intended. She always got snappy when talking about her mother, and was irritated with herself that she couldn't loosen up and take her less seriously. But some sense of daughterly duty prevailed.

Pheely clearly misread it as a loving defence of a great mother and apologised profusely. 'Sorry. I really don't mean it. I said I was a bitch, didn't I? Your mother and I never really hit it off, I'm afraid. No doubt she thought me a terrible slattern and a terrible mother, which I am. That's why I tried to get out of tonight's promise thing – Dilly's doing "A" levels and I really must be there for her.'

'You have a daughter doing "A" levels?' Ellen stopped in her tracks and gaped. She'd been knocking years off her estimate of Pheely's age all the way up the path – she was monumentally unfit, true, but that and the deep voice, which spoke in a curiously old-fashioned manner, were definitely misleading. Her face was fresh and girlish, with its huge baby eyes and lack of crow's feet – after so many summers spent in sun and salt water, Ellen's own skin was far more haggard. And the amazing, gravity-defying body hinted at someone who had yet to find her metabolism working against her. Ellen now put Pheely at about her own age or even younger.

'Yes, Daffodil.' Pheely halted too, with obvious relief, and continued breathlessly. 'Poor darling – I know I can't resist giving people nicknames, but perhaps it was a bit cruel wishing one on my own daughter. Imagine going through boarding-school being called Dilly Gently. Awful. But, of course, I was younger than she is now when I had her, so I can't really blame myself any more. And I must say she's always been terribly good about it. Gosh – look at the village from here! It could almost be picturesque.'

'It is picturesque,' said Ellen, aware that Pheely was changing the subject deliberately. She was starting to get the hang of the topic-hopping. Pheely, vivacious, indiscreet and a babbler, gave information in great dollops, then seized up, like a faulty ice-cream machine. It made her both delicious and irritating.

'It's a seething pit of lies and hatred,' Pheely announced, with only a hint of self-mockery. 'But, yes, maybe it's quite picturesque from here. One forgets when one's lived here so long. All my bloody life, in fact. You never lived here with your parents, did you?'

Ellen shook her head, distractedly doing some mental arithmetic to satisfy her own curiosity. Maths had always been a natural gift – much to her mother's delight and her own embarrassment – and she had never been able to stop herself adding things up. She now calculated that if a daughter taking 'A' levels was older than her mother had been at her birth, Pheely couldn't be more than thirty-three tops. It rocked her back on her heels to discover that someone so close to her own age could have a grown-up daughter.

'Lucky you,' Pheely was saying, throwing the stick that Snorkel had dropped at their feet, which Ellen had been too distracted to notice. 'It was Somerset your parents moved here from, wasn't it?'

'Near Taunton, yes.'

'I thought I recognised that lovely accent. Did you stay on there after they'd left?'

Ellen, who wasn't aware that she had an accent and had suffered hours of elocution lessons at her parents' expense because Jennifer had said once that 'sounding like a peasant' would hamper her chances of getting into medical school, found herself deeply self-conscious. She cleared her throat, and said, in a voice of which Henry Higgins would have been proud, 'I've been mostly based in Cornwall, but I've worked all over the road – I mean, the place. Here and overseas.'

Too busy stick-throwing to notice the enunciated voice, Pheely sighed indulgently. 'Oh, lucky you. What is it that you do?'

'Sports physiotherapist.'

'Wow.' Pheely pulled in her stomach and glanced across at her. 'No wonder you're so gorgeously trim and fit.'

Ellen ducked her head, biting back the comment that she'd piled on weight lately – which she had, misery-eating over Richard. She knew it wasn't the thing to say in front of somebody as curvaceous – however stunningly so – as Pheely.

'Are you working while you're here?' she was asking now.

'No, I'm having a break. I've always worked like mad through the winter – out-of-season training, foreign tours, winter sports, that sort of thing. That way, I can have free summers. Me and Rich—' She stopped herself and tried again. 'I like to surf.'

'Sounds lovely. Makes my life seem very dull,' Pheely seemed wildly envious of any life outside Oddlode. Her butterfly mind, it appeared, was trapped against a window, battering to get out.

Ellen was about to ask her what she did when Pheely clasped her hands to her mouth and let out an excited shriek. 'How perfect! Does being a sports physiotherapist involve giving massages by any chance?'

'It's an important part of the job.'

'Then you can come with me tonight. Yippee!' Pheely was hopping around excitedly, green eyes jubilant. 'You are free, aren't you?'

'Er – sort of. What's happening?'

'Hell's Bells has organised an auction of promises at the manor,' Pheely told her. 'Oh, please say you'll come – please! My friend Pixie can't come now, the bitch, and I hate the idea of going alone, especially with Jasper there, although I'm dying to have a gawp. You can hold my hand and we can gawp together.'

For a thirty-something woman with a voice like a jazz singer and a grown daughter, Pheely could be absurdly childlike, Ellen realised – a spoilt little posh girl who had friends called Pixie and hated going to parties alone. She should be maddening, yet something about her bitchy, witty, frustrated joyfulness was intoxicating. She radiated warm-hearted abandon and instant friendship. Such ingenuous trust was something Ellen had almost forgotten.

'What does it involve?' she asked cautiously, proving her point. She'd become too slow-moving lately, no longer embracing the unknown with the impulsive recklessness that she and Richard had shared for so long, marking them apart from others. She missed it like mad. 'No! Forget that question.' She stopped Pheely before she could open her mouth to answer. 'Where shall we meet and what do I wear?'

'Oh, my darling!' Pheely let out a little whoop and clapped her hands, her smile as wide and sunny as the view. 'You are *such* a welcome addition to the village! Wear anything you like. God knows, looking as sexy as you do in builder's shorts and an inside out T, you could wear a bin-bag and overexcite the locals – although, knowing Hell's Bells, I'd say maybe wear more. Not because she's a tartar for formality, which she is, but because the manor is always freezing, even at this time of year. And come round to mine for a bottle of plonk first so that I can fill you in – Gladys mentioned something about a wine crisis, so we must make sure we've snuffled some back beforehand.' She glanced at her watch. 'In fact – Christ! We must head back and get tarted up straight away.'

Despite having laboured all the way up the hill, Pheely had no such trouble dancing down it again. They were passing the folly and crossing the bridge before Ellen had time to catch her breath, the dogs in hot pursuit.

At the lime tree where the tracks and lanes met, Pheely clasped Ellen's hands, her face pink from running. 'Give me twenty minutes to change, then meet me back here.'

'Can't I just call at your house?' Ellen felt a sudden twinge of panic at agreeing to go to a mysterious village event with a stranger, and to share a bottle of wine beforehand. She didn't even know where Pheely lived.

'It's a bit hard to find the way in,' Pheely said cryptically. 'Much quicker to meet me here. I'll phone Gladys straight away and let her know you're adding a last-minute lot – in fact, Hell's Bells must be back by now so I'll tell her. That'll get the old bag going. Hurry back!'

'A last-minute what?' Ellen called, but Pheely was already dancing away through the evening sun in the direction of the magical arched gateway in the high garden wall, behind which lay the secrets of the beautiful, decaying Lodge. A moment later she had pulled it open, letting an amazing green dappled light spill out as the sun, sinking to the west, poured golden rays through the bottle green leaves of the overgrown garden. It streamed through Pheely's white smock like the beam from the transporter room in the *Starship Enterprise*, silhouetting that astounding, voluptuous hourglass body through the thin fabric before Pheely disappeared through the gate followed by Hamlet, himself dyed green in the light – half dog, half Incredible Hulk.

Ellen smiled to herself. She might have guessed. Ophelia Gently lived in the magical-mystery lodge, in her magical-mystery world of giant dogs, evil villagers and Pixie friends. She wasn't real. She couldn't be real.

Pheely's cottage was a real mess.

It wasn't the Lodge itself, but a ramshackle building tucked behind the big house that its occupant described as a seventeenth-century Nissen hut. Part artist's studio, part open wardrobe, its interior was an installation in itself – something Tracey Emin couldn't hope to achieve in a lifetime of lying in bed sulking.

Having been guided to it through a disorienting maze of over-grown topiary, past astonishing lichen-coated statues, fountains that spurted ivy in place of water, and twisted fruit trees that looked like goblins, Ellen had to look long and hard at Pheely's mess to convince herself she wasn't dreaming. No, dreams didn't contain fifteen-kilo bags of dog food slumped beside a filthy potter's wheel on which stood an open box of Tampax. Dreams didn't feature a row of huge red knickers drying on an empty wine rack, or enough washing up in the Belfast sink to keep Nanette Newman's hands soft for years to come. Compared to this, the Shaggers' mess in Goose Cottage was a dropped sock in a show home.

'I had a quick tidy-up in your honour,' Pheely announced proudly, 'which is why I've only got one eye made up. There's plonk in the fridge – crack it open and I'll daub the other.' She whisked through to the modern lean-to extension, which housed a small bathroom and toilet from which Hamlet was taking a noisy drink.

The 'cottage' was as extraordinary as its wild surroundings. Tucked behind the huge boarded-up Lodge, it was little more than a long, low Cotswold-stone barn with a chimney at each end. With its vaulted roof and hefty oak cross-beams, it felt like the hull of an upside-down ship. Perhaps that was why Pheely's possessions had fallen everywhere when it capsized, Ellen thought, as she picked her way past bags of earthenware clay, and over a carpet of lone shoes and dog chews to the ancient, rust-flecked fridge, which when open revealed nothing but wine and fruit.

Despite the weirdness of the set-up, she found the place surprisingly comforting to mooch around. Like her parents' dishevelled bedroom at Goose Cottage, it reminded her of surfers' cottages in Cornwall and crowded camper-vans on the road.

Looking around for a corkscrew, she wondered where Pheely slept. The cottage was just one big double-height room, the fireplace at one end housing a small, grumbling Rayburn and the one at the other a big kiln – the only sources of heating, it seemed. Beneath the illogical untidiness, there was a logical progression between the two, from kitchen-cum-laundry, past a dining-table-cum-paper-mountain to two very high piles of clothes in the shape of sofas, indicating that there was some sort of seating arrangement somewhere below. To one side, in front of a row of huge north-facing french windows, was a series of clay-crusted benches, shelves, another sink and the potter's wheel with its Tampax installation. Through the open doors, Ellen could see a small terrace cluttered with pots, statues and garden ornaments, some glazed, others left natural and quite a few broken.

But there was no bed. Ellen had no idea where Pheely slept – and she had a daughter living here too.

'Is Daffodil out?' she asked, when Pheely emerged, both amazing green eyes now painted with dark, luscious shadow so that they gleamed from her face like slices of kiwi fruit. Dressed in a purple velvet top that clung to her curves and a fantastically clashing long, burnt-orange silk skirt, she looked amazing. Ellen felt very understated in her best cream cord hipsters, a white shirt knotted tightly under her bust. She'd hoped they showed off her tan, but beside Pheely's colourful presence she felt drab and sepia.

'Away at school,' Pheely explained, carefully extracting two dirty glasses from the crowded sink then finding she was unable to get to the taps to wash them. 'But I have her back here next weekend, mugging up like mad, poor darling. God, they work hard for these exams. Sometimes I'm glad I never went through it. This was Daddy's studio.' She did her change-of-subject butterfly dance as she headed to the sink in the workshop area to clean the glasses. 'Do you like it?'

'Yes.' Ellen wrestled with an ancient, rusty corkscrew as she tried to open a bottle of something that simply declared itself 'Cheap White Wine' on the colourful label.

'It suits me here,' Pheely said, without total conviction. 'I can't possibly afford to run the Lodge – Daddy put it in trust for Dilly, which at least keeps the property vultures at bay. She turns eighteen this August, so I guess I'll be her lodger if she claims her inheritance. The Lodge lodger.' She winked, holding up two dripping glasses, which still bore multicoloured lipstick rims. 'There! Squeaky clean.'

Ellen had dragged out the cork a lump at a time and now splashed out the CWW. 'Were those your father's sculptures in the garden?' she asked, passing Pheely a glass.

She nodded. 'His "bronze meddles" as he called them. Mostly experimental. I can't bear to sell them. Ironic, really – I long to cast in bronze but I can't afford to. One has to be a *very* successful sculptor to go the cold-cast route without a commission, like Daddy could. So I stick to clay pots and gnomes. Selling one of his works would raise the money to make twenty bronzes of my own but I'd need more meddles and less honour. And nobody would buy mine, of course.' She laughed at herself. 'That's the difference. Cheers! To new friendships,' she toasted gaily, almost smashing both glasses in her enthusiasm to butterfly-dance away from the subject and get drunk.

Cheap White Wine was surprisingly good. Because there was nowhere to sit, they wandered on to the little terrace to drink it.

'Okay – here's your brief.' Pheely was already half-way down her glass, the bottle clasped under one arm in anticipation of a top-up. 'Tonight, Hell's Bells has called the great and the good – that's the rich and the talented – of the village to the manor for an auction of promises. The idea is that talented creatures like you and I flog our wares to talentless rich bastards like the residents of Gin Palace Heights to raise money for the restoration of the loo with the view.'

'The River Folly?'

Pheely shuddered. 'As you can imagine, I was not keen, but Hell's has a very persuasive air about her as you'll no doubt see.' She took a long draught of CWW. 'I, for my sins, have agreed to auction a portrait bust, which quite frankly is far too generous of me. Do you know how long it takes to sculpt somebody in clay?'

After a discreet look at some of the earthenware gargoyles and fairies around her, Ellen guessed it took a while.

'You – lucky girl – only have to donate a massage. Very easy. You can knock one off in under an hour, I should imagine, although I wouldn't mind betting that whoever buys it will probably be far too embarrassed ever to claim it. They're a conservative lot round here.' She drained her glass. 'But I had to offer your services to get you in. It's a very select event – strictly by invitation – no blacks, no Irish, no Wycks.'

Ellen raised an eyebrow and opened her mouth to question this, but Pheely was already talking again, topping up her glass as she spoke. 'Now, tonight will undoubtedly be quite a hoot, so please don't worry, I'm not dragging you through the gates of hell – just to the rather fascinating spectacle of Ely Gates sucking up to Hell's Bells. I'll point him out later. And to spice everything up no end, Spurs is staging his first appearance in over a decade.' The bottle clattered against the glass, spilling its contents over the rim.

'Spurs?' Ellen quickly took the glass from her to prevent the lovely purple and orange outfit getting spattered.

'Thanks. Sorry, I'm a bit het-up.' Pheely stepped back quickly and blinked as a thought occurred to her. 'Do you think we have time for a quick joint?' She sounded like a little girl asking if there was time to go to the loo before they set out.

Ellen felt a great big grin wrap itself around her face. 'You have gear?'

'Grow my own.' Pheely looked at her watch. 'Oh, fuck it, we'll be a bit late. I *have* to relax. You're so sweet putting up with me. I will explain why I'm all over the place about this thing, I promise.'

Oh, the heaven of really good grass on a sunny evening in an enchanted garden, Ellen mused cheerfully, ten minutes later, as she perched on a gargoyle head and held a breath of sweet, pure sensimilla in her lungs. It certainly beat the nicotine cravings, and made her first day in Oddlode seem like the best of her life.

'Mmmmmmmmmm.' Pheely had taken the joint and was inhaling a grateful drag. 'God, that's better. Think slow, Pheely, think slooooooow.' She giggled, dropping her neck to relax it and sending a waterfall of dark curls on to the burning spliff. Not seeming to notice, she tipped her head back and took a deep breath, gazing at Ellen with her luminous eyes.

'Jasper Belling – known to all as Spurs, and that's not one of my nicknames, I promise – was a terrible tearaway. You really can't imagine how bad he was. I quite liked him at one time, before he turned too twisted. He did a lot more than cost his father his political career. When he left this village eleven years ago, he left it very, very bitter. I really think that had he stayed a day longer somebody would have killed him. And now,' she took a toke and handed back the joint, 'he's back.'

Ellen let this sink in along with the delicious sensation of total and utter doped-up happiness. It was hard to marry the two. Pheely's homegrown stash was potent stuff. She was already almost too far gone to talk. 'Why?' she croaked.

Pheely shrugged. 'Nobody knows. Glad Tidings has sniffed around like a bloodhound, but the one Oddlode family she can never dig up gossip on is the one she works for. They keep extraordinary close order – probably wise with Gladys keeping house.' She started to giggle, finally falling victim to her potent foliage. When the rush hit, it was like inhaling laughing gas while rocketing around on a bouncy castle. Her green eyes rolled in amazement.

Ellen, suddenly finding this bad joke ridiculously funny, fought to talk through her own unstoppable giggles: 'What did he do that was so bad?'

Snorting and weeping so much that she had to clutch her chest, Pheely stamped her feet in delight. 'Well, he once redesigned Hunter Gardner's disgusting Swiss-chalet garage by burning it to the ground, along with the Mini Metro and the pleasure dinghy inside. That was quite funny, actually. I mean, who has a watercraft in the Cotswolds?'

'I have surfboards,' Ellen pointed out, and they both fell about, howling gleefully as they slid from their pottery seats and knelt on the terrace, hysterical with laughter.

'I – think – I rolled – this – a – bit – strong,' Pheely gasped, between hoots.

Ellen nodded. She was waiting for the stitch in her side to pass. At last, they confined their hilarity to occasional snorts.

'Oh, Jasper did do some wildly funny things.' Pheely wiped her eyes as she ground out the roach, then stood up unsteadily. 'But he did some truly awful ones too. I haven't time to tell you now. We're going to be really, really late, and I *have* to see who gets my lot. If it's Lily Lubowski, I'm leaving the country with you.'

How somebody so stoned could find their way through the tree and sculpture maze was beyond Ellen, but she trusted Pheely as she followed her through the twists and turns that took them over grassy banks, under iron park railings and through tiny openings in wild hedges.

At last they were through the arched gate in the Lodge wall and trotting past the lime tree towards Goose Lane.

Goose Cottage was looking very fairytale princess in the evening sun, despite all her late nights. Every window, apart from those in Fins' barracks, winked open as she gave Ellen a come-hither look.

'Are you sure that's wise with the Wycks on the loose tonight?' Pheely whistled as they passed.

'You think I should close them?'

'No – you're fine. People will think you're in.' Pheely clearly didn't want to be any later. 'Besides, the Wycks' youth are all in the village hall celebrating an eighteenth, and the seniors are in the Lodes Inn.'

As they panted along the lane towards Manor Street, Ellen told her about the Goose Cottage Shaggers. 'I don't really mind – I mean, God knows, Mum and Dad's bedroom could use some action, but I'd like to know who it was. I've got their PlayStation for a start. I want to borrow a game.'

Hit afresh by the dope, Pheely roared so hard with laughter that she had to stop beside the manor gates and bend over to hold back threatened stitch. Her curls swept the blossom on the Tarmac towards her high-heeled sandals. 'Oh, I so wish it *were* Dot and Reg. That would be such joy.' She straightened up, wiping her smudged eye makeup, and let out a delighted sigh. 'I only wish I knew anything that might help – I'm sorry. I don't get to twitch curtains much in my grotto. Was your mother very angry?'

'I didn't tell her.' Ellen was cocking her head to work out where the music she could suddenly hear was coming from. Loud and decidedly unkempt, it seemed an unlikely musical accompaniment to Lady Belling's select soirée. It sounded more like foxes raiding dustbins full of tom-cats.

'Roadkill.' Pheely nodded in the direction of the village hall, which they had just passed and was now hidden by the high wall dividing it from the manor's front drive. 'Local band – playing at the Wycks' party. Tuneful, aren't they?'

Ellen just managed to hold back another giggling fit.

'Hell's Bells was furious when she found out they were playing at the hall tonight.' Pheely winked. 'Come and see her wrath – and wrath's child.' Hooking her arm through Ellen's, she steered her through the huge gateway and they teetered up the carriage sweep, decidedly stoned, decidedly late and firmly decided to be very good friends.

3

'Do I hear ninety? Superb! With you now, Ely, at ninety. Ninety-five anywhere in the room? Is that a bid, Digby, or a nervous twitch? . . . I see. How unfortunate. Now *surely* I have ninety-five? Marcia, you haven't bought anything yet, have you?'

Isabel Belling, or Hell's Bells, was an auctioneer who used her gavel much as she used her beloved Cogswell and Harrison twelve-bore sidelock to shoot pheasant, swinging it around with deadly intent. Standing on a set of library steps in front of a huge stone fireplace, flanked by two sleeping Labradors, she eyed the field for signs of movement. Behind her was her trusty loader for the night, housekeeper Gladys, who clutched a clipboard and made a note of birds as they were shot down. She'd also made a mental note of which guest had knocked back more than one glass of wine at the welcoming drinks and was therefore more likely to break cover.

The great and the good that had gathered in Oddlode Manor's blue drawing room sat on their hands and maintained expressions of serene blankness to avoid being misinterpreted as bidding. Nobody dared catch Hell's Bells' eye, sniff, cough or clear their throat for fear of being saddled with lot fifteen – a meal for two at the Duck Upstream, wine *not* included.

'Three capers skewered on a rosemary twig and no booze. You'd have to pay *me*,' muttered Pheely. 'Ely's only bidding because he's desperate for his wife to lose weight.' She nodded towards a very plump figure sitting beside the bearded man who was currently leading the bidding. 'Poor Felicity gets taken to the Duck Upstream every week for a romantic dinner and has *no* idea that her husband has an ulterior motive.'

Ellen suppressed a giggle. She stared intently at her auction catalogue and bit her lip. The catalogue, which Pheely called the going-for-a-song sheet, listed the lots with a brief description of the promise offered and the name of the benefactor. Hand-written at the end was the unfortunate 'Lot 69 – all-over massage from new local sports physio Ellen Jamieson (as used by England Rugby Internationals and Oxford University Rowing Team)'. Pheely claimed innocently that Isabel must have misheard her when she called through with the information.

'Who will give me ninety-five? Marvellous lot, this – worth every penny.' Hell's Bells consulted her notes and, perhaps realising that it wasn't such good value, cleared her throat, then added, in her forthright baritone, 'And it's in a *very* good cause.'

Looking at her, Ellen decided that Lady Belling was rather magnificent. Her initial impression that their hostess bore a striking resemblance to Ann Widdecombe with a perm hadn't lasted long: Hell's Bells had once undoubtedly been ravishing, and in many ways she still was.

'Who will give me ninety-five pounds towards the restoration of our wonderful River Folly? I *must* have ninety-five!'

Barely five feet tall and probably as wide, she was far from the elegant aristocrat that Ellen had envisaged being married to tall, dishy St John, yet she was as spectacularly eye-catching as the huge house she inhabited. Like the manor itself, she was handsome rather than beautiful and had been enlarged over the years so that she was now a mismatch of styles. The amazing pale freckled skin and silver eyes were original, dressed up with fifties-style makeup that was clearly as rarely used as the Victorian wing in which the auction was taking place. The high-cheeked, square-shouldered bone structure had become buried in muscular annexes and fleshy extensions, but was still symmetrical architecture at its most classic. The hair – a short riot of tight black curls – had defied a hundred different hairdressers' attempts to tame it, just as the huge yew hedge that divided the manor's gardens from its stables and the old hunt kennels had defied generations of gardeners to impose a topiary form. And, like her beloved house, she dominated the village by more than just her age, size and superior heritage: she had a magical, unexpected glamour.

'Ninety-five! Thank you, Mr Hornton,' boomed Hell's Bells, twirling her gavel as if it was John Wayne's pistol at a shoot-out. 'Now, who'll give me a hundred?' She sighted Ellen over the gavel, silver eyes sparkling like bullets aimed at a were-wolf. Behind her, Gladys puckered her lips and gave Ellen a wise look.

Caught in the force of Hell's Bells' stare, like a hare pinpointed by a poacher's lamp, Ellen almost stopped breathing. If Glad Tidings could determine one's DNA structure at a glance, her boss possessed the sort of gaze that could unravel it and bend it to her will. They were a formidable combination.

'Don't move a muscle until she looks away,' Pheely breathed, like a safari ranger issuing instructions to a tourist who'd come face to face with a lion.

Ellen chewed her lips and felt the repressed laughter bubbling in her mouth and throat, like a can of Coke knocked back in a hurry, until at last the silver gaze moved on to a fresh target and she could swallow the froth and fizz. She caught Pheely's eye in relief, and a merry green wink greeted her. They had to look hurriedly at different parts of the ceiling's ornate, crumbling cornicing to stop themselves hitting the laughter meltdown button once more.

Still watching them, Glad Tidings made a couple of amend-ments to her notes.

The auction had already been well under way when Pheely and Ellen had arrived, and the disapproving look they had received from Gladys then was getting sterner by the minute as they whispered like new schoolfriends during the first assembly.

They had settled in the back row of the unusual assortment of seating that Hell's Bells and Gladys had collected together to create an *ad hoc* auction room in the little-used Blue Drawing Room, the more formal of the manor's reception rooms. While Pheely was perched high on a woodwormed Windsor chair, Ellen was just a few knock-kneed inches above the ground on a lumpy *chaise-longue* with books propping it up in place of its missing leg. In front of her, well-dressed locals were lined up on old chintz or leather button-back armchairs, footstools, chesterfields, refectory benches and garden furniture.

'Look at the Surgeon.' Pheely pointed out Hell's Bells' tall husband, balancing uncomfortably on a child's nursery chair. 'I bet the old bat made him sit there to stop him falling asleep. He snores like a trumpet – you should hear him in church.'

Sir St John Belling was no longer the dashing, blond conqueror who had wowed the dog-eat-dog political world with his mix of leggy, Andrex-puppy charm and lean Doberman aggression. He was now an ageing bloodhound, jowly and grizzled, the blue eyes heavily lidded and downturned, the famous mane so thin on top that he looked as if he had two floppy blond ears. Yet he still had enough of the Belling magnetism to send the wives of Oddlode into a powdering, perfuming frenzy before tonight's gathering. The best summer dresses were out in force, hair had been set in his honour, and tens of pairs of eyes secretly studied him as pearls overheated at blushing throats.

To Ellen's alarm, she was attracting a similar reaction from several ageing gents who craned to look at her over the shoulders of blazers and sports jackets, rheumy eyes taking in the bronzed skin, blonde hair and bare midriff.

The great and the good of the village were, on the whole, considerably older than Pheely and Ellen. And because their hostess had maintained such a strict invitation-only policy, there were far fewer bidders than promises. On totting up the numbers, Ellen calculated that even if every single person in the room bought two lots, there would still be half a page of the catalogue to get through before her massage came up. She hoped that by then her several admirers would be feeling too poor to fork out or would have been marched home by their wives at the promised drinks interval after lot thirty (probably the most eagerly anticipated, being '*A day in the Members Enclosure at Royal Ascot as a guest of Sir St John Belling*'). Then she remembered that there was another reason for the curious, hushed atmosphere of statically charged anticipation: 'Which one's Jasper?' she whispered, as she looked around the room.

'Spurs?' Pheely's eyes searched the backs of thirty or so heads in front of her. 'Not here, unless he's lost all his hair or had a sex change in the past eleven years. All these bidders are boffers or biddies.' She let out a low, throaty giggle, but her eyes still scoured the room for the missing prodigal son.

Ellen thought this was a bit of an anticlimax. After Pheely's build-up, she'd hoped at least to catch a glimpse of the village's worst-ever tearaway. 'Maybe he'll pop by later to see his lot come up.'

'What lot?' Pheely consulted her going-for-a-song sheet. Half-way down the last page, Ellen pointed out the short, cryptic lot fifty-four: 'Three wishes to be granted to the winning bidder, kindly donated by Jasper Belling'.

Pheely let out a great snort.

'One hundred! Thank you, Ophelia!' Hell's Bells pointed her gavel triumphantly.

'Oh, shit.' Pheely looked up with a nervous smile, through which she muttered ventriloquist-style, 'Don't tell me I just bid for a meal in the Fuck Upstream?'

'Are we all done at a hundred?' Hell's Bells boomed.

'Please bid, somebody,' Pheely implored, through her fixed smile. 'C'mon, Giles, help me out here.' She stared helplessly at a suave-looking man in a crumpled linen suit who was lounging against a far wall, and who had been bidding on the lot earlier. He smiled back at her with a roguish wink.

'Bastard.' Pheely clasped her hands.

Ellen, who had terrible munchies now that the dope high was starting to pass, was almost tempted to bid herself if she could claim her meal straight away.

'At one hundred pounds, with Ms Gently.' Hell's Bells raised her gavel like a motorist preparing to take out an injured animal with a shovel. 'Going once . . . going twice . . .'

'No, no, please no.' Pheely closed her eyes in horror.

'One hundred and ten,' came a lazy drawl, and the man in the crumpled suit lifted a finger.

'Yes!' Pheely sighed, her eyes springing open.

'Thank you, Giles!' Hell's Bells was jubilant. 'Ophelia?'

'No!' Pheely shook her head hastily then held her breath until the gavel smashed down on a tall mahogany plant stand that had been placed beside the library steps.

While Gladys busily made a note of the lucky recipient of a meal at the village's gourmet pub, Pheely blew Giles a kiss. He smouldered back at her.

'Giles Hornton,' she told Ellen, in an undertone, 'lives in River Cottage. Dilly keeps her horse in his paddock. Giles is our biggest local solicitor in more than one sense of the word. Watch out – that meal has no doubt been bought with the express intention of cross-examining somebody's bikini briefs, and he just *loves* new girls.' Eyes darting around, she stretched up to whisper in Ellen's ear. 'You're probably the only woman in this room he hasn't slept with. He's quite irresistible, my darling.'

Giles, who was the wrong side of forty with a peppery Tom Selleck moustache, Bahamas tan, dissipated blue eyes and very *Miami Vice* taste in tailoring, hardly struck Ellen as irresistible. He gave her a seedy wink, and she lowered her eyes hurriedly to her catalogue.

'Lot sixteen,' boomed Hell's Bells, 'has been kindly donated by Prudence Hornton, and is half a dozen watercolour lessons, paints and paper included.' She gestured towards a slim, scruffy red-head, who was scowling behind dark glasses in a window-seat.

'Is she Giles's wife?' Ellen asked in alarm, not surprised that the poor woman was looking so glum given that she was sitting in a room of her husband's conquests.

'Ex,' Pheely pulled a face, 'and a very silly cow. She runs the gallery in Cider Lane. Only opens the place up when the moon's in the ascendant, and even then she won't let Capricorns in. She hasn't sold one of my sculptures in months.'

This left Ellen wondering whether Pheely's sculptures were only bought by Capricorns, but she didn't get the opportunity to ask because Hell's Bells was already scouring the room for prey.

'Who'll start me at fifty?' she suggested eagerly.

Pru's watercolour lessons were peddled for just forty pounds in the end, which Ellen guessed hardly covered the materials. She was, according to Pheely's *sotto voce* asides, run ragged by three of Giles's many children, knocked back Valium like Smarties and was known as something of an ancient mariner when it came to her problems. 'Whoever's bought that will find themselves trapped on a hill slapping yellow ochre on to rag paper and listening to Pru's tales of woe. Talk about Watercolour Challenged.'

As the lots came up in turn, she cheerfully gave Ellen the low-down on donors and recipients, whispering through her ventriloquist's smile to avoid being mistaken for bidding again.

'That's Lily Lubowski – from the shop,' she hissed excitedly, as the bidding hotted up for a week in a villager's second home in France. 'Married Joel when he was based at Upper Heyford with the US Airforce, then found herself stuck in Little Rock, Arkansas, for twenty years. When he retired, she dragged him back here. She'd always dreamed of running a tea room in Lower Oddford, but for some reason they ended up with a failing post office in Oddlode, hence the vast array of cakes on sale and the baseball bat hidden behind the counter.'

Lily looked innocuous enough, despite the rather startling peroxide blonde hair and obvious face-lift. Ellen wondered why Pheely called her a complete weirdo. 'Does she sell Little Rock cakes?' she asked.

'Lily's *convinced* that every customer is going to stage a hold-up.' Pheely whispered. 'She once even accused poor Dilly of shoplifting. I'd just sent her in there to fetch my paper, which yet again hadn't been delivered that morning, and the next thing you know Lily has the police crawling all over Oddlode. When the constable asked darling Dilly whether a parent or guardian could be contacted, she tried explaining that her parent was lying in bed at home waiting for her *Guardian*, and mad Lily got the

wrong end of the stick and contacted social services. Having lived
on a diet of US reality TV for two decades, she thinks we're all
candidates for *Jerry Springer* or *America's Most Wanted*. She won't
let her paper-round kids near me now. I read Pixie's *Telegraph*
after she's finished with it.'

It seemed that there were few people in the village Touchy
Pheely trusted, or with whom she hadn't fallen out at some point,
although Ellen sensed that affection lay behind the mischievous
nicknames and heated feuds.

'Your neighbour, Hunter Gardner.' Pheely pointed out a
familiar bullish figure, who was bidding for a day's shooting at
the Lower Springlode artificial grouse moor. 'Great chums with
your mother.'

Ellen recognised the stiff-backed, ex-military man and village
complainer, tonight kitted out immaculately in a tweed suit and
golf-club tie. His Field Farm land divided the Goose Cottage
paddock from the manor's fields and consisted of neatly clipped
enclosures housing rare poultry and miserable-looking snowy-
white show sheep. He and Jennifer had happily conspired in
many a campaign, including the one that had closed the footpath
across their combined land. Hunter, as her mother was proud of
pointing out, had a torch-bearing soft spot for Jennifer Jamieson.
Theo loathed him.

'I might bid on his lot.' Ellen looked at the description, which
offered a month's lawn-mowing courtesy of Hunter Gardner's
gardener, Gary. She badly needed some help with sorting out
the Goose Cottage meadow.

'Don't!' Pheely hissed. 'Gary is the Oddlode poisoner. He'll
napalm everything he can't hack to within an inch of ground
level.'

Pheely had reasons why Ellen shouldn't bid on any of the lots,
which was perhaps not such a bad thing because Ellen hardly had
the money to match some of the ludicrous sums being offered.
It seemed that there was an unofficial competition going on
as to who was the most wealthy and generous villager. The
lawn-mowing was snapped up for over two hundred pounds

by one of the residents of Coppice Court, the new executive
development beside Manor Farm, known to Pheely as 'Gin Palace
Heights'.

'They live in Tanqueray,' she whispered, as the winning bidder
gave his details to Gladys. 'I think he's an accountant in London.
The Gordons and Beefeater families are here, too, but I can't
see Bombay Sapphire and I know the Corks are on holiday in
Tuscany this week.'

'Lot twenty.' Hell's Bells consulted her notes with the help of
the half-moon spectacles that dangled from a gold chain around
her broad neck. 'Ah! Rather special, this one. For those of you
with over-productive Bramley apple trees like me, Ely has offered
to have the fruit harvested and make it into cider for you, which
he will have bottled and labelled in time for drinking next year.
Who'll start me at one hundred?'

A furious contest ensued between Joel Lubowski and the Beefeaters, with lots of vocal badinage and laughter thrown in.

Lots twenty-one through twenty-seven were all donated by Ely
Gates and were, Ellen thought, by far the most interesting of
the evening. Among them was a guided balloon ride over the
valley, during which Ely would explain the way that history
had changed the landscape over the years; a wine-tasting tour
of Lower Oddford vineyard, with a crate of the best vintage
thrown in; a month's unrestricted fishing on the Manor Farm
river frontage; and a fresh flower delivery, ready-arranged, every
week for a year.

The tall, thin, bearded entrepreneur and church stalwart occupied a front-row position, sharing a dog-eared chintz sofa with his
small, puddingy wife Felicity, whose very snub nose lent her the
unfortunate expression of somebody with their face permanently
pressed against a window.

'I had no idea Ely Gates was so profligate.' Ellen whistled softly
remembering her mother calling Oddlode's self-styled tycoon a
tight-fisted, puritanical tyrant.

'Hell's Bells might think she runs Oddlode, but Ely is the
real power,' Pheely told her darkly. 'Ever since his father took

advantage of the change in tenancy law to buy Manor Farm from the Constantines, that side of the Gates family has been changing the shape of the village by selling off farmland for profit. They're worth a fortune now. And doesn't he like to show it!'

It was true that, as well as donating so much, Ely had bought over half the lots so far: his hand was raised so often to bid that, from where Ellen sat, he almost appeared to be jiving in his seat. The residents of Gin Palace Heights might be flashing their fortunes as they outbid each other for babysitting, taxi and gardening services, but by far the most generous benefactor was their near-neighbour. Ely must have parted with thousands of pounds already, but Ellen disagreed with Pheely that he was being conspicuous. Compared to the overexcited, vocal bidding of the village 'macho men', he was understated and softly spoken. And this sombre self-effacement clearly wound up some of the other men far more than their own in-joke goading. They were out for his blood.

Lot twenty-eight, donated by Giles Hornton, was listed in the catalogue as 'Ten hours' legal advice from the senior partner of Market Addington's leading solicitors'. But suave Giles interrupted Hell's Bells before she could announce it.

'Change of plan, your ladyship,' he drawled, glancing at Pheely. 'I've been told my lot is rather dull . . .'

'Too right,' Pheely whispered to Ellen, making her wonder whether it was Pheely who had told him this. 'He should have offered a freebie divorce. That would get everybody going.'

'. . . so I am going to change it, if that's agreeable,' Giles was saying – and now looking at Ellen, his blue eyes apparently willing a couple of her shirt buttons to come open. 'I propose to offer use of my Aston for a day, with or without me as chauffeur. I might even be able to arrange an unrestricted road test around Springlode airfield.' He threw his arms wide and smiled at the room.

From the shocked expressions and several whoops that greeted the gesture, Ellen saw that this was quite a coup.

'Bloody hell!' Pheely's eyes were almost popping out. 'Now he really *is* being a naughty boy.'

Giles Hornton's Aston Martin, it seemed, was the one thing in his life to which he had stayed faithful. A rare vintage DB4, which he had had lovingly restored in silver birch *Italian Job* livery, it was the envy of the village. And nobody coveted it more than Ely Gates.

When the bidding started at a thousand pounds, Ellen wrinkled her brow in disbelief. You could hire a fleet of cars for that. She had never understood men's obsession with motors.

At first, Ely was bidding against Hunter Gardner and one of the Gin Palace husbands. But at fifteen hundred pounds, Hunter was forced to drop out and satisfy himself with the fact that he could always drive around ahead of the winning DB4 joy-rider in his Bentley, rigidly maintaining the speed limit and thwarting all attempts to pass him.

The Gin Palace husband, himself the owner of a Range Rover and a Porsche, had a point to prove against the man on whose old milking yard his mock-Tudor five-bedroom house was built. But Ely would not drop out. The bidding reached two thousand, then three without break. Hell's Bells was in ecstasy.

'Three thousand *two* hundred – and *three*. With you, Ely. And *four*!' The gavel spun like a cheerleader's baton.

Lounging against the wall, Giles winked at Pheely and Ellen.

'Crafty bugger,' Pheely murmured. 'He knew this would get Ely going.'

'Ely tried to buy that car from Giles a few years ago – offered him enough to buy a top-of-the-range new one,' she told Ellen, through her fixed smile. 'And Giles was pretty tempted – that car had got him into a lot of trouble when it was spotted parked outside the homes of lonely Lodes Valley wives whose husbands were in London. It's too distinctive for an adulterer. But Giles loves it, so he turned Ely down and bought himself an Audi estate to make his house-calls in. Ely was *livid*.'

'Why does he want Giles's car so badly?' asked Ellen, watching the Manor Farm tycoon jiving discreetly on the chintz sofa, determined to have his DB4 day.

'Sentimental, darling. It belonged to his father – a status symbol the old man bought when he struck it rich, then never really used. He sold it to Giles in the eighties and bought most of Wyck Farm's land with the proceeds. Ely likes to keep things in the family – that's why he wants it back. He loved that car as a boy. My father said that, as a teenager, Ely used to drive it around the old orchard, slaloming in and out of the apple trees. Can you imagine?'

'Three thousand *eight* hundred – against you, Mr Lewis . . .'

There was something curiously intimate about the way Ely indicated his bids to Hell's Bells, as though they were conducting their own private conversation.

Apart from their hostess, Ely was the person in the room who fascinated Ellen most. In profile, his face was noble, the pewter hair contrasting absurdly well with the dark golden brows and neatly trimmed beard. She could imagine him as a young man with film-star good looks – the Peter O'Toole of the village, with intense, troubled eyes that had yet to be calmed by an unstinting devotion to capitalism and Christianity.

Ellen had long suspected her mother of having a secret crush on Ely Gates, although Jennifer had called him a 'common oaf', an 'upstart industrialist' and a 'village wrecker'. The entrepreneur might stand on paper for everything she loathed, yet his name had cropped up in more conversations during Ellen's short stays at Goose Cottage than any other. Until tonight, she'd never clapped eyes on him and, now that she had, she was certain she'd been right. Ely Gates was an ageing hunk. Jennifer Jamieson's scorn concealed a fast-beating heart. She found herself grinning, chuffed as always to find her mother out.

'Does he have any children?' she asked Pheely idly, hoping to hear the magic words 'unmarried thirty-year-old son'.

But Pheely didn't answer as Hell's Bells' gavel hammered down on the plant stand. The Aston Martin treat had been bought by

Ely for four thousand pounds, and Pheely's own lot was next up. She clutched Ellen's arm tightly. 'Please don't let this be another Pru moment.'

'Lot twenty-nine,' Hell's Bells announced breathlessly, her cheeks now high with colour after such an exhilarating battle. 'A portrait bust to be sculpted by local artist Ophelia Gently, daughter of the renowned sculptor Norman Gently OBE. Ophelia will capture the buyer – or a family member of their choice – in clay, requiring several sittings in her village studio. Who will start me at five hundred?'

The great and the good sat on their hands. Most were eager to get on to the Royal Ascot lot and the wine break. Gladys had already crept off to rev up her corkscrew, leaving her clipboard with Sir St John who was reading the notes jotted on it with an amazed expression.

'Four hundred, then?' Hell's Bells didn't want to hang around either. 'Three hundred? Let's see – two hundred and fifty as an opening bid?'

Pheely was turning paler by the second.

'Twenty-five,' offered Giles Hornton, in his come-to-bed drawl.

'Thank you, Mr Hornton. Twenty-five. Do I see thirty?'

'You'll see fucking stars if you sell my promise to that bastard for a pony,' Pheely breathed.

It was humiliation on a grand scale. Ellen hardly dared look at her. 'One hundred!' she bid, wondering what the hell she would do with a huge pottery depiction of herself when she went travelling.

'One hundred from the back of the room, thank you,' Hell's Bells pointed her gavel at Ellen, then swung it towards Giles, who shook his head and smirked.

'Bastard,' Pheely muttered. 'You don't have to buy it, Ellen. Honestly. I don't mind.'

'I want to.' She gulped, hoping Pheely wouldn't make her look like a goblin.

Hell's Bells was asking for more bids. Nobody caught her eye. There was a long pause.

'Are we all finished at one hundred?' she suggested hopefully, and glanced at the big wall clock, which already read a quarter to nine with less than half the lots sold.

'One hundred and twenty-five,' bid the head of the Beefeater household.

'You're off the hook,' Pheely patted Ellen's hand, still mortified that her work was meeting with such little enthusiasm.

'One fifty!' Ellen went straight back in.

'One fif— Two hundred!' Hell's Bells announced a new bid before she'd finished declaring Ellen's.

'Two fifty!'

'Ellen, stop it.' Pheely giggled, but the colour was coming back into her cheeks as she looked around to see whom Ellen was bidding against. It wasn't the Beefeaters or Giles, all of whom were watching silently. Whoever it was had a discreet way of attracting their auctioneer's attention.

'Three hundred!' she announced, and Ellen wondered if the Lady of the Manor was bidding herself.

'Three fifty.'

'Four hundred.'

'Five hundred!' Ellen wasn't sure how much longer her nerve would hold. She really couldn't afford that much. It was a huge cut of her world-adventure savings.

'Seven hundred and fifty!'

'Don't,' Pheely warned her, but it was too late.

'One thousand.'

'At one thousand pounds!' Hell's Bells boomed. 'Any advance on one thousand pounds?' She tapped her gavel menacingly against the palm of her hand.

There was silence.

Shit, Ellen thought in a panic. What have I done?

'Fifteen hundred pounds,' came a deep, deep bass cry in a thick Oxfordshire accent from the front of the room.

Pheely's pale face had flushed almost purple. 'Raise your bid,' she hissed at Ellen.

'I can't. I haven't got the money.'

'At fifteen hundred pounds . . .' Hell's Bells stared at her. 'Young lady?'

'Pleeeeeeeaaaaaase,' Pheely whispered, in her little-girl voice.

But Ellen simply couldn't chance it another time. She wasn't sure what had possessed her to take it so far in the first place, but she certainly wasn't going to spend all her travelling money on a clay effigy, however much she liked Pheely.

'At fifteen hundred pounds then . . . going once . . . going twice . . .' The gavel lifted. 'Sold – to Mr Gates.'

'Bum.' Pheely sagged back in her chair. 'I *hate* doing beards.'

Ellen gaped at her, hardly able to believe that Pheely had wanted her to gamble her entire savings just because she hated sculpting facial hair. 'Maybe he wants you to do his wife?' she suggested.

'My platform would collapse under the weight of the clay,' Pheely said uncharitably, now in what appeared to be a foul sulk.

Ellen sat silently through the next lot, torn between intense irritation and amusement, hardly noticing the battle that went on between henpecked husbands to buy their wives a Ladies' Day at the races with Sir St John.

'At five thousand three hundred pounds . . . going once, going twice . . . Sold to Mr Heaton-Jones! Congratulations. But whatever you do, don't lend my husband any money to bet with.' Hell's Bells looked surprised when this was greeted with guffaws of laughter: she had been quite serious. She tapped the gavel against the plant stand for attention. 'Thank you very much, ladies and gentlemen. We will now break for fifteen minutes' refreshment in the orangery before reconvening here promptly at nine.'

'Let's go to the pub.' Pheely grabbed her bag.

'Don't you want to stay?'

'Not particularly.' She was watching Ely leave the room with the others, all obediently filing out onto the terrace towards the orangery. 'The wine will be ghastly and Jasper's not here to have a squizz at.'

Ellen was finding Pheely's bossiness grating, and dug in her heels. 'I want to see my lot come up.'

'We can come back in an hour.' Pheely was already skipping away, beckoning Ellen towards another door that led to a back corridor. 'You'll only get mobbed here. Come on, Ellen, I haven't been to the Lodes Inn for years. Oh, hurry up – Giles is coming over!'

'I want to stay for a quick drink,' Ellen insisted. Pheely was doing another of her butterfly dances, the fanciful flight of someone who wanted to keep her new friend all to herself.

Anyway, they were already under attack.

'Ophelia! Radiant as always!' The moustachioed Lothario swept in and took her hand to kiss it, naughty blue eyes looking up at Ellen as he did so, X-raying through to her bra, then crossing as they focused on her belly-piercing. 'I don't believe I've had the pleasure . . . ?

'Giles Hornton – Ellen Jamieson,' Pheely muttered, scuffing her toe on the thinning Axminster, not looking at either of them.

'*Enchanté.*' He kissed Ellen's hand too, proving that his moustache was as soft as a teddy bear's head and not bristly at all. He smelt overpoweringly of expensive aftershave and Clorets. 'Now, ladies, may I accompany you through for a drink?' He put a practised arm around their waists.

Within five minutes of finding herself trapped in the stuffy orangery, Ellen was wishing that they had sloped off to the pub after all. The wine – warm sweet Liebfraumilch – was foul, and the company overbearing. As well as suave Giles, she was soon being courted by Hunter 'How is your dear mother?' Gardner, the 'Do you hunt?' joint MFH of the Lode and Foxrush Vale, a camp antiques dealer and even Sir St John himself: 'Are you the young lady coming to Ascot with me?'

When Pheely – who was refusing to talk to any of them – headed out on to the terrace for a cigarette, Ellen excused herself and dashed after her.

'Told you – mob tactics,' Pheely muttered, lighting a Marlboro and offering Ellen the packet.

Ellen shook her head, trying to muster the will-power to keep resisting.

It was a beautiful evening, the last pink streaks of light being stolen from the sky by the ink-spill night. The manor's gardens looked seductive and opulent in the half-light, the roses that crowded around the terrace wafting out their old-fashioned lady's-chamber odour, the huge black yew hedge hiding a multitude of birds wishing one another good night. In the distance, they could just hear the thud, thud of Roadkill playing their second set in the village hall.

Now that she was outside, Ellen no longer wanted to return to the auction. She wanted to sit outside the pub, letting the cool of the evening carry away the stale tiredness of her long day as she sank a long, ice-cold beer and wound down ready to collapse into bed. If Pheely wasn't being so sulky, she'd have grabbed her hand and suggested they make their escape over the lawns. But she really needed to find a loo first. She stifled a yawn, noticing that the roses' subtle scent was being overpowered by Pheely's cigarette and another, more acrid smoke.

'Ophelia.' There was a step behind them.

'Do I smell sulphur?' Pheely hissed, spinning around.

Ely Gates was standing behind a wall of cigar smoke, clutching a very fat Havana in one hand. Close to he was even more overpowering and enigmatic – tall, craggy and sombre with that ageing-hero face and intense navy blue eyes. He nodded at Ellen without interest. 'May I have a word in private, Ophelia?'

'If you must.' Pheely shrugged, eyes downcast.

Ellen waited for a moment, hoping for an introduction to enigmatic Ely, but none was forthcoming. 'I'll leave you to it, then,' she offered, and slipped back into the house by an open door at the far end of the terrace to avoid the mob in the orangery.

She found herself in a huge, shadowy dining room, panelled from floor to ceiling with gleaming oak covered in sporting prints and paintings – most of them macabre depictions of various blood sports. The chairs were all missing from around the vast mahogany table, which was littered with Saturday supplements and paperwork. Ellen glanced around for the most obvious way back into the main house.

An open door directly opposite her led to what appeared to be an old-fashioned billiard room. She could just make out the corner of the table and could hear the tap-click-rattle of cue tip sending white ball on its way to strike a coloured ball into a netted pocket alongside its companions. She was about to pop her head in to ask for directions when a door opened out of sight and Lady Belling's distinctive baritone bark let out a short, exasperated cry of relief. 'There you are! I need you in the Blue Drawing Room in five minutes.'

'Why?' The voice that replied was male, but too smooth and classless to be Sir St John's colonial croak.

'You *know* why.'

'Is she here?'

'No.'

'But *he* is, isn't he?'

'Of course he is. And you must be civil. Five minutes.'

With the cryptic exchange clearly at an end, the door slammed shut again.

The next tap-click of cue against ball was an angry one, followed by a thud in place of a rattle, as the ball flew right off the table and rolled across the floorboards. A moment later it rumbled through the open door into the dining room.

Ellen watched it roll up to her feet, kissing the pink of her nail varnish as it came to a halt. Looking up, she saw a shadow move across the billiard room, but nobody appeared in the door. There was another angry tap-click followed by the sound of balls ricocheting all over the table. Perhaps now wasn't the time to make casual enquiries about the manor's lavatories.

There were two more doors in the panelling to her right. Giving the snooker ball a jaunty kick back into the billiard room, she headed towards them. But when she pulled open the first, she found herself staring at a huge cupboard of silverware.

'She's sold the best stuff,' a smooth voice told her, 'but you might find a couple of decent Asprey pieces left, if you look hard enough.'

Ellen glanced over her shoulder to see a figure silhouetted in the doorway, a red ball held up in one hand. With the only source of light behind him, it was impossible to make out his age or features, but Ellen was pretty certain it had to be Spurs Belling.

'Sorry.' She closed the door and turned to face him. 'I was looking for something more in the – er – porcelain line.'

He tossed the ball up and caught it. 'Minton or Copeland?'

'Armitage Shanks?'

He laughed, white teeth flashing in the shadow, and nodded towards the other panelling door. 'Through there, then immediately left – go to the end of the corridor, through the double doors to the main hall and it's under the arch to your right.'

Grateful that she didn't have to live in a house this huge or complicated, Ellen thanked him and slipped out through the second door. It led to an inner lobby from which there were a multitude of doors and corridors. Taking the first door on the left as she thought she had been instructed, Ellen found herself walking straight into the billiard room. At the same moment Spurs Belling walked back through the dining-room door at the opposite end, so that they appeared like two ballet dancers entering stage right and left.

He looked across in surprise and – now that it was lit by the huge chandelier that hung from the centre of the high ceiling – Ellen saw his face. The moment she did so, she felt a great hammer swing through her chest, splitting her heart wide open.

Ellen had experienced many adrenaline rushes – almost all of them associated with dangerous sports. She had jumped from aeroplanes with nothing but a few metres of silk to save her; she'd thrown herself from bridges and cranes with glorified elastic bands tied to her ankles; she'd ski'd mountains on a plank of waxed carbon, and she'd emerged from twenty-foot wave tubes balanced on a wooden board moving at twenty miles an hour. She knew the taste of adrenaline as well as the taste of cola, and loved the high it brought.

But the first time she saw Spurs Belling's face, she couldn't handle the adrenaline at all. This was all fear with no silk or elastic bands to save her. It turned her into a terrified, frozen plank of wood.

His eyes were dazzling – sterling-silver attraction traps set in a spellbinding face. Without warning, Roberta Flack started crooning in her ears, her deep voice mellifluous with sweet meaning: 'The First Time Ever I Saw . . .'

'Shit!' She wrenched her eyes away and started to back out of the room.

'It's okay,' he called. 'I'm heading in your direction – I'll drop you off *en route*. This way's quicker anyway.'

Not waiting for her – and apparently unaware of the effect he'd just had – he crossed the huge room, beckoning her to follow as he loped past lonely cracked-leather sofas whose companions had clearly been gathered for the auction, then on past a grand piano with no stool. The single room was as big as Goose Cottage, its battered snooker table so dwarfed by the grand dimensions that it seemed no bigger than a butler's tray. Following behind, Ellen was torn between staring around at a tatty upper-class adult playroom and gazing at Jasper's retreating back, grateful that his face was out of sight once more, although his bottom came a close second in the magnetism stakes.

With his scruffy jeans, ancient T-shirt, trainers and unkempt black curls, he looked more like a builder's labourer than a toff's son. He was certainly built like one, with broad shoulders, sinewy sunburnt arms and narrow hips. And he smelt noticeably of horse.

'Here.' He opened a door that led to a high, grand hallway through which the great and the good were milling back towards the Victorian wing, wine in hand. A few turned to look as the door opened, and almost dropped their glasses when they saw Spurs. 'Straight opposite.'

'Thanks.' Ellen couldn't look at him. She dashed through the door and sought sanctuary in the loo, pressing her hot face to the cool wall beside her as soon as she sat down. Nice one, Ellen, she told herself wretchedly. Kick an aristocrat the snooker balls, get caught ogling the family silver, then ask the way to the loo. You are *so* cool.

His eyes still burned into hers, even though she closed them tight and felt the grit of the tile grout scrape her brows.

She might have guessed that the Bellings' prodigal son would possess the best genes this side of a Levi Strauss factory, and that no amount of tearaway, drug-dealing misspent youth would have muted his natural, almost feral beauty. That was just typical of the upper classes, who always got the best deals from nature and nurture. Naturally, Spurs Belling had his mother's amazing silver eyes, freckled skin and wild hair, his father's rugby-player build and beautiful curved mouth. It went without saying that he would be a sublimely good-looking man – probably as beautiful as any man Ellen had ever encountered in a lifetime travelling with some of the best specimens in the world. And he had that easy, arrogant confidence to match. But that was not what had made her feel so giddy that she'd almost passed out.

Spurs Belling had the X-factor. In all her years of travelling with dangerous sports fanatics, especially surfers, Ellen had only met half a dozen who truly had it. And Richard, who had so wanted it, had never really possessed one cell of X.

Spurs Belling was pure, unadulterated X. It made him very, very dangerous. And, as far as Ellen was concerned, it made him someone to be avoided at all costs. She was going straight home.

She waited until the sounds of the great and the good filing past the cloakroom had faded into the distant burble of the great and the good trapped in the Blue Drawing Room. Then she crept out into the hall and headed for the front doors.

'Wrong way,' a voice called behind her.

Closing her eyes, Ellen ground to a reluctant halt.

'You really do have an appalling sense of direction.'

She turned around and smiled apologetically at two long, muscular legs, refusing to let her eyes travel any higher. 'Act-ually, I was going to leave. My dog's already been alone several hours and—'

'Mother will be livid.' He sounded amused.

'I'm afraid I don't know your mother, but please apologise for me. I'm Ellen, in case she asks.'

'You can do it yourself. Mother! *Ellen* wants to apologise.'

'Whatever for?' came an impatient bark, as footsteps rattled down a wooden staircase. A moment later two sturdy female legs had joined the denim ones.

Ellen winced and looked up, forcing a big smile. 'Lady Belling, we haven't met but—'

'You're the Jamieson gal.' She fixed Ellen with the two silver bullets, clearly impatient to get back to her sitting ducks.

'Yes. I was just telling your son I have to get home, so I'll miss the rest of the auction I'm afraid, but—'

'Nonsense!' she bellowed, the silver bullets transforming into harpoons. 'You must come back in. Little Ophelia's been looking for you everywhere. Rude to let her down, eh?'

'I'm sure she'll under—'

'Come on – trot on. You too, Jasper. You can't lurk around out here like a butler.' Five feet nothing of brawn and will-power, Hell's Bells ushered them both through the double doors as though shooing reluctant Aberdeen Angus up a cattle ramp. As they were propelled through, Spurs muttered in Ellen's ear, 'I'll bid on yours if you bid on mine.'

Ellen stared at the room in disbelief. Almost all the assorted bric-à-brac furniture was now empty. Only the faithful few – Ely and his wife, Hunter Gardner and a few of the old-biddy bidders – remained. The Gin Palace residents had gone, as had the Lubowskis, along with suave Giles and his flame-haired ex-wife.

Sitting on an ornate dining chair in a middle row, as close to the door as possible, Pheely shot Ellen a look of panic-stricken empathy, rolling her eyes. While Jasper slumped angrily into a huge carpet sofa near the front, Ellen nipped in behind Pheely.

'Where have you been?' her friend murmured.

'I got lost on the way to the loo. What about you?'

'Frogmarched back by Ely bloody Gates. Who was that you came in with?'

'Jasper Belling, I think. Isn't it?'

Pheely craned her neck, but he was submerged in the sofa several rows ahead. Only one scruffy trainer was visible. The huge green eyes turned to look at Ellen. 'That can't be Jasper. He used to be *so* beautiful. Like an angel, my father always said. Besides, he's blond.'

Dignified in the face of such desertion, Hell's Bells clambered on to her library steps and took up where she had left off as though nothing had changed.

'Lot thirty-one.' She tugged at the half-moons on their chain. 'A weekend at Eastlode Park, full board, all facilities at your disposal. Do I hear a thousand pounds? . . . Five hundred, then? . . . Two? It's in a *very* good cause.'

Ellen could hardly bear to watch as lot after lot was hammered home at knock-down prices, almost all of them to Ely Gates. Gone was the machismo competition among the village men. Most lots flew past with just a single bid, however paltry, securing the promise.

The occupant of the sofa – who might or might not be Spurs – didn't bid on a single item. Neither did Pheely nor Ellen: they were covertly scraping their chairs closer together to discuss escape tactics.

'Do you have a mobile phone with you?' Pheely breathed.

'Yes, but it's switched off.'

'Turn it on and call this number.' Pheely recited her own mobile number. 'I'll pretend it's Dilly having a crisis and that you must give me a lift. Then we can piss off to the pub.'

'I have to bid on something before we go. I feel so mean otherwise.'

'Bollocks you do. Just call the number.'

'Lot fifty-three,' Hell's Bells read from her list. 'A course of riding lessons donated by Rory Midwinter. Who'll start me at one hundred?'

'I'll bid on this.' Ellen made to raise her hand. 'I need to learn to ride so I can trek in Mongolia.'

'Don't.' Pheely grabbed her hand before she could raise it.

'Rory's Hell's Bells' nephew. He taught Dilly to ride and she's always falling off. He's hopeless.'

Since the lot immediately attracted several bids from the biddies trying to get cheap lessons for beloved, pony-mad grandchildren, Ellen acquiesced and reached for her phone.

'Seventy pounds to Mrs Turnball . . . Going, going, gone!' The plant stand took another hammering. 'Right, that means we've reached lot fifty-four.' Hell's Bells cleared her throat and shot the carpet sofa a hard look. 'Three wishes to be granted to the winning bidder, kindly donated by Jasper Belling.'

Buttocks shifted uncomfortably on seats and disapproving murmurs were trapped behind pursed lips.

'Who'll start me at five hundred?' Hell's Bells offered menacingly, hoping to intimidate a hand into shooting up. There was a chortle of amusement from the biddies and the silver gaze slid towards them with deadly intent. 'Is that an opening bid from you, Hyacinth?'

The biddies looked away hastily and adopted stone-statue stances.

'Two hundred and fifty, then?' A winning smile lifted the patrician features, as she willed her guests to bid on her son's lot.

The few buyers left at the auction all shared a common goal: to avoid buying Jasper Belling's lot at all costs. The room was toxically silent, the hatred within it almost palpable.

'Come on. Who'll start me at a hundred?'

Ellen could feel embarrassment tightening the seams of her shirt on Spurs' behalf as she glanced around the static room. It was like sitting in a chamber of cryogenically frozen corpses, all of whom had died from inhaling the same bad smell.

The trainer poking out from the sofa twitched angrily.

Taking advantage of the lull, Pheely glanced at Ellen again, then at the phone she was clutching, and mouthed, 'Hurry up!'

'Fifty?' Hell's Bells growled desperately, glaring with ill will at a hunting crony.

Ellen turned on her mobile, watching the little screen. At the same moment that Hell's Bells announced in a furious voice that she'd take 'any offer whatsoever for this lot', the little phone let out a shrill 'woo-hoo' to announce that text messages were waiting.

'Is that a bid?' Hell's Bells raised her chin triumphantly.

Ellen looked up. 'Um – er . . .' The silver gaze was spellbinding in its power. Hell's Bells knew full well that she had Ellen completely at her mercy. Then a curious, almost girlish smile lit up her freckled face. 'Shall we say five pounds?'

The trainer kicked the sofa arm hard.

Ellen smiled uncertainly, wondering if this was a joke.

'Say no,' hissed Pheely. 'Say no, absolutely not.'

But Hell's Bells had already taken the smile as agreement. 'Five pounds I'm bid for lot fifty-four. Any advance on five pounds? No? In that case, going . . . going . . . gone.' There was an unmistakable sound of splintering wood as gavel hit plant stand. 'Make a note of the name, Gladys.'

'Oh, I have, your ladyship,' Glad Tidings' pink face peered at Ellen over her clipboard, the berry eyes conveying a curious mixture of victory and sympathy.

'You idiot,' Pheely muttered, and then she gasped as, ahead of them, a dark head of curls appeared over the sofa and two compelling eyes studied Ellen.

Snap! Those silver traps claimed Ellen's gaze in return – lapis-lazuli fixed in a sterling hold. She held her breath.

'Blood-*y* hell,' Pheely breathed. 'I don't believe it. We must get out of here.' Grabbing Ellen's phone, she dialled her own number. A moment later, the theme tune to *Roobarb and Custard* was piped into the grand manor drawing room courtesy of a small Nokia.

'Sorry! Emergencies only!' Pheely feigned embarrassment as she answered it. 'Hello . . . *what*? WHAT? *Now?* Oh, my *God*. Of course. Straight away, darling . . . Ssh, ssh. Stop crying. Of *course* I'll come. I'll need a lift – oh, hang on. I have a friend here.' She covered the phone and asked in an overloud voice, given that Ellen was just inches away, 'Can you give me a lift to Trowbridge in your jeep, darling? It's a complete crisis call.'

'Now?' Ellen, a hopeless actress at the best of times, found herself doing her awkward Eliza Doolittle voice as though trying out correct vowel sounds for the first time.

'Yes . . . *now*! We haven't a second to spare.' By contrast, Pheely was really getting into her role as she pretended to talk into the phone again. 'We're on our way, darling. Try to hang on in there until we get to you – and don't do anything silly.'

Ellen hoped the rest of the room – which was agog – couldn't hear Pheely's voice echoing out of her own phone in stereo from the depths of her handbag followed by a shriek of feedback as the call was curtailed and Pheely threw her phone in with it.

'Sorry, everybody!' She stood up, grabbing Ellen's arm. 'So rude to leave like this, but Dilly's in peril. Fabulous night, Isabel. Thanks so much.'

Standing on her library steps, Hell's Bells regarded them with astonishment.

They were almost out of the door when Gladys hopped across the room to accost them. 'Haven't you forgotten something, dear?' She held out her hand to Ellen.

'What? Oh – right.' Ellen fished in her pocket and found a tenner.

'I'll fetch change.'

'Please don't – it's in a good cause.'

Gladys gave her a wise look, which told Ellen that her ten pounds was going to be the most expensive donation of her life.

Looking over the little woman's shoulder, she could see Spurs still watching her from his sofa, his unsmiling face tilted with interest. She rocked as her body took a huge and unexpected G-force jolt. It was like standing at an open aeroplane hatch looking down into pure white cloud.

Then Pheely grabbed her arm and tugged her back into the fuselage, eager for some light refreshment.

'Are you sure we're safe in here?' Ellen asked again, as she sipped her pint at a corner table of the Lodes Inn. The pub was so close to the Bellings' home that they were almost drinking in the shadow of the manor walls. 'What if somebody from the auction comes in?'

'None of that lot drinks in here,' Pheely insisted, knocking back her pint of Guinness with such speed that she gave herself a moustache like Giles Hornton's in negative. 'Neither do I normally, but I thought you'd like it. It's very *authentic*, isn't it?'

It was also certainly authentically popular, the main saloon being so packed with locals that getting to the bar was impossible. Ellen and Pheely were in the 'lounge', which was no more than two sticky tables rammed into a broom cupboard beside a dartboard. Their conversation was punctuated by head bobs as they ducked to avoid the arrows flying past their ears or the sweaty armpits of men leaning over to extract their feathered friends from the target.

To Ellen's surprise, the locals paid the two women barely any heed. If she'd expected the pub to fall silent, *Withnail and I*-style, when they walked in, she had been mistaken. Just like her local in Cornwall, the Lodes Inn was on the tourist trail and accustomed to strangers. Landlord Al Henshall tried his best to discourage them – the pub served no food and was dingily unwelcoming – but a few stray ones always got in. It was assumed that the tanned blonde and her curvaceous friend were staying in one of the village's holiday cottages, or a local B-and-B.

Pheely was almost as unfamiliar here as Ellen, and she seemed impossibly overexcited by the anonymity. 'This was such a good idea – we should have come when I first suggested it. That way you wouldn't have got lumbered with your death wishes and I wouldn't have been asked to cast a magic Godspell in just five weeks. How I'm going to make that girl look human is beyond me – her face is already like a death mask.'

'Godspell?' Ellen recognised the name. 'The little Goth?'

'You *have* picked up village life quickly.' Pheely added a white nose to her moustache as she took another swig of Guinness. 'Yes. Bloody Ely wants me to capture the little monster in clay in time for his garden party – that's just six weeks away. He really does take the pail sometimes. And Godspell is very, very pale.'

'Hang on . . . we're talking about the portrait bust he bought, right?' Ellen was chasing butterflies again.

'Yes. Ely wants his precious daughter encapsulated by these magic hands.' Pheely looked at her broad, artistic fingers, which were scattered with gaudy glass rings. 'Quite frankly I'd rather ring her scrawny little neck. I suppose I should thank heaven he didn't ask me to sculpt Enoch. Ely's son is pure poison.'

'Godspell the Goth is Ely Gates's daughter?' Ellen made the connection with some surprise.

Pheely ducked again as a dart spun towards double nineteen just above her head.

'She doesn't look much like her parents.' Ellen tried to match up the small, vole-faced Goth with huge hunky Ely or her fat, snub-nosed mother.

'I can assure you she probably does.' Pheely giggled, 'but given that neither Ely nor Felicity is one of them, we shall never know. She's adopted – both the Gates brats are. Felicity couldn't have children.'

'Oh.' Ellen blushed. 'Oops.'

Pheely shrugged. 'It happens. I can assure you, they're as spoilt and indulged as any naturally born children would be – more so,' she said, with feeling. 'That awful wailing we heard earlier – Roadkill.' She dropped her voice, aware that she was in Wyck territory. 'Godspell is their lead singer. Ely paid for all their equipment and amps and lets them practise in one of his barns. He's even booked them to play at his garden party, as well as the usual Morrell on the Moor string quartet. Dreadful.'

Ellen grinned at Pheely's somewhat old-fashioned outlook.

'Ely assures me he'll make sure she comes for at least a dozen sittings, but I can't imagine how,' she was saying. 'That girl is a law unto herself and practically nocturnal. When she's not skulking around the graveyard or shouting into microphones, she's fiddling with those creepy pets of hers. Did you know she has the third largest private collection of amphibians and insects in Great Britain?' She shuddered. 'And she's hardly a girl – at twenty-three she's old enough to know better. At that age cock and roach should mean something entirely different to a woman. Another beer?'

Ellen had barely sucked the froth off her Stella. She watched in amazement as Pheely burrowed into the crowd around the bar – like a piglet in a huge litter fighting for a teat – and emerged moments later with two pints held aloft. 'What fun.' She slapped the drinks on to ash-crusted beer mats.

'Is Reg here?' Ellen asked, in a low voice, peering into the throng around the bar in search of the wiry gardener.

Pheely cast a look over her shoulder as she sat down. 'I haven't seen him. Probably whooping it up with his chums at your cottage.' Ellen was appalled, and Pheely giggled naughtily. 'He always moves on to the Legion at nine. You can set your watch by it. Any later and he's too drunk to avoid falling into the duck pond. I've been thinking . . .' she lit a cigarette '. . . with any luck Spurs Belling won't fulfil his promise to you. After all, who would for five pounds?'

'I paid a tenner in the end.'

'Darling, that boy – man, I suppose he is now – lights his cigarettes with tenners. That lot of his was terribly silly, you have to admit. He was obviously only there tonight because the old bag forced him to be.'

'Has he changed much?' Ellen couldn't resist asking about him now that Pheely had brought up the subject. 'You seemed pretty surprised when you saw him.'

The green eyes were shielded with long, painted lashes as Pheely drew a smily face in her Guinness top. 'Mmm. I was.'

'You said he used to be blond?' Ellen fished.

The smily face gained a few freckles, 'Mmm. He was – at least, as a little boy. Now I think about it, he did get darker, but he was always dyeing it strange colours so it was hard to tell. I remember one summer it was shocking pink.'

'Was he a New Romantic?' Ellen remembered her own teenage predilection for blue streaks.

'I don't think you could ever call Spurs romantic.' Pheely rolled her cigarette tip on the rim of the ashtray.

'He must have been quite outrageous by Oddlode standards.'

'He outraged most people, yes.'

'Why?'

'Because he was evil, Ellen.' The sigh that followed this statement made it clear that Pheely didn't want to go there. The
butterfly mind had closed its wings.

Great! Ellen swigged at her lager. The ice-cream pump had
chosen this moment to seize up. All she wanted was a few facts in
case she needed to make three wishes. She hadn't even wanted to
buy them. She found her attraction towards him more annoying
than enjoyable, and had no wish to get embroiled in village feuds.
All she wished for right now was time to get over what had
happened between her and Richard – Richard who was so good
and honest. She knew a bad boy when she saw one – and if Saul
Wyck was dodgy, Jasper Belling was lethal. Why was it she always
found the sinners so much more compelling than the saints? Had
Richard been a sinner, perhaps they would have lasted the trip.

'I just hope, for your sake, that tonight's cheapest lot is forgotten about by tomorrow,' Pheely said eventually, adding fangs to
her smily face.

'What *is* so bad about him?' Ellen asked, although her mind
was only half engaged.

Pheely swept her corkscrew curls from one shoulder to the
other and raised her glass, peering into the black liquid. 'His soul
is this colour, Ellen.'

Ellen stared at the Guinness. It was Richard's favourite tip-
ple. She found it hard to think of it as akin to a black soul.
It reminded her of the Treglin Arms, late-night lock-ins and
doorstep sandwiches.

'My father liked Spurs.' Pheely looked at her over the white
foam. 'Daddy was one of the few to keep believing in him when he
turned bad. He said he was a bird of prey trapped in a gilded cage,
that he was misunderstood and unloved. He encouraged Spurs to
paint. He's a talented bastard, Spurs, but of course he wasted it
on forgeries later on. And he so abused my father's trust. He stole
from him – hundreds of pounds went missing, as well as things

from around the house, but Daddy refused to make an issue of it. I'm a few years older than Spurs – I was perhaps nineteen or twenty at the time, with a toddler to look after – and I don't think I did enough to protect Daddy from him. He had always seemed so invincible and was pigheadedly independent, but I didn't know about the cancer then. He didn't tell me until the last few weeks, when he knew he had little time left to share with me.'

The dark curls drew their heavy curtains across her face as she dipped her head and kneaded her forehead with her fingertips, grappling for self-control. It was obviously something she found hard to talk about without an outpouring of raw emotion, harder still in a noisy pub. But Ellen sensed that the setting had been intentional. Pheely had deliberately sought out a backdrop where she knew she couldn't rant, rage and cry.

When the green eyes reappeared through the curtain, her voice was controlled as she finished the story quickly, in a quiet mono-tone. 'In those last few weeks of Daddy's life, Spurs dominated my father. He was the son he'd never had – my mother died in childbirth, you see. And Spurs spent those precious weeks stealing from him, watching shoot-'em-up films on television while Daddy fought for breath, drinking his whisky, smoking the strong French cigarettes that had given Daddy his death sentence, having loud parties in our house.

'When Daddy died, Spurs vandalised all the sculptures in our garden. I came back from the funeral to find all the stone statues beheaded – the beautiful birds, horses and dogs truncated and mutilated, limbs everywhere. The bronzes were harder to damage, but he'd had a damn good go, gouging out eyes with a screwdriver and breaking anything he could from its plinth. It's as though Spurs wasn't satisfied by hurrying my father to his grave. He wanted to jump on it too, brutalise all the beautiful legacies Daddy had left behind.'

Ellen pressed her fingers to her lips, looking across at Pheely, hardly able to bear the hurt and anger that twisted the innocent-little-girl face into a bitter mask.

'I wasn't quite telling the truth when I told you that I couldn't bring myself to sell Daddy's sculptures.' Pheely's mouth wobbled, and she looked away, blinking at a rebellious tear, her voice barely more than a whisper. 'You can't see the scars so well under all the ivy and lichen that have grown over them now, but they're damaged beyond repair. Daddy left the house to Daffodil and the sculptures to me, but of course they're worth nothing broken. When Spurs went on his demolition course, he turned me into a prisoner at the Lodge. I couldn't afford to get out even if I wanted to.'

Ellen stared into the black Guinness, as dark as tar beneath its snow-white cap. 'And it was definitely Spurs who vandalised the sculptures?'

'Oh, yes, he left his calling card.' Pheely whisked away the tear with a finger and tutted angrily at herself. 'He always left a horseshoe behind when he wrecked somebody's world – hanging upside down for bad luck. I found it on one of the headless dancers, dangling from her outstretched arm with a daisy chain wrapped round it. I suppose he thought it was his funeral wreath. Nice touch, huh?'

Ellen reached out and took her hand, feeling the sharp edges of the bright rings digging into her palm as she squeezed it.

'I don't know what you'd wish,' Pheely stared at their hands, 'but if those wishes were mine, I'd wish Spurs Belling had never met my father, and that he could know what it's like to be trapped *without* the gilded fucking cage. Most of all, I wish that he hadn't come back here.'

The spoilt thatched princess was in darkness when Ellen let herself through the gates, her grubby moonlit windows still wide open like sleepy moths airing their wings. She almost screamed as a ghostly figure leaped out of one, cannoning into her and scrabbling at her legs.

'Snork!' She laughed. 'Are you okay, baby?'

Snorkel sank on to her back and offered her freckled belly to the night, letting out excited whimpers. She smelt foul so had clearly been enjoying some late-night perfuming by the garden pond as she bided her time between the cottage and her big meadow playpen.

Without the porch light on and shadowed from the bright moon, Ellen had to grope around to find the keyhole. She supposed this was nothing compared to Pheely, currently reeling her way through the labyrinth maze to the Lodge cottage. Two pints of beer drunk in quick succession and no food for hours made her feel light-headed. When she heard something metal clatter to the flags beneath her feet, she at first thought it was her mobile phone until she remembered that Pheely still had it stashed in her handbag. She groped around underfoot and picked up something heavy and rough hewn with bent nails or screws poking out, guessing that she'd managed to dislodge the door knocker.

At last she found the keyhole and fell inside with Snorkel underfoot, giggling as she reached for the lights. Then she looked at the 'knocker'.

But it wasn't a piece of black ironmongery. It was an old horseshoe from which three nails still poked like twisted teeth.

'Oh, shit.' Ellen shivered, reaching for the door frame for support.

That's when she smelt a great waft of roses, overpowering the sweet rocket and lavender in the milk bottles and the stale cigarettes lingering in the air.

She closed the door behind her, but the smell remained, even more intense now.

Ellen followed it to the sitting room and switched on the lights.

The PlayStation console had gone. In its place, on the floor, somebody had picked out a word in rose petals. It simply said, THANKS.

4

The next morning, the rose petals on the flagstone floor were already turning brown when Ellen walked into the sitting room, their subtle scent mobbed by the pungent lavender. The deeply set, leaded windows of Goose Cottage let in the rising sun at curious angles so that the pale golden squares of light seemed to melt over the arms of sofas and around the frames of doorways with Daliesque abandon.

Ellen clutched her mug of tea in both hands and cocked her head as she watched the dust and pollen dance in the square spotlights, disturbed by the swish of her dressing-gown as she moved around the house.

It wasn't yet six, but she'd woken as suddenly as she'd fallen asleep, the tight mousetrap lids that had snapped shut six hours earlier instantly pulled back and pegged open, her eyes taking in the unfamiliar room before her mind had registered that she was awake.

She'd slept in the big attic room under the eaves, among the boxes of Jamieson possessions already packed ready to ship to Spain. She preferred it to her parents' old room, with its surfeit of Victoriana and candle smoke, and the official spare room reminded her too vividly of Richard and their rare but difficult visits to Goose Cottage.

Her short but deep sleep had been mugged by dreams of bad witches and good fairies, black-souled forests, stampeding horses and silver-eyed men. She was grateful to be awake and wandering around, enjoying the peace of early-morning birdsong, misty sunshine and warm tea.

Fins certainly appreciated her lengthy visit to his barracks, mewing around her ankles and scraping his teeth and whiskers on her toes as she refreshed his food and water and mucked out his litter tray. He sprang on to the work surface by the long, low windows that looked over the drive towards the thatched barn, watching jealously as Snorkel trotted past on boundary patrol, then cocking his head and gazing at the birds on the telephone wire, little purring growls coming from his throat.

'You can go out soon, I promise,' Ellen soothed him, running her hand along his back and tickling the tip of his tail, which twitched cantankerously.

She looked at all the cleaning cloths and rubber gloves abandoned in the utility sink after her quick blitz the day before. She guessed they'd need to be put to use again, and soon, if the house was going to look in a fit state to show to buyers. The thought of confronting Dot and Reg was not appealing, and she doubted that tackling them on a Sunday would be wise, but she wanted to get on. The day stretched ahead with the promise of sunshine and . . . cleaning. Then, as she stared out of the window, she remembered she had overlooked another potential Shagger den. What sort of state was the bunkhouse in?

With Fins glaring at her from the opposite side of the window, Ellen picked her way across the gravel from the bootroom door, wishing that she had had the sense to put on some shoes. She pulled her dressing-gown tighter around her. It was surprisingly cold in the early-morning mist: the sun had yet to work up strength to share its warmth.

She made her way cautiously up the stone staircase at the side of the barn to the door, looking across to the thatched roof of the cottage and, beyond, to the village, which still slept under its silk sheet of mist.

The bunkhouse had a decked wooden balcony in front of big paned-glass doors, upon which two green plastic chairs leaned on a small table, all covered with dust and fallen catkins. Somebody had certainly been up here to admire the view, Ellen thought, as she counted the cigarette butts underfoot.

When she let herself into the flat, however, it was neat and orderly with no sign of recent occupation. She put down her bunch of keys on the little peninsula unit that separated the kitchen area from the main living room and padded across the rush mats, letting their scratchy softness ease away the indentations on her soles made by the drive's gravel.

Snorkel had followed her up and bounded around, gazing in fascination out of the low windows, which were far better suited for a dog to admire the views than a human. Theo had always referred to the paying guests that stayed in the bunkhouse as 'Legs', asking how many Legs were booked in for Easter, or whether the Legs were taking breakfast that day. This was because from the outside all that could be seen through dormers that poked from the black thatch, like eyes beneath a pudding basin, were the occupants' calves and feet.

The french windows, which took up most of the balcony end, made the little open-plan room bright, but its steep, beamed ceiling reminded Ellen of a sagging tent canvas drooping between a framework of poles. This illusion was even more marked in the bedroom, which smelt musty and damp after months of neglect, its dark corners strung with spiders' webs.

She opened the curtains above the bed and looked out towards the Lodge and its overrun garden, unable to spot a single stone tile of Pheely's cottage roof among the tangled greenery. In the foreground, she could see the lane bathed in early-morning sunlight, in the centre of which one of Hunter Gardner's precious pedigree fowl had decided to go walkabout and was pecking at a discarded crisp packet. A moment later, the little bantam let out a piercing shriek and scarpered as a familiar-looking fat black and white cat sprang out from Goose Cottage's thick hornbeam hedge.

'Fins!' Ellen scrambled off the bed and charged towards the door. 'Fins!'

By the time she reached the lane, there was no sign of him, just a few black feathers.

Ellen called out his name and did a lap of the lime tree, looking along Lodge Farm's driveway, Goose End and North Street, but she knew him well enough to accept that he had no intention whatsoever of showing himself now that he had escaped his confinement. He would come back, she hoped, when he was hungry – which was often, given his lion-like appetite. In the meantime, she guessed it would make more sense to search for him when fully clothed and wearing shoes.

Heading back through the gates, she cut through the open carport space on the ground floor of the barn, which was cold underfoot and smelt of creosote and old tarpaulins, the workshop at one end goading her with its promise of strimmer, mower and weed-killer.

'Snorkel!' she called, as she climbed the bunkhouse steps again, hoping she hadn't lost her too. 'Snork!' She heard a plaintive bark in reply.

Then she saw the blue-eyed clown's face gazing at her rapturously through the french windows, which had clearly closed on Snorkel when she'd scrabbled against them trying to follow Ellen outside. The Yale lock had clicked shut, trapping dog and keys inside.

'Oops!' Ellen crouched down and tapped at the window, persuading the collie to sit. 'It's okay, Snork – I'm sure there are spares inside. I'll go and look. Hang on in there, baby.'

She hopped back over the gravel towards the bootroom door, and found it closed as she'd left it.

'Eh?' Ellen stepped back curiously, wondering how Fins had escaped. Then she spotted that the catflap had been chewed and clawed, its plastic catch broken where Fins had forced his way out.

She tried the door handle, but the latch had dropped into place when she'd pulled it closed earlier. The key was now in the bunkhouse, along with all the rest.

Ellen rubbed her sore feet and went to investigate the outside of Goose Cottage, certain that she'd left a window open. But all of the princess's sparkling eyes were closed and bolted, her doors latched and mortise-locked. With a groan, Ellen recalled that, disturbed by the rose-petal message and the sinister horseshoe, she had been extra-vigilant in her security check the night before.

By the end of her second circuit, she knew that she was well and truly locked out, the only open window being one of the tiny peephole dormers high in the thatch, itself no bigger than a shoebox.

'Bugger.' She sat on one of the garden benches and rubbed her face, laughing despite herself. 'Bugger.'

She wasn't wearing a watch, but she knew that it was probably only about seven o'clock. She had the Wycks' set of keys and the only others that she knew of, apart from those in a drawer in a *finca* on the Costa Verde, were with the estate agent. She wasn't sure that Seaton's office opened on a Sunday.

Snorkel was barking at each of the low windows of the bunkhouse in turn, gazing at Ellen in confusion as she begged to be let out.

Ellen guessed that the easiest solution was to smash the glass in one of the french windows and retrieve the keys.

She went on a quick recce, but the quarter-inch safety glass, which ran the length of the doors, would take more than a woman in a dressing-gown to break – and she risked hurting herself and Snorkel in the process, not to mention infuriating her mother. She couldn't hope to reach round to the low dormers from the balcony, and the hatch that led up from the carport was now blocked off by flooring that had been laid above it.

Ellen needed a locksmith. She also needed a telephone. Then she remembered that her mobile was not locked inside Goose Cottage with her clothes.

Still keeping half an eye peeled for Fins, she nipped across the lane and headed into Goose End, letting herself through the heavy arched doorway to the magical garden. It was even more dreamlike first thing in the morning, swathed in mist and dappled sunlight, the sculptures looming out of dark shadows. As she passed them, Ellen could now distinguish the damage beneath their green boas of ivy, bindweed and lichen. Limbs and heads were missing, noses chipped off and expressions distorted by vandalism.

She tried to remember the way through the twisting foliage

labyrinth, but she was soon hopelessly lost, pushing her way through the same gap in a hedge and ducking under the same rails continually as she wound her way round in ever-decreasing circles. Her bare feet meant that she had to look down rather than around her, careful not to step on brambles, nettles or root clumps. The same sculptures jumped out at her again and again. Eventually she stopped in her tracks, retied her dressing-gown belt and pulled back her hair from her face in defeat. She didn't even know how to get back out on to Goose End. If she'd had Snorkel with her, she was certain the dog would have found her way through to her giant new friend.

Now that she'd stopped, she could hear the wind chimes that hung from the eaves of Pheely's cottage, but it was impossible to determine which direction the noise was coming from. Then she had an idea.

'Meeeoooooow!' she called. 'Mew, mew, meeooooow!'

Nothing.

'Woof,' she tried another tack. 'Woof! Woof!'

'woof!' came the bass reply, terrifyingly loud even at this distance.

Hamlet had answered.

Keeping up the conversation, Ellen hopped over the tangled undergrowth. Within minutes, the cottage was in view, misted in a cool, dark shadow, a thin plume of smoke puffing from the Rayburn's chimney. At one of the big windows, Hamlet's huge face stared at her in wonder; he had been conversing with a funny-looking dog.

As she approached the door, Ellen guessed that at least she'd find out where Pheely slept.

It took ten minutes to rouse her. Accustomed to Hamlet's window-rattling call, Pheely ignored the resounding barks, and was deaf to the door-knocking and cries from Ellen that accompanied them. Making her way round the outside of the cottage with trepidation – there was a surprising amount of broken glass – Ellen peered in through the windows and saw that the huge open room was unoccupied. Then, at the far gable end of the cottage she spotted a narrow window and peered inside to see a small bedroom tucked behind the chimney breast. The bed was piled high with more clutter and paperwork, but it, too, was empty.

'Who is it?' called a sleepy voice above her.

Ellen tipped her head back and saw a lot of dark curls spilling out of an even tinier window, one that made the Goose Cottage attic shoeboxes look like office windows in Milton Keynes. Pheely could barely fit her face through it to peer out.

'Pheely – it's Ellen. I'm really sorry! I've locked myself out and need my phone.'

'Come in, darling – the front door's unlocked. I'll be down in a sec.'

Ellen waited in the huge downstairs room, battling to keep Hamlet's snorting nose out of her dressing-down until Pheely appeared through a door that was almost hidden in the tongue-and-groove beside the fireplace.

'Daddy's secret lair,' she explained, yawning widely and wading through the clutter in the direction of the kettle. 'It would be very romantic to think he bedded local damsels in there, but actually he pickled onions. It was a bit of a passion of his – he'd pickle all sorts of fruit and veg when he needed a break from sculpting. I've never been able to get rid of the smell – stick your head round and have a sniff. Doesn't bother me, but Dilly hates it.'

True enough, the hidden lobby behind the chimney reeked of vinegar. It led to a tiny spiral staircase that curled up to the little bedroom. Beneath it, another doll's-house room – the one that Ellen had seen outside – was accessed by a door no bigger than a coal hatch.

'What time is it? Ten? Eleven? God, I'm hung-over.' Pheely yawned, as she filled the kettle from the workshop sink; the one in the kitchen was still heaving with dirty pans.

As she swept back to the Rayburn, Ellen saw that she was still wearing the same velvet top that she had been the night before and had wrapped a bed sheet around her waist as an *ad hoc* sarong. 'I think it's a bit earlier,' she hedged guiltily. 'I'm sorry about this – Snorkel jumped on the door and closed it. I need to call a locksmith, and I remembered you had my mobile.'

'Of course I do.' Pheely stretched her arms above her head, shook back her hair and went in search of her handbag. 'Who's Richard, by the way?'

'My ex-boyfriend. Why?'

'Can he be my text boyfriend? Your phone kept beeping with text messages from him when I got home last night. The only way to stop it was to send a reply. We had quite a jolly chat in the end. Oh, damn.' She looked at the phone. 'The battery's flat. Do you have a charger?'

'Yes. In the cottage.' Ellen was looking at Pheely curiously. 'Why didn't you just turn it off if the text alert irritated you?'

'Couldn't work out how.' Pheely handed her the useless phone. 'Richard's made it to Cairns and it's raining non-stop. Apparently the apartment's great, although the sea's full of jellyfish and he misses Snorkel.' She went in search of mugs. 'He's thrilled that you're settling in so well here and have made such a gorgeous new friend, and he agrees that you shouldn't be in any hurry to move on. Stay and relax, he says – and I agree. Seems a lovely chap. Shame it went wrong for you two, but I gather the rot set in a long time before you told him it was over. Tea or coffee?'

For somebody who couldn't figure out how to turn off a Nokia, she was a whiz at reading and sending text messages on it. Ellen was too furious to speak, glaring out of the tall windows at the clay hobgoblins and elves, hating Richard for being so perennially indiscreet, and hoping that he got stung by jellyfish in the non-stop rain for at least a month as punishment for talking to Pheely out of context. His text had been a con. Ellen hadn't been the one to say it was over. The truth was far more complicated and messy.

'Can I use your phone?' she asked eventually.

'Of course.' Pheely waved her towards an ancient, clay-encrusted trill phone on the wall.

'Do you have a *Yellow Pages*?'

'I have a lot of yellowing pages, darling.' She laughed, looking

around. 'There might be a *Thomson's* around here somewhere, if
you have a dig . . . Doesn't the estate agent have a set of keys?'

'I don't think they'll be open.'

Pheely was tipping instant coffee straight from the jar into two
deep bowls. 'They always open on a Sunday through summer
round here, darling – catching all that passing tourist trade.' She
splashed hot water on to the granules. 'You would not *believe* how
many people come to visit the Cotswolds for a day trip around
a wildlife sanctuary and a cream tea afterwards, then head back
home having bought a weekend cottage. Give them a ring.'

'It's . . . er . . . a bit early.'

Pheely splashed milk into the bowls of coffee and glanced up
at a lopsided cuckoo clock. The next moment milk was cascading
all over the quarry tiles. 'Aggggh!'

It was twenty to eight. Even accounting for half an hour wandering around the Lodge's lost gardens, Ellen was an early riser.

'Okay,' Pheely said, when she had recovered her composure.
Hamlet began to clear up the spilled milk as she carried the bowls
of coffee across to the phone. 'In that case, try Dot. She's always
up at dawn.'

'I have the Wycks' only set of keys.'

'I doubt that very much.' Pheely gave her a wise look. 'One
of Reg's nephews works at the heel bar in Market Addington.
That couple literally have the keys to the village. Call them.
The number's here somewhere . . .' She searched through an
ancient roto-card device by the telephone. 'Dot used to clean
for Daddy – they still lived at Wyck Farm then, but they kept
the number when they moved . . . Hang on – here!' She reeled
off a number.

Ellen started to dial, then paused at the last digit. 'I'm not sure
about this, Pheely. What about the Shagger thing and the fact
they've not been looking after the house?'

'No need to mention it,' Pheely said breezily, throwing open the
windows. 'What a beautiful morning! I really must get up before
lunchtime more often – thank you for reminding me how lovely
summer is, my darling. Mmm. It smells so – early!'

The phone rang at the other end of the line, and Ellen braced herself.

'Yeah?' The voice was deep, gruff and angry, and accompanied by a splenetic roar in the background. 'Shut up, Fluffy!'

'Er . . . is that the Wyck household?' Ellen asked, because she wasn't sure which of the family she was talking to, and because she always sounded just like her mother on the phone – Hyacinth Bucket meets Margo Leadbetter, with a touch of Clarrie Grundy.

'Whatever it is you're selling, I don't wanna buy it, all right?'

'Oh, I'm not selling anything. This is Ellen Jamieson – Theo and Jennifer's daughter.'

'Who?'

Clearly not Saul, then. It had to be Reg.

'From Goose Cottage?'

'Yeah, I know it. What about it?'

'I'm sorry, but I've locked myself out and I understand you might have a spare set of keys.'

'You already got them, aincha?'

'Er . . . yes, but I was really hoping you might have another set?'

'No.' The reply was very defensive.

'Oh, I see. In that case, I'm sorry to have bothered you, but while you're on the phone perhaps we could arrange to meet this coming week?'

'Why?'

'Well, I couldn't help notice that you and Dot haven't . . . er . . . managed to do much around the house lately.'

'I *am* Dot.'

'Oh, God, I'm really—'

'Reg ain't got up yet, and when he does he'll be straight down the— He'll be indisposed. It *is* a Sunday, you know. We don't work on the Lord's Day, nor do we take his name in vain.'

Ellen felt her face burn. Not only had she mistaken Dot for her husband but she'd offended the poor woman's religious principles to boot. 'Of course you don't work on a Sunday,' she said, mentally adding *or any other day, as far as I can tell.* 'I only mention it now so that I don't have to bother you again. It *is* rather urgent. Perhaps we could meet tomorrow.'

'You accusing us of summit?'

'No, of course not. But we need to have a chat about the state of the house, don't you think?'

'You need to talk to Reg. He runs that side of the business. I'll tell him you called.' With that, the line abruptly went dead.

Ellen replaced the receiver, noticing as she did so that Pheely was standing stock still on her terrace with her arms outstretched and her face tilted upwards. Apart from the bowl of coffee in one hand and the cigarette in the other, she looked surprisingly like the Angel of the North.

Ellen joined her outside and drank her coffee, passively smoking the cigarette with deep, grateful breaths and fretting about Snorkel as she told Pheely about the rose-petal message and the horseshoe.

'God, why didn't you come straight over here, my darling? I'd have been terrified.'

'I think I'd find getting lost in your garden in the dark even more frightening,' Ellen confessed. 'Besides, the message was quite apologetic, if you think about it.'

'Hmm – "thanks" for letting us treat your house like a squat for several weeks? Hardly. And Spurs is definitely behind that horseshoe. Ugh. How creepy.' She shuddered dramatically, spilling coffee and ash.

'Do you think so?'

Pheely wiped sleep from her big green eyes and fixed Ellen with an intense gaze. 'I mean it – steer clear of him. He's poison. Look at all the bad luck you're already having this morning! That's after just a few hours. Throw that horseshoe away, darling. Do it now.'

'I need to get into the house first,' Ellen reminded her. 'Maybe I could borrow a ladder?'

'Mmm, good idea,' Pheely agreed distractedly, stooping to pull lichen from a stone goblin. 'I'm sure Giles has one – he'll even hold it for you and look up your dressing-gown as you climb.'

'Even if I get inside the cottage, I still don't know if there are any more keys to the bunkhouse there.' Ellen sighed, rubbing her forehead. 'I'll have to get a locksmith.'

Having unearthed a three-year-old *Thomson's Local Directory* from its hiding-place beneath a pile of old box files, Ellen found herself flipping past a huge full-page advert for Seaton's. She dialled the number listed for their Morrell on the Moor office, hoping that there was an answer-machine.

'Lloyd Fenniweather, Seaton's. Hello?' said a surprised male voice.

Equally surprised, Ellen recognised his name as one of the contacts her parents had given her. Now that she was away from the horseshoe, it seemed that her fortunes were changing. 'Am I relieved somebody's in the office!' She laughed. 'I need to talk to you about Goose Cottage – you see—'

'*Very* nice property,' Lloyd butted in, sounding like Tim Nice-But-Dim – killingly posh, gushy and softly spoken. 'Needs a lot of work, of course, and probably overpriced, although I have to warn you the owners won't budge in that department. Then there's the neighbourhood disputes and the rather unfortunate right of way.'

'I beg your pardon?' Ellen was astonished.

'We at Seaton's pride ourselves on our honesty,' he announced breathily. 'To mislead is to miss out, that's our motto. But GC really is *very* pretty. Would you like a brochure? We have no colour ones left, I'm afraid, but I can run you off a photocopy. You're lucky you caught me – it's usually only weekend staff here today and they're not in until ten, but I have a viewing this morning and need the keys.'

'So do I. I need the keys to Goose Cottage.'

'We don't allow unsupervised visits, I'm afraid – I might be able to squeeze you in later this coming week.'

'I live there.'

'I think you'll find it's vacant.' Lloyd's voice – which to Ellen sounded affected now, like that of a bad disc jockey – was teasing.

'No – I think you'll find I'm living there. My parents did tell you. My name is Ellen *Jamieson*. I am the owners' daughter, and I have accidentally locked myself out of the cottage. I'm calling you from a neighbour's house, but I obviously need to get in. Your agency has the only set of spare keys in the UK, and I really need to borrow them.'

Lloyd was super-soothing. 'Ellen! Of *course*. How foolish of me. Not a problem at all – if you come into the office with some ID, I'll make sure the staff here let you have the keys for half an hour.'

'I'm sorry, but I can't. All my ID is locked in the house, along with my car keys, my dog and my clothes. I'm only wearing a dressing-gown. I'd really appreciate your help. Can you just detour here quickly with the keys?'

'No can do,' he said, in the same placating tone. 'I have a VIP client viewing a thousand-acre estate at nine thirty. It's an all-morning appointment. I know the properties in this area like the back of my hand, and there really is no other man for the job, otherwise of *course* I'd send a deputy ahead to greet the man's helicopter so that I could personally let you into your house.' His oily tone failed to mask the openly arrogant sarcasm.

Ellen bristled, although she knew that it wasn't *his* fault she was in this predicament. But his 'overpriced' and 'unfortunate right of way' slips played on her mind so she let her anger bubble through her voice. 'In that case, I'll sort it out myself. But I do need you to meet me at the cottage tomorrow morning to discuss Seaton's representation.'

'I don't actually have my appointments diary with me at this juncture.'

'Oh, yes, you do,' Ellen told him. 'At this juncture, it's the back of that hand you know so well. So grab a biro and write "Ellen Jamieson, nine o'clock, Goose Cottage" on it. I'm sure you're aware that you have a great deal of explaining to do, and I'm giving you the opportunity to do it. To misjudge is to miss out, which is why I will see you tomorrow morning. If you're not there promptly, I shall make my dissatisfaction abundantly clear to your superiors. Understood?'

'Absolutely.'

'Good. I look forward to meeting you.'

'And I you.'

Ellen hung up. 'Toffee-nosed idiot.'

'You are so utterly, utterly cool, darling!' Pheely had been listening avidly, now eating chopped fruit from her coffee bowl. 'I'd have burst into tears.'

Ellen glared at the phone. 'Stuck-up twat. Trust my mother to appoint an estate agent who sounds like he's swallowed enough silver spoons to measure J. Alfred Prufrock's life into very old age.'

'Gosh, you *are* refreshing to have around the place.' Pheely giggled. 'Oddlode hasn't seen a Commie since Archie Worthington came home from his first term at university with a Socialist Worker T-shirt.'

'I'm *not* a Communist.'

'No, but you *are* an estate-agent *provocateur*.'

Thank goodness for Pheely's infectious ability to cheer.

AAAA1111 Locksmiths of Market Addington were more than happy to take a Sunday-morning call-out – at triple-time plus VAT plus expenses – and promised that Ellen would be their top-priority emergency.

'Just as soon as they've had a fry-up and read the sports section of the *News of the World*,' Pheely warned, as she saw Ellen out of the garden. 'Are you sure you don't want to stay? I promise they'll be hours. Remember, you're on Cotswold time here.'

'I'd rather wait at the cottage.' She had more faith in the AAAA1111 boys. 'Thanks so much for getting up and letting me hog your phone.'

'Worth it for the dew, my darling.' Pheely took a deep, indulgent breath at the garden door, which was somewhat tarnished by her ongoing cigarette. 'I might pop by with the Dane later to see how you're doing. We can perv around the village spying on weekenders if you have time . . . although you may still be in your dressing-gown then, of course. I once called a local emergency plumber who said he'd be with me in ten – I didn't realise he meant ten days later. Hamlet and I were floating around on the furniture.'

It wasn't a hopeful prognosis.

With Snorkel gazing at her from alternate knee-height windows, Ellen sat in the Goose Cottage garden in her dressing-gown and watched the village wake up, an eye trained at all times for a black and white cat and a locksmith's van.

First to emerge was Hunter Gardner *en route* to the village stores for his Sunday papers. He gave her a hearty wave as he passed and Ellen – who had been trying to hide behind some lupins – managed a vague smile in return.

'Wonderful morning!'

'Yes, isn't it?'

'You tidying up that garden? Awful mess.'

'Yes, isn't it?'

'Rather an odd choice of gardening attire, hum?'

'Yes, isn't it?'

Thankfully this banter lasted only until he had marched beyond the garden wall and started down the Goose Lane hill towards the village green. Ellen had a nasty feeling that he had spotted her loitering in her dressing-gown earlier, which was why he was going the long way round.

Then, half an hour later, came the rather surprising sight of Giles Hornton in very skimpy nylon shorts and a Flora Marathon T-shirt jogging past, sweat already dripping from his moustache.

'Fancy joining me for a run, O sporty new neighbour?' Even at speed he managed to ooze slow, calculated charm as he leered at her over the hedge.

'Another time.'

'I'll hold you to that!'

The white teeth flashed, the moustache glistened, and he tightened his buttocks as he ran on.

While Ellen paced the garden, batting grass with her hand

and huffing impatiently, the village soon emerged in force – the hung-over dog-walkers impatiently rustling empty poop bags in their pockets, the kids on micro-scooters or ponies, youths on bikes, mothers with push-chairs, and ramblers with upside-down Landranger maps. Ellen lurked behind the lupins and watched the shadows shortening, trying to work out how long she had been waiting. It felt like hours. Her skin itched with the heat and frustration. Never a patient person at the best of times, she was starting to harbour fantasies about sledge-hammering the door.

She took yet another lap of the house, hoping to find a way in that she'd overlooked earlier. The hatch to the cellar seemed promising, until she spotted the huge padlock hidden in the weeds that had sprung up between the cracked paving stones around it. She peered through every window in case the automatic locks hadn't engaged, but it was like Fort Knox. She could see the rose petals still lying on the sitting-room floor, her half-drunk mug of tea in the kitchen and the horseshoe on the dining-room window-sill.

Pheely was right. The horseshoe had brought her nothing but bad luck so far. She looked at the twisting nails poking out of it and something occurred to her. She could try to break in. Even though she couldn't pick a lock to save her life, there were other ways . . .

Hunter Gardner was reading his *Sunday Telegraph* on his very clean decking now, a cafetière and a pair of binoculars on the small table in front of him as he enjoyed a little pre-church bird-watching. Ellen crouched down as she passed the gap in the laurels that masked the two gardens and headed for the carport to search for break-in equipment.

An extending ladder was suspended from hooks in the ceiling and conscientiously secured by a bicycle lock so that wannable burglars – or locked-out daughters – couldn't easily appropriate it to shimmy up to an open attic window. But, to Ellen's relief, it had a combination lock. She could hear Snorkel trotting around and whining overhead as she set about trying a few codes that her parents favoured – various four-figure combinations of birthdays and the 90053 'goose' code. At least it passed the time, and made her feel curiously sentimental as she tried out their anniversary and the year she had graduated.

'Bingo!' It was her father's birth year – as always a jolting reminder that he had seen out four more decades than her.

She carried the ladder to the front of the house and set it up by the only open window, stepping back to assess her chances of getting in before she tried out the perilous climb. The window really was very small and would take a lot of contortion to get through. She rubbed her mouth thoughtfully and looked round at the lane, praying for an AAAA1111 van to come trundling along.

The horseshoe's bad luck was playing on her mind now. If bad fortune ran in threes, then she was really tempting fate. First the cat had escaped, then she had got locked out and now she was planning to scale three floors and clamber through a very small window. 'Coward,' she told herself, reknotting her belt and tugging her dressing-gown as far down her bottom as it would go. Then, making sure that the top of the ladder was firmly braced up against the thatch, she started to climb.

It was much easier than she'd feared, the ladder well secured and the thick ivy and wisteria that climbed the house providing plenty of steadying handles in case she happened to wobble. It wasn't until she tried to get from the ladder into the window that Ellen encountered a hitch.

The most obvious way to go in was to clutch the top of the dormer, step away from the ladder and on to the sill then post herself through feet first like a human cannonball into a barrel. But the thatched dormer was almost impossible to hold on to, with its anti-bird chicken-wire hairnet and its alopecia straw. Her weight stayed too far back to maintain a grip for more than a few seconds, which wasn't long enough to get through the window before falling backwards off the roof. After two or three false starts, Ellen concluded that it was way too dangerous.

She tried gripping the window-frame instead, but couldn't get the leverage to move across from the ladder, which pitched sideways dramatically.

'Try going head first!' a voice called from the road.

Ellen glanced over her shoulder, and saw a figure squinting up at her through the sunlight. The curly hair, broad shoulders and freckles were unmistakable. It was Spurs Belling, dressed in ancient jeans and flip-flops. At his ankles were Hell's Bells' two black Labradors, panting.

'You could offer to help,' Ellen muttered, under her breath, as she twisted round again.

'What on earth do you think you're doing, young lady?' bellowed a furious voice. Hunter Gardner had joined Spurs on the lane, now blazered and cravated for church, his bald patch gleaming with Brylcreem.

Ignoring them both because she needed to concentrate, Ellen saw that if she put one foot into the fairly pronounced dip in the stonework to her right, she would have enough purchase to push herself up into the window head first. Years ago, she had done a bit of barefoot rock-climbing in France, and remembered the principles enough to feel sure she'd be safe.

At that moment, Spurs and Hunter were joined by a sweating Giles on the way back from his run. 'Bloody hell – what's she doing up there?'

'Stop her, somebody!' Hunter roared. 'Damn fool woman will kill herself.'

'She'll be fine,' a voice reassured them, then shouted up at her, 'Go for it!'

Ellen took one final glance over her shoulder: Spurs was encouraging her. He was standing to one side of the others – a cyclist and a fellow dog-walker had also stopped to watch – and he was the only one of her audience smiling, not remotely concerned for her safety. Suddenly she found herself grinning back. He understood that, however risky, this was better than hanging around for a locksmith.

'Stop that immediately and come down!' barked Hunter, now half-way along the drive.

If there was one thing Ellen loathed more than waiting around for hours, it was being spoken to as if she was a child. She hadn't clambered all the way up here just to clamber down again. Her blood was up, her ladder was up and she was damn well getting up.

She swung her foot across to the hold, flexing her toes into the crevice until she was happy with the grip. Then, clasping the window-sill with one hand and pointing the other above her head to narrow her shoulders enough to get through, she sprang up into the aperture, twisting her body to get as far through as possible then hook herself in with her elbow.

It worked. She was half-way in, staring at the unmade bed she'd slept in the night before.

The only problem was that her bottom and legs remained outside. With nothing to get her foot on to to hoick herself further up, Ellen's legs flailed hopelessly, acutely aware that any violent move might expose her naked bottom to the village.

'Hang on, I'm coming up!' yelled Hunter Gardner. 'Giles, be a good chap and hold this ladder for me.'

As Hunter laboriously clambered up the ladder beneath Ellen's waggling legs, two cars drew up outside Goose Cottage. One was a tatty white Escort van with AAAA1111 hand-painted along both sides, the other was a smart Mercedes. Both drivers gazed up in amazement at the sight that greeted them.

Unaware of her swelling audience, Ellen was stretching desperately for the corner of the bed to pull herself in.

'Almost there,' panted Hunter, exhausted by the climb and overexcited by the expanse of slim brown ankle now almost within his grasp.

Ellen grabbed the bed end just in time. The prospect of Hunter's clammy paw on her leg propelled her through the tiny hole with only a momentary flash of buttock.

The round of applause that came from outside made her laugh as she gave the room an excited high five, then collected her cut-offs and a fresh T-shirt from a chair.

Hunter was waiting by the front door to give Ellen a lecture.

'Damn fool thing to set about trying to do – young slip of a gel like you – *and* barely dressed.' His big bulldog jowls jiggled furiously. 'What would your mother say?'

'I've done far more risky things in my time, I can assure you.' She grinned, as her audience dispersed behind him. Giles was jogging off, while the cyclist and the dog-walker had already moved on. Only Spurs was still standing in the lane, running a hand through his curls, the smile now dropping away as one eye closed against the sun and the other examined her thoughtfully.

'That's as may be,' Hunter raged on, 'but not in this village. We don't entertain daredevils here.' He glared conspicuously at Spurs. 'The show's over, young man!'

Still flooded with adrenaline and bare-faced cheek, Ellen beamed at Spurs – no longer caring that his horseshoe had brought her bad luck. It had ended, at least, with a fun challenge. And again the G-force jolt rocked her back on her heels, pumping her blood addictively fast.

When Hunter stalked angrily off to church, he stepped forward, but before he could cross the lane, a small man in an AAAA1111 T-shirt emerged from the far side of the hornbeam hedge carrying a tool-bag. Staring bashfully at the gravel, he scuffed up to Ellen. 'Don't suppose you need me now?'

Immensely cheered by her achievement, Ellen was feeling magnanimous. 'I probably do – the keys are actually locked in there,' she pointed up to the bunkhouse, 'along with my dog.' She doubted she could unearth a spare set in the main cottage without a very long search, and Snorkel was barking her head off. 'Do you think you can get in?'

He nodded at Ellen's feet and scuffed his way towards the barn.

Ellen turned back to Spurs, calculating whether she could offer AAAA1111 man a coffee and casually extend the invitation. But to her disappointment he was already sauntering towards the bridleway, shoulders hunched as he lit a cigarette. He glanced over his shoulder and Ellen smiled, then realised that he wasn't looking at her: he was scowling at a man leaning against the shiny Mercedes on the opposite side of the lane. Disappointed, Ellen regarded the stranger irritably.

'Hi.' He beckoned her towards him.

Ellen crossed the road for no man. Staying where she was, she beckoned him in return. But then, as he headed her way, she saw that he was dishy enough to stop traffic, if not to stop her heart clunking unevenly after an encounter with Spurs.

Wearing dark glasses and a big white smile, the Merc driver looked curiously out of place in rural Oddlode on a Sunday morning. He was dressed in an expensive-looking lightweight suit, whose jacket was slung over one shoulder in a decidedly male-model pose. Despite the obvious posturing, he was good-looking enough to get away with it, the rolled-up shirt-sleeves showing deliciously tanned forearms and the loosened tie revealing a neck as smooth and broad as a birch trunk.

Then Ellen spotted a set of house-keys dangling from one of his fingers.

'Thought I'd pop these by in case you hadn't had any luck – but it seems you're resourceful.' He pocketed the keys and held out his hand to shake hers. 'Lloyd Fenniweather from Seaton's International. We spoke on the phone.'

'Ellen Jamieson.' She felt his hand enclose hers in a warm, tight squeeze and breathed in the heady mix of aftershave, sex appeal and naked ambition. She'd guessed from the brief telephone conversation that Lloyd would be charmingly offensive. What she hadn't banked on was that he would be quite so young or so disturbingly good-looking.

'I'm just heading home,' he carried on, standing far too close for a first encounter, head dipped towards her as though passing on intimate scandal. 'My client had to cut today's viewing short. Flying off to see the cricket, lucky devil. So I thought I'd pop by and introduce myself, check you got in okay. And, boy, am I glad I did.' On switched the big neon smile and off came the dark glasses, revealing eyes the same Demerara sugar golden brown as his hair.

Lloyd Fenniweather had been born to sell million-pound-plus properties. He looked as though he would be perfectly at home lounging on chesterfields in front of roaring fires, striding across helicopter pads, plunging into true blue pools and rolling around in four-poster beds. He was absolutely, straight-down-the-line, uncomplicatedly, devastatingly handsome. From his floppy, sandy hair, through his straight nose, big smile, square chin and rower's shoulders to his long legs, he was pin-up hunky. Lloyd Fenniweather was the sort of man Jennifer Jamieson longed for Ellen to bag.

And, rather to her shame, Ellen was superficially attracted to him. He didn't rock her back on her heels, but the thought of standing on tiptoe and kissing him brought a little rush of a smile to her face. 'That's very kind of you.' The AAAA1111 man was hacking his way into the bunkhouse as fast as his specialist tools allowed: there was no getting out of paying the call-out fee now, she guessed. 'As you can see, it's all under control.' A moment later Snorkel almost knocked the locksmith off the balcony as she flew out, free at last. She bounded down the steps and hurled herself at Ellen.

'Hello, gorgeous.' Lloyd was obviously not keen on dogs, but having perfected the art of charming children and animals for professional purposes he managed an awkward pat on the collie's head. 'I haven't conducted a viewing here for a while, and I have to agree that the place does look rather unloved.'

'Exactly,' muttered Ellen, as he took another step towards her so that their shoulders brushed.

'Not that looking a bit rough round the edges puts off the majority of clients,' he added magnanimously, cranking up the dimmer switch on the big smile. There was a curious *double entendre* in the softly spoken sentence, and his eyes bubbled like caramel.

'Not as offputting as being overpriced or having an unfortunate right of way?' Her eyebrows slid up critically, but his smile didn't shift as he carried on gazing into her face. Angry questions about lack of for-sale signs, recent viewings or asking-price offers died on Ellen's lips. It had been a long time since the fast-falling lift of sexual attraction had rooted her to the spot and dragged all her vital organs out of position, but now it had happened twice in twenty-four hours. She felt her stomach lurch, her heart spin cheerfully on its aorta and her legs turn numb. From the way Lloyd Fenniweather's sugar-sweet eyes were tangled with hers like sticky toffee, she knew he was feeling something similar.

'I guess I need to talk you through what's been happening, huh?' he murmured, in a way that clearly suggested *preferably in bed with champagne, massage oil and fur-covered handcuffs*.

As the AAAA1111 man lurked uncomfortably to one side, waiting for a signature on his work docket, Ellen and Lloyd savoured a few more naughty-smile moments of mutual desire.

Ellen knew that what she was feeling was so shallow it wouldn't drown a gnat but, after all the misery with Richard, it was a lovely diversion and far more pleasant than the jolting lurch she felt every time she saw Spurs Belling.

Eventually she dragged her eyes from his, knowing that she'd already been too reckless that day. Being sexually attracted to an estate agent wasn't something she had ever contemplated, but it would probably feature pretty high on her list of 'don't go there', along with a career in accountancy or a passion for cross-stitch. On first impression, she didn't even *like* him – she just wanted to see him naked.

'Right,' Lloyd purred reluctantly. 'I'd better push off if you don't need me. Plenty of time to talk about Goose Cottage anon. Which reminds me, tomorrow morning . . .' He pulled an uncomfortable face. 'I really am flat out until the latter part of the week.'

'I need to get things moving straight away,' she insisted, switching gladly from lust to more familiar irritation.

The lingering eye-meet might be over, but Lloyd was still standing close enough to drop his voice to a soft breath so that only she could hear. 'I wonder . . . can we have a chat about this over dinner, if that's not too forward of me?'

Ellen took a step back. She hadn't seen that one coming. And

Lloyd had asked so charmingly – almost coyly – that it made him seemed absurdly foppish and shy. She had to take a grip on herself not to bat her lashes and press her fingertip coquettishly to her chin. 'That's really sweet of you, but I was thinking of something a bit more formal,' she muttered, knowing that dinner would mean alcohol and mutual attraction and getting caught off-guard. Dinner meant a lot more than chatting about the current property market. 'This is really quite a serious matter, don't you think?'

'Absolutely.' He nodded earnestly, backing off to reassure her, big white smile leaping back into place. 'And believe me, I'm giving it my full attention. Let me go through the file and prepare some full notes, and we'll talk it through. Doing that over supper can't hurt, can it? Have you been to the Duck Upstream yet?'

Ellen shook her head.

'Good.' He was already heading back to his car. 'In that case I'll take you there on Friday evening.'

'Couldn't we make it any earlier in the week?' she asked worriedly, impatient to sort out the cottage situation.

He smiled rather smugly over his car door. 'Sorry – I'm tied up every evening until then – but I'm worth waiting for.' With that, he tipped his dark glasses over his nose and jumped in.

The locksmith cleared his throat noisily as he handed over his clipboard for a signature. 'I've got a free night Wednesday. Fancy the pub quiz at the Grapes?'

'Then the shy AAAA1111 man asked me out,' Ellen told Pheely later, as they strolled with their dogs around the village.

'Shylock Smith!' Pheely snorted happily.

'They must have thought I was gagging for it,' Ellen groaned, 'because I wiggled my bottom out of the window.'

'Oh, darling, how delicious!' Pheely gurgled, swishing her hair back. 'Two propositions on your first weekend, and I bet Hunter's writing an anonymous love-letter as we speak. Still, you are terribly pretty. I'd expect nothing less from the red-bloods around here.'

'I think I need to get a bit more used to being single before I

go out on dinner dates.' Ellen stooped to pick up the stick that
Snorkel had dropped for her. 'I'm going to call the arrogant sod
first thing tomorrow and demand a midweek meeting at his office
instead.'

'The AAAA1111 man?'

Ellen rolled her eyes. 'Lloyd Fenniweather.'

'Oh, you mustn't!' Pheely yelped. 'He's scrumptious.'

'You know him?'

'Vaguely.' She peered over a hedge into a cottage garden
belonging to one of the Manor Lane weekenders. 'Ugh – look at
all those peonies. Foul. Yes, the Fenniweathers are a local family.
Lloyd is their pride and joy. Scholarship boy, first family member
to go to university, that sort of thing.'

'Really?' Ellen found herself suddenly reassessing him. 'Not a
public-school poser?'

'Oh, I rather think he *is*.' Pheely peered into a window as she
passed it. 'Look at those copper pans! Where do they think they
are? Provence? Lloyd,' she turned to Ellen, green eyes curiously
emotional, 'is one of the rare few who could have escaped the
rural backwater but, like me, he's stayed. More fool him. You're
just what he needs.' She whistled for Hamlet, who was lolloping
around in the road. 'And he's just what *you* need.'

'I *need* to find out why my parents' house isn't selling.'

'You need to have fun. When was the last time you had fun?'

'Surfing the Severn Bore in April.'

'With a man?'

Ellen said nothing, thinking about Richard and the recent
misery. As they rounded the corner and headed past the manor,
she glanced up at the big, beautiful house and found her mind
turning to the night before – to the blood-chilling, heart-stopping,
ankle-swiping realisation that Spurs Belling had the X-factor.
Richard only had ex-factor. Lloyd had sex-factor. Maybe Pheely
was right. She just needed to flirt and feel sexy, nothing more.

'It's been a while,' she admitted.

'So, go on a date, darling! Dress up, enjoy your three rocket
leaves balanced on bleeding tuna, flirt for fun, and then give him

hell because the cottage hasn't sold. Don't think of it as a date. Think of it as a perfect opportunity to intimidate.'

She made it sound so simple.

'You look stunning!' Five days later Lloyd ushered her towards his Merc, a dream-date vision of freshly showered hair, shaved chin and toothpaste-ad smile.

'Don't you want to walk?' Ellen suggested. 'It's only ten minutes.'

'I think the storm might break tonight.' He swept back his bronze mane and looked at the sky. 'Besides, I have all the paperwork in the car. Best to drive.'

It was a sweltering evening, the heatwave having slow-cooked the village all week so that the Lode Valley pan had almost boiled dry beneath its hot blue lid.

Ellen was very hot and bothered. Even wearing the thinnest of cotton shirts and a long, wafer-light yellow skirt, she felt as though she was wrapped in tin foil and stewing in her own juices. She longed to throw herself into the sea.

The cool, air-conditioned interior of the Merc was a poor second best to icy brine and surf. Dark, leathery and intimate, it smelt of aftershave and anticipation.

As Lloyd's long thighs and muscular calves pumped the pedals into a flashy reverse out of the drive, Ellen stole a covert glance at him out of the corner of her eye, hoping to cheer herself up and relax a little. He was just as drop-dead dishy as she remembered – more so because he had dressed to impress. The very thin grey silk sweater wrinkled like oil over his broad shoulders and muscular chest; the black designer jeans were beautifully cut for his long, athletic body. With a glistening signet ring on his finger and gleaming Chelsea boots on his toes, his turnout was as impeccable as a guardsman's. Lloyd was iridescent with good health, good looks and bad intentions. Then the Demerara eyes slid sideways to meet hers and he winked.

This, Ellen deduced with a hammering heart, had been a very, very bad idea. She'd let her hormones rule her head when she hadn't argued against meeting him for dinner, but she hadn't anticipated feeling so angry at being kept waiting for five days. Now she just felt like shouting at him. She couldn't even face small talk. She was gunning for a fight. She also badly needed a cigarette, the nicotine cravings from a week of abstinence at their peak.

'Good week?' he asked her, as they pelted rather too fast along North Street.

'I've had better,' she admitted, and stopped herself saying more. Five days of cleaning and hunting for a lost cat hardly made for scintillating conversation. Apart from Pheely, she had barely talked to a soul or felt inclined to. She had kept her telephone chats with her mother to a bare minimum, hadn't answered Richard's text messages, and had avoided the scrutiny of the village shop. This retreat into herself was, she was sure, a form of delayed shock. She had to close down three-quarters of her brain to stop herself mulling over her split from Richard.

'Got out and about much?' Lloyd asked.

'Oh, I've popped over to my neighbour's a few times,' she muttered, entertaining a quick, murderous thought about Hunter Gardner. 'We have a shared interest in chickens.'

'Chickens?'

'Yes. He breeds them, my dog chases them.'

He laughed and Ellen forced a smile, knowing that she really should loosen up.

The evening before, walking with Pheely, she had promised that she would try to enjoy her night out. Overexcited at the prospect of having Daffodil home for the weekend, Pheely had refused to allow a single dark cloud to pass through the blue sky above Oddlode. She clearly found Ellen's glum mood extremely boring. 'You must see the positive side!' she'd enthused. 'And the funny side . . . I mean, you have to admit that Hunter's face was hilarious.'

If the week had started badly with getting locked out and flashing her bottom at her parents' neighbour – not to mention half a dozen other spectators – it had worsened when Snorkel had taken a fancy to Hunter's prize Cochins. These giant feathered ornaments, the koi carp of the chicken world, fascinated the clown-faced collie. Having spent two days gazing at them through the chicken wire while Ellen threw herself into cleaning the cottage, Snorkel had fashioned a way into their pen. The first Ellen knew of it was Hunter's strangled cries of anguish as he chased her around trying to evict her.

No matter how much Ellen apologised and explained that Snorkel was trying to play with them, not eat them, Hunter remained unforgiving. He told her in no uncertain terms that if her dog set foot (or paw) on his property again, he was within his rights to shoot her for worrying his poultry. He then set up watch with his cafetière, binoculars and an air rifle. Ellen thought it a huge overreaction and tried to keep more of an eye on her dog. But it was far too hot to keep her inside, and by then she'd embarked on a never-ending cleaning campaign that she bitterly regretted.

It was only as a result of all the coffee Hunter was knocking back that Snorkel got away with her second visit to the Cochins. He had popped inside his house to answer a call of nature when she slipped under the wire and joined her mesmerising new friends with their feathered bell-bottoms and giant Renaissance-wig crests. Hearing squawks and barks, Ellen dashed into the pens and extracted her in the nick of time – they threw themselves behind the hedge just as Hunter came bellowing outside to investigate the din. After that, Snorkel had to be monitored at all times.

The dog's third visit had been her downfall. As well as their evening dog-walks together, Pheely had taken to popping into Goose Cottage for a coffee *en route* to check Daffodil's horse ('Lord knows why I bother – I go there every day and the stupid thing just stands there, swishing at flies and eating grass. Never changes'). On Wednesday she brought Ellen a lunging rope to tether Snorkel in the garden. In less time than it took to boil a kettle for two cups of Nescafé, the collie had figured out how to undo Ellen's double granny knot and had made her way to the Cochin pen, trailing the rope behind her.

'What's that?' Ellen had turned to Pheely in the kitchen, listening to an unpleasantly familiar squawking.

There followed an equally familiar bellow of fury from Hunter, a bark of excitement from Snorkel, the unnerving crack of an air rifle – and silence.

The two women had run outside in panic, to find Hunter crouching forlornly in his chicken coop, a huge bundle of feathers gathered into his arms. Even more disturbing, he was trussed up like a chicken himself, bound tightly in a long rope trailed by a confused, panic-stricken collie.

Hunter might act as though he had seen more military action than a foot-soldier's blister plaster, but his brief spell in the forces had been, in fact, as a cartographer. He could pinpoint a radio mast to within a yard, but he couldn't shoot it even at point-blank range.

As a result, he had accidentally planted his airgun pellet in the backside of his favourite Cochin and, as the vet later explained, was lucky not to have killed her. He now kept watch day and night, had set traps and bought a high-precision magnifying sight for his air rifle. Snorkel's death sentence hung over her like a black cloud. She could no longer bound through the paddock chasing butterflies or patrol the garden morning, noon and night searching for her friend Fins. Instead, she spent her days tied to the dovecote at the end of a triple-knotted ten foot rope, barking tetchily. Ellen took her on long walks to make up for it – mostly routed via Orchard Close to try to flush out the Wycks.

'So, you've been getting to know some of the village characters, then?' asked Lloyd.

She nodded. 'I learn more about them every day.' The elusive Wycks had still failed to make an appearance and Ellen now found the line permanently engaged when she called; she suspected that they had deliberately left the phone off the hook. Each time she'd visited the house on Orchard Close, she had been greeted by nothing but Fluffy barking her head off through the letterbox.

To her frustration, she'd spotted Reg's ancient pick-up tearing around the village daily, with an ever-changing assortment of goods in the back – one day two old fridges, another day enough greenery for Malcolm's army to approach Dunsinane unspotted, and today enough stones to build Fred and Wilma a two-storey extension. But no amount of waving and cat-calling had attracted his attention. Dot was no easier to track down. Pheely claimed that she was a regular sight in the village on her bicycle, but either she moved at the speed of a Tour de France sprinter, or she had a flat tyre that week.

Ellen knew when she was being avoided.

Which was why, as she and Lloyd made the short journey from Goose Cottage to the Duck Upstream, she found it impossible to shake off her bad mood. It was also why, when she spotted Reg and Dot together, on foot, talking outside the village shop, she screamed, 'Stop the car!'

'Sorry?' Lloyd turned to her in surprise.

'I have to talk to those people – urgently!' She craned round as they cruised past the Wycks, noticing that they appeared to be having a fight. Dot was swinging her handbag around as if it was a mace. 'It won't take a moment. Please stop.'

'Oh, right – fair enough.' He laughed. 'Sounded like you were having second thoughts there.'

Ellen sprang out of the car as soon as it had stopped and ran back towards the shop.

She could hear the couple's argument from fifty yards away, Dot's deep, gruff voice belting out accusations: '—won't let you go over to that pub until you've handed over that hundred quid Lady G give us. I ain't having you drink it all, and we owes Saul thirty.'

'Goodfornothing layabout buggered off come lunchtime,' Reg cackled, in a voice that made his wife's sound refined. 'I ain't giving him nothing.'

'He did most of the dry-stoning! Hand it over. I need to get another key for the 'lectric tomorrow.'

Ellen waded in: 'Hi. Sorry to interrupt, but I really have to have a word. Ellen Jamieson – I called last weekend.'

The two faces drained of colour. Then, in less than a beat, Reg and Dot squared their shoulders fiercely and stared her out. They looked exactly as she remembered them – two small, weathered, stone-faced, sparsely toothed characters that would not be out of place among Pheely's gargoyles and goblins. Reg was still the same curious marriage of a young man's body with an old man's face. Years of hard physical labour had left him with arms and shoulders like a stonemason, the rest of him a wiry taper. His lopsided, battered face, seldom out of the sun, wind or rain, was as tanned and leathery as an old moccasin, and the bloodshot eyes as mistrustful and hostile as those of the Red Indian wearing it. Dot, despite the rusty-nail voice, was barely five feet tall with a tightly permed helmet of unnaturally chestnut hair and a Deputy Dawg expression, belied by sharp blue eyes. This evening they were at their sharpest as they shot her husband a warning look, then narrowed angrily at Ellen. Assuming identical, defensive expressions, the Wycks crossed their arms in front of their chests in unison and only just stopped short of snarling, like two guard-dogs caught napping.

'What d'you want?' Dot demanded, hackles rising.

This was going to be tough, Ellen thought. Having made sure that Lloyd was keeping the Merc's engine running, she cleared her throat and modulated her anger. 'I was hoping you'd be able to tell me why you haven't been cleaning and gardening Goose Cottage for – well, for ages as far as I can tell. Is there a problem?'

'Not as far as I know,' Dot growled, setting her chin.

'So why aren't you doing it?'

The sharp eyes studied her. Apparently Dot was working out which part of Ellen's face to bite off first. 'We subcontracted that job.'

This sounded so ridiculous that Ellen battled not to laugh. 'To whom?'

'A business associate,' Dot said pompously, her hackles creeping higher by the second. Beside her, Reg stared fixedly at the pavement, waiting for the command to attack. He was almost foaming at the mouth.

Ellen took a step back. 'In that case it's your business associate I need to talk to, isn't it? Can you give me his details?'

'He doesn't deal with clients direct.' Dot lifted her chin and glared at Ellen defiantly.

'So who does?'

'He does.' Dot nudged the mute Reg, who carried on staring madly at the pavement. Any minute now Ellen expected him to attack his own shadow, although she suspected that his rabid, let-me-at-it expression had more to do with the proximity of the pub than the argument hotting up beside him.

Lloyd was reversing the Merc, slotting it into a parallel space just a few yards away. Dot jerked her head towards it. 'Friend of yours?' The sharp eyes blinked worriedly.

With its darkened windows and bullet-silver metalwork, the Merc did look rather stylishly sinister – part drugs-gangster, part FBI. How was Dot to know that its occupant was a perfumed, smooth-talking estate agent?

She nodded curtly, squaring her own shoulders and look-ing from growling terrier Dot to her slavering husband – the customer-service manager, it seemed.

'Surely you must *know* that your "business associate" hasn't been doing any work?' she asked him. 'The cottage is hardly inconspicuous – I've seen you drive past it this week. The grass is up to my knees.'

Reg sucked air menacingly through his few teeth, mad eyes darting around – mostly in the direction of the pub.

Ellen felt unpleasantly like her mother lecturing an unruly pupil at Market Addington College. 'This just isn't good enough,' she said, and turned back to Dot. 'My parents have been paying *you* to do the work – not hire some business associate who doesn't look after it at all. Somebody was using the cottage without permission while it was empty. There was mess everywhere when I arrived and—'

'How *dare* you accuse us of that? We ain't done nuthink like that, have we, Reg?' The handbag moved threateningly in Ellen's direction as Dot readied herself for a fight.

'I wasn't accusing you,' Ellen explained hastily. 'I was going to say that had you been cleaning it every week you would have seen the mess and alerted my parents.'

'I'm a cleaner not a security guard, ain't I?' Dot hissed angrily.

However much they knew that they had been caught out, there was no way Ellen would ever get an apology out of them and, as far as she was concerned, it simply wasn't worth the effort. She might have found the fight that she'd been looking for all week, but now that she was being counted down for round one, she suddenly lost the urge to exchange blows. While spending long hours scraping layers of spilled food, drinks, cigarette ash and dust from the corners of Goose Cottage, she had angrily rehearsed the showdown she planned to have with the Wycks. She'd screamed all sorts of angry accusations at the Cif bottle, the Dyson and the block of Vanish. Now, though, having spent the entire week cleaning the spoilt princesses, she was too washed out to fight dirty. Even if Dot came to work tomorrow, there would be nothing left for her to do. Ellen still badly needed help with the garden, but something about Reg's manic silence put her off asking him.

She rubbed her hot face to gather her thoughts. 'As you can't guarantee to do the work personally, I suggest you tell your "work associate" not to bother either. I can cope without you until the house is sold, and I think you can count yourselves lucky that I'm willing to leave it there. I won't mention what's happened to my parents, but you won't be getting a penny more from them.'

Ellen expected them to be sullenly relieved that they'd got away with it. The last thing she expected was vitriol.

Dot launched a full terrier attack. 'You stuck up little madam!' she howled. 'Talk about ungrateful! I've worked my fingers to the bone for that mother of yours, and Reg hates that damn garden and the rubbish mower your dad has. You can't just swan in here like you own the place and sack us!'

Ellen leaped back as the handbag swung.

'You have no right to talk to us like this, you cow!' Dot lunged towards her. 'You wait till my grandson hears about it. Then you'll be sorry.'

Suddenly a trill voice joined in from an upstairs window: 'I'm a witness to this! I am videoing it and I shall call the police if it carries on! Do not attempt to enter the store. My husband is locking the doors.' Ellen looked up to see blonde Lily Lubowski waving a camcorder from the dormer window above the village stores. Below her, Joel's big round face appeared through the security glass of the door as he obligingly sprang the lock and turned the sign to 'Closed', winking cheerfully at Ellen.

Caught off-guard, she didn't see the handbag flying towards her face until it made impact. Thankfully it contained no more than a bus pass and a house key, but the shock made her jump. She landed inadvertently on one of Dot's small feet.

'Owwwww!'

In the ensuing mêlée, Reg sloped off to the pub unnoticed.

'I saw that, Mrs Wyck! That was assault!' Lily was screaming. 'It's on tape. You can't get away with it this time.'

'Shut up, you stupid bitch! She kicked me!' Dot yelled up at her, then turned to Ellen. 'You can't fire us. We need that money. We didn't know that our Sau – that our *work associate* ain't been doing his job. He said he'd look after the place, and we took that in good faith. You can't blame us for that.'

'I'm afraid that's not my problem.' Ellen backed away towards the car.

'Well, I hope you rot in hell!' Dot hopped after her. 'You *and* your posh goodfornothing boyfriend! Stuck-up bitch!'

Ellen jumped back into the Merc, narrowly avoiding being handbagged again, and left Dot standing on the pavement hurling abuse. 'Sorry about this, Lloyd. Would you mind driving away rather fast?'

'Certainly.' He put the car into first gear, only too happy to oblige.

A moment later they were flying past the entrance to the Duck Upstream car park. 'I'll drive round the block to put her off the scent,' he explained, after a glance in the rear view mirror: he was fantasising himself as James Bond staging a getaway from Blofeld, Ellen thought. 'We don't want her following us into the restaurant – I never double-date.'

'Thanks.' Ellen watched the small figure, still hopping around on the pavement, recede into the distance. Then, as they climbed out of the village on the Hillcote lane, she groaned and sagged back in her seat. 'That really wasn't supposed to happen – sorry. I don't think I'm very good at firing people.'

Lloyd raised an eyebrow, still apparently on his Bond trip. 'Why did you need to fire them?'

'Because they weren't doing their job.' She looked across at him levelly, but he just smiled.

'Is that a threat?' His tone was teasing and flirtatious, his big hunky jaw jutting forward.

'Depends if you've been doing yours,' she muttered, and turned to look out at the hot evening, wondering how she was going to tackle the garden alone. She badly needed rain. Even after just a week of unbroken sun, the ground had hardened and cracked. She couldn't hope to get a spade into the earth or pull dock roots from their concrete casing. She was half tempted to ask Lloyd it he'd help – he certainly looked strong enough. Again she was reminded that she only wanted him for his body, and even that urge was waning. It was too hot to get physical.

They drove into the tiny hamlet of Hillcote, which was made up of barely a dozen ancient Cotswold-stone houses clustered around a well. There were chickens wandering free range in the lane and a white goose flapped from an old churn stand. A man watering his garden waved at the Merc and two grey cats watched them impassively from a dry-stone wall. They made Ellen think about poor Fins, fending for himself, not knowing where his home was any more. He hadn't touched the food she'd put out. She hoped he wasn't making a bid to return to Cornwall, *Incredible Journey*-style. He should have asked her first – she'd have tagged along with Snorkel.

'Beautiful round here, isn't it?' Lloyd murmured, as they did a U-turn around the well, ready to head back to Oddlode.

'I prefer the sea,' she said, glaring at the chickens. Trouble-making species: at least seagulls flew away from Snorkel when she tried to make friends.

'You like water sports?' he asked casually.

She nodded, and wondered if he'd spotted the surfboards stacked up in the open barn.

His sugar eyes lit up. 'In that case . . .'

She almost barrelled into him as he took a sharp left along an unmade lane marked dead end.

Half a mile on they arrived at a set of flashy electric gates, beyond which was a huge old house with lots of sculpted garden. Lloyd stopped the Merc in the gateway and reached for the glovebox.

'Pear Tree Farm – on our books for just under one and a half million,' he told her smoothly, a sum he was clearly accustomed to saying as casually as his own telephone number. 'Unrivalled views, twenty-five acres, equestrian facilities, tennis court, pool and guest cottage. Nice little house. Ah!' He pulled out a set of keys and pressed a small button on the keyring. A moment later the gates swung open. 'Want to take a look?'

'I'm not really in the market for a million-pound house,' she mumbled, wondering if this was some sort of psychological game-plan to show her that Goose Cottage – precisely half the asking price of Pear Tree Farm – was very grotty by Seaton's standards.

'Oh, I'm sure I can talk you round.' He steered the car through the gates.

Ellen felt uncomfortable. 'What about the owners?'

'Abroad on holiday.' As they cruised along the gravel drive, he pressed a pre-set on the mobile phone that was plugged into a hands-free kit. It rang through on the car's stereo speakers.

'Good evening, the Duck Upstream restaurant,' came a syrupy female reply.

'Hi, Gina. Lloyd Fenniweather here.'

'Hi, Lloyd!'

'Can you keep my table another half an hour or so? I'm so sorry, but we're going to be late. Unavoidable.'

'No problem.'

'You're a honey.'

God, he was smooth, Ellen thought. He had all the moves off pat. He'd cut the call, cut the engine, grabbed his dark glasses and sauntered round to the passenger door to open it for her in the time it had taken her to undo her seatbelt and reach for the handle.

'Come and have a look round my favourite little bolthole.' He made an extravagant gesture as he led her towards the beautiful farmhouse.

Almost knocked sideways by the stuffy heat of the evening, Ellen bestowed a crabby look on the house and then on Lloyd. She guessed that this routine was well practised, and she doubted it was just from showing genuine buyers around Seaton's most expensive properties. It was probably Lloyd Fenniweather's secret tactic for seducing women. What better start to a date than to bring the girl to a million-pound house and make her feel like she could own it – and him – in one gorgeous deal?

And Ellen needed working on more than most. She'd had an awful week, was six days into quitting smoking, had just been handbagged in the street, and she really only wanted to grill him about her parents' cottage. The sexual attraction that had fizzled between them at their first meeting simply wasn't there this evening – all she felt was over-hot, over-tired, over-stressed irritation at his faked smoothness and his cocky arrogance. 'I'm not sure this is a very good idea,' she said, as he unlocked the front door. 'I don't want to snoop around someone else's house. It feels invasive.' She could almost hear Pheely's voice crying in her ear, *'No! Have a snoop! This is my dream come true!'*

Lloyd looked surprised. Clearly he'd never been refused the opportunity to show off the lifestyle accessories of the rich. 'It's for sale.' He laughed. 'The owners are used to people snooping around – I've shown it to three clients this week.'

But Ellen backed away, gazing up at the pretty sash windows. 'I'd rather stay outside, thanks.'

'It has seven bedrooms.' He raised a suggestive eyebrow. 'And a huge *water*-bed in the master suite.'

Ellen sucked in one cheek as the sugar-sweet gaze watching her hardened excitedly to rock candy . . . quite possibly along with another part of Lloyd's very beautiful anatomy.

Water sports. Of course. She'd heard enough jokes over the years to know that the phrase covered all manner of nefarious games. Lloyd Fenniweather wanted to try out the water-bed. Perhaps meant other water sports too. Had he *really* imagined that he floated her boat that much after she'd spent just ten minutes in a car with him? Well, if he did, he had just burned his own boats and was in very deep water.

'I'm not interested,' she told him firmly. 'I think you got the wrong particulars on this hot property.'

'Suit yourself.' He tried to stay super-smooth but allowed a little petulance to creep into his voice. 'We'll go to the restaurant.'

'Hang on.' Ellen crossed her arms. 'I think we should go through the Goose Cottage situation while we're here. We've got half an hour and it's much quieter than a restaurant. Is there a table or bench we can perch on while we talk?'

Super-smooth Lloyd looked decidedly ragged at this, but he managed an on-off smile. 'If we must – just let me get the file from the car.'

Once he had a smart Seaton's ring-binder clasped under one arm, he led the way round the side of the house to a high-walled courtyard, which glowed in the evening sun. And as soon as she rounded the corner behind him, Ellen saw a sight that made her feet twitch excitedly in their strappy sandals. At one end, separated by a dividing wall, was a very blue, very sparkly swimming-pool. She sat down at a scorched-teak table positively squirming with the need to take a running jump into it. The seat burned her thighs through her thin skirt, and the suntrap courtyard broiled with ensnared heat. The smell of chlorine and the sound of water lapping into the filters made her feel almost faint.

Lloyd took a seat opposite her, pulled his shades into his hair, widened his white fake smile and crossed his hands on the closed file – back in professional smoothie mode, her recent rejection put to the back of his mind as quickly as a lost sale.

'Goose Cottage is a curious little property – far more problematic than we had at first anticipated.' The posh voice purred as soothingly as the lapping pool. 'We set about marketing it in the belief that it would attract offers like wildfire, even given that we were starting out in January. But it hasn't.'

'Why ever not?' Ellen stared longingly at the pool, imagining the cool sensation of chlorinated water tightening her hot, sweaty pores.

'Mixture of reasons – no single factor.' The smile stretched wider and wider. 'People *have* been interested and there's an offer still out on it . . .'

'For two hundred thousand below the asking price!' Ellen reminded him, dragging her eyes from the pool and finding, to her surprise, that he was reaching across the table and fiddling with one of her friendship bracelets. She snatched away her hand and used it to flip her hair back from her sweaty forehead. The courtyard was like a cauldron.

'Which makes you wonder if we've pitched it a little high,' he suggested gently. 'I have suggested this to your parents more than once, but they're adamant they want the full asking price or as near as dammit.'

Now feeling almost too hot to concentrate on what he was saying, Ellen just huffed. It wasn't her place to start demanding that Jennifer and Theo ask less for the asset that they hoped would secure their old age.

'Although exquisitely pretty,' Lloyd was doing his smooth purring thing again, 'Goose Cottage really is only four-bedroom max, and that includes two very awkward attic rooms. People expect more house for that money. The bunkhouse steps make it impractical as a granny flat, and the cellars would make great playrooms for kids, but they have the same frightening stone steps and are a fire hazard. These things put off families with elderly relatives or small children. The garden is a huge responsibility, as is blatantly obvious now that your parents' gardener has – er – given up, shall we say? That puts off weekenders. There's a paddock with no road access, so anyone who wanted to keep a horse or pony would have to lead it through the garden. These all have to be accounted for in the price.'

Ellen was hardly listening to a word he was saying. She blinked sweat from her eyes and noticed that Lloyd was dripping too. The sugary eyes looked into her face with sweet innocence, only the playful smile hinting at a hidden agenda.

'I haven't conducted a viewing in weeks because there simply hasn't been any interest. Now is Seaton's busiest time – long, sunny days, kids still at school, bank-holiday weekends.' He was inching closer across the table, his nose approaching hers as he seemed to sense her frothing over.

Suddenly the sexual energy kicked in again. From nowhere, Ellen found herself fighting a reckless urge to grab him by the scruff of the neck, tow him to the pool, push him in fully dressed and jump in after him. She was craving chlorine, nicotine and the sort of teenage irresponsibility that meant she didn't have to worry about smarmy, male-model estate agents not selling her parents' house. She just wanted to swim and play water-polo and be a kid, like she had been with Richard.

Biting the tip of her tongue hard to make the thought go away, she fanned her shirt, determined get back on track and complete her hot cross-examination. 'Have you advertised Goose Cottage this month?'

Lloyd was glistening all over like an oiled Adonis, licking salty sweat from his perfect lips. He rested his chin in his cupped hands and blinked becomingly. 'Not recently – you have to be aware of the danger of over-advertising.'

Was it her imagination, Ellen wondered, or was his ankle rubbing against hers?

'And the cost, no doubt?' she said lightly, pulling her feet under her and feeling the sweat squelch behind her knees.

'True – but people see the same house advertised again and

again, and start to think there's something wrong with it.' He was
watching her face closely, and added, 'Doesn't that pool make you
want to dive in?'

She felt her toes brace in preparation for a table-upturning
sprint to the diving board. But she held herself down. Nice
try, she thought testily. I'm ready for you. 'Not right now,
it doesn't.' She unglued her shirt from her chest and fanned
it again. 'And getting back to the point, it doesn't help when
the agent tells people, within seconds of their call, that there *is*
something wrong with the cottage, then announces there aren't
any colour brochures left but he'll send off a dodgy photocopy.'

'Ah – yes.' He wiped his wet temples with his palms. 'Sorry
about that, but I *was* in a hurry.'

'And why isn't there a for-sale sign outside?'

'We never put boards up for rural properties over half a million
unless they're hard to find. It gives an air of exclusivity.'

'And it means nobody knows they're for sale!' She wiped sweat
beads off her own forehead. 'Oddlode's full of rich tourists who
might want to buy a house on the spur of the moment.'

'And it's also full of tourists who love to look round properties
for something to do on a rainy day instead of a cream tea.' He
was getting prickly too, the super-smooth banter staccato and
edgy. 'We call them Misguided Tours. They never buy houses
and they waste everybody's time.'

'And estate agents who don't sell houses are a waste of time,
too.'

His handsome face twitched with the effort of maintaining the
big white smile. 'Then tell your parents to drop the price.'

'First, I want a for-sale sign,' Ellen demanded. '*And* I want you
to run adverts for Goose Cottage in the local papers next week, as
well as in *Country Life* and the Saturday *Telegraph* – that probably
means actioning all this on Monday to make the deadlines. I
shall expect to see proof. Did you send press releases to the
property-news pages about Goose Cottage and its history?'

'I doubt it.'

'Then do that too.' She twisted her sweaty hair back from her face. 'I also want you to arrange for more brochures to be printed next week – again, I'll need proof that this has been done.'

'We do charge for these services, you know.'

'If you sell the house within a month, you can charge,' she said simply. 'If not, we take it to another agent and you bear the costs. And if that agent values it at less, we'll sell it at less. *You* valued it at the asking price and you sell at no less than five per cent under that price or you walk.'

'That's unheard-of!'

'So, break the rules. It's either that or I appoint another agency on Monday.' She leaned back in her seat, fanning herself with her shirt.

He cocked his square, pretty jaw, twisted his kissable pin-up lips and stared at her as his caramel eyes bubbled with indignation. 'Is it breaking the rules to call your clients' daughter a total bitch?'

'I'll take it as a compliment.' She raised her chin and smiled.

Sweat was glistening on Lloyd's golden skin, lifting the blond hairs and ruffling his feather-cut fringe. Disgruntled and left-footed, he was far more attractive than when he was trying to charm.

Ping! At last, the attraction she'd felt when she first met him kicked Ellen in the solar plexus. Her libido bounded out to enjoy the sunshine, a little tetchy from so long in the cold and a little uncertain that it was capable of more than a quick outing, but definitely *in situ*.

She felt the big smile pulling at her lips. And it had the strangest after-effect. As she smiled, she felt it tugging her knickers tightly into her crotch. The higher the smile, the tighter her knickers. She found laughter rippling through it too – an irrepressible, joyful release of tension. She was fizzing all over.

And she was impressed and more than a bit surprised when Lloyd suddenly smiled too. 'You really are in a firing mood this evening, aren't you?'

'Firing on all cylinders.' She couldn't stop the sudden crotch-tightening, belly-lurching, hollow-chested feeling. The sexual appeal was back big-time. When you knocked his smooth edges off, Lloyd Fenniweather was pretty desirable. 'So does that mean you'd rather I appointed another agent?'

Lloyd looked at her for a long, long time, the big smile blasting even more heat into the kiln-like courtyard. 'You really are amazing, you know that? You're one of the sexiest women I've ever met.'

Ellen licked her lips, returning his gaze. She still couldn't find him quite as sexy as she had for those few giddy moments on the Goose Cottage drive a week earlier, but she was enjoying herself again. He could forget about water sports in the Pear Tree Farm master bedroom, but there was something else wet and seductive she was desperate to try.

'Are we going to be really late for the restaurant?'

He didn't even look at his watch. 'They like me. They'll hold the table.'

'Good.' She stood up. 'Excuse me – there's something I just have to do . . .'

Kicking off her sandals as she ran and untying the drawstring on her skirt, Ellen left her clothes where they fell on the paving stones and bounded down the diving board.

It wasn't one of her most calculated gestures. As a child of the sea and far too accustomed to clambering in and out of wetsuits to be body-conscious, it didn't occur to her that here, in the landlocked Cotswolds, going for a swim in undies was tantamount to offering yourself on a plate with garnished nipples and sauce on the side.

Lloyd sat transfixed at the table as she pranced along in a white bra and pants then divebombed into the Cambridge blue surface. 'You beauty!'

But Ellen heard nothing but the rush of water and the echoing swoosh of her opening arms as she slowed down and sat on the bottom of the pool. As the air bubbles were forced out from beneath the fine hairs on her body, from her nostrils, ears and clammy skin, Ellen stayed suspended underwater and felt as though she had dived into heaven. It had been a week since she'd swum, and no amount of long warm baths to soothe away the aches of non-stop cleaning had compensated for this sensation. She swam a length of the pool underwater, looking through the clear water at the mosaic tiles and steps at one end, dancing with reflections from the evening sun, in a world of her own.

When she resurfaced, Lloyd was standing, open-mouthed, at the poolside.

'I'll buy it!' she called up to him, wiping water from her eyes and nose. 'Do you think they'll take an offer on the pool? I don't want the house.'

He laughed, and watched her backstroke away, staring hopefully at her undies in case they had gone see-through. But Ellen had swum often enough in her faithful Sloggis to know that they preserved your dignity as well as – if not better than – a bikini.

'Aren't you coming in?' she asked.

Lloyd gave her a wolfish wink. 'No underpants. Besides, I prefer to watch.'

Ellen had a feeling it had a lot more to do with not wanting to ruin his hairdo before their meal, but she let it pass. Teasing him was too easy. 'I'll just do a couple of lengths and then I'll be out.' She crawled her way to the shallow end in smooth, easy movements, unspeakably relieved to have found a way of rinsing away the storm-gathering, nicotine-craving tension. A few more minutes in the courtyard cauldron and she would probably have either clouted smooth, calculated, sexy Lloyd or kissed him, and she wanted to do neither. She wanted him to sell her parents' house ASAP so that she could fly away and find blue seas and pools all over the world to swim in.

So when she mounted the steps, tipping her head from side to side to rid her ears of water, she paused beside him. He was leaning against the west wall of the courtyard in one of his pretty poses, cooling off in the shadows. 'You haven't agreed to my terms yet,' she reminded him, a thousand times more relaxed than she had been when she jumped in. Cooled by the water, her libido had snuggled back into its hidey-hole and refused to resurface.

'I agree.' The white smile beamed out of the shadows. 'Do you

really expect me to say anything else when you're standing in front
of me looking like that?'

'Have you got a problem with it?' she asked.

'Only that I want to kiss you more than anything in the world
right now.' His eyes gleamed, but he didn't move.

Ellen could hardly be surprised. He'd made his attraction to
her very clear, and she was tramping about in wet underwear,
although she no longer felt particularly sexy – just relaxed and
cool-skinned for the first time all day.

She ducked her head away, squeezing water from her hair, and
glanced at him again, thinking how different he was from Richard
– the tongue-tied beach bum, who wouldn't even notice whether
a girl was wearing a microscopic bikini or a full-length drysuit if
she made him laugh, who had no smooth banter or babe-magnet
designer casual wear, whose only girlfriend until now had been
Ellen, and who thought water sports were better than sex, not a
form of it.

Apart from Gavin Grayson at the age of five (school playground, in exchange for a Frazzle), and Damian Atkins at the
age of fourteen (by the ping-pong table in the youth club because
her best friend was snogging his best friend), Ellen had only
ever kissed Richard. She couldn't imagine what another man's
mouth tasted like. She wondered whether their tongues and lips
felt different.

She had no great desire to kiss Lloyd right now, but he was
extremely attractive and looked as though he'd know what he was
doing. She was also pretty certain that he didn't want to fall in
love, get married and have kids. He could make her knickers feel
tight – sometimes – and was far sexier when he wasn't talking.
She could think of worse places to start. It might stop Richard
creeping into her head so much.

'Why don't you, then?' she suggested.

It was certainly nothing like kissing Richard. It was surprisingly
gentle, for a start – his lips were soft and searching, moving
slowly between hers. A cautious hand held her waist as though
her skin was fine silk and another cupped her chin, the fingertips

tracing the curve of her ear. As a practised seducer's kiss, it was unexpectedly timid and passive.

Ellen watched his face as they kissed, the dark lashes closed against the tanned cheeks, the perfect skin still gleaming from the heat of the evening.

To her regret, her knickers didn't tighten. Still sodden from the pool, they drooped like old-lady drawers and started to feel a bit chilly.

Lloyd pulled away, his eyes fluttering open as he smiled, then let out a low growl and tilted his head to the other side to swap nose positions. Now his mouth applied more pressure as he sought out her tongue with his, his chin so much softer than Richard's goatee bristle. Ellen felt her lips yield automatically, allowed her body to be pulled closer to his and tilted up on her toes, but she felt hollow inside. His body was very different from Richard's – taller and less solid, wider at the shoulder and narrower at the hips. When she reached up, she felt a thick, clean mop of hair, not the downy stubble of a balding buzz-cut. The beginnings of his erection – the same familiar, shifting prod – was higher up because he was so much taller, nudging her in the belly rather than the crook of her groin. As it stirred and grew it moved her navel ring from side to side as if it was a miniature door-knocker being rattled.

She tried kissing him back harder, hoping to kick-start something within her, but the only throttle she pressed was his as his tongue leaped enthusiastically in response, probing deeper, his body sliding against hers, the once-gentle hand slipping to her arse and encountering a damp buttock – the erection positively leaped to attention, rattling her belly ring like a hammer on a gong.

Ellen pulled away, wondering what in hell was wrong with her. It wasn't unpleasant kissing him, but it felt no different from getting a shoulder rub while tasting a new wine. In return, he seemed far too eager to pummel her fibroids and down her in one.

'I don't know about you, but I'm starving.' She held him at arms' length, her elbows locking as he tried to lunge forward again. 'Shall we go and eat?'

'Sure.' He let her go reluctantly and flicked on the big white smile.

She turned away, wishing she had just told the truth, that she didn't want to kiss him any more because her experiment had failed, and that while she was actually quite hungry, she was just as happy to go home and eat alone because they had nothing in common, and there was probably some good TV on. At least she'd save him the restaurant bill, so that his wallet wasn't dented even if his pride was.

But Ellen was Jennifer Jamieson's daughter, and while Jennifer would certainly *not* approve of showing your date your underwear then kissing him to see if you fancied him before the meal, she believed in good manners. She had spent years teaching her daughter to be ladylike, gracious and considerate, battling to soften the tomboy edges. It would, Ellen thought, be very bad manners simply to ask Lloyd for a lift home. She would have to spin out her table-talk and try her best to put him off gently by dessert.

She smiled coolly at him over her shoulder as she pulled on her skirt. 'I warn you, I eat like a pig and have no table manners,' she started as she intended to carry on, 'and I'll probably ogle all the waiters.'

Standing on the splashed paving stones beside the pool, watching her stoop down to fetch her clothes and sandals, Lloyd was tempted to stop at his mother's house on the way to the restaurant and warn her that there might be a family wedding imminently.

The moment Lloyd swigged back his first glass of champagne at the Duck Upstream, it was abundantly clear that he couldn't hold his drink. 'You are,' he told Ellen, in an undertone, his accent half-way between mink and manure, '*the* most fantastic thing to come into my life since Seaton's International.'

That was when Ellen discovered that she had misinterpreted Lloyd Fenniweather's smooth, mock-toff banter. He was not as posh as he made out, nor as worldly wise. The smooth-slicker act

– and it was an act – rapidly came unstuck *in vino veritas*, and his egotism grew gargantuan.

'I love this place,' he told her, looking cockily around the room. 'It used to be such a dump, but Pat and Gina – they've the new owners – have turned it around totally. I'd like to own somewhere like this some day – as a hobby, of course. I plan to retire at forty.' His accent was slipping like a teenager's makeup now, revealing the soft, fresh-faced local burr beneath the wised-up drawl.

The Duck Upstream was, as Pheely had warned, a gourmet pub rendered so pretentious by its current owners that it would make New York feel unfashionable, London feel unhistorical and Paris feel like a bad cook, or at least that was its smug belief. When trading as the plain old Pheasant, it had attracted a strong local and tourist following, eager eaters returning again and again for the legendary home-made sausages, the freshly barbecued trout and the beef and ale pies. Now villagers rarely if ever ate there, and most of the custom came from London and overseas. The car park looked like a prestige motor showroom, the coat rack was a small designer boutique and the dining room resembled Harrods' fine furniture repository.

Ellen hated it. Lloyd clearly thought he had brought her to Mecca-on-the-Wold.

'Tonight is really special.' He fixed the Demerara eyes on her and burned every calorie in them. 'You are so sexy. I bet you never thought you'd meet somebody like me while you were here, did you?'

'No – not exactly,' she said awkwardly.

'We're going to be so good together.' He winked roguishly and squeezed her knee with a sweaty hand.

Before Ellen could think of a polite brush-off, an eager hostess had swept in on them like a magpie on a pair of glittering earrings.

'Everything all right, so far?' she asked, in an affected voice, thrusting menus into their faces.

'Divine, Gina.' Lloyd blasted her with the white smile. 'This is

Ellen – you'll be seeing a lot more of her. She's just moved into the village.'

Gina thrust out a paw and arranged her face in a wince-like smile; the Mallen-streak hair and antique jewellery created a theatrical counterpoint to her chi-chi restaurant.

Ellen shook her hand. 'And I'm about to move out again, as soon as Lloyd has sold the house.'

Lloyd let out a little growl. 'We'll see about that.'

'Well, enjoy!' Gina winced her way into a muted gay laugh. 'We like to make our diners feel like members of our special family.' She swooped off through a swinging door to scream at her staff for failing to spot that Lloyd's glass was at a low ebb.

'Lovely woman,' Lloyd purred, giving Ellen a hot look and raising his glass to his lips before he remembered that it was empty.

Rather than go for all-out, wallet-stealing pretension, like the nearby Eastlode Park, the Duck Upstream claimed to encourage a 'friendly, convivial dining experience', but Ellen found nothing convival about the hushed library-reading-room atmosphere, the purse-lipped waiting staff and the modern minimalism that had stripped the old pub of its character.

Diners like she and Lloyd started off (like children in the infant's class) by reading their menus over a cocktail and an appetiser in the Mallard Drawing Room – the old pub saloon, now with natural plaster walls and a seagrass floor scattered with uncomfortable glossy green sofas that required muscular legs to stay on board. Ellen braced her calves to stop her bum sliding off and dipped her head to avoid a nearby spiky flower arrangement as she read the menu and worriedly watched Lloyd order more champagne. 'Don't you think you should go slow if you're driving?'

'I thought I might leave the car here and pick it up in the morning,' he murmured, with a suggestive wink. 'Seen anything you fancy?'

Ellen gripped her menu. Not you, I'm afraid, she thought wretchedly. Oh, God, why do I get myself into these things? Excited, flirtatious Lloyd was about a fifth as sexy as smarmy, calculating-agent Lloyd. Smarmy Lloyd, in turn, was hardly sexy at all compared with irritated, pretentious Lloyd. And that Lloyd, it transpired, didn't really exist at all. She had made him up to satisfy her desire for a little low-level sexual tension.

'We'll have to come here on a Wednesday next time – they have a fantastic pianist, really romantic,' he said cheerfully, as he read the menu. 'Shall we start with oysters?'

'I'm allergic to seafood,' Ellen lied. 'I think I'll just have the warm sardine salad.'

He smiled indulgently and patted her knee again, 'I hate to tell you this, Ellen, but sardines live in the sea.'

'I can eat fish.' She gave him a withering look.

He tilted his head and smiled playfully. 'I love all your curious little ways. You are a creature of mystery.'

He was sounding more and more like Austin Powers. Ellen felt mildly sick.

'What's endive?' he asked, as he read down the list.

'Posh word for disgustingly bitter lettuce,' she said distractedly, checking her watch for the fifth time and wondering how much longer she could stick it out.

'Can you cook, Ellen?' He looked up through sugar-spun brows.

'I do toast,' she said honestly.

He laughed far too much at this, white teeth revealing no fillings and the pinkest of healthy gum. The waiter sallied forth with another glass of champagne and an order pad. Lloyd plucked the glass from his hand and aimed it at Ellen's. 'I do toast too. Let's toast *us*.'

A nearby American couple who had been frantically earwigging, let out loud 'Awwwws' and raised their glasses too.

Ellen steadied hers as it took a side impact from Lloyd's and decided she had two options. She either nipped to the loos now, threaded her way through the window (that was this week's expert ruse) and fled, or she got extremely drunk.

'Madam?' The waiter was tapping his pen on his pad.

Ellen felt a growl in her belly after a week of eating nothing but beans on toast. Casting Lloyd a thoughtful look, she reminded herself that he was (a) selling her house, (b) physically very attractive and (c) paying. What the hell? She was a grown woman. She drained her champagne and requested a top-up at the same time as picking out her sardine starter, a steak and as many side orders as she could find listed.

'I've lost my hunger for anything but your eyes,' Lloyd told her, in a low purr, as soon as the waiter had gone. 'But do I love a girl with a healthy appetite – just so long as she knows how to burn it off afterwards.'

Ellen smiled weakly.

'And you certainly look as though you know how to keep fit.' He ran his eyes over her body. 'I bet you work out all the time.'

'I prefer mental workouts these days,' she said.

'Oh, me too!' His accent was rougher now than a farmhand's. 'When I'm down the gym, I always go mental.' He waited for the big laugh, and when it failed to materialise, he let out one of his sexy growls. 'Relax, Ellen baby. Enjoy yourself. It's not every day you meet someone you want to work out with as much as this, if you catch my drift.' He drew a loose strand of hair back from her face and stroked her neck. 'I can't wait to kiss you again. I bet you feel the same way, don't you?'

Ellen snatched the fresh glass of incoming champagne gratefully and took a swig, working a few things out in her head. It is not his fault, she told herself. It would be the same with anybody.

She'd been right in thinking it was too soon after Richard to start seeing other men, however casually. She hadn't actually been on a date with a stranger since she was sixteen, and the rules had been different then. You went to the cinema, a disco or a party and didn't really talk to each other. You just waited for the lights to go low and 'Careless Whisper' to come on, then snogged each other. All she'd really wanted from Lloyd, she now suspected, was a snog – nothing more. She'd wanted to pick up where she had left off thirteen years ago and build from there. Initially, when faced with Lloyd's obvious good looks, she had liked the idea of snogging him. Now she'd done it, she felt as if she'd eaten too much chocolate – guilty and sick and not nearly as satisfied as she had hoped.

Lloyd, by contrast, had barely lifted the foil from the fruit-and-nut. He was anticipating at least a one-night stand, if not a great deal more. As far as he was concerned, the snogging had barely begun.

While one waiter whisked towards Ellen and Lloyd with two appetisers the size of hula-hoops, which he described floridly as 'aubergine mini-bagels drizzled in oregano-infused oil and topped with pimento tapenade', another was ushering in a large party to try their luck on the green helter-skelter sofas.

Glad of the distraction, Ellen watched as he held open the door, bowing and half kneeling like a medieval courtier, to admit Ely Gates, who strode in with his puddingy wife. Behind them came the lofty, jowly Sir St John with Hell's Bells marching to heel, and to the rear the three children of the combined party – Godspell the Goth, a small, dark-eyed youth, who had to be Enoch Gates, and finally, scowling furiously, Spurs.

Those luminous silver eyes glared around the room as he stalked into it, landing on Ellen and kicking her right to the back of her chair before they moved past her without a glimmer of recognition. This time, the G-force made her reel in shock, because she suddenly recognised why she'd been attracted to Lloyd in the first place. Spurs Belling made her feel recklessly sexual just by looking at her. Men like Spurs, those rare X-factor hooligans with a wild spirit and hearbreaking magnetism, had so much sex-appeal that they made Ellen combust on impact. On the day she had wriggled through the attic window, the knowledge that Spurs was watching had made her blood boil with excitement. And she'd met Lloyd while she was still glowing in its candescence.

Men like Spurs were the reason Ellen's love for Richard had always been compromised, despite their years together. Richard made her feel warm inside, but she secretly craved the sort of intense heat he could never spark. And poor Lloyd just left her cold.

She wrenched her head away and stared at her aubergine mini-bagel, feeling the hole in her heart as clearly as she could see the hole in the doughy hula-hoop before her.

As the party was ushered past her and Lloyd, Lady Belling gave Ellen a curt nod of recognition. But Spurs failed to acknowledge her. Not looking to left or right, he headed directly for his table. He was, she noticed, sporting the same ancient jeans and flip-flops he'd worn dog-walking a week earlier, matched rather eccentrically tonight with a white shirt and striped tie to conform with the restaurant's dress code. The combination would have looked ludicrous on anybody else, but he carried it off with absurd, sullen cool. She felt her heart smash against her ribs and her skin prickle with the heat of pure, intuitive attraction.

'Good evening.'

To Ellen's surprise, Ely Gates had smoothed his Conservative Club tie to his starched shirt and was stopping at their table. 'Lloyd, my boy.' He stooped down to bestow an evangelical double handshake on Ellen's disastrous date. 'Are you in good health?'

'Very well, thank you,' Lloyd was choir-boy gauche in the presence of the village Machiavelli. 'Have you met Ellen Jamieson?'

'Not formally.' Ely fixed her with a gaze that could have burned souls for lesser sins than accepting a dinner date with Lloyd without marriage playing a part in her future plans. 'Although I believe I rudely failed to introduce myself at Lady Belling's fundraising evening.' He extended one long-fingered hand, his eyes lasering into hers so intently he seemed to be checking her optic nerves. 'Elijah Gates.'

'I know.' She smiled nervously up at him as her hand underwent a long, crushing shake with no possibility of shaking in return. He was spectacularly charismatic and scary. With his neatly trimmed beard, smart suit and gleaming shoes, he reminded her of an old warhorse groomed and rugged in plush retirement, yet capable of letting rip and charging that half-tonne powerhouse body up a hill, given half a chance.

'I hope Lloyd has convinced you that my offer is a reasonable one?' He smiled, but his eyes remained arctic with intensity.

'Your offer?' Ellen looked at Lloyd, who was frantically trying to reaffix the big white smile to his face.

'I should have explained.' He glanced awkwardly between them. 'The offer on Goose Cottage came from Ely – hmm – *Mr* Gates.'

'My mother always loved that cottage,' Ely told Ellen, in his rich, old Cotswold accent. 'She said it was a magical place, and that as long as geese are kept on the land, it makes for long marriages, ripe riches and good health.'

'Sounds great,' Ellen wasn't sure her father would agree, 'but surely it would seem very small to you after Manor Farm?'

He let out a bark of amusement. 'I do not wish to buy Goose Cottage for myself, child, simply as an investment.'

'I see.' She smiled awkwardly, feeling silly. 'Well, I think Mum and Dad are holding out for a bit more.'

'And I shall hold out for their agreement,' he said coolly. 'My offer for the cottage remains open, as Lloyd will have explained. I know its value. We'll see who gives in first, shall we? Now, if you'll excuse me . . .' He swept off in a puff of cigar smoke.

Ellen watched him go with wide eyes.

Eating as quickly as possible to hurry the date along didn't present much of a problem to Ellen because the portions were microscopic. Her first course – which appeared to be half a sardine balanced on a potato crisp – disappeared in one mouthful and she was already tapping her fork in anticipation of the main course by the time the Gates and Belling parties were ushered through from the Mallard sofa purgatory to the main dining room. She'd hoped to be able to watch them for entertainment, but they were shown through an archway to the smoking area and when they sat down the only visible member of the group was Ely's wife, who did nothing but blow her nose incessantly on her napkin.

Suddenly Ellen was livid with herself for telling Lloyd that

she preferred non-smoking. What she wouldn't give for a cigarette now!

'More champagne?' he asked, proffering the bottle and rubbing
his ankle against hers.

Ellen nodded, although she was finding it hard to get drunk
– like being too tense for a local anaesthetic to work at the
dentist's.

Lloyd dipped his head beneath the flop of caramel hair and
watched her thoughtfully through it. Having started out by getting
as silly as a teenager on cider, he had now soft-pedalled on the
bubbly long enough to recapture his posh accent and lift his game.
With the help of three glasses of mineral water and a basket of
bread, he was on the attack again, big white smile back in place
as he talked about himself.

'I like sport. I probably could have been a pro – football,
tennis, cricket or something. But I want to make my millions in
business. Now, I wouldn't mind *owning* a football team. That
might be cool.'

Above his head was one of the many strange duck paintings
that were scattered across all the walls, obviously commissioned
by the same artist. In them, each bird was picked out in a brown
ink splat. They reminded Ellen of the hundreds of Coke stains and
spills that she had spent all week scrubbing from the flagstones or
washing and rewashing out of the soft furnishings.

On and on Lloyd droned about his ambitions, the cars and villas
and other status symbols he wanted to own. Not once did he ask
Ellen about herself or her plans, although right now all she wanted
to do was get home as quickly as possible.

'I know you girls find sport boring,' he chortled, 'but it really
is a technical business. I often think that if women bothered to
learn a bit more, they'd get really into it.' The big caramel eyes
blinked sincerely at her.

'Excuse me – I'll be right back.' Ellen went hastily in search
of the loos before she punched him. There was no point telling
him that she probably knew as much about sportsmen and their
technical requirements as he knew about the value of Cotswold

property. It would only increase his esteem, and things were already steamy enough as far as besotted Lloyd was concerned. He had now undressed her so many times with his eyes that he should have coat-hangers dangling from his lashes.

The lavatories – predictably signed 'Ducks' and 'Drakes' – were beyond a candlelit, roofed terrace in which two early diners were enjoying post-prandial cigars and Cognacs overlooking the stream. Ellen eyed the tall, open doors as she passed through, tempted to make a run for it – but she had left her bag and house keys at the table.

To her embarrassment, she found herself walking into the Ducks' wash room at the same time as Hell's Bells, who blustered past with another curt nod and bagged the only cubicle. Ellen studied her reflection while she waited, dragging her fingers through her hair which had dried in rats' tails from swimming.

She had separated every strand and given herself a Farrah Fawcett mane by the time the cistern flushed. Hell's Bells could pee for as long as a horse. Re-emerging with a hunk of loo roll in her hand, she headed for the sink. 'Can't stand those new-fangled blower things.' She indicated the hand-dryer on the wall as she placed the tissues beside the basin in readiness.

Her improvised paper hand towel had, it transpired, been the last of the loo roll. Two minutes later, Ellen tore the cardboard roll from the holder and braced herself for something not very soft, strong or long. She half suspected the old bat of taking it all deliberately – a habitual prank born from years of tomfoolery at boarding school, hunt balls and drunken charity dinners.

Not that she minded. In a curious way, feeling less than savoury hardened her resolve to throw Lloyd off as soon as she could. She was almost tempted to slip it straight into the conversation when she returned to the table – 'you'd think some-where like this would have toilet tissue in the Ladies, wouldn't you? Ugh.'

Smiling at the childish idea, her face flushed from a quick blast with the new-fangled blower, she headed back through the covered terrace. Then, like a soldier given an 'eyes right' command, she found her head twisting to stare over her shoulder before she had time to question why.

Glowing far more brightly than the candles around him, Spurs Belling's eyes pierced the gloom. But they weren't looking at Ellen; they were glaring into his mother's matching silver gaze as the two squared up to one another in the open doorway.

'No way.' He was shaking his head, knuckles white against a cigarette filter as he pressed it to his mouth and took a tetchy puff. 'I won't do it.'

'You cannot change your mind now, Jasper,' Hell's Bells muttered in a low voice, glancing around.

The cigar-smokers had moved outside to look at the stream and the two were alone, apart from Ellen who hovered behind a potted fern, anxious not to be seen.

'I didn't agree to this in the first place,' he hissed.

Ellen had no idea what they were arguing about and wasn't loitering to find out – mother and son were clearly accustomed to locking horns. What rooted her to the spot was the irresistible, voyeuristic urge to look at Spurs for just a few seconds. It was like standing in the eye of a storm, watching it swirl around her – electrically charged, black-souled and unpredictable.

'You know how important this is to me,' Hell's Bells was entreating him, as gently as her angry, bullying tone could manage.

He stared down at her, unblinking, his cheeks sucked in so that every taut muscle in his jaws seemed to have been shrink-wrapped in tanned, freckled skin.

'Frankly, I'd rather die.'

Ellen personally thought that a bit of an overreaction at being forced to dine with the Gateses and their children.

'You're killing yourself already,' Hell's Bells snapped. 'If you keep smoking those ghastly cigarettes, you won't see sixty.'

Recognising her own mother's lecture notes in use, Ellen fought a childish urge to leap from behind the potted fern and beg a Marlboro from Spurs. But instead, she forced herself to turn back towards the restaurant and leave the two scrapping – the babble of diners drowning out the last few moments of the heated exchange.

'That is the plan,' Spurs laughed bitterly. 'In fact, if I smoke hard enough I may be stubbed out before my half century. Thank heaven for Duty Free.'

'It's not a joking matter, Jasper.'

'No, it's a smoking matter.'

'I can assure you, you'll regret this facetious attitude when you are told that you can count out the rest of your life on just one calendar.'

'I already can. There's a date circled in June that might as well be my funeral.'

'You have a duty to the family.'

'Not so Duty Free, then.'

'Do you agree, or don't you?'

'No.'

Diners in the restaurant jumped as there was a loud crash from the terrace. Ellen, who had just settled back into the sugary syrup of Lloyd's gaze, looked up sharply. 'What was that?'

'My heart beating faster,' he purred, his eyes not leaving hers.

'Excuse me – I left something in the loo.' She sprang up.

Stop this, she told herself angrily as she trotted back towards the Ducks. Stop staring into the flames, you stupid idiot. But the storm had broken, and she could never resist watching lightning strike.

The crash had been caused by Hell's Bells sitting down heavily on a wicker sofa and consequently knocking the potted fern from its stand. Crouching on the flagstones, Spurs was scooping soil into the largest piece of pot, a fresh cigarette dangling from his lips. He looked up as Ellen passed, snapping, 'I told you that we don't need any help—'

Realising that she wasn't a member of staff, he shut up and carried on scooping. A moment later, he threw down the crockery and soil and marched outside, muttering. 'Fuck this.'

On the sofa, Lady Belling was looking deathly pale and waxy.

Something about her pallor set off emergency bells in Ellen's head.

'Are you all right?' she asked automatically, unable to pass by without offering help. 'Would you like a glass of water?'

The steely eyes had lost all their shine as they remained staring straight ahead. 'That's very kind,' she muttered hoarsely, 'but I will be quite all right. I just need a few moments to recover.'

There was none of the usual ruddiness in the freckled cheeks and, despite her sturdy bulk and proud, high-chinned posture, she struck Ellen as incredibly frail. 'If you're sure . . .'

'Oh, I am,' she rallied a little prickly spirit and shooed Ellen away towards the Ducks – only to call her back moments later. 'Here,' she drew a small packet of paper handkerchieves from her handbag. 'You'll need these.'

'Thanks,' she wondered if Hell's Bells was trying to make amends, but the dull silver eyes showed no recognition. Whatever had just caused her knees to go had really knocked her for six.

Not needing the loo, Ellen stood in front of the mirror and studied her reflection again, clutching the handkerchieves to her chest.

Nosy Parker, she could hear Richard taunting her. *Can't resist, can you?*

The nickname had come about from her tendency to park the camper van at the best spying vantage points at camp sites. Ellen was notorious for taking hours to go to the loo block because she spent so long dawdling outside tents listening to the conversations and arguments on the other side of the canvas.

'Go away,' she told him. 'I'm not ready to talk to your memory yet.'

Nice dinner date. Very Gilette.

'Go away.'

Shame he doesn't rattle your cage like the posh bastard.

'Shove off. Go on – sling your—' she rapidly turned the mutterings of a mad woman into a cough as a fellow diner came into the Ducks behind her.

'Are you . . . ?'

'No – no, I've finished. Here,' she handed her the tissues, 'you'll need one of these.'

'Thanks – oh, look, there's something stuck to this.'

A piece of tightly-folded paper had become glued to the re-sealable strip on the tissue casing. Ellen took them back and, battling with curiosity, headed out.

Hell's Bells had gone, but Spurs was still framed in the doorway with his back to the room, finishing off a cigarette. Something about the murderous hunch of his shoulders told her to approach with great caution.

'Your mother handed this to me by accident,' she muttered, pulling the piece of paper from the tissues and thrusting it at him with such haste that it ripped, leaving a corner still attached to the glue strip. 'Could you give it back to her?'

He nodded, not turning around, staring fixedly into the bubbling stream.

As she sloped away, he unfolded the remains of the letter and scanned it. Just before Ellen walked under the archway to the dining room, she heard a great, mournful groan and turned to see Spurs bury his face in his hands.

'Find what you were looking for?' Lloyd had already scraped back his chair, standing up and calling across to her.

She nodded as she rejoined him, glancing curiously at the paper that was still dangling from the travel tissues. It was a letterhead – *Foxrush Holistic Veterinary Practice* – with contact details. She pocketed it, wondering vaguely if there was a holistic cure for chicken-chasing dogs and disappearing cats.

'I missed you,' he growled sexily.

'Is that a fact?' She flashed a smile at a waiter as he proudly presented her with her main course, a tiny square of wafer thin bright red beef with charred edges, topped with half a black olive and drizzled with lurid green sauce.

Ellen bolted it in two mouthfuls and waited for Lloyd to demolish a piece of anorexic chicken and strategically arranged pink peppercorns. Even though he was eating slowly because he was talking so much, it was simply too small to spin out very far.

As soon as he had swallowed the last mouthful, Ellen looked at her watch and explained that she had to go, politely refusing his offers of dessert, coffee and Cognac. 'I can't – I have to get back to the dog. I can't leave a window open for her now in case she goes after our neighbour's chickens.'

'In that case, I'll see you home.'

'Oh, I can walk.' Ellen reached for her bag.

'I absolutely insist.'

She relented: she should at least have the decency to go through the motions of fighting him off at the doorstep.

'Thank you,' she said stiffly. 'It's been a lovely evening.' She blushed at the lie.

'It's not over yet,' he purred.

As they stood up to leave, he put a protective arm around her back to steer her away from the table, and Ellen caught sight of Spurs Belling stalking furiously under the archway, heading for the door. As he passed her, the silver eyes locked on hers for a second, almost razing her to the ground. She looked away hastily, hating the reaction that hit her pulses and groin.

'D'you know him?' Lloyd raised his eyebrows.

'Not really.'

'Believe me, you don't want to,' Lloyd whispered. 'I'm glad I'm here to look after you.' He patted her bottom and winked at Gina, who swept over to see them out and wish them well.

Although Ellen didn't entirely trust Lloyd to be sober, she decided to take the gamble of letting him drive her one mile across the village because she wanted to get home.

The leather passenger seat still felt damp from her swimming-pool bottom, although that bottom itself had long-since dried in the warm restaurant. Ellen perched on it, made extra-certain that her seat belt was well fastened, then chewed her lip as Lloyd swung out of the car park, eyes scanning the road.

It was dark outside. The last hot orange fake-tan streaks of a dusky sunset had given way to a muggy navy blue duvet, but villagers were still out and about, walking dogs or lined up along the tables outside the Lodes Inn.

They travelled the short distance in awkward silence, both knowing that they had a fight ahead of them to get what they wanted. When Lloyd pulled up outside the Goose Cottage gates, Ellen burst on to the verge before he could jump out and do his door-opening flourish. But despite her speed he had a secret weapon up his sleeve.

As she turned to close the door and blurt her thanks, he was out of the car and affecting an embarrassed expression over its roof. ''Fraid I need the loo. Would you mind awfully if I used yours?'

It wasn't a very good line. In fact, it was so bad, Ellen stupidly believed him.

As she unlocked the door and greeted Snorkel, Lloyd bounded straight for the stairs.

'It's just to your right on the landing!' she called, then realised that of course he knew where the main bathroom was – he had probably measured it and noted the fittings.

In which case, she wondered, why hadn't he headed for the one beside the bootroom downstairs? It was far closer.

It took half an hour to find out. That was how long Ellen waited before following him upstairs to check that he was all right. She knew somehow what she would find, and it took her that long to pluck up courage.

He'd settled in the main bedroom, draped across the freshly laundered counterpane on the four-poster bed. He was propped up on the pillows waiting for her, wearing just a pair of black jockey shorts and that adorable white smile.

'I lied about the underwear,' he purred.

Ellen felt dangerously close to tears. He was so very handsome – his body magnificent. She'd worked with a lot of athletes and she knew fine-tuning when she saw it. Lloyd Fenniweather kept himself extremely fit. In purely aesthetic terms, he was the most appealing sight she'd seen in years. So why did she want to run away?

'I'm sorry,' she blurted out. 'I really don't want to go to bed with you.'

'You don't?' He looked astonished.

'No.' She backed away. 'I've just come out of a very long relationship, you see. Thirteen years. It's too soon. You're lovely. It's so not you. It's me.' She wanted to close her eyes and scream. For Ellen that was a big-time confession, and it hurt more than her pride to lift the dressing on the wound.

'I know just the thing you need.' He rallied a seductive growl. 'A one-night stand – to be taken lying down.' He patted the bed beside him.

'I'm sorry, Lloyd.' She swallowed. 'I think you'd better get dressed and go.'

'It's just sex.' He held out his arms. 'I'm good at sex.'

'I don't want to have sex with you.'

He sat up and rubbed his designer hair, treacly eyes rolling. 'Okay – okay. I'm sorry. You want to take this more slowly. Of course. You're a lady. We can have dinner again or something. Get to know each other better.'

'It wouldn't work, Lloyd. I'm going away soon, anyway.'

'Where?'

'The World.'

His perfect profile turned away, but his voice held a touch of the old mock-James Bond spirit. 'That's a long way to go to avoid a second date.'

'I know.'

'I've never met anyone as amazing as you before.'

'You should get out more.' She smiled sadly. As far as Lloyd knew, the World began on one ridge of the Lodes Valley and ended at the other.

'Is it because I'm a bit of a fake?' he asked hollowly.

'No.' She swallowed a great lump in her throat.

The huge eyes looked up at her, so full of sadness that Ellen just wanted to break down and cry, hugging him and apologising for leading him on and explaining that she was much more of a fraud than he was, with his phoney accent and big ideas. But then he ruined it.

'I suppose a blow-job's out of the question?'

She went into violent reverse, knowing that she had to bolt before she really did start crying – and that was something she never, ever did in front of a living soul, not even Richard. 'Can you see yourself out? I'm going up to bed. Just don't follow me, please?'

At that moment, Snorkel bounded in and leaped straight on to the bed, one scrabbling white paw landing hard in the middle of the black jockey shorts.

'Yeeeooooow!' Lloyd howled.

Ellen ran. She just made it to the attic before the salt water started breaking through the dam and the tension in her head, chest, shoulders and heart came pouring out. She locked herself into her room, put a pillow to her mouth to muffle the sound, and howled.

It felt like hours before the pressure started to ebb and the tears thinned out. By then, she was so drained that she gasped for breath, mopping her wet face on the pillow and rubbing snot from her nose with her wrist. She snorted with bitter laughter as she remembered how Richard had always known when she'd been crying because she had 'bogey wrists'. He could be such a kid. Between them, they'd stopped each other growing up.

She picked up her mobile from the bedside table and read tonight's messages. Just three. He was slowing down. The first read 'TELL SNORK I MISS HER', the second 'GET SNORK TO TELL ELL I MISS HER TOO', and the third – probably after a few late-morning beers – 'TEXT ME BACK, YOU COW . . . AND PLUG IN YOUR COMPUTER TO DOWNLOAD EMAIL. ARE YOU DEAD?'

Ellen wiped her nose on her wrists again, laughing and crying at once. Maybe tonight she would be brave enough to text him back. She hit the 'reply' arrow. How could she put it? 'HID IN ATTIC RATHER THAN CRY IN FRONT OF SEXY, NEAR-NAKED MAN. SEE? IT'S *NOT* just you.' That would make him laugh.

But the glowing screen fell dark again long before she had typed a single letter and she put the phone back on the table, burying her head in the pillow to chew it again.

It was no good. The moment she had lifted the dressing, the

wound had exploded open and was still haemorrhaging. She couldn't hope to cover it up. Tonight she would have to bleed. It was time to think about Richard at last.

When she heard the car engine start up directly outside in the early hours, Ellen got up and crept to the window just in time to see the tail-lights of the Merc disappearing along Goose Lane.

She'd thought that Lloyd had left hours earlier – when she was crying into her pillow and could hear nothing but her pumping heart in her ears. Since then the house had been silent. She hadn't heard him moving around, or calling up to her or even making himself a cup of tea.

She crept downstairs and looked into the main bedroom, where she found Snorkel curled up on the neatly made counterpane, occupying a recently vacated warm patch. Ellen curled up in it too, soaking up the warmth of another human being's body – albeit at second hand.

'Rich says he misses you,' she told Snorkel, hugging her tightly. 'And me.'

She rolled over on her back and played tailfin with her feet, swimming this way and that as she had as a child.

Richard had been her ocean and now she could only swim in tiny tanks like a trapped dolphin in a sea park. Tonight she longed to swim out to sea and never come back. Had she been in Cornwall, she would have been walking the coast path by now. As it was, she buried her face in Snorkel's ruffed neck and started to cry again. 'I miss Fins,' she wept childishly. 'I miss every fin.'

5

For the first time since she had arrived in Oddlode, Ellen slept late into the morning. And when she did awake, her eyes didn't immediately spring open. They appeared to be broken. They wouldn't open at all.

She lay curled in the twisted duvet battling to separate the fused lids, wondering if Lloyd had crept back into the house with a vial of Superglue, exacting revenge for the disastrous date. Perhaps he had stolen in on her and dabbed the potent adhesive on her eyelashes while she slept fitfully, half dreaming of Richard?

She could feel Snorkel's chin pressing on to her ankles, pleadingly waiting for her morning walk.

At last one eyelid separated just enough for her to make out blurred outlines in the bright room – the corner of the bedside table, the lamp, a discarded sandal on the floor.

She unfolded herself slowly and tottered to the mirror above the basin, then groaned as she saw the blurred, distorted face peering back. Splashed with cool water and rubbed with a towel, her eyes finally opened as much as they could and took in the full picture. Crying late into the night had left her with incredible plump bags and swollen lids, like shiny pink slugs, from which her normally clear blue irises peeped in miniature, the whites marked with tens of bloodshot red contour lines. Her nose and lips were red and flaky, as though she had climbed the entire mountain of her relationship with Richard last night then stood facing the icy wind for hours, not merely camped in the foothills crying into her sleeping-bag.

She turned to look out of the tiny dormer window at the lane, seeing the Saturday-morning village traffic jam – three children on micro-scooters, a dog-walker and two tourists on a tandem. The sun was elbowing its hot rays through a haze of pre-storm mist and vapour high above the valley; once again it was merciless in its strength. To do more than a brisk walk under its canopy would be torture. Ellen accepted the challenge gratefully,

'Sorry, Snork.' She winked one sluggy eye and went in search of running clothes and very dark glasses. 'You can lie in the long grass and wait for me if you get too hot.'

Snorkel was only too happy to bound alongside Ellen as she hammered her way up the baked ruts of the bridleway, climbing through the heat-haze high above the river and its folly, passing fields of ripening corn, yellow rape and blue linseed. As soon as the sweat started running into her puffy eyes, it soothed them, and before long she was scoring an endorphin fix as her lungs gulped in oxygen to pump through her blood and into her muscles.

She was far less fit than she had once been. Two miles of uphill running was all she could take before she flopped on to a thick bed of clover-strewn pasture by a small wood, gasping, puffing and laughing. 'God, that's better!' she breathed, wiping her hot face with her palms and rolling on to her belly to gaze down the valley.

Beside her Snorkel panted in the shade of the wood as they both watched a kite circling overhead, cocking their heads together as it swooped past.

'Don't let me cry again, Snork,' Ellen puffed. 'It doesn't suit me.'

Snorkel turned her clown's face to her, mad blue eyes blinking, a pink tongue lolling from her mouth.

Ellen looked out over the village again, spotting the tall chimneys from the Lodge poking out through Pheely's jungle, and suddenly longed for strong coffee and one of her friend's killer joints. But then she remembered that Pheely had Daffodil staying for the weekend, and also knew that she would insist on hearing all about her date. Given a few more hours to herself, Ellen would probably be able to make it sound screamingly funny, but right now she was determined not to think about it.

She sauntered back at a more leisurely pace, passing a group of ramblers coming in the opposite direction and wishing them a cheery good day. She was safe behind the dark glasses and baseball cap, and knew that while the bright smile wasn't quite matched by the still puffy hidden eyes, it was getting there.

She stretched her arms above her neck and rolled her head to loosen the tension, rounding the corner by the lime tree, ready for a shower, coffee and the battle of the Goose Cottage garden.

Spurs Belling was sitting on the dry-stone wall beside the bunkhouse, smoking a cigarette and kicking an impatient foot against the lichen. He jumped down as Ellen crunched through the gate. 'There you are.'

'Hi,' she greeted him cautiously, pausing on the gravel, fighting an urge to smile stupidly. If a short run was a quick endorphin fix, an encounter with Spurs Belling gave a far faster and easier high. But even though her heart-rate bounded into treble figures once more, his unfriendly, deadpan expression stopped her welcoming him too warmly.

Snorkel had no such hesitation and threw herself at him in her usual flirtatious fashion, licking his ankles ecstatically before upending herself and presenting a speckled belly. Spurs stooped to rub it, looking up at Ellen through the curly fringe, his freckled face unsmiling. 'I came about the auction lot.'

She nodded, not sure what to say. Even standing ten yards away from him in the open made her anxious – not just because of all Pheely's dark warnings, but because he was so totally, unashamedly X-factor that she wanted to turn and run straight back up the hill, dead legs or not. From the tips of his wild curls to the toes of his tatty trainers, he was devilish, decadent and very dangerous – a fallen angel dressed like a tramp. He also seemed to be edgy and impatient.

'The three wishes?' he reminded her, straightening up.

Scruffy, poker-faced and arrogant, he was an unlikely genie. Given that all Ellen wished for right now was a long shower, her eye-mask and a day's solitude, she wished he'd stayed in his lamp

– at least until her eyes adjusted to the light. She'd forgotten just how luminous that silver gaze was.

'Yes, I remember.' She whistled for Snorkel, who was gearing up to plunge through the long grass towards her favourite Cochin-watching spot. 'It was only a ten-pound donation – you really don't have to honour it.' She guided the collie towards the dovecote and clipped the lunge rope to her collar.

He followed her. 'I always honour my promises.'

Still crouching, Ellen smiled to herself as she stroked Snorkel's black ears. She doubted that very much: from what she'd heard, honour had never been one of Jasper Belling's greatest qualities. And at this precise moment, she wanted to forget all about her accidental bid at last week's auction.

'Honestly, I'm happy to let it pass.' She glanced over her shoulder, not wishing to appear rude but anxious to get rid of him.

He crossed his arms and looked down at her, the silver eyes suddenly flint-like. 'C'mon – you can think of a wish, even if it's just that you hadn't drunk so much at the Duck last night. I know a great hangover cure – one wish and it's yours.'

Ellen didn't want to be reminded of the previous night. If she could wish for anything, it would be that she'd never agreed to go out with Lloyd in the first place – but she wasn't about to tell Spurs that. 'I'm not hung-over, thanks.'

He looked down at her for a long time, tapping his fingers against his arms.

'I have nothing to wish for right now,' she hinted.

'There's really *nothing* little Ellen Jones could wish for?' He narrowed his eyes.

It was an obvious taunt. That stony, petulant gaze was practically throwing pebbles at her dark glasses. 'It's Jamieson,' she pointed out. 'And no.'

'Nothing in the whole wide world?' he goaded. 'Spoilsport.'

He was a spoilt brat, spoiling for a flight, Ellen told herself. It wasn't her idea of sport. She knew a red light when she saw one. But she'd always run red lights. It was a lifelong weakness.

'Put like that,' she stood up again and faced him thoughtfully, 'then I guess there would be a few things I'd like – like no wars, no exploitation, no religious bigotry, no racism or sexism or ageism or body fascism. And I wish women could come as easily as men. Do you want to pick out three?' She flashed a smile to let him know she was pulling his leg.

But he didn't return it. He just carried on gazing at her. 'Those don't qualify. The wishes you bought are for personal use only.' He made them sound like recreational drugs. 'Those are just boring. I'm not God.'

He was watching her very closely now, and Ellen was uncomfortably aware that he was looking through her dark glasses and into her eyes. She remembered only too well that Pheely had called his promise three 'death' wishes. Yet, facing him in the bright sunlight, she didn't feel intimidated so much as hot, bug-eyed and flustered. She was irritated that he'd caught her on an off-day and that he was so humourless. She had a curious feeling that he was having an off-day too, which made it doubly annoying that he had come here to vex her.

'All you have to do is make a wish. It's easy. Try it,' he demanded snappishly, still monitoring her eyes through their tinted Perspex veils.

Ellen ran another red light: she refused to drop eye-contact first. She no longer cared how puffy-lidded and cried-out she was. He was far too accustomed to intimidating people, and she'd encountered enough self-styled bad boys over the years to find it – or his village-hooligan reputation – scary. If he really wanted to grant her wishes, then he'd have to stop the Mephistopheles act, brandishing his magic wand like an Uzi.

'Any wish I like?' she asked, pondering her options. Wishing he had a sense of humour might be a start.

'Yup,' he snapped back. 'If I can't make it come true, I'll give you your money back.' Still he stared, until the unblinking, flinty eyes seemed to shower her face with hot sparks and Ellen's sunglasses felt moments away from melting right off her face.

'In that case, I wish . . .' She willed herself to say it. *I wish you'd go away*. But, to her irritation, she found she couldn't. To her even greater irritation, she had to look away before her eyeballs burst into flames. Then, seeking visual sanctuary in the verdigris haze of the garden, she saw a way to get rid of him very quickly indeed.

She ran a hand through her sweaty hair and fanned her T-shirt. 'Okay. Right now, I wish could cut this lot back before the weather breaks.' She nodded at the wilderness. See how you like that, posh boy, she thought with satisfaction.

He followed her gaze, assessing the gargantuan task. 'It looks like it hasn't been touched for months.'

'It hasn't,' she sighed, 'and I've got to make it look like something from *Homes and Gardens* in just a couple of days so that the cottage stands a chance of selling.'

His silver eyes narrowed as he stared across the huge, messy jungle. 'Two days isn't long, but it's a bloody good wish.' Suddenly he smiled – a wide, genuine smile. 'And I thought you were just going to wish I'd piss off.'

Ellen glanced at him guiltily and was almost blinded. She should have just wished for that smile: it was the loveliest thing she'd seen in ages – as cheering, compelling and catching as the giggles. The Belling bone structure, which made a sulk look petulantly beautiful, made a smile simply breathtaking – the broad, high cheeks creasing those big silver eyes, the dimpled chin lifting high above the broad neck like a thoroughbred stallion sniffing the air.

'Okay, I'll grant your wish for you.' He shaded his eyes and surveyed the garden.

'You're not serious?'

'Of course I am – although I'll need your help to get it done this weekend.' He looked around. 'Is there a decent lawnmower?'

Ellen had just dug herself into a very large hole before even investigating the whereabouts of a garden spade. 'It's *way* too much to ask for a tenner,' she said quickly, dragging the smile reluctantly from her own face, but it just sprang back again at the prospect of Spurs Belling stripped to the waist emptying a grass box.

'Three pounds and thirty-three pence.'

'What?'

'Ten pounds for three wishes – that's three pounds thirty-three each.'

Ellen wasn't the only one who couldn't resist playing with sums, it seemed. She scuffed her trainer into the gravel. 'In that case I should have paid a bit more. You can't help me mow this jungle for three quid.'

'You're right.' He rubbed his chin with the palm of his hand. 'What needs doing apart from the grass?'

Ellen stared at him in disbelief.

The silver eyes were dancing now, with infectious excitement as though she'd just offered him a Ferrari for the weekend, rather than a task she had been avoiding all week. 'I can't promise to know a hell of lot about gardening,' he apologised, 'but I picked up some basics when I was on remand.' He watched her face for reaction. When she showed none, he laughed again. 'And the flower-beds here look as though they need some serious attention.' He set off to inspect the closest one, stalking through the tall grass like a leopard slipping silently into the veld.

'I wasn't sure which were weeds . . .' She followed him, wondering what in hell she'd just started. Pheely would be livid with her.

He stooped and pointed at a nettle. 'You know what this is, surely?'

'Ornamental Chinese parsley?' she suggested distractedly, aware that she had unwittingly triggered something she wasn't sure she could handle.

He grinned over his shoulder then leaped up and bounded into the long grass. 'You okay if I look around and throw out some ideas? I know it's your wish, but when I was planting cheap daffodil bulbs in uniform rows, I used to dream of gardens like this.'

'Sure.' She followed him reluctantly. 'My wish is your remand.'

He pulled his hair back from his forehead and strode on down the slope. 'The hedges badly need trimming. This pond looks like it's crying out to be drained and cleaned – and that paddock is way out of control. It should be topped.'

'Topped?' She turned to him alarm, wondering if he planned to kill it off somehow.

'Topping is mowing on a bigger scale – you tow a cutter behind a tractor. There's one at home, but we'd have to bring it through the garden. Then again, it might *do* the garden – there must be half an acre of lawn here, and it'll need at least two cuts.' He strode uphill again.

Ellen watched him for a few seconds before she followed, trying not to notice the way his shoulder muscles moved beneath his T-shirt. This fervent enthusiasm was classic X-factor. For people like Spurs there was precious little midground between passion and boredom. If you found their on switch, it was like starting a firework display, but you usually got your fingers scorched, and the fuses burned out quickly.

He'd wandered round to the back of the cottage now where he was looking up at the walls. 'It's probably the wrong time of year to prune these climbers, but they could be tied back to stop them covering the windows, and I'll clean those while I'm up there. This clematis is being strangled by ivy – and your rambling rose is hosting an aphid orgy. Nice jasmine, though. Mmm – smell.' He held a frond under her nose.

'Were you Lady Chatterley's lover in a previous life?' Ellen joked, as she emerged from the sweetest of breaths.

The silver eyes were almost incandescent now, the soft voice playful. 'Why? Were you Lady Chatterley?'

She looked away quickly. She might run red lights, but green ones were a different matter. She knew his type too well. Flirting with him would be as easy as breathing, but people like Spurs burned so brightly that they stole the oxygen from the air, leaving everyone around them winded. It was better not to go there.

'This is way too much to ask of you,' she said again. 'Three pounds would buy less than half an hour of a professional gardener's time.'

'It's two days' wages in prison.' He smelt the jasmine, eyeing her over its lacy petals.

'You're not in prison any more.'

'Aren't I?' For a moment, he looked flint-eyed again, but then he smiled at her. 'You're right. It doesn't bother you, does it?'

'Not unless it affects your ability to mow a lawn.' Ellen shrugged, then noticed a strange reflection over his shoulder. It was Hunter Gardner's binoculars – trained on them through the gap in the hedge. 'After all, the village guards are keeping watch.' She indicated the sparkling lenses.

Spurs' smile dropped away as he turned to look. 'Bastard!'

'He's actually more interested in the dog,' she assured him.

Spurs thrust up a one-fingered salute and the reflection wobbled furiously.

She grabbed his wrist without thinking. 'Please don't do that – I've pissed him off enough already.'

He snatched away his hand. 'Ashamed to be seen with me too, are you?'

Ellen balked. 'I don't care if you bare your arse at him every time you pass his house.' She laughed in surprise. 'But I hardly know him – or you – and while I could really use some help in this garden, you can bugger off if you're going to wind up the neighbours.'

Slowly the smile lit his face again. It was warmer and more compelling than ever. Within seconds, they were playing 'smile tag', each unable to resist the pull that made their eyes crease and laughter catch in their throats. Then he tilted his head towards hers and whispered in her ear, 'I promise I won't. Please don't tell me to go home.'

He knew she wouldn't. As he straightened up to look at her again, she felt her sweaty T-shirt shrink two sizes. Bugger, Ellen thought, as he drank her in. I fancy you, and you know it. Bugger.

Then, without warning, he reached out a hand and took off her sun glasses, the silver gaze examining her puffy eyes. 'Hay fever?' he asked carefully.

She nodded very carefully in return, reaching out to take her shades back.

His dark eyebrows curled up into his forehead, then he backed off. 'In that case, you'll need to take a few antihistamines before we get cracking. Is there a brush cutter or a strimmer here – preferably petrol-driven?'

'There might be something in the workshop,' she jerked her head towards it and he wandered over to try the door. 'It's locked.'

'Do you have the key?' he asked lightly. 'Or would you rather wriggle in through a window?'

The silver eyes still marked hers as she ducked away in embarrassment, cramming her shades back on and snapping back with a cheap retort because she was flustered: 'I thought that was more your line.'

'Well, I could try forcing my way in with a dodgy cheque if you want,' he muttered, checking the padlock. 'I was banged up for forgery and embezzlement.'

'Not drugs?' she asked, before she could stop the question slipping out.

He let the padlock rattle against the door. 'Good old local legend has me driving a speedboat laden with Thai opium when I was nicked. Slightly more glamorous than trying to use a stolen credit card in Dixons, admittedly, but it means that if I so much as light a fag here, the sniffer dogs are called in.'

'How long did you get?'

'As my mother likes to say, I worked "overseas" for four years.' He chewed at a rueful smile as he turned and leaned against the locked door. 'I forged a bit more than signatures. It was in all the papers – I'm sure Hunter has a scrapbook on the case that he'll let you leaf through if you need my references before I start on the garden.'

'Sorry.' She moved back hastily behind the mark she'd overstepped.

'Forget it. I can't get away from it – especially not here in this village. I might have guessed you'd already know about it. I still get calls from TV shows – *Toffs from Hell* was the last.' He started to look around the car port.

'I'll fetch the keys.' Ellen moved back into the sun, fanning her T-shirt. 'Bugger, bugger, bugger,' she muttered, under her breath, as she left him rootling through the open barn and made her way into the house.

She pulled off the shades and stared at her face in the mirror – still hopelessly red-eyed, but now distinctly red-cheeked as well.

'Bugger.'

This was such a dumb thing to do. She, of all people, should know better than to let someone like Spurs get close enough to play with. He was as energetic, flirtatious and fun as any bad-boy surf nut she knew and loved; he was also dangerous, edgy and reckless. He would probably wreck her parents' overgrown garden and she would help him do it, no doubt, because he was more addictive to be around than Bob Flowerdew and an army of performing garden gnomes.

She knew she couldn't hope to control him. If he chose to, he could play with her as easily as greedy, carefree Fins played with helpless baby rabbits. She'd realised that the moment she'd failed to stare him down. Two days in his company would be two days walking on hot coals. She would have to wear very thick boots.

Suddenly she noticed the horseshoe sitting on the window-sill. She stooped to pick it up, dropped it into an empty plant pot on one of the shelves in the porch and told herself that there was no such thing as bad luck, just bad decisions. She had a feeling this had been one of her all-time worst.

However uncontrollable he might be, Spurs wasn't afraid of hard work. Equipped with Theo Jamieson's ancient two-stroke strimmer, he set to on the Goose Cottage garden like a man going to war, and didn't stop until the engine blew up.

'Jesus!' He leaped back as smoke belched out in front of him.

Ellen straightened up from weeding a bed just in time to see a strimmer fly through the air and burst into flames.

Spurs had managed to penetrate about six feet of long lawn,

leaving it pale and tufted. Half an acre of meadow still stretched in front of him, and then the paddock beyond.

'Dad always said cutting this lawn was a merciless task,' she said as she joined him. They watched the flames die away in cloud of acrid smoke, the dry grasses nearby sizzling.

'Strimmerciless,' he said, seemingly unbothered by the exploding garden tool. He pulled off the unmatched gardening gloves they'd unearthed in the workshop and wiped his sweating forehead. 'This is going to be harder than I thought. Fuck it, I'd better go home.'

He'd got bored even more quickly than Ellen had anticipated.

'For heavy-duty equipment,' he snapped, knowing exactly what she was thinking. 'There's an APV at the manor, and a huge brush cutter thing. I'll bring them over with the topper.'

'Are you sure your mother won't mind?' she asked, without thinking.

He gave her a withering look. 'As long as I don't leave my catapult by the seat, I think she'll be okay. Besides, she's gone to Cheltenham with Father to buy a hat.'

'Special occasion?' Ellen pulled off her own gloves – stupid flowery rubber ones her mother had bought from an upmarket catalogue.

'No – she buys hats all the time,' he said, looking at the tiny impression he'd made on the Goose Cottage wilderness. 'Talk about one man went to slo-mo a meadow. It burns well, though.' He kicked at the scorched patch surrounding the dead strimmer. 'We could just torch it.'

Ellen glanced at him, pretty certain he was joking but not entirely trusting her judgement.

He was waving regally at Hunter Gardner now. 'I hope he has a decent sunscreen – he's been roasting his bald head ever since he put his Panama over his Pimm's. Still, at least he's got his priorities right. There's nothing worse than warm cucumber. And a cold drink's not such a bad idea.'

Then, to Ellen's consternation, he set off across the old footpath that her mother and Hunter Gardner had paid the local councillors backhanders to close. They'd argued that the track – which ran along the bottom of their land as far as the village hall, ending in a little-used gate to the manor – was obsolete, served no purpose and for many years had only been used by riotous children, drunks and ne'er-do-wells.

But today it served Spurs' purposes perfectly, providing him with a short-cut as he jumped easily over the imposing post-and-rail fencing that the Jamiesons had erected to make it clear that the path was no longer in use.

Hunter Gardner, his binoculars still trained as he sat on sentry duty looking out for signs of poultry-worrying, let out an enraged roar. 'What in God's name do you think you're doing, man? You're trespassing!'

Ellen dashed to the hedge in time to see him standing on his decking and waving his air rifle. 'Is that you, Belling? I don't know how you have the nerve to set foot on the property! Get off my bloody land or I'll shoot you!'

Spurs turned to look at him in surprise.

'You have ten seconds or I shoot!' Hunter took aim through his new telescopic sights.

'Stop!' Ellen shouted, then yelped as he swung the gun in her direction. Out of some illogical instinct, she put her hands above her head. 'Spurs isn't doing anything wrong. He's helping me.'

'He is. *On. My. Land!*' Hunter swung the gun back at Spurs. 'I mean it, Belling. Ten seconds.'

'It's a public path.' Spurs looked relaxed. 'I have every right to be here.'

'We had it closed, so you do not.' Hunter strode forward, gun still cocked. 'A lot of things have changed for the better in this village since you've been gone, Belling. And we're no longer willing to put up with your insolent nonsense. Now, get off my land! Ten . . . nine . . . eight . . .'

Still smiling, Spurs folded his arms.

'. . . seven . . . six . . . five . . .'

'For God's sake, get out of there!' Ellen shrieked, but he didn't move a muscle.

'. . . four . . . three . . .'

She closed her eyes.

'. . . two . . . ONE!'

When Ellen opened her eyes, Spurs was running along the path, laughing his head off as he passed the wall that divided the field from the village-hall car park, then leaped the manor gate like a steeple-chaser. He certainly had a swift turn of foot.

'Damned impudence!' Hunter uncocked the rifle and marched up to the Goose Cottage hedge. 'I don't know what you think you're playing at,' he raged at Ellen, 'but from what I've seen so far your mother would be very disturbed indeed to hear of it. Very disturbed.'

'I shook out the pigtails years ago.' Ellen sighed.

'That may be so, but I cannot stand by and watch you entrust yourself to that – that poisonous piece of filth.'

She was taken aback by the vitriol in his voice. 'He's only helping me with the garden.'

'Don't let him into the house!' Hunter warned, his porcine eyes burning into hers.

'What is it about him everyone hates so much?' Ellen asked, then stopped. 'Sorry, I heard about him burning your garage . . .'

'*That*,' Hunter's fleshy neck unfolded as he thrust out his chin, 'was one of his least evil misdemeanours. If you'll take my advice, you'll shut up the house, get into your car, lock the gate behind you and take a *very* long drive.'

Ellen rolled her eyes at him in a way that was better suited to a young girl with pigtails, and wandered inside to make coffee. Then she dug around in her parents' shelves for gardening books. After two cups, a chapter of Alan Titchmarsh and half an hour's more weeding (she was better able to identify the weeds now, thanks to a handy pull-out chart), she decided that Spurs wasn't coming back.

She was surprised at the leaden feeling of disappointment. She had probably been rather unfriendly to him, but the short encounter had cheered her up. And she badly needed his help.

She lobbed Alan Titchmarsh irritably into the long grass, pulled

off the flowered gloves and did a handstand against the wall to
cheer herself up. Just as the blood started rushing to her hot head,
she heard an engine puttering along the lane.

Spurs looked as though he had equipped himself to declare war
on the Goose Cottage lawn and its sniper neighbour. He was riding astride a mini-tractor with an absolutely huge strimmer-type
device slung over one shoulder like a bazooka, goggles propped
up on his forehead and a fag clenched between his teeth. Rattling
behind him was a small trailer laden with spades, forks, backpack
sprays and other useful hardware.

He looked even more bizarre upside-down, and Ellen righted
herself dizzily.

There was nothing self-conscious about him, she realised, as
she went to open the gates. He looked a mess – faded T-shirt
covered in oil, denim shorts grey with dust, scratches on his ankles
and one toe torn from his trainers – yet he was about the sexiest
thing she had seen in years, particularly when he was shooting
her that mesmerising smile.

'Can you believe Hunter Gatherer almost took a pot-shot at
me?' he said, as he swung into the gates and jumped down, cutting
the engine.

'Gardner,' Ellen corrected him.

'I'd rather you called me Spurs,' he told her, eyes sparkling. 'I've never been good at job titles. Did Hunter warn you
off me?'

'Of course.' She checked over her shoulder but Hunter's lookout was shielded from where they stood by the cottage.

'Why were you doing a handstand?' he asked, glancing at the
stone walls against which she'd been tapping her feet.

'It helps with the hay fever.'

'I'll have to try it – although I swear by cold beer.' He reached
into the trailer and hauled out a chill-box, which opened with
a vacuum-packed hiss to reveal several cans of smoking-cold
Stella.

Ellen laughed. 'Isn't it my job to provide the refreshment?'

'It's your wish come true, remember.' He handed her a can.

It was barely midday, but the sweltering heat made beer the kiss of life. 'Perfection,' she gasped happily, after she'd swallowed a draught. She cocked her head and looked at him, taking in the mercury eyes and the sharp, clever features that worked together absurdly well. 'You really are taking this promise seriously, aren't you?'

He leaned back against the tractor and tapped the can with his finger. 'I'm glad you bought it . . . even if you were coerced by my mother. Sorry about that.'

'It was worth it for this.' Ellen raised her beer and patted the bonnet of the little tractor. 'If the others had known they'd get this much value for money, they'd all have been bidding last weekend.'

'Oh, no.' He shook his head. 'Believe me, I am *bloody* glad it was you who bought it,' the silver eyes slid away and creased against the sun, 'because you are the only one in this village who would not use this opportunity to wish me dead three times over.'

'That depends how well you cut the lawn.'

He laughed, toasting her with his can. 'I like you. You're seriously disrespectful.'

She laughed too. 'Why should I respect you? Because you're the lord of the manor?'

'Surely Hunter told you?' He dropped his voice. 'I *am* the devil.'

She drank some more beer and ran a hand round her sweaty neck. 'Is that why it's so hot around here?'

'I've had the brimstone on the hob all week.'

Together they sagged companionably against the hot flank of the tractor, soaking in a moment's sun and relaxation as they geared up for another gardening onslaught.

And that was when it hit Ellen. *She* liked Spurs Belling – on instinct, without questioning it at all. The fear that jabbed fingers through her ribs when she looked at him wasn't the terror that gripped the village, the old unhealed wounds that incensed Pheely, Hunter and the others. She had no reason to feel that. The fear she experienced – and still felt now – was the same exhilarating, freefall fear she had once craved as a daily fix. It was a recurring fear, habitual and addictive, and one that she had long fought to control. It was a fear that Richard had accused her of losing touch with. He'd said that her inability to recognise it would kill her.

Looking at Spurs, she knew Richard was wrong, as she'd told him so many times. It wasn't the fear she had lost touch with: it was her ability to feel it with him any more. Being with Richard stopped her fearing anything, and she craved that fear – pushing herself to greater and greater danger as she strived to feel it. Each encounter with Spurs clamped her chest in a tight vice of apprehension, like balancing on a high cliff preparing to jump into the ocean. But she knew that she had to keep her boots on and stand still. Last night with Lloyd had proved just how ill-prepared she was to test the water, and his salty shallows were barely lukewarm. Spurs' deep fathoms boiled like sulphur.

Thirteen years with Richard and their earthy mutual friends had left Ellen fearless when it came to men, sport and danger. It was her own libido that terrified her. Naïve, undermined, inexperienced and barely used, it sometimes tried to kick its way out of her, aiming at nothing in particular and destined, she was certain, to cause chaos. She fought to keep it rigidly under control.

'Seems a shame to tame it,' Spurs murmured, beside her.

Ellen looked at him in alarm, certain that he had read her thoughts, then saw with relief that he was looking across the garden.

'I know – I prefer it like this to the way it was before,' she agreed. 'But I don't live here. I'm just passing through.'

'Lucky you.' He crunched his beer can and threw it into the trailer.

'I dug out a gardening book,' she told him, and fetched Alan Titchmarsh from the long grass. 'Not sure if it'll be much help – I gave up after three pages on cold frames.'

He took it, flipped a few pages, then tossed it over his shoulder. 'Two rules: we stop every hour for a beer and a chat, and we don't kill anything except weeds and time together, okay?'

'Sure.' She tried to hide the width of her smile and reached for her gloves.

About to head back to the tractor, Spurs stopped. 'Why does your dog have to be on a tether?'

'Hunter has her under death threat.'

'I know the feeling.' He walked over to Snorkel. 'Can she ride with me if I keep an eye on her?'

Ellen glanced at the fence that marked Snorkel's safety zone. She had already lost one pet to God knows where, although she was far more certain of Fins' return than of the collie making it back if she crossed the demarcation zone to her beloved chickens.

'Stupid idea.' Spurs nodded.

'No – it's okay,' Ellen looked across at poor Snorkel, curled up in a tight ball of misery by the dovecote. 'I trust you.'

'You do?' The silver eyes burned into hers and she wondered if she'd misjudged him. Then it struck her that Spurs was so accustomed to being mistrusted that he hadn't been able to believe his ears.

'I trust you,' she repeated.

He stooped to untie the dog, then cupped her clown face in his hands and planted a kiss on her nose. Snorkel licked his cheek with slavish gratitude. Don't get too keen, Ellen warned her silently. He's not the faithful type.

Soon Joni Mitchell was ringing through the garden on Ellen's battered old stereo, almost totally drowned by the drone of Spurs racing through the long grass on his small-scale combine harvester, an ecstatic Snorkel balanced between his knees and the handlebars, ears inside out as she threw back her head and barked. 'One man went to mow, went to mow a meadow!' he yelled tunelessly, waving at Ellen as he passed.

She breathed in the scent of freshly cut grass, which was perhaps the only smell, besides that of the sea, that could make her shudder with uncontrollable happiness the moment it hit her nose.

'"Oh, you are in my blood like holy wine,"' she sang along

to the tape, pulling out ground elder, goose grass and bindweed, '"you taste so bitter and so sweet."' She'd always been a Joni fan, and the tape was one of a little cluster of long-neglected listening fodder from her student days that she had rediscovered during the rushed, messy division of possessions that had taken place at the Shack before they left it for ever.

'"Oh, I could drink a case of you, darling,"' she sang, closing her eyes and thinking about the times she had played it and thought of Richard, more than a decade earlier, '"and I'd still be on my feet. Oh, I would still be on my feet."' She heaved at a huge dock. 'So that I could kick your arse,' she added, falling over backwards with the effort of uprooting it. Lying where she'd landed, she stared at the sky.

'One man went to mow . . .' The engine spluttered past, covering her in grass clippings.

Of course, the track entitled 'The Last Time I Saw Richard' was the one playing when Spurs cut the engine on the little APV and sauntered over for their first break. In an instant the song went from barely audible to deafening, its lyrics ripping through the sultry lunchtime making weekenders look up from their barbecues; a snoozing Hunter woke up and let off an accidental shot from his rifle.

Spurs just laughed as Ellen leaped for the volume control.

'You like Joni Mitchell?' He dipped into the chill box and pulled out two cans.

She shrugged. 'It makes a change from Dead Man's Curve, the Bambi Killers and other quality surf bands.'

'And I thought it was still the Beach Boys.' He settled on the painted bench beside the bed she was weeding.

'Only if you're sixty and live in Hawaii.' She eased herself off her knees and joined him. 'Christ, it's hot.'

'Not as hot as Hawaii.' Spurs looked up at the sky. 'Ever been?'

'Not yet. We surfed in Europe mostly – and a few weeks in South America some years, if there was any money left.' She stared at the sky too, looking for the storm that never came.

'You've done it for a while, then? I spotted the boards in the barn.'

'Almost a decade, although just lately I've been more into kite-surfing – the chute's still in the car.' She watched a light aircraft circling high overhead. 'Before that it was scuba-diving, and before that parachuting. I loved that, but . . .' She stopped. Richard had hated it. He'd never been as brave as she, had never wanted to go up again and again, to go higher and faster, or to base jump – the ultimate dare.

'You couldn't decide whether you wanted to be over the sea or under it?' Spurs suggested.

'Something like that,' she murmured, watching a white chalkmark on the china blue sky. She'd always thought of Richard as her beloved sea – stormy, tidal, ruled by the moon. She was the breeze that ruffled it, the gale that tormented it and the still warmth that calmed it – as light as air and ruled by the sun. 'See that plane there? Eight years ago, all I'd have thought about was jumping out of it.'

'Eight years ago I felt the same way.' He took a swig of beer. 'Only I wasn't too bothered about the parachute.'

They sat in silence for a while, letting the sweat from hard work cool a little, enjoying the silence. Ellen longed to ask why his life had got so bad, but she couldn't break the companionable spell.

'I'll be about another half an hour on the lawn and then I can top the paddock,' he said eventually, putting his can in the shade beneath the bench. 'The cuttings there can just be left, but I'll have to rake all this lot up later.'

'I can do that as you go along,' she offered, stretching her arms behind her neck and turning to smile at him. 'I could use a break from weeding.'

'It's bloody hard work.'

'I'm bloody hard enough.' She grinned.

'I'll bet.'

Just for a moment his eyes traced the stretch of brown belly beside him before the silver gaze flicked away and he stood up to unclip Snorkel again.

Suddenly Ellen felt hotter than ever, the sweat now trickling between excited goosebumps. She pressed her lower arms to her burning cheeks and crushed the feeling down.

Together, she and Spurs worked through the hottest hours of the day in a haze of grass seed, flying cuttings and exhaust fumes. As he towed the big agricultural topper over the contours of the Goose Cottage lawn and then the paddock, Ellen followed behind with a rake, filling the barrow again and again before trundling it to an ever-growing pile beside the field gate. It was tough work, but after endless sweaty journeys, the wide stretches of grass looked civilised again, robbed of their green woolly mammoth pelt. It was still far from Hunter Gardner's trim snooker-baize lawn that ran alongside it, but it was amazing progress. By the time Spurs switched off the engine, all the Goose Cottage land had undergone a thorough buzz-cut.

'Not bad, huh?' he called to Ellen.

'Wow.' She spun around to look. 'Wow.'

She couldn't resist it. She lay down beside the field gate at the top of the long sloping paddock and pushed herself off. Shrieking with laughter, she rolled all the way to the bottom, loose grass sticking to her sweaty arms and legs, face and belly. Snorkel chased her, barking her head off and divebombing Ellen's spinning legs.

Finally coming to a halt by the thick hedge at the bottom, Ellen splatted her arms and legs back against the scratchy grass, stared up at the sky and sighed happily.

A shadow fell over her. 'Idiot.' Spurs' silhouette was all white smile and curly hair. 'Do you know how many nettle cuttings you've just rolled over?'

'I'm starting to guess.' She lifted her now burning legs and winced. 'Hell, it was worth it.'

The shadow only just eclipsed the sun, so that the blinding light flashed on and off her face.

'Hell's never worth it.'

Ellen squinted into the dancing sun and shadow. 'This is heaven.'

She could just make out the white teeth smiling.

'Are you hungry?' she asked.

'Starved.' The shadow moved away.

'I'll fix some food.'

While he started up the brush cutter and began to attack the areas he couldn't get to with the cumbersome topper, Ellen headed back to the house to look through the fridge for something she could offer by way of late lunch. Her staple supplies of sliced bread, baked beans and jam hardly seemed adequate to refuel them after such an energetic morning. She glanced out of the window to watch Spurs moving around an old apple tree, the big brush cutter strapped to his shoulders for stability, so that he appeared to be dancing an old-fashioned waltz with it. He was wearing the goggles, his hair dripping with sweat and full of grass seed, his T-shirt sticking to those broad shoulders and sinewy chest. He definitely needed rocket fuel.

She grabbed her purse and was about to set off for the village shop when she caught sight of herself in the hall mirror. Her own T-shirt was see-through with sweat and covered in soil and grass stains, her hair stood on end and a huge green mark streaked her forehead. Her legs and arms were covered with nettle rash.

She nipped into the bootroom, pulled off her top and threw it into the machine, then leaned over the sink to wash her face, neck and arms in cold water. Then, using a tea-towel to dry herself, she pulled a fresh T-shirt from the top of the pile of clothes she'd washed the day before and dragged it over her head.

It was only when she rattled one ear to release a few stray drops of water that she noticed she couldn't hear the brush cutter's engine. She spun round to find Spurs standing on the quarry tiles behind her, the goggles on top of his head and his T-shirt in his hands.

'Now I know where I've seen you before.' He smiled easily, totally unflustered, as though women took off their tops around him all the time. 'I remember that tattoo.'

Suddenly Ellen flushed red hot as something clicked in her memory. 'It was you driving past the day I was parked near

Hillcote?' She brazened it out, forcing a carefree smile in return. 'I hope I didn't frighten the horses.'

'You certainly shocked my mother.' He headed past her, chucking his T-shirt into the Belfast sink and reaching for the taps. 'She almost drove into a hedge.'

'Does she know it was me?'

'I doubt it.' He pulled off the goggles and tipped his head under the cold tap. 'She didn't take as much notice of the . . . details as I did.'

'I'm going to buy lunch from the shop.' Ellen averted her gaze from his broad, bare back. Her body was doing its hot goosebump thing again.

'Great.' He was twisting his head beneath the cool flood, letting the water run through the thick curls, over his face and down his freckled neck.

'D'you want to come along and choose something?'

'No – that Lily woman presses the panic button if I so much as read a postcard in the window,' he muttered. 'I'll keep Snorkel entertained, if that's okay.' One silver eye opened beneath the cool waterfall and he eyed her over a speckled shoulder.

It was another trust moment, Ellen realised. He was seeing whether she had enough faith in him to leave him alone in the house. Right now, she was more than happy to. She felt far safer at the prospect of dashing away than staying in such close proximity with him and her raging goosebumps a moment longer.

Joel was alone behind the counter, and lifted his arms in praise when he saw her. 'Ellen! Hi! You okay there? Lily was real concerned that Dot Wyck mighta hurt you yesterday – she came on real strong out there, huh?'

'No, I'm fine,' she assured him, smiling politely at a gaggle of tourists gawping at her from behind the Oddlode pottery mug and plate display. 'Nothing I can't handle. Sorry you had to lock the doors.'

'Lily likes to play it safe.' He winked. 'You and the old lady had a difference of opinion, huh?'

'Something like that.' She headed for the cool cabinets, wishing the altercation hadn't been quite so public.

When Joel rang up her purchases his eyebrows lifted comically. 'You sure got your appetite back. We've been worried about you – nothing but bread and beans all week. Your dog eats better. It's good to see you buying some decent food.'

Ellen hoped the Oddlode shopkeepers didn't discuss her consumption of loo roll and tampons in quite the same depth.

She selected her free ice-cream on the way out – now a standard extra, if Joel was serving – and crossed the lane to eat it on Bevis's bench, wondering guiltily as she did so whether she should have bought one for Spurs.

'Am I really mean?' she asked the bench, as she licked the Zoom, which was already melting down her wrists in multi-coloured rivulets.

A caterpillar landed on the banana layer.

'I guess you're right,' Ellen apologised, picking it off. 'I'll get him one tomorrow if he comes back, I promise. I hope he comes back.'

Three caterpillars rained down.

Ellen glanced up at the dark canopy overhead. Then she closed her eyes and thought about her wish. There were so many better things she could have wished for, yet today had been by far the happiest since she had arrived in Oddlode, and it was barely half-way through. That, now she thought about it, was the best thing she could wish for. A truly happy day. There had been precious few in recent months.

'Am I wrong to like him?' she asked Bevis, patting his warm wooden arms. 'I don't think he's so bad.' Looking down through the slats of the bench beside her, she saw a cluster of daisies and picked one.

'Bad – good – bad – good.' She pulled away the petals, aware that she was behaving like a lovesick teenager. She crumpled the daisy between her fingers before she could finish and slapped her hot cheeks with her hands to pull herself together.

★   ★   ★

When she returned Spurs was stretched out on the pale, tufty lawn. Alan Titchmarsh lay open on his face to shade it and Snorkel lay companionably alongside him, tethered to the bench.

Leaving them to their well-earned nap, Ellen carried the food into the house and started to lay it out – fresh fat baguettes, meats and cheeses, pâtés and olives, and a bag of mixed salad. It was about as good as her catering ever got. She put it all on to a tray with a jug of water and carried it out to the table at the back of the house. Then, spotting that the table and chairs were covered with green mould and that Hunter Gardner was monitoring her every move through his bins, she carried it all in again, crossing back through the cool house and emerging at the front to put it on the small table where Theo liked to catch the morning sun. Now almost in shadow, it was probably a better spot anyway, even though it was overlooked by the lane.

Spurs had rolled on to his belly and was completely asleep now, his arms splayed in front of his head, one cheek pressed into the roughly cut grass, his eyelids fluttering in a dream. Ellen knelt down beside him and picked up one of the long, featherheaded grass shafts that she had missed with her rake. She dangled it over his ear.

'If you keep doing that, I'll be forced to kill you.' He didn't open his eyes or move.

Ellen lifted the stem of grass and stared at it minutely. Then she dangled it an inch above his ear. 'How would you kill me?'

'Not sure. I certainly couldn't scare you to death because you're afraid of nothing.'

'What makes you say that?' She looked at him curiously, but his eyes remained closed.

'I can just tell. You jump out of planes for fun.' He rolled on to his back, pushing Alan Titchmarsh out of the way. 'I might be able to bore you to death by reading gardening books aloud.'

'Now, that scares me.' She discarded the grass and lifted the book. As she did so, she spotted the horseshoe beneath it. She picked it up, running her fingers over the three twisted nails, suddenly on edge at the thought that he had been nosing around the house while she was away. 'You found this?'

He opened one eye. 'I needed some empty pots, and there it was. I've never grown a horse from one myself, but adding a bit of compost might be an idea.'

She turned the shoe around in her hand. 'Was it you who left it outside the door on the night of the auction?'

He straightened up and took it from her. 'It's your three wishes.' Gripping one of the three nails with his fingers, he worked it out of its hole. 'Here's your first.' He handed it to her. 'You can give it back to me when I've granted it.'

For a moment, as she took the nail, their eyes tangled and Ellen saw straight through the silver irises to a far more base metal, as twisted and unyielding as the one her fingers encircled.

She tucked the nail into her back pocket and fanned her T-shirt. 'I heard that horseshoes were your calling card.'

He looked away, holding up the shoe to admire it. 'This belonged to O'Malley, a big old Irish thoroughbred that could gallop all day. Long dead now. Who told you about the horse-shoes?'

'Pheely.'

'Ah, the flower fairy herself.' He sighed. 'And I'll bet she warned you to keep away from me too, didn't she?'

Ellen nodded.

'So why didn't you?'

'I didn't have much choice.' She stood up, not wanting to talk about Pheely behind her back. 'Lunch is ready.'

Three children were hacking past on shiny, tail-twitching ponies as they settled at the table. 'Afternoon!' they cried, bobbing the handles of their crops.

'Does the tourist board pay the kids around here?' Ellen waved at them. 'There's more horse traffic than cars in this village.'

'It's the local passion – even I've been known to indulge sometimes.' Spurs fetched two more beers from his cool-box. 'If you grow up here, you wrap your bandy legs around ponies until you're old enough to wrap them around each other.'

Ellen peeled back the foil from the butter. It had melted to dark yellow liquid inside. 'And do you still indulge?'

'In horses or sex?'

She looked up to meet his gaze as coolly as possible. 'Riding.'

'Not often. You?'

'I've never been on a horse.' She set the butter to one side and poured out two glasses of water, annoyed to see her hands shaking.

'That's one dangerous sport that never tempted you, huh?' He reached for the olives.

They were criss-crossing gazes now, silver and blue swordsmanship as their eyes met again and again in sweeping arcs.

'I grew up by the sea. I prefer surf to turf.'

'I could give you a lesson while you're here – see if you like it. Mum's hunters are all out at grass in Lincolnshire, but I'm sure we could borrow something.'

'No, thanks.' She looked away to stop her eyes flirting with his. 'I'll stick to riding waves.' Guiltily she remembered her promises to herself that she would trek on horseback and join a camel caravan as a part of her world adventure. It seemed such a long way off. She'd barely started planning.

'Round here, horses are just a part of growing up,' he explained, helping himself to a forest of salad. 'My cousin Rory and I spent our childhood racing all over the valley on the Welsh cobs his father bred.'

'Do you have a lot of family around here?'

'My aunts still live nearby but their kids have all moved on, apart from Rory.' He reached for a hunk of bread. 'He's five years younger than me – runs a yard in Upper Springlode, and is as wild as his horses. He's always been like a little brother, I guess.'

'Do you have brothers and sisters of your own?'

'No. I don't think my parents took to sex. What about you?'

Again, the *double-entendre* was deliberate and teasing. Again, Ellen prudishly ignored it and shook her head. 'No.'

'I've always been grateful to have Rory knocking around.' He spoke with his mouth full of bread. 'Were you lonely growing up an only child?'

'Not really. I always had a best friend – we'd stay at each other's houses and stuff.'

'You still keep in touch with them?'

She thought about the friends past: Jackie Hemmings, who had married a computer programmer and still lived in Taunton; Emma Butt, who was doing VSO in Kenya; Katy Phillips, who had three daughters and a vast mortgage in Kent. And then there was Richard.

'Not really. We grew apart.' She shook up the vinaigrette. 'What about you?

'I changed school too often to make close friends.' He tore angrily into his bread. 'I had a good friend in the village when I was a kid but he – he's long gone.'

'Did he move away?'

He looked out at the lane, watched the sun dancing on the leaves of the lime tree. 'He had a lucky escape. The Lodes Valley's a great place to be a young kid or an adult, but the bit in between is torture. The teenagers here go mad with boredom.'

'So I gather.'

He looked up sharply. 'What did Pheely tell you?'

'That you were uncontrollable,' she said honestly. 'That you put a lot of backs up and did a hell of a lot of bad things and were eventually drummed out of the village.'

'I can't imagine old Touchy putting it that succinctly. I bet she told you all about my wicked ways.'

Ellen said nothing, her loyalty torn. Talking to Spurs was horribly easy, especially after too much beer and sunshine – she could see herself becoming woefully indiscreet in no time, matching his honesty. And she'd expected far more reticence from Pheely's descriptions of a brooding, manipulative, angry monster. He surprised her.

'Does she still hate me?' he asked now.

Ellen was finding this go-between role uncomfortable. 'It's not for me to say.'

'Do you hate me?' He made the question sound as casual as 'Do you take milk?'

'I hardly know you.'

'You don't have to know somebody well to hate them or like them – or even love them, for that matter.' He helped himself to a slice of pâté, watching her face.

She wondered how serious he was being. The silver eyes were playing with hers again. Hot goosebumps were popping up all over her skin, like the nettle rash coming back.

'Then I love you,' she said evenly. 'I fell in love with you at first sight.'

It was his turn to stare: he was completely thrown.

Ellen ate a slice of tomato and smiled.

'I love you too,' he said eventually. 'Would you pass the salt?'

'Certainly.' She handed it over.

He grinned as he took it. 'I'm so pleased somebody in this village loves me, apart from my mother. It's such a comfort.'

'Well, you're very lovable.'

'I am, aren't I?'

This little patter brought their noses just a few inches apart across the table. Ellen bailed out first, tilted back in her chair and threw a piece of ham to Snorkel.

'People here don't believe I've changed,' said Spurs. 'The old guard in this village live in a time-warp.'

'And have you changed?'

'Yes – enormously. Totally.' He sounded indignant. 'It's been more than a decade. I'm not the same person any more. I just wish they could see it.'

'Maybe they hoped you'd come back wearing a Savile Row suit, with a Sloaney wife and a brace of toddlers?' she suggested.

He nodded and laughed. 'Too right. I could set light to every building in the village now, spray-paint obscenities on the war memorial, smoke dope in the River Folly all day and shag the vicar's teenage daughters just so long as I drove a Volvo and had a respectable job in the City. But I'll never be Giles Hornton.'

She grinned, understanding where he was coming from. And,

talking to him like this, she was certain that Pheely would understand, too, if she were here. He was brusque and forthright, but
his honesty and charm were easy to like.

'Perhaps I can ask Pheely here for a drink one evening?' she
suggested. 'I'm sure she'll see how much you've changed.'

His eyes flashed in warning. 'I don't think that's such a great
idea.'

'Why ever not?'

'She's not known as Touchy Pheely because of her bear-hugs
and love of kissing and making up,' he muttered. 'She's always
been over-sensitive. Of them all, she's the least likely ever to
forgive me.'

Remembering the way Pheely had giggled about Spurs' teenage
antics, Ellen wanted to argue, but this was overshadowed by a very
bleak truth. To her surprise, Spurs 'fessed up without prompting,
dark brows curling together as he studied her across the table.
'You know I vandalised her father's sculptures?'

She nodded. 'Why?'

'I'd drunk a hell of a lot of vodka. I guess I was angry
that he'd died and left me behind. And I was angry that the
bitch hadn't invited me to the funeral – the village and the
art world flocked into Oddlode church and I wasn't allowed
to say goodbye. I fucking worshipped him – he was one of
the few who understood me. But they kept dying. First my
grandmother, then Norman, then . . .' He scratched his chin,
stopping himself before he got too wound up, looking up at Ellen
with an apologetic smile. 'I've never stopped regretting what I did.
You do believe me?'

'I believe you.'

'And you trust me?'

She nodded.

'And you still love me?'

'Don't push it.'

He grinned, but his eyes stayed sad and wary. 'There's no point
asking Pheely's forgiveness.'

'Have you ever tried?'

'Who was it said you should try everything but incest and Morris dancing?'

'I don't know, but I like his style.'

'He should have added "and building bridges in Oddlode".' He looked at her for a long time as he chewed at a hunk of bread, silver eyes assessing her, apparently, for sincerity. Then he laid down the bread and sat back in his chair, dusting crumbs from his freckled chest. 'When I was inside, I saw the guys in group therapy trying to appease their guilt by building bridges, but it never helped their victims as far as I can tell. The damage is already done. It's best to leave them alone to rebuild their lives. Your friend Pheely, in common with a great many people I pissed off in my teens, doesn't want to forgive me for the way I was – and they have every right not to. And I've never asked their forgiveness because I didn't ever think I'd come back here.'

'So why did you?'

'It's complicated.' He looked away, screwing up one eye, then laughed. 'You like to get to the heart of things, don't you?'

'You're the one talking from it.' She watched him, and knew as soon as she'd said it that it had been a mistake.

The laugh gathered force, with a delighted whoop. 'Didn't Pheely tell you? I have no heart. I can assure you, I'm talking from an entirely different part of my anatomy – and so are you. Watching your lips move has been the highlight of my morning.'

Ellen felt her face colour, but she knew too many bad boys to react prudishly. If he'd grown bored with her interrogation and wanted to spar, she could do that. Outwitting and outshocking her was the point of the game, and she wasn't about to let him win. 'In that case, forgive me for not sitting on your face to whisper this in your ear. Sod . . . right . . . off.'

She could see that he was thoroughly enjoying the confrontation. 'But I thought you loved me?'

'I thought you loved *me* until you told me I talked out of my arse.'

'I could listen to you all day. Do you talk in your sleep too?'

'Like a trumpet.'

It was childish, scatological stuff, yet they might have been swapping epigrams in their clipped, light tone. It was only the undertone that got more fiercely competitive and dirty by the moment.

'I gather trumpeters have a novel way of muting their instruments.' The silver eyes were shot through with pure wickedness now.

'Oh, yes?' Ellen could guess where this was going. She knew she should stop, but that would be conceding defeat.

'They like to find something long and hard and insert it carefully.'

'I never mute.'

'Not even on a first date?'

'Especially not then.'

He leaned across the table, dropping his voice to a whisper. 'Did you talk in your sleep last night?'

Ellen stared at him, wondering if he was referring to Lloyd. 'If I did, then I was talking to myself.'

'I'd love to mute you some time.'

'You'd find yourself mutilated in return.'

'I respond much better to a finger pressed lightly to my lips.' He popped an olive into his mouth.

God, he was pushing it, she thought. But she wasn't about to give up. 'And I prefer to be licked on the nose.'

'Did your handsome friend lick you on the nose last night?'

'No, he pecked me on the cheek.'

'Which one?'

'Well, it wasn't all four.'

'Did you want him to lick you on the nose?'

'No.'

'Can you lick your own nose?'

'I've never tried.'

'Try it now.' His voice was loaded with meaning as the olive pip slid from cheek to cheek, silver eyes cornering hers, imagining he was at checkmate.

With an easy smile, she poked out her tongue, stretched it upwards and dabbed her nose.

'That,' Spurs said very slowly, 'was not what I meant when I said, "Try it."'

'That,' she told him, 'is because the sun was shining so brightly out of your – mouth when you said it, I was blinded.'

'And you should wash yours out with soap and water.' He didn't blink. 'I'll happily do it for you.'

'As a public schoolboy and an ex con, I'm sure you'll understand why I wouldn't trust you with my bar of soap.' This time she was determined not to bow down from the staring match.

The silver eyes widened in admiration. 'I could use a cold shower right now.'

She refused to let the hot-metal eyes burn hers into submission. They watched her for a long time, gradually losing their mischief and playfulness until they misted over to a dull pewter.

'Stop it.'

He said it so quietly that she thought she'd misheard. 'Sorry?'

'Stop it.'

'Stop what?'

'Making me want to take you to bed.' He looked away, conceding defeat.

Ellen opened her mouth and closed it again, heart thudding. She'd asked for that. It was, she realised, exactly what she'd wanted to hear when she was playing the game, too competitive to care about the consequences. Victory made her feel charged from head to toe with static and fear. Her trophy for knowing how to flirt with X-factor was tarnished. He'd thrust it at her angrily, and she dropped it at their feet.

He tapped his finger against the table, watching it move, no longer talking from the heart or anywhere else.

They ate in silence, this time uncomfortable and prickly, the heat making the food droop and the wasps swarm. Ellen guessed she'd blown her chance of an easy friendship by flirting.

'Where do you go after this place is sold?' he asked eventually, lighting a cigarette, his mood ten shades darker than it had been minutes earlier.

'Overseas – travelling for a few months, maybe longer.' She didn't look him in the eye, but was grateful that the silence had been broken at last. 'I want to get to Mongolia and Tibet, and maybe China before too many package tours head there.'

'Alone?'

'Yup.' She gave him a 'so what?' look and he half smiled, but the tension remained.

'I travelled for a couple of years.'

'After . . . ?'

'Yes, I thought I'd take a gap year after prison,' he snapped witheringly. 'There are some places you can still go with a criminal record. Half the guys in Cirque de Phénomène were junkies, murderers and wife-beaters. I was small fry.'

Ellen blinked at him in surprise. 'You were with Cirque de Phénomène?'

He nodded warily. 'You've heard of it?'

'I loved it – Richard and I saw a show in Barcelona. It was wild. What did you do?'

'Rode nags – cleaned up their shit, drove an artic, shagged a lot.'

Ellen's awe rose above the awkwardness and she pressed her hands to her hot cheeks excitedly. Cirque de Phénomène was a huge cult on the continent, a wild, anarchic underground circus made up of freak acts, dangerous stunts and a lot of rock-and-roll. It travelled in a huge, ever-changing hippie band, and was legendary for its wild characters, its in-fighting and clashes with the authorities of every country it visited. As far as she knew, no venue in Great Britain had ever hosted the rabble-rousing crew of bikers, horsemen, knife-eaters and fire-dancers.

'I'm *so* impressed.' She pinned her lower lip with her top teeth. 'I talked for months about trying to get into the troupe, but Rich – but it didn't work out. Too many commitments.'

'You'd fit in.' He pushed the olive pips around his plate. 'I could see you there.'

'You really think so?'

'Yup.' He smiled, but he was still on edge. 'I'd have appreciated having you there. Talking French all the time got on my tits.'

'Another lifetime, maybe.' She waved away the regret. 'You were the one who did it. You ran away to join the circus.'

He glared at her, then smiled, as if he had decided her admiration was genuine. 'Yes. I ran away to join the circus. And it teaches you a fuck of a lot more about yourself – and others – than prison, I can assure you.'

'How long were you with them?' She wondered whether he'd been in the show she had seen.

'I left two years ago.'

'Choice?'

'Broke my leg.'

'Falling from a horse?'

'More a case of throwing myself from one. It was either that or being decapitated by a chainsaw.'

'What happened?' She was agog.

'It seems I'd somewhat pissed off Machination – the juggler. One moment I was standing on two cantering nags' rumps, the next I had a metre of fast-moving chain spinning towards my face. My foot got caught under one of the mare's rollers when I jumped. She was only a baby and she panicked – smashed my femur into four equal pieces. Well, actually, I think it was two, but Machination jumped on it afterwards.'

Ellen winced. 'What on earth had you done to upset him?'

'Her.' He grinned. 'Never screw around on a woman who can juggle a chainsaw, a jackhammer and an angle grinder.'

'I'll bear that in mind.'

'Of course, stunt riders are the best lovers.' He couldn't resist trying for another flirtatious rally.

'Is that a fact?' She stayed behind the base line.

'I guess you prefer surfers.'

'I guess.' She couldn't risk playing again.

But their eyes were tangled up once more, the awkwardness gone. This was hopeless, Ellen realised. It was like trying to climb out of a slippery bath only to be sucked back into the bubbles again and again. She either made waves or lay back and soaked in the delicious sensation of drowning in weightless warmth. She could only hope that the water would go cold. Keep your boots on, she reminded herself. Stay in control. 'So what did you do after you broke your leg?'

'I was holed up in an Italian hospital counting wimples for weeks on end, but I got bored and discharged myself. Then I hitched my way back to England and drifted – perfected my limp.'

'You don't limp now.'

'I had an operation last year.' He pulled up the leg of his shorts to reveal a row of dark red dots. 'It hadn't set properly, so they rebroke it and put in pins. My mother insisted on it. She took me from no fixed abode and fixed my bowed legs, bless her.'

'So you'd kept in touch?'

The corner of his mouth lifted and he paused before answering, making it clear that he knew he was being grilled. 'No – she got Father to track me down. He's very well connected.'

Ellen helped herself to more water, now burning with curiosity. She longed to know what he'd done when he came back to the UK – did 'drifting' mean festivals and odd jobs or boxes in doorways? But she'd already overused her Walden cross-examination time. They could only talk for short bursts without flirting, and she didn't trust herself to keep control for much longer.

She looked up as she heard another set of hooves coming along the lane, skittering and stamping, accompanied by a lot of equine snorting.

'Wow.' Spurs looked up too.

Ellen tried not to feel too itchy-skinned at his obvious admiration, and the very obvious reason for it. A leggy blonde was leading a jumpy horse past the cottage. Tall, slim and fresh-faced, she was laughing her head off as the horse – an extraordinary pink-coloured hysteric – leaped this way and that, boggling its big, dark eyes at everything.

To Ellen's even greater consternation, the girl stopped outside the gates, her horse now trotting showily on the spot, and called cheerfully, 'Hi! You must be Ellen?'

She crammed her sweaty baseball cap tighter on her head and stood up. 'Yup. That's me.'

'I'm Dilly – Ophelia's daughter.'

Oh, God, no wonder her mother dotes on her, Ellen thought hollowly, as she took in the cascade of hair spilling from her hard hat – the same glossy curls as her mother's, but russet blonde instead of dark. Her slimmer, younger face possessed the same broad cheeks, upturned nose and amazing green eyes, enhanced by a dimpled, curling smile and a rusty dusting of freckles on chin and nose. She was much longer and slimmer than Pheely, but had the same extraordinary bust – high and round and tightly hugged by the little white T-shirt she was sporting.

'Mum sent me out for some fags, and I thought I'd take the horse – but the bugger won't let me get on him.' She grinned. 'I hoped you'd be around.'

Riding a horse to the village shop was the daftest thing Ellen had heard – especially if you couldn't even get on to it – but Dilly exuded the ditzy, confident charm of youth, where anything was possible. She made Ellen feel instantly prehistoric and deeply dull.

'Great to meet you,' she said, pulling open the gates and stepping back as the pink horse almost went into orbit.

'Don't mind Otto.' Dilly brought him back to a jogging stand-still. 'He's completely hatstand after six weeks off. Mum was supposed to lunge him, but she says she's been too busy – meaning she couldn't be bothered. Hi.' She grinned at Spurs, who had joined Ellen at the gate.

'Jasper Belling – Dilly Gent – er, Daffodil Gently.' Ellen wasn't sure how Dilly had taken to the 'diligently' pun her mother regretted. But Dilly seemed far too preoccupied with gaping at Spurs to notice.

'You're Spurs Belling?' she gasped, green eyes stretched wide as she came face to face with a village legend.

'Nice horse.' Spurs was looking at the pirouetting pink beast. 'Part Arab?'

'Arab warmblood cross.' She nodded as Otto spotted Snorkel and reared back in alarm. 'Totally off his trolley, but I love him. I only wish I could ride the silly idiot.'

'Could use a bit of work, by the look of him,' Spurs walked to the horse's shoulder and ran a hand from his withers to his girth, placing the other at his muzzle for Otto to sniff. 'Beautifully put together, though.'

To Ellen and Daffodil's surprise, Otto stopped jogging and eyed Spurs thoughtfully, his snorting breaths slowing tempo as Spurs tickled his withers and shoulder.

'Have you had him long?'

'Since last summer, but I haven't done much with him. I've been away at school. We had a sharer set up, but she lost interest, so he just loafs around his field.'

'He doesn't look like he loafs much.' Spurs stood back. 'He's pretty muscled up at the front – you just need to get the back end fit enough to match up.' He patted Otto's neck, obviously impressed.

'He's a lovely colour,' said Ellen – hoping that didn't sound too ignorant.

'Strawberry roan,' Dilly told her. 'Mum said we had to have him because he matches my hair. She doesn't seem to mind that his brain's fried, just so long as we look good together when we're bolting across roads.' She returned to Spurs. 'You're Rory's cousin, aren't you?'

'Yup.'

'Is he okay?'

'As far as I know. Why?'

'I can't seem to get hold of him – I, er, wanted him to give me some advice about Otto.'

'I think his mobile's been cut off again. I'll mention you when I see him,' he offered, crouching down to run his hand along Otto's dancing legs.

'Thanks!' She looked thrilled, and turned as pink as her horse. 'Rory was really brilliant last year – I had quite a few lessons. I'm only here for a couple of days now but I'm back for the holidays soon, and I really need to put some work in. I'd love him to teach me again.' She might speak with a forthright manner beyond her years, and look like every red-blooded man's dream date for a week on a Bahamian yacht, but at heart Dilly was still a teenager with a crush on her riding instructor.

Spurs was nodding, silver eyes still focused on Otto's legs. 'Rory knows his stuff.'

'He says you do too.' She looked down at the top of his curly head, going even redder. 'Didn't you win the Devil's Marsh Cup *five* years running?'

'Long time ago.' He rubbed a wrist over his sweaty forehead.

'That's still some record. I thought I might take part this year, but I'm shit-scared. Mum hates the idea. She says someone was killed one year.'

Spurs said nothing, patting the horse's neck and stepping back so that he was brushing shoulders with Ellen.

'Now you're back will you ride in it again this year?' Dilly asked excitedly.

'I don't – I haven't . . .' he glanced at Ellen '. . . I haven't ridden for a while.'

He's hiding something. Ellen realised instantly.

'D'you want a go now?' Dilly offered, patting the saddle.

Ellen saw the sinews lift in Spurs' neck. 'Sure – I'll have a sit on him. Do you want to bring him in off the road – is that okay?' he asked Ellen. The silver eyes were icy with fear.

'Fine.' She wondered whether he needed her to cause some sort of distraction.

But Dilly was already leading Otto through the gates and across the garden towards the paddock. The roan snorted and danced, snatching his head to and fro, his pink ears flattening to his head every time she tugged him on.

'I'll only be a minute,' Spurs told Ellen.

'Are you sure about this?' she whispered.

'Of course. Why shouldn't I be? If you find horses boring, you don't have to watch.' He stalked after Otto, flicking a curl back from his eyes.

Ellen hung back. She could tell that, for some reason, he didn't *want* her to watch.

She glanced at the debris of lunch – now buzzing with flies and wasps. She should clear it away, but she was desperate to hang around and see Spurs ride. She didn't care if he wanted her out of the way. It was her parents' paddock, and Dilly was far too pretty to leave unchaperoned. Pheely would never forgive her, she told herself. She unclipped Snorkel and went to watch.

Already in the field, Spurs was walking slowly round Otto, lengthening the stirrup leathers and talking to him in a low, soothing voice, a hand constantly touching his sweating neck, flank or quarters to reassure him.

Dilly hung over the paddock gate watching them. Her crush on Cousin Rory looked under immediate threat. 'I warn you, he's really, really hard to get on – he prats around all over the place,' she called to Spurs, as Ellen moved in beside her. 'I usually just take a running jump . . . I'm the same with boys,' she whispered to Ellen, winking in a very Goldie Hawn way.

'Good tactic.' Ellen warmed to her daftness and honesty.

'Not very successful so far,' Dilly admitted. 'With Otto . . . or boys.'

'Sometimes you have to jump when they're not looking.' Ellen watched Spurs.

'Have you had lots of boyfriends?'

'I've taken a lot of running jumps,' she hedged.

Had they blinked, they would have missed Spurs mounting. He stepped into the stirrup and swung into the saddle as deftly as a cat springing on to a wall.

Otto's ears flicked back questioningly and he snorted, but he stood stock still, his nose dipping towards his knees.

'Wow – that's rocking.' Dilly whistled.

'Shouldn't you be wearing a helmet or something?' Ellen asked.

He didn't appear to hear. Dressed in dusty shorts and trainers, he rode Otto across the paddock, his bare back taut with controlled muscles, all working in delicate, defined unison beneath the glossy bronzed freckles.

'I had *no* idea Spurs Belling would be so hot,' Dilly whispered, girlish and excited, once he was out of earshot.

Ellen watched him as he and the horse moved easily around the field, Otto's head stretching out in a low, relaxed arc, ears pricked, dark eyes limpid – he looked in horse heaven.

'Mum's always made him sound like Jack the Ripper meets Marilyn Manson.' Dilly giggled. 'And I thought he'd be really old, like her. But he's more our age, isn't he?'

Ellen looked at her in wonder. Dilly was either being grossly flattering, or needed her eyes testing. 'I'm not much younger than your mum.'

'Yeah, but she was middle-aged from birth – you're a babe,' Dilly told her sweetly. 'You look like Cameron Diaz.'

'Thanks.' Ellen checked her eyes for signs of cataracts, then turned back to watch Spurs, who was holding the reins by the buckle now, scratching his thigh and waving cheerily at Hunter. He never let up. The tension, it seemed, had vanished the instant he got on. He looked totally at home and sexier than ever, his back rolling and swaying like a long, muscular shock-absorber as the horse moved, his long legs firm and still against Otto's sides.

Oh, God, oh, god, oh, god, I fancy him, she thought wretchedly. He's badder than bad and I fancy him. She wanted to run across the field and push him off his horse for making her feel this way. 'All he needs is a poncho and a cheroot,' she muttered dismissively, trying to make herself feel better.

Dilly giggled. 'I like his tattoo. What is it?'

'A barcode.' Ellen had spotted it earlier.

'Wow,' Dilly breathed. 'Is that a prison thing?'

'No, it's a fashion-victim thing.' Dating back about three years, Ellen recalled – round about the time Spurs was playing circus daredevil. She hated herself for finding it as sexy as Dilly clearly did – and she certainly wasn't about to admit it. 'If you scanned that at Tesco, you'd find it was seriously past its use-by date.'

'Mum said you were really cool.' Dilly was watching as Spurs coaxed Otto's head up until his neck was rounded like a Lipizzaner then moved him smoothly into a floating trot, circling this way and that to keep his concentration. 'But I had no idea you and Spurs Belling were an item.'

'We're not!' Ellen said hastily. 'He's just helping me out.'

Dilly gave her a knowing-kid smile, propped her elbows on the gate and cupped her chin with a sigh. 'I wish he could help me out. If he's as gangland as they say, I might hire him as a contract killer . . . like in the movie, *Leon*, only gorgeous-looking.' She trapped a plump lower lip beneath her top teeth and gazed at Spurs dreamily. 'I wish bloody Otto went like that for me.'

'That's no reason to have him assassinated,' Ellen pointed out.

'Oh, I don't want Otto taken out.' She looked horrified. 'It's Godspell Gates I loathe.' The green eyes rolled angrily. 'We used to be friends, but now she thinks she's too old and cool to know me. Mum has to sculpt her and she's been lurking in the cottage all afternoon like a ghoul, refusing to talk or even have a cup of tea. That's why I decided to take the Psychotto for a spin.'

'I thought you were on a fag run?'

'That too. Mum's been lighting one from the other since Godspell turned up. And she likes winding Lily up by sending me into the shop for fags – the silly cow trains all her CCTVs on me.'

Ellen had forgotten about the shoplifting incident. It seemed she was playing open garden to the village's crimewave today. She watched as Spurs passed close by, focused on what he was doing. Otto was moving beautifully beneath him so that they seemed fused together into one powerful animal.

'I've never seen him go like that.' Dilly sighed. 'Not even for Rory.'

They broke into a canter, again circling and serpentining, moving around the small field in an intricate dance. Ellen had never taken much interest in riding, but she remembered a huge horse fair in Spain that she and Richard had stumbled across one rainy day in Jerez, and the amazing way that tiny, still-shouldered boys in frilly shirts had ridden huge, fiery stallions as though they were ponies, eliciting total obedience with nothing more apparent than a flick of the wrist, taming half a tonne of brute force with mesmerising simplicity. That was the way Spurs rode. It was spellbinding to watch.

She and Dilly fell into rapt silence.

Soon he disappointed his audience by slowing Otto to a loose-reined walk and returning to the gate, smiling broadly – a bare-chested, wild-haired gypsy, who broke the spell by speaking like a royal prince. 'He's a really nice sort – knows how to use himself, even though he's pretty unfit.' He leaned down to pat the horse's sweaty neck and pull at his ears. Otto was still wearing his horse-in-heaven expression and, to her shame, Ellen found herself envying him.

Dilly beamed up at Spurs proudly, blinking blonde curls from her eyes. 'He jumps fantastically. Do you want to try?'

'I think he's had enough for now.' He pulled a battered packet of cigarettes out of his back pocket and lit one, squinting around as he did so, obviously tempted. 'Besides, there's nothing to jump here.'

'We could build something.' Dilly looked about eagerly, suddenly childlike once more, not wanting the moment to end.

'Maybe another time.' He jumped off and patted Otto, cigarette dangling between his lips as if he were an old ostler. 'Ellen and I still have a hell of a lot to do today.'

'Tomorrow?' she suggested. 'You'll be here tomorrow, won't you?'

'Possibly.' He adjusted the stirrup leathers.

Ellen registered his shuttered look: a big question mark was hanging over 'possibly'. Maybe he'd bored of playing Alan to her Charlie Dimmock now that he could play Mickey Rooney to Dilly's Velvet Brown.

'I'll come by tomorrow, then,' Dilly said excitedly, accepting his offer of a leg up with something close to ecstasy. She was a girl in love. She looked down at him adoringly, then glanced guiltily at Ellen. 'Um – would you mind not mentioning it to Mum? You know what she's like.'

'Sure,' she said uneasily.

Spurs caught her eye and gave a silver wink. She wasn't quite sure how to take it, but it made the hairs on the back of her neck unglue themselves from the sweat there and stand to attention.

As Ellen and Spurs crossed the garden on either side of Otto, Dilly was grumbling about Godspell again. 'She is so up herself. Mum is a wicked sculptor – everyone knows that – and she had the nerve to bring a list from Ely saying that under no circumstances could Mum add(a) horns(b) warts(c) antennae or(d) fangs to the bust. Frankly, I think they'd do that bland little tombstone-face a favour. She is *so* plain. It's no wonder she hangs around in the graveyard.'

Ellen tried to catch Spurs' eye under the horse's neck, but he was glaring at the ground.

'Right – I'm off to the shop.' Dilly turned left at the gate, assuming an affected coolness now that she was back on open ground. 'You guys want anything?'

Ellen was about to ask Spurs if he wanted an ice-cream, but at that moment she caught sight of a black and white shadow springing off the festering lunch and streaking away.

'Fins!' She leaped after him.

He fled behind the bunkhouse, shot through the laurels and vanished. Ellen pulled back her hair and laughed with relief – at least he was still nearby. He'd managed to wolf the rest of the ham and pâté, and most of a melted Brie.

She swung back towards Dilly and Spurs and found – in something of a regretful epiphany – that she was staring at two wildly attractive people who looked disturbingly good together. They also looked strangely conspiratorial, glancing guiltily away from a shared whisper the moment they saw her turn back.

I am paranoid, Ellen reminded herself. I am also not ready to fancy anyone. It's just hours since the Lloyd disaster. Learn, Jamieson, learn.

'See you tomorrow!' she called breezily.

Dilly waved happily and set off.

To Ellen's surprise, Spurs gave her a dirty look as he stomped past her to the workshop, banging the door obviously behind him.

I am no longer interesting, she concluded regretfully. I am a sweaty, dirty blonde who can't ride a horse, and he's just met a ravishing, dewy-fresh one who laughs as her pink prancer poses around the village. If wishes were horses, my two remaining ones would be strapped to a glass carriage and getting me out of this animated postcard as fast as their legs could carry them.

As Otto's hoofsteps faded away, she started to clear the lunch, swatting wasps and glancing around distractedly for Fins. The air was thick with storm flies. This afternoon, she was certain, it had to arrive.

But the sky stayed stubbornly clear, deep blue as she carried the leftover food into the cool of the house, slamming plates into the dishwasher and watching out of the window as Spurs rattled the old petrol mower on to the lawn then adjusted the blades to give it a neater cut.

Angered by his sudden mood-swing and still overheated, she pulled up her T-shirt and gave his freckled back a lengthy, unseen boob flash as he primed the pump. Then she spotted the reflective flash of Hunter's binoculars positively oscillating and dived beneath the window-sill, banging her head against the cupboard below the sink.

Hoping to find a job that provided at least a little respite from the throbbing heat, she donned her mother's spotless navy blue Wellingtons and went into the pond to rescue the few surviving plants before it was drained. It was a disgusting, slimy job and the green, foamy water slopped into her boots, running down to her feet and rooting her anger deep beneath the pond bed. She splashed her face and arms with the green sludge as she worked, slowly turning herself into a swamp monster. By the time Spurs had cut the lawns a second time, she was dripping with green gunk.

'You have no idea how amazing you look,' he said, as he carried the last box of grass cuttings past her to the gate. 'Like a garden statue covered in moss.'

'I'm so flattered.' She was in no mood to spar.

'You're the ultimate pond lifestyle accessory. You should stay there for when buyers come round. Place would sell in a trice.'

'I'll stick to cranking up the coffee percolator, thanks.'

'Not seeing your estate-agent boyfriend tonight, then?' He dropped the box, stretched out his arms and rolled his head.

'None of your business.' She wondered how he knew what Lloyd did for a living.

'You're funny.'

Ellen got the distinct impression he wasn't referring to her wit. 'What makes you say that?'

'Oh, no reason.' He picked up the box again. 'You're just funny.' He stomped off.

What was that supposed to mean?

As the afternoon wore on in unrelenting, humid sunshine, the green algae baked hard on her arms, face and legs. She set up the pump to drain the pond water into a scorched flower-bed and resumed weeding while Spurs went about clipping the hedges. It was no longer companionable work. They tackled their separate jobs at opposite ends of the garden, occasionally casting one another thoughtful glances, which darted away when they crossed. The sun lowered in the sky while they accumulated great piles of foliage and disenchanted tempers.

Having tamed the wild hornbeam at the front of the house, Spurs settled on his favourite bench with another beer, lit up like a bronze in the evening light.

'Fancy one?' He held up a second can, challenging her to another dirty-talk duel of sin and insinuation.

The hard edge to his voice told Ellen to steer well clear. Whatever his crisis before he'd ridden Otto, he'd got on his high horse the moment he had mounted and he was still riding around on it. Right now, he was very dangerous indeed, and he was after a grudge match.

Ellen carried on weeding, pulling out pretty much everything in sight and slinging it over her shoulder in the general direction of the barrow.

'Have you stopped loving me, then?' he called.

She ignored him.

'I still love you.'

She decided that she hated gardening. It was dirty, smelly, thankless work that made your knees ache. She was sweaty, she stank and she was covered in scratches and rashes. As pastimes went, it was all toil and soil with no thrills.

She sat back on her heels, ripped off a glove and rubbed her hot face with an even hotter hand, blinking the steamy mist from her eyes. As she did so, she knew straight away that he was alongside her. It was, she imagined, a similar sensation to knowing that a big cat was breathing hotly down your neck – uncertain whether it was about to lick your ear or pounce for its supper.

He had settled beside her and started replanting the perennials she'd been dragging unceremoniously from their homes. Silently and patiently, he collected them from the barrow, carefully cupping the soil around their roots, and buried them back in the peaty soil that had softened to mulch with the pond water.

He was on his fifth delphinium by before he spoke. His tone was soft and coaxing, deliberately seductive. 'What's up?'

She pulled out a carpet of phlox. 'Nothing.'

'Is it Richard?'

She jumped in surprise and turned to stare at him.

'You mentioned his name. So did Joni.' He rescued the phlox and started to bed it back in.

She snorted and sat back on her heels again, glancing at him warily. 'It's a popular name.'

'Is he your husband?'

Ellen sensed this was another game. 'We never married.'

'But you were together a long time?'

'What makes you say that?'

'Horses and married women.' He laughed softly. 'Two things I know a hell of a lot about. What was it? Seven years – eight?'

He was good – but he wasn't that good. 'Thirteen.'

'Jesus.' He whistled. 'You look bloody good for your age.'

'We got together at sixth-form college when we were sixteen.'

'And you've been together ever since?'

'Until a month ago.'

'Ever strayed?'

'No.'

'Did you have many lovers before him?'

She rolled her eyes at him. So that was the game. Well, she was happy to let him win. 'It was Taunton.'

That, at least, seemed to shut him up. He replanted a few semi-massacred lupins. But he had been biding his time: 'So, let me get this right. You've slept with just one man in your entire life?'

Ouch. Victory. And way too personal. She'd been too hot and bothered to see the sting coming.

'I've done enough for this evening.' She stood up. 'I need a shower, and Snorkel needs a walk before it gets dark. Thanks for all your help.'

'I haven't granted your wish yet.'

'Yes, you have.' She pulled the horseshoe nail from her back pocket and handed it to him. 'You cut the lawn. Three pounds and thirty-three pence well spent.' She detached Snorkel from her lunge line and walked inside without a backward glance.

By the time she'd showered and changed, he and the mini-tractor had gone. To her surprise, he'd put all her parents' gardening equipment neatly back into the shed, including the pump. The black pond liner now held just a few inches of green slime and pebbles, and what appeared to be a paper boat floating in the algae. Ellen fished it out with a stray bamboo stick and unfolded it. Something small and metallic fell out and landed by her feet. She read, 'Only a dark cocoon before I get my gorgeous wings and fly away.'

She creased her forehead, reading and rereading it, trying to remember where she had heard the line before, in a poem or a song.

Then it hit her. It was Joni Mitchell: 'The Last Time I Saw Richard'.

She took a sharp breath and her tear ducts threatened to convulse. Then she crumpled up the note and threw it back into the slime. He was playing games with her head.

Feeling around underfoot, she found exactly what she expected: a single horseshoe nail. One small piece of metal as hard and twisted as Spurs Belling's heart. And he wasn't going to be allowed to hammer it into hers. That was already broken.

She carried it over to the horsehoe, which was lying on the garden bench, and carefully slotted it back into its hole. Then she took the entire thing to the pond and dropped it in.

Ellen's eyes snapped open at dawn, back on the early shift. She lay listening to the birds, taking in the strange strumming top note.

Who the hell was clipping hedges at this time in the morning?

It only took a moment for waking question to connect with waking answer.

Spurs.

She rolled out of bed and looked out of the window. The first thing she saw was a huge pile of hedge clippings, spread out across the lawn to form the word 'Sorry'. Apologising with flora and fauna seemed to be something of a village tradition. Then, as she shouldered the window-frame, her chuckling yawn turned into a groan.

'Why do you need to say sorry?' she asked five minutes later, as she walked outside with two mugs of tea.

He turned round, stopped the clippers and pulled his goggles on to his head. 'For coming back.' His face had caught the sun the day before, his high, reddened cheekbones and freckled nose throwing those pale eyes into even greater relief.

'And why did you thank me in rose petals?'

That sun-kissed face smiled, happy to acknowledge the gesture, making the red dawn hide bashfully behind a cloud as it realised it was being outshone. 'Because you bought my lot.' He put his arm round Snorkel. 'I *was* invited in.'

'And did you take your PlayStation back while you were here?'

The moment Ellen said it, she knew she'd got it wrong. He tilted his head in confusion, utterly baffled. 'I haven't played in stations since I was little.'

She pressed her lips to her mug, steam and tannin waking her, furious with herself for cross-examining a man already on a crucifix. She cast her eyes guiltily around her. He'd already weeded the remaining beds and edged them, as well as training the creepers back from the downstairs windows. She turned back to him in amazement. 'How long have you been here?'

'A couple of hours. I couldn't sleep.'

Snorkel hadn't barked. She was a hopeless guard dog.

'I apologise if I was a bit full on yesterday,' he put down the clippers and pulled off his gloves, not looking at her, 'but from the start, I just madly fell in love with . . .' he paused '. . . this garden.' He looked up, almost knocking her off her feet. Although apologetic, the silver eyes were as playful as the day before.

Ellen met them, blinked, and realised that they were her ulti-mate wake-up call: Play with me and you play with your own wounds, they warned. You know me. You know me. You know me. I am bad. I hurt people, just like you do. Let's be bad together. Let's be bad together. Let's be bad together.

She scuffed her toe against the stubbled grass as she handed him a mug. 'I was in a crabby mood. I hadn't managed much sleep either. Maybe I'm the one who should be apologising.'

'You should *both* be apologising!' snapped a furious voice. They were greeted by the remarkable sight of Hunter Gardner wearing striped pyjamas and a checked silk dressing-gown, glaring at them over his half-clipped garden hedge. 'Have you *any* idea what time it is?'

'Quite early.' Ellen cleared her throat.

'It's a quarter to six!' he snarled. 'And I hardly think you can call this a reasonable time to be running garden appliances, can you?'

To Ellen's surprise, Spurs immediately apologised. 'I had no idea it was so early – don't wear a watch, you see, and I knew we had a lot to do today. I'll do this later. Hope we didn't disturb your sleep too badly.'

Hunter gaped at him, then nodded a gruff acknowledgement of the apology. He turned back to his house. 'And don't let that blasted dog near my chickens,' he called, over his shoulder.

Spurs turned to Ellen and smiled. 'See what a good influence you are on me?'

She narrowed one eye speculatively.

'Do you still love me?' he asked, only a hint of mischief in his voice.

'A bit.' She yawned. 'You?'

'To death – anyone who brings me tea like this wins my heart.' He took a long gulp.

'I didn't think you had one.'

'Grew it back last night.'

'I'll notify the tea ladies of Britain.'

He grinned. 'So I'm allowed to finish granting your wish?'

She nodded. 'Yes, please.'

In the intimate, warm cloak of another humid morning, they worked together, clearing away the huge piles of cuttings and weeds to build a bonfire they would light later. They talked quietly, mostly nonsense, the jokes and games of 'verbal catch' never allowed to get dark and dangerous as they had the day before; the little snippets of information they passed on about themselves scattered like pearls that dropped naturally rather than being prised from shells.

Working before the sun got up to strength meant that they powered through the tasks, hardly noticing the speed at which they were exerting themselves. It seemed laughably easy, compared with the stings, aches, heat and irritation of the day before.

By the time Hunter marched past to fetch his Sunday paper (as always timing it so that Joel would be unlocking the post-office stores at precisely the time he arrived), Ellen and Spurs were sitting on the bench drinking coffee. They waved at him cheerfully. He lifted his chin in return and managed a squinting, unfriendly smile.

'I wonder why he never married?' Ellen mused.

'Gay.' Spurs offered her a biscuit.

'Never! He's always ogled on my mother.'

'Is she very bossy?'

'Fairly. She was a school teacher.'

'There you go. Mother complex. He's definitely queer – tried to grope Rory at the fête when he was eight. Hunter was judging the fancy-dress contest. Aunt Truffle should have known better than to dress him as a sailor. Asking for trouble.'

'Was that why you set light to his garage?'

'Among other things. It was a long time ago.'

'Do you really have an aunt called Truffle?'

'Patricia – yes.'

Not long afterwards, Giles Hornton panted past in his jogging shorts, moustache gleaming. 'Care to join me today?' he called to Ellen.

'Another time.' She waved him on.

He cast Spurs a hard look, and jogged off towards the church.

'Another admirer?' Spurs turned to her teasingly.

'Another?' She wondered, rather stupidly, whether he counted himself as one.

'Your date at the Duck?'

'Oh, him.' Ellen didn't want to think about Lloyd. 'That was just a one-off – I mean, it's nothing serious.'

'Too soon after Richard?' he asked lightly.

She studied his face, wondering if this was a game. But it wasn't. 'Yes, too soon after Richard.'

Later, leaning against the ladder while he cleaned the windows above her head, Ellen watched the sky for signs of a storm. 'It has to break soon.'

'It will. Tonight,' he promised.

'Where do you suppose it is?' She scanned the horizon.

'Now? Throwing its weight around in your old neck of the woods.'

'Cornwall?' She looked up as a cascade of soapy drips rained down on her. 'It'll take hours to get here, then – I took almost four, and I had a jeep.'

'Storms drive faster than women.'

'I drive very fast.'

'I bet you do. But you're not a woman.'

'What am I?'

'You're Ellen.' He passed the bucket down, then hopped off the ladder, lit a cigarette and walked away to admire his weeded flower-beds.

Ellen poked out her tongue at his retreating back, then headed inside with the bucket and splashed her face at the cold tap as she filled it, listening to Joni Mitchell starting up in the garden. Spurs had clearly deemed it a respectable hour to start the noise pollution – although to Ellen's mind there was nothing as pure as Joni's poetry and her sweet, cracked voice.

The soggy piece of paper with its crumpled line from 'The Last Time I Saw Richard' still floated on the pool of slime left in the pond, and hidden below it was the horseshoe. Ellen wondered whether she could retrieve it without Spurs seeing.

When she carried the bucket out, he was playing ball with Snorkel, the cigarette dangling between his lips.

'She needs a walk.' Ellen watched her exploding like a sprung coil after every throw.

'So let's take her.'

'Dilly's coming over,' she reminded him 'Why don't I do it while you finish the windows?'

'I want to come with you.'

'You might miss Dilly.'

Joni was singing about Christmas and longing for a river she could skate away on. Her timing wasn't great. The only thin ice to skate on in steamy Oddlode was frosting Spurs' eyes as he shook his head. 'She'll come at exactly the same time as yesterday. She's a teenager. They calculate things like that carefully. She'll have thought about me all night.'

Ellen pulled back her chin and snorted at his arrogance. It prodded her to ask, 'Did you lose your nerve when you broke your leg?'

'No.' He threw his cigarette butt into the clipped hedge. 'What makes you say that?'

'Yesterday you looked frightened when Dilly asked you to ride Otto.'

'Oh – no, it wasn't nerves. It was something she said.'

'What?'

'Doesn't matter. Just a stupid thing from my past. Haunts me sometimes.'

'So you weren't frightened?'

'No.' He looked at her levelly. 'Horses don't frighten me.'

'What does?'

'You.'

She snorted. 'T'yeah.'

'You're frightened of me too.'

'I'm not.' She laughed. 'You were the one who told me you couldn't scare me to death because I was afraid of nothing.'

'You remember everything I say. That's scary for a start.'

Caught left-footed, Ellen whistled for Snorkel. 'Okay, let's walk.'

'Prove you're not frightened.'

She pulled at Snorkel's ears. 'How exactly?'

'Get your car keys – we can pick up some bedding plants from the nursery while we're out.'

'Oh, that is *so* scary,' she teased, glancing over her shoulder with one eye closed against the sun. 'Bedding plants. Eek!'

Reaching out, he touched her neck with the tips of his fingers, almost making her orbit the planet. 'We have to get out of here.'

Ellen was tempted to tell him to get lost, but somehow when Spurs bossed her about, it didn't feel like being told what to do, lectured or talked down to – her usual fury triggers. It felt like an adventure.

With Snorkel spinning excitedly behind the dog grille, they drove out of the village to the west, then turned right on to the Springlode lane, crossed the narrow bridge over the Odd then immediately climbed a high, winding hill towards Parson's Ridge.

Having followed Spurs' directions, Ellen cast a look at the retreating village in her rear-view mirror. 'This is the opposite direction to the nursery.'

'We'll go there on the way back. There's a great walk up here.'

'The bridleway,' she said gesturing to the right where the track climbed through the fields parallel to the twisting lane. 'We could have walked it from the cottage.'

'It would have taken too long.' He glanced at his watch impatiently. 'Do you have cargo straps for the roof of this thing?'

'In the back, yes.' Was he planning to buy the entire contents of the nursery?

He twisted round to look. 'Where's your kite?'

'My what?'

'Your 'chute. You said it was in the car.'

Who remembered everything that was said now? Ellen wondered, with amusement, as a throwaway comment popped back into her head. 'Under the seat. Why?'

'Turn into the gateway here,' Spurs instructed, and guided her down a long, narrow track that ran along the spine of the dragon, the views on either side breathtaking.

They parked at the far side of a cracked field, under the shadow of a spindly coppice.

'The locals call this Broken Back Wood,' he told her, as they got out and freed Snorkel. 'The hunt draw covert here seven or eight times a season – it's full of fox – and at least once a year a rider breaks their back falling as they chase the pack down there.' He pointed to where the land swept down into the valley, a three-mile, one-in-four terror run of steep, undulating fields separated by dense black hedges and thick dry-stone walls.

Ellen shuddered. 'Now you know why I don't ride.'

'Oh, it's the best feeling in the world galloping from here.' He laughed, did an about-turn and pointed to the more gentle slope down to the Foxrush valley. 'That way, you can have an eight-mile run without crossing a road – can you imagine that? Horses have been known to drop dead of exhaustion.'

Ellen looked at him sharply. 'That's hardly something to boast about. It's sick.'

'I agree. Why d'you think I left this place behind?'

They turned and made their way cautiously down a steep path that led from the wood to a stile in a stone wall, beyond which the Lodes Valley spread out beneath them like a vast, deep green salad bowl, dusted with nutty villages.

Standing on the stile was like standing on a diving-board high above a green sea. Spreading her arms wide and longing to jump, Ellen didn't want to think about cruel bloodsport fanatics riding their horses to death across country. All she could think about was how she craved wings to fly high above it all, the wind rushing in her ears and blood gushing through her veins. 'Where's a parachute when you need one?' She laughed.

'In the back of the car,' Spurs reminded her.

'Sorry?'

'Your 'chute – that you use for kite-surfing – it's still in the car.'

'So it is.' She jumped off the stile and started out across a field of cows, which Snorkel was trying busily to round up.

'Aren't you going to use it, then?' Spurs called after her, still standing on the other side of the stile.

'Don't be daft.' She turned and, walked backwards now. 'It's a *surf* kite – it wouldn't work. There's nothing to surf and no wind.'

'Can't you feel the wind now the storm's moving in?' he yelled, pointing at her hair. 'Look.'

Blonde wisps were being buffeted in a mounting breeze. Ellen carried on walking backwards, shaking her head – windblown hair and all. 'It's a stupid idea. Way too dangerous.'

'You said you'd prove you weren't frightened.'

'I'm not, but I'm not going to jump this hill.'

'I thought you used to base jump?'

'Years ago – it's totally different. There are tons of safety precautions. What are you trying to do? Kill meeeeeeeeeeee-aghhhhhhhh!' Her ankle gave way as her foot landed in a rabbit hole and she tumbled backwards, rolling twenty yards down the slope before coming to a sticky halt.

Eventually Spurs was looking down at her. 'Are you planning on getting up?'

'I could have broken my back,' she snapped, aware that she had been lying down for rather a long time.

'But you haven't.'

'No – I've, er, landed in a cowpat.' Reluctantly, she sat up and peered over her shoulder. It was smeared all over the back of her T-shirt and reeked to high heaven. 'Shit.'

'Literally.' Spurs offered her a hand up, pulling her with such strength that she practically landed in his arms.

'Thanks.' She stepped back hurriedly.

'Here.' He pulled his own T-shirt over his head and held it out. 'Have this.'

When she took it, she could feel the warmth of his body clinging to the folds.

He smiled and waited.

'Turn your back then,' she muttered.

'I have seen you change your top twice before,' he reminded her, still smiling.

'I wasn't frightened of you then,' she mocked.

'Frightened of what?'

'Fine.' She pulled off the cowpat T-shirt, carefully to avoid getting the smelly mulch on her skin or hair, then threw it down before she dived into Spurs' warm, soft replacement. 'Happy?' she demanded.

His smile even wider now, he turned to look out across the valley. 'If you're too chicken, can I use your kite?'

'Absolutely not – it's specialist equipment. Besides, the harness would never fit you.'

'Shame. At least I've got the balls to try.'

'I haven't got balls, remember.'

'Oh, but you have.' He looked at her again.

'Are you insinuating that I am, in fact, a man in drag?'

'Well, you're a drag. Whether you're a man or not – ouch!' She'd clobbered him. 'The tits look pretty real. Ouch!' She'd clobbered him again.

'Glad you like them.' She sniffed, and stooped to pick up her T-shirt. 'I had them done in Singapore. Bloody expensive. Call me Larry.'

'Good to meet you, Larry. Have you been topped *and* tailed?'

'Yes, the full op.' She nodded sincerely. 'I left my dick in South East Asia, along with my last basin of stubble.'

'How romantic.'

'I thought so.' She set off back up the hill.

'Where are you going, Larry?' he called after her.

'I thought I might fly a kite.' Bugger. Ellen cursed herself as she walked. This is so stupid – why does he keep making me feel like this? Like I have to do the things I've always thought about in careless daydreams but which I know are crazy?

Yet she was almost running now, planning the jump, guessing that the wind was just right to skim her low over the hedges and walls with minimal lift or drift. She'd never used her own kite this way before, but she'd seen some of the guys trying them off hills – and even cliffs – without coming to much harm. There'd been a few broken limbs admittedly – at least one concussion that she remembered. But they were far more reckless.

When she reached the car, she pulled the 'chute and harness from the store beneath the back bench seat.

'So you're really going to do it?' Spurs asked breathlessly, as he caught up.

'Why not?' She gathered the silk over one shoulder and handed him the harness. 'Carry that.'

He cast her a look that set her pulses thrumming like overwound metronomes and they set off back to the stile.

'You really are, aren't you?' he asked, as they ran side by side.

'No, I'm going to pretend right up until the last minute.' She scanned the horizon for hazards.

'You don't have to.'

'I want to.' Anything to get away from you, she thought. Anything to get away from my attraction to you.

They stumbled to a halt by the stile.

Spurs scraped his hand through his hair, and drew a short breath. 'If you do this, we might never really get to know each other.'

Ellen admired his courage. She was being far more cowardly by flying away. 'You were the one who suggested it.' She dropped the silk on the far side of the stile, took her harness from him and stepped into it.

He watched her. 'I've changed my mind.'

'Why?'

'Because you might get my T-shirt dirty – ouch! Will you *stop* hitting me?' He grabbed her arm, pulling her round to face him. 'I don't want to be held responsible if you get hurt.'

'Spurs, I want to do it.' She twisted away, tugging up the shoulder straps, then checking the fastenings. 'I'm a grown-up. This is my decision and my risk. Forget you even suggested it – I was thinking about it before you said a word. Now I can't *not* do it. It's the way my head works.'

The corners of his mouth twitched. 'You too?'

'Me too.' She smiled as she realised something. 'Me too.'

Richard had never had X-factor. Richard was a daredevil and a sportsman and a man for whom calculated risks were daily mathematics, but he was also a coward. Cowardice, as he himself pointed out, saved lives – the bravest people in dangerous sports were usually the dead ones. Ellen had learned caution from him over the years, had looked over his shoulder while he did his sums, but it was not something that came naturally to her. She could work out any statistic she liked, except the risks to her own safety.

She clipped on the 'chute, double-checked every fitting and accepted Spurs' high five. The ultimate game was on.

'Stand on the stile and hold the 'chute open from the top – that's right.' She watched him over her shoulder, thankful that he was so tall – his high reach lifting the kite wide open. 'Now I'm going to run like smoke down this hill, and I'll either fall flat on my face at the bottom – probably into another cowpat – or I'll take off in time to clear that dry-stone wall. If it's the latter then the car keys are in the ignition and you might need to collect me from somewhere . . . down . . . there.' She tightened the strapping on her harness and gripped the kite toggles. 'Okay. When I say, "Go", let go.' She held her face up to feel the breeze.

'Good lu—'

'Go! Go! Go! Get out of the way you bloody cooooooooooooo-ooooooows!'

The wind lifted her off the ground long before she had antici-pated, and long before she'd gathered enough running speed to dictate her direction.

Within seconds she was twenty feet in the air and whizzing left at a breakneck pace, high above a dozen surprised-looking cows and a barking Snorkel.

'Bugger.' Ellen dragged at the left toggle and looked around for power lines, pylons and trees as she was blown off course.

She was swept another ten feet into the air by a sharp gust that almost upended the kite, and propelled her even faster in her journey in the wrong direction – rattling along the backbone of the ridge rather than into the valley.

The tiny 'chute wasn't designed to take her far – it was there for spins, jumps and loop-the-loops above the ocean, the board that was normally strapped to her feet coming into regular contact with the waves to gather speed and act as a springboard and counterweight. But now her legs dangled hopelessly as she was buffeted in amazing spirals and swung about like a wind-chime in a storm, letting out less than tuneful squeals of alarm and exhilaration.

She had absolutely no control whatsoever.

The wind had suddenly taken on more strength, changing unpredictably as the storm accelerated closer – something she hadn't calculated on the ground. She could hear Richard's voice in her head: 'You stupid bitch. Watch the weather. You stupid bloody bitch.' He was a meteorologist among surfers.

'Fuck off, Richard!' she screamed, dragging at the left toggle again and executing a complete 360-degree turn through the air. 'Wow! Oh, hell! Wow!'

At last the kite stabilised, finding a kind thermal that lifted Ellen up higher than she would have liked but mercifully kept her level.

Suddenly she could see Spurs again – and the cows, which were now a lot smaller than they had been. She was sixty or seventy feet up, but at least she was travelling in the right direction. She tipped forward to drop the front of the 'chute and lose height – at the same time gathering speed alarmingly. When she passed over Spurs and the cows' heads again, she was swooping faster than a Harrier jump jet. 'Wheeeeeeee!'

Over the stone wall she sailed, lifting in another thermal, throwing another 360-degree turn – far more controlled this time – and flying on down the valley.

At last, she had the green waves she wanted beneath her feet as she soared over hedges and thickets. Far ahead of her lay Oddlode like a stony outcrop in an otherwise peaceful lagoon, its church spire forming a lighthouse to warn incomers of the dangerous undercurrents that waited there.

Just for a moment, she saw herself fluttering all the way to the village – swooping in on Hunter Gardner as he drank another cafetière of coffee and kept watch.

'What a laugh,' she shrieked, her words whipped away by the wind.

But she knew that any attempt to soar, loop-the-loop and thermal ride all the way to Oddlode would be far too high risk.

'Concentrate,' said a voice in her head. 'Think about where to set the 'chute down. You haven't much time.'

'Go away, Richard!' She wailed into the wind. 'I'm having fun. You're out of my life now.'

The valley opened out beneath her dangling feet as she swept down into it much faster than she had anticipated, now feeling like a spinning tiddlywink propelled into a giant green cup. She missed a treetop by little more than inches, startling several young crows who gaped up at her from a high nest. She was flying almost directly over the bridleway now, and recognised the derelict stone barn that marked her turning place on runs from Goose Cottage.

She knew there was a row of telegraph poles two-thirds of the way down so she had to land before them, but she also had to lose speed and height first.

The ground was rushing past far too fast beneath her – faster than she'd ever travelled over the sea, and offering a far less sympathetic landing. She *had* to slow down. But every time she dipped the 'chute to lose height, she speeded up, and every time she gained height she changed direction, spinning dangerously out of control. The telegraph poles loomed closer by the second, along with a large wood and a farmhouse.

'Fuck!' Ellen squeaked. 'It's a lovely way to gooooooooo – nooooooooo!'

The adrenaline rush was an all-time high, but she wasn't ready to die. There was nothing for it . . .

'Backwards,' she told herself. 'Up, over and put your heels down as brakes.'

It was a leg-break move, but she had no choice. It was that or frying on a cheese-cutter wire.

She tugged hard on the right toggle and turned a half-circle until she was facing up the hill again, still hurtling inexorably down towards Oddlode. Leaning right back into her harness and clamping her eyes shut, she tucked her knees into her chest and felt the first bumps or *terra firma* against her backside before she released the 'chute from its harness and tucked in tightly for the roll.

Her roll was swiftly interrupted by a large hillock, which she hadn't seen from the air. It broke her fall with a perfect, soft grass-mattress buttress.

As emergency landings went, they didn't get any better.

Ellen hugged the banks of the hillock and kissed the dry grass gratefully, before jumping up and leaping around in the air.

'Yes! Yes! Yes!'

Far above her, she could just make out two small figures jumping too – Spurs and Snorkel, both barking their heads off. She couldn't hear a word but she waved both arms joyfully and blew a hundred kisses – then ran to the crest of the hillock, doing handstands and cartwheels.

She'd got her spirit back. It felt like falling in love.

Getting her spirit back was one thing, but getting her breath back was another. By the time she had collected her 'chute and clambered back up the hill to rejoin Spurs, she was so puffed out she couldn't speak.

'You beauty!' Spurs hugged her.

She panted into his bare chest and fought an urge to ram her hot cheeks to the freckled skin. She broke away before she could let herself and grinned up at him, shaking her head, still unable to speak.

He cupped her face between his soil-stained hands. 'You are amazing!' The silver eyes danced around her face, a straight-forward, come-to-bed message playing between them.

She knew he wanted to kiss her, and suddenly she felt so turned on that her burning lungs almost imploded. For a split second, as his face moved towards hers, her knees gave way and the burning, buzzing heat between her legs threatened to set light to her harness. But then she twisted her face away so that the kiss landed on her cheek.

'It felt amazing!' she gasped, and turned towards the car as though the near-miss kiss hadn't happened. 'It felt fucking amazing. What a crack.'

The tomboy was back. Ellen, the trouper. Ellen, one of the lads. Ellen, who couldn't allow herself to be attracted to Spurs because that made her vulnerable, and she had no time to be vulnerable. She was going to head off round the world in search of sport and adventure. She had her spirit back.

'We'd better go back – I think Snorkel's had a decent enough run,' she called over her shoulder. 'I have a hell of a lot to do next week, so—'

Two firm hands grabbed her shoulders and spun her round. 'Whoa, whoa. Sssh.'

'What are you doing?' She tried to wriggle out of his grip, but he held on tight, silver eyes searing into hers.

'Calm down, Ellen – sssh. Let it go.'

'What are you talking about? I feel fine. I feel fantastic. That was fucking fantastic!'

'Let it go. Believe me, I know. You have to.'

'What *are* you talking about?'

'I get like this, and I'm sure as hell not getting into a car with you when you're like it.'

'Then walk home.' She jerked back, almost dislocating her shoulders as he held on tight. 'What d'you think I'm going to do? Drive off a precipice?'

'Probably. You've got to let it go, Ellen.'

'Let *what* go?'

He just stared at her, his face twisted with the effort of hanging on.

As the adrenaline and endorphins and lactic acid drained away, Ellen stopped wrestling and took a lot of deep breaths, deliberately calming herself, hating him for robbing her of the high.

Then it hit her like a wall. The pain. It hit her so hard that she almost fell over.

Sliding down to her knees, she put her head into her hands and sobbed.

He sat down beside her while she wept, pulling at the long grasses and looking out at the valley, saying nothing, not touching her or offering sympathy. She was grateful. It was embarrassing enough having Snorkel trying to dry every tear with a sloppy pink tongue, a kind paw on her knee and a little whine constantly playing a violin sonata in her throat.

Eventually Ellen dared to look across at him through the streaming tears, watching his curls dance in the wind and studying the creases beside his eyes where he was squinting into the sun. 'How did you know?'

'I just did.' He didn't look round. 'You've been like an unexploded bomb all weekend.'

'Is this what they call a controlled explosion, then?' she bawled, covering her mouth because the sound of her sobs embarrassed her.

He half smiled and looked down as he pulled another grass stem.

'I hate you for this.' She wiped her nose on the back of her wrist, fighting against the rattling hiccups that were bubbling up through her chest.

'Oh, you'll forgive me soon enough – just as you'll forgive him eventually.'

'Him?'

'Richard.'

She pressed her wet face to the inside of her arms and took a deep breath. 'There's nothing to forgive.'

'In thirteen years?'

'I'm not bitter – I'm just mourning. It's a relief.'

They watched crows rising from a nearby crop like ambush helicopters from a desert haze.

'How do you mean?'

'Our love died in infancy. It's been like living with a corpse.' Ellen let one eye follow the crows until they blurred into specks.

Beside her, Spurs didn't move. 'They say the first day you cry is the first day you can begin to forget.'

'Who says?'

'Some shitty book I read in prison.'

A snotty, impatient snort flew from her nostrils before she could really take this in. 'Did you cry a lot in prison?'

'Only because the books were so shitty.'

They stared out at the valley, watching stormclouds gather on the hills like grey armies preparing for battle.

'I cried a few times,' he conceded eventually.

'Ever cried over a woman?'

'No.'

'So you don't know at all how I feel.' Ellen lifted her face from her sleeve and studied his profile, hating its perfection.

'I've mourned a boy.'

She smiled sadly, dipping her head back into the damp nooks of her elbows. She might have guessed. It was always the ones you least suspected and found most attractive.

'Did you love him very much?'

'Yes.' He turned his face to her. 'I'm not queer. We weren't lovers. We were friends. But I did love him. My first big love, if you like.'

'Like Richard.'

'Well, we didn't screw on a regular basis for thirteen years.'

She snorted, half laughing and half sobbing. 'Neither did Richard and I.'

He scratched his nose with a blade of grass, eyes jumping from point to point on the horizon.

Ellen lifted her head and propped it on her wrists. 'We grew up together and we shared a passion – but it was never really for each other. We evolved this odd life that only we understood – working through winter, playing through summer. And we like each other – we can talk all night.'

'Just not screw?'

She tilted her head. 'Oh, we had our fair share. I'm only thinking of the last couple of years when it was birthdays and Christmas, and we both had to be pissed to do it.'

She didn't see his eyes press carriage return on her face.

'Why did you stay together so long?'

'We relied on each other. We had the same job and loved the same sports. My parents hated him, which gave me a reason to prove it could work. Besides, we *wanted* to make it work. We're best friends. We're – we *were* like a little self-contained unit, a camper-van couple who only needed a small backpack and each other. And we did *need* each other,' She thought about it afresh, her analysis clumsy with the post-mortem of renewal. 'I was the brave one who made things happen, he was the sensible one who always made sure we had cash, a home and decent jobs.'

'I could use his number right now.'

'Me too.' Ellen laughed tearfully. 'He's in Australia.'

He pressed his chin to his shoulder as he turned to look at her. 'Long way to go to get away from you.'

'He wanted me to go too. It was an ultimatum.'

'But you're still here.'

'I'm still here.' She nodded, eyes sliding towards his. 'Turned out he was braver than me all along.'

'I doubt that.'

Ouch, ouch, ouch! Ellen fought to pull away from the silver A and E gaze that was mugging her eyes, ripping Richard from her head and replacing him with big electric defibrillator jolts to her heart.

She shook her head repeatedly. 'Our loopy little life suited me. It had no ties.'

'Except to each other?' He kept her eyes trapped. 'You never tied the knot.'

'I was always hopeless at knots. It's why I never took up sailing or mountaineering.'

'They're easy to tie when you're frightened you'll lose something.'

'Like horses?'

'Like horses. I always tie them up very carefully.'

They were pattering again, and Ellen was grateful. Her chest and eyes hurt, and she was ashamed and angry with herself. Her magnificent, spiralling flight down the valley seemed petty and attention-seeking now. The emergency landing had been a crashing fall after all.

She looked down at her scratched, grass-stained legs and tattered clothes. If yesterday in the garden had turned her into a swamp monster, this morning's escapades had dragged her from the primordial soup and pulled her through a hedge backwards.

'You're not seeing me at my best,' she apologised.

'Does that matter?'

'I guess not. Most bomb-disposal experts don't admire the casing before they defuse the detonator.'

'You have fantastic casing.'

She rubbed the sticky sweat from her eyebrows.

'Come and meet my cousin.' He stood up. 'I want him to admire your casing.'

They drove into the village of Upper Springlode, one of the tiny limpets that clung to the flank of the dinosaur crest, a scattering of old, honey-coloured houses divided by sheep-filled paddocks and windswept woods. They turned into a bumpy, potholed drive and stopped by a cluster of ramshackle farm buildings. Several droopy-lipped horses peered out at them suspiciously from mismatched stables as they jumped out of the jeep. A transistor radio was blaring the latest manufactured-band hit from an open doorway.

'Bloody hell – he's teaching.' Spurs was looking across at a sand square behind a rusting horsebox. In its centre a grumpy, good-looking youth was watching a fat middle-aged woman bouncing around with no stirrups on an equally fat cob. 'That must be a first. Rory!' he called.

The youth looked up, then called to his pupil, 'Carry on trotting, Ann. Won't be a tick.

'What d'you want?' he asked suspiciously, when he joined them.

'Jumps.' Spurs patted him on the back. 'Rory – this is Ellen.'

''Lo,' Rory reached straight into Spurs' rear pocket, pulled out his cigarettes and lit one. He gave Ellen little more than a passing nod, although she was staring at him in amazement.

He was a Spurs in miniature. The resemblance was uncanny – the same eyes, mouth, nose and high cheekbones. Rory was finer and lighter than his cousin – the hair blond and straight, the freckles like gold dust and his frame narrower. Yet the similarity was eerie. 'How many d'you want and how long for?' he was asking Spurs. His voice also held the unmistakable Belling drawl. Or was that Constantine?

'A couple – just today.'

'Sundays are my busiest teaching day.'

'Aw, c'mon. Ann there hardly looks ready to try her luck over the sticks.'

They all watched red-faced Ann as she bounced past, big bottom crashing unevenly on the saddle.

'I have other pupils.' Rory shrugged, then called to Ann, 'Terrific! He's really tracking up.'

'Bollocks! She can't even sit to the trot properly.'

'It's what they like to hear. That's what they pay me for – that and the good looks.' He managed a short, sweet smile. 'If she thinks that she and her carthorse are capable of getting to the Olympics then let her.'

'Rory hates teaching *ordinary* people to ride,' Spurs explained to Ellen, in an undertone.

Ellen thought it hardly surprising that the yard was doing so badly.

'You can have the old rustics,' he said to Spurs. 'Do you have a trailer with you?'

'No. They can go on the roof of the Jeep.'

Rory raised an eyebrow and looked at Ellen. 'You ride, then?'

'I think they're for Dilly,' she explained.

'Dilly?' He cracked a huge, stale yawn.

'You know her.' Spurs watched him. 'Has a nice roan.'

Rory's arrogant face lit up. 'From Oddlode? Pheely's girl?'

'She says she fancies you too.' Spurs laughed.

'Really?' Suddenly he appeared quite goofy.

'Think she could use your help with her horse – when she's back for the summer holidays.'

'Sure – absolutely. She can bring him up here any time.' He grinned.

'Come down this afternoon if you like,' Spurs offered.

'Can't.' He pulled a regretful face. 'I'm on my own today. Sharrie's taken a couple of the youngsters to a show.' He glanced towards Ann, who was now struggling to breathe. 'I guess I'd better get back. The jumps are in the flat field behind the barn, okay?'

'Thanks.' Spurs slapped his back again and set off to fetch them.

As they heaved a heavy wooden upright on to the jeep roof, Ellen tried not to feel jealous that he was going to such an effort for Dilly, or resentful that he was using her diesel, strength and time to do so.

With the jumps secured to the roof, they left Rory being circled by poor, red-faced Ann and set off again, driving out of Springlode and into the valley once more.

'Fuck – he's pissed already.' Spurs rubbed his eye sockets with the balls of his hands.

'He was drunk?' Ellen turned to him in surprise. She hadn't spotted it.

'Probably from last night.' He lit a cigarette, and cranked down the window. 'Although you can bet he's already topped up his coffee. Fuck.'

Rory hardly seemed old enough to drink, let alone to have a problem.

'We start young round here,' Spurs laughed bitterly, 'and having me around didn't help the poor little sod.'

Ellen negotiated the hairpins as the jeep groaned down the hill, its roof creaking beneath the load.

'He must have been pissed not to fancy you.' Spurs flicked his ash out of the window.

'I look like sin.'

'Exactly – you're irresistible. My beautiful sinner.'

Ellen narrowly missed cannoning into the bridge over the Odd. 'What about Dilly? They seem pretty well suited.'

'He'll have to sober up before I let that happen.'

'What are you? Her father?'

'In this village,' he threw his cigarette butt out of the window, 'anything is possible. Let's go and pick some strawberries.'

'I thought we were going to buy bedding plants?' Ellen asked distractedly as she pondered Dilly's paternity.

'I never bed anything on an empty stomach. The nursery has a market garden. We can pick strawberries for lunch.'

On cue, Ellen's stomach let out a hungry growl and she remembered that she hadn't eaten all day.

'Hear hear.' Spurs patted his bare, brown belly cheerfully. 'I hope they don't mind topless fruit pickers. When I was a kid, the place was run by a band of Christian brothers, but the new owners are a bohemian lot, I gather. Mother disapproves so much that she sends Gladys to the farmers' market in Morrell. They're both convinced the couple there run it as a cover for a cannabis farm.'

'Pixie and Sexton,' Ellen recalled.

'You know them?'

She shook her head. 'Pheely's good friends with Pixie.' The name had cropped up more than once. And, according to Pheely, Pixie's husband Sexton indeed grew so much illegal produce in the hothouses that he was known to his select clients as the British Hempire.

When they drove into the little organic market garden and nursery, which was offering Pick Your Own on large, lopsided signs at the gate, they were greeted by a rabble of dogs and children. The pack circled the jeep as it bounced across a rutted field to park by a vast greenhouse.

'You tourists?' the children demanded.

'Woof, wooooooof, WOOF!' The pack jumped up at Snorkel, claws skittering against the paintwork.

'No.'

'Not from London, then?'

'No.'

'Wooooof!'

'Can your dog play with ours?'

'Okay.'

'Jesus.' Spurs stood back as Snorkel joined the rabble and they all tore off behind the greenhouse. 'Are you sure that was wise?'

'She can look after herself,' Ellen said, but wondered exactly the same thing.

They took their empty strawberry punnets from a distracted, blue-haired woman who was reading an Open University prospectus by a long potting bench, a wilting courgette plant in one hand.

'The best fruit is up by the sheep, to your right,' she said dreamily, waggling the courgette towards the door. 'Enjoy!'

That, Ellen guessed as they headed outside again, had to be Pheely's chum, Pixie. In the flesh, she was far less ephemeral and menacing than she had imagined. Ellen only wished the same could be said of Spurs, who got more bewitching by the second.

Ten minutes later, he laughed at her. 'You have to eat them!'

'I can't.' She dropped another strawberry into her punnet.

'You can.' He held out a plump red heart, tracing it tantalisingly across her lips before burying it in his own mouth, drawing it in with those white teeth.

And she did steal strawberries, unable to resist his lures or the moreish taste of the red fruit.

Pink juice dribbling from their lips, she and Spurs picked one and ate one in the traditional way, trying competitively to fill their own punnet first, while at the same time greedily incapable of stopping themselves cramming the best of the crop into their mouths.

'I always think these places should weigh the punters along with the punnets before letting us loose,' Ellen said, as they worked their way along opposite sides of the same row, bumping heads as they looked for hidden gems beneath the shark-toothed green leaves.

'How much does a guilty conscience weigh?'

'More than a bellyful of strawberries.' Ellen watched as Snorkel and her new pack charged up to another car bumping across the ruts in the parking field. 'Why?'

'Just wondering. How much soft fruit does a thought that weighs on your mind weigh?'

'Three strawberries and a loganberry.'

'And how many strawberries does it take to pull your weight?'

'More than a weight off your mind but less than it takes to throw your weight around. Is this going anywhere?'

He looked up, holding the fattest, juiciest strawberry Ellen had ever seen. 'No. I like going nowhere with you just as much as I like going places.' He put the strawberry to her lips.

'Stop it,' she breathed, and turned her face away.

'Sorry?'

'You heard.'

He tapped the strawberry against his nose, then laid it carefully on top of his punnet. 'You're funny.'

'If you say so.' She wiped the sweat from her forehead, longing for the storm to break.

Blue-haired Pixie had gone when they walked back into the glasshouse. In her place was the eldest of the many elfin children, scribbling doodles on the OU prospectus and chatting on her mobile phone. She watched Spurs with interest as he gathered several trays of bedding plants from the tables in the centre. Then he spotted a big bucket filled with citronella torch candles in the shape of stars and gathered up the lot. He marched to the till and gave her his devilish smile.

She weighed the strawberry punnets and rang them up, along with the bedding plants, chatting all the time. 'Yes, he's *still* with her, although fuck knows what he sees in her, and she has a singing voice like a cat that's just been sat on by a pensioner. Thirty-five pounds sixty.' She looked up at Ellen and Spurs.

'*How* much?' Ellen hastily hid the twenty she'd fished from her shorts.

'Thirty-five pounds sixty. Thanks.' She took the fifty-pound note that Spurs was offering and gave him a ravishing smile as she rang his change through the till. 'Dilly reckons Ely Gates is still trying to split them up – her mad mum is like a witch or something and she always knows what's going on. Yes, I know she's a bit stuck-up, but I reckon Dilly's quite cool as it goes. Fourteen forty.' She handed Spurs his change with a wink.

As he and Ellen headed towards the doors again, the girl whispered into her phone, 'I just had a *right* stud buying stuff here. Shame he has a wife. You should *see* him. No – definitely not local.'

'That,' Spurs breathed as walked outside, 'is manna to my ears.'

'Being a right stud?' Ellen cuffed his arm.

'Nope.'

'Oh, you mean the fact she didn't recognise you as local?'

'No.' He looked at her through the bedding plants, silver-bullet eyes scoring direct hits. 'She thought you were my wife.'

'Ha ha.'

'We could be married,' he pointed out, dead-panning her. 'We're at a garden centre, after all.'

'We could be brother and sister,' she retaliated. 'You dared me to jump off a hill and made me cry.'

'We could be mistress and gardener,' he offered.

'Or colleagues in a strawberry-jam-manufacturing business?' She looked at the overflowing punnets.

'Or just greedy bastards?'

'Fly-hating arsonists?' She propped the citronella torches against the jeep bonnet.

'Lovers.' He leaned against the car while she unlocked it.

'Strangers,' she reminded him. 'We hardly know each other.'

'Oh, we do.' He smiled. 'We so fucking do.'

'Friends.' She looked at him levelly.

He shook his head, still smiling. 'I don't do friends any more.'

Ellen left him laying the trays on the back seat and went to gather Snorkel, who was happily joining in her new gang's attempts to mug a well-dressed couple with a pair of furious pugs on their parcel shelf.

'You tourists?'

'Woof, wooooof, WOOF!'

'Yes.'

'You from London?'

'No – Ashbridge.'

'Wooooof!'

'Can your dogs play with ours?'

'Absolutely not – shoo! Shoo!' they told Ellen furiously. 'Your children should learn a little respect.'

Spurs laughed his head off when she told him as they drove back. 'So you're my wife and we have uncontrollable children – why am I seeing my future flashing in front of my eyes?'

Ellen put her foot down, ignoring the rattling above her head and in it.

While Spurs was unloading the jumps from the jeep, Ellen stashed the strawberries in the fridge, then walked through the house, letting herself out of the low cellar-steps door so that she could creep to the pond and fish out the scuppered paper boat and the horseshoe. She rinsed both under the outside tap, but the paper shredded and fell apart in her hands.

She clipped the hose on to the tap and went back to the pond to wash the last of the algae from the liner, first scooping out the slop with a bucket.

'What is it with you and that pond?' Spurs asked, when he came to find her.

'I like to be near water,' she explained, poking a stick into the fountain nozzle to remove the gunk that had built up there.

He picked up the hosepipe and she thought he was going to drench her with water, but instead he directed it at one of the big flower-beds under the hedgerow, showering it with great spectrums of droplets to soften the earth for planting.

'My father dug this pond himself,' Ellen told him, her pride fierce, not knowing where this outburst was coming from. 'He'd just had a heart-attack, but he was still out here with a shovel day and night. He could never stand still.'

'Like you.'

'Maybe.'

'Is he okay now?'

'So-so – he still pushes himself too hard, and I think my mother is terrified that he'll drop dead the moment this place is sold and leave her alone half-way up a Spanish mountain. She thinks he's on borrowed time, but Dad never borrows anything he can't repay. He'll be around for years.'

Spurs was creating another small water feature now as one corner of the bed filled up with dark, swirling earth. He hardly seemed to notice that he was watering the same spot continually. 'How can you be so sure?'

Ellen looked up from poking at the fountain. 'Because I want it to be true.'

'Don't you think it's better to prepare yourself?'

She threw the stick into the reeds and clambered out of the pond. 'I've seen him attached to tubes and monitors and machines that kept him breathing. We were told he wouldn't survive the first attack. I was prepared then, but he wasn't. He thinks he's immortal. Why shouldn't he be allowed to live for ever if he wants? I'm not going to stand in his way.'

He was still soaking a tiny patch of bed so that muddy water spilled out on to the grass. 'I only ask because my mother is quite ill. Very ill,' he corrected himself. 'My mother is dying.'

'Oh, Christ, I'm so sorry,' she breathed.

He was soaking his own feet now. 'She refuses to tell anybody that she's terminally ill. I only found out by accident,' he grimaced at the enormity of the secret. 'Christ knows, I should have guessed. She's so driven now. And she's in such a hurry – she has an awful lot to sort out before . . . before she . . . goes.'

'I'm so sorry,' Ellen said again, standing beside him, her feet sinking in his man-made bog. 'Do you know how long?'

'Not longer than six months, I believe.'

'Is it cancer?'

'I don't know – maybe.'

Ellen gently took the hosepipe from him and twisted off the sprayer. It seemed so strange that he knew so little compared to the way her family had coped with her father's illness, acquainting themselves with every medical fact at their disposal, reading books and searching the Internet for information until they were better versed than the cardiologist.

'Nobody in the village knows, so I'd be grateful if—'

'I won't tell a soul,' she promised.

'Thanks.' He looked down at his wet feet. 'She's always said they're made of clay – and here's the proof.' He laughed bitterly.

'But you came home to prove otherwise?'

He stepped out of the loamy puddle and prised off the sodden trainers. 'I guess so. The prodigal son and all that. Take your shoes off.'

Ellen sensed there was a lot more to it, but he wasn't saying. He took the hose back and rinsed first her feet, then his own before leaving the water running into the pond.

'Have you thought about your other two wishes?' He stared at the bubbling water, desperate to move away from his tragic secret.

'You've granted more than three already.'

He stared into the black depths, a crooked smile on his lips. 'Oh, you don't get away with it that easily. That's just wishful thinking.'

'Then I wish I didn't think so much,' she said idly.

'Wish I couldn't read your thoughts?'

'I was thinking just that.'

'I know.'

With their trainers drying side by side they knelt in front of the bed and started to dig in plants. Ellen couldn't bear Spurs' sadness. She longed to cheer him up, however temporarily. 'Let me buy you a meal tonight to thank you for this,' she insisted. 'If you don't mind eating at the Duck twice in one weekend?'

'You'll never get a booking.'

'Somewhere else, then – the Oddlode Inn?'

'I'm under a lifetime ban,' he admitted, not looking her in the eye. 'Besides, they don't serve hot food. You can cook for me if you like.'

'I don't really cook,' she confessed, the customary fear gripping her at the prospect of anything involving a pan, a hob and a smoke alarm.

'In that case I'll just have to settle for strawberries and lot sixty-nine.'

'Lot . . .' Ellen's heart hammered as she recognised the number only too well. 'You bought *my* promise?'

'It was a fair trade. Mind you, I had to fight for it – Giles had bribed the auctioneer, I gather. Thankfully, I have her ear.'

Oh, hell. Ellen buried her hot face in a tray of garish dahlias.

Ellen tried to cram back as much lunch as possible in the hope that there wouldn't be enough supplies left for supper so they'd have to go out after all. But they had picked more strawberries than the Wimbledon crowds could consume on men's finals day, and the huge hunk of cheese that had survived from the day before was still as big as a brick, even after she'd stuffed her face with the doorstep sandwiches she'd lobbed together.

'Worked up an appetite flying around earlier?' Spurs watched her bulging cheeks with amusement, no longer melancholy.

'Something like that.' She thought about the way he had made her cry afterwards and found she couldn't swallow.

He threw the crust from his sandwich to Snorkel. 'It's a beautiful place. I haven't been up there for years. We used to go there as kids – play dare.'

'Ever do that dare before?'

'That was at least a double dare,' he teased her, silver eyes egging her on to play verbal catch. 'And no, we never got the girls to do double dares.'

They eyed each other childishly, and Ellen felt the sparks light her touch-paper as always. 'Does that mean I get to dare you?'

'If you like.' He smiled, but his eyes hardened warily. 'What did you have in mind?'

The tension stretched out between them like taut elastic. He knew her well enough already to guess she wasn't going to challenge him to naked mud-wrestling in the flower-bed.

She fanned her T-shirt and chewed a corner of her lip, risking a wild card because time was running out. 'I dare you to apologise to Pheely.'

'That's not fair.'

'I think it is.'

He ate a strawberry, threw the stalk on to his plate. 'I'd rather gallop Daffodil's horse down from Broken Back Wood.'

'I doubt she'd let you do that.'

'Want a bet?' His eyes sparkled.

'No. You mustn't ask that of her. It's not fair. The horse might get hurt – then Pheely would never forgive you.'

'Otto's Dilly's horse. I bet she'd let me.'

'You could kill him.'

'And me? What if I got hurt?'

'You'd be more likely to get hurt apologising to Pheely.' She was suddenly incensed. 'That's what you're really frightened of, isn't it?'

'Fuck Pheely.'

Ellen felt her arteries boiling, all pity abandoned. 'I *dare* you.'

'To fuck Pheely? No, thanks.'

'To apologise to her!'

'Never. I'll ride that hill every day and kill a hundred horses until I shatter my spine first.'

She looked at him levelly. 'You're such a coward.'

'I'm not!' He hulled half a dozen strawberries, laying them out in front of him like ducks in a shooting gallery. 'They'd love it round here if I broke my back.'

'Maybe it would break the rod you've made for it?'

'The only rod I can feel is the one between my legs that wants to fuck you.' He popped the strawberries into his mouth one at a time as he stared her out.

'Oh, grow up.'

He laughed. 'I thought you loved me?'

'Not when you're like this, I don't.' Ellen stacked the plates together, grabbed the strawberry bowl and carried them inside.

'I haven't finished!' he complained, following her and snatching strawberries. 'And what d'you mean "when you're like this"? Like what?'

'Where do I start? Self-pitying – reckless – headstrong – crude as oil.'

'Just like you, then?'

'I'm not crude.'

'Oh, you are. And you want to get a whole lot cruder with me right now.'

She slammed the plates down on the kitchen surface. 'I didn't know you before, but frankly I'm finding it hard to swallow the "I've changed" line. You don't seem to care about another soul – human or animal – apart from yourself.'

'Don't you believe I love you, then?'

'That joke's worn thin. I've enjoyed your company these past couple of days, and I'm really grateful for your help. Honestly. But you are one of the most changeable, unpredictable and screwed-up individuals I've ever met.'

'So are you.'

'Excuse me?'

'I'm not surprised Richard pissed off. Two days with you is hell – how the poor sod lasted thirteen years is a miracle.'

'You bastard!'

'You bitch.'

She threw a strawberry, which bounced off his chest. He lobbed a tea-towel back. She launched a handful of strawberries and half a baguette. He retaliated with a kitchen roll. She scored a direct hit with the cheese. He played an underhand shot with a wax lemon from the artificial fruit arrangement and laughed when it ricocheted off her forehead into the sink.

'This is *not* fucking funny!' she howled, then hurled a plate, which he only just managed to duck. She stormed outside to the pond, which had filled to overflowing. Picking up the hose, she turned back to stop him chasing her outside. '*Don't* come any closer!'

'Or what?' He slowed to a walk.

'You get wet.' She held up the hose.

'Oh, I am *so* scared.' He carried on walking towards her.

'I mean it!'

'How wet would I get?'

'Bloody wet.' She turned the jet from a trickle to a blast and wagged it in the air, inadvertently showering herself with drips.

'As wet as you are now?' he asked.

Thinking he was referring to her lack of hose control, she glowered at him.

'As wet and slippy and hot and bothered and horny and turned-on as Ellen?' He spoke in a hypnotic chant.

Ellen felt the hosepipe wobble as her hands started to shake.

'Deny it.' He was still walking towards her. 'Deny you're so wet you don't know what to do with yourself.'

'Get lost.'

'You can't, can you? You can't deny it.'

She thrust the hosepipe in front of her and let him have a gallon full in the face.

'Yeaaaaaaawwwwwwwwww!' The next thing she knew, thirteen stones of muscle-power had rugby-tackled her and she
was flying backwards, his arms around her waist, straight into
the pond.

'You b-b-bastard!' she spluttered, choking on the water.

'Bitch!' He held her under.

She hammered at his chest and kicked out, convinced for a
moment that she was fighting for her life. She should never have
crossed him. He was capable of murder. He'd tried to kill her once
already that day – sending her off on a crazy parachute jump for a
dare. Now he was drowning her. Well, she wasn't going without
a fight.

'Owwww!' he wailed, as she scratched his face hard. 'Get off!'
He was still laughing.

Splashing away from him, Ellen realised that perhaps he hadn't
been trying to kill her, after all. Breathless, heart hammering, she
managed to stand upright, only to find his hand on her ankle,
pulling her over again.

She kicked out as she fell and caught him hard on the chin.

Totally submerged, she felt the water rush through her nostrils
and down the back of her throat as she gulped it into her windpipe
by mistake. In the gloom, she could see a hand reaching out close
to her face and she batted it away, kicking back with her legs to
get as far away as possible. Her head burst out of the water, and
she made a lunge for the bank, dragging herself up on to the reed
bed and spluttering as she fought for breath, laughing and gagging
as she went. Then she turned back to the pond.

'You bast – oh, shit!'

He was lying face down in the water, motionless.

'Oh, shit!' Ellen plunged back in, realising that she must have
knocked him out when she kicked him. She turned him over in
the water and cupped his chin, towing him to the edge before
heaving him out by the arms.

'Spurs! Spurs – can you hear me?' she called, hauling him into
the recovery position and prising his mouth open to check his
airway. It was clear. She reached for his pulse, looking urgently

around for help – but Hunter Gardner was not at his lookout for once, and the lane was empty. She could hear children playing in a distant garden and a lawnmower moving further away.

His heart was beating hard and fast.

'Spurs. Wake up!' She slapped his cheeks and rubbed his back to encourage him to cough.

That was when she realised he was faking. She'd been through enough life-saving dummy runs to know the difference between practice and the real thing. She'd only done the real thing twice – both times assisting rather than life-saving – but she knew that people on the verge of drowning didn't open one eye when they thought you weren't looking.

'Oh, Spurs, don't die,' she begged melodramatically, stroking his forehead. 'You might be an unmitigated shit with no morals, but I would miss you.'

He started to splutter.

'That's it! Live, my darling,' she encouraged. 'How else am I going to beat you to a pulp? I can't do it when you're dead.'

He spluttered some more, but his eyes stayed shut.

'Spurs, if you think I'm going to give you the kiss of life, you can lie there faking it as long as you like – this laughing gear is going nowhere near your pond breath.'

He spat out a great shower of water and opened his eyes. 'Damn.'

'Feel better?' she asked sweetly.

'You really wouldn't care if I died, would you?' His silver eyes glittered.

'Not right now.'

'I'd have cared if you'd died running down Broken Back Hill like a lunatic with an oversized handkerchief tied to your arse.'

'Only because you thought you'd get the blame if I did.'

'True.'

They exchanged a long look of understanding.

'Don't ride Dilly's horse down it.'

'I wasn't going to.' He sat up, shaking his wet hair and spitting out more water. 'I wouldn't dream of it.'

'Fine.' She squeezed the water from her own hair and pulled at her T-shirt, which was clinging like an Ibiza nightclub competition winner's. Then she went to switch off the hose, which was dancing like a maddened snake and drenching Hunter's chicken pen.

Finally, she lay down at a safe distance from Spurs to dry off a little too. However alarming, the dunk had cooled her off. She could hear the storm rumbling in the distance, but overhead the sun still scorched out of big blue gaps in the gathering clouds.

'We'd feel a lot better if we got it over with, you know,' he called.

'Got what over with?'

'Screwing each other's brains out.'

She hoped nobody was walking along the lane. That drawling voice carried. 'Forget it. It's not going to happen.'

'Shame.' He was doing his light, clipped, play voice again. 'Too soon after Richard?'

'Yup.' She closed her eyes, adding silently, *and I've lost my nerve*.

'Dare you.'

'It's your turn to do a dare, not mine.'

'Name it.'

'I already have.'

'Can't do that one.'

'Do a circus trick, then,' she muttered impatiently. 'Disappear.'

He laughed. 'On Psychotto?'

'If you like.'

'If I do, will you kiss me?'

'No – but I'll cook tonight.'

'Just who's being dared here?'

As predicted, Dilly turned up at exactly the same time she had the day before. Otto exploded through the gates and almost charged straight into the replanted beds when he spotted the sparkling pond now bobbing with lilies, the little fountain trickling at one end.

Dilly had gone to a great deal of effort with her appearance, her hair braided with ribbons, mascara daubed on her long pale lashes and her pink T-shirt even tighter than the one she'd sported the day before.

Ellen was again acutely aware of her own scruffiness, still dressed in Spurs' T-shirt and her filthy denim shorts, now dry but smelling distinctly of pond.

'Wow – you got jumps!' Dilly shrieked, sending Otto exploding off in the opposite direction. 'That is *so* cool.'

Spurs – still bare-chested and every teenage girl's fantasy horseman – headed across the paddock to slot cups into the uprights he'd carried across earlier. 'Rory lent them – he says he'll help you out over the summer.'

'Really?' She almost let go of dancing Otto in her excitement. 'You saw him already?'

'Yup.' He hauled a pole into a cup to create an imposing crossbar. 'Has Otto jumped much?'

'Well, he jumps out of his skin every time a car passes.' She giggled.

'Okay.' Spurs dropped the cup a few holes. 'I'll just pop him over some small stuff to see what sort of shape he makes. Can you two hang around and be jump judges in case we knock everything flying?'

Dilly was already pulling down the stirrups and checking the girth.

'Sure.' Ellen glanced at the approaching storm, now darkening the sky by the second. 'Do you think the weather will put him off?'

'It'll rumble for at least two or three more hours before it breaks.' Spurs looked up too. 'Seven o'clock – I bet you a fiver. I grew up with the weather here. It's like everything else in this village. Takes twice as long to happen as anywhere else.' He gave her a meaningful look and went to mount Otto.

While Spurs worked the horse in, circling at trot and canter and getting him to listen, Ellen and Dilly took up sentry duty by one of the jumps.

'I wanted to come earlier – but Mum insisted on cooking a fancy lunch.'

Ellen swallowed hard at the thought of cooking and eyed Spurs for signs of circus tricks, but so far he was playing it safe.

'Godspell's back again, perching in the corner of the studio like a crow,' Dilly grumbled. 'I'm catching a train at six, and I bet she's still there. Oh, look, Spurs is going for it.'

The moment he saw the jump, Otto thrust his nose into the air and set out at a blind gallop towards it, almost falling over it because he couldn't see his feet.

'Whoa – whoa, steady!' Spurs laughed. 'Sssh. Take your time, baby.'

Something about the deep, languid, reassuring voice kicked Ellen in the solar plexus. He was right. He did turn her on like mad – even more so when he was sitting on half a ton of overexcited animal. She tried and failed to kick away the image of him sitting on nine stones of overexcited Ellen.

Over they went again, this time a little more slowly, taking a big turn afterwards before coming again with even greater control. Soon Otto was clearing the fence like an old hand, snorting out great excited breaths, joyful expression on his face.

'It can go up six inches,' Spurs called out, slowing to a walk. 'He's pretty green, but he's willing.'

Ellen knew how he felt.

'The thing you have to understand about horses,' he told Dilly, 'is that they are fundamentally frightened of everything. That's their instinct. They are creatures of flight, and millions of years of evolution can't be changed by a human in a hard hat. So you have to work with them and harness that instinct.' He looked straight at Ellen. 'Make them feel they can bloody well fly if they want to.'

Ellen felt a blush threaten to spill on to her already hot cheeks. She had a feeling he wasn't just talking about horsepower here.

'But I always think I'm going to fall off,' Dilly was saying.

'If you think that, you probably will,' he said bluntly, as he set Otto off into a canter again and called over his shoulder, 'The trick is to get straight back on again.' A moment later he had kicked out the stirrups and thrown himself out of the saddle.

'Bloody hell!' Dilly cried in alarm, as he disappeared from sight behind the snorting roan.

But Spurs had landed on his feet and was running alongside Otto, still holding the reins in one hand and reaching out to grip the pommel with the other. With barely any perceivable effort, he sprang from the ground and landed back on board, steering the horse in a wide circle. 'See? You just get straight back on.' They bounded over the jump.

Shrieking with laughter now, Dilly jumped up and down on the spot. 'Oh, please, do that again!'

He shook his head as they cantered past. 'I don't want to give this poor boy too much to think about. Let's concentrate on chilling him out a bit.' He cast another long look at Ellen over his shoulder, and his face was a picture of victory.

She couldn't help smiling back. It looked as though she was cooking supper, after all. Watching the muscles moving along his back, she gripped one of the fence wings and tried to breathe normally.

For half an hour Spurs came at the jumps from different angles and made Ellen and Dilly create different shapes with the poles, until Otto was completely relaxed about what he was doing, his pink ears pricked happily despite the storm rumbling on the horizon. 'Okay,' he told Dilly. 'You have a go now.'

'Me?'

'Yes. We'll take them down again so they're only small and you can pop over them. Give you some confidence.'

'I'm not sure.'

'Go on,' Ellen urged. 'You'll feel great – something to make you smile when the exams are getting you down.'

'Okay.' She grinned up at Spurs.

'Atta girl.' He kicked out his stirrups. 'Hold his head a sec, will you? Try not to let him move. There's something I have to do for Ellen.'

He swung one leg over as though he was going to dismount but then, with both palms down on the saddle, he locked his arms and pulled himself up into a handstand.

'Bloody hell,' Dilly gasped.

Otto snorted in alarm and stepped sideways, but to Ellen's amazement, Spurs kept his balance, moving his palms so that he was walking a circle on his hands, his arms leaping with veins at the effort involved. Finally, he gave Ellen an upside-down wink and flipped elegantly off.

'That,' she laughed, 'was amazing.'

'I used to do a hell of a lot more – but the animals were trained for years, and they were a bit calmer than our friend here.' He patted the pink rump.

Dilly was speechless with admiration, Spurs' antics fuelling her burgeoning crush.

Ellen looked away, angered by her own jealousy.

Flying as high as her heart, Dilly sailed over the jumps on Otto, shrieking and laughing for joy.

'D'you want a go?' Spurs asked Ellen, as they watched.

'Not on your nelly.'

'I wasn't offering you a ride on my nelly.'

She cast him a withering look and he grinned. 'So you liked my tricks?'

'Two tricks – I'm honoured,' she conceded a smile.

'One was for dessert,' he cocked his head. 'What did I score? Lobster bisque? Boeuf bourguignonne? Summer pudding to follow?'

'Sausage casserole.' She'd seen Richard cook it enough times. 'Then ice-cream.'

'My favourites. Shall I dress up?'

'Oh, do. I always insist upon formal attire.'

'Do I have to keep my tie on for my massage?'

'Absolutely. Tied on your nelly.'

'Do you wear one of those tight white coats with buttons that unpop when you stretch across to massage my shoulders?' he asked.

'No, I wear protective headgear and a boiler-suit.'

'I can't wait.' He turned to look at her, the silver eyes full of mischief.

Ellen guessed that, however she played it, tonight would be difficult to control.

He left with Dilly, walking alongside Otto as she hacked him back to his field. Ellen listened to Dilly chattering as they went, trying to persuade Spurs to ride Otto for her during the last few weeks of her school term.

'It would make all the difference – he's desperate for exercise. Just a couple of times a week. Mum doesn't need to know – she never checks him. I'm sure you've got some tack that fits at the manor.'

'I'd be arrested for rustling if she saw me.'

'Why? Do you have paper pants or something?'

'Ha-ha.'

Their voices trailed away companionably.

Fanning her T-shirt and leaning against the porch, Ellen tipped her head up to the hot sky and watched a cluster of storm-flies dancing around the white light casing.

'He's gorgeous,' she breathed. 'Christ, he is *so* bloody gorgeous.'

Had she been a horse, it would have been time to toss her head, fan out her tail and gallop to the hills.

'Bugger, bugger, bugger.' Ellen stood outside the closed village shop. She'd forgotten that Joel and Lily shut at lunchtime on a Sunday, instead of their usual dawn until dusk hours. Without sausages and beans, there wasn't much of a casserole. She guessed she would have to raid the Goose Cottage freezer.

She went to sit on Bevis's bench, and did not notice the caterpillars dropping on her. A fine thank you dinner this was going to be, with a storm about to break and only defrosted leftovers to eat. She was desperate for the weather to hold just a couple more hours so that they could spend the evening outside, enjoying the garden they had made over together, away from the clammy intimacy of being alone in a room. Every time she'd been in a room with Spurs – even for just a few minutes – she entered meltdown. The more she thought about the evening ahead, the more nervous she became, like the build-up to a big, bone-breaking wave for which she knew she wasn't competition-fit.

She walked back to the cottage and took a shower to help herself think, pulling on a slip dress and pinning her hair up to stay cool, then slipped her feet into clogs and clacked downstairs to examine the contents of the freezer.

Two ice trays and the blue cooler bottles from a chill-box greeted her. Jennifer Jamieson had cleared her freezer efficiently, switching it to minimum and keeping it running to stop mould building up. Ellen slammed the door and went to peer into the larder. It was almost empty, apart from her one remaining can of baked beans and some old Kilner jars of rices, pulses and pickles, which were more for ornament than consumption.

The fridge housed nothing more than what was left of the strawberries, and the cheese – both rather battered after being used as missiles. There wasn't even any bread because Snorkel had stolen it while the pond fight was going on.

'Bugger.' Ellen sat down at the kitchen table and bit her knuckles fretfully, wondering if the Duck Upstream did takeouts. Then she remembered the takeaway containers that had greeted her arrival at Goose Cottage.

She looked up at the kitchen clock. If she drove like the clappers, she might just make it.

The Peking Garden in Market Addington was extremely swift in filling two white plastic bags with silver trays and handing them over to Ellen, who bolted next door to the off-licence for beer. But despite her speed Spurs was waiting in the garden when she turned the jeep into the gates, sitting on his favourite bench with his head bowed. Dressed in a crisp white shirt and suede jeans, he looked very different from the scruffy, laughing horseman who had left earlier. Shoulders hunched and one heel tapping impatiently, he looked more like a drug-runner waiting for the drop.

He didn't look up when Ellen cut the engine. He had a box of matches in his hands, which he was striking randomly.

'What do you think you're doing?' She leaped out in a panic, imagining the tinder-dry thatch going up in a roar of flame and smoke.

'I thought you'd chickened out.' He narrowed his eyes as he looked up at her, the cigarette that he had been trying to light dropping from his lips

'No, I went out for chicken.' She took a step back, trying to read his expression. Gone was the easy, teasing warmth of earlier. His cheeks were pinched and the silver gaze suspicious.

He looked up as a rumble of thunder boomed through the sky. 'If it rains, I'll never get the torches lit.' He stood up, rattling the matches.

'What torches?'

'You said you wanted to eat outside.' He beckoned her towards the back of the house. 'We'd better hurry. The storm's not far off breaking. We can watch it.' He had arranged the garden torches to form an avenue leading to the rear terrace, and in a circle round it. Only two or three were lit, smoky flames rippling like yellow ensigns. The table and chairs, now washed down and spotless, were arranged under the clematis awning, looking out over the lawn and paddock to the village roofs. More candles – nightlights that he must have brought from the manor – were licking hot little flames in every windblown direction on the walls and railings, and in the centre of the table. It was still far from dusk, but the stormclouds made it dark as an eclipse and the little flames lit up the magical bower.

'These torches are a bitch to get going.' Spurs lit his cigarette from one. 'I was taking a break just now. Didn't think it was worth it if you really had done a bunk with the sausage casserole.'

Ellen bit an embarrassed smile from her lips. 'Sorry,' she turned to him, 'I thought—'

'You thought I was going to burn your parents' cottage down because you'd blown me out?' he suggested.

She looked away, turning red because, put like that, it sounded very silly indeed. 'I haven't blown you out.'

'No,' he smiled, 'and I really don't huff and puff and blow houses down any more.' He sounded like a grown-up teasing a child.

And that, Ellen realised, was exactly how she felt – young, vulnerable and scared stiff. However hard she tried to shake them, her nerves were starting to get to her. 'The wind's doing a pretty good job of blowing everything down – there are branches all over the lanes,' she prattled, tying Snorkel's lunge line to one of the wooden uprights before heading back to the car for the takeout.

'Coward,' he said, over her shoulder, as she pulled out the bags, making her jump because she hadn't heard him following. 'You said you were going to cook.'

'I decided not to kill you quite yet.' She fumbled for the off-licence bags, which had fallen off the seat. 'I have two more wishes to be granted, after all.'

'Good point. You look beautiful, by the way.'

'What?' She almost dropped a bag of prawn crackers and sauces, as she spun round to find his face far too close to hers, those disturbing eyes as stormy and electrically charged as the sky overhead.

'You look beautiful – you *are* beautiful. I should have said it before.'

Ellen couldn't tear her eyes from his, reading the desire in them with hopeless excitement. The bangs and whistles all started going off at once in her body, along with a warning siren in her head. 'We'd better eat this before it gets cold.' She handed him a bag and scuttled towards the terrace, heart pounding.

'Don't you want to put it on plates?'

'It'll be fine like this. I picked up some chopsticks. We've got everything we need.'

'Have you locked yourself out again or something?'

'I prefer to stay outside.'

'If I'd known you were that keen, I'd have brought a tent round for us to camp in the garden.' He went to light a few more torches.

'My mother could get Gladys to bring us out Marmite sandwiches and Bovril.'

Her childishness obviously irritated him. The tomboyish flirt Spurs had got dirty with all weekend was showing her flipside. Knowing how he wanted the evening to pan out made Ellen feel fifteen again, those pre-Richard years when being adult meant driving *Miami Vice* cars, having Jackie Collins sex every night and tall, dark strangers giving you Milk Tray.

A rumble of thunder made Spurs look up at the menacing sky. 'Ever made love in a storm?'

'Not recently,' she mumbled.

'A great uncle of mine was struck by lightning while screwing his mistress against an oak tree on the ridge. Killed them both.' His cold, angry laugh made Ellen jump.

Almost hyperventilating with nerves, she scattered the foil containers randomly on the table and took a seat at the far end, deliberately placing herself between two sturdy plastic legs. I can, and I will stop this happening, she told herself. This is just a friendly thank-you meal, nothing more, however much spin he tries to add to it.

'Did you agree to ride Dilly's horse while she's back at school?' she asked chattily, determined to set the tone.

'I said I'd think about it.' He cursed under his breath as another match blew out the second he struck it. 'Depends how busy I am.'

'What do you do during the week?'

He looked up at her. 'I'm a professional prodigal son.'

'Meaning?'

'I prod a gal here, and prod a gal there.'

'And you think you're going to prod me tonight?'

'No. I don't think that.' His eyes burned into hers.

Ellen looked away. If her flipside was stupid, schoolgirl gaucheness, his was far more dangerous and threatening. She'd been so obsessed with her own nerves that she hadn't noticed how tense he was, and getting more so by the minute.

'Tuck in!' she offered brightly, pulling the lids off the foil dishes.

He was still trying to light the torches, battling to keep a match alight in the wind, his own fuse almost burnt through. 'What's the hurry?'

A great rip of thunder split the sky, followed seconds later by forked lightning diving out from a cloud above the church. The first torch flared, its great yellow flame writhing in the wind. Spurs pulled it from the ground like a knight with a medieval sconce and set about igniting the others with it.

By the time he'd enclosed the terrace in a fiery circle, the food was cold and the beer bottles Ellen had opened dripped with condensation, their labels sliding from their green shoulders.

'Cheers.' He stepped back on to the terrace and lifted one.

'To wishes coming true.' Ellen lifted hers, looking at his face anxiously.

Another thunder roar rippled through the sky. Spurs' silver eyes gleamed. 'Why d'you have to make it so difficult?' he asked quietly.

'My wish?'

'No. That was the easy part.'

'And this is the Chinesy part,' she joked feebly, not at all certain how to read his intense expression. 'Sit down and eat.'

She looked at the trays of food and knew for certain that she wouldn't be able to eat a single grain of rice.

Spurs didn't sit down. He paced between the torches then faced her. 'I have a confession to make,' he blurted. 'On Friday night – at the restaurant. I . . . I – oh, fuck.' He laughed, the wind tossing his hair every way and flattening the white shirt against his chest. 'I agreed to something so fucking awful.'

Ellen felt her blood freeze. Every bad word she'd heard about him echoed in her head – violence, drugs, gangland, danger, merciless.

The torches were roaring up in the wind, sending great sparks across the lawn and threatening to set light to the clematis. By contrast most of the tea-lights had blown out as the sky blackened, ready to unleash the downpour.

'I have to tell someone – no, I have to tell you.' He wrapped his arms round himself and stood facing the wind, so close to the torches that Ellen thought he'd shoot up in flames. 'I don't know what the hell to do.'

'What did you agree to?'

He pressed his hand to his mouth and stared at the stormclouds, the torch flames turning his eyes from silver to molten gold.

Ellen stood up cautiously and moved behind him. 'What, Spurs?'

He dipped his head and turned to her, his face in shadow, half covered with his hair. 'Do you love me?'

'A bit.'

His lip curled for a second and he reached out a hand for hers.

The moment their fingers connected, Ellen lost all sense of time and place.

Had another bolt of lightning shot from the sky and delivered a direct hit she couldn't have been more charged. It literally rocked her on her toes, propelling her forward and against Spurs, as if they were two magnets slamming together, skin against skin, muscle against muscle, lip against lip. It wasn't a kiss. It was too angry and too urgent.

'Ellen!' a voice called excitedly. 'Dilly's just left and I have a *huge* bottle of vino and a joint for us to guzzle while we watch the storm. Gosh – those torches are wonderful!'

Ellen broke away, sending a chair flying. Spurs gripped her hand tightly. 'Get rid of her,' he breathed, stepping back into the shadows.

'Hang on – I'm coming round.' Pheely's voice was approaching fast. 'I have been *desperate* to talk to you all weekend about lovely Lloyd – I saw his car still parked here in the early hours of Saturday, you naughty minx. Didn't I say you'd be perfect together?'

Ellen turned to Spurs in a panic, but he had already slipped between the torches and on to the lawn.

The silver eyes flashed for a second and then he was gone, darting through the gap in the hedge and across Hunter's fields faster than a hare. By the time Pheely rounded the corner of the cottage with her bottle of wine, he'd disappeared.

'Wow! What a feast! Can I pick? I am *livid* with Daffodil. You will never *guess* who she's asked to ride her horse . . .'

7

Ellen didn't see Spurs for days. She thought about him obsessively on long walks with Snorkel, searching the village and hills for Fins while her head searched for equally elusive answers. But both her black and white cat and her black-souled friend were lying low, and her head remained hopelessly muddled.

She wasn't sure whether to be angry with Spurs for running away before she could explain that Pheely had got the wrong end of the stick, angry with Pheely for interrupting before Spurs could tell her what he had agreed to do, or angry with herself for letting him go.

In the end she settled for being angry with Fins for not coming home when the storm broke as she'd expected him to. He hated rain. She needed to know that he was safe.

After the storm that had raged through the Lodes Valley on Sunday night, pulling branches from trees and tiles from roofs, the week was blustery and overcast. Bad-tempered clouds moved moodily over the hills, rushing from Morrell to Maddington to Ibcote to soak the tourists as they moved between antiques and collectors' fairs at the three towns' corn-markets. The Oddlode pensioners congregated by the post-office counter, shaking out Rain Mates, patting perms and grumbling that it was horribly wet and windy, just as they had grumbled that it was horribly hot and humid the week before. To Joel and Lily's ongoing fascination, Ellen bought an increasing array of tinned fish, fresh smoked salmon, cheeses and hams. They thought she had really got her appetite back, but they were all left in Fins' bowl by the bootroom window to lure him in. Several local rats and a fox took advantage, but there was no sign of free-agent Fins. Nor was there any sign of her estate agent.

Lloyd Fenniweather was 'out of the office' every time Ellen

called to check on progress with the second Goose Cottage marketing wave; nor did he respond to her messages. No for-sale sign appeared, all the advertising deadlines came and went, and there seemed to be no sign of new brochures or – most importantly – viewings.

'I think you should let me appoint another agent,' Ellen told her father, when he called to see how she was. 'Seaton's have lost interest, and this is the perfect time to sell. Three houses have sold in the village in the last month and they're far less attractive than the Goose. I've checked out which agents they used.' No need to mention that two of them had sold through Seaton's – the other through a rival agency.

'Let your mother and me talk about it, duckling,' was all Theo could promise, in his cider-and-haymaking Somerset brogue. Jennifer, he explained, was in a bad mood, having sent him out for milk and eggs only to find him bearing a goat and half a dozen laying hens when he returned. 'I've always wanted livestock. I loved the idea of having geese at Goose Cottage, but your mother wouldn't tolerate it, said they'd ruin the garden. How is the garden, by the way?'

'Great. Lots of action.'

'Always at its best at the end of May. Reg keeping everything from running riot?'

'I – er – I don't really think you need him and Dot any more. I can do everything.'

'Are you sure?'

'Absolutely. It's not as though I've anything else to do and it saves you the expense.'

'Oh, you are a duck, trying to stop the aged parents ending up in penury. I'll call them and let them know.'

'No need – I've already had a word, sown the, er, seed.'

'Were the Wycks okay about it?'

'They took it on the chin.'

'They're a stoic old pair.'

'Aren't they? Dad . . .' Ellen chewed her lip. 'How are you feeling – I mean, your health? How is it?'

'Rude, just as it's rude of you to ask.'

'Sorry.'

'No, no need. I know you worry, duckling, but it's fine. I'm feeling great.'

'Well, you take care of yourself.' She tried not to think about Hell's Bells and the terrible secret that Spurs wasn't supposed to tell a soul. Her father, she was certain, would tell her if something was wrong.

'I will. I've got your mother to look after – and Gladys Knight and the Pips.'

'Who?'

'The goat and the hens.'

'You don't want a collie to round them up and a cat to keep the rats at bay, do you? You can rename them Tina and Ike.'

He gave a laugh as sweet as clotted cream. 'I don't think I'd get that one past your mother – more chance with a new estate agent. You really sure Seaton's aren't up to the job?'

'Absolutely.'

Ellen tried Lloyd's mobile when she'd finished speaking to her father, and was again diverted to his voicemail. She shuddered at the fawning, super-smooth outgoing message that promised to 'catch you later'. She suspected it wasn't the only thing people caught from the over-friendly agent.

'You have until tomorrow to return this call or you and your agency are fired,' she fumed, then added 'and thanks for dinner on Friday. It was food for thought.'

She dug out an old photograph of Fins, looking thinner but no less despotic, stuck it to a piece of A4 and wrote out a 'Missing' notice, detailing his gigantic proportions and advising the public not to approach him, then took it to the post-office stores to photocopy.

'Aw, your sweet little pussy has slipped away, honey?' Lily Lubowski cooed over it as she bore it off behind the counter to the Xerox. With her mad peroxide hair and love of frills, she was disturbingly like Mrs Slocombe from *Are You Being Served?*

but with what Theo called a 'translangtic' accent – three parts California waves to one part estuary sludge.

'Yes, I thought he'd be back by now, but he's still missing.' Ellen gathered an armful of local papers in case, by a miracle, Lloyd had followed her instructions and run adverts for the cottage.

'Is he neutered?' Lily asked.

What was it with this village and domestic animals' sexual capabilities, Ellen wondered.

'Only my Abyssinian is going through her . . . *girl thing*,' Lily whispered, so as not to be overheard by her husband at the till, 'and I'd hate her to get raped.'

'Fins isn't a rapist,' Ellen assured her. 'He's gay.'

'Really?' Lily's plucked eyebrows shot up. 'When did you find out?'

'He came out of the closet about a year ago.' Ellen cast a guilty look at Joel too, but he was being chatted up by the Oddlode Pensioners Collective, and wasn't listening.

'Oh, my. How amazing. Have you taken him to a pet therapist?'

'No, but he never misses an episode of *Animal Hospital*. He adores Rolf.'

'How cute! You must miss him so. Ten copies okay for you?'

'Great.'

The door pinged and Glad Tidings bustled in. She trotted straight up to the posse beside the till with a self-important air. 'You'll *never* guess what young Jasper's done now,' she panted, having clearly run all the way from the manor to tell the news. 'It's nothing short of heinous.'

'What?' Her audience surged around her. 'Do tell.'

'He's persuaded that no-good cousin of his to lend him a horse to race the Devil's Marsh. Ely's accepted the entry – says he won't stand in the lad's way. Probably hopes he'll go and kill himself proper this time.'

'No!' There was a chorus of shocked gasps.

'After what happened and everything.' Gladys clutched her

quilted bosom disapprovingly. 'He has no shame. Her ladyship is beside herself.'

'Can't she stop him?'

'Handsome is as handsome does in her eyes – always has been,' Gladys clucked. 'Besides, she can't risk him running off again, not with her wanting to marry him off.'

'You sure that's why he's back, Glad?'

'Oh, yes, dear. Lady Belling has plans for that young man. We've had the vicar to dine every month because she wants a church wedding, and God's still having a spot of bother forgiving Spurs all them misdemeanours, it seems, especially the ones involving the east transept. I told her a nice ceremony in a marquee at Eastlode Park is just as good. They do a very good fork buffet, I hear.'

Ellen found herself clutching the post-office counter.

'Are you saying she's gotten someone to take him on?' Joel chuckled. 'From what I hear, he'll be one helluva handful to take in marriage.'

'Some fool flibbertigibbet with eyes on that house, I'll fathom.' She sniffed, suddenly catching sight of Ellen and giving her a beady look that made it clear her spies had caught all the weekend action in Goose Cottage. 'She'll have to be a good breeder, though, to get rid of that bad blood. Shame her ladyship preferred breeding them darned horses. If Jasper had a brother, the Surgeon could disinherit him and favour another but, as it is, he's stuck with that good-for-nothing. I just hope they've found a nice young brood mare for him.'

'She'll need a bob or two and all, I reckon,' laughed one of the pensioners. 'Rumour has it the Surgeon ain't got as much as he once had.'

'Where did you hear that?' Gladys demanded defensively.

'Dot Wyck told me he borrowed a tenner off Reg in the bookie's last week. His credit card had got rejected, she says.'

'Don't believe anything that sister of mine says,' Gladys snapped. 'She always was a liar. She taught young Jasper everything he knows.'

*　　　*　　　*

'Didn't you know Gladys and Dot are sisters?' Pheely laughed when a shocked Ellen told her about the overheard conversation later while patrolling the village on a dog-walking and postering campaign. 'They're twins, but they're barely on speaking terms. Not only did Gladys get *the* plum job in the village, working at the manor while her sister has to clean up after the rabble, but she married a Gates, and Dot married a Wyck. It's like Aclima and Jumella.'

'Who?'

'Cain and Abel's twins – married their own brothers,' Pheely explained in an oddly good-girl voice, as though reciting her times tables.

Ellen, who had patiently endured endless scripture with her church-going mother, didn't remember them. 'Are you sure?'

'Oh, yes. Bear in mind that Adam and Eve didn't have an awful lot of eligible bachelors around to choose from – and neither does any Oddlode parent trying to palm off a brace of girls.' She let out a delighted cackle.

'What about a devoted mother trying to palm off her black sheep of a son?' Ellen tried to steer the conversation back on track. She had only mentioned Gladys's outburst because she was telling Pheely the far more disturbing news that Spurs was on the marriage market.

But Pheely was eager to impart one of her local history lessons – something akin to a potted *Dynasty* plot set against a bucolic backdrop.

'Granville Gates and Reg Wyck aren't *officially* brothers, of course,' she murmured, 'but local legend firmly hints at bad old Constantine Senior squiring both their poor mothers. If that's so then they're not members of the rival Oddlode clans at all – they're actually Hell's Bells' half-brothers. Oh, it gets even more complicated.' She laughed at Ellen's boggling eyes. 'You have no *idea* how entangled the family trees are around here. They make Ely Gates's orchard look like bonsai. There's more mixed blood than a field hospital.'

Ellen was already completely lost. 'So is Gladys's husband . . .'

'Granville,' Pheely helped her out.

'Is he one of Ely's brothers?' She paused by a lamp-post to Sellotape up a 'missing' sign.

'Granville? No, he's an uncle. He used to be the manor groundsman, but he was dismissed when he went mad.'

'Mad?'

'Yes – good old-fashioned mad. There's no delicate mental-health descriptions applied around here, and the poor bastard has probably never been referred to a psychiatrist in his life. He's just mad. I do *so* envy him the freedom.' She sighed.

'He's still alive?'

'Very much so. He lives in an old railway carriage in the cutting by Eastlode Heath. Glad Tidings still takes him his supper every evening after she's finished work – carries it across the fields with a tea-towel wrapped around the pot and delivers it to the door before going home to her tithe cottage. Come hail or storm, she does her meals-on-heels run – unless the Bellings are entertaining, in which case she leaves it at the edge of the orchard to save time, and mad Granville collects it.'

'Does he ever come into the village?' Not for the first time Ellen suspected her of embellishing the truth, however delectably.

'Not often, as far as I know. He train-spots – I'm not making it up,' she said, as Ellen looked sceptical. 'He sits in his carriage and watches the trains go by although, God knows, after ten years, you'd think he'd get bored of the regular Paddington to Hereford service and take a day trip to Clapham Junction or Crewe.'

'What made him go mad?'

'No one knows. It was around the time Spurs left.' She gave Ellen a weighty look, practically mowing her down with those huge green eyes.

Ellen bit the tape from the reel and fastened the last corner of the poster. At last they had got to the point. The butterfly had landed.

'I can't see Hell's Bells finding him a suitable wife,' Pheely opined. 'None of the grander families around here would touch him, and she's a frightful snob about marrying "down".'

'Won't Spurs have any say in the matter?'

'I doubt it. Isabel's class are of the opinion that you can fuck whomsoever you like – discreetly – but you marry the person you are told to.'

'I can't see Spurs buying it.'

'He can always bugger off again. Maybe he already has. Have you seen him yet?' she nosed.

Ellen shook her head.

'Good.' Pheely had only heard edited highlights of Ellen's weekend in the garden with Spurs, but it was enough to sign her new friend's death warrant as far as she was concerned.

'Has he ridden Otto yet?' Ellen couldn't resist asking.

'If he has, he's done it bareback. I've locked the saddle in the woodshed.'

He had a bare back before, Ellen thought wistfully, remembering the muscles moving beneath the tanned, freckled skin.

'I'm so glad I turned up to rescue you that night.' Pheely kept pace as they moved on to another lamp-post. 'God knows what would have happened otherwise.'

I'd have found out what Spurs is hiding, Ellen thought wretchedly. We'd have carried on kissing. And I wouldn't have lost his trust.

Yet she couldn't feel angry with Pheely: she valued her company and good humour too much to blame her. If anyone was to blame, she knew that she was wearing her skin. She had thought about calling Spurs, but she had no number and was too much of a coward to turn up at the manor in person, uncertain of her reception. She was far more certain of Pheely, who always greeted her with a smile as warm as a hearth and stories of village births, marriages and deaths.

They made their way across the green, deserted today beneath the grey, threatening skies. Ellen gave Bevis's bench a friendly nod as they passed it, then called the dogs away from eyeing up the nervous ducks on the pond before walking under the row of horse-chestnuts and crossing towards Manor Lane.

'The mill-race has been throwing itself about like a white-water run since the storm.' Pheely went to take a look at the violent swirling beneath the bridge. 'One day it's going to sweep all those old vans and cars right into Ely's orchard.'

'Who lives in the house?' Ellen studied the shabby old mill, its grandeur slipping away a stone tile at a time, like a lizard with alopecia hunching its scaly shoulders as it clung to the banks of the swirling stream. Its forecourt was filled with an extraordinary collection of ancient cars and rusting farming machinery, as it had been for as long as Ellen remembered. One Land Rover had been up on bricks for so long that it was overgrown with ivy, like one of Norman Gently's sculptures.

'Ely's younger brother Noah inherited it from Pa Gates's estate.' Pheely continued her lesson in the Gates family tree. 'This is known as Noah's Car Park – although I prefer to think of it as Mills and Baboon. Noah is *very* unreconstructed, rather like his house.' She eyed the grubby windows for signs of life. 'Ely's dying to get his hands on the building to develop it, but Noah refuses to budge. Sometimes you see him leaning out of his attics, scanning the horizon for a dove with an olive branch, poor sod. Ely can make it very difficult for somebody if he wants to buy them out.'

'Like you?' Ellen asked, thinking about the much-envied beauty of the Lodge.

'I wasn't thinking of me.' She glanced at Ellen pointedly then moved on and yelled for Hamlet, who had cornered a cat across the road in the Lodes Inn car park.

'Do you know something I don't?' Ellen hastily checked that the cat wasn't Fins then hopped after her.

'Only through deduction.' Pheely was pulling clematis flowers from stone walls to thread through her curls. 'You say Ely is behind the one and only – and very silly – offer on the cottage. Nobody else seems remotely interested, despite its obvious charms. QED, he's putting the kibosh on any other deal. Take it from one who knows, you can't rely on sly Ely. He has money in his pocket and God on his side. The whole village is under his spell. And some are under his Godspell – mostly teenage boys.' She giggled wickedly, adding a fat red rose from an immaculate front garden to her Ophelia tiara.

'How's the bust going?' Ellen sensed mutiny.

'Don't ask.' Pheely marched along Manor Lane, then proceeded to tell Ellen all about it. 'That child is so unpleasant, these days. We've had three sittings so far, and she just plugs herself into that ratty-tatty impersonal stereo and sits staring into space. I shall immortalise her with wire coming out of her ears, whatever Ely says. It's her only distinctive feature. In fact, I may try something a little abstract to express the solitude of stereo,' she mused thoughtfully, as they paused by a dog-poop bin to attach a poster above it.

Ellen looked at her fifth Sellotaped photostat of Fins, with his furious face and puffed-up black and white chest. He looked like a waiter who had been told that the steak was overdone.

Suddenly it hit her that he might have gone for ever, that he might not return when he was hungry and cold and wet. Because he would be all three right now, and he still hadn't come back to her. Like Spurs, she thought illogically. He was like a feral cat – independent, wilful, prone to disappearing acts and unwilling to make friends.

'She's such a curious child.' Pheely was still venting her spleen about Godspell. 'Always has been terribly backward. Never mixes with others her age, and still thinks she'll be a pop star. She was bearable when she was younger – cripplingly shy, of course, and totally spoiled, but sweet enough, and great chums with Dilly. Now she's withdrawn into herself, become furtive and bad-mannered. I'm surprised Ely can't see that the apple of his eye has gone sour.' She glanced across at the gnarled old orchard. 'But he always was blind where his children were concerned.'

'Dilly said that the two of them were no longer friends.' Ellen pocketed the Sellotape, trying to drag her mind back on topic.

'Yes, they both shared the pony-mad thing at one time, but

Godspell lost interest.' Pheely led the way past Cider Lane, with its peeling board advertising the antiquarian bookshop that never opened and Prudence Hornton's failing gallery. 'She was never very brave, and her father persuaded her to ride the Devil's Marsh race last year – no Gates has ever taken part, and child Enoch is allergic to horses, so Godspell was to champion the wonder family. But she was so frightened, she fell off at the start and humiliated Ely, who had his camcorder trained and a vast bet laid. Godspell hasn't been on a horse since, and rather let us down because she was supposed to ride Otto during term-time.'

'What exactly is the Devil's Marsh race?' Ellen asked, distractedly Sellotaping Fins' poster upside down on a silver birch.

'Oh, don't mention that Godawful cavalry charge.' Pheely shuddered, forgetting that she was the one who'd brought it up. 'Dilly's got it into her head that she should take part this year – probably as one in the eye to Godspell. I know there are always plenty of kids on fat ponies and housewives on cobs bringing up the rear, but she can be *so* reckless.'

'Is it like a gymkhana race?' Ellen persisted.

Pheely laughed. 'Not quite. Come and look.' She beckoned Ellen from the lane into Manor End, which led past Ely's beautiful farm to his less aesthetic money-spinners. Casting furtive looks up at the glossy, Bible-black sash-windows, they passed the tall, wisteria-covered Queen Anne house and went on towards the trout farm, hooking a stealthy left through a gate marked 'Private', which was opposite the back entrance to the little industrial estate. Some way along the overgrown farm track that wrapped their calves with wet nettles and grasses, they reached a rickety wooden footbridge across the river Odd. On its far side was a huge flat water-meadow, which stretched from the railway line on the right across acres of wildly tufted terrain to a wooded coppice far to the left, which hid it from the Goose End bridleway and prying ramblers' eyes. Pimpled with clumps of sedge and rush, and dusted with marsh marigold, ragged robin, yellow iris and cuckoo-flowers, it stretched like a ravishing beaded velvet hem beneath the uniform rape and corn in the hills above.

'Beautiful, isn't it?' Pheely breathed. 'Unchanged for centuries because it can't be farmed – it's only dry for three months a year. The rest of the time you could drown crossing it. Ely's father spent years trying to drain it, but it just sucked up the ditches and spread itself back out like crème caramel when you draw lines through it with your spoon.

'There's been a horse race across Devil's Marsh for as long as anyone can remember,' she went on. 'The Romanies held it every year before the big summer horse fair in Morrell – they'd tether their horses on the land here, get tanked up on Manor Farm cider and gallop all over the place causing havoc. Somebody once told me they called it the dragonfly race because there are hundreds here and it takes a fast horse to catch one – the gypsy who caught the most got the highest price for his horse. I hope it's true. It was a wonderful sight, by all accounts, and the local daredevils would join in – from dashing Constantine sons on hunters to farmhands on shires. But Ely's father put a stop to it when he bought the farm from the Constantines and banned the gypsies from his land.

'When Ely inherited the farm, he started holding his ridiculously show-off garden party during Ascot week.' She scooped up a handful of blossom and scattered it into the river, playing her own dreamy game of Pooh Sticks on the bridge, 'and he decided to resurrect the race to rival the action on the royal turf, at first inviting a very select group of riders, who all wore proper silks and tried to horsewhip each other into the river when they learned the prize was a thousand pounds.'

'A grand?' Ellen whistled, half tempted to enter herself. That would pay her way into a few nice hotels on her world tour.

'Oh, yes.' Pheely gave Ellen a wise look. 'Ely doesn't think a competition is worth running without a decent pot – and his parties are always *very* lavish. He even had a gold-plated cup made, *so* ostentatious, like a Formula One trophy. That was about fifteen years ago, and it's been going ever since, attracting more and more riders every year. It's more chaotic now than it was when the gypsies held it, I imagine. Someone always gets hurt.'

Ellen remembered Dilly saying that somebody had been killed

one year, but before she could mention it her mobile rang in her pocket. She grabbed it hurriedly, hoping the feckless Lloyd was getting back to her at last. But it was her father, with an even more satisfying result. 'Your mother agrees that you can appoint another agent, duckling,' he told her. 'Just get them to fax us through the details. They'll have to work fast, mind you.'

Ellen couldn't wait to get on the case.

Seaton's great rival, Fox-Day's, were only too happy to give a valuation that afternoon. To Ellen's amazement, they suggested increasing the asking price. 'The property market has boomed in the last six months,' explained Poppy, the eager agent. 'I really think we can sell this in no time – I have clients I can bring round straight away. It's a smashing little cottage.'

Telephone calls and faxes flew back and forth between the Costa Verde and Morrell on the Moor that afternoon, until everyone was satisfied that Goose Cottage was now the new gem on Fox-Day's books and Seaton's were history. Theo Jamieson made the call personally to Lloyd to break the news.

Within an hour Lloyd was on Ellen's doorstep, abandoning his Merc at an angle across the lane, the engine still running and Kylie chirruping from the stereo.

'You can't do this!' he blurted, when she opened the door.

No longer lifestyle-advert slick, he looked as though he'd leaned down to adjust the volume on his Blaupunkt car stereo and found his hair sucked into an air vent. The treacle-coloured floppy fringe was on end, his tie was skewiff and he'd spilled coffee down his shirt. 'I thought we had an understanding,' he wailed.

'That you would pull your finger out to try to sell this cottage, yes,' Ellen agreed, 'and you haven't even started.'

'You've hardly given me five minutes!'

'You had seven days to get things moving. You blew it.'

'This is completely unreasonable. Let me come in and talk about it, at least.'

He tried to shoulder his way past her, but Ellen stood her ground. 'Why haven't you returned my calls?'

Suddenly that big white smile sprang up, calming the chaos running across his handsome face. 'Is that what this is all about?

She stared at him, wondering what she had ever found attractive about him. His eyes were too close together, his thick hair showed a decidedly threadbare patch at the crown, and the square chin, now that she looked at it again, was distinctly Jimmy Hill. 'I'm sorry, Lloyd, but my parents aren't going to change their minds. You've had your chance.'

'You don't understand.' His eyes darted over both his shoulders, as though they were being watched, and he dropped his voice to a whisper, the pseudo-accent long gone. 'You can't do this to me. I'll lose my job.'

'You should have thought of that before. I'm not surprised your job's on the line if the dotted ones on all the sales contracts you handle are as blank as this one.'

'Ely Gates's offer is still on the table,' he rallied, thrusting out the huge square chin.

Ellen took a step back into the porch and blinked as it suddenly hit home. 'He bribed you, didn't he?'

Lloyd looked shiftly, his chin swinging backwards and forwards like a great bulldozer bucket.

Ellen realised what Pheely had been hinting at, and could have hit herself for not seeing it earlier. 'He bribed you to make sure nobody else wanted Goose Cottage so that he could get it cheap, didn't he? It was his mother's favourite cottage – a sentimental addition to his property empire, just so long as he gets it at a bargain price. He probably bribed the Wyckses too.'

'He's my uncle,' Lloyd confessed, his big chin hanging loose as he gave up the show. 'I had no choice. He's bailed Mum and Dad out loads of times. We owe him. If he doesn't get this place, you have no idea how bad things could get for us.'

'He can have it,' Ellen said simply. 'He just has to pay the asking price.'

'He won't do that.'

'He can afford it.'

'His pride can't.' Lloyd sounded defensive. 'He doesn't like outsiders to profit from the village.'

'My parents lived here for over a decade.'

'My mother's family has lived here for twenty generations.'

'Then we have nothing more to say.'

'Please!' he begged. 'For my sake – I thought you liked me. We kissed.'

'That was a mistake.' Ellen looked away guiltily. Then she took a deep breath. 'You *are* a nice guy, Lloyd – or you could be. You just have to start thinking for yourself. You're bright enough and good enough at your job to rise above Ely and twenty generations of bigotry. You have to break free from your family some time.'

'You don't understand life around here!' he exploded. 'If you'd got to know me a bit better, you would. We have so much in common, Ellen. I think we're made for one another. I think—'

They both turned to the lane as a clatter of hooves heralded a bitter laugh. 'Before you set about making the earth move, would you mind moving your bloody car?'

Spurs was riding Otto, his long legs wrapped around the speckled pink back with no saddle for support or balance as Otto spun round, boggling at the badly parked Merc and its blaring stereo. Yet Spurs barely moved a muscle as he sat out the hysteria and settled the horse, no longer laughing, his huge eyes pouring molten-silver scorn on to Ellen and Lloyd.

'Bloody gypsies!' Lloyd fumed, marching up to face Spurs over the hedge. 'We're not buying anything, *okay*?' he snapped, then turned back to Ellen. 'Shall we go inside?'

Ellen was staring at Spurs, her heart crashing. He hadn't shaved in days, and the dark stubble made him look more wild and beautiful than ever. His faded red T-shirt was ripped at the shoulder so that one brown bicep showed through, and his jeans were coated in dust, as though he'd been sleeping in a barn.

'Shall we go inside, Ellen?' Lloyd repeated anxiously, not liking the way Spurs was reining back the big horse.

'Piss off,' she snapped.

'Lovers' tiff?' Spurs asked nastily, glaring at her. He looked murderous.

Before she could answer, he and Otto had clattered away towards the bridlepath.

Kylie called after him, entreating him to confide in her.

Ignoring Lloyd, Ellen watched the distant path until she saw a pink streak thundering along it, heading for Broken Back Wood.

'Go home, Lloyd,' she said eventually, and turned to go into the house. 'You're fired.'

'You bitch!' he howled after her. 'I hope your pain-in-the-arse parents get a pittance for this naff, dingy little rat hole. And I hope their cock-tease daughter gets—' suddenly his tirade was interrupted by an even louder rant.

'Move this bleedin' contraption afore we drive right into the bugger!' screamed a hoarse voice.

Ellen turned at the door to see Dot Wyck leaning out of the cab of a familiar red pick-up that had pulled up beyond Lloyd's Merc, engine revving. At its wheel, Saul glowered at Ellen and Lloyd through a dusty, fly-flecked windscreen.

'You think you own this village, doncha?' Dot yelled at Ellen, her face turning as red as her grandson's Arsenal shirt. 'You and your flash boyfriend!'

Gulping nervously, his big caramel eyes blinking as they took in Fluffy the sabre-toothed dog mutant slavering ferociously from the back of the pick-up, Lloyd bolted towards his car.

Ellen watched him go, momentarily grateful to the Wycks for bringing an end to an unpleasant encounter. But then her heart sank as Dot Wyck took advantage of Lloyd's clumsy manoeuvring to hurl a few more insults for good measure.

'People like you don't deserve to live round here, you stuck-up cow!' she pointed a finger. 'You go round acting all high and mighty, taking away our livelihoods. You don't care if the likes of me and Reg starve just so long as you get what you want.'

Ellen marched out onto the lane, temples throbbing. 'Please don't shout.' She stopped a safe distance from Fluffy's high-rise hackles. 'I thought we'd been through all this.' At that moment, Saul leaned on the horn to hurry Lloyd along.

'You ain't no better than us!' Dot carried on shouting above the horn. 'Everybody knows you've been putting it about like a tart already. Your boyfriend know you been knocking round with Spurs Belling?' she jerked her head towards the Merc, which was now executing a twenty-five point turn as Lloyd crunched the gears in fright.

'That is none of your business,' Ellen fumed, refusing to fuel the argument by defending herself.

But Dot seemed to be enjoying herself now, slanging matches clearly a recreational pastime. 'I ain't having a cheap tart bad-mouthing my family!'

'I haven't bad-mouthed your family,' Ellen sighed as Saul's horn-leaning stopped and Lloyd finally drove away in a series of panic-stricken kangaroo-hops.

'Not what we heard.' Dot didn't bother dropping the volume. 'You bin calling us lazy Pikies and goodfornothing inbreds and all sorts, ain't she Saul?'

The blue eyes flashed beside her and Saul nodded, casting Ellen a look that could have frozen hell and carved it into an ice sculpture of Medusa. Dot's vitriol held no fear, but one look from her broken-toothed grandson made Ellen step back in alarm. Something about Saul was deadly. Then she spotted a gun case in the back with Fluffy and backed away further.

'Whoever told you that was lying,' she spluttered. 'I've said nothing about you.'

Dot dropped her voice to a threatening growl, only just audible above Fluffy's snarling. 'I think we know who the liar is round here. Sounds like you been lying all the time lately. Most of all, lying with Belling, you little fool.' She cackled, tugging at the sleeve of Saul's red football shirt and telling him to drive on.

As the pick-up rattled away, Ellen closed her eyes and thought of Spurs galloping up into the hills on Otto, still seething with misunderstanding about Lloyd. What had he been saying about her?

8

As an evening downpour started in earnest, Ellen set up her laptop on the kitchen table, plugged the modem into the socket on the wall and waited for Windows to greet her with the sound of a crashing wave, as Richard had programmed it to do.

It was all very well for him to send irate text messages demanding that she read his emails, she thought, but he was the one who had cancelled their service provider. Oddlode was hardly over-subscribed with Internet cafés. It had only just occurred to her to use one of the thirty-day free-trial CD-roms that littered the junkmail which had accumulated during her parents' absence.

Richard had persuaded her to buy the little computer three years earlier with money left to her by her grandmother. He'd loved the new slimline machine, which travelled with them across Europe, its batteries charged from every conceivable outlet, the three-pin plug inevitably carrying a caterpillar of wonky adaptors like mismatched Lego. He connected to the Net via his mobile, played online backgammon and subscribed to surfing newsgroups; he bought and sold his gear on auction sites; he emailed friends and swapped digital photos of competitions; he spent more time tapping keys than talking. It had been his biggest escape when the relationship went truly stale. In despair, Ellen had been forced to email him and request a real-life conversation. Richard didn't get the joke.

Then, just before the split, he announced that her laptop was hopelessly out of date and had bought himself an all-singing, all-dancing Sony with the money they had saved for a new van. The new computer played DVDs and received radio stations all over the world and could be used to edit the photographs of Richard surfing to make the waves look bigger and his belly smaller. Looking back now, Ellen should have guessed what was to come – in the same way that she should have read signals into the fact that he started auctioning off almost all his possessions on eBay, updating his palmtop with addresses from her bulging old Filofax, and checking out property values in North Cornwall.

Ellen had barely ever used her not-very-old reject laptop, except to print out her CV. The picture that greeted her as wallpaper was the one Richard had left there – a photograph of him emerging from the tube of a vast wave near Torquay, a small, wetsuited acolyte in a water-vaulted cathedral. It was a fantastic shot. She hastily slotted the free CD-rom into the sliding drawer. The computer whirred into action and welcomed her to the World's Favourite Internet Provider.

Five minutes later, she was online and ready to make contact. Pulling up the Outlook Explorer window, she knew that she had to face the music and check her Hotmail account to read the messages Richard kept texting her about.

She typed *www.Hot* . . . then paused as the scroll bar dropped down to suggest shortcuts to sites recently accessed, which started with 'Hot'. Richard, it seemed, had liked a lot of hot sites, but he hadn't checked his mail as often as he'd checked *Hotsex*, *Hot-xxx-action*, *Hotporn* and *Hot_teens*.

Ellen's hands slid away from the keyboard, her heart pounding hollowly in her ears along with the rain rattling on the windows.

'Oh, God, Richard.' She let out a sad laugh.

. . . *mail.com*. She typed the end of the address, logged in with her username and password, then groaned as her inbox cheerfully downloaded with fifty-seven new messages.

They weren't all from Richard, but he had written almost every day. The first few messages were cheerful and upbeat, deliberately chatty if a little stilted, regaling her with stories about his journey and his first few days in far-north Queensland, including a few digital photographs of sandy beaches and an apartment with palm trees outside its windows.

But his tone soon changed. By the fifth or sixth message, the recriminations began: the angry post-mortem of the thirteen-year-old corpse. It was bitter stuff, full of blame and self-justification, no longer caring to maintain a semblance of friendship. Initially, he'd clearly thought a great deal about what he was writing, carefully constructing his sentences, balancing his argument, trying to see her side – even putting himself down occasionally, a very unRichard thing to do. But it didn't last.

From the increasingly erratic typing, constant repetitions, contradictions, and appalling spelling, Ellen could tell he'd had a skinful when typing the later emails. He'd made some great friends, he said, was going out on the town every night, the weather was picking up and he didn't miss her at all. Then he told her what a bitch she was. Then he accused her of throwing away something special. Half a page later, he was writing that they had both wasted the past thirteen years and should never have started going out in the first place. Then he told her he missed her, and hated her, and couldn't live without her, and never wanted to see her again. He called her a frigid bitch, then accused her of being unfaithful a hundred times over because she 'couldn't get enough'. He told her she'd lost her looks; he told her that she was beautiful and that he'd never wanted anyone else in his life. He told her she was too good for him, rotten to the core, intelligent, stupid, reckless and a coward. He said again and again that she was just like her mother.

i bet you're judging this email like a fucking essay, arent you, he typed, having long since dispensed with punctuation and capitals. *you think <what a dickhead he never could write a decent letter> well, i hope you find some idiot who can. this will be my last email. you will never hear from me agaon.*

But he had written again, unable to stop himself boasting about a one-night stand with an eighteen-year-old called Lali: *she said i was the best lay she ever had. see what you are missing. then again <she> was better than <you>*

His final email had been written that morning – last thing at night in his time zone – and was a page of non-stop, badly spelled, repeated apologies. He said he was crying. He missed her. He missed the Shack and Snorkel and their friendship. He wished it hadn't had to end.

Ellen's head sank into her hands. She felt utterly drained, clueless how to answer or whether even to answer at all, terrified that it would open another can of worms for the worm who'd turned. This was Richard's way of working it out. She mustn't screw it up for him.

She trailed to the kitchen to fetch a pint glass of water and stared out at the rain-lashed lawn, wondering what life would have been like had they been brave enough to call it a day five or six years ago. She guessed there would have been more tears, less certainty, yet probably the same overwhelming sense of relief.

Hearing of Richard's one-night stand had only stirred the smallest spark of edgy jealousy, like a sharp electrostatic shock. She had no reason to feel hurt. That they had stayed faithful to one another until the bitter end was surprising, and she guessed that it was born of fear on both sides. After thirteen years, jumping off a cliff was far easier than jumping into bed with a stranger. Richard hadn't been a virgin as she had when they'd started going out. He boasted a torrid past: he had had sex twice with Tracy Coal on her parents' sofa.

Hugging herself, Ellen returned to the laptop and thought about her reply.

She thought about it as she searched Google for cheap flights, looked up accommodation, safety tips and travellers' tales for her world trip, requested brochures and free guides, ordered several books from Amazon and added useful sites to the favourites file.

She thought about what to reply as she scrolled further down that list of favourites and found yet more porn sites, wondering whether Richard had been deliberately brazen about leaving the evidence of his after-hours Internet passion, or whether he'd just been stupid. That she hadn't noticed said a lot.

She played with a few opening sentences in her mind as she clicked on the links to his favourite sites, accessing a world she'd never known.

Hi Richard. We're both to blame here . . .

Hi Richard. I'm to blame here . . .

Hi Richard. You're to blame here . . .

Hi Richard. No one's to blame here . . .

Hello Richard. The cat's gone missing and the neighbour wants to shoot the dog. I think I may have fallen in love. I blame the weather.

She fanned her T-shirt away from her belly as she took in the sites with which Richard was so well acquainted. The World's Favourite Internet Provider kept warning her that she was entering Over-18 Areas Containing Material of A Sexually Explicit Nature and she clicked the *OK* box over and over again as she sped past pixillated screens that took for ever to download, boasting cum shots, lesbian shots, anal shots, triple-penetration shots, black-on-white, Asian babes, teen temptresses, big boobs.

'Jesus wept!' She tilted her head this way and that to try to work out what was going on, starting to feel hotter and hotter.

Dear Richard. I had no idea porn could be such a turn-on. Why did you never show me this stuff?

But she wasn't really thinking about Richard. His face was blurring in her mind, to be replaced by another, the face that for the past few nights had stayed with her as she twisted in her sheets unable to sleep.

She fanned her T-shirt again, her nipples suddenly so hard that it felt as though she was clouting them with a cricket bat every time the cotton fabric landed against her hot skin.

OK, she clicked. *OK. OK. OK. OK. OK.* Her head tilted, tipped back, pushed forward, her eyes like saucers.

There was a clatter just outside the window.

'Shit!' Ellen cricked her neck looking over her shoulder, suddenly drenched in the cold sweat of shame. The computer screen was in full view of the window that faced the front garden – anyone coming to the door could have glanced in and seen the hot dot com action she was browsing through. She slammed the lid and waited, holding her breath, but there was no knock on the door.

Jumping up, she rushed through to the bootroom to turn on

the outside lights, peering through the windows at the needles of
rain jabbing down and catching in the gleam, the black shadows
of the climbers as they were buffeted by the wind. She scoured the
shadows for signs of life, jumping out of her hot, prickling skin.

The gate was ajar, when she had definitely closed it, but it might
have been caught by the wind. She could see the poster that she
had Sellotaped to it flapping, now secured by only one corner.
Something black and white was lying on the bonnet of the jeep,
sheltered from the rain by the barn awning.

'Fins!' she breathed ecstatically, pulling on some shoes and
racing outside.

She slowed as she rounded the corner to the barn, anxious not
to frighten him away. Rain whipped her face with huge warm
drops, like an Asian monsoon.

Hooking her hair behind her ears, she made the low, cooing
noise that always soothed him, chirruping his name: 'Fins. Here,
baby. Prrrrruuuuu. Good boy. Who's a good boy? Fins.'

Even ten yards away, Ellen knew that he was dead. The matted
black and white coat was streaked with dark blood, and the
unnatural twist of the body and its rigor-mortis stillness made
her cry out in horror. Somebody had left a note under the
windscreen wiper behind the sodden corpse, the angled corners
of which flapped over it like angel's wings.

Dropping to her haunches where she stood, she pressed her
face into the crook of an elbow, fighting a great wave of nausea.
'No, no, no!'

Having scrabbled her way out through the bootroom door,
Snorkel blasted alongside Ellen's crouched body, barking furiously, demented with fear and confusion.

It was several minutes before Ellen was brave enough to move
any closer. Even then, she returned inside first, leaving Snorkel
howling and barking, to fetch rubber gloves and a cardboard
box in which to put the poor warrior cat, feared by all in North
Cornwall, the best ratter in Treglin.

It was only when she finally moved out of the rain and under
the gloomy roof of the barn, badly lit by a spotlight in one corner,

that she realised the dead animal on her car bonnet wasn't Fins. It wasn't a cat at all.

It was a badger – huge, bloated in death, its yellow teeth grinning from peeled-back lips. It stank of decay, and the fleas that were drowning in its wet pelt crawled in great armies over the bony shoulders and domed head. Dark blood soaked its twisted, chewed-out throat, which was crawling with maggots.

'Oh, Jesus.' Ellen covered her mouth and fought not to retch as she stretched across to pluck the note from the windscreen.

'ROT IN HELL YOU INTERFERING BITCH!' read the big black marker-pen capitals.

'Gosh, you *have* pissed off a lot of people.' Pheely's eyebrows shot up as she refilled Ellen's whisky glass and then her own. She crossed the Goose Cottage flagstones to peer out of the window and check that the gate was still secure. 'Well, I really don't think young Lloyd would be up to such a thing – carrying a dead badger would ruin his expensive designer clothes. And I agree that the Wycks probably have a better knowledge of musteline mammals, but I can hardly see Dot trundling through the village with one slung across her bicycle rack, can you?'

'What about Reg?'

'Far too drunk to manage a trick like this.' Pheely was reading the note again, holding it with her fingertips. 'Besides which, the poor bugger can't read or write.' She held it up. 'Whoever penned this can spell "interfering".'

Ellen hated whisky, but she managed another sour mouthful to try to anaesthetise the fear and anger raging within her. It was such a horrible thing to do. She knew that she'd been pretty harsh with both the Wycks and Lloyd, but surely she didn't deserve this?

'I can tell you *exactly* who did this.' Pheely settled beside her on the sofa, spreading out the note and tapping it. 'Spurs.'

'I don't believe you.'

'It's just his style. And you said yourself that he had a go at you earlier today.' Pheely probed darkly.

'Only because Lloyd thought he was a gypsy.' And that we

were some sort of item, she added silently, still not believing Pheely.

'How anybody could mistake a four-thousand-pound horse for a gypsy's is beyond me.' Pheely tutted. 'Unless, of course, he thought Otto was stolen – which I suppose, technically, he was. Dilly might have asked Spurs to ride him, but I am his legal owner and I forbade it – I've even hidden his tack. I wonder if I should report it?'

She wasn't taking this very seriously, Ellen thought, starting to regret her panic-stricken call. An overexcited, panting Pheely, plus a spliff and a bottle of Scotch, had arrived within minutes, covered with greenery from a hasty dash through the Lodge gardens. She claimed nothing so thrilling had happened in the village since Prudence Hornton had driven drunkenly into the duck pond after a furious argument with Giles about alimony.

'I just don't believe Spurs would do this to me.' Ellen read the angry black words. 'I haven't done anything to merit this.'

'With Spurs, it doesn't take much.' Pheely lit the spliff. 'There was a time when he'd do far worse just for giving him a dirty look. You have no idea the stupid little things that incensed him.'

'Like what?'

Pheely gave her a wise look. 'Hurting his warped libido, dealing a blow to that mountainous pride, making him think he's in with a chance of a quick tupping session then turning out to be a tease. He's very sexually driven.'

'I did no such thing.' Ellen felt her face flame.

'I did once.' Pheely drained her Scotch. 'Awful.'

'You did?'

She nodded. 'When Daddy was ill – before it got really bad, but he'd started to sleep a lot – Spurs and I smoked a couple of joints while Daddy was taking a nap upstairs. I admit I did find him rather attractive then. Dilly had just started at playschool, and I hadn't had a boyfriend since she was born – I suppose it dents your confidence. When Spurs made a bit of a play, I was very flattered. Okay, I was completely bowled over.' She giggled, refilled her glass and toked again, too carried away by the memory to offer Ellen a drag.

'He was *very* grown-up for sixteen – six feet one and a husky broken voice, that magnificent mane savagely cropped for school like an OTC recruit. He was so beautiful. You have no idea. I just thought, wow, wow, wow – this is going to be wonderful! I know it's shameful – looking back, I feel like a terrible cradle-snatcher for even contemplating it although, God knows, he was probably far more sexually experienced than me even then and not that much younger. Glad Tidings got very tight on sherry at Hell's Bells' Christmas drinks once and told me she'd caught Jasper in bed with a girl when he was just thirteen.' She took another deep draw and laughed again, her butterfly mind dancing back to the topic in hand.

'We had *the* most amazing kissing session – it went on for hours – and I suppose I got a bit emotional, what with the dope and being so relieved to be fancied again, and I told him how beautiful he was and that I would do anything for him. Then he got this malicious look in his eye and said in that case could he call a friend who'd like to watch. He was on the telephone before you could say "peepshow". I lost my nerve – I really wasn't that experienced. Dilly's father was my first – well, my only lover at that point. There was something about Spurs that was so dirty and dangerous. I was hopelessly excited but I just couldn't go through with it. He was livid – stormed out on me that night and didn't reappear for ages.

'Every morning that bloody awful week I found a dead crow outside the kitchen door alongside the milk. Can you imagine? It scared me half witless. Spurs was behind it, of course – he used to shoot them out of the corn with his air rifle for a couple of quid from local farmers.'

'It was definitely him?'

She nodded. 'I stayed up one night and saw him delivering one of the wretched things. I so wanted to have it out with him, but I flunked it. He had his gun with him.'

Ellen chewed her thumbnail. The thought of Pheely and Spurs

kissing all those years ago made her veins clog and tangle, her lungs fold in on themselves and her head pound. Stop it, she told herself. Stop it. He's bad. He's done awful things. You hardly know him. He's just scared you half to death to amuse himself. Feeling so jealous is crazy.

'Don't you see that he *must* be behind this?' Pheely was saying, picking up the note again, the spliff dangling from her lips. 'If you and he had a dodgy dalliance over the weekend, you mustn't keep it to yourself. You could be in a lot of danger, darling. Is there something you're not telling me?' The green eyes blinked through a miasma of dope smoke, almost but not quite concealing the desperate desire for hot gossip.

Ellen nearly pulled the nail off her thumb as she gnawed at it, looking from Pheely to the note and then to the window, beyond which lay the garden where, for a while, she'd thought that not just one but all of her wishes were going to come true. She had been such a fool.

What had he been going to tell her on the night of the storm? she wondered hopelessly. All week she'd toyed with a hundred ideas, but her stupid, dreamy imagination had lingered lovingly over the notion that he had been on the brink of saying that he had agreed to go away again, but that now he couldn't leave her. This was so dumb, and obviously so far from the truth, it was laughable.

She stood up furiously. 'I'm going round to see him. I need to have this out.'

'What – now?' Pheely looked groggily at her watch. 'It's after eleven.'

'I don't care.' She went to fetch her coat. 'Can you stay here until I get back?'

'What if he's hanging around in the garden with more dead animals?' she yelped, peeing out of the windows.

'Lock the doors, finish the joint and you'll be fine,' Ellen assured her. 'Please, Pheely? I have to do this.'

'God, you're brave.' Pheely shuddered, biting the spliff for safekeeping and leaning back from the smoke as she buttoned

Ellen's denim jacket for her as if she was a child, her fingers shaking.

'He doesn't frighten me as he does you.' Ellen smiled, but her skin was tightening like a wetsuit in cold water.

'Not yet.' Pheely brushed a long blonde hair from the jacket. 'But if you two carry on like this, he will.'

'He started it,' Ellen hissed, 'and I'm going to put a stop to it.'

The rain had eased to a warm drizzle as Ellen splashed through the puddles on Goose Lane, wishing she'd remembered to bring a torch. This side of the village was deserted, although she could hear raucous laughter beyond the manor as the last few drunks were dispatched from the Oddlode Inn.

Two shadowy figures were lurching across the village green as she turned the corner into Manor Street, at last reaching the part of the village that was illuminated at night, albeit dimly, its few lights set between thick trees that hunched like pallbearers beneath the lead-lined-coffin clouds, casting huge ominous shadows. The rain had brought out the sherbet smell of the cow parsley that sprouted beneath the laurels in front of the village hall, and the sweet reek of the lilac bush above them, which drooped under the weight of the water it had collected.

Ellen took a deep, scented breath, and faced the manor gates. The house was in darkness, all its big mullioned windows showing blank faces.

Either the Bellings were out, or they had gone to bed.

She looked at the buzz-box on the gatepost, reluctant to summon fearsome Hell's Bells or grand Sir St John from their sleep. She wished she knew which of the windows was Spurs' so that she could bombard it with pebbles. She eyed them speculatively. She didn't even know if he lived in the house with his parents.

Frustrated by her cowardice – and by such an unsatisfactory anticlimax – Ellen prowled the outer perimeters of the high Cotswold-stone wall for ideas, passing the now silent Oddlode Inn and turning into Manor Lane. Her heart lurched as she spotted one of the Missing posters she'd Sellotaped up earlier. The ink had run in the rain so that Fins' angry little face slid off the page like Munch's *The Scream* with tufty ears.

Moving into the black water of unlit darkness once more, Ellen stalked past a locked garden door in the eight-foot wall and an equally impenetrable set of tall double gates.

The rain started to fall harder again, sliding through her hair and on to her face, soaking through her denim shoulders and thighs as she dipped her head and plodded into it, losing some of her enthusiasm to bawl Spurs out. She blinked it out of her eyes as she reached the corner of North Street, where the high manor wall gave way to a lower one, which bordered the paddocks. In the middle of it, there was an inviting little rail. She clambered over, and landed with a splash in an unseen water trough.

Now spurting water from her trainers and jeans, she squelched across the dark field, burning her wet ankles with nettles and cursing all the way. He'd better be in after this. Her weakening anger staged a comeback, fuelled by an unpleasant encounter with a huge pile of gently steaming manure.

On the other side of a five-bar gate was a Tarmac yard skirted by old open barns containing Hell's Bells' horsebox and a sheep trailer, along with an assortment of agricultural devices with great spikes and rollers. It looked like equipment gathered from a torture chamber. Beyond another padlocked five-bar gate was the stableyard with its grand archway leading to the old hunt kennels. One bright streak of light cut diagonally across the gloom beyond the arch and Ellen jumped as a shadow moved across it.

She crept through the arch, hearing the water drumming hard overhead as she moved momentarily out of the rain, pressing her back to the wall and shuffling sideways to crane towards the source of the light.

Set high in a steeply pitched roof was what appeared to be an old grain hatch, now converted into an ivy-fringed window, revealing a heavily beamed ceiling and an old model aeroplane dangling from an unshaded lightbulb. Even standing on tiptoe, Ellen couldn't make out anything else – the window was far too high. Nor could she see an obvious entrance to the flat: no front door or stone staircase to that storey.

She squelched crossly to the other side of the yard, where another archway led to a weed-strewn back drive that culminated in the tall, locked wooden gates she'd walked past earlier. To the left, a vegetable plot had gone to seed, and to the right, a row of potting sheds and tall yews divided the drive from the manor's sculpted gardens. She darted past them and, feeling more and more like a mad stalker, found her way to the opposite side of the kennels, tucked away behind the yews along with down-at-heel rows of broken cold frames and mildewed glasshouses with few intact panes remaining. On this side, there was a line of brightly lit skylights in the building's steep stone roof, and beneath them a vast black door with no handle.

Ellen fought down a wave of panic that told her to go home, dry off and save this until morning. But she was damned if she was going to lie awake stewing. She hammered on the door with her fist, hoping it didn't open to reveal a wizened old gardener in his pyjamas, or a strapping stablehand.

Rain drummed her shoulders as she hammered again and again. The more it beat on her temples and soaked into her clothes, the more angry she felt that Spurs could play such a childish game. He was a spoilt brat, a twisted excuse for a human being whose charmed birthright of wealth and sheer beauty had rotted his soul to black tar. He wasn't worthy of all the hot, cold, steamy, tingly and downright disturbing thoughts she'd had about him in the past few days. The only reason she'd felt so hopelessly out of control and excited during the weekend was because of the building storm, she told herself angrily. He'd blown hot and cold on her sweaty skin, had been as changeable as the weather – sunny one minute and stormy the next. Well, now it was time to rain on his paradox.

She stepped back and glared at the cheery skylights, aiming a hard kick at the door and stubbing her toes on the stone step through the sodden trainers. Hopping around, she wished she'd brought his rusty horseshoe with her so that she could hurl it through one of them – preferably the one that was open so that she didn't have to pay for the glass to be replaced.

She stood still and looked again. Aha!

Struck with an idea, she cast around for something to throw, but the grass around her was devoid of useful missiles. Hell's Bells obviously didn't go in for Pheely's characterful garden statuary – just banks of lush bedding plants and roses.

She dragged off one of her waterlogged trainers – now a good throwing weight – took aim and hurled it. She hadn't lost her touch. It sailed through the gap in the open skylight and landed on the other side with a satisfying clatter.

She was still staring up at the window, waiting for a head to poke out, when the door in front of her was wrenched open.

'What the fuck do you think you're playing at?' Spurs stood tall and furious in front of her, silhouetted in light like a demon emerging from a hell pit, roaring like the fires within.

'That should be my line,' she snarled.

For a moment he said nothing as he registered the drowned rat in the buttoned-up denims standing on one leg in front of him. The whites of his eyes gleamed as his gaze moved up and down the rain-blacked Levi's, the mud-splattered ankles and the flattened, dirty-blonde hair. 'You came to see me,' he said at last, the anger evaporating. He sounded as though he'd been expecting her.

'Was that your intention?' she demanded. 'Because you didn't need to go to such elaborate lengths. You could have just invited me over for tea in the usual way.'

'How did you get in?' He was looking over her shoulder at the dark house. 'My parents are away. No one's around to open the gates.'

'I can walk through walls,' she muttered, in no mood to describe her water-trough dunk.

'And drive people up them.' A smile lifted the stubbled cheeks.

'And line people up against them to shoot them if they wind me up.'

'Come in out of the rain.' He stood back, laughing now, delighted by his unexpected visitor. 'You're soaked through.'

'I'm fine out here.' Ellen felt safer in the garden. She hopped back a few paces and balanced herself with her bare toes. 'This won't take long. I'd have brought your friend badger back, but he has a sore throat.'

'You what?' He creased his forehead, stepping out into the rain.

'I can't believe you could do something so foul,' she raged. 'Why, Spurs? What have I done to offend you?'

'I don't know what you're talking about.'

'The sodding great badger carcass that I've just hauled off my car bonnet, that's what. And the gift-tag. Nice touch.'

The rain was easing off again, jewelling Spurs' black curls and speckling his grey T-shirt to match his freckled face. The silver eyes watched Ellen as she hopped around the grass like a furious fairy who'd burned her toe with her magic wand.

'And you think I have something to do with it?' he asked eventually.

'Of course you bloody did – Pheely told me all about the crow milk-round you once made, just as she told me about the horseshoe. You really should vary your routine.'

'Interfering *bitch*!' he exploded.

Ellen gasped, taking a few stumbling hops back. 'What did you say?'

'Interfering bitch,' he snarled again, eyes darting furiously. 'You can't deny it. You should keep away from her. You should keep away from me, come to that. You should never have fucking well come here, turning me inside out and giving Pheely an excuse to get her cauldron out.'

Ellen couldn't speak. She seemed to have forgotten how to breathe too.

'*What?*' he snapped, taking in her white face.

'I didn't believe it was you,' she breathed eventually. 'Even coming here to "confront" you I was fooling myself because I just wanted to prove it *wasn't* you. And it was. Oh, God, it was.' She clasped a shaking hand to her mouth.

'It *wasn't* me!' He charged up to her, so livid that the veins leaped from his skin like cobwebs as he spoke. 'How many times? It wasn't me! I've changed. I don't do things like that any more.'

Looking at that beautiful, corrupt face, Ellen was reminded of the parable of the boy who cried, 'Wolf!', only in Spurs' case it was 'I've changed'.

And she so wanted to believe him that it hurt like a body-blow. She cast her eyes to his hand, remembering how she had taken it in hers and almost lost consciousness because of the force that had exploded through her. She had never been so attracted to anyone in her life. Even now, certain that he would wilfully terrorise her because she had let him down, she was shot through with longing. But he was a stranger, she reminded herself. Their few hours together meant nothing compared to her thirteen years with Richard, and the chemical combustion between them was far too life-threatening to analyse. To look into the flames would blind her. Self-preservation took hold.

'I just want you to leave me alone,' she said.

'My pleasure!' He held up his arms and took a step back.

Ellen stumbled back too, looking up at his molten eyes.

'What do you think I've been doing all week?' he yelled, backing away still further. 'You're the one who's come here to crawl under my skin again. Believe me, you are so much better not knowing me. Go play with your Ken-doll boyfriend.'

'He's not my boyfriend!'

'Sorry. My mistake. Call me old-fashioned. You're fucking him, therefore I assume he's a boyfriend. What would you prefer? Lover? Playmate? Re-bounder?'

Ellen couldn't stop the punch of recognition that winded her, bringing pleasure with its pain. He was jealous. He was jealous!

'What bloody business is it of yours who I sleep with?' she breathed.

He didn't answer, eyes gleaming furiously.

'I haven't fucked Lloyd.' She squared up to him. 'But that doesn't mean you can lob dead wildlife on my bonnet just because some jumped-up estate agent happens to offend your precious pride by calling you a gypsy.'

'Jesus! Read – my – lips. It wasn't me!'

'And read mine.' She turned away and pointed defiantly at her bottom. 'I don't believe you.'

But before she could walk away, he grabbed her shoulders, twisted her round and glared down at her. 'I am so – so – glad that Touchy Pheely popped by last weekend to ask all about your sordid night with Ken-doll. To think I almost mistook you for someone I could trust. Someone who could have fallen from the sky, she was so different.'

'I did fall from the sky,' she howled, wriggling frantically. 'You happily dared me to do it. I could have been killed.'

'I was trying to mend that sodding great hole in your heart.' His fingers dug into her skin.

'You weren't interested in mending holes; just accessing them.'

'You were the one who wanted to jump. You wanted to fly away, with your fairy wings on your back.'

'I guess I flew too close to the son of a bitch.'

'And I had no idea you were after another sort of jump entirely.'

'Bastard!' She fixed her eyes on his.

'Bitch!' He locked back on target.

But they were no longer arguing. Their mouths moved closer together, not caring what words were being uttered through them.

'I love—'

'I hate—'

'I love—'

'I love—'

'I hate—'

'You . . . you . . . you . . . you . . .'

Lip slammed lip, body slammed body, bones clashed, muscles played washboard friction and fingernails dug hard into leaping skin. Mutual mistrust, desire and adoration conspired as they kissed, freefalling from their ivory towers.

When Ellen felt the blow against the back of her skull, she

thought at first that Spurs had coshed her. She was vaguely aware, as she slumped forward under the impact, that whatever had hit her smelt bizarrely of oranges, before also realising that she wasn't falling over as expected.

Woozily, she sagged in mid-air, head throbbing, held up by Spurs' tight grip on her shoulders, wondering how he was planning to finish her off. That's when it occurred to her that he couldn't have hit her at all – both of his hands were stapled to her shoulders. They had been all along.

Pressing her face into the crook of his neck and moaning because it smelt like home, she passed out.

When she opened her eyes again, she was lying on a very wet bench on her own in the manor garden. She groaned and felt around her pounding head, exploring carefully for open wounds and splintered skull but, apart from a disappointingly small bump, there was no evidence that she had been crowned by an evil manor burglar streaking away after looting Hell's Bells' remaining silver.

Moments later, Spurs appeared from behind the yew-tree curtain.

'They've scarpered.' He was clutching a Hooch bottle, catching his breath from running. 'Thank God you're all right.' He crouched down beside her, taking her hand. 'Does your head ache? Is your vision okay?'

'Did you go for a takeout?' she asked blearily, as she tried to focus on his bottle. 'Nice of you to hang around and make sure I was still alive.'

He watched her face with concern. 'Are you feeling groggy? I'll drive you to Cheltenham General – ambulances take hours round here.'

He was rubbing her hand now, his fingers against her knuckles, sliding up to her wrist and stroking his thumb against the soft skin beneath it. Ellen watched for a moment, mesmerised by his sudden gentleness.

'God, I'm so sorry.' He pressed his forehead to her hand. 'It shouldn't have happened.'

'You weren't the one who hit me over the head.'

'I wasn't talking about that,' he breathed into her fingers, wet hair tickling her arm.

Still dazed, she wondered what he was talking about. Instinctively, she reached out her other hand and stroked his damp curls. For a moment his whole body seemed to relax, yielding into the caress. Then he jerked back his head. 'We'd better get you checked over by a doctor.'

'I'm fine – I don't need to go to hospital,' she insisted, standing up and battling not to sway, noticing as she did so that Spurs was still holding the bottle. 'I'm not a big Hooch fan, thanks all the same. I thought one was supposed to have hot sweet tea at times like this.'

'This is what hit you. It came over the wall.'

She went cross-eyed as she studied at it, watching the bottles multiply. 'Makes a change from ten green ones.'

'Or talking to a brick one.' He sighed, put the bottle on the bench and straightened up.

'Eh?' She blinked a few times.

'I didn't leave the dead badger.' He pulled his hair back from his face. 'I swear on my life.'

'Of course. The badger. Shit.' Ellen started to feel nausea grip her belly, her head throbbing painfully. 'I'm going home.'

Spurs moved closer, watching her face worriedly. 'You look bloody pale. You have to come inside and sit down for a bit, at least.'

'No, I don't.' She held her head with one hand and the back of the bench with the other, waiting for the garden to turn the right way up again. 'I take it that was intended for you?' She nodded at the spinning bottle.

'Probably just kids – with the pub so close, we've always had a lot of empties hurled in. Mother thought about employing a potman at one time, before the money ran out. Are you really okay?'

'I'll live.' She was peering groggily at her bare foot, trying to remember where her shoe had gone. Then, it all flooded back – the badger with the cut throat, tramping across fields in the rain, throwing her shoe, the heated argument, the kiss and then the knock-out. She swayed as she remembered that they had kissed. How could she forget? She couldn't trust herself. She had to get away and lie down.

'May I hop you home?' He offered his arm.

Now unable to look at him, she shook her spinning head. 'I'd rather have my trainer back.'

'Then come inside and fetch it.' Spurs made to take her hand and steer her towards his door.

Ellen took a nervous hop back.

'Don't worry, I've already gift-wrapped the dead weasels and hedgehogs ready to deliver in the morning,' he muttered. 'There's a fallow-deer carcass on the coffee table, but I can cover it with a tea-towel.'

'It's not funny.'

He laughed softly. 'Ellen, I wouldn't dream of frightening you like that. Not you, the woman I love.'

'Cut out the love crap.' She took a few deep breaths, fighting to find a place where the world would stop spinning.

'Would you like me to cut my heart out and leave it on your bonnet to prove it?'

'It's so small, I'd probably drive off without noticing it.' She forced herself to look up.

His eyes moved between hers, silver linings to black clouds as his pupils stretched wide in the darkness to take in every feature on her face.

And suddenly Ellen realised that the world wasn't about to stop spinning. However many bottles hit her on the head, her life would keep revolving while he could make her feel like this just by looking at her.

'Fuck off back to where you came from, Belling!'

Ellen and Spurs both spun round to see several more bottles sail over the high wall towards them.

'Get down!' He pulled her out of the way, tucking her under the crook of his arm and deflecting one with his back.

'You should have been left to rot in prison, you murdering

bastard!' yelled a voice from the lane, followed by the sound of running feet.

Pressed hard against his body, Ellen could feel Spurs' angry breaths punch air in and out of his lungs. She glanced nervously up at him. 'Kids?'

He swallowed, and gazed at the shattered glass where one bottle had crashed on to a stone path.

'I don't want you to have anything more to do with me,' he said suddenly, standing up.

'What?' She rubbed her head and struggled to her feet, too.

'You heard. I want you to keep your distance.' He stared at her, his face in shadow, his voice hard. 'Don't try to see me again before you leave. We agree to forget about the auction lots. You'd be better off if we'd never met.'

'Why?'

He let out a hollow laugh, turning away from her. 'I knew coming back here would mean facing a whole new punishment. And now that my life sentence has been passed, I find something I've been searching for all my useless life. If there is a God, I hope he's bloody well cracking up.'

'What do you mean by that?' Ellen asked, her arteries flooded with a heartbreaking wave of rushing blood – the biggest tube she'd ever surfed through, sweeping her off her high horse, her board and her wet feet.

'Just do as I say, Ellen. You need me like a hole in the head.' He started walking back towards his kennel flat.

'At least tell me why.' She stumbled after him. 'What do you mean by "life sentence"?'

'Go away, Ellen.'

'No! Tell me what's going on.'

'What do I have to do to make you leave?' he stormed, turning back to her.

'Tell me what you were going to say on the night of the storm. Tell me the truth.'

He stared at her for a long time, his eyes unblinking. Then he shouldered the black door open. 'Don't glorify this with any great

significance, Ellen. You were right all along. I only ever wanted
to fuck you. Then I found out that the estate agent had already
dropped off a deposit and I withdrew my offer.'

'You don't mean that,' Ellen gasped.

He closed one gleaming eye. 'Oh, I do.' As the door opened,
spilling light past him, his face disappeared into shadow. 'You're
not that hot.' With that, the door closed.

Ellen saw red, not even thinking before she started screaming
at the door, 'Yeah, and I'm going round the world as soon as I
leave this dumbass backwater!' She hopped rabidly on the spot.
'So you can just fuck off and play with your dead badgers, you
twisted bastard!'

Heart hammering, she stumbled back through the kennels
towards the old footpath that led directly to the Goose Cottage
paddock. Had she glanced up at the grain-hatch window as she
passed it, she would have spotted her trainer swinging from the
model aeroplane.

A moment later, Spurs removed it carefully and then slumped
on his sofa, hugging it to his chest.

Late that night, long after Pheely had been dispatched to the
Lodge, stoned and whisky-soaked, rambling that Spurs should
be arrested for leaving a potentially concussed woman to walk
home alone, Ellen wrote to Richard.

> *It is over, but I'll never, ever be out of touch if you need me.*
> *Thirteen isn't always an unlucky number. There were more*
> *good years than bad, and there are more good memories than*
> *bad ones.*
>
> *Believe me, it's best that we finally came to this decision. I'm in*
> *bits, but I know that every little bit will eventually glue itself back*
> *together and I know that we did the right thing. Every little bit of*
> *me loved you at one time. That love still lives in a corner of my*
> *heart and will be treasured there as long as I live. You are my sea*
> *and my ocean. Exxx*

Those two paragraphs took her hours to write and she found

herself weeping stupidly over them, hardly able to bear to part with them because it was like ripping out her hollow heart, knowing that another had filled it. Pressing 'send' was switching off a light that could never be turned back on.

Which made it doubly galling when a blunt reply came winging straight back.

*you bitch. i bet you don't fakey it with him. you always did
with me.*

Far beneath her leaden feet, Richard was online, reading between lines and playing back old lines.

There was nothing like the shorthand between a long-term couple, the greatest of friends and the longest of rivals. He always knew when she was in love. Although never unfaithful, Ellen had fallen in love many times in recent years.

Fakey – riding the board with one's left leg in front of the right, as Ellen surfed – had been a private, pillow-talk joke. Richard, a notorious stayer, could take hours to come – and Ellen occasionally faked orgasm to hurry him up. Her fakeys were something they'd laughed about once. Until she had done it every time they had sex. Then it was no joke.

She looked at the kitchen clock, and saw it was past four – early afternoon in Oz – Richard's favourite beer and alternative surfing hours. In Oddlode, it was almost light, the birds chorusing. She hadn't even noticed. Her head was still throbbing from the flying Hooch bottle and from staring at a small, flat computer monitor.

Not always.

She sent the reply and closed her eyes. 'You're not that hot,' she whispered, wincing at the memory of Spurs' final taunt. He was right. She was far from hot. Richard had spent hours twiddling and stroking and licking, and she had remained as cold as ice.

Within seconds a window popped up on her screen, to the accompaniment of a seagull call. Above a little text box, a message read

Surfdood21 wants to chat. To reply, type below. This private chatroom is not monitored. For your own safety please do not exchange home addresses.

Below it, in a jaunty red font, Richard had decided to open his heart, his secret Internet world and the can of worms she'd dreaded.

how often?

She closed her eyes. Too often to count.

Hardly ever
   is he better than me?

The reply flew back and then, seconds later, another line appeared.

forget that. i miss your body
   I miss

Ellen looked at the flashing cursor and realised she didn't really miss him at all. She just missed talking to somebody who knew her so well – better than her parents or her greatest friends. It was a horribly selfish reason to miss someone. More so because Richard only knew who she was when she was with him, and she already felt estranged from the Ellen who had shared his life.

She tapped the backspace button for six strokes and typed,

Be happy
   Do you want cyber sex?

A little icon appeared beside this message, a face with a tongue hanging out and an animated winking eye.

She looked at the empty box waiting for her. Was this how easy it was to turn thirteen years of friendship into a disturbing conundrum of two strangers typing into small out-of-context boxes?

Slowly, she closed the lid of her laptop, sealing the time capsule, and went upstairs, leaving Richard alone in his chatroom.

The phone started ringing as she was cleaning her teeth. Ellen looked at her guilty reflection and rubbed her gums raw as she let it ring on for minutes before he gave up.

★   ★   ★

Three fields away, a damp trainer flew out of a skylight. Inside it was a mobile phone. As it crashed into a wet flower-bed, it went into redial.

When the phone rang again, the birds on the telegraph wire outside Ellen's bedroom window launched into a competitive impersonation chorus until they resembled the BBC switchboard after a heated lesbian handbagging in the Queen Vic.

Pulling the pillow over her head, she wished with all her heart that it was Spurs calling and not Richard. But that was one wish he couldn't grant. He had pushed her away, rejecting her big-time. He might excite her more than a thousand Richards, but to him she was just a horny blonde on the rebound and not worth the effort.

It rang on and on.

'Hello?' she answered wearily.

Nothing but birdsong greeted her. Clutching the receiver to her chest, she buried her face in the pillow and dreamed of her gorgeous wings.

9

Poppy, the eager young estate agent, suited her name perfectly. Her dark eyes popped out of their sockets with enthusiasm, her poppy red car was always parked outside Goose Cottage and she took to popping in when Ellen was least expecting it. As soon as she had secured the appointment to sell Goose Cottage, she appeared daily in her glossy scarlet Golf to 'spruce things up' for the procession of buyers to follow. She liked to add a personal touch, she explained, and always insisted upon being present at the viewings. Soon every vase was filled with freesias and stargazer lilies from Morrell on the Moor Tesco, real coffee bubbled in the Jamiesons' filter machine throughout the day, the toilets all acquired little scented rim blocks and never had their seats left up, the dining-table was laid for six and the breakfast-table for four – and Snorkel found herself tethered to the dovecote come rain or shine. Poppy was, as Ellen had promised her parents, very good at her job. But she set Ellen's teeth on edge.

'An absolutely *enchanting* cottage with medieval origins . . .' She'd wave would-be buyers from room to room in a waft of Givenchy, her sing-song voice resembling a fifties fashion commentary. '*Lovingly* restored by the current owners, who now live overseas. It has *wonderfully* versatile space and, being in such a premium Cotswold village, it represents a *superb* investment.'

'*Lovely* people,' she said, after every visit. 'I think they're keen.'

Each enthusiastically hosted viewing brought a new spin to her patter: 'As you can see the garden is *beautifully* established and provides almost total privacy, although the neighbours are *terribly* nice.'

'Yes, *lots* of wildlife – birds, deer, foxes, hedgehogs. Have you seen much during your stay Ms Jamieson?'

'Mmm – a badger.'

'How *gorgeous*!'

When Poppy suggested politely that Ellen might like to tidy herself up a bit, as though she were a dog-eared sofa that needed a neutral Ikea throw to hide its garish upholstery, she decided to steer clear of the daily influx.

At first, the sulky clouds continued emptying their loads on the thatched princesses, not showing them off to their best advantage and making it hard for Ellen to find somewhere to escape to when families came to look around. The jeep had a flat battery, and trips to the village shop or to walk Snorkel around the block were rarely long enough to allow eager punters to investigate the ancient, exquisite cottage and her outbuildings. Some spent hours. From the cameras slung around necks, the guidebooks on the back seats of cars and the holiday wardrobes, Ellen understood what Lloyd had meant when he'd said that viewing houses up for sale had taken over from visiting churches on the tourist trail, particularly in bad weather.

'Are you a writer?' they asked her, spotting the laptop on the kitchen table, excited at the prospect that they might be looking at a cottage immortalised in a historical saga or a racy romance.

'No, I'm just planning a trip,' she told them.

Spurs' unpleasant revelations, the badger threat, and Poppy's confidence that Goose Cottage would now be sold 'in a trice' had prompted Ellen to plan her trip properly, eager to set off as soon as an offer was accepted. She'd started drawing up an itinerary, plotting a route on the blow-up beach-ball globe she'd bought from a tourist shop in Bude the day Richard had said he was going to Australia.

She made endless enquiries by email, using the new address given to her by the World's Favourite Internet Provider to avoid downloading any more of Richard's bitter missives. She knew it was cowardly, but she couldn't face his aggressive rhetoric. To her even greater shame, she rarely thought about him at all. It was Spurs' face she saw when she closed her eyes and lay back in the bath each evening, feeling her heart crashing so hard that the foam around her popped, and the water seemed to boil and bubble. She was humiliated by the enormity of her self-destructive crush. That he obviously felt so little for her tripled the shame but did nothing to curb the obsession. She saw nothing of him, although she learned from Pheely that he rode Otto daily. Given her random and regular excursions around the village and bridleways, he was clearly working hard at avoiding her.

When the sun staged a watery reappearance over the Lodes Valley, Ellen made sure that she and Snorkel were well out of the way for Poppy's hosted viewings. Several families had come back for a second look already – one couple were on their third visit. Ellen found a patch of four-leaved clovers by the River Folly and plucked one every time she passed, pressing it into her world atlas when she got home and hoping that, with their luck, she would soon be far away from Oddlode.

As well as walking daily laps of the village in search of Fins, or high on the ridge in search of solace, Ellen also spent an increasing amount of time on the Lodge cottage terrace with Pheely, drinking ludicrously strong coffee, watching her sculpt, and listening to her larger-than-life, embroidered tales of village life, which cheered them both up like mad.

'I can't do anything to Godspell's death-mask until she comes in for another sitting,' she complained, 'and Lord knows when that will be. I gather Ely has her under house arrest for after-hours drinking at the Lodes Inn.'

The half-finished bust of Godspell Gates sat conspicuously under wet sacking while Pheely concentrated her attentions on a sculpture of a curvaceous mermaid. 'For Pru's gallery,' she explained gaily. 'Trade always picks up there in summer.'

'Surely she's old enough to drink in a pub?' Ellen asked.

'Good grief, yes. Pru's probably eligible for the British Legion supper club,' Pheely said bitchily. 'Do you know she's had two face lifts?'

'I meant Godspell.'

'Oh, Ely likes to exert his paternal authority from time to time. Being gated by Gates is a way of life for those children – Enoch was once confined to barracks for the entire summer for bringing a copy of *Penthouse* back from school. I imagine they'll still get locked in their rooms at night when they're in their thirties. But I do wish Ely had thought it through on this occasion. He's the one who wants this wretched bust finished so quickly, and my memories of his wretched daughter are so tainted I can hardly be expected to sculpt from them.'

Her village tales often centred on Ely and his family, Ellen noted.

'Ely's definitely got something up his sleeve for the garden party this year,' she confided one day. 'You must *promise* me you'll still be here.'

'I might,' Ellen hedged, thinking about the Devil's Marsh race and imagining Spurs galloping across that jewelled grass on a sweating thoroughbred – all the village booing in his wake.

'I think he might have a rather grand announcement. He's probably bought the Manse from the bank that repossessed it from the cult – or he might have found a way to get Noah out of the mill at last,' Pheely mused. 'Whatever it is, Ely's cooking something up. You can always tell when he's on to a deal, because he starts putting twenties in the church collection – paying God guilt money.'

Ellen hoped it had nothing to do with his desire to buy Goose Cottage at a knock-down price. Poppy had already reported a call from Ely, who had been acquainting the new agents with his silly offer. 'He couldn't be behind the dead badger could he?' she gasped.

'How many times, Ellen?' Pheely laid down her sculpting trowel and rolled her green eyes in exasperation. 'It was Spurs.'

Ellen watched a squirrel dart bravely onto the terrace to pick a wild strawberry before scampering up one of Norman Gently's headless stone figures and leaping into a tree. She thought about the day she'd hurled strawberries at Spurs and he'd pushed her into the pond, accusing her of having the hots for him. He'd been right. She still couldn't cool down.

'Has he left any more gifts?' Pheely asked.

'No. I haven't seen him at all.'

'Too busy treating poor Otto like a trail bike,' she grumbled. 'Dilly is thrilled – says she asked him to get the horse fit for the Devil's Marsh, but Pixie was in Upper Springlode yesterday delivering organic veg and she saw poor Psychotto tethered outside the Plough while Spurs and Rory lolled in the beer garden.'

Ellen smiled sadly and then remembered something. 'I still have two of Rory's jumps in my paddock.'

'Don't tell Dilly when she gets back – she'll insist that we ferry them up to his yard on the moped as an excuse to see Rory, although, I have to admit that boy is *very* dishy. He has his mother Truffle's looks, unlike the lumpy daughter.' She was clearly all set to launch into another history lesson in Oddlode genetics.

'He looks incredibly like Spurs,' Ellen said mindlessly.

'He looks nothing bloody like him,' Pheely retorted, and gave her mermaid buck teeth. 'Hyperion to a satyr, my darling. And satyr is the lowest form of dimwit.'

Remembering Spurs' worries about Rory's drinking, plus a throwaway comment that his feckless, forgetful cousin slept with the eager female stablehands when he was drunk, Ellen wondered just who was the dimwitted satyr.

As always when the topic touched upon Spurs, she found herself keeping the conversational plate spinning for as long as she could before Pheely's butterfly mind alighted on a more fragrant flower.

'What exactly happened to make him leave the village all those years ago?'

'Well, getting sent to jail meant it was pretty pointless renewing his Pony Club sub.'

'He didn't go to jail until he was nineteen. I thought he left Oddlode before that.'

'A couple of years, yes.' She popped a wart on the mermaid's nose.

'I got the impression that something specific made him go?'

'You could say that.' The green gaze was warning her off, but Ellen was desperate to know.

'What did he do?'

'What's the worst thing you could possibly do? Think Oedipus, only racier.'

Ellen thought about it, remembering her father's fondness for Greek tragedies, her eyes boggling. 'Sleep with your mother and kill your father?'

'Close.' Pheely removed the wart from the mermaid's nose and calmly lobbed it over her shoulder. 'Try again.'

'Sleep with your father and kill your mother?'

'It may have escaped your notice, but both Spurs' wretched parents are still alive.'

'Sleeping with both your parents and killing the Labrador?' Ellen was getting bored of playing games. 'Tell me.'

'You have a long, hard think about it.' Pheely swung round crossly. 'Think about the fact that everybody hates him. Think about the trouble he caused, the hearts he broke, the lives he wrecked and the mess he left this village in. He left in one hell of a hurry. He didn't come back for twelve years, and we still hate him. Think about that. And when you have, you might find you stop talking to me about him like he's the hunkiest Little Lord Fauntleroy you've ever met. Because he's not. Believe me, he's not – I'm fed up of telling you this. He is a very, very ugly character.'

Ellen quailed, dismayed that she had upset her so much.

'I'm sorry.' She moved into the sun beside Pheely, terrified at the thought of losing her friendship, more terrified still by the thought of what Spurs must have done.

Pheely sniffed, equally fretful. 'Please don't let's fall out over it. You're such a lovely new chum.'

'Of course not.' She quickly changed the subject. 'Is Dilly due back soon, then?'

'Last exam tomorrow – the school lets them go home as soon as they've finished. She's getting a lift back with the Fullertons' daughter – Lord knows where we'll put all her stuff. In the old house, I suppose – if I can find the keys.' Pheely turned back to stroke her mermaid's hair for comfort, still jumpy from her outburst. 'I'm going to cook her a fabulous meal to celebrate getting through her A levels – I thought I'd do a Thai creation with salmon and eggs. Eggs-salmon-Asian. Ingenious, huh?' Her jokes were always appalling when she was nervous.

Watching her wide, kind face, Ellen realised that whatever Spurs had done, she should leave it well buried. It was already stirring in its grave without her help.

Yet that evening, checking her emails, she couldn't resist typing 'Jasper Belling' into Google's search engine. Pages of matches flashed up, mostly press articles about Sir St John's fall from Tory grace and Spurs' prison sentence. He was right that he had forged more than cheques. It seemed the young, wayward Spurs had forged everything from historically important letters to prescriptions, VAT invoices and Munnings' sketches. Norman Gently's recognition of his final protogée's artistic talents had been well-founded.

Ellen read on late into the night, determined to hate him.

He'd said she needed him like a hole in the head. And he was right. Ellen's head had always been ruled by her heart, and the hole in her heart had grown so large in their brief acquaintance that a meteor could have landed in it. But, try as she might, she couldn't hate him.

'Ellen! Thank goodness. I need your help!'

Ellen tucked her mobile phone under her chin and reached for her coffee. 'Pheely, where are you?'

'At the Maddington market fish stall. I've just seen the nine-thirty bus go past without me on it, and I'm not going to get back in time for Godspell's sitting unless you rescue me.'

'I can't,' Ellen apologised.

'You have no idea how hard I had to work on Ely to release her on early parole. It will only take you twenty minutes.'

'The jeep's battery is flat.'

'Damn – no, *not* that fatty one, it looks as though it took a taxi upstream. I want that gym-fit salmon at the back.' Pheely broke off to issue instructions to the fishmonger. 'Damnedy damn. I don't have her mobile number, and the Manor Farm line is permanently engaged.'

Ellen could see Poppy's red Golf pulling up outside.

'Would you like me to go round and tell her you'll be late?'

'Oh, darling, that would be terribly kind – no, I want it *gutted* – do you mind?'

'Snorkel could use the walk.' Ellen waved as Poppy headed towards the house with yet more Tescos flowers and coffee. It was a good excuse to avoid another one of the estate agent's gushing misguided tours.

'You are super. I'll get the ten-thirty bus.'

'I'll let her know.'

The sun had returned to drench Oddlode in its melanoma furnace as Ellen set out along North Street, half expecting to meet Godspell coming the other way with a black parasol shading her pale little face. But the lane was deserted except for Hunter's rebellious bantam pecking at an abandoned crisp packet.

The village was unusually quiet, caught in the lull between children being walked to school and tourists arriving to nose around. Ellen fanned her T-shirt uneasily. It felt like a museum – unreal and unoccupied, a period film set awaiting its costumed players.

The haunting peal of Manor Farm's echoing old door bell seemed to accentuate the antiquation when she pulled it – fading away through the house as it summoned a shuffling housekeeper of days gone by.

The image was shattered when Felicity Gates' pudgy face appeared over the security chain, her mottled chins propping up a walkabout phone.

'Yes?' she asked suspiciously, not eager to find herself talking about insurance, double glazing or the Second Coming.

'Hi. Is Godspell in?'

Her face lit up and she opened the door to reveal an apron covered with alarming blood splatters. 'Are you one of her friends? How lovely. Come in! You can tie the dog to the boot scraper. Jonathan Cainer's recorded horoscope just said today would bring fresh faces.' She waggled the phone and pressed her ear to it once more as she led the way.

Before she could explain why she was there, Ellen found herself ushered through a dark panelled hallway, past a ticking long case clock and along a lobby to a narrow back staircase. 'I think she's in her room. She's going out any minute, so do—' Felicity cocked her head as the voice in her ear told her that today was good for romance '—do go straight up. Excuse me – I'm must finish cutting this pig up for the freezer before Lady Belling's coffee morning.' One ear still glued to Jonathan Cainer, Felicity waddled away.

As Ellen opened her mouth to ask directions, she was distracted by the sound of disembodied screaming coming from upstairs.

'Is that . . .' she asked, before realising that Felicity had disappeared, '. . . normal?' The screaming from above was soon accompanied by the sound of a cleaver hacking through tissue and bone in the nearby kitchen.

Without thinking, Ellen bounded the steps two at a time and found herself on a tiny landing, presumably some sort of old servants' quarters, its whitewashed walls hung with an alarming number of crosses. The screaming was coming from behind an arched doorway. She tried the handle and found it locked. Stepping back, she saw that it was fitted with a Yale.

'Hello? Hello! Are you okay?'

She listened in trepidation as the screaming continued, along with a maddened series of bangs and metal thrashes.

Moving along the landing, she found a tiny bedroom containing nothing more than a single bed, a small wardrobe and a wooden chair. Yet more crosses adorned the wall. It looked like a nun's cell.

To the left, a connecting door with another Yale lock led to the screaming room. It was ajar.

'Jesus!' Ellen stepped back when she pushed it open.

The first thing that hit her was the heat, closely followed by the smell. The room – as dark and moist as a witchdoctor's loin-cloth – smelled as though somebody had died in it.

The windows were shuttered and it was lit only by the dimmest of Anglepoise lamps. The gloomy walls were stacked with glass tanks, some of which possessed their own little lights, giving the impression of miniature skyscrapers with only a few of the offices occupied.

But as Ellen stepped cautiously into the room, she realised that all the tanks were very much occupied. They housed insects of every description – armoured, hairy, diaphanous, as big as hands and as small as eyelashes, gangly-legged and stumpy – all shuffling around in temperature-regulated, light-monitored high rise flats containing earth, leaves, mealworms, rotting flesh or fresh locusts. And all these insects were listening to the deafening, agonised screams being belted out of two stereo speakers that hung from the ceiling.

Covering her ears, she started to back away. As she did so, she tripped over a strip plug and accidentally yanked it from its wall socket.

Instantly the screaming stopped and the dim light bulb went out, plunging Ellen into near-darkness. She reached for the door, which had swung closed behind her, and realised to her horror that it must have latched itself from the outside.

'Shit!' she looked around in a panic, her eyes battling to adjust to the gloom.

That was when she heard the hissing.

One of the tanks was hissing at her.

'Eugh!' She leaped back as she realised that it contained half a dozen cockroaches as big as mice. From the tank above, two scorpions looked down at her thoughtfully, wondering what she had done to disturb their neighbour.

Rubbing her face with the balls of her hands to summon strength, she tried the door once again to no avail. Now that her eyes had started to adjust, she could see the locked door that must open on to the landing, and a further door on the opposite wall.

That was unlocked, leading to a room in pitch darkness. From its depths, Ellen could distinctly hear the fluttering of insect wings. This was getting way too *Silence of the Lambs*, she decided as she hastily closed the door once again and called out. 'Hello? Can anybody hear me? Hello? Godspell? Felicity? *Hello*?'

The hissing cockroaches increased their efforts and were joined by the rasping sound of cricket wings being rubbed together. The heat and stench were stifling.

Ellen banged on the door that led to the landing. 'Hellooooo! HELP!'

Nothing. Outside, she could just make out the sound of a car turning on gravel and its engine being cut.

She peered through a tiny slit between the window shutters and realised that the room overlooked the driveway. Ely Gates was climbing out of a black Range Rover. For a moment, he looked up at his house and seemed to stare straight at her, but then he heard Snorkel barking and disappeared from sight as he went to investigate.

'HELP!' Ellen tried again. 'Can anybody HEAR me? HELP!'

The hissing cockroaches gave up and shambled away to eat some rotting fruit.

She cast her eyes along the rows of tanks, totally failing to understand the appeal of such a hair-raising array of pets. A praying mantis cocked its skull-like head as it watched her from its illuminated cube. In the glass case beside it, several vast shiny beetles with great armoured horns on their heads formed an excited rugby scrum, kicking up sand. She was grateful for Snorkel's simple ball-catching pleasures.

Groping around on the floor, she located the socket strip and plugged it back into the wall, lighting up the small lamp in one corner and inadvertently cueing in the screaming once more.

'Waaaaaaaaaaa!' wailed the voice on the stereo.

She hurriedly crossed the room to silence it, too deafened by the racket to hear the feet marching up the stairs and a key being inserted into the lock.

'*What* have I told you about playing that—' Ely Gates' silhouette towered in the light pouring in from the landing, the crosses on the walls behind him dancing as Ellen blinked at the sudden brightness. 'May I ask what you are doing in my daughter's insectarium?'

Ellen could make out the arctic blue eyes gleaming in the dark face and quailed. 'I came to give her a message, and I got locked in by mistake.'

He rubbed his beard as he considered this.

'Pheely asked me to let her know that she's going to be late for their sitting.'

He said nothing.

'Is Godspell – er – here?'

He nodded towards the door that led to the pitch-black, wing-flapping room.

'In there?'

'You'll find her through the lepidoptery, yes.' He nodded. 'I shall ask my wife to make coffee. You may join us downstairs.'

Ellen was still staring nervously at the door. Lepidopterists collected moths and butterflies, as far as she remembered. 'Really, there's no need to –'

'Five minutes. No longer. Bring my daughter with you.' As he turned away, Ellen registered that this was an order.

Bracing herself, she walked into the blackened room, feeling, like Clarice Starling without the gun.

Now partly illuminated by the light that was spilling through the insectarium from the landing, the wing-flapping moths turned out to be safely contained in huge floor-to-ceiling tanks on two sides and mostly immobile, taking their daily naps. One or two big hawk-wings flew into action at the sight of daylight, thumping dustily against the glass as Ellen rushed past and knocked on yet another door in Godspell's creepy labyrinth. There was no answer.

'Christ,' she gasped as she let herself in. 'This just gets better.'

The secret room, decorated entirely in splattered gore red and widow black, was wallpapered with macabre posters for bands boasting names like The Parricide Parasites, Blood in my Vomit, Sisters of Myra Hindley and – most charmingly – Abba's Abattoir Abortion. A real gravestone was propped up against one wall, its pale stone face without inscription. Ellen looked around for a matching coffin, but saw only pointy gothic chairs covered with piles of black clothes topped with spilling ashtrays. The dusty black floor was littered with CD, video and PlayStation cases, and the room reeked of stale tobacco.

If the nun's cell was Godspell's bedroom and the rooms of tanks her pet sanctuary, then this appeared to be her playpen. It was mercifully devoid of live arachnids, mantids and cockroaches. But it was also apparently devoid of Godspell.

Scratching her head, Ellen wandered up to a long bench draped in dark red velvet, cluttered with spiky jewellery, photographs, Hooch bottles with black lipstick smudges around the necks, and notepads covered with scrawling handwritten verse – Roadkill's lyrics, she presumed, although she couldn't make out a legible word. Yet the manic black handwriting was strangely familiar.

Standing out among the gothic paraphernalia was a brightly coloured glass snowstorm – the sort peddled at tatty gift shops and souvenir stalls. Ellen picked it up and shook it, watching the gaudy glitter disperse and dance around a prancing plastic unicorn.

'Put that down!' ordered a husky little voice, and she spun around to see Godspell peeling a pair of headphones from her ears and casting a PlayStation controller to one side. Hunched amid the folds of a vast black velvet sag bag in the corner and dressed in her customary black, she'd been perfectly camouflaged as she silently fought blood-sucking zombies on a small portable television.

'What are you doing here?' She stood up, reaching across to turn off the set.

'I brought a message from Pheely . . .' Ellen hastily explained her mission.

Despite the gloominess of her lair, Godspell was wearing dark glasses. Her pale, pointed face didn't move as she listened and, afterwards, she said nothing. She had her father's gift for silence, it seemed.

'Ely asked that you come downstairs with me,' Ellen muttered awkwardly, studying what appeared to be a ghoulish shrine that formed a vast cross on one wall, where shelves of insects were entombed in Perspex.

Godspell appeared at her shoulder and reached for a dusty cube containing a stick insect. 'My first baby.'

'What was he called?'

'She,' Godspell corrected, 'was called Sticky.'

Ellen tried not to laugh. With the dark glasses in front of her eyes, it was hard to tell whether Godspell was looking at her or not.

'You really love them, don't you?' she asked.

Sticky's little plastic tomb was rolled between two pale, bony palms like a die about to be cast, the heavy gothic rings clinking. Godspell Gates – who had few friends and rarely spoke a great deal – was about to confide her great passion.

'They are my life.' She turned Sticky the right way up and held her up to the light. 'They really are very beautiful when you get to know them. Like angry men.' She pressed her dark lips to the cube and closed her eyes in silent prayer before placing it carefully back onto the shelf. 'We had better go,'

Ellen nodded, heading for the door, grateful to be leaving.

'This way.' Godspell indicated a huge black hanging cloth painted with a giant red spider on the opposite wall. 'I don't want you to disturb my pets again. They were listening to my music.' She held back the cloth to reveal an archway that led through to a tiny, neat study complete with iMac and shelves of reference books – mostly about insects.

'This is an amazing part of the house.' Ellen followed her through another archway to yet more stairs. 'You'd never know it existed from outside.'

'Dad calls it the Moth Wing,' Godspell muttered, neatening a framed set of exotic butterflies on the stairwell. 'It's not that big – we had to move the snakes to a garage.'

'Reptiles too, huh?' Ellen tried to sound chatty.

'It's a sideline – I prefer bugs.' Godspell opened a door that led out onto a formal landing, with button-backed ticking chairs and framed oils of flower arrangements. They were back in the main house. Again, there was a Yale lock on the door.

'The farmhouse is even more complicated than the manor house.' Ellen looked around, trying to work out how the Moth Wing fitted – a mathematical puzzle that she had to solve to satisfy her curiosity.

'I heard you liked it there.'

Ellen stopped dead. 'Liked it where?'

'At the manor.' Godspell stopped too. Then she swung around, dark glasses reflecting Ellen's questioning face. 'Do you know why he's nick-named Spurs?'

'Jasper – sper – Spurs?' Ellen suggested, wondering what she was driving at. 'And he rides horses.'

'Football,' Godspell informed her, running her tiny hand around the wooden turning post at the top of the stairs. 'Tottenham Hotspurs.'

'Oh.'

'I support Arsenal.'

'Really?' Ellen wasn't quite sure where this was going. Was Godspell's village nick-name Arse?

'Dad doesn't approve.'

'More of a rugby man?'

She shook her head. 'Arsenal is the Wycks' team.'

Ellen remembered that the last time she'd seen Saul Wyck, he'd been wearing a Gunners shirt. Pheely had mentioned that several Wycks were in Roadkill too. Ely was bound to disapprove.

'People round here say Jasper Belling only played at the football hooligan thing when he was a kid to wind the family up,' Godspell was saying. 'He used to graffiti cocks on the barns at Wyck's Farm.'

'Cocks?' Ellen had no idea that Spurs had been such a childish rebel.

'A cockerel is the Tottenham emblem.'

'Of course it is.' She coloured, still wondering why Godspell was telling her all this.

'The Wycks hate him for that – and other stuff he did back then.' She pushed her dark glasses higher up her nose. 'That's why . . . the thing is, they didn't realise someone else got hit by a bottle. Pheely says it knocked you out.'

Ellen crossed her arms angrily, torn between cursing Pheely's indiscretion and intrigue at what it had thrown up – or rather thrown over the garden wall. 'So you know who was behind the bottle that hit me?'

'A friend.' Her voice was deadpan.

'One of the Wycks.' Ellen knew not to push it. 'Were you there?'

She nodded.

'Was that why your father –'

'Dad doesn't know,' she muttered, glancing down the stairs. 'He's just mad at me for staying out late. Still thinks I'm a kid.' Her mouth twitched. 'Sorry you got hurt. You had enough grief with the badger that night.'

'Pheely told you about that too?'

She looked away. 'Yeah. That's right. Pheely told me.'

'Well, thanks for apologising. It wasn't your fault.'

'It was my bottle.'

Ellen thought about the Hooch bottles that lined Godspell's lair – along with the PlayStation games and brimming ashtrays. The same things had been amongst the mess that had greeted her arrival at Goose Cottage. Was Godspell Gates one of the Shaggers?

Before she could think of a suitably subtle way of finding out, Ely bellowed Godspell's name from below and the little Goth skittered downstairs.

In the Gates' sombre drawing room, Felicity – now minus blood-stained apron – was pouring coffee from a smart porcelain pot and glancing fretfully at the clock on the mantel. 'I really must leave for the manor, Elijah. You know how Lady Belling loathes to be kept waiting.'

Ely looked up as his daughter entered the room, his arctic gaze melting a little. 'Why not take Godspell, pudding? She is not required to sit for Ophelia until later today.'

Felicity looked flustered at the thought. 'Well, Lady Belling didn't actually –'

'Young Jasper will be there.' Ely stood up and removed his daughter's dark glasses, smoothing a few of the spiky black hairs that sprang from her crown. 'It's about time they got to know one another better. Go with your mother, Godspell. I shall have coffee with Miss Jamieson.'

Godspell let out a low noise that sounded remarkably like one of her hissing cockroaches, but Ely had complete control over daughter and wife, both of whom melted obediently away to apply black and pink lipsticks respectively, ready to transfer to the Belling Royal Doulton.

Ellen swallowed rising bile, not at all comfortable with the thought of hanging around as Ely indicated for her to sit and placed a cup of weak coffee on a walnut table in front of her, pinning her in. She glanced at her watch. 'I really must get back soon – I have people looking around the house. This is very kind, but I only popped by to let God –'

'You have not reconsidered my offer for the cottage?'

'My parents haven't, I'm afraid, no.' Ellen tried to be tactful, wishing her cup and saucer wouldn't rattle so much when she picked them up.

'They will.' Ely smiled confidently, settling in a leather wing chair nearby.

'I rather think not.' She cleared her throat. 'They're aware that you paid Lloyd to keep potential buyers away, you see.'

One grey eyebrow lifted like a seagull's wing above his choppy blue gaze and there was a long pause as he stirred a lump of sugar into his coffee.

Ellen studied a huge, dark oil painting of a dying stag that hung above the fireplace. Something about its wild, angry eyes, still fighting for every second of life as dogs tore at its neck, reminded her of Spurs.

'I do hope that you will be able to join in the garden party that Felicity and I are holding.' Ely broke the silence. 'It is always a very jubilant village occasion. Lloyd will be attending. I'm sure he would like to speak with you again.'

'I doubt I'll still be in Oddlode,' Ellen muttered, hardly able to believe his gall. 'Lots of people are interested in the cottage. It should be under offer within days.'

'What a shame,' he gave her a chilly smile, leaving her uncertain whether he was referring to the cottage's sale, or her likely pre-party departure.

There was another awkward pause and Ellen glared at a photograph of Ely shaking hands with Thatcher.

'You are a brave girl, are you not, Miss Jamieson?'

'Call me Ellen,' she muttered, her cup and saucer clattering like mad now that she returned his gaze. 'And I'm not brave. I just like to be honest about things.'

'You are brave,' he assured her, blue eyes freezing into hers. 'And foolhardy.'

'To expose your underhand tactics?'

He shook his head and smiled, looking into his own very steady cup. 'To befriend Jasper Belling.'

Ellen balked. 'I don't see that our friendship – and it hardly counts as that – can be any business of –'

'Leave him alone, Miss Jamieson.' He looked up, his glare crashing against her face like a tidal wave. 'He's evil.'

'It's Ellen. And I am leaving him alone, believe me. I want nothing more to do with him.'

'Good.' He adjusted his spoon on the saucer. 'I hope that, being such an *honest* person, I can take your word in this matter.'

She stared at him, cup rattling as she matched his formal tone. 'May I ask why you are encouraging your daughter to get to know this evil person better?'

He didn't blink. 'As you will no doubt have gathered, Godspell is rather fond of evil things.'

'I'm sure she loves her father very much.' She spoke tersely.

He took a sip of coffee, watching her over the rim, his gaze blood-chillingly steady.

Ellen put her cup down with a splash, knowing she had gone too far. 'I'm sorry. I must go.'

Without another word, Ely saw her to the door and she burst gratefully out into the sunshine.

Gathering Snorkel from her tether, she called Pheely from her mobile as she jogged home. 'I am *never* going to that house again,' she gasped. 'They are mad.'

'I did warn you that the girl is disturbed.'

'No wonder, with a father like that.'

'He's just old fashioned,' Pheely said cheerfully, market traders still calling out for custom in the background. 'Do you think Dilly would prefer treacle tart or lemon meringue pie for pudding? There's a stall here that does the most amazing cakes.'

'Shouldn't you be on the bus?' Ellen looked at her watch, wondering how on earth Pheely could still be grocery shopping.

'Damn! I knew I shouldn't have popped into the solicitors after I bought the fish.'

'Solicitors?'

'I was making my will abundantly clear.' Pheely giggled mellifluously. 'I'll have to catch the next bus. Could you possibly –'

'Godspell has gone – er – somewhere with her mother,' Ellen fluffed hastily. 'You have loads of time.'

'Goodie. Oh, I'll get both puddings. And I have time to buy vodka. Tonight is going to be so special!'

Pheely's A-level signature dish didn't quite work out. Dilly had already agreed to go clubbing with her schoolmates to celebrate the end of an era, leaving her mother glaring furiously into the dull eyes of the salmon and murderously lowering her vodka bottle's level below the A for Absolut. The following morning Dilly finally poled up at the same time as Godspell Gates. The former crashed into bed to sleep like the dead; the latter perched on a chair to pose for her sculptor, looking like the living dead.

To her consternation, Pheely found herself too busy with

Godspell's bust to spare her daughter much time over the coming days, and Dilly got increasingly bored, seeking entertainment by venturing across the road to see what Ellen was up to.

'Bloody Ely came over the morning after I got back,' she complained, taking Ellen's laptop into the garden to play with it. 'I couldn't possibly have a lie-in with the racket he and Mum made, arguing about that bloody bust. He says she's not pulling her finger out, and she started yelling that his fucking daughter was the one to blame. When I charged in to tell them to lay off, you should have seen their faces! Adults are so funny. Then Ely did his big, formal churchwarden act, asking after my exams and my "future plans". I told him I wanted to train to be a vicar just to wind him up – he's completely anti female clergy. Mum got terrible giggles. I wish she didn't have to do this bloody sculpture. I wanted this summer to be special.'

'There'll be lots of time after the garden party.'

'I suppose so.' Dilly lay back to sunbathe. 'But I might be in traction from the Devil's Marsh Cup by then. Spurs says Otto's seriously fast.'

Ellen picked up the discarded laptop and closed it. 'You've seen him, then?'

'Yes, I take him a bunch of carrots every morning. I haven't ridden him yet, though.'

'I meant Spurs.'

'So did I.' Dilly snorted, getting the giggles as she rolled on to her belly and looked up at the glossy new for-sale sign. 'How's it going? *Please* tell me Jamie Oliver is going to buy it after a messy divorce.'

After a promising start, Poppy had reported a hitch. One or two low offers had already dribbled in, but almost all of the buyers had commented on how offputtingly dark the cottage was, with its low, hooded windows and the Jamiesons' love of rich, sombre colours.

'It is dark – old cottages are,' Ellen grumbled. 'I know Mum and Dad's taste is a bit traditional, but they had an army of decorators to do all this.'

'I could help you repaint it!' Dilly sat up excitedly. 'It wouldn't take more than a couple of days to cover those dreary down-stairs walls.'

'I don't know if it's worth it – whoever buys it will redecorate straight away.'

Dilly had an obvious ulterior motive. 'We could get Spurs to help. He helped you before, didn't he?'

Ellen tried to imagine Spurs' face if she turned up saying, 'Let's forget about the badger and the fact I'm not hot enough to sleep with. My second wish is that you make over the cottage.' She still hadn't caught sight of him all week, although she looked up with sickening excitement every time she heard horse's hooves passing by, and her walks inevitably seemed to take in the loop past the manor. 'I'm sure he has better things to do,' she said quickly. 'And the cottage really isn't that bad.'

But Dilly was inspired, already bounding inside to take a look at the project, alarmingly like Lawrence Llewellyn Bowen in a curly blonde wig. 'If you painted all these walls white, it would show off the stonework and the beams,' she pointed out. 'It would make it look really medieval.'

'That William Morris wallpaper cost my parents a fortune.'

'But it's *so* gross. This place is so gloomy and depressing. And it looks like a chapel of rest with all these flowers lit-tered about.' There was nothing like a teenager for summing things up.

Ellen started to laugh, cheered by her energy.

'Oh, come on,' Dilly pleaded. 'I'll help you for nothing – I'd just be grateful for something to do.'

'What about riding Otto?'

'Spurs is far better at that than me. Actually, I get a bit freaked out by him. He scares me.'

'Are we talking Spurs or Otto this time?'

'Both.'

Having convinced Dilly that they really didn't need Spurs' help, Ellen took her to the bizarre higgledy-piggledy hardware store in

Market Addington where they bought several litres of one-coat emulsion, two trays and two rollers.

'You are *so* good at maths.' Dilly whistled, as Ellen calculated how much paint they'd need.

'My mother read me times tables in bed instead of stories,' Ellen joked, although it was closer to the truth than she cared to admit.

'My mother told me about her boyfriends,' Dilly giggled, 'so I only ever got up to the two-timed table. She has a crap love-life. It's the only thing we have in common.'

With the stereo blaring and all the doors and windows open to disperse the fumes, they slapped on paint and found a tremendous ability to render each other senseless with giggles. To Ellen's shame, the source of a great deal of this laughter was Pheely's eccentric attitude to motherhood.

'She didn't bother getting a push-chair when I was a toddler, just used the wheelbarrow to take me out, trundling me back from the village shop with a crusty loaf and a *Daily Telegraph*. I always smelt of compost and potash. She says we had to beg, barrow and steal the show because we were so poor after Grandpa died. She's such a bloody exhibitionist – apart from when she has an exhibition and she gets so nervous she hides.

'When I was little, she used to give me lumps of clay to play with because she couldn't afford toys,' she told Ellen, as she trailed masking tape along the wooden skirting-boards, 'and I'd just poke my fingers into them. Mum glazed and fired everything I did because she couldn't bear to throw it away. That was around the time the Spring Open Studio Week started in West Oxfordshire and art-lovers would troop in. She was furious that my stuff sold out and hers didn't. That was when I got my first pony.'

Ellen couldn't help wondering how a mother who couldn't afford to buy her daughter toys could find the money to keep a pony or send her away to school. She must have charged a fortune for the finger sculptures.

'That was the year we moved out of the Lodge and into the cottage,' Dilly explained. 'Mum simply couldn't run the big house any more. Things became a lot easier after that, although I missed the television.'

'Couldn't you move that to the cottage?'

'Mum's work was getting very experimental at that time, so she smashed the screen and filled it with little clay people trying to fight their way out. It was pretty cool, actually, but nobody bought it.'

Dilly clearly had a classic love-hate relationship with her mother. Given such a Bohemian childhood, she was wilful and more than a little spoilt, and she patently resented the lack of luxuries that her schoolfriends had taken for granted.

'She's not mean, but she just doesn't understand or want the same things as other people. She's never seen a soap opera in her life, or worn a pair of trainers. She thinks entertainment is reading a favourite chapter of Iris Murdoch or playing a Carpenters' LP – an LP! I ask you! Who has vinyl any more? Most of my friends' parents are *much* older than Mum, but they know what a DVD and an Mpeg are. They have cars they can teach their kids to drive in, they watch *Big Brother*, and they have a social life.

'We hardly ever went on holiday – Mum can't drive and we've always had a dog, so it was hard to get away. We took Gertrude – that was our old Labrador – to Wales once on the train to go camping. It was only when we got there that Mum admitted we didn't have a tent. She'd brought the drain rods and a couple of old tarpaulins because she thought she could "fashion" something, but it was a total disaster and all the B-and-Bs were too expensive, so we caught a train straight home.'

Her funny stories and her extraordinary blend of innocence and cynicism made her beguiling company, although she lacked her mother's naughty but wise wit and self-deprecation. Ellen was reminded again and again of how childlike both women were, little girls who had grown up in a fairy grotto and been sent away to old-fashioned schools, destined to spend holidays playing solitary games and only conversing with one – very eccentric and equally childlike – adult. And, just like Pheely, she got the impression that Dilly longed to break free from the spell that had trapped her in time. Her vivacious energy had a curious anger to it.

'Do you want to be an artist?' Ellen asked, as she watched her slapping on emulsion with gusto.

'God, no – it's so lonely. Mum wants me to become a doctor or a solicitor. *Boring!* I've always had other plans.'

Ellen expected her to announce the desire to be rich and famous in common with her sometime-friend Godspell. But, to her surprise, Dilly said, 'I want to get married as soon as possible.'

'And . . . ?'

'And have *lots* of babies.' She loaded her roller and attacked a fresh wall. 'I want to make a big, boisterous family to fill the Lodge. Mum can live in the cottage and baby-sit when she's not sculpting. It'll be perfect.'

Ellen couldn't see Pheely taking to an annexed-granny role, but she kept schtum. 'What about university? I thought you had a place?' She remembered Pheely boasting proudly that Dilly would have the academic opportunities that young motherhood had denied her.

'Yeah, and I'll take it if I don't meet my husband this summer – it's a good hunting ground for husbands, and I'm bright enough to get a degree while I'm at it. But I'd rather not go away again. I love this place. I belong here.'

Ellen couldn't have got it more wrong. Dilly just wanted to share the magic Lodge with a proper family at last, one of her own making.

'It's a shame Mum hasn't ever married – she just borrows other people's husbands.' She gave Ellen a mischievous look. 'But she's still young enough to have more babies, so maybe we can do it together. That would be beyond cool. Can a mother and daughter marry a father and son, or is that illegal?'

Ellen tried not to laugh. 'Who did you have in mind?'

'I'm not sure yet.'

'Well, it would certainly get Lily Lubowski going.'

'Too right!' Dilly shrieked with laughter. 'I might put an ad up in the post-office window. They'll need to be local, ideally, and very rich – the Lodge needs thousands of pounds of work.'

Ellen was having trouble getting her head around Dilly's plans. She couldn't tell whether she was extraordinarily naïve for seventeen or wise beyond her years. She certainly had a strange attitude to men. 'Do you have any contact with your father?'

'He died when I was a baby,' Dilly said flatly.

'I'm sorry.'

Dilly sent showers of paint over herself and the floor as she overloaded the roller and drew great white zigzags across the dark blue flowered walls. 'He was an artist like Mum, one of Grandpa's students. Mum says he was the most beautiful man in all the world. He was the love of her life, her true soulmate. If he hadn't died, they'd still be together, living at the Lodge with hordes of children. He was killed in a motorcycle accident.'

'I'm sorry.' Ellen saw the sting in Dilly's childlike fairytale plans. She wanted to create the life that a tragic death had stolen away. Her heart went out to Pheely, who had never breathed a word, or shown any self-pity for the love that had been taken from her.

Dilly dipped her roller again. 'I never knew him, so I don't really miss him – like Mum not having a mother to look after her when she grew up. I want to meet my soulmate while I'm still young, so that we can have our whole lives together. I planned to do it when I was sixteen, like Mum, but I'm crap at flirting and exams got in the way. Bloody all-girls' schools are hopeless. Did you go to an all-girls' school?'

'No, I went to the local comp.'

'God, I envy you.' White paint splattered over the T-shirt Dilly was wearing. 'I wanted to, but Mum said I had to go away and get a proper education – so she could get sloshed and behave badly while I wasn't around to see. Did you have lots of boyfriends at school?'

'No. I met a boy at sixteen and we were together until quite recently.'

But you never married or had children?'

She shook her head.

'In that case, he can't have been your soulmate.'

'He was once.' Ellen thought about Richard. 'But I was very different at sixteen. We both were. Souls grow up too, you know, and they can grow apart.'

'Yeah, well, I'm seventeen now – so I know more about what I want. I'm ready to get married.'

'I'm twenty-nine, and I'm not.' Ellen laughed. 'Are you sure you'll feel the same way in ten years?'

'Absolutely. I know it's time. I think Rory might be my soulmate. Or, at least, I did,' she heaved a deep sigh, 'until I met Spurs. Now *he* is gorgeous. Do you think he fancies me?'

Ellen's roller hissed against the wall as she waited to breathe normally, anxious not to react with a stupid, jealous blurt that would give away her feelings. 'Bound to,' she said finally, looking across at the blonde curls spilling from their scrunchie and the pretty face covered with paint speckles, forcing herself to give Dilly a cheery smile that said, 'What man wouldn't?'

'Really? Has he said something?'

'I haven't seen him lately.' The goosebumps sprang to attention as they always did when she spoke about Spurs.

'I see him around all the time.' Dilly sounded surprised, then thought about it, pressing the roller to her chin. 'Maybe it's fate.'

'Maybe.' Ellen painted carefully around a light fitting.

'I believe in fate. Like him coming back to the village this summer. *And* I've just studied *Romeo and Juliet* for A level.' She waved the roller excitedly, revealing a white beard where it had been pressed to her chin.

Ellen was too jumpy at the subject matter to risk arguing about the spurious connection between the two. The Bellings and the Gentlys were hardly the Montagus and Capulets of Oddlode, but Dilly's romantic interpretation was pure teenage Juliet, and Ellen was a reluctant Nurse, listening to her flights of fancy. Somewhere in the outskirts of her mind, this triggered a thought she couldn't quite grasp – something or somebody Dilly reminded her of.

'I can't see Spurs making a very reliable husband,' she mused, before remembering suddenly that Glad Tidings had said Hell's Bells was determined to marry him off. She felt spiteful fingers pinching her heart.

'I don't want a stockbroker, I want a soulmate,' Dilly said petulantly.

Ellen tried to imagine Dilly having anything approaching a normal marriage, and couldn't. It would be wild and wonderful, and almost certainly disastrous unless she found somebody wild and wonderful enough to take her on. Then her pinched heart turned over as she registered that she was being handed a golden bow and a poisoned Cupid's arrow.

They did look beautiful together, Ellen conceded, thinking back to the day in the garden. They would have stunning children. Perhaps Dilly was the angel Spurs needed to lift him from disgrace. They could be eccentric and lawless together in the decrepit old Lodge. He could paint and ride and revel, and she would have his babies. If only the mothers-in-law could see the sense in it . . .

'I thought you two got on really well.' Dilly was fishing, radiating as much heat as a Ready Brek kid.

'I hardly *know* him.' Ellen turned to look into those sparkling green eyes, caught up in a frenzy of goosebumps and heart rush. 'But I know his soul very well indeed. I recognised it straight away.'

'You did?' Dilly didn't think this odd at all. 'And what's it like?'

Ellen bit the corner of her mouth before saying truthfully, 'It's very like mine.'

'You fancy him, then?' The plump lower lip was thrust out huffily.

'Oh, Dilly, he's not my soulmate,' she lied. 'We're sole survivors from two separate shipwrecks that washed up on the same shore – or, in our case, the same landlocked village. I'm leaving as soon as I can float this boat.' She jerked her head around the room. 'Spurs only stopped by to help me put it back together – like you are.'

'Like me.' Dilly drew in a little breath. 'That is *so* beautiful.'

Ellen coloured against the white wall she had just painted, aware that she had got thoroughly swept up in Dilly's ingenuous fairytale world of love-ever-after.

'It *is* fate, isn't it?' Dilly smiled widely, cracking her painted white beard. 'Village fate!'

Ellen nodded. It was, in fact, a village fate worse than death, as far as she was concerned. Meeting Spurs was confusing enough, but playing the Good Witch to his wizardry and to Dilly's Dorothy made her want to join Richard in Oz.

By late evening, they had painted the dining room. Dilly dashed home to check whether Godspell had gone and to invite her mother back for a drink, leaving Ellen to scrub paint splashes from the flagstones. A strong wind blew blossom in through the open door and drew long, mournful breaths in the chimneys.

Ellen folded up the old sheets that she had used to cover the furniture and carried them through to the sitting room, ready to tackle it the next day. Dilly had been right. The white walls transformed the dining room, so that moving between it and the dark reds of the sitting room was like walking from heaven to hell. Fitting, then, that she was in hell when she heard hooves on the lane and looked out to see Spurs riding past on Otto with Dilly walking beside them, chatting eagerly. Spurs was dressed in an old hay-covered sweatshirt with a rip in one shoulder and jeans so faded they were almost white. His cheeks were high with colour and, from the dark sweat glistening on Otto's neck and flanks, he had clearly been for a gallop.

He reined Otto to a halt at the gate and Ellen ducked down to peer out through a vase of orange chrysanthemums strategically placed by Poppy, cursing Snorkel who was barking an ecstatic greeting from her tether. The wind was buffeting Spurs' curls

and whipping Otto's pink mane into a Mohican as he snorted
nervily, nostrils flared like two red trumpets.

'Ellen? Are you there?' she heard Dilly call, and ducked down
again, accidentally catching the lip of the chrysanthemum vase
with her baseball-cap peak and knocking it over so that a litre
of smelly flower water cascaded into her cleavage. She lunged
just in time to catch the vase as it rolled off the window-sill and
clutched it to her dripping chest, holding her breath. Why was it
that every time she saw him, she got absolutely soaked? Still, at
least it cooled her down.

'Ellen?'

When she took another peek, she could see Spur's forehead
creased as his silver eyes watched the window. He said something
to Dilly, and shook his head.

Dilly was clearly trying to persuade him to hang around,
pointing first at the cottage, where Ellen was lurking, then down to
the paddock where Rory's jumps were still set up from a fortnight
earlier. But Spurs just laughed and reached down to ruffle Dilly's
hair before he rode away.

Ellen felt a stab of pain so sharp in her fast-pumping heart that
she gasped. She couldn't believe how jealous she felt, just because
Spurs had made an affectionate gesture towards Dilly. She was in
agony, and close to tears. It was pathetic.

'Oh, wow, oh, wow!' Dilly gasped, as she dashed inside. 'Ellen?
Where are you? Something so fantastic has just happened! Oh –
you poor thing. You're all wet. Jesus! You're bleeding!'

Ellen looked down to see red marks spreading through the wet
fabric of her grey T-shirt. 'Shit!' She'd been clasping the vase
so tightly to her chest that it had cracked, a sharp edge cutting
into her skin. She put it carefully to one side and pulled up
her T-shirt to look. 'It's okay – it's just a scratch.' She watched
the little beads of blood gathering in a fringed line along her
breastbone.

Dilly dropped to her haunches beside her and started gathering
the orange flowers from the flagstones, breathless with excitement. 'Spurs has just asked me out!'

'Really?' Ellen asked in a strangled voice, mopping up water with one of the sheets, burning with envy and self-loathing.

'Yes – I just met him coming down the bridleway when I was walking out of the gate with Godspell. Mum says she'll be over in ten minutes, by the way, she's just taking a shower.' She was talking far too fast in her excitement. 'You're so right – it's fate! It's fate! I just stepped out and there he was, like magic, asking if I was busy tomorrow night.'

Ellen closed her eyes for a second. 'How . . . fateful.'

'I know! Oh, God, Ellen – Rory's going to be there so I really, really need your help. Oh, please, say yes. You see, it's a sort of double date . . .' The big green eyes watched her pleadingly.

Ellen's heart crashed so hard at the thought of a night out with Spurs that she expected showers of blood to spring from her T-shirt. 'I'm not sure, Dilly. I'm pretty busy at the moment.' Who was she trying to fool?

'Oh, please, Ellen. I'm helping you paint.'

'Your mother will be livid.'

'You mustn't tell her!' In alarm Dilly let the chrysanthemums fall to the floor.

Ellen knew she must come across as an ageing stick-in-the-mud, but she was sinking into emotional quicksand. 'Won't she want to know where you are?'

'That's where I need your help.' Dilly bit her smiling lip. 'Can you say you're taking me to the cinema or something to say thanks?'

'I don't like lying – especially to a friend.'

'You're *my* friend too,' Dilly whined. 'It would mean *so* much to me.' She snatched up the flowers again. 'I haven't seen Rory since I got back from school – Mum still won't get the moped fixed and it's too far to walk to Upper Springlode, particularly if he's not interested.' It seemed that even a soulmate didn't merit a three-mile uphill hike. 'I don't know how I feel about him any more, but I'm dying to see him.'

And I'm dying to see Spurs, Ellen thought wretchedly. I know

I shouldn't. I know we're bad for each other, and he's up to no good.

But she couldn't help herself. The moment he reappeared from the shadows, the socking great torch she was holding for him lit up with a million candlepower, searching him out. It was all very well teasing herself with the idea that he and Dilly were the Bryant and May of perfect matches, but she couldn't make herself forget the inevitable fact that she and Spurs were as combustible as a lead azide detonator and a lump of gelignite.

'So you really want to see Rory?' She wondered if she could cope with Spurs playing her off against Dilly, if that was his game. She doubted she'd last five minutes, and poor drunken Rory wouldn't have much fun either.

'Totally.' She nodded. 'Can't you see how kismet this whole thing is? This way, I can decide whether I fancy him or Spurs most.'

And, meanwhile, I do what exactly? Mark them both out of ten for you? Ellen wondered murderously, regretting her earlier encouragement.

'My only worry is that bloody Godspell will snitch.'

'Why should she?' Ellen turned to look at her.

'Because she'll be there, stupid.' Dilly giggled, burying her face in the broken chrysanthemums. 'Didn't I say? She's the other girl coming on the date.'

'Godspell?' She wanted to throw herself on the broken vase. She was, it seemed, a wrong-end-of-the-stick in the mud.

'Yes – I can't believe she agreed to it, but I guess it's impossible to say no to someone as gorgeous as Spurs, and it'll make a change from staying in her room watching horror movies on satellite. I had no idea Spurs knew her. In fact, I'm sure he doesn't. Oh, he is *so* fantastic – he must have remembered that I said Godspell and I had fallen out and is trying to mend the rift for me. You don't think he fancies her too, do you?' She looked worried.

'I'm sure you'll have Spurs and Rory clamouring for your

attention – along with Godspell.' Ellen was staggered by Dilly's egotism.

'Oh, I do hope so, that would be *so* cool.' Dilly smiled happily, and Ellen realised who she reminded her of: Queeny from *Blackadder II*, a joyful narcissistic caricature of girl power, winding up Nursey and Lord Melchett with her capricious demands and her petulant reminders 'Who's queen?'

'So will you help me?' Dilly cocked her head winsomely. 'And can I please, please borrow something to wear? You have such trendy clothes and Mummy's been such a bitch about money lately – she won't let me buy anything.'

Ellen only wished she had a trendy chastity-belt.

'I'd love a tattoo like yours. Will you do a temporary one on my shoulder for me? I got a henna kit for Christmas.'

'How about a badger?' Ellen suggested evilly, overcome by an urge to write a message warning Spurs off.

'That would be lovely! A badger catching a butterfly – I can sketch it out for you first if you like.'

'Sure,' she agreed reluctantly, trailing into the bootroom to rinse off the flower water, aware that she smelled as foul as her thoughts.

That evening, Ellen knocked back an uncharacteristic three glasses of wine with Pheely in the Goose Cottage garden while Dilly – as high as a kite caught in a whirlwind romance – threw Snorkel's ball again and again, doing handstands and cartwheels like a six year old.

I did a handstand the day Spurs granted me my first wish, Ellen thought angrily. He did a handstand the next day. Now he's got Dilly at it. Perhaps circus tricks are catching.

'Isn't she beautiful?' Pheely sighed indulgently. 'I was never that pretty.'

'I'm sure you were.' Ellen decided that Pheely was, in fact, far more beautiful than her buxom blonde daughter – who was, in truth, immature and rather gingery. 'You're still absolutely stunning.'

'Oh, you are sweet – like the loveliest little sister – but I'm going to seed faster than the cabbages in Reg Wyck's allotment. I just wish I had your looks.'

Ellen, who had never been confident of her beauty, particularly after years without a single compliment from Richard, found herself asking vainly why Pheely would want to look like her.

'Oh, come on!' Pheely reacted a bit snappishly, already working her way through a second wine bottle. 'Look at you – blonde, blue-eyed, tanned, a figure to die for. Most women must hate you. You could steal half the husbands in this village if you wanted to.'

'I don't want a husband,' Ellen said idly. 'I want a soulmate.'

'Bollocks.' Pheely giggled, reaching for the bottle again. 'No such thing – just lovers and other animals. And very good friends.' She chinked it against Ellen's glass.

'Dilly told me,' Ellen started cautiously, checking that the girl was still doing gymnastics out of earshot, 'about her father. She said that he was your soulmate.'

'Did she?' Pheely said archly, spilling wine over her knees.

'Sorry. You probably don't like reminding. It's terribly sad.'

'What exactly did she tell you?'

'That he was killed in a motorbike accident when she was just a baby.'

'Oh, that one – I didn't think she used it any more.' Pheely smiled fondly at her daughter, who was dangling her feet in the pond now and teasing Snorkel with the ball so that the clown-faced collie plunged in and out of the reeds, sneezing at the water in her nose.

'You mean it's not true?'

'It is, if she wants it to be.' Pheely raised her glass as Dilly turned to wave at them, blowing kisses, two butterflies dancing above her blonde head. 'She absolutely doesn't want to know her real father, so she likes to make up imaginary ones.'

'You mean he's still alive?'

'Oh, yes. Unlike this topic of conversation.' The green eyes hardened.

Ellen knocked back her glass of wine in one and suddenly wondered if it could be Spurs. She tried to do the sums, but she was too drunk. Whatever was going on, something definitely didn't add up.

> 'Lavender's blue, Dilly Dilly,
> Lavender's green.
> When you are King, Dilly Dilly,
> I will be queen . . .'

Dilly sang happily as they painted the sitting room walls the following day. 'Godspell winked at me this morning when she turned up for her sitting. I think that means she's cool about tonight.'

She could talk about nothing but the double date and the agonising decision that faced her.

'I had this huge crush on Rory last year, but he never showed any interest,' she lamented. 'And I know Spurs is much older, but the way he looks at me just makes my hairs stand on end, you know?'

Oh, I know, Ellen thought uneasily. No amount of Frizz Ease and hairspray could stop her skin prickling like a hedgehog whenever he was near.

'I think he'd be thrilling to lose my virginity to – he's so experienced, he's bound to be a really thoughtful lover.'

'Don't bet on it,' Ellen said, goosebumps popping. 'Loving and leaving a lot of women isn't a great indication of thoughtfulness.'

'Rory's always shagging Sharon.' Dilly's pretty face tightened. 'She's his head girl – in every sense. She's so madly in love with him, she doesn't mind that he can never remember her name or afford to pay her just so long as she gets to share the horrible bed in her mobile home with him once or twice a month. He walks all over her.'

'A plimsoll mate,' Ellen muttered.

'He would *never* treat me like that, of course.' Dilly stretched to paint a high corner. 'But that reminds me, I need to ask you about sex just so I don't end up looking stupid.' She made it sound as if she was about to sit another exam.

'What about it?'

'Well, I know the basics, but could you show me how to give a blow-job? We could use a bottle or a banana or something.'

Ellen painted a light switch without noticing. 'Take my advice and don't even think about sleeping with Rory yet. Just go and have a fun night out, and make friends with Godspell again.'

'Godspell didn't lose her virginity until she was *twenty*,' Dilly told her indiscreetly, not at all interested in Ellen's advice. 'That was last year. We were close then – we used to hack out together at weekends. She got fed up waiting, so she drank half a bottle of her mother's Amaretto before the village barn dance and propositioned Archie Worthington. They did it in one of Ely's holiday cottages. She said it was quite nice – a bit uncomfortable to start with, but very grown-up and sexy, like getting your first bra.'

Ellen remembered her first bra – a Lycra and scaffolding creation that had pinched her small but burgeoning double-A bust into submission while she continued competing in her school's sports teams. It had not been remotely sexy.

'And are Godspell and Archie soul-mates?' She tried to keep the conversation on love-song.

'I don't think they ever actually talked.' Dilly snorted in amusement. 'She only did it with him to get experienced enough to chase The Candle.'

'What is the Candle?'

'That's what she calls a guy she's always been mad keen on – she wouldn't even tell me his name.'

Ellen's thoughts turned briefly to the Shaggers. She now strongly suspected Godspell of being one, in which case perhaps this mysterious Candle was the other? They had certainly burned enough of his namesakes while lighting their romantic encounters in the Jamiesons' four-poster.

'I doubt it worked.' Dilly clearly didn't want to distract herself with an ex friend's love-life for long. 'Archie told Dickon Hewitt that she wasn't up to much.

'What was your first time like?'

'Awkward, painful – it took a few tries before I started to enjoy it.'

'Do you know lots of different positions now?'

'A few.'

'Which is the best? For a beginner, I mean.'

'Sitting down with your legs crossed all night.'

'You sound like Mum.'

'Have you told her about tonight, then?'

'God, no! But she's always lecturing me about sex. I think she was a bit pissed last night because she kept insisting that she had once been the most beautiful creature in Oddlode.' She sniggered. 'She put on her favourite Carpenters LP when we got home and told me that Spurs had been "in awe" of her.'

'He probably was.' Ellen hadn't forgotten Pheely confessing the failed teenage seduction.

Dilly mulled this over as they took a toast-and-coffee lunch break and Ellen drew a rather lopsided badger chasing a butterfly on her smooth-skinned shoulder, which ended up looking as though it was playing host to a duck-billed platypus waving its webbed claws at a pterodactyl. Dilly's increasingly single-track line of conversation distracted her reluctant tattooist. 'Do you have a condom I could borrow? I don't want to get pregnant straight away like Mum, but Lily Lubowski would tell the entire village if I bought a packet of three from the shop.'

'Aren't you planning to wait until you marry?' Ellen asked, bearing in mind the romantic whimsy behind Dilly's plans. Twisting her soulmate into a sexual back-flip and slipping a condom on with her teeth on a first date hardly seemed to fit in with flower-fairy families in the Lodge.

'God, no! The sooner I know what it's all about, the better. I was thinking about it in bed last night, and I decided that I really should start out by getting rid of the big V ASAP.' She giggled at the accidental rhyme. 'I'm sure Spurs would be up for it – he's so sexual. Mum says he'd slept with hundreds of people by the time he was my age. And if Rory really is my soulmate, being broken in by an expert like Spurs would make him jealous enough to 'fess up to his feelings.'

Her attitude appalled Ellen, as did the information about Spurs' early sexual voracity. 'It doesn't work like that, Dilly.'

'I don't see why not. I fancy Spurs and he is a *very* naughty man, as everybody keeps telling me. He might well be my true soulmate, in which case Rory's missed the boat. I have a very special feeling about tonight – I did the tarot and got the Lovers three times.'

'That doesn't mean you should set out with the intention of having a shag, Dilly. Sex should be a lot more special than that.'

'That's *such* an uptight attitude. And you can talk – Mum told me about your one-night stand with the estate agent.'

Bloody Pheely, Ellen thought darkly, wishing she hadn't given her so much wine the previous night. 'I'm at least ten years older than you – and it wasn't a one-night stand, it was just dinner,' she insisted, frantically casting around for a change of subject. 'Where are you all going tonight?'

'Just the Plough in Upper Springlode – nice and handy for Rory's cottage. Actually, most pubs have condom machines in the loos, don't they?' Dilly was still thinking about sex – albeit safe sex.

'Often only the men's loos,' Ellen muttered.

'I always use the gents – after all, I am a Gently.'

When they gathered up their rollers again, Ellen painted as quickly as possible so that Dilly would go home and leave her alone.

I want to be going out with Spurs, she thought unhappily. I want to go out to a country pub on a sunny evening and sit in the garden, flirting and joking and thinking about what he'd be like to go to bed with. I want to go on a double date with him, Rory and Dilly – if only to ensure Dilly keeps her knickers on. The thought of Spurs and the ravishing teenager entwined in a haystack was crucifying, both because it made her wildly jealous and because she was frightened for Dilly. She was tempted to run straight round to Pheely and scream, 'We have to stop her getting hurt!'

At last the sitting room was as angelically bright, white and pure as the dining room, the paintings, flowers and furnishings providing bright splashes of buyer-friendly colour.

With a heart as heavy as a songbird full of lead shot, Ellen dispatched Dilly with her favourite little floral slip-dress, a short blue leather jacket and her strappy clubbing sandals.

'You're such a good friend, Ellen – I wish you were my big sister.' Dilly hugged her at the door. 'And you're really okay if I tell Mum you're taking me out to the cinema to thank me?'

Ellen was sorely tempted to warn Dilly that if she didn't tell her mother exactly what was happening, Ellen would. Caught in a strange mid-generational gap between the two, she was uncertain with whom she identified most or to whom she owed her loyalty. But Dilly's increasing obsession with Spurs cast her in the role of secret, guilty, voyeuristic empathiser. It was horribly addictive.

'Call round any time, if you want to talk,' she found herself saying, and instantly felt like a creepy old hag.

'Thanks – I might.' Dilly grinned, unfazed by her ambitious plans to lose the big V ASAP. 'I'll check what film's showing at Maddington Corn Exchange tonight so that we can synchronise stories if she asks,' Dilly promised. 'I'm meeting Spurs under the lime tree at seven, so don't forget to hide your jeep and make it look like you're out – Mum is bound to go out for a walk with Hamlet before it gets dark.'

'The battery's flat . . .' Ellen remembered. Too late: Dilly had already danced away beneath the lime tree and through the magical gate.

Pheely, in fact, set out for her evening perv around the village at a quarter to seven, popping in on Ellen on the way, big green eyes blinking warmly because she knew she'd been testy – and a little drunk – the evening before, plus wildly indiscreet afterwards.

'Gosh, this looks *so* much better. Heavenly – apart from the smell.' Her nose wrinkled against the paint fumes as she wandered from the dining room to the sitting room. 'You and Dilly *have* worked hard – the evening light looks just amazing on here now.

I might loan you a sculpture to put in that corner . . . It would really set it off.'

'How is the bust going?' Ellen trod water, trying not to look at her watch and wondering what the hell to do.

'Ghastly. That girl hasn't spoken one word since we started, although she winked at me twice today, which was frankly creepy – it works rather well in clay, mind you, lends her face a teensy bit of animation.' She smiled impishly. 'Dilly is *so* jealous and attention-seeking, poor duck – it must be rotten after all her hard work to come home and find Mum so distracted. Thank you, darling one, for keeping her out of my hair. You are my fairy godsister and her fairy god-aunt.'

'She was a great help and great company,' Ellen said honestly, glancing out of the window at the lime tree. She didn't feel very godly – more guilty, duplicitous and anxious.

'Shouldn't you be getting ready?' Pheely had finally taken in Ellen's paint-stained shorts and old denim shirt. 'Dilly's really going to town. She's been locked in the bathroom for hours – says you're treating her to a meal at the Turnpike afterwards, the lucky thing. You might have invited me.'

'I – er – was going to, but— Oh, phone!' Ellen leaped on it in relief.

'Help!' It was Dilly. 'Mum's out on the prowl.'

'Yes, I know.'

'Is she there?'

'Mmm.'

'Oh, no! What are we going to do?'

'Not much I can do about it, I'm afraid.'

'You've got to get rid of her.'

'That might not be very easy.' Ellen looked round to see Pheely floating through to the kitchen and rooting a bottle of red wine out of the larder, mouthing, 'Quick drinky?'

'I'm going to call Spurs. Please, Ellen, think of something!' Dilly begged.

Ellen cut the call, took a deep breath and turned to Pheely, who had found two clean glasses now and was eager to impart a bright idea. 'I might stay here to look after Snorkel this evening and watch the box,' she suggested, searching the drawers for a corkscrew. 'I haven't watched television in years, and if I'm here you can leave the windows open to get rid of the smell of paint. Dilly says you have three viewings tomorrow.'

'I'm not taking Dilly out tonight. Spurs is.'

'What?' A drawer clattered shut.

'He wants to thank her for letting him ride Otto,' Ellen improvised, trying to make it sound better and hating herself. 'Rory and Godspell are going too – just for a drink in Upper Springlode. It's all perfectly innocent, but Dilly was afraid that you would get the wrong idea, which is why she lied to you.'

'How dare she?' The bottle crashed on to the surface, making Hamlet quail and Snorkel dive for cover behind her mistress's legs. 'And how *dare* you collude? I thought you were my friend.'

'Which is why I'm telling you the truth.' Ellen bit her lip awkwardly.

'Only because I mucked up your plans by deciding to stay here.' Pheely was a wizard lie-detector.

'No!' she yelped, feeling torn. 'I wanted to tell you from the start, but Dilly begged me not to.'

'I'm not surprised. She knows how I feel about Spurs. I absolutely *won't* allow it. He'll eat her alive.' She rushed towards the door.

Following, Ellen was just in time to see the Bellings' vast Land Rover pull up at the lime tree, and Dilly – looking ravishing in Ellen's dress – leap inside before it accelerated away. Through the driver's window and the spitting dust haze, Spurs' silver eyes glared at Ellen.

It was all rather *Dukes of Hazzard*, she thought, spellbound by the getaway needed around here to go for a drink in a local pub. It was a far cry from wandering lethargically to the Treglin Arms, and she felt a great, ill-timed pang of homesickness. She longed to scoop up Spurs, Rory, Dilly, Pheely and even silent Godspell straight to Cornwall to share a table, six scrumpies and sea-flanked mellowness.

'We *must* follow them!' Pheely shrieked, turning back to Ellen. 'Get your car keys.'

'The battery's flat.' Ellen closed her eyes and tried to visualise the sea, instead seeing Spurs' angry face as he drove away.

'Don't lie!' Pheely found the keys and frogmarched her to the car.

With Hamlet and Snorkel play-fighting happily in the back of the jeep, Ellen tried and failed to start the engine. 'I meant to replace it in Cornwall.' She sank back in her seat. 'It really isn't going anywhere.'

'We'll take the moped. The dogs can stay here.' Pheely leaped out again. 'You put them in the kitchen while I bring the bike round.'

'I thought it was broken . . .' Ellen's words died on her lips as Pheely sped towards the Lodge cottage, flip-flops slapping. She looked like she was running for her life.

The weekenders in the Corner House were having a barbecue, sending great clouds of hickory-chip smoke across the lane as Pheely dived towards her magic gate. Mungo Jerry was singing 'In the Summertime' on a reedy stereo.

Ellen pressed her head to the steering-wheel, using every iron girder of her willpower to breathe life into the car's battery and make it start. If it did, then she, Snorkel and a kidnapped Great Dane were going to drive to Cornwall to escape and breathe the sea.

But the engine just groaned. So did Ellen when she heard the spluttering of a frail moped engine.

When two scruffy women – one paint-stained, the other clay-encrusted – set off through Oddlode at a whining putter on an ailing moped, a few heads appeared over garden walls and hedges to watch in amazement. Pheely was wearing an ancient khaki army helmet and goggles, and had equipped Ellen with Dilly's riding helmet for safety, the pink hat-silk flapping like a camisole strapped to a tortoise.

The ancient Vespa, which Pheely called Pompeii because it was an Italian death-trap, wasn't capable of speeds over fifteen miles an hour.

'I didn't see Godspell in the car, so they'll have picked her up from somewhere on the way – we might not be far behind,' Pheely yelled over her shoulder. 'I suggest we try to catch up with them without arousing their suspicions so that we can spy rather than intercept.'

Ellen thought that the likelihood of them staying inconspicuous on the noisy moped in sleepy Upper Springlode was unlikely, but the chin-strap of Dilly's helmet was so tight that she couldn't open her mouth to speak. It took all of her concentration to stay aboard as Pheely careered unsteadily around the hairpin turns, bouncing on and off the verges and gathering large amounts of greenery in their wake. Trailing cow parsley and willowherb like a small, unstable carnival float, they laboured up the steep hill towards the ridge.

'Pompeii's not feeling herself,' Pheely shouted, as they started moving more slowly than their cloud of midge outriders. 'I think you might have to get off and walk.'

Ellen was only too glad to oblige, feeling far safer on her own two feet than on Pheely's bald tyres. She pulled off her helmet and wondered why on earth she had agreed to this.

'I'll see you at the top.' Pheely revved the engine and puttered away.

Although sorely tempted to start running fast in the opposite direction, Ellen set off behind her at a brisk jog and, to her surprise, found herself catching the frail moped within seconds, then keeping pace. Pheely, her chin set determinedly, took this opportunity to brief her like a training coach with a runner.

'We'll check the car park of the Plough first,' she called. 'If the Bellings' Land Rover is there, we can probably sneak in and get a couple of drinks, then spy from the other side of the beer garden without them knowing we're there. It's very wooded around the stream so lots of good places to hide – all the local adulterers take their mistresses there.' She winked at Ellen as the moped racketed over potholes. 'If they're at Rory's cottage, it won't be so easy.'

'I thought you wanted to fetch Dilly home?'

'I can't do that – she's seventeen and she'd just tell me to go to hell.' The moped was coughing and belching alarmingly. 'But I have to look after her. We'll be her guardian angels for the night. It might even be quite fun. That doesn't mean you're forgiven.' She cast Ellen a reprimanding look and almost mowed down a panic-stricken pheasant.

Guardian angels with dirty faces, thought Ellen, as sweat started to run down her forehead, dislodging the paint splatters. She tried to imagine how she would have felt at being pursued by her mother and a friend on a moped when she and Richard had started drinking in the pubs of Taunton. However much Jennifer Jamieson had disapproved of Ellen's boyfriends, she'd never followed in their wake to spy on them.

As she dropped back to run behind the moped and let a car come past in the opposite direction, she felt more and more stupid for agreeing to this, and increasingly certain that there was something Pheely wasn't telling her. That Pheely hated and mistrusted Spurs wasn't in doubt, and she'd made it clear there

were things he'd done that could never be spoken about. And that
Dilly intended to 'lose the big V' tonight played on Ellen's mind
like non-stop, discordant jazz. She was both jealous and worried
sick, but she still needed to know more before she set up skulking
surveillance on the double date.

Muscles now heavy with lactic acid, she battled to catch up with
the moped once more.

'Is Spurs Dilly's father?' She had to ask.

Pheely zigzagged the moped precariously across the road,
almost taking out Ellen's tired legs. 'No! Dear God! Whatever
makes you say that?' To Ellen's surprise, she started to hoot with
laughter.

Having lost their running rhythm, Ellen's legs were going dead,
her chest was burning and her steering less controlled as she
stumbled after the whooping Pheely.

'What's so funny?' she panted, tripping over a loosening lace.

'You have no idea how much better that makes me feel! Imagine
if she was out on a hot date with her father!'

This was a bit far-fetched even for Oddlode and, light-headed
from running, Ellen started to laugh too. They meandered up the
hill like two spiked Wacky Racers, terrifying the sheep in the fields
to either side, who bleated noisily as runner and rider clipped
alternate hedges and gathered hawthorn-blossom dandruff until
they resembled sheep themselves.

Just before the turning to Upper Springlode, the moped engine
cut out.

Ellen collapsed, panting, on the verge while Pheely tried to start
it again. 'It's always bloody doing this – should start again in a tick.
I think it overheats.'

But even after several minutes, the engine refused to fire.

'When did you last put petrol in it?' asked Ellen.

'I don't know – about a month ago? I don't use it much.'

Standing up, Ellen gripped the handlebars and rocked the
little bike, listening to the tank. A few drips of fuel swirled
around inside.

'Damn.' Pheely clambered off again and propped it up on its

rest, scanning the lane above and below. 'The nearest petrol station is at least five miles away. We'll just have to hope somebody
comes along with a jerry-can.'

'I can run on to the village,' Ellen suggested.

'Or we could stash the bike behind a gateway and walk to the
pub.' Pheely looked around fretfully for a handy opening in the
high hedges. 'I know this must seem silly, but I just need to know
she's okay. She is terribly innocent for seventeen.'

Ellen thought about the big V and looked away guiltily.

'Wonderful! Look! A car's coming!' Pheely leaped into the lane
and started to wave her arms at the big offroader roaring up the
hill towards them. Then her arms dropped hurriedly to her sides
as she recognised the muddy blue Land Rover. It was too late
to hide.

'Oh, no.' Ellen groaned, and pulled down a shirt cuff to wipe
the sweat from her face.

Coming up the lane towards them was Spurs, his silver eyes
widening in surprise, a furious-looking Dilly glaring out of the
fly-specked windscreen beside him. Silhouetted between the two,
Godspell Gates's head carried on bobbing as she listened to her
personal stereo.

'What are you doing here?' Dilly wailed at her mother, when
Spurs pulled up on the verge.

'Just out for a run,' Pheely said breezily, battling not to give
away how mortified she was. 'A run out of petrol, as it transpires.
Hello, Godspell. Spurs.' She averted her gaze as she spat out his
name as if it were snake venom.

'Need help?' He got out, glancing at Ellen, who was trying hard
to blend into a hedge.

'Not unless you have a can of petrol,' Pheely snapped. 'You
always had one handy at one time, as I recall.'

Spurs didn't react. 'The Land Rover takes diesel. Where are
you trying to get to?' He was still looking at Ellen, the pale eyes
unable to tear themselves away.

She swallowed uncomfortably, clutching Dilly's riding helmet
to her chest as she tried to calm her rib-kicking heart, the

goosebumps leaping to attention all over her skin. 'The – er – pub in Springlode.'

'The Plough?' He feigned good-natured surprise, but there was an edge to his voice. 'We're going there too – I can sling the scooter in the back and we'll give you a lift.'

Ellen wondered what he was playing at. 'You don't need to—'

'That would be very kind of you, Spurs.' Pheely cleared her throat, sounding like Boudicca accepting a lift from a passing Roman.

Lifting the moped into the Land Rover was a great deal harder than it first appeared. The little machine was hot and cumbersome, and only just fitted through the tailgate. Spurs groaned as he and Ellen manhandled it inside, watched by Pheely and Dilly on the verge and Godspell in the back seat. None offered their help.

Pheely and her daughter were having a stiff-jawed whispering argument, like two ventriloquists. Ellen couldn't hear what was being said, but it was pretty obvious that they were livid with each other.

Taking advantage of their distraction, she whispered to Spurs, 'I'm sorry about this.'

'Forget it,' he muttered, not looking at her.

'You could have just driven past.'

'No, I couldn't.' He scraped the bike against the tailgate, the last few drops of petrol leaking out of the tank all over him.

Ellen couldn't help herself: 'But I thought I wasn't that hot?'

'Ow – Jesus!' Spurs howled, clutching his neck and dropping the weight of the moped so that Ellen was left propping it up.

'What happened?' She steadied the bike.

'Pulled something, I think.' He grimaced.

'So I can see.' Ellen's eyes flashed from beneath a hundred kilos of metalwork as she looked from Dilly to Godspell.

He smiled nastily and, still wincing, helped her push the Vespa the last few feet.

*   *   *

'It's all right, we'll sit over here! Thanks for the lift – hello, Rory.' Pheely dashed to a far table in the garden of the Plough, covertly within eye and earshot of the one that Rory had already bagged and, from the empty glasses on it, had obviously been waiting at for some time.

'Don't you think we should at least buy Spurs a drink to say thanks for the lift?' Ellen followed Pheely.

'I haven't got any money on me,' she murmured.

'Neither have I.'

They looked at one another.

'Bugger.'

If not blown, then their cover was looking almost as windswept as the beer garden of the Plough: gathering clouds and a blustery breeze augured another downpour, despite the flirtatious sunshine. Set around one of the springs that gave the Springlodes their name, the roughly mown green acre was, as Pheely had promised, dotted with little clusters of trees that provided individual lairs for drinking parties and couples up to no good, who only broke cover to teeter into the tiny thatched stone pub and gather another round.

Sitting at the more exposed tables, which had views of the valley, tourists gritted their teeth and tried to keep salad leaves on their plates as the gale picked up. Ellen and Pheely sat conspicuously with no drinks and a filling ashtray, teeth chattering as twigs rained down on them.

'It's a popular spot.' Ellen looked around.

'Some famous American travel writer called this "the least spoilt hostelry in the Cotswolds" and they've been coming in droves ever since,' Pheely grumbled, eyeing Spurs' table as she lit yet another cigarette. 'Dilly is on her third drink already *and* she's smoking.'

'So she's having a good time.' Ellen only wished *she* was. She fanned her shirt.

'Aren't you cold?' Pheely asked.

'Not particularly.' Ellen craned to see Dilly's table. As though alerted by a siren, Spurs immediately caught her eye, his expression too guarded to read.

'You must be cold,' said Pheely. 'You have goosebumps.'

Ellen escaped to the beer-garden loos, which were housed in a collection of outbuildings, and was appalled at her appearance in the mirror. Her hair was so tangled from the wind and the helmet that she couldn't even get her fingers through it, her shirt was filthy and she had paint on her face, neck, arms and hands. To cap it all, a large spot was starting to swell on her forehead like a bindi mark.

As she headed back along the narrow corridor between the buildings and the pub, wishing that she had some cash for a stiff drink, she slapped straight into Spurs. He'd been idling in the shadows, smoking a cigarette and waiting for her.

'Hi.' She ducked her head and edged past him, but he barred her way with a broad forearm.

'What exactly do you think you're up to, Ellen?'

She set her jaw. 'Having a drink with a friend.'

'I haven't seen you drinking much,' he said softly.

'I'm working up a thirst.'

They were directly behind the pub kitchens. Wall filters were belching out the smell of cooking fat and sealing meat, along with chemical-filled steam from a busy dishwasher and the banter of kitchen staff swearing at each other.

'Does Pheely think I have nefarious designs on her daughter?' He raised an eyebrow.

'*Do* you?'

'She's very beautiful.' He smiled slowly. 'Rory is completely smitten, if not terribly sober, the idiot.' He pulled a face and glanced towards the garden. 'He'll have to get his act together if he wants to keep her keen.'

Ellen watched his throat, taking in the lifted sinews and veins that ran from one ear to his shoulder in the tanned, freckled skin, like ripples in a luxury truffle. He was a lot more tense than he made out. 'He's so lucky to have you on hand for advice and guidance,' she said cattily.

'Isn't he?' He matched her tone. 'I do like to keep an eye on things. Rather like you.'

'But I'm sure you'd never dream of stepping in and taking over.'

'Oh, I don't know.' He ran his tongue over his top teeth. 'Needs must when the devil's designated driver.'

'And let me guess, Godspell sucks on your familiars when you want to change gear?' She knew she was getting bitchier, but she couldn't stop herself.

'Leave her out of it,' he said lightly, swinging round to look at her. He seemed to be focusing on her bindi spot. 'You need a wash.'

'At least I've got a clean conscience.'

Without warning, he dropped his face to her unwashed neck and breathed deeply. 'I want to wash you.'

Goosebumps flared in the most unexpected of places – even in her ears. Ellen battled to pretend he hadn't just said that. Twisting away and feeling his teeth graze her skin, she spluttered, 'You'll have to clean up your act first.'

'I suppose you want me to beg Pheely to forgive me so that my soul is cleansed?' he sniped angrily, backing off.

'It might make up for lusting after her daughter.'

'Does that bother you?' He marked her eyes with his.

'It bothers Pheely.'

'Admit you love me and maybe I'll do it.'

'Cut the love crap. You're the one who told me I wasn't hot enough for you.'

He bit away an emerging smile and whispered, 'Surely you know I'm a compulsive liar? Enough people must have told you that by now.'

Ellen snorted sarcastically. 'So you really *do* desire me with all your soul?'

'I've wanted you from the moment we met.'

She laughed. 'Which is why you're out with Dilly and Godspell, I suppose.'

'I have to do something to keep my mind off you.'

'Ever thought of trying Morris dancing?'

His smile sprang back. 'No – nor incest, as it happens.'

'Hard to tell around here, I should imagine.'

'I'm told the bells usually give it away.'

They had edged towards each other again, voices lowered to an intimate, teasing whisper.

As they looked at one another, eyes tracing eyes tracing lips tracing eyes again, Ellen felt a blade of longing run its way up her spine, then slide beneath her chin and against her throat. She couldn't resist her attraction to him, however much she tried. Spurs watched her face, his cheeks quilted with tension. 'I told you this can't happen,' he muttered.

'Nothing's happening,' she said, goosebumps popping out on her goosebumps until she was convinced she must look like a figure in a Seurat painting.

He dragged his eyes from hers. 'I want you to keep your distance.'

'And I haven't come looking for you,' she said hoarsely.

'So why are you here?'

'We're just watching out for Dilly. Pheely insisted. I didn't ask to be here.'

'T'yeah.' He let out a sharp breath through an uncertain smile. 'Then go home.' He walked away.

Ellen rose on tiptoes of frustration as she battled not to chase him down and demand to know what the hell he was playing at. Instead, she threw up her chin and threw the best missile she had to hand: 'I do love you. Now ask Pheely to forgive you.'

He didn't even look round.

Pheely clutched Ellen's arm like a vice when she said she wanted to go home. 'We can't leave her here. Besides, he has Pompeii hostage.'

'Ask for it back – you can freewheel it home. It's all downhill from here.'

'That's what I'm afraid of.' Pheely sighed in despair, looking at Dilly who was shrieking with laughter and stealing one of Rory's cigarettes, irresistible body spilling out of Ellen's dress in all the right places.

Ellen sat in a cloud of Pheely's cigarette smoke, watching the equally unwelcome rainclouds gather overhead. She refused to look at Spurs and tried to blot his soft, drawling voice from her consciousness. She reminded herself again and again that he wanted her gone. Whatever his reasons, it wasn't going to happen, chemistry or no chemistry.

He doesn't want me here, she told herself, wondering why the back of her neck was burning up, as though the sun were shining brightly through the overcast sky.

'Don't look now,' Pheely lit another cigarette, 'but Spurs can't keep his eyes off you.'

Loitering under the trees in a beer garden without a drink was one thing, but when the heavens opened and they were forced to cram inside the small, heavily beamed pub, it was obvious that something was missing. Spare tables, chairs and any cash to buy a drink being key among them.

Spurs' posse had gathered at a bowed table in a window recess by the time Ellen and Pheely reluctantly squelched and dripped inside. Dilly was talking non-stop – already very tight on Archer's.

'. . . *totally* cool.' She was giggling, determinedly ignoring her mother and Ellen as they passed.

'Still here?' Spurs looked up at Ellen, rubbing the shoulder he had hurt earlier. His face seemed guilty somehow, anxious to convey a message that she couldn't read.

'Erin! Hi!' Rory raised his glass, spilling most of the contents, his sleepy grey eyes crossed as he grinned up at her. 'Joinush!'

Ellen looked at Spurs again and suddenly saw a green light. She opened her mouth to accept, but Pheely pinched her arm hard. 'We'll be fine at the bar!' she insisted, dragging Ellen along. 'You'll just have to bat your eyelashes to get us free drinks.'

'What?'

'Hi.' Pheely smiled at the landlord as she plonked herself down on a bar stool.

'What can I get you, ladies?' he offered affably, as he filled a pint glass for another customer.

'Ellen?' Pheely turned to her mischievously.

Thrown, Ellen looked at the friendly, bearded face behind the bar and smiled awkwardly. 'What do you have?'

'We're a public house, madam. We have the usual selection.'

'Could you just talk me through it?' Ellen asked, trying not to hear Pheely's groan beside her.

Suddenly she felt a warm, hard body pressing against her back. 'I'll get these, Keith.'

Ellen's skin performed a Mexican wave as Spurs leaned across her. She half expected her popping goosebumps to spring him back against the far wall like lead shot.

Beside her, Pheely was glaring at the towels lined up on the bar. 'Really, there's no need.'

'I'd like to buy you a drink, Pheely,' Spurs said softly, trying to catch her eye, his chest still pressing hard against Ellen's back.

Acutely aware that he'd said she needed a wash and that she probably smelt foul after a day's painting and an impromptu run, Ellen tried to lean away but, short of clambering right over the bar, she was trapped. She could feel his heart beating against her shoulder-blade and was surprised by its speed – it was racing as fast as her own.

'In that case,' Pheely was saying, in an arch, childish taunt, 'I'd like a glass of champagne.'

'We don't sell it by the glass,' Keith said apologetically.

'Then we'll have a bottle,' Spurs said easily, although his heart still hammered Ellen's back. 'Ellen?'

'I'll just have a mineral water.'

'Oh, c'mon – help Pheely out.'

She glanced over her shoulder, met his eyes and immediately felt as though she had drunk Dom Perignon dry. Champagne fizzed and popped in her veins as she read the message in his face. I'm sorry, his eyes pleaded. I'm sorry, I'm sorry, I'm sorry. And I'm scared of Pheely. 'Have a glass of champagne, Ellen,' he persisted.

'Sure.' She smiled: she had a small victory to celebrate. She had read his mind. Only the opening line, admittedly, but it was a start.

'Come and join us.' Spurs turned to Pheely as Keith fetched a bottle of dubious-looking champagne from a fridge in a back room.

'We'd just cramp Dilly's style,' she said sharply, glaring at her clay-embedded nails.

'I'd really appreciate some adult conversation,' he joked uneasily.

'I'm sure if you practise enough you'll start to get the hang of it,' she muttered.

He carried on smiling, eyes boring into hers. 'Give me a chance, Pheely.'

That smile was still as devastating as it had been twelve years earlier, the silver gaze as hypnotising, and try as she might, Pheely's resolve started to melt.

'I suppose if we joined your table, I could study Godspell's funny little face in animation.' She thought about it. 'She's so deep that her personality rarely surfaces, don't you find?'

'Quite.' Spurs cleared his throat, and they all looked back at Godspell, who was looking as deep and animated as a puddle in a hard frost while she studied her dark fingernails in minutiae.

Pheely shot Spurs another look of mistrust, then cocked her head as Keith popped the cork with tell-tale lack of practice, firing it into the tankards above the bar. 'Well, maybe for a moment,' she conceded, hopping off her bar stool just in time to avoid several pieces of pewter falling on her. 'I guess it can't be any more dangerous than it is here.'

Ellen found herself sitting as far away from Spurs as possible, tucked tightly at the far end of the window-seat between Godspell and Rory, whom she soon discovered were not great conversationalists. Rory managed 'Hello, again,' and Godspell stared blankly when Ellen asked after her insects. Any subsequent attempts at striking up banter fell flat.

Evidently livid that her double date had been hijacked by the motorcycling double act, Dilly ignored her mother and played up to the men. She hadn't been wrong when she'd told Ellen she was a hopeless flirt. Now reeling from an alcopop sugar high, she was about as tactful as a red-top photo-strip and didn't so much flirt as spurt.

'Where's Sharrie tonight?' she asked Rory.

'Out, I think,' he told her sleepily.

'I bet she has loads of boyfriends. She doesn't strike me as too fussy.' She sniggered. 'And she'd be quite pretty if she lost some weight. Then again, she probably has fantastic breasts. Big girls always do.'

Rory looked instinctively at Dilly's huge gravity-defying tits jutting from her slender chest as she launched into giggly tales of how awful it was having a bra so much larger-cupped than the other girls' at boarding-school. 'I just don't understand why they all tease me, then stuff their baggy Wonderbras with socks and loo roll, do you? I mean, it's not as though I'm *fat*. God forbid. I just got given these darlings as a part of the great handout, and I *do* find them a bit of a handful. I used to want to be flat, like you, Spelly,' she sighed with mock-envy at Godspell's plumb-line chest, 'but now I've grown rather used to my puppies.' She cupped her cleavage and batted her eyelids as she aimed it innocently at Rory.

Watching it all impassively, Godspell didn't say a word. Neither did Rory, whose eyes were crossing even further as he stared at Dilly's assets.

He was, Ellen realised, very drunk indeed, the beautiful pewter Constantine eyes glazed, the dreamy smile soporific and the long, lounging body close to sliding off its chair.

Spurs, by contrast, was sharp-witted and sober, totally focused on gaining Pheely's trust, his knuckles white as they clutched a pint of Coke.

Ellen had never seen him nervous, and it made him look more like a beautiful fallen angel than ever. The sinews in his neck leaped, muscles slammed in both his cheeks and he pulled back his hair from his forehead again and again to reveal wide, anxious eyes as he spoke in a near-whisper, oblivious of Dilly's big-breast debate. 'I know I've done the shittiest things alive, but I can't bear the thought of you hating me . . .'

He's going for it, she thought in disbelief, looking away as guiltily as a tourist stumbling into a cathedral confessional, her throat choked with emotion.

Swiping angry tears from her eyes before they spilled, Pheely wasn't making it easy for him, and neither was Dilly who, irritated by the amount of time Spurs was spending talking to her mother, brought up her favourite topic of the day. 'I think people are really *far* too uptight about sex,' she told Rory loudly, stilling the entire pub with her joyful, sing-song 'Who's queen?' voice.

'Too right.' He raised his glass.

'I mean, I can't *wait* to have a go.' She looked coquettishly towards Spurs, but he carried on talking to Pheely in a low, earnest tone.

Straining to hear what he was saying, Ellen almost jumped off her seat when Dilly slapped the table with her palm and demanded, '*Why* am I still a virgin at seventeen? Ellen was much younger when she lost it, and she's only ever slept with one man. I'm not going to bonk the county or anything. I just want to know what it's like.'

Spurs didn't react, still talking to Pheely, his head bowed in concentration.

Rubbing her forehead with her fingers, Ellen glanced worriedly back across the table. To her surprise, Godspell caught her eye and winked heavy black lashes.

'Is that a fact?' Rory was slurring.

'Yeah – I bet it's *really* good fun.'

'Oh, it is.'

'You know that from personal experience?' Dilly tilted her head coquettishly.

'Yeah.'

'Have you slept with lots of girls?'

'A few.'

'I wish I was one of them.' Dilly reached coolly for her glass, missed it several times then tipped most of its contents down her front as she aimed randomly for her mouth. Unperturbed, she smiled at Rory. 'I bet you're really good in bed.'

Ellen winced. When Rory stood up, she half expected him to suggest that Dilly and he pop back to his hay barn for a quickie, but instead he burped loudly and lurched off to the loo. Ellen slid across into his chair and tried to calm Dilly down a bit. 'You look lovely. That dress really suits you.'

'Sssh,' Dilly hissed. 'I don't want anyone knowing it's yours. But thanks.' She wrinkled her nose in appreciation, young and drunk enough to know that she looked a hell of a lot better in it than Ellen ever had. Then her eyes crossed and uncrossed as she gave Ellen a beady look and whispered, 'What on earth were you thinking bringing Mum here? It's the last thing I need.'

'It was a misunderstanding,' Ellen hedged.

'You *followed* us. And look at the old cow now – all over Spurs. I thought she hated him.'

Spurs and Pheely were nose-to-nose at the opposite end of the table, but the conversation hardly looked flirtatious or friendly. They looked closer to having a punch-up. Ellen turned back to Dilly. 'Maybe,' she told Dilly gently, 'they've decided that it's time to forgive and forget.'

'Hmmph.' Dilly glared at Godspell. 'Forgiving people is totally wet.'

But her erstwhile friend didn't react. Godspell was too busy taking in the action at the end of the table, her dark-painted eyes hooded as she watched Pheely and Spurs exchange bitter whispers, her narrow purple lips pursed.

'I never forgive,' Dilly told Ellen, still glowering at Godspell. 'I just forget. I find forgetting people really easy. What's your name again? Helen? Eleanor?'

Ellen looked away in despair, caught Godspell's eye again and was graced with another wink. The little Goth was drinking pints of bitter – which secretly Ellen found quite impressive – and didn't seem at all bothered by her own silence, despite her exclusion from everything going on around her. Her passive, watchful presence was disquieting.

'So, you two used to go riding together?' Ellen asked her brightly hoping to recapture the fleeting affinity they had shared in her lair, but blowing it by sounding false.

Godspell nodded silently.

Beneath the table, Dilly gave Ellen's ankle a sharp kick. 'Godspell gave up,' she sneered. 'She lost her nerve.'

Godspell didn't react. Close to, she looked older and less malevolent, with giveaway laughter lines around the coffee-bean eyes, but she had yet to try out a facial expression. Her only animated feature was one selective winking eyelid, which stayed determinedly unbatted when Ellen tried for a conversation. 'I heard your band playing the first night I was here – Roadkill, isn't it?'

Another nod.

'Sounded great. Have you been together long?'

''Bout a year.'

Victory! She was talking at last.

'And do you write you own material?' She remembered the note pad, in Godspell's playpen.

'Some.'

'I'd love to be able to write lyrics.' Ellen lied shammily, then tried eagerly to drag Dilly in. 'Wouldn't you, Dilly? I bet you'd be wonderful at it.'

But, apparently furious that she was no longer the centre of attention, Dilly had already started looking around for a distraction. Rory was still in the loo and her mother and Spurs were hissing away like two snakes in a basket. When she overheard Pheely say, 'You have some nerve thinking you can breeze back in and charm my daughter into thinking—' she had her cue.

'Stop dredging up ancient history, Mum. I don't care what Spurs did. He's been really cool.' She widened her eyes at him and let a few curls drop over her face. The lurching sway of her shoulders gave away how sloshed she was.

'Shut up, Dilly,' Pheely snapped.

'Don't talk to me like that! You weren't invited here. Spurs asked *me* out.'

Spurs reached for a cigarette, glancing anxiously at Ellen as though to remind himself that she was there, before he addressed himself to Dilly. 'I asked your mother to join us,' he reminded her.

'Only because she followed us,' Dilly huffed, waving her arms around and knocking her glass over. 'And because you want to get into Ellen's knickers.'

'Dilly!' Pheely's green eyes bulged in warning.

'You were the one who told me he and Ellen had the hots for each other!' Dilly taunted. 'Anyway, Ellen says it's rubbish. She told me that Spurs wasn't her soulmate, didn't you?' She turned to Ellen, who was close to mortified combustion. 'So you're wasting your time.' She smiled naughtily at Spurs. 'Ellen says *we*'d be perfect for one another. You and I.'

'I didn't say that,' Ellen bleated.

'How *dare* you set up such a perverted match?' Pheely stormed at her.

'Spurs is *not* a pervert,' Dilly yelped. 'He's bloody lovely.'

Lifting her pint of bitter to her purple lips, Godspell let out a strange, disembodied wolf-howl of laughter.

'And you can shut up!' Dilly wailed, in the grip of her alcohol and sugar high. 'You only came along so that you could gloat at me because you think you're so grown-up and superior. You might be too bloody cool to talk nowadays, but you're a freak.'

When Rory lurched back from the loo, Dilly was in full swing, laying into her mother again, now chemically hyperbolic to the point of meltdown. 'You're just jealous because Spurs and Rory fancy me, and I get to choose between them and you only get wrinkly old has-beens with beer bellies – and I'll probably be fabulous at sex and you're hopeless. I know because I read your diary and you wrote that you faked your organis – organ – origam—'

'You fake your ORIGAMIS!' she announced victoriously as Pheely turned purple. 'And you!' Dilly wagged her finger at Rory. 'You probably don't even remember yours because they're wasted on fat Sharrie. She's such a minger, I don't know how you could bear to do it. I mean, loads of girls must fancy you, even though you're not that bright . . . Rory . . . Rory?'

Raising his eyebrows in drunken alarm, Rory sauntered straight past the table and out of the door, pitching into the coat hooks before he fell into the re-emerging evening sunshine, muttering to no one in particular that he had to do the evening yard check.

'Where d'you think you're *going*?' Dilly yelled, at his departing back.

'Getting away from you, I should think,' Pheely told her, with surprising dignity, given the recent revelations. 'Few men like to witness children's temper tantrums.'

'Piss off, you old cow!' With a sob, Dilly fled to the loo.

'Oh dear, I suppose I'd better go after her.' Pheely grabbed her champagne glass for a swig. 'She's been very emotional – exam stress, you know.' She spoke loudly to appease the pub at large, her voice drenched with maternal patience and understanding. But her hand shook, belying her humiliation and reluctance to face the monstrous, hormonal, drunken, jealous, immature mess that awaited her.

But before she could stand up, Godspell unfolded herself like a waking bat and fluttered silently after Dilly, shooting one of her killer winks over her pointed shoulder.

Pheely sat down gratefully and reached for the bottle. 'I'll let her deal with it. Maybe they'll make friends again.'

'Like us.' Spurs steadied her glass, which was rattling under the bottle neck.

'We were never friends.' Pheely waited for the froth to subside as she poured, her eyes brimming with tears.

'I thought we were.' He was trying to get her mind away from what had just happened, his own petition for peace immaterial. 'You were like a goddess to me. You bought me my first pint in a pub, taught me to roll a joint, introduced me to Hendrix when I still thought Duran Duran were real musicians. And you helped me finish graffiti-ing Nazi Nigel's garage wall.'

'Ssh.' Pheely shot Ellen a guilty look, aware that she had been caught out. Then, despite herself, she let out a little gurgle of laughter at the memory.

'I'd like to be friends again,' Spurs entreated.

The laughter died in Pheely's throat. 'I don't think that's possible.'

'Please forgive me.'

'You should have asked that a long time ago.'

'I was too fucking scared,' he said quietly.

'You aren't afraid of anything.' She laughed hollowly.

'I am now.' He gazed at Ellen, eyes haunted.

Pheely cleared her throat. 'What do you think, Ellen?' She stretched across to top up Ellen's glass, spilling champagne everywhere.

'It doesn't matter what I think.' Ellen resurfaced from trying to merge with the furnishings.

'Oh, yes, it does.' Pheely's green eyes trapped hers, and her hypnotic voice growled, 'You're the reason we're sitting here, my darling. You keep telling me that Spurs has changed – something you have obviously gleaned from your short horticultural acquaintance. And you've certainly been happy to let him set out to seduce my daughter under your garden guardianship.'

'That's not fair!'

'It's the truth,' she pointed out bluntly. 'As Dorothy Parker said, you can lead a horticulture, but you can't make her think. Why are you digging up old graves like this?'

'My garden angel,' Spurs murmured, reaching for his glass. But his eyes remained haunted.

Ellen looked from him to Pheely, feeling cornered and exposed, knowing she was to blame for this if it all blew up.

'I'm stirring because I can,' she said truthfully. There was no point in procrastinating. 'I don't know about the past or the future because I'm only passing through. That's why I can burn bridges and boats saying that you two should get on like a house on fire.'

'Perhaps an unfortunate analogy, given Spurs' arson record,' Pheely murmured, but her eyes were brimming even more.

'Everyone deserves a second chance.' Ellen resorted to another cliché.

'If not a second generation,' Spurs said drily.

'Quite.' Pheely let a wary smile dawn over her champagne glass as she studied him. 'You should leave Dilly alone. You're not Wordsworthy.'

He raised his eyebrows. 'Okay, so I was never cut out to be a host of daffodils. That doesn't mean you and I can't be civil to one another.'

Pheely cast Ellen a thoughtful look, then started to giggle. 'Maybe the Oddlode outlaw can come in from the cold at last,' she conceded. 'But that's not a reason to set me up as this wretched renegade's mother-in-law, Ellen. What *were* you thinking of?'

'I didn't set anything up,' Ellen bleated, eyeing Spurs, who shrugged nonchalantly.

Suddenly she, too, found the situation ludicrously funny. 'That'll teach me to go gardening with a reformed rake.'

'Digging up the past can be the best way to lay new paths,' Spurs said smoothly, looking at Pheely. 'Does this mean you forgive me?'

'Only if you leave my daughter alone.' Her eyes twinkled, the freshly wiped tears replaced with renewed spirit.

'I'm only interested in riding her horse,' he declared, tipping his chair back. 'Not her.'

'As long as you mean that.' She glanced towards the door to the ladies'. 'She needs you like a hole in the head.'

'I couldn't agree more.' Spurs looked at Ellen, who registered the echo and swallowed uncomfortably.

'Is Rory okay?' she asked, anxious to move on.

'Probably passed out in a ditch.' He didn't seem remotely concerned, but picked up her cue and played the subject-change game. 'Sold the cottage yet?'

'Almost.'

'I've told Ellen she must at least stay for Ely's party.' Pheely was watching them contemplatively, still feeling her way back into talking to Spurs like a normal human being.

'Oh, absolutely,' he agreed, with a strange edge to his voice too. 'I certainly wouldn't miss it for the world.'

'Surely you're not going?' Pheely was amazed.

'On the contrary, I'm guest of honour,' He replied, as Godspell came back with a very grey-looking Dilly. 'Your father's party is set to be quite remarkable, isn't it, Witchy?'

Godspell flared her pale nostrils and settled back in her seat to fold up her black layers, indicating for Dilly to sit next to her.

'Sorry Mum, Ellen – Spurs.' Dilly spoke very carefully because she was frightened of slurring. She hung her head, unable to look at them. 'I think I've had too many Archers.'

'Maid Marion felt exactly the same way, darling.' Pheely raised her glass, eager to bestow forgiveness while she was feeling conciliatory. 'Let's all forget about it.'

Dilly managed a wobbly, grateful smile. 'Should I go and check if Rory's okay? I think I upset him.'

'I'll go.' Spurs sprang up and edged his way around the table.

Suddenly Ellen felt a warm hand clasp her fingers. 'I need a word with you.' Before she could protest, he was spiriting her towards the door. As she stumbled past Godspell, Ellen was almost certain that the little Goth shot her another killer wink.

'Never double-date with a blonde,' Pheely told the two girls cheerfully, and reached for the champagne bottle. 'This always bloody happens. Bubbly? It's the best thing for sobering you up, Dilly darling. If you're not going to chat, can you just turn your head to the left a bit, Godspell? I'm still not intimate with your wretched chin.'

'So I'm not your soulmate?' Spurs laughed as they climbed the short hill through the village towards Rory's yard.

'It was just some silly teen stuff Dilly was spouting,' Ellen lied, remembering with shame that she had been the one spouting it.

'She's absolutely adorable, isn't she? Especially when she's pissed.' He looked at her. 'Pheely was the same at that age.'

'Thank you for apologising. It meant a lot.'

'I didn't do it for you.'

'It doesn't matter. It was a noble thing to do.'

'I did it for Dilly.' He watched her reaction.

'Oh.' She let this sink in. 'Good.'

Overhead, damp birds were having frantic conversations before bedtime. The sun had come out again, low and red, burnishing the wet leaves.

'You like her, don't you?'

'I like them both.'

'There was a time,' he plunged his hands into his pockets and turned to walk backwards so that he could look out across the valley at the rainclouds moving away, 'when I wanted Pheely more than anyone else in the world. I had this unbelievable crush on her. I thought I'd die without her.'

Ellen fought down the jealousy demons. 'And now?'

'Ancient history.'

'She's still young.'

'It was only ever a kid thing, although at the time it felt like the world would stop if nothing happened.'

'But it did almost happen, didn't it?' she reminded him awkwardly.

'Of course – you know about the crows. I really screwed up there.'

'As opposed to screwing Pheely.'

'God, but I love it when you're crude.' He cackled, then looked at her profile for a long time as they walked. 'A friend of mine said I'd never get her to bed in a million years. When she agreed, I wanted to show him he was wrong.'

'Slightly unsubtle actually inviting him to watch, don't you think?'

'I was stoned, I was sixteen. Besides, I've always been an exhibitionist. I think I did Pheely a favour. We'd have been disastrous.'

'You were pretty young to become a step-parent,' she said pointedly.

'You never know, it might have straightened me out.'

'I doubt that. You'd just have been one step-parent closer to incest.'

He laughed. 'Which would only leave Morris dancing.'

'Poor Morris. So sad dancing alone,' Ellen hated how easy it was to patter with him. 'Is this what you brought me out here to talk about?'

'No. I like talking to you. I know I can say anything without shocking you.'

'Like what? That you fancied Pheely when you were sixteen, but now you fancy her daughter?'

'Yes.'

Ellen's heart sank.

'But that's not what I wanted to talk about either.'

They started crossing the green – smaller and wilder than the one in Oddlode – wading through long wet meadow grass and wild flowers that waved in the wind beneath a row of creaking elder.

'What do you want to talk to me about?'

'This.' Without warning, he cupped her face in her hands and kissed her. But this time his mouth took hers with the softest, sweetest impact. As their lips yielded, a strawberry fresh tongue tasted hers, making a great husk of longing loosen inside her, tickling her inside out with yearning.

For a moment the loud roaring in her ears made Ellen panic that they were destined to be run over by a maddened local farmer on a tractor. And then she realised it was just the sound of blood rushing in her ears. The goosebumps almost popped right off her skin, like ball bearings in a magnetic storm, as she felt the electricity rip through every muscle and staple her to the spot.

'Tell me to stop.' He kissed her lips, her face, her ears, her throat.

Ellen said nothing because she couldn't speak. She could barely breathe for freefall exhilaration. If he threw her down on the spot and took her there and then she wouldn't protest, despite the close proximity of several sheep and a farmhouse.

Then she kissed him back and the elders seemed to close in around them like blossomed curtains as the world disappeared.

'Christ, Ellen,' Spurs breathed into her mouth, 'we could be so good together.'

'So why stop it happening?' She kissed him harder and deeper, loving the way their bodies fused.

'I can't.' He groaned, tasting her teeth. 'I can't. I begged Pheely's forgiveness for you, not that bloody kid of hers. I admit it. I don't give a fuck if I've known you a day, a week or a year. I don't care that you're going away. I *want* you to go away. I just want to love you before you go.'

'I want to love you too.' Their hands slithered beneath clothes on to hot skin.

'Do you?'

'Yes.'

'You love me?' His fingers traced her burning-man tattoo.

'I could.' She shivered.

A moment later he'd pulled away with a violent jerk, starting off across the green once more. 'Tell me we're not soulmates now!' he threw over his shoulder.

Ellen reeled as the elder curtains opened and the sky fell down.

'You bastard!' She ran after him, grabbing his arm. 'How dare you?'

'How dare I what?' He swung round, walking backwards towards a dewpond. 'Prove you wrong?'

'There's a world of difference between wanting to pull each other's clothes off and being soulmates – if such a thing exists.'

'Oh, do explain,' he taunted girlishly, skipping to the edge of the pond, which was a sheet of burning orange in the evening sun. 'Explain it just like you did to Dilly.'

'Fuck off!' She stalked to the other side of the pond to give herself a safety zone. 'You can't just pounce on me because you've got wood over her.'

'Is that what you think?' He sank to his haunches at the water's edge, staring into it.

'Yes. You admitted you have the same feelings about her as you did for her mother all those years ago. You're dying to get into her knickers.'

'And you're jealous as hell,' he said victoriously.

'Bollocks,' Ellen fumed, then slammed on the brakes and shrugged in defeat. 'Why should I be jealous of a ravishing teenager with no side to her, breasts like tennis balls and her sex life ahead of her?'

'And why should *I* possibly want to get into her driven-snow white little knickers?' He stood up, smiling wickedly.

Despite herself, Ellen laughed. 'You are so bloody scruple-free.'

'I need to get inside someone to get you out of my head. You take up a lot of room.'

'Don't use Dilly. She needs looking after.'

'Maybe you're right. If she and Rory become lovers, I'll be chuffed for him. If you took a lover, I'd just want to kill him. And you feel the same way about me.'

'That's such rubbish.'

'I fancy Dilly, Ellen, but I love you.' He started wading through the pond towards her, hamming it up. 'I love you.'

'Cut the love crap.' She laughed nervously.

'I'm trying to – I've *been* trying to, haven't you noticed? I keep climbing up to higher ground, but the tide rises and you wash up on my fucking beach all the time.' He stood in the middle of the pond, up to his knees in glowing red water. 'You're like the little mermaid who traded her immortality for legs and stalked into my life at just the wrong moment.'

'Don't tell me, I've been running through your mind ever since?' She snorted.

'Yes!' He spread his arms wider. 'I want you to go away. I want you to walk into this water towards me and dissolve.'

'Go jump off your high ground.'

He rubbed his wild curls and looked up at the sky. 'The little mermaid was a hell of a lot nicer than you. For a start, she was a mute. That prince was a bloody idiot marrying somebody else.'

'Are you planning to get married to a mute, then? Might be hard to exchange vows.'

He closed one eye, watching the bustling clouds and letting out a bitter laugh. 'Will you marry me?'

'Don't believe in it.'

'In that case, will you organise my stag night?'

'I won't be here.'

'I might get married this month.'

'I might leave tomorrow.'

'You see? You're going to dissolve, after all.' He scanned the sky one last time before dropping his chin and looking at her. 'You know, I haven't been able to cool down since we met. I'm boiling hot all the time. Are you?'

She pressed her thumb to her mouth. 'Actually, I'm not so hot. You said so yourself.'

'Oh, you are very, very hot.' He watched the ripples on the water. 'We both are. What does that mean?'

'That it's been unseasonably warm for the time of year.'

'No. This is what happens when you get sent to hell.' The silver eyes blazed as he looked at her again. 'And I am in hell.'

'Why?'

He didn't answer.

'What did you agree to do that's so awful?'

He looked down at the water and kicked up an angry wave. 'To find that out, my little mermaid, you'll just have to solve the riddle before you dissolve for ever.' Then he looked up at her once more, blew her a kiss, thrust his arms out again and then fell backwards into the water, sending up a great tidal splash. As the turbulent ripples subsided, he floated on his back, staring at the sky. 'I want you to make another wish.'

Ellen kicked off her shoes and waded in to her ankles. 'I thought you wanted to forget about the wishes?'

'We can't forget. That's why we're here. A promise is a promise.'

'Okay.' Ellen licked her lips, still tasting his mouth on hers. 'I wish you'd tell me what it is you've agreed to do that's making you so fucked up.'

'That's not a proper wish.' He bobbed around in the water. 'That's therapy.'

'And?'

'And I told you, you've got to solve the riddle. Dissolve the riddle.'

Ellen pulled her sweaty hair from her face and huffed in frustration.

She waded back out, and stalked around the pond with her arms folded against her chest, boiling hot and longing to plunge in too. The sun, even redder now, made the pond look like molten lava. 'Don't be so bloody obtuse.'

'Are you going to make a proper wish?'

'No,' she snapped, reaching boiling point. 'I'll take the six pounds sixty-six pence.'

'Six six six. How apt. I'll have to write you a cheque.'

'Will you sign it "Beast"?' She matched his coolness, wishing he'd put up more of a fight.

'I'll sign it "love from Beast",' he floated into some reeds, 'with three crosses – one for every time we've kissed.' He waited, watching her across the red water.

Ellen tried to stop her heartbeat jazz free-styling. She had to concentrate very, very hard not to blow her refund by wishing that he would kiss her again. 'What's zero point six six six?' she asked, resorting to her favourite ardour-cooling pastime.

'Do tell.'

'The number of the millibeast.' She crossed her arms and kicked water from her trainers. 'One six hundred and sixty sixth?'

'Enlighten me.'

'The common denominator of the beast.'

'What's the binary of the beast?' he mocked.

'One . . . zero . . . one . . . zero . . . zero . . .' she screwed up her face in concentration '. . . one . . . one –'

'Christ, I wish I'd brought my chequebook with me.' He

started to backstroke out of the reeds, wincing as he found it hurt.

'. . . zero . . . one . . . zero!' she finished victoriously. 'Now do I get my money back?'

'Maybe. But I still want my massage. My shoulder's killing me.'

'Sure.'

'Can I have it tomorrow? Before you go?' he teased.

'If you like.' She stared out across the valley and noticed that the raincloud was dumping its contents on Oddlode now.

With a great splash, Spurs stood up, water pouring from his clothes as he waded out. 'You do realise that if you touch my skin, I'll get third-degree burns.'

'I'll wear oven gloves.'

He stood close to her, turning to watch the distant rain too. 'I'll come round tomorrow, then.'

'I have people viewing the house all day,' she said, avoiding his gaze.

'I'll wait till they're gone.'

She stole a glance across at him. He was ridiculously wet and smiling. 'What's so amusing?'

'You know we'll end up in bed.'

'No, we won't.'

'Try to stop yourself.'

The door to Rory's tumbledown cottage was locked, the key still under the pot where he always left it when he was out. Spurs checked on the horses while Ellen went in search of Rory, looking in the tackroom and the horsebox, trying to stop her heart beating between her legs and relocate it to the usual place.

'No sign.' She met Spurs at the edge of the tatty stable-block. 'He must have gone back to the pub.'

He shook his head. 'He was so nervous about seeing Dilly, he was already caned when we arrived. You saw him, he could hardly walk. We must have missed him on the way over here. He'll have keeled over somewhere.'

'Who lives there?' Ellen gestured to a rusting caravan behind a huge manure pile.

'Sharrie the groom. She's out.'

The windows were steamed up. Listening carefully, they could hear groaning.

When they made their way closer, it was obvious that Sharrie had stayed at home after all. Through a dusty, steamed-up window, a pale muscular bottom was bobbing up and down. To either side lolled Sharrie's mottled thighs.

'He might not be able to walk, but he's certainly managing to fuck,' Spurs said dispassionately.

At his shoulder, Ellen tried desperately not to stare, but it was impossible.

However squalid and unloving, the sight of two people connected together shot a great jolt into her already electric pelvis. She could tell that Spurs was feeling exactly the same hot, angry excitement as he watched beside her.

When she turned to walk away, he grabbed her and twisted her back to face him. 'Don't be too hard on him. He doesn't think he's good enough for Dilly – which he probably isn't. Imagine that as an introduction to sexual pleasure.'

Given that Richard had always demonstrated a very similar technique to Rory, Ellen said nothing, pulled away and headed back to the pub as fast as possible, hating herself for her grubby thrills and for the seething jealousy that told her Spurs planned to break Dilly in far more gently.

He lit a cigarette and followed at a distance, dripping water all the way as he scanned the sky again.

In the window-seat of the Plough, the bottle of champagne had been drained and replaced by a bottle of house white – all Dilly could afford with the ten pounds she'd brought with her. She and Pheely were absolutely plastered and laughing like drains.

'There you are. Take a pew.' Pheely waved her arm around. 'We were just talking about you.'

'Where's Godspell?'

'Disappeared in a puff of smoke,' Pheely said airily. 'People to see, places to go. Where are the boys? Have you eaten them?'

She and Dilly dissolved into giggles, and Ellen got the uncomfortable feeling that she had just been dissected. On closer inspection, Pheely had clearly been working her way through the wine by herself while Dilly drained pint after pint of tap water in a bid to sober up and keep the nausea at bay. The tactics had brought mother and daughter to identical levels of giggliness.

'Rory had a horse to – er – see to at the yard.' Ellen wished she knew more about horses so that she could lie better. 'Spurs is helping him.'

'Should I go and help too?' Dilly offered, swaying as she stood up.

'No need.' Spurs sauntered in. 'Just a touch of colic. He's keeping an eye. Says he's sorry to bail out, but he had to get the bales out to feed the beasts.'

'Darling! Did you get caught in the rain again? You're all wet.' Pheely was wickedly magnanimous. 'Come and sit next to me and tell me what you've been up to all these years. When you were a toddler,' she told Dilly, 'Spurs used to read you fairytales.'

'He's not that old,' Dilly snorted in disbelief.

'Oh, I am.' Spurs looked at Ellen. 'My favourite was *The Little Mermaid*.'

'Talking of which, you're absolutely soaked through!' Pheely jumped away as he settled beside her. 'I'd no idea it was raining *that* hard.'

'It isn't.' He carried on looking at Ellen. 'I just needed to cool off.'

'I might walk home.' She dragged her eyes away and smiled apologetically at Dilly and her mother. 'It's a beautiful evening now, and I've got an early start.'

'We'll all go!' Pheely insisted, terrified at the thought of policing Dilly and Spurs on her own.

'I'll bring the car round,' said Spurs, clearly thinking the same.

As soon as they reached Goose Cottage, Pheely remembered

Hamlet. 'Oh, the poor darling! Let's give him a run in the garden and we can share that bottle of wine.' She was clearly eager to spin out the evening. 'Spurs?'

'I'll pass.' He and Ellen lifted the moped from the back while Dilly drooped on the verge, yawning widely. 'And, besides, I think this poor kid is bushed.' He winked at Ellen, leaving her uncertain whether he was referring to her or Dilly.

'You're right,' Pheely blustered, as easily offended as ever. 'I'm obviously boring you all to death. I'll just get the Dane and take Dilly home.' As soon as Hamlet exploded from the kitchen like a huge harlequin missile, Pheely scuttled away guiltily, dragging her moped creakily with her, trailed by the yawning Dilly.

Spurs slammed the tailgate closed and turned to Ellen. 'Tomorrow?'

She nodded, watching his face warily through the gloom, wondering what his secrets were.

Suddenly his teeth flashed white as he smiled. 'You don't want to know.'

Ellen tilted her head curiously and concentrated her mind on an image of the sea to test whether he really could read her thoughts.

He couldn't. When he stepped forward, she realised that he was planning to kiss her, and hastily moved her face to one side so that he had to peck her cheek. Then, in a curiously unexpected gesture, he reached out and rubbed her shoulder comfortingly before he turned and got back into the Land Rover.

She started to move to the house, then spun around. 'Why did you change your mind about our promises?' she asked. 'About keeping away from me.'

He looked at her for a long time. 'You know the saying "Out of sight, out of mind"?' he said eventually.

She nodded, and jumped as the engine started with a diesel roar.

'Well, it should be "Out of sight, out of your mind",' he shouted, finding first gear. 'Try to think of a wish. I hate giving refunds.'

As he drove the short distance to the manor, headlights flashing behind her neighbours' houses and between trees, Ellen threw the ball for Snorkel and did her now customary patrol of bushes and borders for Fins, then put out some food for him. She heard Spurs cut the engine in the distance, imagined him shouldering open the big black door and bounding up to bed.

Then, in the secluded gloom of the lower slopes of the garden, she stripped to her underwear and waded into the pond to float on her back, letting the cool water lap over her hot skin as she watched a sliver of new moon drift in and out of the clouds. 'I wish,' she breathed, 'that soulmates really existed.'

By the time she went back to the house, it was anthracite dark. The horseshoe sat on the front step. The first wish nail was missing; the second had been prised from its hole and was lying on the step, ready to be exchanged.

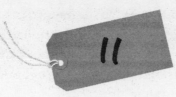

11

Ellen's decision to go out for a run while Poppy showed the first of the day's potential buyers around Goose Cottage on Sunday morning was not a wise one, as it turned out. She pounded out of the gates with Snorkel at her heels and set off past the bright red Golf straight into the oncoming path of Giles Hornton. 'You decided to join me today!' He beamed, and sucked the sweat that was already forming on his moustache as he jogged on the spot.

'No – yes. That is, I'm headed in the opposite direction.' She indicated the bridleway, knowing that Giles always jogged along the village lanes towards the church.

'Make a nice change going off-road.' He did an about-turn. 'Don't worry, I'll take it easy so that you can keep up.'

'Sure.' Ellen blasted off and he tripped hurriedly after her.

Behind, and struggling to keep pace, Giles was soon far too puffed out to strike up a conversation, but was more than compensated by the glorious view of Ellen's bottom.

The morning mist had yet to burn out of the valley bowl, but the sun was already glowing warmly through it as Ellen ran along the grassy stripe between the two tractor-wheel furrows, still sticky in places from that week's rain. Crows flapped out of ripening barley as she passed an open gateway, and Snorkel dived in and out of the ditches to either side of the track, covering her piebald coat in grass seeds and hogwort pollen.

She was high above the valley by the time she eased off, more for Snorkel's sake than her own. Yesterday's sprint up Springlode Hill had pumped up her energy levels and loosened her legs. She turned to look back at the hazy village as she stretched away the small cramps and saw Giles a hundred yards below, weaving all over the place as he broke through the pain barrier. Further in the distance, a horse was crossing the grassed bridge over the Odd, leaping in excitement at the prospect of a gallop. As soon as it drew level with the River Folly, its rider loosened the reins and they exploded forward.

She watched, entranced, as the horse streaked up the wide track, catching up with Giles so quickly that he seemed to be going backwards. Had he not stumbled into a hedge, the horse would have cannoned straight into him as it charged past at high speed, spooking at Giles's shiny red running shorts, which poked out of the willowherb, and letting out a series of squealing bucks, pink rump skipping into the air and black hooves sending up clouds of dust.

Ellen knew only one horse with such acute fashion sense that it had a coat in this season's must-have shade.

Spurs reined Otto to a halt a few yards from her. 'Are you okay?' he called breathlessly. 'I saw that old bastard following you.'

'We're running together,' Ellen explained, trying not to laugh.

'Oh.' He looked over his shoulder as Giles picked himself out of the hedge. 'In that case, watch him – he has a bloody awful reputation.'

This time she did laugh, and he had the grace to spot the joke, the silver eyes creasing as he looked away. Still blowing hard from his exertions, Otto threw up his head in alarm as Giles started to stumble along the track again, calling, 'It's okay – no harm done. Wait there!'

Ellen stepped forward to pat Otto's hot neck and scratch his shoulder, her hand tantalisingly close to Spurs' thigh. Her goosebumps were developing a dance routine now, moving around on her skin like bubbles in a river.

'Hop on,' Spurs offered suddenly, holding out a hand.

'Don't be daft.' She glanced up at him, as hot-headed temptation tried to squeeze her heart out between her ribs.

'We could be in Broken Back Wood in ten minutes.'

'Or I could have a broken back in two.' She watched Giles panting the last fifty yards.

'Let's make the beast with two backs,' he whispered, making the bubbling goosebumps rush excitedly up and down her spine and between her legs.

'Back off,' she muttered. 'You owe me a back-dated cheque signed "Beast", remember?'

He laughed. Beneath him, Otto stamped a front leg and bobbed his head. 'My shoulder's killing me.' He rolled his neck. 'Can you make it better?'

She nodded.

'Good – I'll come round at about six. Don't dress up. In fact, don't dress at all.' He gathered up his reins, and kicked Otto away in a canter just before Giles reached them.

'Bloody idiot tried to kill me,' he gasped. 'D'you see that? He ran me off the path.'

'Yes, it was close,' Ellen said vaguely, watching Otto thunder away.

'He wasn't bothering you, was he, my dear?' Giles removed fronds of hawthorn blossom from his moustache before clutching his knees to catch his breath.

'No – I'm fine.' Ellen fanned her T-shirt and watched the pink horse disappear into the mist.

'Good job I was here. Hate to think what might have happened had Belling encountered you alone up here. He has a bloody awful reputation.' He glanced up at her, his leathery forehead creased. 'What's so funny?'

'Nothing.' She kicked her trainer into a clump of dandelion clocks and sent up a little puff of lost time. Had Giles not been around, she suspected she and Spurs would be flattening that clump right now.

'Bad enough having the bastard rolling up my drive every day to ride the Gentlys' horse without him mowing me down. Poor Ophelia is in a terrible stage. Apparently he's making a dead-set for Dilly.'

'Is he?' Ellen kicked another feathery clock.

'Awful business – of course, you wouldn't know, being an outsider.' As he got his breath back he managed a more intimate tone. 'Such a shame we're not going to have you here for long. You do brighten the place up.' He made her sound like decorative bunting.

'What do you mean "awful business"?' Ellen asked.

'Best not talked about.' Giles flashed his teeth; clearly deeming whatever it was far too macabre for Ellen's pretty little head and likely to ruin his chances of some sunny flirtation. 'Jolly attractive spot, this.' He sniffed. 'We must bring a picnic up here some time. What are your plans this week?'

Ellen definitely didn't want to go there. 'Pretty busy, I'm afraid. Have you recovered enough to run on?'

He pulled up his T-shirt to rub his hot face, revealing a very tanned, hairy midriff with a staunchly controlled middle-aged porn-star six-pack that was clearly intended to make her go weak at the knees. When he looked up again, the blue eyes were on the seductive attack and he edged closer. 'It's not wise to start out so fast. You'll blow up before you've got into a rhythm. Much better to take it slow, allow recovery time and enjoy the view.'

They loped a little further at barely more than a walk, frustrating Snorkel who was accustomed to Ellen at full pelt.

'Wonderful for working up an appetite, running.' Giles huffed alongside her. 'How about a spot of lunch in a pub later?'

'Sorry, I have people looking around the house all day.'

'Supper?'

'I have plans.'

'Another time.' He smiled his big-seducer smile. 'You really are a ravishing creature.'

'Thanks.' She put in a burst of acceleration to escape the cheesy lines, but Giles had found his rhythm and was getting into his stride.

'I have a Jacuzzi at home. Great way to cool off after a jog.'

'I'm sure.'

'Come and have a dip now. With people looking round the cottage, you'll get a bit of privacy.'

Ellen doubted that. 'I'm fine, thanks.'

'I have champagne on ice.' He wasn't about to give up.

'I prefer something isotonic.'

'I can do ice and tonic – and gin if you're feeling frisky. It *is* Sunday. *And* I have some fantastic grass, if you indulge.'

By the time they had jogged back down the bridleway he had offered her the entire contents of his drinks cabinet on ice in the Jacuzzi, bath and shower, with optional recreational drugs on the side.

Ellen gratefully spotted Pheely wandering back along Goose End as they ran the last leg, her arms full of Sunday papers and croissants, a jaunty headscarf covering her dirty hair. 'Treats for Dilly – she's feeling a bit jaded, poor darling. Hi, Giles, giving Ellen the runaround?' There was an edge to her voice, which Ellen put down to a hangover. The big green eyes were hooded and her usually glowing skin was tinged with grey.

'Darling!' He kissed her sweatily on both cheeks. 'You're up early.'

'I was working on Godspell's bust,' she said grumpily.

'Ely should really fork out for a decent plastic surgeon to do that.' He guffawed and ogled Pheely's naturally generous cleavage. 'I was telling Ellen what a shame it is she's not going to be here long.'

'Isn't it?' Pheely glanced at him suspiciously, then turned to Ellen. 'Whatever you do, don't sell the cottage to the couple who've just left,' she warned. 'They brought five children and a pack of yappy dogs that crapped all over your garden. And she was pocketing cuttings left, right and centre. Glad Tidings says they're called Radish and they own that ghastly olde-worlde theme park in Maddington. I just bumped into her in the shop.'

'How does she know?' Ellen was, as ever, baffled by Gladys's spy network.

'Their nanny is going out with the man who delivers the oil. Are you in later? I might pop round.'

'Not this evening.'

'Earlier, then.' She looked even edgier, glancing from Giles to

Ellen again before she vanished through her magic-garden door.

Despite heavy hints, Ellen didn't invite Giles into the cottage for a cool drink. Poppy had left a note saying she would be back in an hour with a Mr and Mrs Crabtree. Ellen grabbed a quick shower, shaving her legs, armpits and bikini line, making sure she removed any stray hairs and soap stains from the glass cubicle beneath the attic beams and opening a window to disperse the steam. As she dried herself with a beach towel, so as not to disturb the fluffy white ones on the rail, she heard Otto skitter past the cottage from the direction of the church – they must have come down the valley by a different route. Spurs had him on a loose rein and was smoking a cigarette. He blew Snorkel a big kiss as he passed and she barked appreciatively.

Ellen sat on the bed, her heartbeat pounding in her groin. She reached for her aloe cream and smoothed it on to her legs and bikini line to stop them reddening post shave, and noticed that her tan had dropped its tidemark from swimsuit to shorts level since she had arrived in the Cotswolds; the smooth skin at the top of her thighs was now butterscotch to the strong coffee beneath.

You mustn't sleep with him, she told herself. It would complicate things far too much. He's told you nothing can come of this, and while he might want to scratch the mutual-attraction itch by having sex, it would just open your wounds. He's had hundreds of women. He has no scruples or inhibitions. You've just had Richard and a decade of frustration, and it's too soon to take big risks. Lloyd was a safe bet and that bombed. This has far higher stakes and lower morals.

But as she sank back on the counterpane, she closed her eyes and groaned. Just the thought of Spurs' lips against her skin made the goosebumps dance quadrilles and her nipples point furious fingers towards the ceiling. Her skin prickled hot and cold, the beat between her legs pounded and twitched and she squirmed with frustration. She was going to explode if she didn't sleep with him, with someone – anyone – soon.

'It's not him,' she told herself. 'It's hormones. It can't be him.'

She laughed as she imagined chasing after Giles Hornton and body-slamming him in his Jacuzzi to appease the craving. A bubbling tub and that big tanned hairy body would be a perfect padded cell in which to get rid of her caged-tiger libido without releasing it into the wild.

Rolling over so that her hot face was pressed against her damp hair, she banged her head against the mattress and groaned.

She'd left the radio on in the bathroom and the latest summer smooch ballad floated in through the open door. Ellen couldn't shake the naughty thoughts from her head. Suddenly her mind was full of sex, cocks springing up like a pink cacti – wide, narrow, small, huge, veined, smooth. Men's heads between her legs – blond hair, dark hair, bristly crew-cuts all poised above her, parting her labia and dropping their tongues towards her.

She longed to be as sexually experienced as Spurs. Her mind, now devoid of principles as it roamed the fiery depths of her fantasy world, ran back through all the missed opportunities, the temptations over the years that would have been so easy to follow through. Those X-factor boys with their hard bodies and fast lives that had come and gone, trying to bed her. She'd stayed true to Richard, but it hadn't been easy. She'd felt none of the white-hot attraction for him that she did for others. When drunk, stoned or just low, she had come so close, but she had only ever gone all the way in her mind.

And now she went there again. She had quick, urgent, scruple-free sex in the backs of cars, behind sand dunes, in pub car parks, in the sea, in Cornish cottages and rain-hammered tents. She was on top, in front, alongside, above, below and twisted every which way. She crouched on her knees and sucked off beneath tables, unseen by all those gathered around, she lay back and took warm, lapping mouths between her legs in cheap B-and-B bedrooms and the backs of transit vans.

Her hands crept between her legs as she took cock after cock into the welcoming, hot, oily warmth there, the muscles gripping and releasing every shape and size coming at her from every direction.

As she climaxed with a short, sharp, convulsing release of energy that was almost more painful than it was pleasurable, she rolled over again, burying her face in her wet hair and biting her lip hard to stem the tears.

She felt dirty and self-loathing, wildly ashamed of her own mind and disappointed that such a maelstrom of hard-core thoughts had resulted in such a literal anticlimax. She wondered if it would be better if she had slept with all those men, if she had got to know her own triggers better. And far from ridding her head of thoughts of Spurs, he was now watching her from the corner of her mind, the silent voyeur, silver eyes mocking her pathetic lack of true, free-spirited passion.

'Fuck you,' she said.

'Yes.' He smiled that rare, kneecap-shooting smile. 'Fuck me. You know you want to.'

When she closed her eyes to try to make him go away, she was floating in the dewpond high on the ridge above the valley, staring up at a red-streaked sky, listening to the ripples coursing towards her as Spurs waded in, spread out his arms and fell backwards on to the burnished water beside her. Automatically, her hands fluttered up to her naked breasts to cover them from the splash, encountering the hard little nipples.

'Oh – my – God!' Ellen gasped, shuddered, and came as unexpectedly as sneezing. Then again. And again, a delicious unstoppable procession of ever-decreasing circles. Her eyes snapped open and the oak beams spun above her head like helicopter blades. 'Jesus! Wow! Blimey!'

'Miss Jamieson!' a voice called cheerily from below. 'I have the Crabtrees here. We're just dashing round quickly, if that's okay?'

'Bugger!' Ellen fell off the bed in shock, grabbed her towel and called, 'Fine! I'll be down in a sec.'

Far below, Poppy was already extolling the virtues of the house as she chased after the impatient Crabtrees. 'All original features – these beams have been treated for woodworm, of course. Doesn't it *smell* wonderful? No, it's not new paint, it's years of love and family life. Old properties like this have *so* much personality and so many stories to tell. Just look at that inglenook! Er, yes, I'm sure it could take a coal-effect fire if you wanted to go that route.'

Dressed in her denim shorts with only half of the fly buttons done up and a red T-shirt that stuck to her still-wet skin and matched her face, Ellen greeted the aged and fastidious Crabtrees at the top of the attic stairs.

'We're seeing five properties today so we're in a bit of a hurry,' the vulture-faced wife explained self-importantly, nosing in the eaves cupboards. 'I really think this place is too old and labour-intensive. It would take ages to dust, and I'm sure I can smell damp. And these stairs are a nuisance. I prefer bungalows.'

Her husband, who looked even more like a vulture, with massive shoulders, a scraggy neck and a bald head, gave Ellen an appreciative look as he followed his wife on her whistle-stop inspection. 'I hope we didn't disturb you?'

'No – no, I was just – er – getting changed.' She knew she was looking flustered and caught out, but she couldn't stop her face burning and was still catching her breath as the echo of those delicious ripples tickled her belly and thighs.

Poppy gave Ellen an apologetic look, whispering, 'We're a bit early.'

'This is a sweet little guest room.' The female vulture peered beneath the low beam into Ellen's bedroom. 'Oh, I hope that's not from a leak in the roof.'

In the centre of the antique bed's very crumpled pale blue counterpane there was a dark patch.

'No, that just happened a minute ago,' Ellen said hastily, then blushed. 'I lay back on it with wet hair.'

The Crabtrees gave the bed a wide berth, and Poppy's eyes boggled.

'I do apologise.' Mrs Crabtree cleared her throat disapprovingly, as she peered out of the window. 'You've obviously got company.'

'No, I'm alone. It really was wet hair that did it,' she bleated.

'I *mean*,' Mrs Crabtree sniffed, 'that somebody is at the door.'

Ellen escaped downstairs and encountered Pheely who, having wandered straight in, was looking as usual for a corkscrew.

'It *is* after midday – just,' she justified, waggling a bottle of Cheap White Wine, lowered eyebrows showing that she was in an even blacker humour than she had been earlier. 'Bloody Dilly eschewed my croissants and buggered off to see if Godspell's all right. She's in a foul mood. She still hasn't forgiven us for last night.' She rolled her eyes, then looked up before mouthing, 'What are this lot like?'

They could hear creaking overhead and Poppy desperately assuring the Crabtrees that thatch was just as warm and water-proof as 'nice, modern tiles'.

'Retired, pernickety – I don't think they like it.' Ellen switched off the bubbling coffee-maker, which was threatening to boil dry.

'Good.' Pheely smiled naughtily, seeking out glasses. 'I might get to keep you longer. Now, you obviously don't listen to a word I tell you. What do you *think* you're doing agreeing to go out to dinner with Giles this evening?'

'I didn't.'

'Oh. Are you sure?'

'Yes.'

Her face lit up. 'That's a relief. So what *are* you doing tonight?'

'Taking Spurs Belling to bed.'

Pheely was prevented from saying anything by the reappear-ance of the Crabtrees, looking more disapproving than ever as they spotted the wine.

Poppy ushered them towards the cellars, switching the coffee-maker back on as she passed it and mouthing to Ellen, 'They're getting keener.'

With the voices now floating up from beneath them, Pheely stared at Ellen open-mouthed.

'It doesn't mean anything. It's just sex.' Ellen tested her new resolve in a whisper. 'I have to do it, Pheely. We're burning our skins off, Spurs and I. And we're both adults.'

Pheely was in a very strange mood indeed. She pulled out a cigarette and lit it before exhaling tetchily. 'I agree.'

'What?' Ellen was astounded.

'You *should* sleep with him. Christ, I envy you.'

'After everything you've said?'

'It's such fun going to bed with somebody new. As long as you don't fall in love with the bastard, you can eat him for breakfast as far as I care.' She threw her dead match into the sink. 'At least it'll keep him away from Dilly while she's on heat. He's such a tomcat.'

Ellen tried not to react.

'Of course she'd be devastated if she found out. She doesn't understand that some adults can quite happily have sex with no emotional attachment.'

She swallowed uncomfortably. 'You're not going to tell her?'

'She's young. She'll get over it.'

'She doesn't need to know.'

Pheely backed down: 'Of course I won't tell her – although, God knows, she needs taking down a peg or two. I'm absolutely furious with her for reading my diaries.' She rolled her eyes. 'And I do *not* fake my origamis as she so delicately put it. I have *no* idea where she got that from.' There was clearly a lot of pride at stake, given the topic of conversation. 'I'm actually rather fantastic in the sack.'

'She was just trying to make herself feel better.' Ellen kept her voice low, hoping to encourage Pheely to do the same. That deep baritone carried.

'Well, she was the one who came out of it looking like an idiot, as I told her this morning,' Pheely huffed, the volume still on the rise. 'Spurs may have mellowed a little, I'll grant you, and I think he was rather charming last night, but he is still a big, predatory, feral tomcat. That much hasn't changed.' She popped the cigarette between her teeth and pulled the cork with a grimace of effort. 'He needs sex like other men need televised sport. And he's probably fantastic in bed – I've always thought that. Potentially heartbreaking for a teenager with a crush, of course, but perfectly adorable recreation for a woman on the rebound like you, who simply wants some hot nookie while she's stuck in the sticks. You love dangerous sports, after all. I thought I detected a sexual frisson between you two last night.'

'You did?' Ellen watched her pour the wine, pulses pounding at the thought, too distracted to remember to ask Pheely to keep her voice down.

'God, yes. And I do envy you having such a positive body image,' she went on, in a booming voice. 'I have to get into training six months before I go to bed with a man these days – dieting, getting rid of the fluff, paring off the bunions, applying verruca plasters and slapping vanishing cream on the stretchmarks. You're *so* lucky. I long to be as carefree about screwing as you are.'

Ellen cleared her throat, hoping she could start being carefree after all these years.

'You're both free agents,' Pheely gurgled, then practically shouted, 'and, as you say, you are consenting adults. As long as you know the only thing he's ever going to be committed to is a criminal hearing or a mental institution, and you make sure he wears a condom, I think you'll have *huge* fun. Good luck to you, darling. Or should that be good fuck?' She raised her glass. 'To good luck, and a jolly good fuck.'

At this moment the shocked Crabtrees reappeared from the cellar and gaped at Pheely. 'You'll love this village,' she told them cheerfully. 'Everyone is *so* friendly.'

'So I can see.' Mrs Crabtree sniffed archly. 'I think I might take a turn round the garden.'

'Have a funny turn in it, more like,' Pheely said, after Poppy had ushered them outside. 'Stiff-knickered old bat. I think I might take your lead and find that new lover I keep promising myself. Mine is getting rather wearying.'

'You have a lover?'

'Absolutely. I simply can't survive without at least one origami a week. It's a staple, isn't it? In fact, do let me know if Spurs is as good as I suspect. I may even toy-boy with him myself once you're gone. Now that *would* put bloody Dilly in her place.'

'It's a staple,' Ellen reminded herself, as she took yet another shower between Poppy's viewings, this time scrubbing every inch of her body with walnut exfoliant, removing the little islands of hair that she had left after her first hasty shave, rubbing scented gel into her skin and adding half a bottle of conditioner to her wind and sea-ravaged hair.

Right now the only staple she could feel was the nervous one piercing her stomach, like a centrefold, as she made her body as smooth and glossy as its naked content.

The final family coming to see the cottage that day were called the Brakespears and had travelled specially from Essex, according to Poppy. They didn't want to view any other properties in the area, and she said that she had a 'good feeling' about them.

Ellen had very bad feelings towards them because they were late.

She'd put her hair in Velcro rollers and covered them with a bright scarf as she bounded around the house, deciding on the best spot for the massage. There was nothing as good as a proper massage table, but the kitchen table was long, narrow and a good height, she decided. If she put a duvet on it, it shouldn't be too uncomfortable, and she could close the roman blinds to avoid being gawped at by Hunter on one side and anyone walking along the lane on the other.

She put some more wine to chill, knowing that she would be shot down in flames for offering an alcoholic drink to any of the sportsmen she normally treated. But she for one would definitely need it to stop her hands shaking. She also sought out the few candles that the Shaggers hadn't burned, along with pretuning the kitchen radio to a mellow station and lining up her massage oils.

'Hellooo! Sorry I'm late. Are they here?' Poppy breezed in with some biscuits and a fresh packet of coffee. Ellen sometimes wondered if she secretly craved a job in Starbucks.

'I thought you were bringing them with you?' She glanced worriedly at the clock. It was already past five.

'They wanted to meet me here. Know the village quite well, apparently.' Poppy headed for the filter and started spooning in coffee, glancing rather worriedly at Ellen's Hilda Ogden hair accessories.

Ellen dashed upstairs to remove the rollers and check her appearance, guessing that the dreaded Brakespears might still be hanging around when Spurs arrived. Her hair tumbled in glossy ash waves around her tanned face, her eyes sparkled between rare licks of mascara and her cheeks glowed from a hasty dusting with blusher. She rubbed salve shakily on to her lips and squirted on some Eau Dynamisante, the closest thing she had to perfume. She didn't want to make it look as though she'd gone to too much of an effort – and she wanted to give Spurs a decent treatment without being hobbled by a stupid outfit – so she'd stuck to her faithful frayed denims matched with a little gypsy shirt and flip-flops that showed off her freshly painted toes, but she had shamelessly dug out her best underwear combo of a lace G-string and matching bra covered with dancing butterflies.

She stood in front of the mirror and drew an anxious breath, telling herself that she looked okay, not too tarty, not too scruffy – just the Ellen that Spurs had already got to know, only a bit sharper. She touched the burning-man tattoo for courage, then reached inside her shorts to touch the silver surfer on her butt, finally making it three for luck with the stud in her navel.

'It's a staple,' she told her reflection, with a wink.

Then, feeling mischievous as confidence and anticipation started coursing through her, she undid two top fly buttons, knowing that when she bent over, the top of her G-string would show.

They would have sex all night, she decided. First, she'd make him wait until the very end of his massage, when he was lying on his back. She knew he'd have a huge wood – they always did. She would climb on top of him and take him on the table. Then they could have a shower together and do it again standing up. Then perhaps outside as it was getting dark – up on the bunkhouse balcony overlooking the village, or under the apple trees. They could come inside and have a food fight – they were bound to have worked up an appetite. She must check what was in the fridge that could be eaten off a naked body. That would probably be the cue for another wash – a bath this time. She could show him how long she could hold her breath under water and challenge him to do the same. Finally, they'd fall into bed and stay up all night, talking and kissing, touching and caressing.

Tomorrow morning they would have one last, long, delicious session before getting up, getting dressed and wishing one another farewell. If he chose to keep his secrets and lies to himself, then that was his prerogative. He could go back to being a prodigal son. She would leave him far behind as soon as the cottage sale was secured. Her two remaining wishes were simple: she wished that one night of scruple-free sex and sin with Spurs would help her put a decade of hammer-drill action with Richard behind her; and she wished that she could forget about both of them afterwards.

Positively radiating wantonness, Ellen paced around impatiently as she and Poppy waited for the Brakespears, watching the clock get closer and closer to six. Poppy's attempts at polite conversation were greeted with a series of increasingly distracted and dislocated replies.

'Are you excited about your trip?'

'Mmm – yes.'

'Where do you plan to go first?'

'Nirvana.'

'Oh, lovely. Are you going to Las Vegas, then?'

'That's Nevada.'

'Oh. Silly me.'

'More whorehouses, more marriages, more gambling,' she explained idly. 'Nirvana is less rock and roll – you don't get a three carat rock or to roll the dice. You just go to heaven.'

Poppy's bulging eyes almost fell out of their sockets.

At last a big luxury people-carrier pulled up outside and a family of five spilled out – a huge, middle-aged rugby prop forward and his tall, thin wife along with children of different heights and sexes who separated faster than an SAS unit casing an enemy outpost the moment they were through the gate.

'Mr and Mrs Brakespear!' Poppy rushed out to greet them. 'You found it okay then?'

'Please – he's Graham and I'm Anke,' the woman said, in a northern-European accent, looking up at the cottage with shining blue eyes. 'I am sorry we were delayed, but my father, he did not want to go out to play bridge as he usually does – it took time to change his mind. He must not know about this. He thinks we are on our way back to Essex.' She let out a little sigh loaded with meaning.

'Mrs Brakespear's father owns the little antiquarian bookshop in Cider Lane,' Poppy explained to a distracted Ellen, who had come out to scour the lane for signs of Spurs.

'Oh, yes?'

'We want to move closer to him – to a house that has somewhere he can join us when he grows too frail to care for himself.' Anke smiled. 'We stayed here many times when visiting him, with your lovely parents. They are well?'

'Fine,' Ellen muttered, hoping that, as they knew the house already, their visit would be fleeting.

'This weekend, we stayed in Lower Oddford, which makes it hard to come and look here without him noticing.' Anke seemed happy to stand and chat on the gravel while her children raced around and her husband leafed through the particulars Poppy had handed him. A tall thin daughter was already in the paddock, sizing it up; an even taller son was smoking a cigarette and eyeing up the dovecote. 'Would this make a recording studio, d'you reckon?'

'If Morfar doesn't come to live with us, can I have the garage?' asked a younger son, who was built more like his huge father and bounded up the steps to peer into the bunkhouse.

'The children have already decided we will move here,' laughed Anke, lighting a cigarette of her own and looking up at the thatched princess. 'We always loved it here, and now that Graham has sold the company and found an interesting project in the Cotswolds, we really might be able to do it.'

'So, what line of business are you in?' Poppy asked gushily, while Ellen glanced at her watch and wished they'd bloody well go inside.

'Haulage.' He looked up from the brochure with a big, bearlike smile. 'At least I was until two months ago – sold the business on to an old mate. It was time to get out. I've found a little agricultural distributor's up on the ridge here that's going broke so I thought I'd buy it as a hobby. Farming sure as hell needs a kick up the arse, and I like to fly by the seat of my pants. It keeps me young.' He winked at Ellen.

Graham Brakespear – a swarthy Lancashire lad who clearly wore his heart on his Ralph Lauren sleeve while flying by the seat of his designer pants – took a long look at Ellen and closed the brochure. 'I see a lot I like here. A lot.'

'Would you like a cup of coffee while you look round?' asked Poppy. 'Or a glass of wine?' She'd seen the classy sauvignon in the fridge.

Ellen gritted her teeth.

'Wine would be lovely.' Anke smiled tiredly. 'We have had a difficult day.'

'Got any beer?' asked Graham, admiring Ellen's legs. 'And the kids'll have Coke.'

'I'll check.' Poppy danced inside, evidently smelling buying signals galore.

Why not watch some television and try out the beds? Ellen thought murderously. Poppy's make-yourself-at-home sales spiel was getting out of hand.

'So you're on your way back to Essex tonight?' She looked at the lane again. 'I'm sure you don't want to leave it too late.'

'Oh, it doesn't take long if you drive like Schumacher.' Anke gave her husband an amused little smile and watched the tall daughter loping back from the paddock. 'What do you think? Will Heigi and Bert like it here?'

'It's smaller than I remember, Mum,' she fretted. 'And there aren't any stables.'

'We can build those.' Graham patted his daughter's back and smiled at Ellen. 'This is Faith – Laurel and Hardy over there are Magnus and Chad.'

Ellen nodded in acknowledgement, then felt her heart slam her several paces back as she saw Spurs idling along the lane in scruffy shorts, dark glasses, bare feet and a pork-pie hat. He looked like an Italian rent-boy.

'I'm from Denmark,' Anke was saying. 'My father moved here to live with us when my mother died, but he did not like the village near Burnley where we were living then so he bought a little shop in Oddlode and started selling books. Now he is very old and he needs help, so we want him to live with us. But he is also very stubborn, so we must not tell him our plans. This is your friend?' she asked, colour leaping into her pale cheeks as Spurs ambled through the gates.

'Hi.' A dark eyebrow curled above the very dark glasses, and Ellen sensed that his mood had blackened. It made him sexier than ever, but also potentially highly explosive.

'These are the Brakespears – they're looking around the house,' she explained uneasily. 'This is Jasper Belling.'

When Poppy came back outside with a tray of drinks, Spurs dragged Ellen to one side. 'I had no idea you'd arranged a cocktail party,' he hissed, as the little group sorted out whose glass was whose. 'I'd have dressed up.'

'They arrived late,' Ellen explained in a whisper. 'They'll be gone soon.'

But the Brakespears, who knew that they had a safe two hours to look around while Ingmar played bridge in Hillcote, were in no hurry.

'I was under the impression that you were travelling down from Essex today?' Poppy tittered merrily, getting chatty.

'Change of plan – I wanted to look through Dulston's paper-work and he could only see me on Friday so we came down for the weekend.'

'Dulston's of Springlode?' Spurs asked Graham. 'James Dulston?'

'Yep – you know him?'

'He was married to my aunt for a couple of years. Used to screw his secretaries and diddle the VAT man. Wears women's underwear.'

It was an awkward moment but, to Ellen's relief, it prompted the Brakespears to head inside and start looking round.

She turned to Spurs, goosebumps raging. 'Drink?'

'I can't stay long.' He turned his face towards the sun.

'Got a hot date?' Her banging heart was firing great shots into her ribs.

'Yes.' He looked up over the rims of his glasses, silver eyes dancing. 'Christ, you look divine.'

She took a step towards him, breathing in his untamed smell, looking at the lean, muscular chest, the tatty shorts slung on his narrow hips, the long legs and dusty bare feet. Later she would get to explore every corner of his beautiful body. She couldn't wait. This was her gig. She was going to call the shots. 'I warn you, sports massages can hurt.'

'I always knew you'd hurt me.' He retreated behind his dark glasses.

Without thinking, she reached up to take them off, but he grabbed her arm to stop her. 'We need to talk,' he muttered, stepping away.

'Miss Jamieson?' A window shot open and Poppy's eager face shot out. 'Would you mind explaining exactly how the wood-burning stove works?'

Ellen watched Spurs worriedly, but his eyes were still hidden by the shades and he shrugged. 'Later.'

Reluctantly leaving him stretched out on his favourite garden bench with a bottle of beer, Ellen trailed around with the Brakespears, who wanted to know every last detail about the house, what was included in the sale and how her parents were getting on in Spain. In turn, Anke told her companionably all about her eccentric father who so rarely opened his shop, her worries about his health and their decision to move to the area to keep an eye on him. Ahead of them, the children squabbled about who would get which room and complained about the lack of telephone and TV aerial points upstairs.

Ellen looked out of every front window as she passed it to check that Spurs was still there, spotting the top of his camouflage hat and the long, tanned legs sprawling out in front of him. She was feeling hotter and hotter.

'Is this something to do with the alarm?' Anke pointed out a little socket hole by the skirting.

Ellen bent down to look. 'No, I think it's a vent.'

When she straightened up, Graham, Magnus and Chad Brakespear were all gaping at her adoringly because she'd just flashed her butterfly G-string and her silver surfer.

Back outside, she delivered another beer to Spurs as the Brakespears took a turn round the garden and outbuildings. 'Not much longer,' she promised.

He glanced up over his glasses, silver eyes troubled. 'Get rid of them.'

'I can't. They seem really keen. We've got all night – I mean all evening.' She flushed.

'No, we haven't,' he muttered, but before she had a chance to ask what he meant he added, 'What's in hell's got into you?'

Too much wine, heat and sexual frustration made Ellen feel reckless. 'Nothing yet,' she murmured, 'but I'm hoping you will later.'

A smile twitched on his lips but didn't break cover. Then he grabbed her wrist and she thought he was going to pull her on to his lap and kiss her, but he was just looking at her watch. As he did so, his fingers curled through hers. 'We really have to talk. There's something I need to tell you.'

'And there's something I need to tell you.' She bent over and spoke in his ear. 'I think we should fuck each other's brains out.'

His fingers tightened in hers and he pressed his lips to her collarbone, making the skin leap and burn. Then his other hand strayed momentarily up her thigh and between her legs, and she had to grip the back of the bench tightly to stay upright. Her whole body drummed and buzzed like an apiary in an earthquake, cleaving towards his.

'Miss Jamieson!' Poppy rattled past with another tray of drinks and Spurs' hand was swiftly removed. 'Sorry to drag you away, but can you tell the Brakespears about the barn conversion? I understand there are some old plans from when it was done.'

During a lengthy inspection of the bunkhouse and a worried discussion about the practicality of steep stone steps for an eighty-year-old man, Ellen looked out of one of the knee-height windows to see Spurs heading into the main cottage. Her heart leaped around like a squeezebox on elastic, hoping that he would head straight to her room and strip off.

The Brakespears stayed a further half-hour, chatting, laughing and hanging around in the garden in the lowering sunlight to admire everything. Every time Ellen tried to creep inside in search of Spurs, she was called back to answer a question or hear more tales of Magnus's band, Faith's pony and Chad's desire to be a fighter pilot. The wine was polished off, along with all the beer and every soft drink in the house, plus three bags of crisps and an apple. Only Poppy's fresh coffee bubbled untouched when they finally made moves.

'We'll be in touch,' Anke promised Poppy and Ellen, as they headed towards their car. 'Thank you so much!'

'My wife loves the place.' Graham winked. 'I'm sure I'll be calling you tomorrow, Poppy. Great to meet you.' He gave Ellen a hot look.

'Have a safe journey home!' Poppy called then whispered to Ellen, 'Lovely family. I must say, I thought he wasn't going to be keen, but he seemed *very* switched on. I think they'll offer, but we'll still have to watch out for him. He likes a bargain, I feel. Do you want to set negotiating perimeters over coffee?'

'Not right now – that's up to my parents. Call me when you know anything.' Ellen ushered her hurriedly towards the gate and bolted inside.

But Spurs wasn't in the house. On Ellen's bed, he had left a note. 'Wish Two expires in 24 hours. So will I without you. S.'

Ellen left the house unlocked and ran across the closed footpath, ducking out of sight of Hunter Gardner until she'd clambered over the gate to the manor's courtyards, hurried through the arches and around the yews. She hammered on the big black door, all set to rip off her clothes in an instant.

'What d'you want?' demanded a furious voice behind her, and she swung round to see Hell's Bells clutching a pair of secateurs and glaring at her. One look at the panting, flush-cheeked blonde in the half-undone clothes had clearly told Spurs' mother that she wasn't out collecting for Christian Aid.

'Lady Belling, I'm sorry to interrupt but I need to see Spurs.'

The big jaw lifted away from its cushioning chins and she fingered the secateurs menacingly. 'I've sent him on an errand this evening. He won't return until *very* late. How did you get on to the grounds?'

'I – er – know the way in,' Ellen said vaguely.

'Then you'll know the way out again,' she snapped.

Remembering that Hell's Bells was very ill – and that she was technically trespassing – Ellen apologised again. 'You see, I was supposed to honour the promise he bought at the auction, but I got held up and he left without rearranging a time.'

'Yes, well, he's gawn out. And I doubt he'll find the time again. No doubt he can gift the lot to someone else. What was it?'

'A sports massage,' Ellen muttered. And a night of hot loving, she thought silently, the goosebumps stealing away to be replaced by twitching anger.

'I'll mention it to his father,' Hell's Bells was saying. 'St John gets rather troublesome backache, which might benefit from a rub-down.'

'Why won't Spurs have the time?' Ellen asked.

'I don't see that that is any business of yours.'

'I still have to claim my lot from him. We have lots in common,' she joked, nervously because Hell's Bells was advancing at speed now, her rolling stride alarmingly like that of a Sumo wrestler heading for his first grip. Her G-string certainly wasn't up to a power hold.

Thankfully she stopped a yard short of Ellen and thrust the secateurs under one arm like a sergeant major's swagger stick, then pulled off her gloves. 'I think it best if you forget about that little bit of nonsense. In fact, I suggest that you forget about my son altogether.'

'But we're friends.'

'I rather think you're not.'

Ellen was surprised by the vehemence in her voice. 'I appreciate that I don't know him very well,' she said quickly, 'but I still think that we count ourselves friends.'

'Assuming that you can count at all after what has doubtless been a pitiful education at the state's expense,' Hell's Bells rose up to her full five feet three in sensible gardening shoes, 'then I suggest you count your blessings that we are having this little chat. You are *not* friends with my son, nor will you be. You are not welcome on our land or in his life. The sooner you leave this village the better. Do I make myself clear?'

Ellen wondered why she was being so cantankerous. 'I hear what you're saying,' she said carefully.

'Well, I suppose one should be grateful that you're not deaf as *well* as dumb,' Hell's Bells tutted. 'Now, would you kindly leave this garden?'

Ellen thrust her hands into her pockets to stop herself taking a swing at the old bat. 'Will you at least tell him I was here?'

'Very well.' The familiar silver eyes were like steel traps.

She trailed back to the cottage despondently and took her third shower of the day. This time it was a cold one.

First thing the following morning Poppy was on the telephone to tell Ellen the good news that the Brakespears had made an offer just a few thousand below the new asking price, which had already been fifty thousand higher than the one put forward by Seaton's. Having already called Theo and Jennifer in Spain, Poppy reported that they were thrilled and had decided to accept. She thought that it would be a straightforward sale: 'The Brakespears already have an asking-price offer on their property, and they're not seeking a new mortgage, so there's no reason why we can't exchange within the month.'

'Thanks,' Ellen said hollowly, wondering why she wasn't more relieved. 'You've done a fantastic job.'

'You can book your flight to Nirvana now.'

'I've changed my mind. The Foreign Office is warning against travelling there. I think I'll start somewhere a bit less remote.'

When Ellen carefully replaced the handset, she caught sight of the massage oils still waiting on the sill in the kitchen, and felt a heavy bolt of regret slide across her head, heart and libido. It was over. It had to be over. It had never really started.

She fired up her laptop and set about confirming her flights – starting with the one from Heathrow that left in a fortnight's time, on the day of Ely Gates's garden party.

Snorkel watched her worriedly from a corner of the kitchen, black ears flicking backwards and forwards, blue eyes blinking.

'I'll find you a lovely home,' Ellen promised her. 'And we'll bloody well track down that antisocial mog too.'

On the table in front of her was the nail from the horseshoe and Spurs' note. Ellen turned them over and over in her hands as she waited for her online credit-card transaction to be confirmed.

'You've got to solve the riddle before you dissolve,' Spurs had said.

But Ellen couldn't take the heat. She'd always stood a snow-ball's chance in hell with someone so loaded with X-factor. He had warned her off more than once, knowing that she was flying too close to the prodigal sun. Melting his heart was like being burned at the stake. And now she was dissolving the partnership instead.

12

At her parents' instruction, Ellen started boxing up many of their more personal possessions on the same morning that the Brakespears' offer was accepted.

'Don't you think I should hang fire until it's all more definite?' she'd asked her mother, during their early-morning call. 'After all, if this falls through you won't want it full of packing cases for more viewings.'

'Don't be so lazy,' Jennifer snapped. 'You've already told us you're swanning off in a matter of days, and while I'm sure the removal company are very capable, there are certain items that your father and I would prefer to be handled by you.'

'I thought you might change your mind and come here for the final move?'

'You know how much your father hates travelling these days, and now he has the wretched animals as an excuse. It might be better just to leave it to the experts.' Her voice was tight with emotion, which Ellen at first read to be ongoing anger about Theo's poultry and goat purchases. It was only when she'd rung off that it occurred to her how upset her mother must be that the dream cottage would soon no longer be hers.

And at least packing things away took Ellen's mind off Spurs. Ever efficient, Jennifer had already sent her a copy of the detailed itinerary listing what was to go to Spain with the removers, and what was to be taken away by the house-clearance company – both of whom were poised to descend the moment contracts were exchanged.

She was stashing another box of trinkets in the cellar when she heard footsteps in the kitchen above her. Hoping blindly that it

was Spurs she raced up the narrow stone stairs so quickly that
she cracked her kneecaps.

But it was just Dilly, returning Ellen's clothes and in desperate
need of advice. 'Oh, God, I made *such* a fool of myself on
Saturday night, Ellen. Was I completely and totally uncool?'

'No.' She made them both a cup of tea. 'You were just a bit
caned. Nobody could blame you for being upset that your mother
and I gatecrashed. I'd have reacted in exactly the same way.'

'But I told everyone that Mum fakes her orgasms, then started
banging on about Rory and Spurs both fancying me in front
of them. Mum says that I behaved like a big kid and it's no
wonder Rory walked out.' Dilly sat on the kitchen table and
swung her legs, looking every inch a big kid. 'She's being so
bitchy. She says you probably hate me because I told everybody
that you set Spurs and me up. She says that you're *her* friend,
not mine, and that I should leave you alone, but I told her she
should too. It was her fault you got dragged along on Saturday,
wasn't it?'

There had been a huge mother–daughter confrontation when
they'd sobered up, Ellen realised. No wonder Pheely had been so
crotchety the day before. She smiled awkwardly. 'She *is* looking
out for you, I promise. We both were. You did set out on a bit
of a mission.'

Dilly hung her head and looked at Ellen through her lashes
as she watched her milk the tea. 'I know. A missionary-position
mission. Did you and Spurs fight when you went to check on
Rory? Mum thinks you pushed him into a water-trough for having
designs on me.'

Ellen laughed. 'No, he just waded into the pond.'

'He's a bit crazy sometimes, isn't he?'

'Sometimes.'

'He really likes you, I can tell.'

Ellen grabbed the mugs and carried them outside, barely
noticing that the scalding china was burning her hands.

'Did he say anything to you?' Dilly followed her. 'About me,
I mean.'

'Only that he thinks you're adorable.' Ellen settled on Spurs' favourite bench.

'Really?' Dilly's face lit up and she stooped to rub Snorkel's belly. 'Godspell was really funny about him. She calls him Squire Hard-on. I don't think she likes him much.'

'So you and Godspell are friends again?' Ellen didn't want to talk about Spurs.

'Sort of. She still won't tell me where she disappeared to on Saturday night. She kept getting these text messages, and then just before you and Spurs got back a car horn beeped outside and she upped and left so fast she forgot her purse. I went round to Manor Farm yesterday to return it and she showed me her new boa. We sort of talked.'

Ellen had a brief image of Dilly and Godspell sharing girly confidences, makeup and accessories before the notion was shattered.

'She's called him Noose,' Dilly went on. 'I had no idea snakes were so warm and smooth. Mum's wrong about her. She might not say a lot, but she's really bright and funny. And you can't blame her for being a bit odd with a father like Ely. He's horrible. You know he makes his children sign contracts about everything? Their allowances, their education, even the amount of work they do around the house. He's always done it. Giles Hornton draws them up.'

'Blimey. Is that legal?'

'Dunno, but they're too scared of him to argue.' Dilly chewed her thumbnail nervously. 'At least Mum's pretty easy-going, even if she does spy on me when I'm out on the pull. Oh, heck, I am *so* embarrassed.' She put her face into her hands. 'Spurs must think I'm such a baby. He's taking Otto out for the last time today. Rory's found him a horse to ride in the race, and he says it's about time I got to know Psychotto better. I'm sure it's only because they're both too disgusted by my behaviour to ever want to see me again.'

'Rubbish. If you want to ride in the race too, you're going to have to get on Otto again soon. I'm sure they'll both help you – Rory and Spurs.'

'I can't bear not seeing him. Please, Ellen, I need your help.'

'What can I do?'

'Talk to him for me. Tell him I'm sorry.'

'You have nothing to be sorry for.'

'I was really horrible to him. I said horrible things. I think I'm in love with him, Ellen.'

Ellen rubbed her face tiredly. 'In that case you should talk to him, not me. I have a lot to do, Dilly. I'm leaving soon. It's really better that I'm not involved.'

'Mum was right.' She stood up huffily. 'You're just playing with us for fun – like dolls. I can't believe I thought you were so lovely. You're horrible and selfish. I'm glad you're leaving. I hope I never see you again. And leave my mother alone!'

'Dilly!' Ellen called after her, as she sprinted away.

'Screw you!' she called, starting to run backwards. 'You were right when you said you were like Spurs. You're both so easy to fall in love with, but you have no souls. You're not soulmates. You're soulless, both of you.'

Why? Ellen asked herself wretchedly, as she wandered up Giles Hornton's hot Tarmac drive, trying to stay in the shade of the poplars. Why am I doing this?

River Cottage, a low-slung, white weatherboard boathouse conversion, was tucked well back from North Street and faced out over the Odd towards Devil's Marsh. Otto's field spread out beyond the poplars to the right.

Thankfully the flashy Aston Martin was missing from the triple garage when Ellen skulked past the house to greet Otto at the gate. The crotchety strawberry roan was already waiting for Spurs, head bobbing and tail twitching against the flies.

They greeted one another warily. Ellen offered him a Polo and he nudged her shoulder with his pink lips as he ate it.

'You know him pretty well by now.' She looked at the suspicious dark eyes and then, remembering Spurs telling her that horses found that intimidating, looked up at his ears. 'What do I say?'

He snorted unhelpfully and tried to nip her. Then she noticed that his ears had pricked and, as she heard an engine approach, she followed his gaze, her ribs curling anxiously in on themselves.

Spurs was puttering along the drive on the Manor's mini-tractor, a saddle and bridle slung over the carrying rack in front of him.

'Down, boys,' Ellen hissed at her goosebumps.

He braked hard when he saw her. 'Come to see Giles?' he shouted, over the noise of the engine. 'I think he's out.'

Looking at him, Ellen was almost winded by a sadness so acute that it took all her willpower not to run away. She knew the moment she saw him that he had slid the same bolt across his feelings as she had. His haughty, freckled face was a guarded mask, his shoulders yoked by heavy self-control and his back rigid with a rod of his own making. He had doused the fire as surely as she had, leaving the coals to smoulder and spit, the red-hot heat still broiling deep beneath the hissing surface, now starved of oxygen in which to burn.

'No.' She fished in her pocket and pulled out the twisted nail. 'I've come about this.' And I'm about to bang it into my own coffin.

Still astride the tractor with the engine switched off, he listened warily to her request. When he heard what it was, he burst into sardonic laughter. 'You want me to *what*?'

'Treat Dilly to a night out,' she repeated, 'for a proper dinner date. Wear a suit, spoil her rotten, flatter her, take her home, kiss her on the check and then leave. That's my wish.'

'Bollocks it is. She's put you up to this.'

'It's my wish. You gave me twenty-four hours to make it and there it is.'

'You said you wanted your money back.'

'So I changed my mind. I wish you'd take Dilly out.'

He sucked in one cheek and looked away, silver eyes glaring at Giles' poplars. 'Why?'

'To make up for Saturday night. Pheely and I ruined it for her – for both of you.'

'And last night?' He swung his leg over the tractor and jumped down.

She turned away and stroked Otto's soft muzzle. 'Let's forget about it.'

'I'm sorry, Ellen.' He carried the saddle over to the field, not looking at her. 'I couldn't stay.'

'Sure.'

He hooked the saddle over the gate and leaned on it, rubbing his forehead beneath the dark curls. 'I had to go out on an errand.'

'So your mother said.'

He turned away, taking the head-collar from his shoulder and buckling it on to Otto. 'You spoke to my mother?'

Hell's Bells clearly hadn't passed on the message. 'She suggested that you didn't need my friendship.'

'I don't "do" friends.'

'I didn't want to be friends last night.' Her heart hammered in indignation.

'That,' he glanced over his shoulder, the flints in his eyes sparking with that familiar amusement, 'was pretty obvious.'

Lanced by rejection, she looked away.

Spurs handed her the lead rope, pulled the cuff of his sleeve into his hand and brushed the dust from Otto's back, then went to fetch the saddle. He paused when he spotted the nail and picked it up. 'Mother sent me to London to see the Queen.'

'Rather late for a social visit?'

'The Queen is nocturnal.' He smiled sadly at her baffled expression. 'It's what we call Uncle Belvoir – keeper of the Belling family jewellery.' He tapped the nail against his nose. 'We had quite a chat. I told him all about you – I was rather fucked off with myself at the time – and he agreed that I mustn't let it happen, *dear boy*. The family's future is at stake if I don't behave myself, after all. Too much passion is a very bad thing, you see. One should never let oneself be swept away by a mere popsy when one has one's heritage to protect.' He recited the lines bitterly.

Ellen could hardly believe her ears. 'Are you saying I'm too common for you?'

He laughed, holding up the nail. 'Oh, Ellen, my little beggar-girl, if this were a horse, maybe I'd get you riding after all.'

Ellen felt her adenoids crackle with fury and hurt, a red mist forming in front of her eyes as the red carpet was pulled from under her feet.

It had been simply a matter of class all along. She was from the wrong social drawer. She needed him like a hole in the head because her silver spoon was missing. That's why Hell's Bells had been so rancorous. Ellen Jamieson, with her Somerset accent, her state-school education and her tattoos would sully her prodigal son now that he'd cleaned up his act. Last night, when she'd been ready to offer herself on a plate, had he bolted because he'd thought she wanted the wedding breakfast and the full Crown Derby dinner service on the gift list as well?

'The Queen is just looking out for the family,' he was explaining, still strangely cheerful. 'He's always tried to keep his brother's wayward son on the straight and narrow, much as it pains him that I'm not gay. He says popsies can never give the same pleasure as one's own sex.'

'Next time you see him, tell him to sit on his orb.' She was almost incandescent with indignation.

He laughed. 'Tell him yourself. He's coming down for Ely's garden party.'

'I won't be here. My flight leaves that evening.'

There was a long pause. Spurs stared minutely at the horseshoe clench. 'So you're getting your gorgeous wings to fly away?' he said eventually.

She was tempted to point out that she was in cattle class, along with the rest of the beggars.

The corner of his mouth twitched. 'They're buying the cottage, the Swiss Family Robinson?'

'She's Danish and they're called Brakespear.'

'Forgive me for not giving a fuck who they are. I hate them.'

'I was always going to leave as soon as the sale was agreed.'

He nodded. 'Fuck.' He turned away and glowered at the gatepost, then kicked it. 'Fuck.'

Otto jerked his head back in alarm and Spurs turned to soothe him, laying a hand on his neck. 'I told you you'd dissolve.'

When she didn't answer, he turned back to her and ground the horseshoe nail into the soft wood at the top of the gate. 'Forget friendship. We'd just be running in new shoes.'

Ellen watched the nail dig out splinters.

'Do you know how to shoe a horse?' he asked suddenly.

She looked at him curiously.

'You say, "shoo, shoo."' He tushed with fake laughter at the bad joke, looking up into the trees. 'D'you know how to shoo an Ellen?'

'Tell me?'

'You tell her you love her.'

'And?' There was a catch in her throat.

'She runs away so fast her feet don't touch the ground.' He watched a magpie chatter and flap from the trees. 'Who needs shoes when you can fly?'

She stared at the ground, her heart pinching.

He didn't ask where she was planning to go. Instead, he pocketed the nail. 'Where do you want me to treat Dilly to this meal?'

Ellen struggled to drag her mind back to her wish. 'Somewhere sophisticated. But I'll pay.'

'Won't you need all your money to hire camels and sherpas?'

'I can just about cover it if you don't drink Krug all night.'

He took the saddle and lifted it on to Otto's back, but then he pressed his cheek to the black-leather knee-roll, sliding his eyes round to look at her. 'We couldn't have let it happen, you know. *Us*. Too messy.'

'I'm glad it didn't,' she lied.

'No, you're not. Neither of us is.' The clipped voice was pure Belling. Only the eyes remained untamed and vivid with emotion.

Ellen couldn't hold the stare for more than a few seconds. 'I must go – let me know how much I owe you for the meal,' she said. 'And treat Dilly gently.' She was so wound up that she didn't even notice Pheely's teenage indulgence slip out. Ignoring his shouts, she sprinted along Giles's drive.

Snorkel positively bungeed her lunge rope in the Goose Cottage garden a few minutes later when Spurs dragged the unwilling Otto into the garden and up to the pond, into which Ellen was staring with murderous intent.

'I won't grant your wish. I'm not taking Dilly anywhere, Ellen.'

She opened her mouth and closed it again. Something about his expression told her not to say a word.

'You can be so blindly, stupidly selfless, you know that?' he said angrily, loosening Otto to let him graze. 'I bet you gave all your toys away as a kid, let the losers win to make them feel better, had friends you only kept up because you felt sorry for them, and let the ugly boys kiss you because you knew no one else would put up with it.'

She felt numb with shock that he could sum her up so cruelly and succinctly. 'If you say so.'

'Was that why you stayed with Richard all those years? Out of kindness?'

'I don't want to talk about it.' She took a step back, but he marked her, cornering her by the bulrushes.

'Maybe not,' his eyes narrowed, 'but let me tell you something as your newest "friend" – one who you no doubt feel sorry for because I have no others in this fucking village. You're a brave, sassy woman, Ellen, but you won't get round the world on kindness. You'll be mugged for it everywhere you go. You'll keep meeting bastards like me who fall in love with you for your kindness as much as that beautiful arse, and will want to steal it away from you.'

'I doubt that.' She laughed hollowly. 'I don't think I'll ever meet anyone like you again in my life.'

As she started to walk away, he called after her. 'I won't grant your wish, but I *will* treat Dilly to her posh nosh. I just won't be there in person. Rory can do it.'

She turned around. 'That's not what I wished for.'

'Dilly is mad about Rory, Ellen – he's all she ever talks about and vice versa.'

'But I thought . . .'

'That she was mad about me? No, she just got caught up in your enthusiasm because you're so bloody gorgeous she wants to be exactly like you.' He leaned back against Otto. 'And you *are* mad about me, just like I'm mad about you.'

Ellen felt every vertebra in her spine exchange a high five. 'You're mad about me?'

He nodded. 'I'm a thief. I covet what I can't have. And I can't have you, so I decided to steal your kindness as a memento.'

She cocked her head and blinked, torn between anger and fascination. 'Explain.'

'I think Dilly is very pretty, but she's just a kid. And Saturday night certainly wasn't the hot double date Pheely thought it was. Rory's banned from driving right now so he asked my help to get them together – she is obviously nuts about him too, the foolish child. I was simply the free taxi. And Godspell had to get out from under her overprotective father's nose to catch up with her dealer, so she tagged along.'

Ellen's eyes boggled. 'What does that make you? Robin Reliant Hood?'

He gave a brittle laugh. 'They call me the wild Land Rover.'

'Oh, shit.' She covered her mouth. 'You mean I was giving Dilly lots of encouragement over you and it was Rory she pre-ferred all along?' Playing back the conversation she'd had with Dilly earlier, she suddenly suspected that she hadn't been talking about Spurs at all. 'Poor thing. I must have really confused her.'

'Poor bloody Rory.' Spurs patted Otto's neck. 'He was nervous enough before Dilly started spouting lyrical about your prediction that she was my bloody soulmate. No wonder he fled into Sharrie's arms. I looked like such a fucking cad after that, and all I wanted to do was spread a bit of loving like my guardian garden angel. I had no idea you'd already been laying it on with a trowel about the reformed-rake business.'

Ellen hung her head. 'I didn't mean to interfere.'

'Yes, you did,' he said, but not unkindly. 'This isn't some fairy tale you can manipulate to give us all happy endings before you fly off on your star-encrusted white-witch broomstick. I was never destined to be Dilly's gent. She and Rory will probably get it together with or without anyone's help this summer – he'll break her hymen then her heart before she heads off to university to meet a nice middle-class boy, sell the Lodge and move to London. Meanwhile, Rory stays behind to shag his grooms and drink himself to death by forty. It's all predetermined. Life is more of a pantomime than a fairy tale when you think about it.' The voice was getting more clipped and disdainful.

'You don't really believe that?' she asked.

'I believe in fate. You can't change the script, but that's no reason not to stage it differently. All your wish needs is a cast shuffle. Rory will never be Prince Charming, but at least he can press all the right buttons to start Dilly off. They just require a little help from the wings. I'll keep him sober if you keep her calm.'

'We can't go too,' she yelped.

'I'm not suggesting we do.' He checked Otto's girth. 'But they're going to need a lift to this "sophisticated" restaurant.'

'I'll pay for a cab.'

'No, you won't. You'll drive them, Fairy Godmother.'

'It's *my* wish.'

'Not any more. You're hopeless at wishes.'

Ellen started to laugh despite herself. 'And what will you do while I'm driving the coach and foreplay, Squire Hard-on?'

He looked at her sharply. 'Why did you call me that?'

She watched his face, her laugh instantly put out. A muscle was twitching tiredly under his eye and his cheeks were hollow. His snappishness worried her, like a rattling lid on a pan of boiling oil that was about to ignite and burn the house down. Neither of them was finding it easy to run in the new friendship shoes, but Spurs was sprinting away and dragging her along in an awkward, unnatural three-legged race.

'Just something I heard.'

He looked at her for a long time. 'I'll come too.'

'Is that wise? Won't your mother disapprove?'

His eyes flashed a warning, but then he smiled. 'I'll shimmy down the drainpipe after my lights-out curfew.' Something about his tone told her that he wasn't entirely joking as he stepped into the stirrup and mounted. 'I think we might manage a friendly drink if we try really hard.' He looked down at her. 'In fact, you owe me supper.'

Remembering the abandoned Chinese, Ellen looked away. 'I don't think that's such a good idea.'

'Afraid I'll squander all of your camel-trekking money on calamari and chips?'

'What if "us" happens?'

'There is no us.' He rode Otto towards the gates. 'Get Dilly geared up for Wednesday – I'll find out where Rory wants to take her. Make out that it's coming from him, for Christ's sake.' He stifled a yawn, and Ellen following behind realised that he couldn't have slept much if he'd driven to and from London to spend the night talking to the family uncle who'd given him treasures and pearls of wisdom.

'We can have a last supper.' He smiled down at her. 'A first-date last supper. Your treat.'

She leaned back against the gatepost as Otto exploded past her, knowing that she would have put up a far greater fight had Spurs not been prancing around on a horse.

And yet she still couldn't leave it there. 'Spurs!'

Otto pirouetted on the spot, but the silver eyes didn't leave hers.

'Why did you go to London?'

'To fetch my jewelled manacle before it ends up intestate. It's very pretty. It could have been yours.'

'I'm sorry?'

'I asked you to marry me, remember?'

'You were joking.'

'Was I?' He and Otto set off along the lane at a thundering trot, sending up sparks in their wake.

★   ★   ★

Pheely was admiring the UNDER OFFER sticker that had already
been plastered on to the Day-Fox sign outside Goose Cottage,
a huge bunch of irises in her arms. 'Pixie brought them round
– aren't they divine? I thought you'd like some to help set the
place off, but it seems I'm too late.' She thrust them at Ellen.
'Sorry I was a bit of a cow yesterday. Mind you, I think I swung
the sale, huh? People love villages with lots of sex scandals
going on.'

Ellen smiled wanly. 'You were magnificent. But they're not
buying it – someone else is.'

'Really?' Pheely, who would have been agog at any other time,
seemed barely to care. 'Now, tell me about Spurs. Was it origami
galore?'

'Not worth the paper.'

'*Really?* But I've heard he's *huge*, my dear.'

'It didn't happen.'

'God, how awful – had he drunk too much?'

'Helloooo there!'

Ellen looked up as Hunter Gardner bustled up, twirling his
walking-stick at the prospect of new blood. 'I see it's gawn off
the market at last. Anyone I know?'

'Lovely couple. They run Balinese-trance workshops,' she
snapped. 'I hope to catch one before I leave – apparently you
get to bite the head off a live chicken. Excuse me.' She stormed
inside.

'Not enough sex,' Pheely told Hunter cheerfully, before heading home to break the news of the sale to Dilly.

'He really wants to take me out for a meal? Just the two of
us?'

Ellen nodded. She and Dilly were sitting on Bevis's bench
eating a Zoom and an M and M Cornetto respectively.

'Wow.' A very pink tongue delved around the wafer rim.
'That's really cool. Isn't it?'

'Yeah. Really cool.'

'Wow.'

She didn't sound quite as enthusiastic as Ellen had hoped. 'Are you still in a bad mood with me?'

'No! No.' Dilly nudged her to show they were mates again.

'You do want to go for a night out with Rory, don't you?'

'Yes! Totally. Absolutely. It's just . . .'

'Just what?'

Dilly stared at the pond, watching the ducks craning round to clean their feathers. 'Will it be a very smart restaurant?'

'I'm not sure where he wants to take you. I should think so.'

'I'm a vegetarian – well, I eat fish, but not anything with eyes that look at you.'

'I'm sure they'll have vegetarian options – and fish dishes without stary eyes.'

'Oh.' Dilly was still looking worried. 'Will there be lots of people there?'

'I don't know. Depends how popular it is.'

'Only Rory gets intimidated by crowds, and very posh places. His mother used to take him along to very smart society dos when he was younger and it freaked him out. He can't stand anything pompous. I'd hate him to take me somewhere really smart just because he thinks it'll impress me. I'd rather he was relaxed.'

'I'm sure he'll find somewhere cosy,' she promised, looking out over the roofs of the old chapel triangle towards the Hillcote shank of the valley, where the rape-fields had returned to green having lost their flowers, and the butterscotch gold of the ripening wheat now formed new layers in the terrine.

'The thing is,' Dilly went on, 'Rory called me just after I saw you. His phone's been reconnected. He was so sweet – he said I wasn't rude to him at all. And he suggested tomorrow night in the Plough without – er – so many people. He didn't mention anything about a restaurant on Wednesday.'

'Oh? I must have got the wrong end of the stick.' Ellen blushed furiously. The one thing she and Spurs hadn't accounted for was Rory using his own initiative.

'I'd still appreciate a lift if that's okay.'

'Sure.'

'And will you lend me something to wear again?'

'Of course. Come round early and I'll sort stuff out for you to try.'

'Thanks.' Dilly pressed the last hollow inches of her Cornetto to her nose. 'Sorry I was so horrid to you.'

'Don't worry about it. I'm glad you were. I needed to talk to Spurs.'

'Rory says he's acting really funny.'

'In what way?'

'Dunno – he didn't say.' She crossed her eyes looking at the wafer cone. 'He doesn't say a lot. I like that about him. Spurs is far too talkative, and I can never tell when he's being serious. I thought he was totally amazing at first, but I don't fancy him half as much as Rory now. And I've had a bit of an idea.' She pressed the little cone to her lips and looked at Ellen coyly. 'Can I tell you it?'

'Fire away.'

'Mum . . . and Spurs!' she announced, with a flourish. 'What do you think?'

'I think – well, I don't know what to think, really.' Ellen reeled.

'It's perfect, isn't it? Now that she's forgiven him – oh, I know she's still a bit edgy about it, but you've done the most amazing thing getting them talking, Ellen – they should maybe go out to dinner or something romantic and see what happens. Perhaps you could suggest it and give them a lift tomorrow night too?'

'That might be a bit soon,' Ellen stalled, trying frantically to think of a good reason to put a stop to Dilly's thinking.

'Maybe.' She crumbled her cone and threw it for the ducks. 'But it's still a fantastic idea, don't you think? You could say something. It would just sound silly coming from me.'

'It would sound equally silly coming from me, I can assure you.'

'No, it wouldn't. They knew each other as children – Grandpa adored Spurs. I think Mum secretly fancies him, and you saw how desperate he was for her to forgive him on Saturday. He even used to read fairy tales to me as a little girl. Can you imagine a double wedding?'

Ellen closed her eyes and smiled. 'In a fairy tale, maybe.'

'So, will you say something?'

'I'll think about it.'

'Are you walking back to Goose Cottage?' Dilly asked.

'Not just yet.' Ellen opened her eyes. 'I'll hang on here for a bit. Got some of that thinking to do.'

She watched Dilly wander away across the green, so beautiful and fresh-faced and full of vigour.

'So much for playing fairy godmother.' She sighed, patting Bevis's bench. 'I bet you'd rather have gone to a pub with a girl at your age, wouldn't you?' Chatting to his bench always reminded her of being seventeen or eighteen, as though her years with Richard hadn't run away with her until she'd found herself almost thirty and no more romantically experienced than a teenager.

She picked one of his shady daisies and plucked idly at the petals, wondering if Spurs would still want the friendly meal. Her remaining days in Oddlode stretched out ahead of her like the empty boxes she had to pack for her parents, hollow and only to be filled with nostalgia and regret. What she wouldn't give to have the sea and the waves nearby, to be able to grab her board and spend her days racing the surf.

Not wanting to go back to the empty cottage, she unhooked Snorkel's lead and headed along the lane towards Hillcote, intending to buy some more strawberries from the market garden as a present for Hunter Gardner to apologise for being so rude. Her mother would never forgive such belligerence towards the neighbour who had been her stalwart chum for over a decade.

Just as the pavement gave way to wide verges laced with cow parsley on the outskirts of the village, Ellen spotted Reg Wyck's pick-up roaring along the lane towards her, with Fluffy snarling manically in the back. At the wheel was Saul, nodding his head to the loud drum 'n' bass track belting out of the stereo.

Ellen pulled down her baseball cap in a hopeless attempt not to be recognised and stepped into the cow parsley, making Snorkel sit beside her.

But the pick-up stopped twenty yards short of her in the middle of the narrow lane and Saul watched her through his windscreen, revving his engine.

Ellen waited.

Saul revved louder, the battered rusty metal grille of the old pick-up like bared yellow teeth. Fluffy was going demented in the back, contained by a chain tied to the roof of the cab, which rattled and strained as she tried to throw herself out to get at Ellen and Snorkel.

Ellen felt a muzzle glue itself nervously between her calves. She glanced around; but she was a hundred yards from the nearest house and there was no sign of life nearby or another car coming.

Fine. He could play games, she decided, but there was no way she was going to join in. Tugging at Snorkel's lead, she set off along the lane again, in the direction of the pick-up.

Without warning it launched towards her as fast as it could accelerate.

'Shit!' Ellen leaped into the cow parsley, dragging Snorkel towards a dry-stone wall as the pick-up mounted the verge and headed straight at her. She could have jumped the wall in time, but she couldn't leave Snorkel in its path so she did the only thing she could think of. She threw out her arms and dared him.

The hot radiator scalded her knees as the pick-up screeched to a halt just an inch short of them.

'Just *what* is your problem?' she raged, slamming her fists on the bonnet.

'Didn't you get the message?' Saul yelled over Fluffy's barking and the drum 'n' bass. 'Piss off back to London you interfering cow!'

Ellen marched to his window, not caring that Fluffy's drooling hackles were just inches from her ear. 'I am *not* from London.'

'Yeah – no matter. We still hope you rot in hell.'

'It was you!' She rounded on him. 'You left that bloody badger.'

'Can't prove it.' He thrust out his jaw. 'You should just get out of here. You were totally out of order speaking to old Gran like that. Nearly give her an 'eart-attack.'

'You hadn't done a stroke of work there for months.'

'The mower was busted.'

Ellen couldn't be bothered to start scrapping over garden equipment. 'Well, Goose Cottage has just been sold, so if you wouldn't mind cutting out the dead-wildlife routine and the dangerous-driving act, I'd be grateful. I'll be out of your hair before you know it.'

'Oh. Right you are. Ely got it, then?' Suddenly he seemed quite chatty and amenable. Ellen would have laughed if she hadn't been in such a foul temper. She eyed him angrily. 'Did he give you a backhander to let it go to pot?'

'I wouldn't do nothing for that bastard,' Saul snarled. 'I just knew he was after it. Wedding present or summink.' The bright blue eyes watched her face.

But Ellen couldn't care why Ely had wanted it. 'He didn't get it. A new family will be moving in soon,' she said wearily, 'and I'm sure they'll be happy to hear about the services you offer.'

'That a fact?' His boxer's face twisted thoughtfully. Then he licked his lips and leaned out of the window. 'Is it true Spurs Belling's boning you?'

'Who said that?'

'Everyone's talking 'bout it. Gladys has bin telling all the biddies you two've been at it since you got here. Her ladyship's in a right state. She wants you out of this village 'n' all. I should watch your back.' Giving her a menacing, broken-toothed leer, he put the pick-up into reverse, then belted away in a plume of black exhaust fumes.

'It's all your fault,' Ellen told her mobile, when it rang as she trailed back from the organic gardens with her strawberries, having taken half an hour to extract Snorkel from the wild pack of children and animals. 'Why don't you have a silent alert?' If the pesky little device hadn't rung at the charity auction, she would never have got to know Spurs. Had Hells Bells not taken its trill ring as a bid, she would never have bought Spurs' wishes at a knock-down price.

'You could at least vibrate,' Ellen told it, as she fished it out of her pocket. 'Yup?'

'Ellen?'

She clutched the phone so tightly to her ear that her earring tapped tunefully on the number four button. She had never spoken to Spurs on the phone before, and the sound of his voice deep in her ear made her sway into the verge. Her mobile was vibrating like mad now.

''S me.'

'This is Spurs.'

I know, she thought, as the goosebumps raged. I bloody know. 'The answer's still no.' She managed to sound calm.

To her consternation, he just laughed, knowing immediately what she was alluding to. 'I warn you, I'll ask you again. What's that noise?'

Ellen took out her earring to stop the four button intoning. 'My mobile does that sometimes.'

'I'm having a drink with Rory. He says he's already asked Dilly up here tomorrow night.'

'I know.' She leaned over the stone wall and watched a herd of cattle drift aimlessly in the afternoon sun. 'I've told her I'll give her a lift to the pub.'

'Good. Because I told Rory about your pantomime idea—'

'It wasn't my idea—'

'—and he told me he thinks it's fucking crap.' He laughed, ignoring her interruption. 'But he's now come up with some thoughts that I have to admit are frighteningly camp, so we're on for a bit of set-dressing at least.'

'Spurs, I don't want to play the back end of your panto horse any more.' She kicked the wall.

'What?'

'You're right – us trying to be friends would be like running in new shoes, only worse because we have nowhere to run except out of time.'

He dropped his voice: 'At least try them for size.'

'I don't see that there's any point. We're being . . .' she cleared her throat '. . . talked about.'

'By whom?'

'The entire village, as far as I can tell.'

There was a long pause.

'Does that bother you?'

'No, but then I'm not staying much longer, am I? You have more at stake.'

'I don't give a shit what they say about me.' He let out an angry tut and muttered something at Rory in the background. 'You still owe me dinner, and Rory here could use our help. You don't get out of it that easily.' The arrogant clip in his voice made it clear he had no intention of losing face. The slight slur to his voice was even more worrying.

Ellen watched two magpies rise up from the field and chatter into a tree. Far beyond it, bathed in hazy sunlight, was the Springlodes, perched high on the ridge. She could make out the huge house, which sat in a wooded park between the two villages. Somewhere, in that little cluster of stone dots to the right, Spurs was breathing vodka fumes into her ear.

'Please, Ellen. Wear the new shoes.' He had lowered his voice huskily. 'I *need* you to keep me good. You're my garden angel. My avenging angel.'

'*No!*' she shouted, sending the cows into a panic-stricken stampede across the field. 'I'm *not* your good fairy or Dilly's fairy godmother or Pheely's *Guardian*-reading angel or anybody's anything else. I just want an easy life, not a hard-luck story. You're *so* wrong about me, Spurs. I don't believe in fairy tales – I don't even know most of them because I never heard them as a kid, just as I never went to pantomimes or played at make-believe.'

He started to laugh, offending her even more. 'Are you serious?'

'Yes. I never got to do that stuff. And I'm too old to start now.'

'No, you're not. We can do it together.'

An elderly couple on a tandem had wobbled into sight from a breakneck descent down the Hillcote one-in-four, both pale-faced and sweating as they cycled unsteadily along the lane towards Ellen.

'I'll come round at seven tomorrow,' Spurs was saying.

'Please don't.' Ellen tried to return the couple's smiles, but she had to turn her face away as tears bobbled on her eyelashes.

Spurs breathed deeper in her ear. 'I love you.'

'Cut that out,' she muttered, staring blurrily at the distant Springlode specks.

'I'll make everything better,' he whispered. 'I'll make-believe everything better.'

It was only after she'd pocketed the phone that Ellen wondered how he had got the number. She'd never given it to him.

13

'This is *such* a balmy evening, isn't it?' Pheely sighed as they took their customary walk around the village.

'I know – it's crazy,' Ellen agreed, fanning her T-shirt.

'I was talking about the weather.' Pheely glanced at her. 'I think it's rather lovely that you and Spurs have rallied on Dilly's behalf. She's terribly chuffed.'

Ellen said nothing, pausing to reattach the loose corner of Fins' Missing poster, which was drooping from the poop-bin post.

The cottages along Manor Lane were glowing gold in the late-afternoon sun, their little front gardens bubbling with colour, the swathes of honeysuckle climbing the walls curling open to waft sweetly across the lane. Swallows looped showily overhead, watched by a lean tortoiseshell cat lying bravely in the centre of the lane, batting its disapproving tail as Hamlet and Snorkel strained towards it on their leads.

'And I think it's terribly brave of you going out for a chummy meal with Spurs,' Pheely was gurgling indulgently. 'I'd be so hurt if somebody had given me the brush-off like that – I'd avoid them like the plague.'

Ellen glanced worriedly at the manor's back gates. 'We've come to an understanding.'

Pheely snorted. 'If you understand him you're doing a hell of a lot better than anyone else around here. We just stand under the big black cloud of doom that rolled in when he came back.' She glanced up and looked rather disappointed that no clouds had conveniently appeared in the blue sky. 'Everybody's waiting for him to spontaneously combust.'

'Why should he?'

She shrugged. 'Something's going on.' She turned her huge eyes on Ellen. 'Something brought him back here and whatever it is has made him a very meek boy. He even turned you down.' She looked rather too pleased with the thought.

'It wasn't like that.' Ellen cleared her throat awkwardly, glancing around.

'Extraordinary.' Pheely was shaking her head. 'Maybe you're just not his type.'

'We might as well have been at it non-stop, for all the village thinks,' Ellen muttered, noticing heads turning at the tables outside the Oddlode Inn on the opposite side of the lane.

'Yes, the grapevine *has* been having a vintage season at your expense.' Pheely laughed.

'Why didn't you tell me?'

'What would have been the point? You ignored my warning that he was mad, bad and dangerous to know – you were hardly going to change your behaviour as a result of pensioner tittle-tattle.'

She had a point, Ellen thought, as they crossed towards the village shop and looked at the new cards in the window in case there was a 'Found' one describing a cat resembling Fins. But apart from someone advertising an old Fiesta, and yet another 'friendly local family' desperate for a cleaner, there was nothing new. Lily Lubowski moved conspicuously into view with a duster and glowered at Pheely over a display of local produce.

'You do know,' Pheely said idly, as she gave Lily a cheery wave, 'that there's another rumour going around claiming Saul Wyck tried to mow you down on the Hillcote lane last night?'

Ellen turned to her in surprise. 'So lovely that whoever saw it came to help,' she murmured bitterly, starting to harbour seriously evil thoughts about every inhabitant of Oddlode.

'So it *was* you?' Pheely was agog. 'I thought it was just another case of him driving at ramblers. He and Reg have a competition going.'

'Yes, it was me,' Ellen confirmed. She told Pheely about her encounter with Saul. 'He was the one behind the badger and the note. And I'm pretty certain it's not just about firing his grandparents – I think Ely was bribing him to let the cottage go to pot. I wouldn't mind betting Saul was one of the Shaggers too.'

'How thrilling.' Pheely's eyebrows shot up. 'To think that I've spent thirty years ruffling feathers in this village and I've never managed to elicit much more than disapproving looks. You have half the locals on a hate campaign after just a few weeks. I suppose that's what you get for befriending Spurs. When you're tarred with that brush, the ruffled feathers are bound to stick.'

'Saul's pranks had nothing to do with Spurs.'

Pheely shook her head wisely. 'Around here, you only have to stop to talk to him in the lane and he'll get the blame for everything from your bad double-parking to your anti-social bonfire. Believe me, the fact you two are in cahoots means that *you* are perceived as troublesome. And you *did* want to take him to bed, darling,' Pheely reminded her with a naughty gurgle.

'It would have been too messy,' Ellen said flatly.

'Oh, don't be such a prude.' She winked at Lily who was still glaring at her. 'I love messy sex. It's the threat of being thrown to the hounds after he'd taken his pleasure that would put me off Spurs. You had a lucky escape.'

'That's what he said about you.'

'Was it?' Pheely looked thrilled. 'How sweet. I wonder if he still hankers a little?'

Ellen started walking away from the shop, thinking tetchily about Dilly's latest absurd plan to get her mother together with him.

Pheely followed, checking the lane so that they could cross over to the green. 'I'm stunned that he didn't take up your offer of a night of sin. By God, even if nothing else convinced me, that shows he *must* have changed. Either that or he's fallen in love at last.' She laughed uproariously. 'But with whom, I wonder. Probably himself. All that therapy has created the great love of his life.'

Sometimes Pheely's delight in dissecting Spurs infuriated Ellen. Having expended so much effort in revving her up to talk about him over recent weeks, she now regretted that he'd latterly become the most common topic of their conversations. Pheely's combined fascination and hatred was unhealthy. 'So Dilly's excited about this evening?' she asked, to get her friend off topic.

'Very much so. Although I do still entertain doubts about that haughty horseman she fancies, however pretty he looks. He was very louche the other night, I thought. And he mumbles terribly. Do make sure she comes to no harm.'

'I'll try my best,' Ellen promised.

'Where are you going while the youngsters moon?'

'A pub in another village, I guess. I promised Spurs supper.'

'Let's hope they have very long-handled spoons.' Pheely gave her a shrewd look. 'Don't go too far from Springlode in case Dilly needs rescuing.'

'Are you going to sculpt this evening?' Ellen had worrying visions of Pheely taking up pursuit on her moped.

'I should. That wretched bust really isn't coming together. I long to start again, but I'm running out of time.'

'Is it that bad?'

'My work is *never* bad, but I sense it might be too interpretive for Ely's taste. I don't suppose . . .' She gave Ellen a sly look. 'Could Dilly sleep over at the cottage? She'd love that, and it means I can sculpt uninterrupted all night.'

'I – er—'

'Oh, please, darling. It's not as though you and Spurs are going to get up to anything naughty, are you?'

'No, we're not.' Then Ellen gasped with alarm as she remembered that the jeep was out of action. 'Oh, God, I must fit the new battery.'

'Steady on.' Pheely giggled. 'You do know those devices can make you go blind?'

Having wired in the replacement battery, Ellen decided to give Dilly's carriage a quick valet. She plastered the jeep with foamy water, then washed it off with the hose and gave it a chamois polish. Then she dragged out the vacuum cleaner and sucked up enough Cornish sand from the upholstery and footwells to make a twenty-four-hour egg-timer. When she straightened up and switched it off, she heard a familiar engine rattling along North Street and walked to the gates just as Spurs rounded the corner into Goose Lane, riding the mini-tractor. Its front racks were piled so high with bags and boxes that they almost obscured him, and it wasn't until the oversized quad ground to a halt on the gravel beside her that Ellen saw he was wearing a suit.

'Evening.' He jumped off and brushed dust from his legs.

Ellen watched him warily, rubbing the rebellious goosebumps from her arms and telling her heart to shut up. Instantly she felt very, very ill-at-ease.

It might have been the very first time he'd appeared in the Goose Cottage drive telling her that she had to make a wish there and then. There was something unfamiliar about him, an impatient, intimidating mood that seemed to make the air spit hotly around her.

She told herself firmly that it was just because he looked different. He had always been impossibly scruffy, apart from that one interrupted evening when he'd worn pretty sharp rags, but they had had nothing on this. The suit – immaculately tailored pale grey silk, matched with a purple shirt and tie – wouldn't have looked out of place on a shady Soho boho or a fashion icon at a première. It made him seem strange and formidable, as did his narrowed eyes and brutish smile.

'I've got the props,' he announced, as he started to unload the tractor. 'Open the boot.'

Ellen silently watched bags and boxes being transferred into the freshly vacuumed space, unable to talk around the lump in her throat. Despite her mental battle, she was almost wiped out by how attractive she found him. And yet it felt wrong. The entire thing felt completely wrong.

'Rory gave me a shopping list – he's really into your bigged-up romance idea.' He laughed. 'When I went to see this new horse of his this morning, I checked all over the house for vodka in case he's on one of his benders, but I think he really is inspired. He's okayed it with Keith Wilmore – the landlord at the Plough.' He handed her two boxes. 'These are for you. It's your costume, and your new friendship shoes.'

She laid the boxes carefully on the garden bench and went to unplug the vacuum. She couldn't bring herself to look, frightened of the emotions welling up inside her, knowing she had to hold it together.

Spurs eyed her edgily, reluctant to acknowledge that she wasn't playing along as he had hoped. 'Shame you haven't time to try them on.' He heaved the biggest of the boxes – marked 'Easy Assemble Oriental Pagoda' – on to the roof and went in search of the cargo straps under the back seat. 'We have to run everything up to Springlode and then you need to come back here for Dilly. I'd have dropped this lot off myself, but I was giving Pa a lift back from Cheltenham Races and I couldn't risk taking him anywhere near a pub. After all this effort, Rory sure as hell doesn't want his hot date screwed up by the old man drowning his sorrows at the bar all night.'

She stooped to wind the flex back into the vacuum, watching it slither across the gravel like a snake. Then Spurs stepped on it, forcing her to look up. 'Cat got your tongue?'

'Cat's still missing,' she muttered.

He untangled the cargo straps, winding them around his hand as he looked down at her. 'So what's wrong?'

'I told you I didn't want this.'

'Well, I do,' he snapped, stepping off the taut flex. 'I want to be good.'

'This isn't good.' She laughed hollowly as the plug rattled into its plastic well. 'This is interfering.'

He unleashed a cargo strap over the car like a long whip, then stalked round to the other side to thread it under the running rails.

Ellen stood up, ruffled by his insolence and the way he was hijacking the evening. 'You shouldn't have filled Rory's head with stupid ideas about big romantic gestures,' she rounded on him. 'They should be allowed to get to know each other without us imposing a great theatrical happening on them.'

'I'm not imposing anything.'

'Yes, we are – you are. You were the one who started banging on about fairy tales and pantomimes and acting as set-designer and stealing my kindness. You're the one who grants wishes and lights fire circles around Chinese takeaways, who buggers off for days, then gallops up on a horse to tell me you've sold your soul but, hey, now I've sold the gingerbread cottage, let's be mates.'

'Don't be so unromantic.' He pulled back on the first cargo strap to snap it tight, bracing his legs against the car so that he looked like a sailor mending rigging.

'I don't want to be romantic!' she howled, knowing that there was absolutely no point. Nothing was going to happen between them.

'You made that abundantly clear on Sunday.' He reached for the second strap and lassoed it over the roof. 'When you announced that we were going to – now, how did you so delicately put it? – "fuck each other's brains out"?'

Ellen glanced nervously at the lane in case anybody was within earshot. 'Was that why you left?' she asked hoarsely.

He looked at her over the roof, his eyes giving nothing away.

'I thought that's what you wanted all along,' she muttered.

'Maybe, at first,' he sighed, 'but it's like wanting to be mortal then finding you have no voice.'

'Sorry?'

'*The Little Mermaid.*'

'I told you. I don't know the story.'

'I'll tell you it over supper. We don't have time now.' He fixed the second strap.

She sighed, defeated by his indomitable mood. It was the same mood she'd left him in the day before, and she didn't understand it at all.

'All this must have cost a fortune.' She looked at the bags with their designer tags.

'Don't worry, it's all going back tomorrow. I told the department store that I was borrowing it all for a fashion shoot for *Cotswold Living* mag.'

'That's fraudulent.'

'Not as fraudulent as using your credit-card details for security.'

'What?'

'You really shouldn't leave your drawers open.' He smiled easily. 'I have a wonderful head for figures.'

'What's got into you?' she demanded.

'Oh dear.' He blinked up at her. 'Am I straying from the straight and narrow?'

Ellen drove Spurs to Upper Springlode in silence while he smoked a cigarette broodingly beside her, the window wide open so that ash billowed around them, flecking his expensive suit. He turned the stereo on full blast and kicked his foot against the glovebox in time to Robbie Williams' 'Let Me Entertain You'. It was partly like driving a small, sulking, hyperactive boy, Ellen decided – and partly like driving a wild animal.

When Rory opened his cottage door, he was wearing nothing but a grubby towel and had a toothbrush poking out of his mouth. Spurs thrust several of the carrier-bags at him and muttered something in his ear, then jumped back into the jeep and told Ellen to drive on to the pub car park.

'This really *is* his idea.' He was kicking the glovebox in time to the Prodigy's 'Firestarter' now. 'I'd never suggest something so completely crass as the surprise he's got lined up.'

'What is it?' she asked.

But Spurs had spotted Keith, the bearded landlord, waiting for them in the car park and jumped out before Ellen had pulled up.

'I've kept it for you like you asked,' Keith greeted them cheerfully, beckoning them into the beer garden, which was already full of evening drinkers enjoying the sunshine and the views.

Ellen and Spurs carried the boxes to the furthest cluster of trees, beside the bubbling stream that gushed noisily from the spring, masking the sound of conversations nearby. In a clearing on the bank was a lone table, quite hidden from the rest of the garden, on which Keith had placed a handwritten reserved sign.

'Bring Dilly to this table at half past eight – no later,' Spurs told Ellen, taking her wrist and glancing at her watch. 'That should give me enough time to lay everything out and get Rory in place. And don't forget to change into your costume.'

When Ellen lifted the tissue paper on the first of the boxes Spurs had left with her, she wondered what on earth Rory had cooked up that required Spurs to wear a slick suit and her to dress in . . . She gathered it up and walked to the mirror . . . This. Oh, wow! Layers of white chiffon fluttered against her in the breeze from the open attic window.

It was heaven. But how on earth did you put it on, she wondered.

She was crouching on the carpet searching frantically for her strappy sandals when Dilly arrived downstairs, complaining bitterly the moment she was through the door. 'Ellen! Can I have a quick shower? Mum's been hogging the bathroom for the last hour, slopping around like a great hippo saying she needs to soak away her stress to get into the right frame of mind to spend the night reworking the bust. I couldn't get in there. Ellen!'

'Help yourself,' she called down the stairs.

A few minutes later, hair still in a shower cap, Dilly trailed scented drips into the room and ground to an amazed halt. 'Bloody hell! Like, bloody, bloody hell!'

'What's the matter?' Ellen smoothed the chiffon nervously.

'Oh, God, can you make me look that sexy? No, forget it. I could *never* look that sexy in a million years. Bloody hell.'

'You like it?'

'You are *so* beautiful. I had no idea you could be that beautiful.'

'Get outta here.' Ellen laughed. 'It's just a posh frock.'

She looked in the mirror again, still uncertain that she had the balls to go anywhere dressed like this. The layers of bias-cut chiffon clung delicately to every curve of her body, like steam from a shower. The long bell sleeves constantly slipped over her worriedly adjusting hands as the dress fell off each shoulder in turn. Slashed almost to the waist in front, it barely maintained her dignity with a few fragile cross-laced ribbons, but the narrow margin of fabric that separated her nipples from the wide expanse of brown chest shifted dangerously if she so much as breathed.

'It suits you so perfectly,' Dilly was burbling excitedly. 'Not sure about the shoes, though.'

Ellen looked down. 'The ones that go with it don't fit and I can't find my strappy sandals.'

'Oh, Hamlet chewed them up. Sorry. I meant to tell you yesterday when I brought the rest of your stuff back. I can give you the money if you let me pay you in instalments. You will still lend me something, won't you?'

She smiled. 'Take your pick.'

Dilly looked at the clothes spread out on the bed and her face lit up.

'Dilly!' Ellen burst out laughing when she started to pull on her choice. 'You don't want to wear those. They're only there because I just took them off.'

'I love them.' Dilly buttoned up the ancient denim cut-offs that Ellen almost lived in. 'These are far more me than dresses and high heels. I'll leave those to old bags like you and Mum.'

Ellen went to swing a good-natured thump at her shoulder, but stopped when her boob fell out of the great cleavage divide.

'You'll have to watch that.' Dilly sniggered, trying on a bootlace top while Ellen tucked herself back in.

Ellen looked at her reflection dubiously. 'I thought Cinderella was the one who got to wear the beautiful dress, not the fairy godmother.'

'Eh?' Dilly abandoned the bootlace top and pulled on the gypsy shirt, holding Ellen's red suede bustier up against it and tilting her head at the mirror. 'Do you think this would look too tarty?'

'No, it'll look great. Like a medieval wench.'

'So where are you two going on to tonight?' Dilly started to put the bustier on over the gypsy shirt. 'Mum says you're taking Spurs out to dinner while Rory and I are at the pub.'

Ellen helped her do up the studs at the back. 'I left it to Spurs to decide.'

'Must be somewhere *really* fancy to merit a dress like that. Maybe Tewcott Castle, where you watch the jousters and eat roast hog? Spurs could joust for your honour.' She sat more upright so that Ellen could reach the lowest studs. 'Actually,' she added, 'now I think about it, I'd really rather have liked Rory to take me somewhere like that tonight. I know the Plough is more familiar, but it's not very . . . special, is it?'

'You said you wanted to go somewhere he could be relaxed,' Ellen reminded her, 'so that you can get to know each other properly.'

'I know, but it's just a bit odd, isn't it, that Rory and I are having our first proper date together in a smelly old pub and you and Spurs – who are just friends – are probably going out somewhere really amazing?'

Ellen looked into the mirror over her head: both boobs had fallen out of the flimsy fantasy dress now. 'If there's magic between you, it doesn't matter where you are,' she said, almost to herself. 'The simplest of places can seem like paradise. You just have to look into each other's eyes and forget the real world exists.' She remembered her first long, hot weekend with Spurs when every time she'd looked in his eyes the world had disappeared, as had her desire to go and see it.

'God, Ellen!' Dilly sneered. 'That is so, so schmaltzy. I thought *I* was a hopeless romantic, but you should hear yourself. And there was me thinking you were a super-cool surfer chick.'

Ellen caught her own eye in the mirror. 'I've been accused of being completely unromantic.'

'By whom?'

'The man I looked at and forgot the world existed.'

'He can't have seen you in that. If I was wearing that dress, Rory would never look me in the eye. He'd be far too distracted, poor darling. Mind you, he's a bit of a shoe-gazer, so I must be prepared. Perhaps you should rethink your footwear too?' she reminded Ellen kindly.

As Dilly jumped off the bed to start trying on Ellen's small collection of mostly clumpy, urban-chic footwear, Ellen spotted her neon pink diving fins leaning up against the old wardrobe. Perfect for the Little Mermaid. She started to laugh.

'What's so funny?' Dilly looked up from strapping on Ellen's red wedges.

'Nothing. I've just realised I've been swimming against the tide.'

'You can drop me here,' Dilly insisted excitedly, as they drove into the Plough car park.

'I said I'd see you to your table.' Ellen checked her watch. They were bang on time.

'It's just a pub, Ellen – more's the pity.' She pulled a goofy face, jumped out and checked her face in the wing mirror.

But as they walked into the beer garden, it became apparent that one part of it, at least, wasn't just any old pub. Ahead of them, an avenue had been created with sparklers poked jauntily from the grass, all of which spat and frothed their hot little shards far more brightly than the sun sinking behind the trees. Several tourists had whipped out cameras and started forming a small crowd to either side of the burning path that led into the secret grotto where Rory had reserved a table.

'Bloody hell!' Dilly started to laugh, turning to Ellen. 'Did you know about this?'

Carefully keeping her hands clamped to her side to stop her tits popping out, Ellen shook her head and indicated for Dilly to follow her.

Breathless and babbling eagerly, she followed Ellen along the fizzing corridor, waving happily at her audience. And then, as

they walked under the tree canopy and into the privacy of the
little streamside bower, she let out a shriek of delight.

The ordinary picnic table had been transformed. Now set
beneath a tented garden pagoda, it was swathed in silk sarongs
and covered in hurricane lamps glowing with every colour of
candle. Crystals dangled from the branches to either side, creating
dancing prisms of light in the clearing as they caught reflections
from the stream. A small self-important Jack Russell, wearing a
bow-tie, was sitting on one of the bench seats.

Waiting beside the table were Rory and Spurs. The former had
a fiddle pressed under his chin, the latter a guitar slung round
his neck.

Dilly and Ellen looked at each other as the duo launched into
'Will You Come To The Bower', both men whistling the tune
and the Jack Russell barking along.

'Shut up, Twitch, you're ruining it,' Rory hissed, out of the
side of his mouth, as the bow danced on the strings. Dressed in
a retro black suit, with a long-lapelled flowery shirt unbuttoned to
the chest, very clean floppy blond hair and pointy-toed boots, he
had transformed himself from the stable tatterdemalion into the
ultimate young rock god.

Ignoring him, Twitch barked all the more. Dilly clapped her
hands in delight and rushed over to gather him up and start
dancing along to the tune.

Just for a moment a bewildered, laughing Ellen caught Spurs'
eye before he looked fixedly at his frets once more. Purple tie
loosened and hair flopping over his face as he struck out the
chords, he was disturbingly unfamiliar again, showing aspects of
himself he'd never even hinted at.

'This is so, so cool!' Dilly danced around. 'I'm going to have
the best night ever!'

As soon as the song was over, Spurs twisted the guitar round
to his back on its strap like a banderol, made a quick bow, then
took Ellen's hand without looking at her.

'Enjoy yourselves, kids. We'll pick you up later.' He led her
back down the spluttering sparkler path, ignoring the excited

cheers of the other beer garden occupants, some of whom had
noticed that Ellen's chest was threatening to stray out of its chiffon
because Spurs was towing her along at such speed.

'Quietly understated for a first date, huh?' he said, when they
reached the car and collapsed against it.

'Certainly different.' She pressed her hands together and lifted
them to her chin so that she could discreetly pop her assets back
into place.

'Oh, it's cheesy as hell, but the boy wouldn't be told once he
latched on to the idea.' Spurs was shaking his head in amusement.
'I tried persuading him that the musical turn was too much, but
he had his heart set on it.'

'It was good. I didn't know you played the guitar.'

'Aunt Til taught us to play Irish jigs at family parties – much to
my mother's pique.' He looked at his fingers. 'Rory's sister played
the tin whistle, and Aunt Til was a demon on the bodhran.'

'Well, Dilly loved it. She loves it all.'

He pulled the guitar from around his neck and put it into the
back of the car, not looking at her. 'And you?'

'I'm sorry I doubted you.' She hauled the slipping dress back
on to her shoulder.

'All Rory's idea.' He swung the door shut.

'And the costumes? Were they his idea?'

'No.' He checked that the door was shut properly, then tweaked
his shirt cuffs from his jacket sleeves in a curiously formal gesture.
'They're for a different show. I have a lot more style, you see.'

At last he looked up at her from under his brows, his face
expressionless. 'It suits you.' He nodded curtly.

It was hardly in the premier league of compliments. It was
years since Ellen had worn anything so dressy, and she felt
deeply self-conscious in the little bare-fronted number. She felt
even more insecure when the dress chose that moment to plunge
off her shoulder once more and reveal a tiny crescent of dark
areola before she retrieved it. 'I think the usual method is to
attach toupee tape to stop things falling out,' she mumbled.

'I think the usual method,' he said calmly, 'is to wear it the other way round. The criss-cross bits were at the back on the mannequin.'

'No?' Ellen looked down and laughed. 'I'd better go and change it round in the loo.'

'Wear it like that,' he insisted. 'It looks much better.' Then he looked down and saw that she was wearing clogs. 'Was there something wrong with the friendship shoes?'

'I couldn't walk in them.' The very high, strappy mules had been three sizes too big.

'I got an eight.' Spurs was indignant. 'That's what was written in the trainer you threw at me. I still have it.'

'Those trainers are American – an American size eight is an English five.'

'Trust the Americans to exaggerate.' He glared at her tatty clogs. 'I bet Big Foot just has slightly high insteps. Couldn't you have found something a bit smarter?'

'Hamlet chewed up my best shoes. I'm sorry.' She tried not to laugh at his indignation. 'Are you supposed to be the footman or something?'

'Almost,' he said grumpily, crossing the car park to a big barrel full of blue irises and tugging a bunch. Keeping one for himself, he handed the rest to her before opening the jeep's passenger door. 'Your carriage awaits.'

'I thought I was chauffeur?' she asked uncertainly, clutching the pilfered flowers.

'I'm in the driving seat now.' He attached the iris to his lapel and pulled his signet ring from his little finger. 'Hold out your hand. No – the other.'

She held out her left hand and he slid the ring on to her third finger, the Constantine crest facing into her palm so that only the plain gold band showed.

'This evening,' he closed her fingers tightly round the ring, 'it's the cygnet's turn to become a swan.'

Ellen looked up in confusion.

'It's a fairy tale, Ellen.' He pressed his lips to her fingers. 'The ring's on your finger – and bells on your toes are part of the costume.'

'Are we morris dancing?' she asked.

The smile almost gobbled up her fingers. 'Tonight I'll try anything for you. Even that.'

14

'Mr and Mrs Gardner. Many, many congratulations!' The maître d'
fluttered around them. 'Have you had a splendid day?'

'*Wonderful,* thank you.'

'On behalf of all the staff at Eastlode Park, may I wish you a
very enjoyable evening with us? If you'd care to go through to
the Green Drawing Room where my colleague will bring you
complimentary champagne . . .'

Ellen clutched her irises tightly to her exposed chest as she
followed the waiter through to the grand reception room, Spurs'
hand on her back. 'Mr and Mrs *Gardner*?' she hissed over her
shoulder, already feeling the cold sweat of deceit prickling in
her hair.

'Yes, darling. You'll have to get used to your new name.'
He spoke through a fixed smile, silver eyes dancing around
the room.

Such was Spurs' magnetism and charm that the historic hall's
staff were completely won over by him and his pretty bride,
despite her strange choice of footwear. Waiters rushed over to set
coasters and bowls of finest Japanese crackers on the dainty walnut
and ormolu table between two velvet-backed Chippendales.

Eastlode Park was just as grand as the write-ups proclaimed
in the brick-thick glossy magazines: they eulogised the priceless
antiques, impeccable service and outrageous luxury. From the
moment a liveried staff member had glided across the raked
gravel to valet park the jeep – by far the scruffiest vehicle on
the grounds – Ellen and Spurs were attended to unmarried hand
and cloven foot. Struck dumb by its sheer scale and extrava-
gance, Ellen had never seen anywhere remotely like it in all her

life, not even when trailing dozens of National Trust properties after her parents on holiday as a girl. The house – a titanic, beautifully preserved eighteenth-century palace – had been built for a famously lavish dowager duchess, who had died before it was completed. Gaudy, opulent and dripping with gold leaf, hand-carved cupids, ornate columns and frescoed ceilings, it had survived into the twenty-first century to become pure Baroque and roll.

Run as one of England's smartest and most exclusive hotels for many years, with a Michelin-starred restaurant, a nine-hole golf course, fishing lakes, shoots, helipad and even suites with private indoor pools, it was as famous for its outlandish prices as its luxury. Only the wealthiest film stars, rock legends, oil barons, gun-runners and Japanese tourists stayed there.

'What better place to stop off on our wedding day?' Spurs pointed out cheerfully as they settled in chairs as valuable as small Islington flats and watched a waiter pour vintage Bollinger into Bohemian lead-crystal flutes.

'Indeed,' Ellen said, through gritted teeth, as she attempted to achieve a sitting position where her boobs didn't immediately spill out of the dress. This wasn't quite the fairy tale she had envisaged.

Another simpering waiter, ogling Spurs discreetly, swept over to open velvet-covered menus with no prices, and place them reverently into the newlyweds' hands. '*May* I recommend – he started.

'No, you may not,' Spurs snapped, waving him away, then casting Ellen a roguish smile. 'Are you looking forward to the honeymoon?'

'Where are we going?' She cleared her throat awkwardly.

'Secret,' he whispered. 'Such a bind chartering a private plane that can't get a take-off slot until eleven.' He opened the wine list and one eyebrow shot up. That clearly *did* have prices. 'Still, I've always meant to drop by here and see what the grub's like. Heard it's rather good. See anything you fancy?'

She licked her lips, glancing around at others in the room,

which was so huge that the furniture formed tiny priceless drift-wood islands in a great sea of Persian rugs and runners. She could just make out the cotton-covered heads of a group of Arabs under one window, and hear Japanese being spoken nearby, along with at least two groups of Americans. Expensive cigar smoke floated around a Chinese vase the size of a large man. 'What's this in aid of?'

'Don't be so ungrateful, darling.' He kept up his clipped, upbeat pitter-patter voice.

'I'm the one paying, *dar*ling.' The meal would set her back about four months' travelling money, if not her entire budget. She was only thankful the Shack had commanded such a profit.

'Well, I was *going* to say this is in aid of friendship.' He lifted his glass. 'But it seems the shoes didn't fit after all—' He almost fell off his chair as a great pat on the back propelled him forward in a plume of cigar smoke.

'Belling, my boy!' boomed a walrus-yowl voice, which ema-nated, rather surprisingly, from a man the size of an ageing jockey, with beady black eyes and very sharp teeth. 'By God, I *thought* it was you. Looking good. This the new fiancée?'

Spurs was momentarily thrown, his face as shifty as a car thief caught twiddling with the heated seats. 'Er – yes. No. I mean, Sir George Hampden, this is Ellen.'

'Delighted to meetcha.' Sir George bowed his head and clicked his little polished heels together, eyeing the open-fronted dress with obvious appreciation. 'Heard Spurs was in line for the dreaded shackles, but I had no idea she'd be so easy on the eye, eh?'

Ellen tried to tuck her scruffy shoes under the chair.

'Been at the races?' Having regained his composure, Spurs gave his mile-wide smile.

'Indeed. Saw your father there.' Sir George cleared his throat and examined his cigar. 'Best not mention you saw me tonight, eh? Might be offended I didn't invite the old boy over for a drink.'

'Of course.' Spurs glanced across at the six-foot blonde who was waiting for Sir George by the huge vase. 'I'm sure you'd rather be alone with your—'

'Financial adviser.' He tapped his nose cheerfully. 'Like to bring her here because it's so damned expensive there's nobody British around, if you know what I mean.' He nodded to them and marched off jauntily to rejoin the blonde *en route* to their room.

'Fuck,' Spurs muttered under his breath, dropping the smile and checking over his shoulder in case any other of his father's friends were floating about.

'Who's he?' Ellen asked, longing to lean towards him for discretion's sake but unable to move for fear of her dress shifting.

'Hampden was my brief.' Spurs was still checking out the room. 'Known then as the Editor because if he couldn't get you off he could get a sentence reduced to almost nothing. That was before he became a QC. He and Pa shoot together sometimes.'

'Afraid he'll say something?' Ellen watched his darting eyes.

'Christ, no. I'm just pissed off that he buggered up the ambience.' A self-mocking smile danced on to his lips.

She stretched out a clog and kicked his ankle. 'Hard to get into the make-believe mood when your barrister pops up and your "wife" complains about the prices, isn't it?'

He cast her a dirty look from under his brows, then laughed. Slouching back in the chair, hair flopping over his silver eyes, he rubbed his chin against each shoulder in turn. 'Maybe I should take tips from Rory?'

'Maybe you should.' She wasn't about to make him feel better for making her a hell of a lot poorer.

'Would you rather have gone to a pub and pretended to be friends?' He creased his brow.

She watched the suave, silent waiters gliding around the room communicating with discreet nods and asides. 'I'm more of a spit-and-sawdust girl at heart.'

He let out an irritable sigh. 'I wanted you to see what it's like really living in a fairy tale. If we can't make love I thought we could at least make-believe.'

'This is just on-the-make believe.' Ellen looked around the

ornate room again, taking in the old masters clashing with new money. 'As in, they make up the prices as they go along, and we can't bloody believe them.'

'Are you suggesting I'm trying to fleece you?'

'I guess that's what they mean by shear class.' She remembered only too well his cheerful account of his uncle's advice to avoid such a common 'popsy'.

As Spurs watched her with troubled eyes, Ellen saw a vein steal up his neck and a muscle twitch in his cheek. He's about to detonate, she thought. 'Tell me about the Little Mermaid,' she said quickly.

'Too fucking romantic for you,' he whispered.

'I want to know the story.'

He picked up his champagne glass and looked at her over the rim, his eyes accusing. When he spoke, his voice was deliberately drawling and monotone. 'As far as I remember it, the little mermaid grew up among the pearls on the sea-bed. The day that she was finally old enough to be able to swim to the surface to sing on the rocks with the other mermaids, she encountered a drowning man and saved his life. She fell madly in love with him and couldn't be happy singing when she could see him high in the castle above the cliffs, looking out to sea each day. So she sold her exquisite voice to the evil sea witch in exchange for the most beautiful legs ever created, under the strict condition that should she ever return to the sea, she would become nothing but foam and her soul would be claimed too.

'But when she went ashore,' he went on, his voice losing its flatness and gaining a husk of emotion, 'she found that the man she had saved was none other than the castle's good-for-nothing prince. And while he was grateful that she had saved his life, he was betrothed to another. Try as she might, she had no voice to tell him of her love, and eventually his wedding day arrived and he married a very pretty and eligible princess. Heartbroken, the little mermaid waded back out to sea on her beautiful long legs and dissolved into the foam.'

Ellen looked away and studied an ornate ceiling carving, which divided several times and danced around in her watery gaze. She waited a few seconds until she'd got a hard grip on her emotions and said, 'Couldn't she have just written him a note?'

Spurs snorted disparagingly. 'I don't think he loved her.'

'Probably a tits man.'

He gave her an angry look. 'You are *so* unromantic.'

'Did he love the princess he married?'

'Unlikely. It was probably a political match. I doubt they even spoke the same language.'

'The Little Mermaid couldn't speak at all.'

'So she got a bad deal from the witch. She should have negotiated.'

'What would you trade in?'

He loosened his tie and undid the top button of his shirt. 'I wouldn't have saved him from drowning in the first place.'

Up swept their two obsequious waiters, one to refill the champagne flutes, the other to take their order.

Ellen looked at the florid descriptions on her menu, complete with the inevitably baffling array of French culinary terms and new foodie fashion trends. There seemed to be about eight courses to choose.

'For you, Madame Gardner?' The waiter gave her a chivalrous nod, knowing that to use her new married name would make her feel very special.

'You decide for me, darling.' She closed the menu and smiled at Spurs. 'Anything but fish.'

'We'd like sausage casserole, please.' He closed his menu too.

'I am sorry?' the waiter queried, in a nasal French accent.

'Sausage casserole,' Spurs repeated very politely.

'I am afraid that dish is not on the menu.'

'Oh, I'm sure Chef can rustle something up.' He reached for the wine list. 'And to go with it, we'd like a bottle of,' he glanced up at Ellen, 'Clos de Vougeot Leroy 'ninety-five. And sparkling mineral water.'

The waiter tried and failed not to look absolutely staggered as he gathered their menus, flashed a wary smile and backed away.

'You're such a thug,' Ellen told him, unable to resist smiling.

'I know.' He sighed with mock-regret. 'Are you sorry you married me?'

'Distraught. Is it too late to annul?'

'We haven't consummated the marriage . . . yet.' He slouched back in his chair and tipped his chin to one side, eyeing her with such wickedness that her loose-cannon nipples almost forced their way out of the chiffon of their own accord.

Whoa. Whoa! Ellen thought, in a panic. We are not meant to be doing this. 'We should have ordered consommé.' She threw out a bad joke to play for time. 'Then we could have consomméd the marriage.'

'Far too cheap.' He shuddered.

'I knew you only married me for my credit limit.' She tried to calm her nipples down as they rallied their goosebump friends and her entire body began popping like a Rice Krispie Kid bathed in milk.

'Of course I did.' He picked up his champagne glass. 'Do you mind?'

'My lord and Mastercard.' She narrowed her eyes. 'I suppose it's unique to have a husband who can forge one's signature on the register.'

'Ah, yes.' He watched her through the cut crystal. 'I should mention that I had to book a room to get a table tonight.'

Ellen's goosebumps burst out angry little flames. 'On my card?'

'Of course. This *is* your treat.'

She had to work very hard indeed not to throw her glass at him. 'I could kill you for this.'

'Divorce is less messy.'

'In that case, I definitely want an annulment. And then I'll kill you.'

'I'm sure there are grounds.'

'There *are* grounds.'

'Yes, three thousand acres,' he gestured towards the window, 'including a deer park and a big lake. We drove past it.'

'How convenient. We can drown each other in it.'

'Far better to shoot one another on the clay-pigeon range, don't you think?'

'I prefer drowning.'

They locked eyes and drowned far from the lake.

'I wanted to take you to the sea,' Spurs whispered, and touched her knee with his finger, 'but there wouldn't have been time.'

Ellen's knee developed a mind of its own and started shaking stupidly. 'Oh, any old place that serves sausage casserole is fine by me.' She could see the waiter, having emerged from the kitchens, having frantic words with the maître d'. 'This is okay.'

Fighting to break the spell, she uncrossed her legs and crossed them the other way to trap the disobedient knee and hastily rerouted a boob as it fought to peep round the chiffon curtain. Anxious not to lose it again, she sat more primly than ever.

Spurs slumped back in his chair and stared up at the ebullient ceiling fresco of fat cherubs cavorting with even fatter goddesses. 'You're like one of those women up there with just a tiny piece of gauze covering your wicked delights.'

'Is that why you choose this dress?'

'No.' His eyes levelled with hers. 'I chose it because I knew you would look more beautiful in it than any other woman could ever hope to. That's because you look more beautiful in anything than other women. And probably in nothing.'

'Stop it,' Ellen muttered.

'But you're my wife. I'm allowed to desire you.'

The waiter chose that moment to stalk up with delicate little appetisers and the news that the chef would comply with their request for sausage casserole. He spat the two words as though they'd asked for boiled babies, but he was under strict instructions to cater to the volatile newlyweds' every whim from the enchanted maître d', who firmly believed they were Brit Pack actors. At least this simple dish meant they wouldn't be in the dining room very long, offending the more delicate of the overseas visitors with their white-hot looks and her (very) dirty shoes. Forcing a sickly smile, he melted away to deal with a neighbouring group of Arabs.

'Why don't you want to play?' Spurs slouched even further into his chair as soon as he'd gone.

Ellen looked down at the beautiful dress that meant she had to sit like a little girl at ballet school, and the tatty shoes beyond. 'You were right when you said that you can't "do" friends, Spurs. Friends don't pretend to be married, defraud their mate's credit card, then order bottles of wine which cost as much as a month's rent at the other's expense to boot.'

'You saw the wine-list then.' He clicked his tongue guiltily in his cheek.

'I saw the waiter's expression.'

His silver eyes, shaded by black lashes and wild curls, moved round her face. 'I want to spend all your money so that you can't go away.'

Ellen felt the goosebumps perform a Mexican wave from neck to toe once again. 'I've already paid for my flight. I leave a week on Saturday.'

There was a long pause.

'What if you have no money left for a taxi?' he asked lightly.

'I've found somewhere near Heathrow that's happy to buy the jeep for cash, then run me to my terminal.'

'What if I torch it before you can set off?' Something in his expression told her he wasn't altogether joking.

'I'll hot-wire Giles' Aston Martin.'

'You'll have a fight on your hands. Ely Gates is driving it that day.'

'How do you know?'

'I'll probably be under it.'

The waiter swooped a tray down between them to pluck up their glasses. 'Your table is ready.' He eyed the untouched appetisers. 'These did not meet with your approval?'

'We're saving ourselves for the sausage casserole. Big wedding breakfast, you know.' Patting his belly, Spurs stood up and took Ellen's hand. 'Come on, darling, must eat up. We can't miss our flight, can we?'

As they walked through the double doors to the famous ivory-panelled dining room, he held her hand so tightly that she thought her fingers would snap off.

The wine, which had been decanted and was poured for them with religious reverence, was so incredible that Ellen couldn't talk for a moment after sipping it, letting the complex, delicious tastes steal any words from her mouth.

'I bet you taste just as good.' Spurs was watching her obvious pleasure.

'So bitter and so sweet,' she muttered.

'I'd like to drink all your cases so that you have no baggage.'

'I'm only taking a backpack away with me.'

That smile twisted on his lips again and he stared into the blood red wine. 'Would you stay if I asked you to?'

'Are you asking me to?'

He dipped his finger into the glass and watched a drip form on it. 'No.' Then, breaking the whispered stillness, he sucked his finger and looked up at her sharply, 'What will you do with the rest of your things?'

'There isn't much.' She matched his steady gaze. 'I can give most of it away. I don't get attached to things.'

'Can't fit a dog into a backpack.'

Ellen felt her heart thud unhappily. 'Would you like her?'

His eyes glowed molten. But then he shook his head. 'She'd remind me of you.'

'See? We can't be friends. Even man's best friendship is too much.'

He nodded slowly. 'I know. It was worth a try, though, eh?'

She twitched a corner of her mouth in silent accord.

'What people don't realise about fairy tales,' he said suddenly, 'is that they were far more macabre in their original form. There were no happy endings. Little Red Riding Hood's grandmother, for example, was murdered by the wolf and he stored her blood in a bottle before killing the little hooded one in her bed.'

'Is that why you like the Little Mermaid?' she asked. 'Because it doesn't have a happy ending?'

'I was in Denmark with Cirque de Phénomène – the first and last time the troupe will be asked to perform in Tivoli Gardens. I followed the tourist trail and read the little plinth on the statue – she looked funnily like you, with her graffiti tattoos and her bubblegum studs. I just fell in love with her because she blew it so damned sweetly. An innocent scarred by modern life, swimming up to the surface after all those years trapped in a childhood idyll, only to fall in love with a bastard like me.'

Two spectacularly over-elaborate high-rise sausage confections were lowered simultaneously over Ellen and Spurs' left shoulders and the waiters stepped back in unison, waiting for awed comments, but Ellen and Spurs just gazed at one another.

'I love you,' he said urgently. 'I love you more than anyone else I've ever met in my entire life. I love you more than my bloody life. Christ knows, it's been one long, fuck-up journey from cage to cage so far – totally, mindlessly pointless until I met you. Then I spent two days with you. Two days of freedom with you, and I finally knew what prison really was because I'd already agreed to go back in for life this time and there's no getting out.'

Ellen stared at him, not understanding, her heart burning its way out of her chest.

'I just want one more day,' he went on. 'I just want one night. Tonight, tomorrow, this moment, today – fucking now. I can't watch you go without telling you how I feel. I don't care if one night in heaven makes hell even hotter. I can't wait any longer and I can't just walk away.'

She took his hands over the table, wine tipping over, nipples spilling from her dress, chair scraping against the polished floor, not caring about or even noticing the chaos in her wake.

'I *love* you.' He gripped her hands, eyes bubbling with mirth and relief. 'This cynic's got quixotic and the devil's been born again. I believe in soulmates, I believe in love at first sight and in sweet Jesus Christ right now because whatever it was that put you and me together should be worshipped by millions of people around the world and hated and loathed by just as many. *I believe,*' he shouted, '*in Jesus!*'

More waiters rushed over, forming a human wall around them like desperate German defenders given a Beckham free kick from the edge of the box.

Ellen was laughing. Laughing and crying and not noticing the frantic activity around her. A pair of sausage casseroles were swept from the table as Spurs made his way across it towards her and took her face in his hands. 'I married the most beautiful, good, kind, sexy, fucking amazing woman in the world today. I married the love of my life. It will be a short marriage, but they don't get any finer.'

Fellow diners turned in amazement. Two discreet Japanese women sidled up to take photographs, certain that this had to be two very famous people to look so good and behave so badly. An ageing American beauty demanded to know the name of Ellen's plastic surgeon because 'I *must* have those breasts.'

'Perhaps,' the maître d' hustled up urgently, 'you would like to finish your meal in your room, Mr and Mrs Gardner?'

Ellen reached out to touch Spurs' face. Her hand traced his high cheekbones, his dimpled chin, his creased, worried forehead and his noble nose down to his beautiful mouth. She slipped her fingers between his lips and touched the smooth teeth beneath. 'Where are we?' she asked dreamily.

'Fuck knows. Together.'

'Somebody here says we've got a room.'

'Let's go there.'

The hand-painted Chinese wallpaper in the bridal suite went unnoticed, as did the matching raw-silk-upholstered *chaises* on either side of the vast floor-to-ceiling bay window overlooking the park, as did the complimentary fruit and champagne chilling in frosted silverware above the antique veneer cabinets housing minibars and a multi-channel entertainment centre. The vast fireplace spilling with fresh damask roses was overlooked, the seductive original Klimt sketches went unspotted and the bed

– a riotously ornate carved French oak four-poster, acres wide, layered with silk counterpanes and topped with a love heart picked out in orchids – might have been a footstool in the corner of the room.

'Thanks. Fuck off.' Spurs thrust a fifty-pound note at the porter.

Kicking the door shut, he and Ellen set about ripping. White silk chiffon frayed, suit buttons popped, knickers tore, a ruptured zip gave way to a splitting seam, cotton shredded and shoes spun in the air. A tatty clog took out several crystals from an antique chandelier.

'I love you,' Spurs breathed into her mouth, body slamming against hers as they backed up against the door. 'I thought I'd die if I let you go without doing this,' they spun round again, 'without tasting you, without—'

'I love you too.' She shut him up with a kiss and jumped, knowing he would catch her. She could jump from the highest cliff and he would catch her.

Dilly and Rory shared another cigarette and another long kiss, and scratched their mosquito bites distractedly as Keith shambled up to refill their glasses with 'charity' rum. Lips not leaving Dilly's, Rory dropped another fiver into the good-causes bucket and gave him the thumbs-up.

'No sign of your lift, I'm afraid,' Keith told them cheerfully, looking at his watch. 'Ten past midnight. Stay as long as you like. Mary and I will lock up at half past, but the key's under the lupin tub.'

Dilly and Rory kissed on, legs tangling under the picnic table as candles guttered and midges gathered around them.

Fat on untouched chops and chips, Twitch the Jack Russell let out a contented burp and curled up between their feet, snapping at moths.

'When does Dilly get home?'

'Oh, she'll be tucked up in bed soon.' Pheely pressed her cheek indulgently to the pile of clothes she was lying on as her right nipple was sucked into a frothy peak. 'She's not coming back here tonight.'

'Good.'

She gurgled approvingly as Oddlode's greatest law-suitor pressed her breasts together and took both nipples into his mouth at once, chewing playfully with his very white, very expensive veneers. The bristling hair on his lip made the soft, puckered skin around them burn sensationally. 'Can I take a cast of your cock tonight?'

'No.' He kissed on.

'But you are so magnificent.'

'I keep telling you,' he let her breasts slide back under her armpits and reached for his glass of Cheap White Wine, 'I am allergic to plaster-of-paris. I got a terrible rash when I had to have my ankle set after I tore a ligament playing cricket at school.'

'In that case I'll have to sculpt it from memory.'

'What are you doing?' he asked in alarm, as she started to wriggle beneath him.

'Memorising it.'

'Where are we?' Ellen asked, as she stretched across a silk-soft woven rug to a magical luminous doorway that housed all manner of treats including the small cold bottle of water she grabbed now.

'Home.' Spurs ran his cheek up her thigh and sank his face between her legs.

The water bottle rolled on the woven rug.

'No, no, no, no!' she howled, as the circles rippled inwards from her fingers and toes to his beautiful, ever-kissing, ever-tasting mouth, plunging down between his lips and tongue to a never-ending, bubbling stream of pleasure.

Later, he walked a satin trail of kisses to her throat and she rolled over to grip him beneath her.

'Why do you say that when you come?' He looked up at her, reaching back for the water and handing it up to her.

'Say what?' She opened it with her teeth.

'No. You say no.'

Ellen took a long draught and handed the bottle to him to drain. 'Because I know this is make-believe,' she said. 'It's not real. That's why it's so lovely. So easy.'

He crumpled the empty water bottle in his hand and threw it angrily at the wall. 'It *is* real. Tonight it's real. Feel.'

She howled with indignation as he pinched her hard on the thigh. 'Okay,' she grabbed his wrist, 'I believe you. Cut that out.'

'Not unless you say yes when you come.' He teased, using the other hand to slap her arse. 'Say yes, Spurs! Yes, I love you!' He smacked her again, 'Yes, I want to spend my life with you!' Slap. 'Say, yes, yes, yes!'

Shrieking with laughter, she slapped him back and they wrestled over and over on the rug until he had her pinned beneath the heavy curtains at the window – impromptu covers for another delicious coupling.

'Yes,' Ellen gasped. 'Oh, yes. Yes, yes, yessssssirrrreeeeeeeee!'

Spurs cupped her breasts in his hands and arched up to kiss one, then the other as he finally exploded inside her. 'We have to stop coming together like this.'

'You shouldn't be so hard on yourself.' She shifted as she felt him stiffen again almost immediately.

'It's you who's making me hard on you.'

The huge windows had been thrown open, the heavy tapestry curtains dancing awkwardly to either side like a pair of foot-shuffling wallflowers at a disco, watching the best-looking couple kissing on the dance-floor. Despite the night air, the room was only just cool enough to be bearable.

Ellen watched his fingers move around her body as he familiarised himself with every curve and crease and crevice, like Pheely working with her beloved clay. He tilted his head this way and that as he traced her contours, his hair brushing softly against her skin as he examined her in minute detail, telling her how beautiful she was, that he'd never forget her.

Then, suddenly, that skin started to change, making him smile. 'You've got goosepimples. Are you cold?'

'No. Just frightened.'

'Frightened?'

Ellen couldn't explain. She stood up and headed into the cool, marbled bathroom, not bothering with the lights because its huge window already let in so much of the luminous moon that it already felt too bright. Her skin was jumping with fear now, crawling anxiously closer to her muscles, tweaking at her belly stud and twitching between her legs where Spurs had fitted so perfectly minutes earlier and propelled her to such crazy, uncharted heights.

It was the biggest bathroom she had ever seen. A double-sized claw-footed bath sat beneath a mullioned window looking out to Oddlode, the church spire gleaming in its lottery-funded flood-lights. At the end of the room there was a blue- and white-tiled walk-in shower that could have taken a football team, with vast nozzles at either end, and even a tiled bench against one wall.

Ellen set the hot tap running in the bath, feeling the steam hit her face as she tipped in the contents of every glass bottle lined up on the window-sill and fought to breathe.

'I'm having a piss, okay.'

Jolted, she looked round to see Spurs standing beside the lavatory; Michelangelo's *David* in an upmarket water-closet.

In thirteen years with Richard, she had never seen him urinate. The very idea would have creeped her out. Yet suddenly she wanted to stick around while Spurs took a pee.

'Sure.'

As the hard flow hit the porcelain, she turned back to the bath, blushing despite herself, dipping her hand into the scalding water.

'Why are you frightened?' he asked, over his shoulder.

Ellen watched the foam rise up in the bath, enchanted cloud castles full of dreams that fizzled away. 'Because this isn't real.'

'It feels real to me.'

'It does while you're pissing in the same room, yes.' She

scooped up a frothy beard and popped it onto her chin. 'But it can't last.'

'Because it's make-believe?' He flushed the lavatory and walked across to her, stepping straight into the bath.

'I haven't put any cold in yet!' she yelped.

But Spurs sat in the scalding water, taking her face in his hands. 'This isn't make-believe, Ellen. We haven't been making believe at all.'

'What have we been making, then? Merry? Hay while the sun shines?'

He leaned towards her and bit her lower lip, the sweat that was already forming on his upper lip touching saltily against her teeth. 'I love you.'

Ellen pulled back, staring at him. '*Do* we love each other?'

'Oh, we do.'

'If this is love, I didn't love Richard.' She started to cry.

He reared out of the bath and took her into his hot, wet, slippery arms.

'If this is love I've never done it before either. Ssh, baby. Ssh.'

They hugged tightly, consumed by steam and terror.

Suddenly Spurs pulled back, staring at her intently. 'We're not making believe at all.' He started to laugh. 'We're making love. Don't you see? We're making love! Two fucking virgins.'

Ellen found herself laughing too, dancing around the tiles, her face wet with steam and tears.

'Will you come to the bower o'er the free boundless ocean?' Spurs sang the jig he and Rory had played earlier.

'*Where the stupendous waves roll in thundering motion.*
Where the mermaids are seen and the fierce tempest gathers,
To love Ellen the queen,' he bastardised, '*the dear love of our lathers.*
Will you come, will you, will you, will you come to the bower?'

The boilers in Eastlode Park chugged and rattled in overtime that night as the bath in the bridal *en suite* was topped up with hot

water again and again. Then the shower powered out its hot flow
for hours.

When they finally fell back into the bedroom, Spurs and Ellen
were as wrinkled as raisins.

'If we can't grow old together,' He kissed her creased hands,
'this is the next best thing. This is what you'll be like old. I'd love
to know you old.'

'Will you come away with me?' She pressed her crinkly thumb
to his lips and watched his silver eyes.

'To see the World?' He dipped his face so that the thumb traced
his nose and forehead, tangling into the wet curls.

She nodded, goosebumps edging between the wrinkles.

Spurs pressed his face to her belly. 'You are my world. I don't
care where the fuck I go or where we are. Where are we?'

'The most expensive hotel in England.'

'Can we stay here for ever?'

In the early hours, while Spurs napped on a *chaise-longue* –
they still hadn't got round to using the bed – Ellen dialled an
outside line.

'Hi,' she whispered. 'I booked a flight a few days ago in the
name of Jamieson . . . BA373 leaving on the twentieth. Yes,
thanks . . . That's right. Is it possible to get another ticket? . . .
Yes, I'll hold.'

She looked out of the window, at a beautiful park emerging
slowly from the dawn mist, its ancient fat-trunked trees and
metallic lake, which had been the backdrop to ancient hunts,
gallant duels and small-waisted damsels giggling beneath silk
parasols as they threw scraps at swans. And the huge bedroom
– once the master's chamber in this grand old house – now housed
the most beautiful and noble sight it had ever seen. Naked and
glorious, lit by the blond morning haze, Spurs slept more soundly
than he had in all his life.

Ellen abandoned the piped classical music in her ear to fetch
the note that had been thrust beneath their door. It was a polite
message from the porter, explaining that when they had fetched

the Gardners' luggage from their car, they had only found the items that were now outside the room.

Ellen opened the door a fraction and dragged in two smart carrier-bags. One contained her surf kite, an ancient jumper that Snorkel slept on when she travelled and a pair of very cracked flip-flops. The other housed her neon pink fins.

She pulled on the fins, flapped back to the phone and gave her credit-card details. Then she flapped to the window and struck a pose.

'Do you really love me?'

Opening his silver eyes, Spurs smiled a wide, sleepy smile. Then he saw the flippers and laughed so much that he fell at her webbed feet. 'I love you, Little Mermaid.' He looked up at her. 'I love you.'

15

'What *are* you doing?' Spurs yawned, watching her over a freckled arm. Behind him, the sun had risen another twenty degrees above the lake and was pouring sharp gold light through his hair.

Ellen blinked in amazement, suddenly seeing the young Spurs with his blond curls and dangerous smile. For a moment, she was too blown away to speak.

'Am I dreaming?' He eyed her groggily, still surfacing from sleep.

'I was the one about to ask that.'

'Yeah, but I'm the one whose world has just turned upside down.' He pressed his smiling mouth to his forearm.

'No.' She cleared her throat, wishing he hadn't chosen quite this moment to wake up. 'I really *am* doing a hand-stand.'

'Why?' He rolled over on the *chaise-longue* so that his face was upside-down too, and they regarded one another across the vast room, blood rushing to their heads.

'Because you're right. The world has turned upside-down. I thought it would make more sense from this angle.'

'Does it?'

'No.' The sides of her mouth turned down, creating a topsy-turvy smile. 'I still don't want to wake up – and I haven't slept a wink all night.'

'I'm not surprised. Bloody hard to sleep at that angle.' He raised his eyebrows towards the floor.

Ellen took a deep breath, forcing herself to start breaking the spell. 'Was this a one-night stand?' she asked.

'A one-night hand-stand?'

'If you like.'

'Well, we made love standing up.'

'True.'

'And I have asked for your hand in marriage.'

'You didn't mean it.'

'You're wearing my ring,' he pointed out, head still lolling from the *chaise-longue*. 'Do you have any idea how desirable you look right now?'

Ellen looked down at the signet ring on her finger, hair falling across her face. Naked and inverted, she felt a blush steal across her skin. 'I just need to know where we stand.' Then, realising how stupid that sounded, she laughed. A moment later, Spurs had rugby-tackled her and they fell to the floor together in a shrieking tangle of legs, arms and hot skin.

'And I won't stand for this sort of talk.' He kissed her face. 'Last night was ours.'

'And who does today belong to?' She surfaced from the embrace and propped herself on one shoulder to look down at him, hating herself for still trying to break the spell.

'The highest bidder, I guess.' He clearly didn't want to talk about it.

But Ellen had to. For all the giddy, delirious happiness she was feeling, she knew that if she didn't resurface and start breathing again she would drown.

'Now that we've been to bed together, should we pretend it never happened?'

'We didn't go to bed together.' He reached up to kiss her again. 'We didn't even sleep together. We just made a hell of a lot of love.'

Ellen laughed into the kiss, feeling his teeth against hers. 'And did we make believe?'

'Maybe a little.' He ran his hand up her side.

'So we're still in Never Never Land?' she said, gently pulling away.

He nodded. 'We should never have done this because we can never take it back. He cupped her head and drew her ear down to his mouth. 'I love you.'

'I love you too.'

For a moment they clung to each other, heads pressed into the crooks of necks, letting the fairy tale blot out reality.

'It's a weird feeling, isn't it?' he whispered. 'Not like I expected at all. It's like fear, only nice. Can you feel it?'

Pulling away, Ellen looked at the silver eyes and was almost wiped out by their intensity. She felt a great churning inside, fear blending with almost overwhelming happiness. 'I feel it.'

They stared at one another, ribcages touching, great anvil-and-hammer heartbeats exchanging high fives beneath the bone and sinew.

'So it wasn't a one-night stand?'

'No.' Spurs blinked up at her.

Ellen pressed her forehead against his, breathing him in, a smell already so familiar and precious. 'Did you know that we were going to spend last night together when you decided to bring me here?'

She felt the forehead move from side to side. 'No. I just thought that if I spent all the money you've saved up, you might not go away. It was a spur-of-the-moment thing.'

'Well, you're certainly the Spurs of my moment.'

'Am I?' He started to kiss around her ear. 'Then we'll have to make this moment last for ever.'

Feeling her cheek reddening against his, Ellen thought about the extra ticket. 'How do you mean?'

'I can't let you go. I'm not going to let you go.'

She shivered with happiness. 'You don't have to. We can go away together. We can—'

'No.' He pressed his fingers to her mouth. 'I can't go away.'

'Do you want me to stay?' She jerked her head back, struggling to look him in the face. But he carried on holding her so tightly that she felt her ribcage groaning.

'If you do,' he muttered, 'we'll have to keep it a secret – "us" a secret.'

'For how long?'

There was a long pause. When he finally spoke, the words were barely audible. 'For ever.'

She laughed, wondering why he was teasing her. 'So the wedding's going to be pretty low-key, then?' She rubbed her ring against his neck.

His hot skin leaped as the gold touched it. 'We can never marry. That was the make-believe.'

'What are you talking about?'

'In the fairy tale, we get married and have babies and make love until we're very, very old.'

'I thought I swam back out to sea?' She was struggling to understand what he was trying to tell her.

He didn't answer.

'Spurs, you have to explain what's going on.'

For a moment, she felt the sinews of his neck harden against hers. Then he let out a long sigh. 'Let's not talk about it now, little mermaid. I can't bear to talk about it now. Besides, if your legs are going to dissolve into the sea, I think I should part them a few more times first.' His hand was already sliding downwards.

Ellen wriggled, desperate to get to the truth before she lost all care and tipped into the pleasure zone again. 'Spurs, I need to know—'

A knock on the door made them both jump.

'Let's tell them to go away.' He held on to her wrist: to open the door would be to let in yet more reality.

But Ellen broke free, grabbed a towel and went to answer a second knock.

'Your breakfast, Mr and Mrs Gardner.' A liveried room-service waiter rattled in a trolley laden with silver-hooded goodies.

As she stood back to let him pass, Ellen had a vague recollection of Spurs ticking everything on the breakfast chit before hanging it outside their door in the early hours, dragging her with him so that they'd almost been locked out of their room during a protracted kiss on the landing.

'Is everything to your satisfaction?' The waiter arranged their feast, then loitered for a tip, eyeing the perfectly made bed in surprise.

Spurs had retreated, naked, behind the *chaise-longue* and pulled the long lining muslin from the curtains across him like a mosquito net. Only his head poked out, silver eyes assessing the fully laden trolley. 'Impeccable.' He smiled from his tent.

'Thanks.' Ellen found her purse and discovered that all she had were twenty-pound notes.

The waiter took one without batting an eyelid, clearly accustomed to tips at least as large, and nodded politely as he retreated from the room.

'Did they remember the Frosties?' Spurs came out as soon as they were alone once more, pulling silver domes from plates. 'Yum, smoked salmon and scrambled eggs, kedgeree, bacon – oh, God, kippers. What *were* we thinking of?'

Ellen watched his excited appraisal, knowing that he was trying to spin out their happiness for all it was worth. And suddenly, as he looked at her suggestively over a jar of honeycomb, she didn't want the bubble to pop either. She didn't want to think about the ticket she had bought, about going away, secrets and lies, feuds, fairy tales or harsh facts. She just wanted him to touch her again. Right now, she wanted to make the Spurs of the moment last every precious second.

He looked up with a wicked smile. 'Lie back on the bed.'

She did as she was told, catching his eye and smiling back as he started to lay strawberry slices along her thighs.

'These are my strawberry fields for ever.'

When Pheely emerged from her magical-garden gate into a sharp, sunny morning to stretch deliciously under the lime tree, she didn't notice at first that there was something odd about the Goose Cottage barn. It was the best of June mornings, already as crisp and fresh as a lettuce heart, dusted with dew and sparkling under a Wedgwood blue sky. Wood-pigeons called sleepily from the firs along the Lodge Farm drive, the banks of foxgloves outside North Cottage buzzed with bees and one of Hunter's bantams strutted along the lane, cocking its head at Pheely and, she was certain, winking at her.

Feeling rather splendid after a pleasant, if not mind-blowing, origami the night before, she had decided to buy a breakfast feast at the shop and share it in the Goose Cottage garden with her daughter and her new best friend over talk of first love and second chances.

The Oddlode Pensioners' Collective were in full force at the post-office counter, with Glad Tidings at their helm, dressed in her flowered tabard and still wearing rubber gloves, having hotfooted it from the manor on her Dr Scholls with the juiciest bit of gossip that the village had heard in years. She gave Pheely such a knowing look when she first pinged in that she was convinced her lover must have been espied leaving the Lodge in the early hours. But this news was far more shocking than the revelation that Touchy Pheely was enjoying relations with a village legend.

Muffins and fresh juice forgotten, Pheely hurried through the village, her flip-flops slapping as she rounded the Lodes Inn and headed up Manor Lane to the farm.

Ely himself answered the door, and looked appalled to find her panting on his rush mat.

'I thought I told you never to come here,' he hissed gravely, glancing over his shoulder and taking a step outside so that he could pull the door closed.

'This is urgent.' Pheely was so out of puff, she had to clutch her knees.

'You could have telephoned.'

She ignored him, staring at her painted toes. 'Glad Tidings is telling everybody the news.'

'What news?'

She had to admire his cool. One sandy eyebrow lifted and his beard bristled only slightly.

'About your future arson-in-law,' she snapped.

The blue eyes flashed, and she knew she had him.

'I think you must have misunderstood some village tittle-tattle,' he rallied.

'And I think not,' she snarled. 'I've always said your daughter could benefit from better manors, but what you're doing to her is unspeakable.'

'In which case, I suggest you stop speaking, turn round and go home,' he said darkly. 'I am certainly not willing to discuss it with you.'

Pheely flinched, too frightened of him to stand and fight. A great lump welled in her throat. 'To think that face once gave me such pleasure.' She reached up and touched his beard then turned away hastily.

The flip-flops now slapped all the way to the lichen green front door of Goose Cottage, on which she hammered urgently. When no answer came, she called, peering in through the windows. A white clown's face met hers and Snorkel barked thankfully, desperate to be let out.

'Oh, you poor little poppet! Are those girls still lazing in bed?' Pheely said soothingly, then dashed round to check the back door.

Which was when she noticed that the jeep was missing from the barn.

Rushing home, she rang her daughter's mobile number. 'Where are you?'

'In Upper Springlode,' Dilly announced cheerfully. 'At Rory's yard.'

'Where's Ellen?'

'I don't know. She sort of forgot to fetch me last night.'

'Christ! Hell! Dilly!' Ellen sat bolt upright, slices of kiwi fruit flying from her nipples. 'We left her stranded!'

Spurs looked at up her, nonplussed, a raspberry seed on his nose.

'Dilly?' Ellen reminded him. 'Had a hot date with your cousin last night? We were supposed to pick her up.'

'Oh, she'll be fine.' He plunged back down again.

'Snorkel!' Ellen yelped, as the realisation hit that her poor dog was still home alone.

'No, I'm fine – I can hold my breath under water for hours.' Spurs carried on licking. 'I can put on the pink flippers if it adds something?'

'I . . . meant . . . the . . . do – oooooh, my life!' She sank back on the berry-strewn counterpane.

'You taste so beautiful.' He pulled her thighs on to his shoulders.

'We mustn't do this . . .'

'Stop trying to wake up.' He spoke with his mouth full. 'We're still dreaming.'

'We have to stop. The maid's knocked on the door three times now.'

He reached up and put a huge slice of orange into her mouth to shut her up.

'We *can't*,' his fingers, sticky with juice, slipped between her buttocks, 'we so can't. We haven't got much longer, and you're all mine.'

'Oh, don't stop,' she moaned. 'Please don't stop.'

He made her so bad, she realised. So utterly irresponsible and downright wicked. But she didn't care. Right now, with hardly a pinch of shame, she couldn't care less about man or beast or life or death. Right now, all that mattered was being here with him.

The telephone shrilled.

They ignored it, guilt losing the battle to pleasure.

It carried on ringing and eventually Ellen dragged it from the bedside table, spilling starfruit and bilberries in her wake as she reeled it in by the cord.

Spurs rolled her over, laying the last of the fruit on her buttocks as she listened vaguely to the caller.

'It was Reception.' She dropped the phone from the side of the bed, moaning deliciously as a physalis was succulently removed from its resting place. 'They're demanding the room back.'

'They can go to hell.'

'The people who've booked it are due here any minute – it's almost lunchtime.' She barred the peach slice that was about to slide up her spine. 'They were pretty insistent that we vacate.'

'Spoilsports.' Spurs sulkily threw the peach out of the window and sucked his fingers. Seconds later, without warning, he'd slid one of those slippery fingers into her. 'We can't possible vacate before I've filled this delicious place.'

Fighting lust with all her pious willpower, Ellen wriggled away. 'We have to wake up.'

'I don't want to.' He held on to her thigh and pulled her back hard against him, angry hand pinching her skin while the other – infinitely gentler – reached beneath her buttocks once again and delved into the wet, bubbling welcome lying there.

'We mustn't,' she gasped.

'You want to.' He bent over and bit her arse. 'There's nowhere we can't go, and we can't stop ourselves. We belong to each other.'

'Tell me your secret,' she whispered, shuddering as his fingers drew long, slippery lines from her clitoris to her anus.

'Later.' He gripped her by both hips and sank smoothly inside her, forcing both their heads beneath the water again as they drowned in scruple-free pleasure. 'When we've left the palace and the fairy tale is over, I'll tell you everything.'

Ellen carefully reread the hotel invoice at the cashier's desk, trying hard not to give away her sheer terror. It was far worse than she had imagined. Her credit-card limit would barely cover it, and she had already bought two airline tickets with her savings. She cast her eyes down the list, boggling at its itemised contents.

The stylish gold shirt and Bermuda shorts, exclusively designed for the hotel by La Coast, cost as much as a package holiday. Buying them had seemed a better option than stealing the bathrobe or trying to patch together the chiffon dress, but Ellen resented paying several hundred pounds to look like a staff member at an exclusive Essex gym

'Is there a problem, Miss Jamie– I mean Mrs Gardner?' the cashier asked kindly, examining Ellen's charity credit card and smiling at the picture of a puppy whose life would be enhanced thanks to exorbitant hotel bills put on plastic.

'No – no, it's fine!' Ellen glanced over her shoulder to see Spurs smoking a cigarette by the doors and squinting out at the hot sun on the raked gravel sweep. The arrival at their room of the porter, politely but firmly insisting that this time they *must* leave, had plunged him into a strange, edgy mood. He had insisted that Ellen was 'dissolving'. She longed to mention the ticket, but knew she had to wait until he explained what was going on. Her stomach churned with fear.

And yet, as he caught her watching him now, his face relaxed into a smile of such mesmerising trust and elation that she felt invincible. She smiled back, her throat so cram-full of emotion that she expected it to puff out like a bullfrog's. I love him more than anything else in my life, she realised in amazement. I can forgive him anything. He can't let me go, and I can't even begin to think about losing him. I can forgive him anything.

'I do hope that you'll both find your plane ready for you now.'

'Sorry?' She turned back to the cashier.

'I gather it wasn't possible to leave for your honeymoon last night.'

'Oh, yes. I think it's fine now.' Ellen's pen hovered worriedly over the empty space in which she could add a staff gratuity. Even ten per cent of this bill would be a month in China. But she couldn't leave it blank. Then she smiled. What the hell? She had just been to heaven and back several times in one night. 'We really enjoyed our stay here.' She added an extravagant tip.

'So I gather.' He watched her hand as she signed the receipt and then – clocking the gratuity – forgave Spurs and Ellen for hogging the room all morning. 'What an unusual ring.'

The Constantine crest was showing on her finger. Hastily Ellen whipped away her hand and glanced back at Spurs. He was talking to somebody at the door now, a short and very round figure in a summer dress carrying a trug, hair covered with a silk scarf. From Spurs' anxious, quilted cheeks and the lowered brow, it was obvious that the encounter was a regrettable one.

'Anthony is bringing your car round to the front of the hotel,' the cashier was saying. 'May I wish you a wonderful honeymoon?'

'Thanks,' Ellen said distractedly, the churning returning to her belly as she remembered that the honeymoon was already over. She no longer cared what it had cost her financially. That was a fraction of the price she and Spurs would pay when the fairy tale ended – and she had an uncomfortable feeling that 'Anthony' was driving a big pumpkin on to Eastlode Park's carriage sweep. Meanwhile, Prince Charming had found himself collared by one of the Ugly Sisters.

She took her credit card and printed receipt and crammed them into the bag with her tattered dress and the pink fins, then turned back to Spurs. But his silver gaze was waiting for her over the trug-carrier's plump, sunburned shoulder.

Ellen stopped in her tracks and raised her eyebrows inquiringly. His eyes said it all. They were pleading with her to stay clear. He looked ashen.

She hovered uncertainly on the marble-tiled floor, clutching her bag and making a bad attempt to look casual while shuffling sideways to see who the hell he was talking to.

The small, headscarfed figure was practically bouncing up and down on the spot, and indicating the door. Then, as she got a look at the woman's profile, Ellen recognised Ely's puddingy wife Felicity, with her piggy little face and very pink cheeks.

'. . . always let me have their leftover flowers for the church,' she was saying in her soft lisp, 'which is terribly kind. They always have lots of life left in them.'

Spurs was snacking on a thumbnail, his neck criss-crossed with anxious veins as he glanced at Ellen again, tortured with unknown demons.

Why is he bothered about Felicity Gates seeing us together? she wondered. Then again, from the excitable, adoring look on Felicity's plump face, she might almost be as much in love with him as Ellen was. The thought made her snort with laughter.

Spurs almost shot through the roof, so finely tuned into Ellen's every move that he could probably hear her heart beating. But Felicity even didn't look round. '. . . better get a move on,' she was saying. 'The lilies are wilting in the back of the car. I'll drop you on the way. I can't believe you forgot the lunch. You are a one! Your mother has been telling me all week that you'll be there. Come on, then.' She trotted off, trug swinging, nodding gratefully as the liveried valet who was emerging through the doors held them open for her with a touch of his cap.

As soon as the doors closed, Spurs dashed to Ellen, eyes wild, sending the valet flying as he tried to present her with her car keys. He grabbed both her hands. 'I'm sorry – I'm so sorry. I have to go. I'll explain later.'

'Go where?'

'I'll explain later.' He pressed her knuckles into his teeth, staring at her over them, the silver gaze tarnished with guilt. 'I'll come to the cottage. I'll explain everything, I promise.'

'You can't just—'

'I love you.' He kissed the signet ring on her finger. 'You're my life, and you're the one secret I just can't keep.' With that he sprinted away, sending a Japanese family flying.

By the time Ellen had grabbed her keys from the dishevelled valet and picked her way over ten matching Louis Vuitton suitcases, Felicity's Volvo was half-way along the Eastlode driveway, passing the lake where two swans were stretching their wings together.

Swans mated for life, Ellen recalled, as her mind jerked uncertainly between extremes of confusion, happiness and fear. *Last night, I was the signet that became a swan. Just my luck to pick a black one.*

She looked at the ring on her finger, wondering what possible reason Spurs could have for abandoning her in favour of the church stalwart and local do-gooder, plump, boring Felicity.

You are the one secret I can't keep.

Did that mean he wanted to tell everyone that they were in love, or did that mean he couldn't keep her?

'I love him, I love him, I love him.' She stared at the swans, who were now gliding serenely on the lake, waltzing in their own watery ballroom. And Ellen laughed as it hit her what love really meant. What had Spurs said? Like fear, only nice.

*   *   *

When Ellen drove up the potholed drive to the yard, Dilly was leaning over the gate to the sand school, yawning widely as she watched Rory riding a youngster. Dressed in Ellen's hot pants and one of Rory's shirts, her hair piled under a baseball cap, she turned to wave at the jeep and mimed cutting her throat.

'Oh heck.' Ellen chewed her lip as she parked beside a huge pile of plastic-wrapped haylage bales. She glanced anxiously out of the window, watching Dilly brush noses with the ginger stable cat that had teetered along the gate to join her.

Deep breaths, Ellen told herself. You can always lie.

Dilly bounded over as soon as she got out of the car. 'What happened to you? Did you break down? We tried the mobile but you didn't answer. Where's Spurs? God, what *are* you wearing?'

Ellen looked down at her discreetly logoed gold Eastlode polo shirt, but thankfully Dilly was too preoccupied with chattering to pursue the subject.

'Mum is *so* mad at you. She called ages ago, when she discovered nobody was at your place. She said something about ordering a taxi, but I think she must have got distracted because nobody's turned up – a bit like last night.'

'I'm so, so sorry, Dilly.' Ellen felt clammy with embarrassment. 'Were you okay? Rory looked after you, didn't he?'

She nodded, looking across at Rory, who was cantering around the sand school. 'I've had the best night of my life ever. We stayed up talking most of it, and Rory made me banana sandwiches at four in the morning, and we watched the dawn and saw fallow deer and I helped him muck out and . . .' She looped her arm through Ellen's, babbling like a happy toddler. 'We kissed for *ages*. He says I'm really special.'

Ellen gave her a hug. 'You are.'

'We didn't do *It*,' Dilly whispered in her ear. 'We did lots of other things, but Rory thinks I shouldn't lose the big V ASAP. He thinks we should take our time.' She pulled away, glancing at him with unconcealed rapture, then took Ellen's hands. 'You

were so right when you said that if it's truly magical you could
be anywhere in the world.'

Ellen bit her lip.

Dilly was watching her face closely. 'Where *did* you get to
last night?'

'I went round the world.'

Pheely was beyond livid. Furious with herself for blithely letting
Dilly stay away all night because she wanted privacy with her
lover, she turned the force of her wrath on Ellen, whom she
decided had abused her trust for the last time. Touchy Pheely
was about to show how she had earned her name.

Bow-legged, exhausted, and wantonly bonked half to death,
Ellen was an easy target when she brought Dilly back. They
had walked together to the Lodge cottage, with Snorkel in tow,
so that she could apologise in person.

'Mum!' Dilly charged out of the wilderness on to the terrace,
almost knocking Godspell's bust from its plinth as she gave her
mother a huge hug and spun her round. 'I have had the *best* night!
Rory had done the table in the Plough's garden like a magical
grotto, and he played the fiddle and Twitch sang and then—'

'That's enough, Dilly darling.' Pheely prised away her arms and
caught Ellen's eye over her daughter's shoulder. 'I'd like a word
with Ellen. Go and have a bath.'

'But—' On seeing her mother's expression, Dilly knew it wasn't
wise to argue and sloped inside, followed by the tussling Hamlet
and Snorkel.

The green lantern eyes almost seared the skin from Ellen's
face. 'How *dare* you abandon my daughter overnight with Rory
Midwinter?'

Ellen hung her head. 'It was completely thoughtless and selfish
and I can't excuse it. I'm sorry, Pheely, but at least she was okay.'

'Okay? *Okay?*' She mocked Ellen's Somerset accent, drawling
out the slang word with a snobbish sneer. 'She's a little girl!'

'Pheely, she's seventeen,' Ellen reminded her kindly, not picking up on the severity of Pheely's anger. 'I was living out of a

rucksack in Europe with my boyfriend at seventeen. My parents were lucky if they got a postcard a month.'

'That's because you're a tart,' she snarled.

Ellen reeled.

'At seventeen,' Pheely seethed, 'I had a eighteen-month-old child because I'd been so naïve and desperate to fall in love that I willingly gave myself to the first man who treated me like a grown-up.' She paced over to a crowded table to extract her cigarette packet from among sculpting tools and empty wine bottles. 'I can't *believe* I trusted you and you let me down not once but twice, in the worst possible way. You have encouraged my sweet, open-minded daughter to open her legs and her heart to any man that comes along. You might live like that, but I can assure you not everyone wants to be known as the girl who fucks like a stoat.'

'Steady on.' Ellen caught her breath.

But Pheely was on the rampage, assuaging her own guilt by attacking. 'First you put all sorts of ideas about Spurs – Spurs! – into the child's head, and then you turn her special night out into a grotty sleepover. You are completely unreliable. Worse than that, you're manipulative and selfish and really quite evil. It's no wonder you and Spurs are so close.' Satisfied with her outburst for now, she kicked a pot of chives and crossed her arms, waiting for the backlash as she took a cigarette break to regroup.

But Ellen felt no anger, just desperate shame that the friendship was crumbling when she needed it most. Pheely deserved her honesty, at least.

'I was with Spurs last night,' she confessed hoarsely. 'We love each other, Pheely.'

'Ha!' Pheely lit her cigarette. 'Ha!'

'I love him.'

'You bloody reckless idiot, how can you possibly love someone you've known barely five minutes?'

'I've known him all my life.'

'Oh, no.' She tutted patronisingly, '*I* have known him most of my life, and I think you'll find you've barely scratched the surface.

You've just scratched an itch. You wanted to shag him, you told me yourself. And last night you did just that, I take it?'

Ellen's skin still burned from every kiss. She looked up at a streak of white where a plane had just crossed the blue sky and tried hard not to give into the urge to shriek happily and dance around Pheely's terrace. 'I know it was totally irresponsible, but we couldn't stop, and it was . . . Oh God, it was the most breathtaking thing that has ever happened to me, Pheely. It felt like nothing on earth.' She hugged herself tightly. 'I love him totally.'

Pheely laughed bitterly. 'Hooray, hooray, Spurs is a great lay. Well, bully for you, Ellen. But please don't mistake what's just happened to you for *love*.'

Ellen closed her eyes and felt Spurs beside her and within her, a magical force that she had lived a lifetime in possession of, never knowing how to harness it until now. And she knew for certain that this wasn't a case of mistaken identity. This was love. She'd never experienced anything like it before in her life.

'He'll break you up into pieces.' Pheely sighed, with deliberate dispassion. 'Which is probably the least you deserve after what you've done to Dilly. He can smash you to bits.'

'I was already in pieces when we met,' Ellen kept her eyes closed, longing for Pheely to understand, 'but I didn't see it – nobody did except him. He's made me see that my pieces fit with his.' She pictured two fractured vases that combined to make a stained-glass window depicting a fairy tale.

But Pheely interpreted the perfectly fitting pieces differently: 'Please don't go into the sordid details of your smutty night spent shagging in some ditch,' she huffed.

Opening her eyes, Ellen looked at Pheely's generous face, twisted with anger. 'I know I've let you down, and I know that you'll never trust Spurs as I do. But he and I understand one another. From the moment we met, it's been like trying to deny my own identity. I feel like I've been under water for thirteen years and have only just come to the surface.'

Her cigarette break over, Pheely ground out the butt into the terrace and dusted her dress down, a nasty smile curling on to her plump lips. It was time to launch the cannonball.

'It's rather a shame that Spurs is marrying somebody else, then, isn't it?'

Ellen froze. Was this some sort of absurd joke?

Pheely widened her eyes and spoke very slowly and clearly, as though addressing a halfwit. 'That's why Spurs came home in the first place, Ellen. He's getting married.'

Unable to speak, Ellen shook her head stupidly.

'I do love good old-fashioned arranged marriages.' Pheely was relishing her revelation, her anger at last sated by a satisfactory revenge. 'There's something rather sexy about a Machiavellian union arranged by ambitious parents. One imagines the innocent victims torn from true lovers and forced to endure their lives of wealth and privilege together far from love.

'Then again,' she cocked her head, happy to be swept away, 'it could be rather *Kiss Me Kate* – two strangers sharing a wedding bed on the first day they meet, only falling in love after months or years of marriage.'

Ellen wasn't taking any of this in. She was unable to believe that Spurs was getting married.

'I'm not surprised Spurs is devoting himself so avidly to screwing around right now,' Pheely mused. 'That's where you came in – he must have been thrilled to find a wannable Pamela Anderson on his doorstep, fresh from the beach-bum, rebounding like a bouncing beach-ball, and swooning over his pathetic circus tricks. He won't be able to have casual sex much longer, after all – one can hardly be unfaithful with Gladys as a housekeeper. God knows, the Surgeon's tried hard enough. Spurs will have to be a faithful husband. With any luck, that means he'll drink himself to death fairly soon.' She peered at Ellen. 'Have you got a fly in your ear or something?'

Ellen stopped shaking her head and just stared at her.

'I'm sure he told you he loved you.' Pheely feigned understanding as she fluttered back to the table to search through the bottles for one with same wine left in it. 'Most men say that when they want to take a girl to bed, don't they? But this wedding has been planned for a very long time.' Finding her search fruitless, she turned back to Ellen.

Slumping down on to an earthenware gargoyle, she battled not to be sick. 'Wh-wh-who . . . is . . . he . . .' She stopped in horror as Pheely stepped towards her latest work of art.

Very slowly, she turned Godspell's bust to face Ellen. 'Dracula's bride. I think it's rather fitting, don't you?'

'*Godspell Gates?*' Ellen gasped.

'The engagement – which, I gather, will be extremely short – is going to be announced at Ely's garden party. This little creation,' she tapped the top of the horribly lifelike head, 'is to form the centrepiece of one of Felicity's floral displays, a huge tribute to Ely's little girl who has so dutifully agreed to unite Oddlode's two great families by marrying Jasper Belling. So romantically feudal, don't you think?'

'This is a joke.' Ellen stood up, clutching her head. 'A bad joke.'

'Ely wanted to buy Goose Cottage as a wedding present for the young couple,' Pheely went on. 'He is *very* disappointed that you've scuppered his plans, and he'll be even more irate if he finds out that you've been playing with the bridegroom. You really should watch your back.'

'I don't believe you. Spurs would never agree to do something like this.'

'No?' Pheely dusted ash from Godspell's nose. 'Why don't you ask him yourself?'

Ellen stared at her.

A stricken look crossed Pheely's face, but she held it in check. 'Where exactly *is* Spurs, Ellen?' she asked lightly. 'I thought you were so madly in love that you couldn't leave one another's sight.'

It was as though her own shadow had disappeared. Ellen turned and stumbled into the wild garden.

Ellen ran along the old footpath, deaf to Hunter's bellows, the rush of blood in her ears like an approaching tidal wave. Still dressed in her disgusting gold Eastlode Park sports separates, she stumbled over the gate and through the archway to the kennel yard.

Spurs had shown her the answer to the riddle all along, she realised. It was in the story of the Little Mermaid; the prince had married somebody else. Not all fairy tales had a happy ending, he had explained. He'd agreed to marry Godspell Gates.

'Oh God, no,' Ellen raced past the yews, her windpipe so atrophied with panic that she thought she would suffocate.

There was no answer when she hammered on the big black door. Looking around frantically, she spotted that the french windows leading from the terrace into the manor house were open, and she darted inside, searching each room in turn for Spurs.

The dining-table was laid for six at one end. At the other a large open folder spilled details of marquee-hire companies, caterers' sample menus, toastmaster's CVs and mobile-disco playlists.

Yelping, Ellen pinched herself hard. 'Wake up,' she gasped as she ran on. 'Wake up, wake up.'

But she was already awake, and however hard she pinched herself, it was nothing to the thousands of mousetraps that were snapping shut on her heart.

Spurs wasn't in the big games room with the billiard table, or the huge hallway. The Victorian drawing room, which looked completely different without the rows of mismatched chairs that had been laid out for the auction, was deserted, its heavy curtains drawn against the picture-fading sun.

She ran back along the winding inner lobby, looking into each room in turn. And ground to a halt as she heard raised voices at the far end of the house.

'I won't stand for this!' Came Hell's Bells' familiar baritone, snarling with anger. 'I'm going to get your father in here!'

'You can get the household cavalry for all I bloody care,' Spurs' voice yelled back.

Ellen followed the racket and found Spurs and his mother

squaring up to each other across a huge kitchen table covered with Cellophaned quiches, pies and salads. They were arguing so furiously that, at first, they didn't notice Ellen standing in the doorway.

'We have the Gateses coming to lunch in ten minutes' time. What am I supposed to tell them?'

'That it's off.' Spurs laughed at the simplicity of the solution. 'Tell them it's off. I won't do it.'

Ellen let out a strange squeak as her hands flew to her mouth in relief.

'What's she doing here?' demanded Hell's Bells in a boom that would have stripped a horse-chestnut of conkers.

The black Labradors who had been making waggy-tailed progress across the flagstones to greet the newcomer sloped hurriedly back to their baskets.

Spurs ran his hand shakily through his curls and looked at Ellen, his face pale.

'I've just heard,' she croaked. 'The whole village knows you're marrying Godspell Gates.'

He sprinted across the room and drew her into his arms. But before he could say a word, Hell's Bells squawked, 'The village can't possibly know! We've gone to great lengths to keep it from Gladys. She even has this afternoon off so she can't listen in to our lunch. All we've told her is that Ely is going to announce Godspell's engagement at his party, no more.'

'It's true, then?' Ellen looked up at Spurs.

He pulled away and rubbed his forehead with white-knuckled fingers, unable to look at her. 'I tried to tell you, but I couldn't. God help me, I just couldn't.'

'What business is it of hers, anyway?' snapped Hell's Bells.

'Is it true, Spurs?' Ellen repeated.

He sucked in one cheek. 'That was the plan.'

'My son,' Hell's Bells told Ellen, fixing her with the steeliest of gazes, 'is indeed to marry a lovely local girl later this summer. Such a shame that you won't be in the village to witness the celebrations – I gather you'll be leaving us soon?'

Ellen stared at her in disbelief. 'And Godspell's agreed to this?' She looked from Hell's Bells to Spurs.

He nodded.

'They make a delightful couple,' Hell's Bells said, with great force if little conviction. 'Of course, you probably won't understand the way we do things around here, Miss Jamieson, but one *must* put duty to the family first, and that is what Jasper is doing.'

Ellen gaped at them both. 'It's medieval. It's crazy. It's the stupidest thing I've—'

'How *dare* you come into this house uninvited and start questioning our lives?' Hell's Bells raged.

'No!' Spurs turned to his mother. 'She's right. It is medieval.'

Hell's Bells was purple with indignation, 'I hardly think that you should listen to the opinion of some tramp you've been—'

'*Shut up*, Mother,' he snapped. 'I love her.'

She didn't miss a beat. 'Don't be ridiculous.'

'I . . . love . . . her,' he repeated.

'Very well.' She unfolded several chins, undefeated. 'I accept that you think you are in love with this . . . *person*,' she cast a beady silver eye over Ellen, 'but that does not and *can*not alter your duty to this family.'

Spurs shook his head. 'You don't understand. It alters everything.'

'Explain.' She tapped the toe of her court shoe.

He walked to the far end of the kitchen and leaned against the Aga, as though desperate for its heat despite the sweltering day.

'When you suggested this idea, Mother, I no longer believed that I deserved any sort of happiness.' He spoke quickly and quietly, forcing them to listen. 'All I knew was that here was a chance to make amends at last, that even though I've given you and Father so much bloody suffering with my actions, you were willing to entrust me with a legacy. I ruined Father's career, I made this family a laughing-stock, I practically bankrupted you, I turned you into an alcoholic, which is probably why you're now—'

'We don't talk about that,' Hell's Bells reminded him, glancing uncomfortably at the large bottle of gin poking out from behind the toaster.

He stared at his feet for a moment, his cheeks hollow. 'I'd got to a point where I no longer cared what I did with my life,' he went on. 'I'd been running away for so long that I'd forgotten what I was running from – I was just following the white lines on the roads. When I came back, I was willing to sign on whatever dotted line you wanted me to. I am a professional prodigal son.' He laughed bitterly. 'My first proper job.'

'You are a good son,' Hell's Bells' voice cracked with emotion, but she stood firm, her chin still aloft as she reminded him, 'a *dutiful* son.'

'I felt no sense of duty, honour or responsibility to the family, the house or our history when I was younger.' He turned to Ellen, silver eyes tortured. 'It seemed archaic – those draconian schools, being told *who* and *what* I was all the time, as though breeding and heritage superseded any individuality. It's a job, you see – even today. With bugger-all left of the estate and no farms to manage, being a Constantine is still a vocation.'

'But you're a Belling,' she muttered.

'This family is Constantine!' Hell's Bells boomed. 'The Constantines have lived in Oddlode manor for three hundred years.'

Spurs watched her wearily. 'I'm sorry, Mother, but I've never wanted it – the house, the history, the lifestyle. I came home to save it because I felt that was the only way to make sense of my life . . . and then what you asked me to do seemed to make sense of your death.'

Her eyes bulged. 'My what?'

He looked away. 'There's no point in hiding the truth. I know.'

'Know *what* exactly?'

Ellen had to admit that Hell's Bells was doing a good job of bluffing. She looked utterly stupefied.

Spurs walked to his mother's shoulder. 'I have the letter . . . *It is with great regret that I must inform you that there is very little that we can do for the terminal condition you describe, especially at this advanced stage*".' He quoted from memory. 'I've read that bloody letter a hundred times or more, I read it every night before I sleep, wondering why you can't bring yourself to tell Father and I.'

Hell's Bells pressed her gold-encrusted ring finger to her lips and watched him with troubled eyes. 'I read it a hundred times too,' she said hoarsely. 'I kept it in my handbag and read it in the car, trying to believe it. I thought I must have dropped it. I turned the dratted car upside down.'

'I found it by accident.' His eyes shot to Ellen's face for a moment.

'You should never have read it.'

'"*I am sure this comes as a very great disappointment,*" Spurs carried on quoting in little more than a whisper, '"*but it would be unprofessional of me to advise otherwise. We do have treatments which will greatly ease the discomfort and pain during the later stages of the disease, and I am happy to talk these through with you at greater length should you wish to pursue the matter. But as regards curative treatment, then I am afraid the outcome is unavoidable.*" I think I deserved to know that my own mother is dying.'

Hell's Bells stifled a throaty sob and blinked. She looked guilt-striken. 'You mustn't tell your father about this.'

'Was it from your consultant?' he asked.

She shook her head, rattling her rings against her teeth, her eyes racing around the room. Revealing her secret seemed to be tormenting her. Ellen's heart ached for them both.

'It was some quack Hilary Winston-Black mentioned – I thought he might be able to help.'

'Hilary the dog breeder?'

'One is willing to try anything at times like this,' she mumbled, her fighting spirit draining fast. 'It was my last hope.'

'Can't the doctors do anything?'

She turned away. 'It seems not.'

She paced the flagstones before stopping to seek sanctuary in the chunky, seal-soft necks of her Labradors as they lay anxiously

in their baskets. She pressed her forehead to the greying muzzle
of the senior dog and muttered something under her breath. Ellen
couldn't be sure, but it sounded like 'Forgive me.'

'"*I hope that these last few months do bring some joy and understanding amongst the inevitable heartache*",' Spurs finished bitterly,
a shaking hand raking his hair from his face. 'I guess I'm still
working on the understanding part, but it was pretty obvious that
my marrying Godspell would bring you great joy. And at the time
I agreed to it, that was something I wasn't capable of feeling so it
was easy to give away. That night, I read the letter and thought
that if all the king's horses and all the king's men couldn't put my
mother back together again, then at least my horse and carriage
could make it up the aisle before the funeral procession.'

'It means so much to me,' Hell's Bells breathed into a domed
Labrador head. She cleared her throat, suddenly sounding more
like her old self. 'It is my dying wish.'

'Even if it makes me the most miserable man on earth?' Spurs
asked gently.

Her eyes narrowed as she straightened up, turning her gaze to
Ellen. 'This . . . creature . . . cannot be allowed to compromise
our family.'

'She already has,' he laughed. 'She was there the night I agreed
to do this – sitting a few tables away, dripping water everywhere
as though she'd just walked out of the sea.' He shook his head
at the memory, as though it still astonished him. 'I was watching
her while you and Ely banged on about grand unions and family
ties. She couldn't see me looking, but I wanted to walk out of my
own body and join her, leaving just the name and the heirlooms
for Godspell to marry because she sure as hell will never get
my spirit.'

Ellen remembered that tortuous date with Lloyd. She had no
idea Spurs had been watching her. He had barely seemed to
notice her. She remembered witnessing his argument with his
mother, and recalled how ill Hell's Bells had looked when she'd
thought Spurs was refusing to bend to her will. Had she known
what his mother was asking of him then, Ellen would have thrown

over tables in protest. There was something else about that night lurking in the shadows of her mind, another champagne-muddled memory, but she couldn't pin it down.

'You have no idea how close I came to walking out that night, Mother – to leaving Oddlode and your life and death wishes far behind,' Spurs was saying. 'But I stayed and I listened to the whole, ridiculous marriage idea because I know how much I owe you and Father.' As his eyes found Ellen's, a smile lifted his face and he walked towards her. 'Then I read that letter and felt a thousand thorns in my side. But I only agreed to do it because I was drunk and tired and I'd just seen the girl I'd fallen madly in love with making eyes at another man.'

'Don't be fatuous!' Hell's Bells raged.

'It's the truth,' he didn't take his eyes from Ellen's as he stood in front of her. 'When I saw you for the first time and fell straight through that big hole in your heart, I thought you'd been sent to punish me. There you were, eyeing up the family silver for a pot to piss in, like a fallen angel at an auction room. And I just fell in love.'

Ignoring Hell's Bells' outraged turkey gobbles, Ellen laughed. 'I thought *you* were the fallen angel.'

'We were falling too fast to think straight, weren't we?' He took her face in his hands. 'I spent years looking for you, and just as I stopped believing you existed, along with God and Father Christmas, there you were. I never imagined you could love me back. I agreed to this bloody marriage as the ultimate sacrifice, but I couldn't leave you alone, even when I thought you still loved Richard.'

'I fell in love with you the moment we met,' she admitted.

Unselfconsciously, he drew her towards him and slid his thumbs into her hair, his eyes moving between hers. Then he dropped his mouth to her ear and whispered, 'We fit inside each other's heads and bodies and minds. It's as though you've always been there, and losing you would be dying. I want to die with you at my side – whether now or at a hundred and ten doesn't matter.'

If Ellen's heart could have burst out of her chest, it would have done. She gripped his hands to stop herself breaking down. 'I want to *live* my life with you, not die. I want to start living.'

A low rumble across the kitchen provided only the briefest warning of the outburst to follow. 'I cannot and *will* not condone this childish nonsense! You are getting married to the Gates child, Jasper. This – this – *creature* is about to leave the village and mercifully never return. And *I* am the one about to die.'

'I can't go through with it.' He cupped Ellen's face again and looked at it. 'This is the face I can't live without.'

'You gave me your word, Jasper!' Hell's Bells raged. 'A Constantine never breaks a promise. Remember the family motto!'

'"To break a promise is to break one's sword,"' he recited flatly, and his hands fell to his sides.

'Only a coward goes back on his word.' Her voice shook as she marched to his shoulder. 'Only a coward lets his mother die upon a thousand broken swords, knowing that the son she has never stopped believing in has failed her in her final wish. Only a coward follows the selfish, dilettante route to earthly pleasure knowing that the souls of his forefathers will never rest. If you break your promise, Jasper, you will break this family. You will show yourself to be the same pathetic coward you always have been.'

'I am not a coward!'

'Prove it,' she hissed, into his ear. 'Do the first noble thing in your Godforsaken life and let me die in peace.'

Watching Spurs' face, Ellen's heart ruptured. Hell's Bells had him in her clutches again.

He bowed his head. 'Don't make me do this.'

'You – gave – me – your – word!' his mother intoned.

'I was prepared to die then.'

The once-beautiful face fell. 'I'm preparing to die *now*,' she said hoarsely.

They stared at one another, absurd replicas, sharing the same features set in different clays.

'I love her,' he murmured.

'Are you saying you don't love me?'

He stared at the ceiling. 'You're my mother. Of course I love you. But I love Ellen too, and I can't lose her. I can't lose both of you. I think I'd lose my mind.'

She twisted her mouth angrily. 'Very well. If the girl agrees to be discreet, we may be able to accommodate her in the arrangement. It's far from ideal, but time is not on our side, and I can see that you are infatuated to the point of lunacy. When Ely arrives, we will discuss the possibility of a rented cottage in which the girl can live for the time being. Somewhere tucked away and inconspicuous. His nephew should be able to rustle something up.'

'The "girl" won't agree to that,' Ellen gasped. 'The "girl" can't stand back and watch this crazy, loveless marriage take place.'

'Oh, do dry up! Love has nothing to do with this union. I've never loved Spurs' father, and we have a very good marriage.'

'I don't want a good marriage,' Spurs snapped, taking Ellen's hand. 'I want Ellen.'

The court heels clicked away, and Hell's Bells' broad shoulders were pinned to her ears with tension as she gathered her fiercest force. 'This marriage *must* and *will* go ahead, Jasper. If it doesn't, I'll die with my spirit and heart broken along with the family sword.' Hell's Bells crashed a firm hand on the table. 'By God, I've forgiven you a great many things, but this would haunt us all beyond the grave. You cannot throw this away for a rebellious crush, boy! If you love her more than me, then go – go now and never come back. I hope you both die happy, because I certainly shan't.' Her eyes lit up as a thought struck her. 'And I won't be the first to depart this life cursing you, will I, Jasper? We both know that.'

Ellen waited for Spurs to retaliate, but it was as though he had been shot with a tranquilliser pellet – the sometimes fierce, sometimes playful, always dangerous big cat reduced to a subjugated, trapped victim with no fight left in him.

Sensing victory, Hell's Bells rubbed her fingers together and drew several restorative breaths. 'I want you to leave.' She glowered triumphantly at Ellen. 'Leave this house, leave my son and leave this village.'

Ellen looked at Spurs in a blind panic. His eyes were tortured, caged, and no longer told her his secrets. He had, she saw in horror, conceded defeat.

'I think you know why I am not being as civil as protocol might dictate,' Hell's Bells was saying, as she indicated the door. 'Alas, I have no time left for civility, pride or convention. My son is a wilful idiot, but I do love him and I have loved him a great deal longer than you have. You will cry for a short while, no doubt, but young hearts mend easily – especially those that are rather . . . *easily* won. But I'm afraid that your brief acquaintance with my son is at an end. Come along, now – I'll see you out.'

One by one, Ellen released Spurs' fingers. It was like pulling harpoons from her side. Each one ruptured another artery, dragging nerves and blood and fibre through her skin as she let him go.

'I *forbid* you two to meet again,' Hell's Bells was saying, quite cheerfully, 'I absolutely forbid it.'

'Go to hell,' Spurs muttered. 'She leaves Oddlode in a fortnight.' But his voice carried an echo of farewell.

'She leaves your life this very minute, Jasper. You will not see one another again before she leaves.'

Again, Ellen waited for Spurs to protest, but he nodded curtly. Without warning, her welling anger and resentment burst through in a great geyser of spit and passion.

'I hope you realise that by making your son marry for Mummy and money you are wrecking his life!' she screamed at Hell's Bells. 'You'll be taking his soul to the grave with you. That will be your legacy – not this bloody house, which Ely will grab for himself the moment you're dead and turn into a hotel or a convention centre.'

Having said nothing at the thought of her son's life being wrecked, Hell's Bells wailed at the prospect of her beloved manor suffering a similar fate, incensing Ellen more.

'No wonder you're called Hell's Bells! I bet they're ringing out a welcome for you down there already. And you,' she turned to Spurs, 'you're a—' She couldn't say it. She couldn't call him a coward. One look at his face told her that he was the opposite. He was the bravest man she had ever met.

'Stay, Ellen,' he entreated, his eyes alight. 'Stay with me. We'll find a way.'

But she was already backing away, knowing she would never be as brave as he was. 'I'll leave you to your duty. You leave me to my duty-free.' She turned and ran.

'Wait!' Spurs came in pursuit, but Ellen was too fast for him. Sprinting out of the house, she was through the yard and over the old footpath gate before he'd jumped from the terrace.

With the devil at her heels, Ellen ran straight past Goose Cottage and on to Goose End, crossing the bridge and heading up into the hills.

It was only when she reached Broken Back Wood that she could cry, but by then she was too breathless to sob: she simply drew in great dry gulps of hot air and looked back across the valley, a simmering, corn-ripening crucible in which she had burnt her fingers and broken her heart.

Isabel Belling rang through to Ely Gates without delay. 'Lunch is orf, I'm afraid, Elijah. We have a situation. I need your help.'

'A situation?'

'It's the *girl*. Such an inconvenience. I shall be ordering Spurs to help his feckless cousin at the Springlode yard to keep him out of harm's way. I have alerted my network and trust you will do the same, but I must warn you that this may require us to move on to Plan B.'

'Good God, is it that serious?'

'I've never seen anything like it in m' life.' She shook her head. 'They call it love, but I rather think it smacks more of mutual lunacy.'

Ely drew a sharp breath. 'In that case, we must alert the registrar and consider taking other measures.'

Hell's Bells gasped. 'You don't mean—'

'No, Isabel, I was thinking of something a little less bloodthirsty than breaking the sixth commandment. Leave it to me.'

16

Poppy was breathless with excitement as she made an early-morning call to Ellen: '. . . a quite *exceptional* offer. Of course, the Brakespears are terribly disappointed, but I can quite understand why your parents had no choice but to accept. Gazumping is a very broad term, these days, and this hardly even slips under the wire. Market forces dictate new rules all the time and . . .'

God, that woman loves her job, Ellen thought irritably, as she crammed the receiver under her ear and filled the kettle from the kitchen sink, watching Hunter Gardner feed his chickens.

Two sleepless nights were blurring her brain and she rubbed her temples and fought to keep pace, dragging her mind from the why-why-why to the here and now.

Her mother had already pre-empted Poppy's call with the news that a last-minute – and simply irresistible – offer had been made on Goose Cottage, blasting the Brakespears out of the water. After such months of static, it seemed everyone wanted Oddlode's prettiest cottage. Ellen's parents attributed this turnaround to their clever daughter, and claimed that she had always been 'very lucky'. And despite Ellen's protestations that it was unethical, Jennifer refused to feel guilty about the Brakespears. She and Theo had already eagerly accepted the new offer.

'. . . I am only sorry that it involves you vacating the property even earlier than anticipated,' Poppy went on. 'That is the only requirement we really must adhere to.'

'I'm flying a week on Saturday,' Ellen pointed out. 'That's not a problem.'

'Oh, joy!' Poppy piped.

Ellen was glad that Poppy found it such a cause for celebration. She would probably be the only person willing to wave her off, although the rest of the village would be there in spirit.

'Mr Gates will be thrilled,' Poppy announced cheerily.

Ellen felt like a sword-swallower with hiccups as she fought to talk round the steely lump in her throat. 'Mr Gates?'

'You must remember him – the man who made the silly offer early on?' Poppy confided chummily. 'Well, be prepared to fall off your seat. He's the purchaser! He *has* changed his tune, literally tripled his offer to secure the property at this late stage. He *really* wants it.'

And wants me gone, Ellen thought wretchedly, propping the phone beneath her chin and wrapping her arms around her shoulders as she slumped her head to her knees and fought a wave of nausea. Ely was even willing to pay a ridiculous trumped-up price for Goose Cottage to ensure that a greater des. res. was within his grasp – the manor house. He was ruthlessly determined that nothing would stand between him and his dream – not his daughter's happiness, not Spurs, and certainly not Ellen.

'His one stipulation,' Poppy went on, 'is the hasty completion date. His solicitor, Mr Hornton, has even been instructed not to bother with searches. The draft contract is already being biked to your parents' solicitors.'

Ellen rang off and went to fetch the horseshoe from the mantelpiece, looking at the single nail still lodged in a hole.

So Spurs and Godspell would have their wedding gift of a gingerbread cottage, after all, she realised.

She sank forlornly on to the window-seat in the dining room and pressed her cheek to the deep sill, looking across at the polished table and trying to visualise Godspell, resplendent in gingham oven gloves, settling a steaming hot-pot on a trivet while Spurs waited, knife and fork poised.

She laughed tearfully. It was ludicrous. The whole marriage was ludicrous, concocted by an ambitious social-climber and an impoverished landowner. That their children had agreed, in this day and age, was astonishing.

She had no idea what drove the strange, withdrawn Godspell, and why she would co-operate with her father's plans. But Spurs, whom she understood only too well, had an overwhelming debt of guilt and duty to fulfil. She knew that he loved her as recklessly and ill-advisedly as she loved him – something undeniable that had caught them unawares, hitting them at such velocity that they had crashed together in a tangle of heartstrings and volatile chemicals, too shocked to realise what was happening.

Ellen sobbed as she laughed. 'You bloody idiot. You complete, bloody idiot.' She was speaking for both of them.

She picked at the nail in the horse shoe, remembering Hell's Bells incanting the Constantine family motto. *To break one's promise is to break one's sword.*

Right now, she longed to pull the sword from her throat and run it through the entire population of Oddlode, with their kowtowing hierarchical hypocrisy and their total deference to a family that no longer existed. Most of all she wanted to run around the manor, cutting down the tapestries and the velvet curtains, slashing the macabre hunting oils, carving graffiti into the oak panelling and sending up sparks from the flagstones. She wanted to leap upon the dining-table, twirling her longsword and screaming, 'Monkey!', a small, incandescently angry Samurai warrior, declaring war on Hell and all her Bells.

Spurs had tried to warn her, despite his infatuation. He'd invited her to love him, but never to honour or obey because that, after all, was his job. He had told her from the start not to get involved with him. And she had returned fire by believing that it was far too soon after Richard, by claiming that her heart was frozen along with her desire.

And, as the ultimate irony, he had only agreed to marry Godspell because she had been on her disastrous date with Lloyd the estate agent in the same restaurant.

Ellen threw the horseshoe across the room and howled in fury.

'You're the one who believes in fairy tales.' She watched the shoe spinning on the flagstones. 'You make the wish.'

*   *   *

'He's helping Rory at the kiddies' riding school until you go,' Gladys told Ellen breathlessly in the post-office stores, feverish with the secrecy of it all. 'Fred the kennelman gives him a lift at dawn, and he's there all day until Stan Baker drives him back to Oddlode again. After that, they watch him like hawks in the big house. He's been told that if he's so much as seen walking past your cottage, he'll lose a finger for each step he takes closer.'

Ellen, who had sloped guiltily into the shop for her first packet of cigarettes in weeks, took a few bewildered moments to take in what was being said. She looked from Gladys to smiling Joel, who gave her a big wink. 'Spurs is working at the riding school?' She caught up dimly.

Gladys nodded. 'But I wouldn't try to get there if I was you – more chance of getting to the moon. I think it's ever so mean keeping you two apart like this. That's what I was just telling Mr Lubowski. I mean, you're both adults, aren't you?'

Ellen nodded, remembering Hell's Bells' insistence that her housekeeper had no idea Spurs was the one Godspell was to marry. 'We are.'

'Unfair to keep you apart, then.' Gladys tucked in her chin. 'I mean, telling the poor man he'd lose a finger coming near you. This ain't the Lebanon. You might be a bit tarty, but I think we should all be a bit more tolerant in this day and age. I've told Lady B that if she don't buck up her ideas, I'll be applying for a job at the Waitrose in Minster Bourton.'

'Thanks.' Ellen was touched by her support, if appalled that everybody seemed to know her business.

Sitting on Bevis's bench afterwards, she tipped her face to the tiny pinpricks of sun penetrating the horse-chestnut and wondered how many fingers she could live without if she were in Spurs' place. She stretched up her hand and looked at it, shocked to find it shaking.

The speed with which Glad Tidings had stalked her between manor and post-office stores disturbed Ellen, as did the heavy trade that the little shop encountered during their brief conversation. Every pensioner in Oddlode had decided to buy their local paper at the same time as Ellen went in to buy cigarettes. They had shuffled around her in a formidable group detachment, tuning in hearing-aids and peering over half-moons.

'What was that about?' Ellen asked Bevis, as her ice-cream melted on her knee, seeping into the fabric of her capri pants.

Above her the horse-chestnut whispered in the breeze, suggesting that love and thunderstorms were in the air. No caterpillars descended this time. Instead, Ellen watched the leaves move inside the canopy, her own personal comfort umbrella, reassuring her that this was her safe place.

'I don't want to be in a safe place,' she suddenly realised out loud. 'Safe is somewhere you lock things in. Bugger safe. Bevis, we have to *do* something!'

The leaves shook under a gust of breeze and Ellen ducked as something resembling confetti tumbled towards her. But then she saw that it wasn't a paper cascade – it was butterflies. Dozens of white butterflies flew from the horse chestnut and across the village green.

'"This is the self-preservation society!"' she sang as she ran back to Goose Cottage to fetch the jeep. '"*This is the self preser –*" oh, bugger.'

The Wycks barred her path at the gate. Like two of Pheely's weathered gargoyles propping up a row of goofy garden gnomes, Reg and Dot played sentry to a rabble of ape-shouldered youth, Saul at their centre. Ellen quailed, knowing that she couldn't talk her way out of this one.

'You bin gallivanting with Belling?' Dot demanded, fingering her handbag.

Ellen nodded, not trusting herself to speak.

'Ely bin interfering?' she persisted.

Amazed at the way news travelled around here, Ellen nodded again, noticing that Saul's blue eyes were shooting out of his face like gas flames.

'Go talk to the nutty potter,' Dot told her. 'Tell her you needs to know the truth.'

Ellen glanced over her shoulders anxiously. 'I'm sorry?'

'Talk to Ophelia Gently.' Saul translated for his grandmother. 'She knows why Ely's doing this.'

'They was good kids,' Dot lisped, through her missing teeth. 'Not like most round here. Belling ain't never bin as bad as they all makes out. The nutty potter knows the truth. You talks to her, girl.'

Ellen swallowed uncomfortably. 'Thanks. Would you mind my asking why you are telling me this?'

'Saul!' Dot summoned her grandson, making the entire Wyck contingent quail.

He scuffed the ground. 'Nan reckons as I owes you an apology,' he told Ellen, glancing at his diminutive grandmother. 'For the badger.'

Ellen stared at him in amazement. 'Accepted.'

He scratched his shoulders self-consciously beneath his T-shirt arms, revealing his muscled biceps and the unicorn tattoo. Ellen studied the bareback nymph for a moment, vaguely recognising the pale-faced temptress, although she couldn't place her.

'Ely made me do it.' He didn't look at her.

'Ely was behind the badger?' Ellen gasped.

'He din' kill it or nothing. He caught me with it and said he'd report me for baiting – then he said as how I could make up for you mucking Nan about. He said he wouldn't do nothing about it if I left it here for you.'

'Did he write the note?' Ellen wondered what Ely planned to leave her next – a wildebeest in her bed, perhaps, or a pony carcass in the bath?

He shook his head. 'I got someone else to do that.'

Ellen was too distracted and weary to care. 'Let's forget about it.'

'You're okay, you are,' he muttered, glancing at her shyly. 'We'll make it up to you.'

She looked at all the Wycks, wondering why they had changed their tune so suddenly.

'Talk to the nutty potter,' Saul repeated his grandmother's words.

Ellen caught Dot's eye. 'Okay. I'll talk to her again. Thanks.'

Pheely, rather embarrassingly, was in the loo when Ellen found her way out of the choked garden maze and into the Lodge cottage.

The sound-effects were not good. A tinny transistor belting out Radio Three failed to mask the noise of a loose bowel movement being evacuated at speed, followed by a long, mournful groan.

Ellen wavered, tempted to bolt back to Goose Cottage and continue walking the carpets bald as she had been all morning. But Hamlet had already lured Snorkel into the undergrowth for a game of rough-and-tumble, accompanied by great growls and shrill barks.

'Who's there?' Pheely demanded, through the bathroom door. 'Is that you, Dilly?'

Ellen chewed her lip and looked anxiously around. Godspell's bust had been moved inside to shelter it from the spits of rain that were dancing out of the tall pines. It was even more mesmerising now that Pheely had started to add the final touches before glazing. The limpid eyes watched her suspiciously, the narrow mouth was pursed with disapproval and the spiky hair exploded from the frowning forehead and crown, as wild and black as a thick cloud of crows rising from a crop field. But what Pheely had really captured in that severe, passive little face was the sadness. There was something heartbreaking about it, an unspoken energy that seemed to crack the many angles, gouges and swirling marks in the clay. Compared to the gnarled gnomes and flowery fairies, Pheely had created a masterpiece. It was incredibly powerful.

Dragging her eyes away, Ellen noticed that Pheely had been working on another sculpture on a second stand, this one covered with wet muslin and a bin-liner. She went to take a peek underneath.

'Don't look at it!' howled a frail voice behind her.

Pheely had emerged from the bathroom, looking grey, her bloodshot eyes slitted. 'My work is private,' she enunciated. 'You have no right to snoop. Have you come to apologise?' She reached for her cigarettes. 'Make it snappy if you have – I'm not feeling too good.'

She and Ellen squared up to each other, the recent shift from new friendship to enmity awkward and unyielding.

Ellen wanted to wade in with accusations and demands, but instead watched her pale face worriedly, wondering how long she had been ill. 'Where's Dilly?'

Pheely misinterpreted the question. 'If you came to see her,' she muttered, reluctant to show how disappointed she was to come second best, 'she's staying with a friend in Kent for an eighteenth birthday party. She'll be back at the end of the week. I'll tell her you popped by.'

'I came to see you.'

Pheely lifted her chin. 'Yes?'

'You were right. Spurs has agreed to marry Godspell.'

'Of course I was right,' Pheely snapped impatiently, glaring at Godspell's bust.

'I think you know why.'

For a moment the huge eyes were unshuttered and frightened. Then they blinked and reappeared cast in cucumber cool. 'They must be in love.'

'No! It's farcical,' Ellen raged. 'They don't love each other – they barely know each other. Hell's Bells and Ely are blackmailing their own children.'

'They could both walk away if they wanted to.' Pheely touched her belly as it let out a great roar of complaint.

'No, they can't. Their hands are tied. Their hands in marriage are tied.' She laughed hollowly. 'They're being held behind their backs while they're marched up the aisle.'

'Spurs will leave long before it happens. He ran away last time.'

'Not this time. He's got this crazy guilt thing going on, atoning

for the past. And this time his mother is d—' Ellen remembered
that she had been sworn to secrecy and stopped herself. She stared
at the capsized-hull ceiling. 'His mother is putting him under a
mind-blowing amount of pressure,' she burbled feebly. 'I think
he's close to cracking up.'

'He's hardly got a reputation for stability. What exactly do you
expect me to be able to do about it? Suggest a good therapist?'

Ellen felt the tears bubbling. 'I just need you to forgive me for
being a lousy friend,' she whispered hoarsely. 'I can't leave this
bloody place having screwed up both love *and* friendship.'

Pheely cleared her throat archly. '*I* was being a very good
friend when I told you not to go near him, and now look what's
happened.'

'I know. I let you down, I let Dilly down—'

'You've let yourself down,' came the sanctimonious interruption.

'No!' Ellen protested hotly, no longer caring if the tears spilled
– she couldn't hope to control them these days. 'I don't regret
the fact that I love him. Loving him has made me feel alive
again. I've found a part of me that I thought I'd lost and it's
the best thing that has ever happened to me. It might have cost
me my pride, my heart, my savings and my bloody self-control
but, Christ, I love him. And don't you *dare* tell me that what we
feel for each other isn't love. I don't care if it's days, hours or
only minutes. Thirteen years with Richard never left me wanting
to die for him.'

'You want to die for Spurs?'

'I was dying of suffocation with Richard. Now I'm just dying
of love.'

Pheely's own eyes filled with tears, but she set her chin determinedly and looked away. 'I don't think I can help you, Ellen.'

Ellen nodded silently.

'I don't know what you're going through, you see,' Pheely
admitted suddenly, in a small voice. 'I thought I had a working
knowledge of love until I saw you and Spurs. How can I help you?
I don't know the first thing about love. Just motherhood.' She let

out a stifled sob and immediately batted out a don't-go-there hand as she battled to regroup her emotions.

Ellen chewed back the questions, knowing that to ask any of them would excite the full Pheely armoury of defensive fire. Instead, she settled for the simplest and most truthful of facts. 'You could be my friend again.'

'Lord, no,' Pheely muttered, in a choked voice, 'you'd only mope about being miserable.'

Ellen snorted with unexpected laughter.

Pheely's huge sad eyes watched her speculatively as they regarded one another with closely guarded affection. 'Thank you.' She mustered a pale smile.

'For what?'

'For not asking.'

'Not asking what?'

'Stay and have a drink,' she offered, still very much on edge, 'and I might just tell you.'

'Is everything all right?' Ellen asked cautiously, looking at her deathly pale face.

Pheely stubbed out her cigarette and immediately lit another *en route* to the fridge. 'Fine – I've just been working rather hard, and Dilly's been ridiculously theatrical about everything. Then I ate some old mackerel pâté that gave me a terribly upset stomach and the stress rather got to me. I'll be fine. Nothing compared to your heartbreak. Cheap White?' She held up a bottle.

It was far too early in the day for Ellen, and she doubted Pheely was wise to booze on food poisoning, but she was too grateful for the reprieve to refuse.

They sat on the floor by the open terrace doors, looking out at the gathering rainclouds above the wooded garden. Ellen told Pheely about her confrontation with Hell's Bells, and Spurs' defeated concession. To her surprise, Pheely's face lit up as she listened. 'This might sound foolish, but I envy you,' she said. 'Knowing what it's really like to be madly in love with someone who's madly in love with you is a very rare experience. It's what we all dream about, isn't it?'

Ellen looked at her in bewilderment. 'It doesn't feel that great right now, I can assure you.'

'But you don't really think he'll go through with it?'

She didn't hesitate. 'He'll see it through. He has to.'

'Really?'

'He sees it as the ultimate sacrifice to make amends.'

Pheely whistled, pressing the cool wineglass to her pallid cheek. 'He hasn't found religion, has he?'

Ellen shook her head. 'I'm sure his father-in-law will be working on that.'

'Oh, yes, Ely the social-climber will not be satisfied until he makes it to heaven,' Pheely said bitterly. 'He once told me that religious devotion was three parts devil to one part emotion.' Her eyes flashed.

Ellen watched her curiously. 'You know him quite well, then?'

'No better than anyone in this village. I can take him or leave him. In fact, I find him rather comical.'

And yet when Ellen told her about Ely gazumping the Brakespears and buying Goose Cottage for an inflated price, Pheely exploded. 'The bastard! How *dare* he?' she ground her teeth. 'Ely is so damned conniving. You might think Hell's Bells has her son in manacles, but she's nothing on Pearly Gates. The pig. He told me he had hardly a penny spare, that the auction had almost wiped him out.'

'Does he owe you money, then?'

'And the rest! That bloody *rat* is refusing to put Dilly through university. I can't possibly afford to, and I simply can't bring myself to tell her that the pot is empty. She's so looking forward to going.'

Ellen looked into the unsipped amber depths of her wineglass and felt her mind swimming up to the surface of self-obsession, hauling itself on to the bank and shaking itself dry.

'Ely Gates is Dilly's father, isn't he?' She tried not to laugh.

Pheely sucked in her lips and looked at her for a long time. 'He seduced me when I was sixteen – and it's not the first time. Don't believe for a moment that he is the bastion of morality around here,' she snarled. 'He's kept mistresses for years. Just ask yourself how Pru Hornton survives in that gallery without selling a thing. Ely keeps her. And he kept me. To my shame, he still keeps me.'

In sobs and gulps and shudders of embarrassment, the story was revealed. Pheely told of her unexpected pregnancy after a tipsy teenage night with Ely, not long after his marriage to wealthy but dull Felicity. The decision to keep the baby had infuriated him, and his subsequent financial input, sternly regulated and carefully overseen, had been under the strict proviso that their secret was never revealed.

'Poor darling Dilly was so devastated when she found out who her father was – he completely rejects her on a personal level, and still has precious little to do with her. He might keep a close eye on her running costs, but he can't bring himself to admit how wonderful she is. I'm such a pathetic woman, relying on his pitiful handouts.' She sobbed harder. 'Dilly is determined that we can get away from him, that we can somehow turn this place round and escape him. But how can we possibly do that, when he denies her the education she deserves? Sinking every damned penny he has into this wretched wedding, the cottage his mother loved and his dream of one day owning the manor.'

She got up and paced around the cluttered room. 'For a man over-familiar with scripture, Ely covets everything from Hunter's bloody chickens to Giles's Aston. I always rather adored his ambitious, envious streak until my daughter started to suffer as a consequence.'

She buried her face in her hands, long black curls catching in her rings. 'Oh, God – admit it, Ophelia, you still adore him. I think if he could only bring himself to love Dilly as I do, I would lay down my life for him. There! We're both wretched bloody women in love.' Opening her arms, she swept forward and captured Ellen in a tight hug. 'Oh, God, I wish Ely and I loved one another as you and Spurs do,' she bawled.

'Are you still lovers?'

Pheely snuffled tearfully into her shoulder. 'Not for years. He went off me. I was *so* insulted.'

They hugged tightly, and Pheely gradually pulled herself together, with a series of heartfelt sniffs, pressing her forehead to Ellen's collarbone. 'I shouldn't have told you all this. You'll probably try to use it to get Ely to put a stop to the wedding now, won't you? By threatening to reveal his love-child to the village unless he puts the brakes on?'

'Do you want me to?' Ellen asked, sage enough to know that a part of Pheely secretly longed for her to do just that.

But Pheely wiped her nose on the back of her hands, leaning back to look Ellen in the face and shaking her head like a small child faced with a scary fairground ride. 'I stand to lose everything if you do. We hardly make ends meet as it is. Without Ely's love-child maintenance, we'd have to sell up.'

'It might not come to that.'

'I can't risk it.'

'So why tell me?'

'Because you're a friend – a true friend.' Pheely stroked Ellen's cheek. 'I knew that the moment we met, just as I guessed that you'd fall for Spurs no matter what I said. He was right, you know – you were dying inside when you met him, I saw that. You so needed to know that your wings still work. And they do. That's what he wanted for you. You have permission to fly away, can't you see that? You can escape.'

'Not without Spurs.'

'He and I grew up here. We've been branded. I have no doubt that he loves you – it's eating him away – but it won't stop him going ahead for the sake of the family.'

'Ely might stop it if we threatened him?' Ellen suggested desperately.

'He'd make us suffer all the more, believe me. Spurs would be lucky to walk away from it alive.'

Ellen felt a dozen hypodermics inject her veins with iced fright. 'What are you talking about?'

Pheely avoided her eye. 'Leave it with me, darling,' she offered vaguely. 'I have an idea – in fact, I've been working on it for a while now. I can't promise anything, but it's worth a go. Are you and Spurs meeting later?'

'He's been exiled,' Ellen said angrily. 'He's working at Rory's yard all this week, mobile confiscated. Hell's Bells has rallied all Gladys's spies and the warning klaxon sounds the moment I leave the village so that she can put obstacles in my way until he's safely removed.'

'You *are* kidding?'

'No. When I tried to drive there this lunchtime, I found a herd of sheep in the road. Fifty yards further on, a horsebox had its ramp down in the middle of the lane for no reason. By the time I got to Springlode, the yard was deserted except for Sharrie, who said that Rory and his cousin had both been hustled into the back of a Land Rover five minutes earlier. So I came here.'

'Good old Hell's Bells,' Pheely gurgled, sounding more her old self. 'I never knew she had it in her.'

'Oh, she's thought of everything. I can't get beyond the manor gates, the shortcut via the old footpath is suddenly blocked with barbed wire and electric stock fencing.'

'Amazing to think that two people can be kept apart in a small village, but if anybody can do it Isabel and Ely can.'

'I can't bear not seeing him.'

'You'll find each other,' Pheely assured her. 'You're like two explorers with no sense of direction crashing around the same jungle. You might never find your way out, but I can guarantee you'll cross paths again and again.'

17

When Ellen made her way woozily back to Goose Cottage, she hesitated beneath the shadow of the lime tree and looked back along the bridleway, wondering whether to turn heel and run to Upper Springlode.

She had drunk far too much wine, she realised, as she clutched her temples and gathered herself together. She was even starting to see things. Parading past on tippy-toes, a very fat and self-satisfied-looking black and white cat turned to wink at her, a dead rat in its mouth.

'Oh, Fins!' Ellen closed her eyes. When Snorkel let out a bark of recognition she snapped them open again. 'Fins!'

The conceited piebald bottom swaggered through the gates opposite her and straight into Goose Cottage.

Ellen gave chase. But when she raced into the kitchen, a tall figure turned towards her, framed by the sunlight pouring through the windows.

Ellen let out a yelp of fright.

It was the matchmaker himself, Ely Gates, his clipped beard bristling with hostility.

'What are you doing here?' she demanded.

'I think you'll find that I own it.' He eyed her with dis-taste.

'Not yet. You can't just walk in here without permission.' Ellen felt her tantrum touch-paper go up as though struck by lightning. Her blood started to boil, her ears to thrum with accelerating heartbeats, her chest to creak with deep, unexhaled breaths. Oh, God, she was going to explode *any* –

'Indeed.' Ely was still bristling. 'And I telephoned your parents this morning and confirmed that I would be inspecting the property.'

'Well, it's not convenient.' – *second* –

'I'm afraid that you have no choice in the matter.'

—*now!*

'You PIG! You total and utter pig! Get out!'

Caught unawares, Ely took a horrified step back, his eyes boggling as though she had just drawn a hasty pentagon around herself, lit a few black candles and started trying to summon Lucifer.

'There is no reason to be—'

'Uncivil?' she raged. 'Rude? Oh, I think there is. I think that right now I would be quite justified in ripping up the fucking floorboards and burying a whole set of dead badgers beneath them, along with a hundredweight of rotting kippers and a freshly bludgeoned property owner.'

'Dear child, you may have grown attached to this little cottage during your brief stay here, but I'm afraid that—'

'It's not the cottage I'm attached to!' she stormed, Snorkel barking in furious support behind her. 'It's Spurs. How could you blackmail him – and your own daughter? It's inhuman.'

'They are a young couple very much in love.'

'Bollocks! At least Lady Belling has the honesty to admit that the marriage is nothing more than a glorified property deal. The only love story going on here is between you and the manor.'

He barked a great wolf's laugh and turned away to inspect the doorway through to the bootroom. 'I believe my little girl will be very happy here.'

'How can you possibly imagine that the marriage will last more than a week?'

'I think you'll find that marriages in this village last a great deal longer than the sort of sordid trysts that you are accustomed to.'

'I got the impression that you were the one more familiar with sordid trysts,' she spat.

He took a long time to answer, the blue eyes searing into hers and, just for a moment, Ellen glimpsed the towering sexual ego.

But he wasn't about to reveal his true colours and, apart from a streak of red on both cheeks, he remained stony-faced. 'I have no idea what you are talking about.'

Ellen narrowed her eyes. 'Have you no interest in your daughter's feelings?'

'I care for her future and for her welfare.'

She continued staring at him fiercely, refusing to back down. 'You're twisted. Seriously twisted. You think you can play God to this village, manipulating people with your wealth and influence – even your own family.'

'Young lady, I—'

But Ellen had the bit between her teeth, forty-eight hours of sleepless anxiety and helplessness distilling into blind rage. 'Supposing they *do* marry – what then? Do you expect him to fuck her? Do you?' she yelled, over his outraged protests. 'Are they supposed to have children and somehow bring up the poor wretches happily? Spurs might talk about duty and honour and atoning for the past while his mother's alive, but the moment she's gone, he'll self-destruct. You must know he'll turn in on himself, turn on Godspell and the village and anything he can damage. You might as well hold a gun to his head.'

There was a flicker of excitement in Ely's cool blue eyes that made Ellen gasp. 'Christ, that's what you're *hoping*, isn't it? You *want* him to self-destruct, leaving your daughter with the Belling legacy!'

'He will serve his purpose.'

Ellen was hardly able to believe his calm, calculated bloodlessness. Reining in her fury, she tried to match his tone, but her voice caught with emotion. 'I guess it's rather fitting that your daughter already dresses like a widow, then, isn't it?'

Ely rubbed his white beard and drew in his hollow cheeks. Just for a split second a look of such hatred passed between them that it almost knocked Ellen back off her feet.

'You think that you're an astute judge of character, don't you, young lady?'

'I think you're a charlatan, yes.'

'And do you think you would know a murderer if you met him?'

Suddenly Ellen was acutely aware of the knives poking from their block within his reach. She watched his face, her skin crawling with icy fingers of trepidation. 'Why?'

The spots of colour on Ely's cheeks darkened and he clenched his bony hands into tight fists. 'Spurs didn't leave Oddlode a decade ago simply because he had driven the villagers to despair with his wretched hooliganism.' His level gaze didn't leave hers. 'Spurs left because he couldn't live with the guilt of a young boy's death.'

Ellen started to shake her head, but he held up a finger. 'Please don't call me a charlatan. I am a religious man, Miss Jamieson, and I believe in forgiveness. I also believe in divine justice. God will decide what fate befalls young Belling. I am simply his humble servant.'

Ellen turned and fled, Snorkel at her heels.

The hood of Ellen's sweatshirt was whipped right across her face by the wind as she climbed towards Broken Back Wood, stumbling blindly over ruts and rabbit-holes, wrapping her arms around her to keep out the chill. The wind was chasing away all the warmth of the sun, and when the scudding clouds covered it, it felt like a winter's day.

Ahead of her, Snorkel's ears blew inside out as she scooted along.

They passed the strange mound that had broken Ellen's fall when she had flown her kite down the hill – a curious man-made grassy knoll that could have been anything from a Bronze Age burial mound to modern landfill. She didn't want to remember that day, the day she had let Richard go, acknowledging the anger, regret and finality of it all. Richard had been safe. Spurs was pure danger.

Now her reckless freefall seemed like a small step in the dark compared to the Armageddon taking place all around her. She kicked the mound and screamed at it. Her dreams seemed to be buried in there, far from her reach.

It was a long, long walk. She abandoned running and staggered on as best she could, hardly noticing when the rain started to lash down.

Rory was in the tackroom soaping a hanging straggle of bridles when she finally burst in, her lungs burning. 'Where's Spurs?'

He looked up in shock, blond locks tangled in his eyelashes. 'He set off about an hour ago – along the bridleway. I told him not to, but he said he had to see you.'

'I came that way. I'd have seen him.' Ellen noticed a vodka bottle propped beside him.

'Shit!' He dropped his sponge and jumped up. 'I told him Hercules had no brakes.'

'Oh, God, is Hercules a horse?'

'No.' Rory dashed for the door. 'It's Sharrie's mountain bike.'

They searched the bridleway, looking in ditches and behind walls. The ground was too hard for tyre-tracks, and there was no obvious sign that Spurs had passed along it. As they looked, Rory filled Ellen in on the extraordinary curfew under which his cousin was living.

'He's moved into the manor – his parents won't let him stay in the flat above the kennels in case he tries to creep off to see you. They have him under close arrest, poor sod.' He offered her a swig from his hip flask

Ellen refused. 'But he can come and go when he's with you at the yard?'

'Not likely.' He took a gulp, then screwed the lid back on. 'She's a canny old bat, Bell – always popping by to check on him, sending all her cronies to me for lessons, telling her chums in the village to keep an eye out for him. Every time we hack past the Old Vicarage, Marjory Whittaker logs it in a notepad, then makes a call to HQ.'

'HQ?'

'The manor.' Rory pocketed the flask. 'Aunt Bell's done every-thing short of having him electronically tagged. The only reason

he got away today was because he borrowed Sharrie's old mack-
intosh and bush hat, along with about ten of my sweaters to make
him look fat. He was sweating like a pig.'

Ellen, who couldn't stop shaking, wished she had had a few
jumpers when she'd stumbled along the path.

'I must say, you took your time coming up here.' Rory followed
her, fuelled by the vodka. 'Spurs has been falling apart all week.'

'I did try,' Ellen explained, 'but there was a surprising amount
of agricultural traffic blocking my way.' She glanced back at him.
'And forgive me for not persisting, but last time we spoke he gave
me the distinct impression that he's marrying Godspell Gates.'

'Yeah, and you have to help him out,' Rory pointed out,
making it sound as simple as persuading him not to wear an
unflattering hat.

'He chose the devil over the deep blue sea,' she muttered.

'You can work something out.' He grabbed her arm. 'If you
don't help him through this, I think he'll crash and burn big-
time.'

'I am *not* helping him.' Ellen glared at him. His silver eyes were
so like Spurs' that she felt her arteries rattle under the pressure
of pumping blood. 'I can't help him. If he truly loved me, he
wouldn't do this.'

Rory pulled back. 'You have no idea, do you? Of course he
loves you. He fucking adores you. He talks about nothing else –
it's driving me nuts.'

'So why side with his mother?'

He reached for his hip flask again without answering.

And then Ellen remembered Hell's Bells telling Spurs that hers
would not be the first unhappy death he had caused. She grabbed
the flask from Rory and downed a long, dribbling draught.

'Tell me about the boy who died. The one Spurs is supposed
to have killed.'

'How the—' Rory backed away.

'Tell me, Rory.'

He backed further away. 'You mustn't talk about that. No one
talks about that.'

So Spurs had kept his darkest secret from her all along. Murderer – that's what Ely had called him. Murderer. She watched the word flash up behind her closed eyes, garish red-top headlines, graffiti on walls, accusations on lips. She turned her face to the wind and tried to wash the love from her veins, scour the blind forgiveness from her heart, bleach the besotted trust from her head. Murderer. You can't love a murderer.

But her mind chanted its hypnotic mantra. I can forgive him anything. Anything. Anything. I love him. I love him. I love him.

When she opened her eyes again, Rory had gone. She spun round, disorientated, but he had disappeared – doing a bunk for fear of being interrogated, she thought. She still held his flask in her hand – a battered silver one bearing the Constantine crest. Ellen drained its contents and tried not to gag as the vodka burned her throat. Then she almost jumped out of her skin as she heard a strangled howl just beyond the thick bramble hedge. Tripping over Snorkel, who was cowering at her feet, Ellen ran to the open gateway ahead of her and found Rory perching on a stile.

'What is it?' she gasped, almost too terrified to look.

But when he pointed into the valley, he was smiling widely. 'Now tell me he doesn't love you, you stupid cow.'

Ellen climbed on to the stile beside him. The rain was lashing the far ridge of the valley now, and a circle of blue sky had opened up above Oddlode, letting out great rays of sunlight. Ely Gates's halo, she thought bitterly, as she strained her eyes for signs of movement lower down the path.

And then she saw what Rory was pointing at. In the huge cornfield beyond Devil's Marsh, an intricate series of crop circles had been carved, forming words in the ripening wheat. I LOVE YOU. FORGIVE ME.

Rory patted her shoulder, jumping from the stile. 'And I thought I was having a hard time getting Dilly on a second date.' He loped away.

Ellen clasped a hand to her mouth, laughing and sobbing.

'I love him. I can forgive him anything,' she said, scrambled off the stile and ran as fast as she could.

She raced along the bridleway, her lactic-acid-filled legs cramping as she sprinted towards the cornfield. Breathless and almost demented with excitement, she danced around the words, flying between avenues of wheat as she ran from 'I', through 'LOVE', around 'YOU', up 'FORGIVE' and down 'ME'. Standing in the final leg of the E, she spun round and called Spurs' name.

But he didn't answer.

Ellen paced around 'ME', getting her breath back and running her hands though her hair. The sun, blasting between bustling clouds, lit up the wet crop like a sheet of pale gold.

After ten minutes, she walked back through the hollow words and hurried along the path towards home, her tired body kept going by a faint hope that he would be waiting for her there.

But then, as she passed the River Folly, she heard a flint strike.

Camouflaged by nettles, goosegrass and brambles, he was sitting between two pillars, his face as white as the clouds circling overhead.

Ellen went straight into his arms, not caring that bramble barbs ripped at her legs and nettles burned her ankles.

The moment their lips touched, it was a silent pact. Spurs clutched Ellen as though he would never let go and she clung to him in return. They were fused together like molten solder. They kissed on and on, unable to stop, think, pause for breath, words or laughter.

At last, starved of oxygen, they pulled apart.

'I have to do it.' He took her hands in his. 'But it doesn't change anything. I want you to stay. You *have* to stay. I can't live without you.'

'Come away with me. We can get away from here.'

He pressed his forehead into the crook of her neck. 'You don't understand. I must do this. It's the only way to make things right again.'

'There's nothing right about what you're doing, Spurs. It's all wrong.'

'Ely is prepared to forgive me.'

'No, he isn't.' She pulled his head up, forcing him to look at her. 'He says you're a murderer. Don't you see that he can never forgive you?'

His head jerked back as though she'd applied a cattle-prod to his temples and he stumbled away, crashing into the brambles.

'You know,' he breathed, staring up at the sky. 'You fucking know.'

Ellen hugged herself tightly. 'I don't know anything about it.'

'You—' He stopped, brows furrowed. 'What?'

'I'd trust you with my life,' she sobbed. 'I love you too much to care what you've done in the past. It doesn't matter. *I* trust you with my life.'

'Even though Ely told you I'm a murderer?'

She nodded. 'I get to choose where I put my belief, Spurs. And it's not in God, duty, justice or village scandal. It's in this great pumping lump in my chest. That's what tells me never to doubt you, and I'll believe that until it stops beating.'

He stared at her, the silver eyes so wide that they seemed to take up most of his face. 'But Ely was telling you the truth.'

She didn't move, not even daring to breathe.

'I killed his nephew,' he whispered. 'I was the reason Bevis never made it to his eighteenth birthday.'

Ellen's vision tunnelled and twisted as she leant against a column for support. She could hear herself speaking before she even realised what she was saying. 'Bevis Aspinall?'

'Ely must have told you.' He looked up sharply.

'I sit on the bench that's dedicated to him. I talk to him sometimes. We were born on the same day.' She trapped the palm of her hand against her forehead trying to force her thoughts to settle. 'Christ. Oh, Christ.'

Spurs crashed back through the undergrowth leaped straight over the ledge that Ellen was sitting on and went into the folly.

His voice was distorted by the strange acoustics, words tumbling out and rattling around the domed ceiling. 'Bevis was my best friend in the village – we'd known each other since we were toddlers. His mother is Ely's sister Grace, who looked like Greta Garbo. He was something else – Ely worshipped him, and so did I. He was the golden boy – funny, clever, good-looking, a bit soppy and shy sometimes, but the girls always fell for him. He kept me sane – like you do.' He looked at her over his shoulder. 'I gave him hell, but I'd have cut my heart out for him.

'He died during the Devil's Marsh race,' he told her, his voice echoing in the stony chamber as he paced from wall to wall, caged by his guilt. 'His horse stumbled on the riverbank and he fell in. It was very high that year, like this – there had been storms all summer. I went after him. I thought he was drowning – pulled him out, tried to revive him. But what I did killed him. I didn't realise he'd broken his neck. A splinter of vertebra had entered his spinal cord. By dragging him on to the bank so quickly, I caused it to lodge right in and kill him. I killed him.'

'But it was an accident!' Ellen scrambled round to face him. 'You were trying to save him.'

'Ely called me a murderer and the village believed him.' He looked away. 'There was an inquest, of course. Accidental death, although nobody cared to accept it. They all blamed me and they were right. That day, I'd wished him dead in front of everybody.' He clamped his wrists to his head as he remembered. 'I wished him dead – and then he fucking died on me. He went ahead and died, the idiot.' He slumped against a wall in the shadows, engulfed in barbed brambles.

'That summer, we'd argued for the first time.' He was speaking in little more than a whisper now. 'He fell for the only girl who couldn't care less about him. She was from another planet, but he couldn't see that. He was besotted. He was such a romantic fool that he would have slain a dragon for the tiniest little bit of her, but of course he just made a fool of himself. I even set them up, knowing she wasn't interested – I thought I was helping, but he accused me of ruining everything. So did she.'

Ellen held her breath, suddenly knowing who he was talking about.

'I guess I loved her too.' He stared at his hands. 'And I thought

I was being so noble – offering to share her like a bloody chocolate bar. Shows how much I knew about women then.' He laughed bitterly. 'Bevis knew a hell of a lot more and he couldn't forgive me for hurting her. It was a huge falling-out. We were barely speaking by the day of the race. And then I said the dumbest thing of my entire life. I stood up in my stirrups at the start and wished him dead. But I still loved the fucking idiot. He should have known that. Instead he went ahead and granted my wish.

'After he died I was sent to Coventry. I got hate letters and was beaten up. Even my parents thought I was to blame for his death.'

'Was that why you caused so much chaos around here?'

He looked up from the shadows. 'I was causing chaos before then, but I upped the ante. I just didn't care any more. I could hold my hand over a flame and not feel the pain. I left before I was tempted to hold anybody else's hands over it.'

'And that's when you started forging stuff?'

He moved one cheek around with his tongue. 'Pretty pathetic, huh?'

'Yes.'

He snorted, pulling a flower from a bramble and shedding its petals. 'You really share Bevis's birthday? That figures.' The petals scattered on the floor. 'Christ! If Ely has summoned the forces of good and evil to try me for murder, he's done a damn fine job, I'll give him that. He couldn't have found somebody that I'd love more.'

'This isn't a medieval morality play,' she gasped. 'This is life.'

'Is it?' He looked up, haunted by ghosts. 'In that case, I'll lay mine down for you. All you have to do is wait for me to make sense of it. And I can only do that by going through with this. I can't break my word.'

'Do you really think marrying Ely's daughter will make up for Bevis's death?'

'Of course not.' He laughed bitterly. 'That's the whole point. Marrying the princess and uniting the kingdoms of Oddlode is just the first of my tasks. Ely has issued a far more difficult challenge and he's banking on the fact that I won't succeed.'

'What are you talking about?'

'I ride in the Devil's Marsh race, remember? And by all accounts Ely's paid an army of locals to try to ride me into the river. Most of the field aren't racing for the cup at all – a grand is nothing compared to the pay-off they'll get if I'm despatched.'

She clasped her spinning head. 'Are you saying he wants to kill you?'

'Conveniently crippled would be better. It's in his interests to have the marriage last longer than half an hour, after all. Godspell will doubtless exercise rights over the estate if it's left heirless so soon after we marry, but it would be better to wait until the ink's dry on our paper anniversary. I'm sure Ely's taken *very* good advice from Giles.'

Ellen stared at him, not understanding, her heart racing so fast that she had to clutch a lichen-crusted pillar to stop herself passing out.

'There's been a change of plan,' he spelled it out flatly. 'Ely's not just announcing Godspell and my engagement at his party. We're getting married.'

'No!'

'Ding-dong. A bit of a rush job, I gather, but the registrar was *very* accommodating – the vicar was having none of it, alas, although he might be swayed for the funeral. He hasn't opened the Constantine crypt in ages.' His cynicism was blistering now, although whether he was referring to his mother's death or his own was uncertain.

Ellen's hand flew to her mouth.

'It's a huge secret, naturally – breathe a word to anyone and Ely will have us both shot,' he warned. 'And that would be very unfortunate – far too hasty and painless a death for me as far as he's concerned. He has a more melodramatic dispatch in mind.'

She stared at him in disbelief.

'Godspell and I will trot obediently up the aisle shortly before the start of the big race,' he explained. 'And then, if Ely has anything to do with it, I gallop obligingly into the river and break my neck "showing off" for my new wife. That would be a nice touch.'

'Oh, God, why did you agree to ride?'

He seemed to find this hugely funny. 'Quite frankly, it didn't seem to matter whether I lived or died at the time.'

'And now?'

'Rory's found me a bloody good horse, but he'll have to sprout wings to get me out of this one.'

'You can't go through with it!'

'Oh, I can.' He smiled suddenly, and moved towards her. 'Don't you see that it's the one part of the whole Godforsaken day I'm looking forward to? I won't be riding for my wife, or my mother, or even poor, wretched Bevis.' He cupped her face in his hands. 'I'll be riding for you.'

'But I won't be there, Spurs.'

'Not even going to risk an each-way bet on me, then?' he looked over her shoulder at the lowering sun. 'I must go.'

'No!' She grabbed hold of him as he jumped out of the folly. 'You can't tell me all this and then just walk aw—'

He shut her up with a kiss that stole away her furious protests and tears, panic and confusion, their tongues coiling together with desperate, silent complicity.

When they resurfaced he took her hand and played with the signet ring, which she was still wearing. 'Will you meet me here at the same time tomorrow?'

She nodded.

'It's Ascot week,' he said. 'Mother's leaving her spy network on full alert, but I think I can fool them for a couple of hours. Bring the horseshoe.' He pulled away and picked up a pile of discarded sweaters from beside a tree stump, and started to pull them out his head.

'Why?'

'You still have wishes left for me to grant.'

'Just one.' She couldn't bear the thought of them being separated again.

'Two,' he insisted, from the depths of a tatty polo-neck. 'Your second wish didn't count.'

'None of them count any more because you can't grant the one thing I wish for.'

His face popped out, hair on end, silver eyes stormy. 'Then you can at least wish me luck.'

Crashing through the undergrowth once more, he grabbed the ancient bicycle that was propped up against the folly and pedalled away.

Ellen and Spurs met at the River Folly each evening in the build-up to Ely's garden party and the surprise wedding. He would appear dressed in a bizarre assortment of Sharrie's clothes, rattling down the hill at breakneck speed. Despite the awfulness of their situation, he seemed to take pleasure in his ludicrous costumes and disguises. And they made Ellen laugh. No man but Spurs could look sexy in bright pink fluffy knitwear and bobble-hats. She couldn't wait to rip them off.

They bathed in the river under the canopy of weeping willow. They made love and talked. He stemmed her tears with his fingers and told her he would die for her.

'I don't want you to die,' she would wail.

'And I have no intention of croaking just yet.' He held her closer. 'But I want you to know that I might vow to be with Godspell till death us do part, but I will love you for eternity.'

'Come away with me,' she tried again.

'I won't run away this time.'

'And I can't stay.'

They lay in the long grass far from the path, listening to dog-walkers idling past, ponies' soft hooffalls on the dried mud as they enjoyed evening hacks, and the occasional clutch of ramblers yomping along a well-planned hiking route. None were aware of the lovers so close by, the evening sun on their naked skin. Nor did the light aircraft and gliders soaring far overhead spot two entwined bodies as gold as their sedge-grass bed far below. Only the birds kept watch, along with Snorkel, who curled up on their clothes and kept her mad blue eyes trained for anyone or anything that might stray too close.

On the night before the garden party, Spurs forfeited Sharrie's bicycle and rode the horse Rory had lent him down to their meeting place.

'This is White Lies.' He introduced her to the huge grey thoroughbred.

Ellen put a hand on his hard white neck and willed him to look after his rider the next day.

'Will you be here to watch the race?' Spurs asked.

She didn't answer, just pulled the signet ring from her finger and held it out for him to take back.

'Keep it.' He looked away.

'I'm lousy at goodbyes.'

'I have something else for you.' He reached into his pocket.

It was the horseshoe nail she had given him the day she'd asked him to take Dilly out. 'I still owe you this.'

Ellen stared at White Lies' stamping feet, filled with so many wishes. 'You know I'll never come back once I leave.'

'I know. But I will find you. One day I promise I will find you.'

'Or you'll break your sword?' She fought not to break down as she looked at the nail, then reached into her own pocket, pulling the horseshoe from it along with a crumpled envelope.

'Here.' She thrust the envelope at him with shaking hands, then tried to wrench the final nail from its hole.

'What's this?' He pulled out the airline ticket.

'It's in your name.'

He pressed it to his forehead, his eyes clenched shut. 'You know I can't do it.'

Ellen scrabbled at the stubborn nail, ripping her fingernails and grazing her skin as she fought to free it.

At last she had both nails in her hands and shakily held them up to Spurs. 'These are my two remaining wishes. You have to choose between them.' She pressed the first nail to his palm and closed his fingers around it. 'I wish with all my heart that you would come away with me tomorrow.'

He looked away, almost crucified.

Blind with tears, she pressed the second nail into his palm. 'If you don't, then I wish that we had never met . . . and that our paths never, ever cross again. You decide.'

18

Frantic preparations for Ely Gates's garden party had been going on all week, with smartly liveried vans trundling along Manor Lane at regular intervals, boasting catering, cleaning, marquee erecting and gardening services from their waxed and polished sides.

Pheely, who had been enjoying a thoroughly good perv at all the activity during regular walks with Hamlet, took every opportunity to pop in on Ellen and update her in the hours building up to her departure. 'At least three hundred gold-painted chairs went into that marquee today,' she reported excitedly, on the morning of the party. 'Dear God, I hope Ely isn't planning on delivering a sermon.'

Pheely evidently knew nothing about the surprise wedding ceremony. Nor had Ellen told her of her evening trysts with Spurs, although she didn't doubt that Pheely had guessed about them. Since returning from Kent, Dilly had been riding Otto to the Springlode yard every day to see Rory and reported back to her mother that Spurs was behaving very oddly indeed, cross-dressing and disappearing at odd hours on an ancient bicycle. Pheely predicted happily that Spurs was about to go all-out, old-fashioned, Granville Gates mad, and concluded that Ellen was leaving the village in the nick of time. But on the whole she'd preferred not to dwell upon Spurs during the build-up to Ellen's departure. She found the party far more diverting as she sought to pretend that Ellen leaving the village meant nothing to her.

'You could have lent Ely some chairs, come to think of it.' She wandered about Goose Cottage, checking the labels on every piece of furniture. 'I must say you're terribly organised.

I'm sure you've got bags of time to pop in on the party before you go.'

Ellen, who had woken up with a lump the size of Yorkshire in her throat, was finding difficulty in making even monosyllabic answers.

'Don't forget that Dilly has bought a bottle of champagne for us all to share to see you off,' Pheely reminded her. 'It cost her practically every penny she has, so I expect you at the Lodge later this morning on pain of death.' She stooped to collect the ball Snorkel was offering. 'And you, my darling girl, can settle into your new pad while we toast Mummy on her big adventure.' She waggled the ball, making the collie leap excitedly in the air. 'Are you coming to live with me? Are you?' she teased. 'Yes! Oh, *yes*, you *are*.'

Snorkel barked adoringly.

Ellen turned away her head to hide the tears.

Pheely had insisted on giving the collie a home, pointing out that Snorkel and Hamlet were madly in love and adding that she loved Snorkel's sense of humour. It was a huge source of relief for Ellen, who had agonised over what to do about the dog when she left, although it made it no easier to face the final farewell.

If only saying farewell to Fins were possible, but the great black and white hunter was still out on manoeuvres. At least Ellen could comfort herself with the thought that his welfare was no longer in doubt – in fact he seemed more concerned about hers, delivering regular gifts in the early hours that she discovered waiting for her on the doorstep each morning. That week's total already ran at three voles, several fledgling birds and a fat rat. Yet she longed to see him properly ensconced in a new home before she left. Life al fresco in Oddlode might be a riot in summer, but winter was another matter. She needed to know that he would be safe, and loved.

'I'll look out for him, darling,' Pheely had promised. 'You're the one whose safety I fear for. As if it's not enough to spend most of your life jumping from planes or riding waves, you're now flying long-haul to uncharted waters to become a back-packing drop-out. God, I envy you.'

Pheely had also asked if she could have Ellen's surfboards to incorporate into a sculpture that she had been commissioned to undertake for the new leisure centre in Market Addington. And she had been impossibly touched when Ellen gave her laptop to Dilly. In exchange, she now gave Ellen the parting gift of a necklace wrapped in an oversized red-spotted handkerchief. It was a chunky pendant made up of intricate Celtic silver knotwork, tarnished with age and neglect, the burnished pink stone at its centre dark-edged with dirt. 'Watermelon tourmaline,' she explained. 'It's quite rare and has amazing properties – I call it the "funny side" gemstone, because it helps one see happiness in adversity. It opens the heart chakra.' She winked, knowing that Ellen didn't believe in that sort of claptrap. 'And it's a locket – you can put something in it. I kept a little recreational party grass in it at one point, but the clasp is a bit loose and I was always finding my bra full of best home-grown sensimilla.'

'Thanks – I'll treasure it.' Ellen pressed it to her cheek.

'Rubbish – you'll trade it for a taxi-ride in Kazakhstan.' Pheely giggled. 'I'd far rather you treasured the kerchief. That was Daddy's. I thought it was rather fitting – you should bundle your possessions into it.'

Ellen forced a smile: the oversized handkerchief was pure Disney runaway cliché. 'I'll tie it to my backpack,' she promised.

'You do that.' Pheely boffed the ball against Snorkel's nose. 'Mummy's seeing the funny side already, isn't she?' She glanced up at the kitchen clock. 'God, I must go back and glue Godspell's clay facial piercings back on.' She sighed and threw the ball. 'My work cannot be hurried, and Ely is getting rather fractious. How was I to know all that body jewellery would drop off in the extreme heat of the kiln?'

She had insisted that she must work on the party's sculptural centrepiece until the very last minute, and had appalled Ely by arranging for two junior members of the Wyck family to transport it to Manor Farm in Reg's pick-up later that morning.

'I can hardly carry it myself,' she pointed out, smiling naughtily, 'and they've promised they'll be careful. Besides, they need a way of double-crossing Ely's threshold, bless them. His gate policy beggars belief, and he believes the Wycks are beggars. Do you know he's hired West End bouncers to man his manor this year?'

In the interests of appearing benevolent and a true Christian, Ely always invited the entire village to his party and could not exclude the Wycks although, according to Pheely, he tried his best to discourage them from lowering the tone.

'Daddy used to call the Gates jamboree Royal Faux Pas-scot because they are such dreadful *nouveau* snobs.' She was heading back out into the garden. 'Ely *insists* that men wear ties and ladies hats. He only relaxed the rules on morning suits when a few drunken revellers from the Lodes Inn deliberately misunderstood and came in their birthday suits. And who wouldn't, given glorious weather like this?' She tipped her face up to the sun. 'What perfect party weather.'

Always held on Saturday, the only non-royal day of the famous Ascot race meeting, the annual garden party at Manor Farm boasted endless champagne and Pimm's, lavish catering, a grand raffle, live music and – of course – the now legendary local horse race. Part village fête, part horse show, part open house, the day was one of the most eagerly anticipated in the Oddlode social calendar.

This year, the village ladies, who had spent months planning their outfits, were in for a treat. Great secrecy surrounded Felicity's celebrated floral display, which reportedly took up an entire end of the huge open-sided white marquee and was concealed by a vast white screen of cotton sheets until the time came for the dramatic unveiling.

'Oh, my darling, they are in for *such* an eyeful.' Pheely clapped her hands eagerly as she danced out of the Goose Cottage gates. 'I refuse to let you fly away before you see it. I guarantee you will never forget it, even if you can't remember my name in a month's time.'

Ellen said nothing as she watched her go, knowing that the butterfly had been fluttering cheerfully from pupa to pin-board, avoiding the nectar that had almost poisoned their friendship.

Pheely had not mentioned Spurs once.

Holding the locket to her cheek once more, Ellen sat down on his favourite garden bench and watched the lightest of angel-wing clouds scud across the blue sky. Not long until her plane cut through it, she thought, imagining feathers floating to the ground as she soared into the air. She would have an empty seat beside her, of course.

The lump was almost cutting her throat now.

It was perfect wedding weather. Across the county, brides were patting their barrel curlers worriedly and knocking back champagne to calm their nerves.

Ellen tried and failed to envisage Godspell under the caring attentions of hairdressers and beauticians, fretting about her veil, a stress spot and the chances of her lipstick lasting.

She climbed up the bunkhouse steps and looked across to the manor, just able to make out a few attic windows. Slumping down on the steps, she pressed the locket to her lips and kissed it for luck.

It sprang open. Pheely had packed it full of her killer grass.

Smiling despite herself, Ellen snapped it shut again and watched two magpies having a heated argument on one of the manor's chimney stacks.

Two hours later, now somewhat stoned, Ellen watched a procession of colourful hats and dresses float past as she stuffed her rucksack with the few things she planned to take with her. Her more precious possessions were packed in one of the boxes to go to Spain, but most of her stuff had already been donated to a local jumble sale.

Snorkel watched her from the bed, blue eyes troubled.

'You'll be fine.' Ellen ruffled her thick coat, unable to look at her. 'You'll love having a live-in boyfriend and a wild garden to play in.'

Horses were clattering past now, already *en route* for the race. Ellen checked her watch and winced. It was after eleven. Her heart spun on its aorta. Time to go. Time to go. Time to go.

She'd planned to put everything in the car and lock up the cottage before making the trip to the Lodge to say farewell. But as she packed up the jeep and checked around the house, making sure that every box was arranged ready for the removers, that the furniture was cleared of clutter, the beds free of linen and the cupboards emptied of contents, she felt a great ball of panic welling up inside her.

I can't leave him here, she realised. I can't leave him.

She stopped in the dark turn of the stairwell and took deep, gulping breaths. But the lump in her throat was strangling her now.

During the previous sleepless night, she had made the decision to get as far out of the village as possible before the wedding, even though her flight wasn't until late evening.

It was already much later than she'd promised Pheely that she would drop Snorkel at the Lodge, but she didn't trust herself to leave the cottage without breaking down. If he really loved me, he'd be coming with me, she told herself firmly, trying to pull herself together. He doesn't love me enough to leave.

'And black is white.' She heard a voice in her head – brusque and argumentative, too authoritative to deny.

'Bugger off, Mum,' she moaned, burying her head in her hands.

'If *you* really loved him, you would bloody well go there and stand up to be counted. Remember Emily Davison.'

Ellen groaned: Pheely's dope had got her a lot more wired than she'd planned. She had only smoked the tiniest toke, tucking the rest of the stash into the airing cupboard with a note as a treat for Spurs and Godspell. It was her wedding present to them – God knows, they'd need it. But now her head reeled, as she heard her mother's imaginary voice in her head.

'Typical!' the voice lectured. 'Getting high on wacky tobacco at the most important moment in your life. *And* you're driving. Have you *read* the statistics?'

Ellen watched Fins trot up the stairs towards her, eyes shining.

'Oh, God.' She covered her own eyes to stop herself seeing things. 'Any minute now, Richard will demand cybersex.'

On cue, her mobile phone rang.

'Ellen, dear!' the brusque voice rang in her ear. 'Just calling to wish you *bon voyage*. Everything okay?'

Was this still a dope daydream or was that really her mother's voice, Ellen wondered vaguely. She reached out to tickle Fins' neck, feeling soft fur slide beneath her fingernails. He purred and pushed against her, collapsing on his back, paddling his paws into her wrist and head-butting her ankle.

'Mum,' she felt Fins dig his claws into her arm and watched the beads of blood appear, 'why doesn't anything add up any more?'

Jennifer Jamieson coughed. 'I'll get your father.'

Ellen cocked her head as a drop of blood landed on her frayed cut-offs. She could hear her mother saying something about '. . . must be having second thoughts.'

'Ellen?' Theo came on the line.

She burst into tears.

'Sssh . . . sssh, duckling. What is it?' her father soothed. 'Is it Richard? . . . Are you frightened about going away? . . . What is it, my little duck? What can I do to make things better, eh?'

Ellen was sobbing so hard that it took her a while to answer. When she got the words out, they sounded so embarrassing that she laughed as she wept. 'T-tell me a fairy tale, Dad.'

Theo stalled. 'A what?'

'A f-fairy tale.'

'I don't know any,' he confessed eventually. 'I can tell you a joke . . .'

Ellen sobbed all the harder, ripping the locket from her throat. Pheely had been wrong. She couldn't see the funny side.

'An Englishman, a Scot and a Spaniard walked into a bar—' her father started buoyantly, desperate to cheer her up.

'Once upon a time,' Ellen interrupted, watching Fins stalking back down the stairs. He was fatter than ever. 'There was a little mermaid, who grew up on the sea-bed. Are you with me so far?'

'Um, yes . . .' Theo answered cautiously.

'When she came of age, she swam to the surface of the ocean to sing upon the rocks with the other mermaids. But before she could join them, she saw a man drowning and she saved his life . . .'

'The cottage door is wide open, Snorkel is rollicking around in Hunter Gardner's paddock, there's a rucksack on the bed in the attic and she's written the weirdest message on that lovely white wall you painted.'

'Oh, yes?' Dilly was barely listening to her mother's breathless report as she tacked up Otto, her head full of thoughts of the race.

'Yes. It says MERMAIDS RULE. Oh dear, perhaps giving her that dope wasn't such a good idea. Where do you suppose she can be?'

'At the party?' Dilly suggested, buckling up the throatlash with shaking hands. 'I told you she wouldn't be able to leave without watching Spurs ride. Oh, God, I wish Rory was here. Why did I say I'd meet him there? I'm too nervous to do this right.'

'Here, let me.' Pheely removed her hat, plonked it on the gatepost and took over.

On the manicured Manor Farm lawns, the garden party was already in full swing, and there was an excited air of anticipation as guests held on tightly to their hats in the buffeting wind. Word had got out that Ely was set to make an announcement, and wild rumours had started to pass between the clusters of eager locals. Only a few had heard the engagement story doing the rounds among the pensioners. Most assumed that it was connected to the Gateses' burgeoning empire.

Almost everybody was aware that Ely wanted to set up a hotel in Oddlode, and villagers knew that he had his eye on his brother's dilapidated mill. The most popular train of thought was that he had found a way of getting his clutches on it. He was very close to Gina and Pat, the ambitious owners of the Duck Upstream, so it would make sense if they had all got into cahoots and staged a buy-out.

'The bounder's planning to set up a theme park, I hear,' muttered Hunter Gardner, his low-slung chin disappearing angrily into his cravat.

'Possibly.' Pru Hornton smiled winsomely, draining her third glass of champagne-and-Valium, convinced that today, at last, Ely would announce he was leaving fat Felicity for her. He had been behaving very strangely lately.

'Look at him, showing off in that ridiculous car of Giles's,' Hunter grumbled as Ely performed another circuit of the huge circular drive that cut through his garden, loudly reminding his guests that there would be a very special surprise shortly before the race. 'And why, in God's name, has he put ribbons on it? The chap's gone totally barking mad.' His hat flew off in a gust of wind.

Trapped in the Aston Martin with her husband, Felicity was looking anxiously at her watch. The centrepiece of her floral display had still not arrived, and Pheely was not answering the phone at the Lodge cottage. She clutched her mobile to her chest.

'Fear not.' Ely patted her large thigh. 'It will be here.'

'And what about Lady Belling? She and the Surgeon were supposed to arrive hours ago.'

'The Belling boy is here,' he muttered under his breath. 'He is all we need.'

'But her ladyship won't let the ceremony go ahead without them.'

'Be silent, woman! Today, my little plum pudding, everything will be perfect.' He started to laugh, running over Hunter Gardner's Panama hat as he accelerated along the driveway. 'Welcome, welcome, guests!' he called out benevolently. 'Today is a *very* special day. Welcome!' He parked the Aston at a rakish angle by his gateway and sprang out to greet new arrivals, feeling a young man again.

In the marquee, Lily Lubowski tried very hard to peek round the white sheeting that covered Felicity's floral display, certain that it housed a scale model of a vast new estate Ely planned to build to house immigrants or dangerous criminals. But she was foiled by the arrival of several Wycks, buckling under the weight of a shrouded object on two sturdy planks.

'Out the way, missus,' Saul growled, sweat dripping from his buzz-cut.

At the opposite end of the marquee, Roadkill were performing a sound-check amid screeching feedback and ear-splitting guitar chords. Saul almost dropped his planks as he saw Godspell appear on the stage. Dressed in a long black dress with a fishtail skirt and high pointed collar, she was deathly pale, her witchy white face covered with a black lace veil. She reached out her spiky black fingernails to the microphone, stared straight at Saul, and opened her small black-lipped mouth:

'Let the ANTICHRIST of HATE that is SITTING on your GATE take your SOUL . . . YEAWWWWWWW-AUGHHHH!' she sang, knowing that it was his all-time favourite. Saul's blue eyes filled with tears.

On a little raised platform beside the rose garden, the Lower Oddford string quartet also had tears in their eyes as they raked their way through Vivaldi, completely drowned by the wailing from the tent.

Indulgent Ely, who was tone-deaf, thought the discord rather charming as he towered beside puddingy Felicity at the head of the drive, welcoming their guests who were crossing from the temporary car park set up in the orchard.

'There you are, Ophelia.' He greeted Pheely with a steely smile. 'I must say, I had hoped the bust would be here a little sooner.'

'Have you seen it?' Pheely panted breathlessly, having chased her commission all the way to the farm, furious with Ellen whose no-show had made her so behind schedule.

'Not yet,' he muttered. 'Your porters used the back entrance from the farmyard. They're setting it up in the marquee now, I believe.'

'Oh, how thoughtful of them!' Pheely gasped with relief. 'I'll go and check it's okay.'

'I'll come with you,' Felicity offered, but her husband took her pudgy little hand.

'Later, Pudding, later – we must greet our guests.' He nodded pointedly at a shiny little Mini pelting towards the orchard. At its wheel, a large woman in a navy blue suit was waving a piece of paper cheerfully, almost crashing into the horsebox in front of her. It was the registrar with the last-minute paperwork permitting a marriage ceremony to take place in Ely's gardens that afternoon, and which she had agreed, after a little cajoling, to conduct. The backhanders involved had cost Ely a great deal, and Felicity let out a little squeak as he squeezed her hand tightly and shuddered at the thought of the expense.

'Oh, right, yes – well, I know it will be just super.' Felicity flashed her auto-pilot smile at Pheely. 'All your work is, Ophelia. Is Daffodil not coming?'

'She's taken her horse straight round to the collecting ring.'

The paddock beside the trout farm was already almost filled with horseboxes and trailers, from which fit, excitable mounts were being unloaded and walked around in anticipation of being tacked up and crossing the private bridge on to Devil's Marsh for the traditional one o'clock start. In one horsebox, a grey, shaking Spurs was being comforted by Rory and now Dilly too, as he asked over and over again whether he was doing the right thing.

'Oh, yes! Of course, Dilly's taking part this year, isn't she?' Felicity looked up at her husband proudly. 'It's a big field. Quite our biggest yet.'

'Indeed. We expect a very competitive race.' Ely's eyes sparkled.

'Not long until the start.' Pheely looked up at the clock-tower on Ely's old coach-house. 'Will you be unveiling the bust afterwards?'

'No, that will be done very shortly – we have a rather special celebration.' He glanced over his shoulder and nodded at one of his hired bouncers, who set off along the lane to fetch Spurs. He tutted angrily beneath his breath as he spotted yet more Wycks spilling from an ancient Ford van.

'Oh – how lovely!' Pheely gurgled. 'The Oddford Wycks. Word *has* got around. What *are* you celebrating, Elijah? Beatification at last?' Not waiting for an answer, she skipped away to check her work of art, her long curls flying back in the wind because she had lost her hat somewhere along the way.

Now temporarily without his bouncer, Ely cleared his throat nervously and contemplated the unenviable task of turning away the new arrivals.

But the Oddford arm of the Wyck family – by far the most rabble-rousing – took the most direct route to the party. Ignoring their hosts waiting at the gates, they crossed the lane from the orchard and climbed straight over the dry-stone garden wall as they homed in on the free bar. Ely couldn't give chase because their arrival coincided with Hell's Bells sweeping up in a vast ostrich-feather hat that buffeted around like Pheely's wild curls. She had brought along her two sisters Til and Truffle, one as gawky and scruffy as the other was chic and beguiling. 'Sir St John apologises, but he will be coming straight on after the last race at Ascot,' she droned regally, extending a gracious gloved hand. 'He is entertaining some Arabs and can't *possibly* leave early.' She could barely conceal her fury, but her sheer stage presence stood her in good stead and Ely fell for it, despite the reek of sherry whenever she spoke.

'You mean he's in *Berkshire*?' He gulped, seeing his plans falling apart around him.

'Thereabouts, but he promises he will get here *very* speedily afterwards. No need to panic. We can just jiggle the running order.' Her silver-bullet eyes gleamed with irritation. Far from entertaining anybody in Berkshire, St John was glued to the television in his study. A week of course-side betting at Ascot had left him in even greater debt, owing old friends to the tune of thousands. That morning, to Hell's Bells' absolute fury, she had discovered his *Sporting Life* marked up as usual with his choices from the Ascot race card, although he was absolutely *verboten* to attend the fifth day, or visit the local bookie's. He had, however, found another way of gambling. Desperate to win back the money he had lost, he'd placed a telephone bet, using the only source of ready cash at his disposal – his son's Switch card. Having emptied Spurs' account, Sir St John Belling now had all his hopes riding on an accumulator and refused to budge until he knew the outcome. Having emptied the sherry decanter, Lady Belling had told him that if he missed his son's wedding, she would empty her shotgun into him.

'Will he be here for the "announcement"?' Ely was hissing in an undertone.

'We shall have to wait for him,' she murmured back, waiting for her sisters to engage fat Felicity in conversation. As soon as they had – admiring her garish flower-beds – Hell's Bells drew Ely hastily to one side. 'The race must be run before the wedding.'

'We can't do that.' Ely thought of all the ambulances and paramedics he had laid on especially. 'The wedding ceremony will take place first.'

'Spurs' father *must* be here,' Hell's Bells insisted, blasting his face with sherry fumes. 'It's correct form.'

Ely summoned the charisma of both his religions, virtuous and venal, and tried to stare her down with a dagger glare. 'They will marry at one.'

But when Hell's Bells' twin-barrelled gaze returned fire, her silver eyes cornered him like a hunted serf in open moorland. 'They will marry at one's convenience, Elijah, or they will not marry at all. Let the race be run first. Should Spurs win – which is very likely, I gather – we will have even more reason to celebrate.'

'Indeed.' Ely swallowed uncomfortably and glanced across to the paddock where the city bouncer was picking his way nervously around horses in search of Spurs, pausing to exchange words with one of Ely's farmhands as he performed a tack check on a nervy chestnut.

Ely raised his hands to attract their attention and get them to stop. Waving back at him, the bouncer unwittingly terrified the chestnut and suddenly disappeared from view. Moments later the St John's Ambulance crew were in attendance.

Ely looked up at the sky wearily. 'Very well. It's in your hands now.'

Ellen ran round the O of 'FORGIVE ME' one last time. Spurs' crop circles were barely visible now, the wheat having sprung back up in recent days. Her legs were itching from wading through its scratchy ears and she had lost her way in 'LOVE' several times, finding herself back at 'I'.

But now, puffed out and pumped full of endorphins, she was ready. The dope was out of her system. She was going to face them all.

Ahead of her, the Devil's Marsh laid out its tempting carpet of wild flowers. One or two competitors had already made their way over the bridge to warm up and check the course. The St John's Ambulance was back – it had disappeared for a while – and was taking up a hopeful position close to the start. On the opposite side of the riverbank bright dresses and hats milled around in front of the huge white marquee, which was still emitting the odd disembodied wail as Roadkill checked their levels to wind up the string quartet.

Ellen made her way to the edge of the cornfield, looked through the hedge on to the marsh and wondered whether she should just walk out on to it, Emily Davison-style, as her mother had suggested.

No. That had been the dope speaking. She had no intention of getting flattened in the stampede. Breaking into a run, she found her way back on to the bridleway and crossed the river by the folly before darting through the courtyard of new barn conversions and on to the bank on the village side – private fields and paddocks belonging to the plush cottages of North Street.

One of them was Otto's field and Ellen stopped in wonder when she reached it, stealing through Giles's garden. A bright red hat was swinging from the gatepost, trailing a long purple scarf in the breeze. It was as though somebody knew she was coming.

She crammed it on to her head and jumped the gate, running alongside the bubbling Odd and darting behind Gin Palace Heights.

She could now clearly hear the chatter of guests and the spirited bow work of the windswept string quartet, as well as smell roast hog and barbecue smoke. Overhead, the clouds were pelting past, switching the sun on and off like a strobe show.

Hesitating by the high, impenetrable hedge that separated Ely's ancient lawns from those of his yuppie neighbours, Ellen glanced across the river at the jewelled marsh. More horses were gathering on it, snorting excitedly, spooking and whinnying, their riders struggling to keep them under control. She couldn't see Spurs among them.

'Ladies and gentlemen!' announced a jolly, gin-soaked voice, and Ellen realised that Giles Hornton was taking over on the PA. 'If I can have your attention! I'm sure you'd all like to join me in a round of applause to thank Ely, Felicity and their family for inviting us here today.'

There was a paltry smattering in response and Ely's peacocks shrieked mournfully.

'Hear hear.' Giles rallied bravely. 'And the Gates family have a *very* special surprise that they would like us to join them in celebrating today. I have been asked to tell you all that, before today's race takes place, there will be – oh – one moment—' There was a shriek of feedback as a hand covered the microphone and a muffled exchange took place.

'Immediately *after* the presentation for the big race,' Giles said, sounding shell-shocked, 'there will be an announcement in the marquee that I can assure you nobody will want to miss. Ely asks that you all gather promptly for the unveiling of the traditional floral display along with a specially commissioned piece of art created by our beloved local sculptress, Ophelia Gently. We will be entertained by local band – er – Road Drill.' The microphone was muffled again as the running order was checked.

'And *then*, I am told, there will be a quite magnificent surprise celebration that we simply cannot miss. All guests are asked to refrain from photography, smoking, consuming alcohol and swearing at that time.' There was another blast of feedback and, thinking that he was off-air, Giles swore a great deal. 'I'll personally be pissed, stoned and videoing the lot. Jesus!' he cackled, puffing noisily on a freshly lit cigar.

'But first, fellow Oddloders, to the event I know you've all been waiting for!' He returned gratefully to his script. 'The Devil's Marsh Cup! Today's race will take place on the opposite side of the river in twenty minutes' time, so could you all gather your glasses and assemble on the banks to watch the jockeys parading for you. Bets can be placed with "Honest" Al Henshaw, who is running a small charity bookmaker's from the pagoda. A full list of runners and riders is on the large noticeboard beyond the marquee, so please do make a note of the combination you would like to win and – don't – forget – to – CHEER!'

Ellen felt her throat constrict in terror as she watched the crowds drift towards the riverbank beyond the high hedge. They were running the race before the wedding. What was going on?

Crashing through one of the Gin Palace gardens, she sprinted out of Coppice Close and on to the lane, following the sound of whinnying and clattering hooves as she raced towards the trout farm. Late arrivals queuing to get into Ely's garden turned to look as she belted breathlessly past the farm gates dressed in frayed hot pants and an outlandish hat.

'I do like her style.' Truffle Midwinter turned to her sister Til. 'Rather reminds me of you at that age.'

'Nonsense,' Til muttered brusquely. 'I was far more gauche.'

'Not too gauche to meet Reg Wyck in the River Folly after lights out.'

'Patricia!' Til blushed crimson and checked over her shoulder to make sure nobody had overheard. With so many Wycks swarming about it was very dangerous territory.

Every family member from the valley seemed to have gathered in Ely's garden for a rare clan reunion. And they all seemed unexpectedly distracted. They weren't raiding the food and drink or watching the race as would be customary. Most of them were in the marquee, taking an unexpected interest in Felicity's shrouded floral display like eager mourners at a wake.

'Do you know? I definitely think something fishy is going on here,' she whispered at her sister.

'Oh, I agree,' Truffle scooped a raspberry from her Pimm's and popped it into her mouth. 'Very, very fishy.'

Ellen made it to the horsebox field as the last of the competitors were mounting and making their way towards the bridge. Spurs was nowhere in sight. Then she spotted Dilly hopping around a hugely overexcited Otto with one foot in the stirrup.

'Where's Spurs?' Ellen gasped, as she rushed up to them.

Otto took one look at her hat and almost passed out.

'Oh, thank goodness you're here!' Dilly hopped even faster as Otto dashed away from Ellen's hat. 'Can you hold his head for me? Bloody Rory and Spurs have already gone ahead so that they can be at the front of the start. That stupid man spent ages checking my tack and I got left behind.'

'Can I ride Otto?' Ellen begged, assessing the stirrup for height as she worked out how to get aboard.

'What?' Dilly was almost flattened as Otto barged forward while her attention was distracted.

'Please, Dilly – lend me Otto! I have to stop Spurs killing himself.'

'Don't be daft. You can't ride.'

'I'll pick it up as I go along.'

'No, you won't.' Dilly scrambled into the saddle and looked down at her. 'Spurs will be fine – honest. He's a better rider than anyone. He'll win like everybody says he will. Wish me luck!' She bounced away on the pink snorter.

Ellen looked around desperately for an unguarded horse to steal, but all had been gathered up and were being directed towards the start. On the other side of the farmhouse, Giles was on the PA again, announcing the favourites and telling the crowds excitedly that they could count many professional riders among the field that day.

She ran towards the bridge, where one of Ely's burly farm-workers was counting the runners and riders past with a clipboard, ticking off numbers and checking girths.

'Nobody on foot beyond this point,' he told Ellen sternly.

'I'm First Aid.' She tried to push past.

'No, you're not – my brother Jack is in charge of St John's and you ain't from his blood wagon.' He gave her a wise look. 'If you want to cheer your boyfriend, do it with everybody else, love.' He nodded towards the gates that led to Manor Farm's courtyard. 'Nice hat, by the way.'

Ellen sidled into Ely's lair, pulling the brim of the red hat down over her face and darting past chattering guests. The riverbanks were crowded with eager spectators. Only one section was empty where the marshy rushes made it too wet to stand. Ellen ran towards it.

The competitors were already lining up for the mass start across the river. She gasped as she took in the number of horses. There had to be close to fifty, from huge snorting shires to fat little ponies. Most of the riders were white-faced with fear, but determined to acquit themselves with honour.

And then she saw the bravest of them all. At their fore, Spurs sat very still on the huge grey White Lies, whose flanks were dark with sweat as he waited, boggle-eyed, for the signal.

As Ellen waded in to her knees, pulling her hat from her head so that she could see, he turned to look at her and the silver eyes seemed to dim the sky. His smile stretched between his horse's ears, wide and proud and victorious.

'You came!'

She couldn't speak for emotion. She wanted to scream at him to stop, not to do it, but when she opened her mouth, nothing came out.

'I'm riding this race for you,' he shouted to her.

Tears slid from her eyes. She knew he was riding for so much more. He was riding for his life, and Bevis's death. He wasn't riding against fifty other horses. He was riding against unseen ghosts, against prejudice and hatred, and a village made up of rumour and envy.

The crowd had turned to stare at Ellen, agog at the sudden pre-race distraction. And she suddenly realised that history was repeating itself. Spurs was shouting his head off as he had on the day Bevis had died. She shook her head, clasping her hand to her mouth, willing him to stop. But it was as though unseen hands had closed around her throat to strangle her. She couldn't say a word.

'If I win this, I deserve to be happy.' He stood up in his stirrups and told them all. 'If I win, I deserve Ellen. If I win, you can all go fu—'

At that moment, Giles's PA let out a deafening shriek as he switched it back on. 'Testing, one . . . two . . . three. Test-*eeeeeeeeiiiiiiiiiiiii*!'

White Lies reared up, almost throwing Spurs. It spun in fear, nostrils trumpeting red, ears flat back like a fighting cat's. A woman in the crowd screamed.

To Ellen's horror, Spurs simply dropped the reins and spread his arms wide, laughing his head off.

'Oh, no, Spurs, no,' she murmured, as he blew her a kiss.

I would die for you, his silver eyes transmitted a silent message.

Ely's guests murmured and gasped in surprise as the huge grey horse suddenly planted itself stock still, dipping its nose to its chest and letting Spurs calmly gather the reins.

'It's TIME, ladies and gentlemen!' Giles announced theatrically as, further along the bank, Ely clambered on to a riverside podium holding a flag. 'When Mr Gates gives the signal, the thirty-seventh annual Devil's Marsh Cup will be under way. It only remains for me to wish the very best of luck to all the brave souls taking part, and to remind them that there are no rules – the first horse across the line wins. Over to you, Ely.'

Ellen waded up to her thighs, her legs dragged back by river weed that tangled around her ankles, almost pulling her over. Ahead of her, Spurs turned the big horse, jostling for position.

With gothic aplomb, Ely held his flag aloft and glared at Spurs. 'Under starter's orders,' he hollered, 'and . . . AWAY!'

The thundering of hooves across turf was deafening as the field exploded into action. Horses galloped the wrong way, reared, refused to go. Several riders fell off, others found themselves clinging blindly to their galloping horses' necks, and one hairy Shetland calmly turned on its heel and started trotting determinedly back towards the bridge, despite its rider's furious protests.

But Ellen didn't notice any of this as she watched, tethered to the riverbed, her eyes not leaving Spurs and his white charger as they raced along close to the front of the field.

'Oh, please, no.' She dragged her legs free and stumbled back to higher ground to keep him in sight.

Although he headed the stampede, it was obvious straight away that something was wrong. He kept looking down at his left leg in concern. With one hand on the reins, he tried to reach down beneath his boot, cannoning into the horse beside him. Gripping handfuls of white mane he readjusted his balance and tried again.

But then, without warning, he slumped over the horse's neck like a soldier shot in action.

'No!' Ellen screamed, her cry drowned in the passing cavalry charge. 'No, no, no!'

The big white horse veered dramatically away from the field and bucked, desperate to rid itself of the dead weight on its back.

Ellen heard somebody wailing like a battered dog, then realised that the noise was coming from her own throat – an unstoppable, agonised cry of anguish.

But Spurs stayed put. There was no blood, no lifeless deathslide to the hoof-hammered turf below. Ellen splashed back into the river again: he wasn't unconscious or paralysed by a gunshot. He was clinging on for dear life.

She heard a shout of laughter in the crowd. 'Belling's girth's broken. Christ, he'll be mincemeat in a moment.'

A long strap was flapping around beneath the big grey's belly – the girth. Even at speed, it was obvious from the sheared ends that it had been cut almost right through, the little that had been left to hold the saddle in place breaking as soon as the horse was galloping.

'Good God! The cynical voice took on a different tone. 'Will you look at that?'

Still at full pelt, Spurs pulled the saddle from underneath him and cast it aside, kicking on to steer back on course and catch the leaders. The whole manoeuvre – lightning fast but precision perfect – was over in the blink of an eye. He barely seemed to move a muscle on the horse's back, but it was a feat of horsemanship that left the doubter in the crowd reeling.

Ellen tried, and failed, to breathe again.

'You're *here*!' Pheely had appeared at her side, clasping her hands together tightly as she watched the action. 'Look at Dilly! She's doing so well. And lovely Rory is riding alongside her to make sure she comes to no harm. He really is a sweet boy.' She calmly took her hat from Ellen's shaking hands and plonked it on her own head, as thought it was the most natural thing in the world.

Ellen was too terrified to say a thing, chattering teeth eating her hands a knuckle at a time as she waded back out of the water.

'I think Spurs might win it – as long as he doesn't come unstuck round the bend. That's where a lot of them lose it. Why on earth is he riding without a saddle?'

At the very far end of the water-meadow, the field was expected to turn back on itself and charge the length of the marsh again in the race to the finishing post opposite Manor Farm. It was a notoriously tricky feat on a horse travelling at close to thirty miles an hour. Over the tannoy, Giles reminded the crowd cheerfully that most years the field dwindled in carnage as riders were dispatched, or horses refused to turn back and instead careered on over the hedge and out across the valley. 'Get those cameras ready!' he suggested, as Spurs reined back White Lies and balanced him ready to turn.

Pheely locked her arm through Ellen's and crossed herself as the first of the field – including Spurs – executed the turn safely and started hurtling back along the marsh.

'They used to turn anti-clockwise, towards the river, but since the – accident – they turn away.' She craned so far forward to keep an eye on Dilly's progress that she almost pulled them both down the riverbank. 'Here they go. Oh, slow down, Dilly! Oh, God—' She covered her eyes and then, a moment later, peeked through her fingers. 'Oh, hooray! Clever girl. She's made it. Lord – Spurs is a long way ahead. Who's that upsides him?'

Spurs was already a third of the way back to the finish and kicking White Lies on as though his life depended upon it – which it almost certainly did.

Having stayed out of the barging, bumping horse traffic because of his horse's sheer speed, he could not shake off one rival, a huge dark bay ridden by a hunched determined figure in red silks and shaded goggles. Whipping his horse frenziedly, the opponent started edging closer and closer to Spurs' grey steed.

'Good God, don't tell me they're trying to ride one another off? That's madness.' Pheely let out a little squeak as the rider in the red silks lifted his crop even higher.

Down came the whip on Spurs' back. And again, trying to knock him off balance.

The two horses' huge shoulders crashed together and they stumbled, heads bobbing towards the rushing turf, swerving in shock and flattening their ears.

Galloping, body-slamming and fighting in a blur of speed and colour, they raced dangerously close to the river. On the inside, Spurs glanced across to the point where the bank dropped away, just inches from his horse's hooves and kicked on hard. His rival wielded his whip directly at White Lies' rump.

'No!' Ellen yelled.

With a great surge of effort, the grey pulled ahead just in time to avoid the blow, and the man in the red silks struck out into thin air. Unable to keep his balance, he tumbled out of the saddle and rolled down the bank, causing Spurs' big grey to swerve away and its rider to hang on by just a lower leg. The man in red silks threw down his crop in disgust as he struggled muddily up to chase after his horse.

'And we have another faller!' boomed Giles, who had been keeping up an excited commentary throughout. 'The Patriot has dispatched his rider, leaving White Lies alone out front. Can Belling keep this up to the finishing post? He looks pretty precarious having lost his saddle. This is a very brave ride indeed,' he conceded reluctantly, clearly willing Spurs to fall, along with most of the crowd. Then his hyena screech of laughter said it all as the huge grey horse stumbled and Spurs lost his grip, disappearing from sight.

'Oops! He's gone!' he announced, with more relish than necessary, before taking in a surprised breath. 'Or is he . . . ?'

Ellen found the scream dying in her throat and re-forming as a laugh: she had recognised his favourite trick. 'Oh, please, yes. Please do it. You can do it!'

Spurs had landed on his feet and was running alongside the horse, a great hunk of white mane clutched in his hand. Letting out a banshee howl, he jumped back on again.

Pheely's jaw hung open. 'Tell me I'm not seeing things!'

'You're not seeing things.' Ellen was bursting out of her skin with love and pride. 'You're seeing my wish come true.'

As he galloped the last hundred yards he turned to salute her. He was riding for her now, and her alone. Beneath him, the huge white horse pricked his ears, mane flying, froth flecking the air, legs blurred as he carried his rider to victory. Spurs was standing on the highest wave in the ocean, forcing the tide to stand still.

'Belling is past the post!' Giles was cackling a moment later. 'With that circus trick of his, Belling has won the Devil's Marsh Cup. Whoa! Whoa, Spurs. It's over now.'

But Spurs carried on driving the huge horse onwards. They plunged on, checked, then turned towards the river.

'Good God!' Giles squeaked, losing his composure as Spurs headed straight towards his commentary spot. 'What is the man doing? You can collect the cup later, Belling – there's a bridge to come over. Wait! Shit!' With a final shriek of feedback he fled his post.

The brave grey didn't falter as Spurs asked him to take the huge leap over the river. Even at its narrowest point the Odd was a bubbling torrent, with deep, uneven banks and a gaggle of screaming hat-wearers on the landing side. Trusting his rider implicitly, White Lies leaped from the Devil's Marsh to the Oddlode bank without hesitating.

The only person to keep her eyes open as he did so was Ellen, and those eyes filled with tears as he landed safely and thundered across the garden towards her.

White Lies halted and danced beside her, steam rising from his flanks and foam flying from his mouth. On his back, Spurs held out a hand that danced too. 'I love you! I'll grant your wish. I'll grant every wish you make from now on.'

Ellen stared up at the blur of muscle and sweat and power and love, and no longer cared whether it was sport or whether it was dangerous. It was love.

He stretched his hand lower. 'Need a lift?'

She nodded happily. 'We have a plane to catch.' Then she stepped forward, took his wrist against hers and jumped.

'Stop!' Hell's Bells shrieked, huffing up as fast as her short and sturdy legs would carry her, curls springing out from beneath her ostrich hat. 'What about the wed—'

But Ellen had her arms closed tightly around Spurs' waist and they had already turned to gallop away, jumping over the garden wall and clattering along the lane.

19

Desperate to cover up the mortifying sideshow that had just taken place in the middle of his garden party, Ely wasted no time in regrouping and adopting damage-limitation tactics. Booting Giles back on to the PA podium to announce the beginning of Roadkill's performance, he hurried to the marquee to cue his daughter and prepare a placatory speech.

Hell's Bells hopped after him, ostrich feathers flying. 'We can still save face,' she panted. 'Jasper won't get far. He has no money and no passport. I'll arrange roadblocks.'

'Already in motion – Giles is making some calls,' Ely muttered into his collar. 'My girl will stay true. She may be broken-hearted, but she is brave. She will sing through her sorrow while we fetch him back. This wedding will go ahead.'

'Yes – quite.' Hell's Bells cast him a doubtful look.

But when Godspell took the microphone, she was singing from a different hymn sheet. It was the moment she had been preparing for all week, coached by a professional rebel. Instead of launching straight into the band's first number, she started to talk, addressing the crowd – an unfamiliar husky voice that was far more compelling than her cat-on-heat vocals.

'It's time to tell the truth about this family,' she told the bemused guests, her words amplified across the village by a great stack of speakers. 'It's about time somebody fucking did.'

The Wyck clan – who made up almost half the audience – let out a great raucous cheer. A small smile twitched at Godspell's black lips as she winked at them.

'A good friend told me recently that love is like clay – you can only mould it once, when it's new and impressionable. As soon as it's fired, you're stuck with it until it shatters.' She looked at Pheely for reassurance and received a hearty thumbs-up from beneath a battered red hat. 'And this friend wisely says that people who play at matchmaking aren't sculptors at all, as you might think, but bulls in china shops.

'A month ago,' she rasped, crashing a tambourine on her bony hip for emphasis, 'my father made me sign a contract. He told me that if I refused to, he would burn all my . . . all my beloved pets alive.' She closed her eyes, thinking of her precious snakes, lizards, insects and arachnids. The tambourine hit the hip again. 'Today, ladies and gentlemen, you were all supposed to witness a wedding organised by a bull in china shop. My father,' she pointed him out with the rattling tambourine, 'Ely Gates, your so-called upstanding villager, a Christian and a family man, is so desperate to get his hands on Oddlode Manor that he blackmailed me into marrying Jasper Belling. Today was to be our wedding day, although it felt like both our funerals.'

There was a shocked intake of breath from the rapidly gathering crowd

'Oh, yes.' Godspell lifted her pointed chin over the microphone. 'But it seems Jasper's just got even over Oddlode at last.' She started to giggle. 'You all thought he had feet of clay, but he doesn't. They have wings, like Hermes'. It was his heart that was made of clay, until he fell in love.

'Only he didn't fall in love with me. He fell in love with Ellen, who has wings on her feet and her heart and her back. Seeing Spurs with her just for one night taught me that love isn't something you can manufacture. It's a one-off, like a sculpture. And I'm grateful. My life, am I grateful – I could almost marry the bastard for teaching me that!' Her loopy laugh echoed around the marquee. 'You see, I love somebody too. I want to introduce you to my love, my hero and my one-off . . .' She turned to her drummer and blew him a kiss, crashing the tambourine against her hip. 'Ladies and gentlemen, I give you Saul Wyck!'

He gazed at her over his snare, one hand automatically seeking out the unicorn tattoo on his bicep with its dark, sultry rider, the other hand rattling out a loud drumroll between bass and tom with shaking sticks.

Uncertain if this was some sort of theatrical sideshow, there was a smattering of applause throughout the marquee. Then the Wyck clan let out another raucous round of cheers and the tent exploded with a delighted, clapping ovation.

Godspell stilled her rattling tambourine against her chest and waited to get their attention back. 'This is a song I wrote about what's been going on. It's called "Ma Rage and Pa Son Money".' A moment later Godspell had clutched the microphone to her twisted black mouth and emptied her lungs, causing women and men to flee the marquee as it almost collapsed under the deafening cacophony of Roadkill's opening number. 'WHY did you STAND back and WATCH the LAMBS to the SLAUGHTER? Was it because HE worships at another's ALTAR? He was a PIMP and a WIMP to a SLUT in a RUT, but I AM YOUR DAUGHTER! WHEAAA-AAAAAAEEEEEEEEE-IEEEEEE!'

Pheely clenched her fists in victory and started to head-bang along so excitedly that her hat flew off and was trampled by the pogoing Wycks family. Beside her, Ely had pressed his fevered brow to Hell's Bells substantial shoulders and was openly weeping like a child.

'Oh, do dry up,' Hell's Bells snapped.

Giving Godspell a victorious thumbs-up, Pheely joined the mass marquee exodus, dashing to greet Dilly and Rory, who were trotting across the lawns on their horses, oblivious of Ely's gardener's irate protests.

'You wonderful, loved-up children – well done!' she gurgled. 'Now go after Spurs and Ellen and, for God's sake, catch them before they leave. Tell them we have plenty of time for that farewell drink. Godspell is going for bust – which reminds me.' She turned to the Wyckses, gave them a Dick Emery wink and shouted, 'Cue the unveiling, boys!'

When the white awning finally fell from Felicity Gates's floral arrangement, the few loyal guests still tolerating the decibels in the marquee turned away gratefully from Roadkill's performance, then drew in a collective breath of even greater shock.

The blooms were perfect, the arrangement divine and the colours exquisite as always. But the centrepiece was as shocking as it was beautiful.

It was obscene. It was flagrant. Nobody could take their eyes from it.

For nestling among the orchids, Asian lilies and cabbage roses was a bronze of a couple, an inseparable couple, giving off so much white-hot heat that each and every person who saw it stepped back.

The figures depicted were unmistakably of Spurs and Ellen.

Pheely cocked her head critically. 'You know, I think I need a bit more research before I tackle erotic work again.'

At her shoulder a smooth voice said, 'Only too willing to oblige.'

She looked up and smiled. 'You have river water in your moustache.'

Giles wiped it away.

'And, by the way, I think I'm pregnant.' She sighed dreamily, looking at her sculpture again and patting her stomach, immensely proud of the portrayal, even if she'd been forced to sell the last of her father's sketchbooks to afford the casting.

'It's *terribly* good.' A hunky youth sidled up to her other shoulder and Pheely excitedly recognised Ely's nephew Lloyd, the dishy estate agent. He had artist's muse written all over him, she thought languorously.

'Yes, isn't it?' she batted her eyelashes at him, wondering how Ellen could possibly have chosen Spurs above such an Adonis. 'Watch out where you tread – our local lawyer has fainted down there. Tell me, do you know anything about origami?'

The big grey horse looked up at the dark windows of the spoilt-princess cottage and whickered before he sank down to roll in the paddock, covering his coat in grass stains.

'He'll be fine,' Spurs turned back to the room. 'Rory can pick him up later. We should go. They'll be after my blood.'

'You have no passport,' Ellen reminded him, sitting on the mattress and flicking one of the clasps of her rucksack open and closed.

He reached out to take her hand, his eyes downcast. 'I don't want you to miss out on the World.'

'It doesn't matter.' She found herself laughing. 'The World's right here.'

Starting to laugh too, he suddenly launched himself on to the bed.

'We'll go to Cornwall.' She kissed him.

'Or Scotland.' He unbuttoned her shorts.

'Or Yorkshire.' She pulled his T-shirt over his head.

'Or the Isle of Wight?' He slid his hands beneath her knickers.

'I've heard the Cotswolds are very nice at this time of year.'

'Really? I've heard that too.'

'There's the most exquisite little cottage vacant at the moment – the sale has fallen through, apparently.'

'Is that so? Perhaps we could stay there? Where is it?'

'Oddlode – very picturesque, I gather.'

'I know it well. There's a sport's physio based there at the moment who comes very highly recommended. She promised me a massage, but she hasn't kept her word.'

'How remiss of her. Do you have any particular ache you'd like her to treat?'

'Well, now you mention it, my heart was aching like bloody mad, but it seems to have got better all of a sudden. Now the ache is rather lower down.'

'Let me check it out . . .'

Dilly and Rory stared up at the Goose Cottage windows from horseback and tilted their heads in amazement as the top one started to steam up.

'I don't think they're going anywhere in a hurry, do you?' Rory suggested.

Dilly shook her head pinkly.

He turned to her. 'I'll win the race for you one year.'

'No – I'll win it for you.'

'I'll win it first.'

They turned to hack back to Manor Farm, arguing happily.

'Me.'

'No, me.'

'Dead heat?'

The cry that issued from Oddlode Manor just after the three forty-five at Ascot could be heard half-way across the valley.

On the nearby lawns of Manor Farm, Ely Gates's guests looked up, sensing yet more village excitement in what could only be called a truly vintage year.

Hell's Bells set off wearily along the drive to investigate her husband's latest losses, but he was already sprinting up Manor Lane towards her. He appeared to be carrying an outraged cat under one arm.

'Oh, for God's sake, St John!' She stepped back in distaste. 'Must you carry that foul feral mog around with you everywhere? I've told you, I hate cats. If it's unwell, dispatch it with an air rifle.'

'It's not unwell – far from it.' He panted up to her, his face alight in a way that Hell's Bells hadn't seen since he was on the front bench exchanging badinage with Kinnock. 'I've told you, cats decide their owners and Godfrey has chosen me.' He kissed the overweight cat's black and white head and it looked at him adoringly, then shot Hell's Bells a dirty look. 'And he has brought me luck.' St John rained more kisses on his head. 'I *told* you he was lucky.'

'What *are* you talking about, St John?'

'It came in!' he shouted, dancing around with the cat. 'They *all* came in – five long-shots, one after the other, romping home, the beauties.'

Hell's Bells' noble face went very still. 'Tell me this isn't a joke?'

He shook his head, still laughing. 'It is no joke m'dear. We're rich. WE . . . ARE . . . RICH!'

'Oh, my house. My beloved house.' She clasped her chest, turning paler and paler. 'It doesn't need to be sold.' She battled for breath, reaching out to his arm for support. 'We can mend the roof. We can keep the horses. We can save the River Folly.'

'Don't overexcite yourself, m' dear.' He patted her hand, lowering his voice to a broken whisper. 'I know that you are unwell.'

She looked up at him sharply and he shrugged, the spaniel-ears hair flopping over his face. 'Gladys overheard you talking with Spurs. She thought I knew. My poor Bell.' The big, faded blue eyes looked away, distraught. 'I would happily give away every penny if it brought your health back.'

Hell's Bells nodded curtly, then smiled suddenly, very wickedly. 'Actually, I'm in rather rude health.'

'You mean you lied to the boy?' He spluttered.

'I simply let his misguided interpretation of the facts pass unchecked,' She was not married to a politician for nothing. 'He found a letter from the homeopathic vet and seemingly mistook the identity of the patient. He thought I was Gladstone.'

'You led him to believe that you were a Labrador with advanced cancer of the spleen?'

She closed her eyes for a moment, 'Don't ever let me hear you say that in front of the puppies. It is haemangiosarcoma. Gladstone doesn't understand long words.'

'Sorry, m'dear,' St John humoured her with a kindly pat before chortling. 'Good grief. I know that Jasper has done some very bad things, but don't you think that was a little harsh on the lad?'

'I was testing his grit.'

His eyes softened with love as he remembered why he had married her. She was a formidable woman. 'And?'

'It's rather gritty.'

'Perhaps it's best that he didn't marry the Gates child, then?' He hooked his arm through hers.

'God, yes – especially now we don't need the money. It would have been quite frightful. Are we really terribly rich?'

'Rather.'

'Richer than Elijah?'

'I'll say.'

'What fun! Shall we throw a party?'

Ellen pressed her palms firmly into the muscles to either side of Spurs' spine, watching the bronzed, freckled skin wrinkling as she leaned into the pressure, stretching forward to roll the stroke up to his shoulders. 'This would be better with oils,' she apologised.

'It's beautiful like that.' He eyed her over his shoulder.

Sinking the length of her body into the hollows of his back, she touched her nose against his. 'I kept my promise, after all.'

He kissed her. 'And I kept mine.'

Their lips formed words and laughter that were kissed away before they shared unspoken happiness on a mattress labelled 'Spain'.

Hours later, Spurs propped himself up on one elbow and looked out of the tiny shoebox window to where an aeroplane had left a white scar in the blue sky. 'I think we've missed our flight.'

'There'll be others.' She stretched up to kiss him. 'I'm flying too high to wear a seatbelt.'

He laughed, pressing her back against the mattress. 'You know you still have one wish left?'

'Not *still*?' She groaned, laughing.

'You wished we'd never met. I can't grant that. You'll have to pick another.'

She reached up a hand and traced the curve of his jaw with her finger, knowing that she would be able to examine it from every angle and in every season – tanned, pale, stubbled, grey-bearded, laughing, tense and relaxed in sleep – until she grew too old to see.

'I wish we could live happily ever after.'

'I think that can be arranged.'